CW01149842

THE SOLDIER'S SON

Books 1-3

MALCOLM ARCHIBALD

Published 2024 by Next Chapter

THE NOISE OF ZULU BATTLE

THE SOLDIER'S SON BOOK I

For Cathy

So, all day long the noise of battle rolled
Among the mountains by the winter sea.
Idylls of the King, by Alfred, Lord Tennyson

PART I

CHAPTER 1

ZULULAND, JUNE 1877

Jama halted and raised a hand. Obediently his small *amabutho* – regiment [1] - the Abanonya, stopped, crouched down and rested on the rustling grass of Zululand. Each man held an oval shield of stiffened cowhide, three foot six inches tall and two feet wide. The shields shared a pattern, with a black fringe around a white interior containing two black smudges. The warriors also held the *iKlwa,* the short stabbing spear the great King Shaka had introduced. With a shaft thirty inches long and an eighteen-inch long, one-and-a-half-inch wide blade, the *iKlwa* was lethal in the hands of a trained warrior, and each of Jama's men had been highly trained since youth.

As well as the stabbing *iKlwa*, the warriors held one or more throwing assegais- spears- and some carried knobkerries, heavy club-like weapons with a long shaft and a heavy knob used for braining the opponent. Only one carried a firearm, an ancient Brown Bess musket that had travelled a long way since its original owner, a British soldier, deserted from his regiment some forty years before.

"There is the king's *imuzi* – his homestead," Jama announced to his men.

Jama's *amabutho,* a mere hundred and twenty strong, looked and nodded solemnly. They were familiar with King Cetshswayo's royal *imuzi* of oNdini but paused to admire the spectacle before advancing.

oNdini, which the white people called Ulundi, was vast, far more extensive than the *imuzi* where they lived. Sitting on the quiet slopes easing from the valley of the White Umfolozi River, it was composed of thousands of *izindlu* – the local grass-built houses - behind a vast thornbush barrier, with an inner hedge enclosing a huge open space for cattle or ceremonies.

When he was satisfied his men had looked their fill, Jama led them down the slope to oNdini. He listened to the disciplined tramp of hard feet behind him and fought to contain his pride. These were his men, his warriors he was taking to meet Cetshwayo.

oNdini's gate was open, and the royal *amabuthos* of the Undi Corps lined the interior. Jama recognised each regiment by their shields, regalia, and the age of the warriors. He saw the uThulwane, 1,500 strong, and each man forty-four years old. He saw the Nkonkone, five hundred strong and two years younger than the uThulwane, with each man staring at his tiny *amabutho*. The Ndhlondhlo were there; the same age as the Nkonkone, they looked an impatient bunch of veterans. Beside them were the much younger inDluyengwe and finally the twenty-three-year-old inGobamakhosi, six thousand warriors all yearning for a chance to prove themselves in battle.

Jama studied each *amabutho*, comparing them to his Abanonya. The youngest regiments had all-black shields, and the most experienced carried all-white. Most regiments were in between, while mixed or married *amabuthos* carried red shields. Every warrior wore the *umuTsha,* a cord around the waist, with lengths of fur dangling in front and cowhide at the back. More senior regiments also wore extra fur and hide attached to the *umuTsha*. Decorative furs, feathers and hides augmented each warrior's basic clothing, each piece proudly worn, men proclaiming their allegiance and regiment.

Jama glanced back at his warriors as they trotted past the assembled Undi corps. They looked splendid with their leopard skin headbands, red cow tail necklaces and feathers that rustled beneath the knees. Each man of the Abanonya held himself proudly erect, ignored the jeers of their rival regiments and took their place in the assembly. Jama's oldest friend Ndleleni stood in the centre, with his necklace of *umzimbeet* seeds proving his bravery. Cetshwayo had granted Ndleleni the honour of wearing that badge of honour after the battle of Ndondakusuka over twenty years before.

After a few moments, Cetshwayo emerged from his *izindlu*; tall, broad-chested, and handsome with a neat beard, the king possessed the bearing of royalty and the powerful thighs common to his family. Every warrior in oNdini raised their spear and shouted the royal salute.

"*Bayete! Bayete!*"

Jama shouted with the rest, proud to be in the same *imuzi* as Cetshwayo, a descendant of Shaka, who was, in turn, a descendant of Zulu, the progenitor of the nation. As the name Zulu meant heaven, and all the clans and sub-clans within the Zulu empire adopted his name, they became the Children of Heaven.

King Cetshwayo was a proud man in a difficult situation. His kingdom bordered the Boers of the Transvaal on the northwest and the British colony of Natal on the southwest. To the north was Swaziland, while the Indian Ocean washed the western shore. Trouble could erupt across any of his borders.

"*Bayete*!" the warriors roared the royal salute. "*Bayete!*"

Cetshwayo knew his warriors wanted the opportunity to fight and were supremely confident of their ability to win against any enemy, yet the king did not want a war. His men carried assegais and shields, frighteningly lethal weapons at close quarters, but both British and Boers had firearms and fought at a distance. To defeat either, the Zulu warriors would have to endure concentrated rifle fire.

"*Bayete!*" the warriors shouted in a full-throated chorus. "*Bayete!*"

Cetshwayo acknowledged his people with an upraised hand.

Jama watched with awe as the king ordered the royal cattle herds to enter the vast central area. With cattle the mainspring of the Zulu economy, Cetshwayo was displaying his wealth.

The herds moved in unison, black cattle with black, white with white and red with red. They entered the *imuzi* in a ground-shaking rumble of thousands of hooves, with dust rising and the ground shaking. The assembled warriors stared in admiration. They knew their king was a powerful man and respected him even more for showing them his herds.

"*Bayete*!" an induna, the head of a regiment, shouted, and the others joined in, thrusting their spears to the sky. "*Bayete*!"

When all the warriors had witnessed the royal herds, Cetshwayo ordered the cattle away and addressed the *amabuthos*. Jama listened and watched as the king called the indunas to him and spoke to each man personally.

Eventually, Cetshwayo summoned Jama, who ran forward and prostrated himself on the ground.

"You, Jama, are induna of the Abanonya, the Vicious Ones."

Jama did not move, although he was proud that the king had recognised him, a minor induna of a small sub-clan.

"You are of the Quangebe clan." Cetshwayo displayed his impressive knowledge of his people and events in his kingdom. "Your chief Sihayo has his *imuzi* in the Batshe Valley, near the border with Natal."

Jama remained still, unsure whether to respond or not. As Cetshwayo continued, he knew it was better to stay silent.

"I want you and the Abanonya to keep watch on the Batshe Valley, Jama, and do not allow intruders into the land of the Zulus."

Jama allowed the words to burn into his soul. Serving the king was a warrior's duty; he had no other purpose in life.

"The white men in Natal, the British, are not to be trusted, Jama," Cetshwayo said. "Do not give them an excuse to start a war. Do not cross the Buffalo or the Tugela River into their lands."

Jama remained still until Cetshwayo dismissed him when he rose. The young woman behind the king smiled at him, and Jama recognised Thadie, one of Cetshwayo's relatives. He returned the smile, wishing he could make Thadie one of his wives, and trotted back to the Abanonya. He was proud his king had singled him out and knew his prestige and standing amongst the Abanonya had increased.

❄

"This river is the Great Kei." Sergeant Ashanti Smith of the Frontier Armed and Mounted Police gestured with his right hand as his left held his horse's reins. "It is the boundary between British Kaffraria and Kaffirland, that is, the land of the free Kaffirs."

"What does Kaffir mean, Sergeant?" Andrew asked, looking across the river at a tangle of ochre and green hills scattered with trees. He could make out a small herd of cattle but no people.

Smith shrugged. "It's the name the Arabs give anybody who is not a Moslem, Constable Baird. I suppose it means unbeliever."

Andrew nodded. "We're Kaffirs too, then. It's not what the tribes call themselves, then?"

"No." Smith shook his head. "They might think of themselves as Xhosa, for they all speak that language. There are various tribes."

Andrew borrowed Smith's field glasses and stared across the river. "How many different tribes are there, Sergeant?"

"If you mean tribes, sub-tribes, and clans," Smith said, "There are probably hundreds. The main tribes are Galekas, Tambokies, Pondos, Bomvanas, Pondomise, and Fingoes." He paused for a moment. "To them, you may add the Gaikas under their chief Sandili, a drunken, dissipated old rogue who is waiting for somebody else to start trouble so he can raise his army. He hates us, of course."

"Do they all hate us?" Andrew asked.

Smith laughed, produced a pipe, and began to stuff tobacco into the bowl. "Probably," he said. "Kreli, the chief of the Galekas, certainly does. Gangeliswe of the Tambokies might do, and Moni of the Bomvanas. I'm not sure about Umquiqela of the Pondos. Umquiliso of the Pondomise is undoubtedly ready to attack."

Andrew stared across the Great Kei, wondering how many Xhosa warriors were watching him and whetting their assegais. "How about the Fingoes?"

Smith scratched a match and put it to his pipe. "They don't have a chief as such, but their head man is Veldtman, who is semi-educated. We can nearly trust the Fingoes on a good day." He puffed out aromatic blue smoke.

"It's reassuring that we have one friendly tribe in South Africa," Andrew said.

Smith smiled around the stem of his pipe. "Whatever they think of us, Baird, the tribes all have one thing in common. They all hate and fear the Zulus, the most powerful force in Black Africa."

"My knowledge of South African geography is vague, Sergeant," Andrew admitted. "Are the Zulus in Transkei as well?"

"No," Smith told him. "They are hundreds of miles north of here, bordering our Natal colony."

Andrew smiled. "I won't lose any sleep over them, then."

Smith removed his pipe and gave a gap-toothed smile. "Only a fool doesn't lose sleep over the Zulus."

"I'll bear that in mind," Andrew said. He watched others of the Frontier Armed and Mounted Police ride line up along the Great Kei River. Most were in their twenties and thirties, and, to Andrew's eyes, their horses seemed overburdened for the duties they had to perform. In front of their leather saddle, they carried a waterproof coat, a valise, and an oversized blanket. These items of equipment reached nearly as high as their chin, impairing their vision. Behind the saddle, each rider carried two saddle bags, which banged against their flanks, while the troopers added personal equipment, such as a camp kettle, axe, or spare carbine.

"Are you all set, Baird?" Smith asked.

"As set as I'll ever be, Sergeant," Andrew replied.

Smith smiled. "The tribes are volatile at present," Smith told him. "I've knocked about across Africa for some years, Baird, and I've learned a thing or two. When the natives are insolent in the trading stores, and their witch doctors begin to doctor them, there is trouble in the wind."

"What do you mean, doctor them?" Andrew asked.

Smith removed the pipe from his mouth and added more tobacco, tamping it down with a calloused thumb. "When the witch doctors buy ox tails and skins from our stores or cut the tails from farmers' cattle, they are preparing some disgusting concoction to make their warriors invulnerable to our bullets." He replaced his pipe.

"Does it work, Sergeant?" Andrew asked.

"Not so far," Smith said, puffing blue smoke into the air. "But they're a superstitious bunch and believe in all sorts of charms and magic. They believe that wizards, *abaThakathis,* cause all illness and everything bad. These *abaThakathis* are like spirits that infest a plant, or a rock, an animal, or a human."

Smith removed the pipe from his mouth. "What's worse is that people don't know these spirits infest them. However, the witch doctors or witches can smell *abaThakathis.* As you may imagine, that gives the witches a special place in society."

"I can imagine," Andrew said. "A bit like our witch-finders in the seventeenth century."

"An apt analogy," Smith agreed. "As all the tribes fear the Zulus, even the bravest of Zulu warriors fear the witch doctors in case they smell an *abaThakathi* in them. Once the witch doctors condemn a warrior, his death is singularly unpleasant, so it's best to keep clear of those particular devils." He grinned. "You're a new chum here in Africa, Baird, but there's something about you I like. Stick with me, watch the skyline for movement and keep your carbine handy, and you'll be all right."

"Thank you; I'll do that," Andrew said. "I can't see any Xhosa here, though."

"Don't you?" Smith indicated a prominent hill beside the road. "This hill is Maunder's Kop," he said, guiding his horse with his knees and leaning back in the saddle. "Not long ago, a group of British officers rode to the top to view the countryside. It was a pleasure excursion, not a military expedition, but the local tribesmen took their chance."

"What happened, Sergeant?" Andrew asked.

"A horde of warriors scrambled up the side of the hill," Smith pointed to a nearly perpendicular track, "and attacked the officers. After a terrific struggle, the natives killed all the officers. Those they did not assegai, they grabbed and threw down the hill."

"Why?" Andrew asked.

Smith shrugged. "Ask the Xhosa, for I am sure I don't know. Presumably, because they were white men and vulnerable to attack. The moral of this story, young Baird, is never let your guard fall. However innocent the situation looks, danger could be lurking."

Andrew nodded. "I'll bear that in mind as well."

Smith lifted his Snider carbine. "This little beauty is your best friend out here, Baird. Its .577 cartridge is good; it's a man-stopper like the Martini-Henry and better than anything the enemy has. Keep it clean, oiled, and well-maintained, and it will repay you by saving your life."

Andrew nodded. "I know a little about guns," he said.

"You're fresh out from home," Smith said, more curtly than usual. "All your knowledge is theoretical. Until you've seen how your rifle acts in action, you know nothing about it and little about yourself. Did you shoot back home?"

"I did." Andrew did not want to give away his background.

"That's a start," Smith gave grudging praise. "Targets, clays or hunting?"

"All three," Andrew said with a faint smile.

"Even better." Smith seemed surprised. "Have you ever shot a man?"

"No, Sergeant." Andrew shook his head. "British law tends to frown on such things."

"It's one thing to fire and another to be fired at," Smith told him, "As you'll soon find out. The Galekas have attacked the Fingoes, who appealed to us for help." He tapped Andrew's shoulder with the stem of his pipe. "Why did you think we are on this patrol?"

"I wondered," Andrew said. "What happens now?"

"We help the friendly Fingoes, give the Galekas a bloody nose and hope the whole frontier does not explode." Smith puffed out smoke from his pipe. "You'll need a decent horse as well. Where did you get that beast?"

"The police supplied him." Andrew patted the neck of his raw-boned grey. "He's only temporary until I buy my own mount."

"Good." Smith nodded. "When you choose your horse, make sure he's salted. Distemper is rampant here, and you want one that's survived that disease." He removed the pipe from his mouth. "Do you know anything about horses, Baird?"

"A bit, Sergeant," Andrew replied cautiously. "I've been around horses all my life."

"Come on, Baird, you've been a frontier policeman for a month now. Time to earn your corn."

❄

"That's a rum lot of beasts." Andrew walked around the horses the dealer had brought to the barracks.

"You have two trials," Inspector Robert Fraser was a slender, straight-backed man with a florid face. "If you don't like either of the horses you choose, we'll allocate you a mount. Understood?"

Andrew, Hitchings, and Simpson, the three recruits, nodded.

"You have to pay for your horse," Fraser said, "so choose carefully."

Andrew circled the animals, inspecting each one. Most were in poor condition, underfed, undersized or nervous. When he asked about ages, the dealer shrugged and said, "Cape age," which meant anything from six to sixteen. Andrew stopped at one small, shaggy-looking animal of indeterminable age and looked into its eyes. "What's the provenance of this beast?"

The dealer, a thin-faced man with a loud checked suit and bowler hat, stepped closer. "A British officer brought that one from India," he said casually.

Andrew moved on as Hitchings and Simpson examined the taller, faster animals. He returned to the shaggy pony. "Has he been salted?"

"All my horses are salted," the dealer boasted.

"Let's see." Without bothering to saddle the horse, Andrew mounted and rode around the barrack square, whispering into the animal's ears. He returned within ten minutes, dismounted, and patted the horse's neck. "I'll take him," he said. "What happened to the previous owner?"

"He died of fever," the dealer said as Simpson and Hitchings laughed at Andrew's choice.

"That's not a horse," Simpson sneered. "It's only a pony! It's a girl's mount."

Hitchings spat on the ground. "Can't you manage a real horse, Baird?"

When Andrew said nothing, Inspector Fraser approached him. "Are you sure, Baird?"

"Yes, sir," Andrew replied. "He's a Kabul Pony, used to rough territory and with the heart of a lion. My father owned one."

Damn! Why did I say that? Andrew continued quickly to cover his wayward tongue.

"He's not the fastest horse in the world, but he'll ride through snow or heat in the worst conditions imaginable and keep going when thoroughbreds or Arabs give up." He patted the horse's neck. "I'll call him Lancelot."

"Lancelot, he is," Fraser said as Hitchings and Simpson looked on, sneering.

On the 18th of September 1877, the Frontier Police assembled at Ibeka, right on the border between the Fingoes and the Galekas. They fed the horses and erected their tents, ready to help the beleaguered Fingoes as they wondered what the future held.

There was nothing much to the tiny settlement and a potentially hostile nation on their doorstep, so for seven gruelling days, the men laboured to secure the camp. Using picks, spades, and a great deal of sweat, they dug trenches and threw up mud walls in case of a Galeka attack.

"There's nothing the Xhosa like less than attacking entrenchments or defended laagers," Inspector Fraser informed the toiling police. "The harder we work now, the easier life will be later."

Smith waited until Fraser was away before he grunted. "You'll notice the man giving the orders is not the man wielding the spade." He stopped to fill his pipe. "If you aim to make a career here, boys, don't stay at the bottom. Get a commission, and then you can give the orders rather than taking them."

Andrew said nothing, digging his spade into the stony ground and wondering why he was there. He looked across the narrow path that marked the boundary into the Galeka's territory and contemplated what sort of people lived there.

"Are you all right, Baird?" Fraser asked cheerfully, running a hand down his long face.

"Yes, sir," Baird said.

"You were looking pensive there. Cheer up; once we get the place more secure, we'll have a look into Fingoland. Tour a little, show the flag and eye up the opposition." He winked, raised a hand, and walked on with his hands behind his back. Andrew noticed the inspector had unbuttoned the flap of his pistol holster while the carbine across his back was ready to use. For all his flippant tone, Inspector Fraser was prepared if the Galekas attacked.

Andrew lifted another spadefuls of stony dust and piled it on the wall. He had not expected to be a navvy when he joined the Frontier Police. That thought raised the question: what had he expected?

Andrew shook his head. He had joined to escape his family heritage rather than search for a bright future. He did not dislike his family, but neither did he wish them to control his life. Andrew continued to dig, with the hot African sun bringing sweat to his body and a host of flies tormenting him.

"That's looking good," Ashanti Smith approved, studying the trenches and embrasures. "I doubt any Galekas would wish to rush us now."

Andrew estimated Smith to be in his late thirties or early forties, with a face that showed the years had not come easily to him. He walked warily, balancing on the soles of his feet, and his eyes were rarely static as he surveyed the surrounding terrain.

"Have you fought the Galekas before, Sergeant?" Andrew asked.

"No." Smith shook his head. "I've fought Ashantis in West Africa and Paythans in India, but never Galekas. I reckon that will change soon."

Andrew brushed away a persistent fly. "How soon, Sergeant?"

"Very soon," Smith told him. "Top up your water bottle and make sure your carbine is oiled and clean. We're joining Number Five troop on patrol."

"Whither bound, Sergeant?" Andrew asked, glad of something to break the monotony of digging trenches and rifle pits.

"Ours not to reason why," Smith replied. "Ours but to bleed and die. In other words, young policeman, I have no idea. Pack up your bags and keep your powder dry."

"Yes, Sergeant," Andrew said. He felt an unusual mixture of apprehension and excitement. *I wonder if my father felt like this before he went on a campaign.* He shook his head. *No, he'd be calm and relaxed, looking for the opportunity to be a hero.*

At nine that morning, Andrew joined the little column of a hundred and forty men, a seven-pounder mountain gun and a handful of officers as they rode through the gate, around the newly completed entrenchments and into the brightness of the day. A handful of local Xhosa watched them, holding shields and assegais and saying nothing. Andrew eyed them, wondering if he might be fighting them soon.

"Me too," Smith murmured. "Keep your finger near the trigger, Bairdie, and watch your back."

Inspector Chalmers halted the column ten minutes march from the camp. "Gather round, gentlemen."

Andrew joined the others in crowding close to Chalmers while Smith kept a wary watch on the surroundings.

Chalmers gave them a few moments to settle down. "You may have heard that the Galekas attacked our friends, the Fingoes, on the government reserve near Guadana Hill. We are going to have a look and make peace if we can." He nodded to a bearded, sun-browned colonial. "Sergeant Duncan, you're a local man and know the tribes better than most. Take your section and ride in front. I don't want any surprises."

"Well, now we know," Smith said as they resumed their march along the main road, with the horses kicking up dust and the African sun beating on their heads and shoulders. Ochre-tinted or green hills surrounded them, with the occasional trees, small groups of round, thatched-roofed *izindlu,* and some grazing cattle. A woman, her face daubed in white clay and smoking a home-made pipe, stood outside one of the *izindlu*, watching them without responding to Andrew's wave.

"She's probably counting our numbers," Smith said.

"Or wondering who we are, passing her house." Andrew remembered the curiosity of people in rural Northumberland and Berwickshire. He tried again.

"*Molo*!" he shouted, using one of the few Xhosa words he knew. "Hello!"

"*Molo! Ujani*!" the woman replied, lifting her pipe in greeting. Her wide smile took Andrew by surprise. "Hello, how are you?"

"*Ndiphile enkosi unjani wena*," Andrew completed his Xhosa vocabulary. "I'm fine, thank you, how are you?"

When the woman replied with a long sentence Andrew could not grasp, he waved again.

Inspector Fraser gave Andrew an approving nod. "You've learned some Xhosa then, Baird."

"Only a few words, sir," Andrew said.

"More than most new chums learn in such a short time," Fraser said and rode on.

"While you've been sweet talking to the ladies," Smith said, "the natives have been gathering." He nodded to the skyline. "Somebody's watching us."

Andrew saw a small group of natives behind a clump of trees. As the police patrol drew near, two men broke away and sprinted to the north, with the sun glinting from the points of their assegais.

"They're off to warn Kreli," Smith said calmly, filling his pipe. "Don't be surprised if the whole Galeka army appears within the hour."

"Sergeant Smith," Inspector Fraser shouted. "Take two men and apprise Duncan of the situation. Scout ahead and be careful."

"Sir!" Smith responded. "You're with me, Bairdie, and you, Hitchings."

Hitchings was a tall, brown-haired, smooth-faced man to whom Andrew had taken an instant dislike. The three men kicked ahead of the column, with Andrew feeling suddenly vulnerable. The friendly locals of the morning had altered in his mind to predatory warriors waiting to attack him. He checked his carbine was secure in its bucket beside the saddle.

"Gunfire!" Smith held up his right hand. "Careful now, lads." He glanced around, quartering the ground with suddenly hard eyes.

Andrew became aware of the crackle ahead and shivered with a mixture of excitement and apprehension as he reached for his carbine.

"Is that gunfire, Sergeant?" Hitchings asked.

"It certainly is," Smith said tersely. He raised his voice. "Hitchings, you're rear guard. I'll go in front and, Baird, you're the meat in the sandwich. Watch the flanks and warn us if you see anything untoward."

They walked their horses forward, with Andrew's nerves jangling, expecting the Galekas to shoot him or charge with poised assegais at every step. He smelled smoke drifting in the faint breeze and heard what might have been the murmur of insects.

"There!" Smith said. "Half a mile ahead!" He halted his horse and motioned Andrew and Hitchings to join him. "Look!" He passed over his field glasses.

Andrew focussed the glasses and saw a confused mass of men, with sunlight flashing from the blades of assegais and smoke rising from burning *izindlu*.

"Here comes Duncan," Smith said as three horsemen thundered into view.

"Smith!" Duncan shouted. "There's trouble ahead! Don't go any further!"

"We've seen it," Smith said. "You two, Baird and Hitchings, ride back to Inspector Chalmers and tell him the Galekas are burning the kraals and killing the Fingoes," Smith said. "I'll wait here and observe."

Andrew hesitated for a moment, not wishing to leave Smith in danger.

"Go!" Smith snapped. "That's an order!"

Hitchings was already away, and Andrew followed, allowing Lancelot to stretch its legs on the dusty road. Duncan rode at his side, glancing behind him from time to time.

"I'll make the report, Baird," Duncan said.

"Yes, Sergeant," Andrew agreed.

The inspector considered for only a moment, then sent Hitchings two miles back towards Ibeka. "Find Mr Ayliff," Chalmers ordered. "He's there with a company of Fingos. Tell him to hurry along with his Fingo warriors."

"Now what, Sergeant?" Andrew asked.

"Now we wait," Sergeant Duncan said and winked. "Welcome to the Frontier Police, my boy, where we have ninety-nine hours of routine and waiting, followed by one hour of terror."

Andrew forced a lopsided grin and looked ahead, listening as the wind carried the faint popping of musketry.

CHAPTER 2

The police waited in the heat, listening to the distant crackle of gunfire.

"What's the to-do?" Smith cantered to Andrew with his forage hat pushed to the back of his head, puffing smoke from his pipe. "I thought Chalmers would bring the boys up."

"We're waiting for Ayliff's Fingoes, Sergeant," Andrew said.

"Are we, now?" Smith said. "By the time they arrive, the Galekas will have massacred half of Fingoland." He shrugged. "Not that it's any of my concern, but the women and children might feel a little miffed."

"Here they come now, Sergeant," Hitchings said.

The Fingoes marched or rode up the track, seemingly in no hurry to fight the invading Galekas. Some were dressed in cast-off European clothing, others in the traditional native blanket, while a few wore a mixture of both. While a few carried the usual assegais and shields, most had firearms, from ancient muskets that looked as if they would explode if fired to more modern Sniders as good as the carbine Andrew held.

"They're actually called Fengu, not Fingoes." A slender, gaunt-faced constable gestured to one warrior who wore European clothes, a broad-brimmed hat and carried a long rifle. "And some of them are a damned sight better marksmen than we are."

"Is that so?" Andrew asked.

"It is so," the slender man said. "Walter Abernethy, by the way." He proffered his hand.

"Andrew Baird." Andrew shook the hand. Abernethy's grip was frank and powerful.

"The Xhosa tribes called them amaMfengu, which means "wanderers," and say that the Fengu, or Fingoes, came from the tribes the Zulu king Shaka shattered. They fled from the Zulu and settled here." Abernethy tamped a quarter inch of tobacco into the bowl of his pipe. "The Xhosa, particularly the Galekas, or Gcalakas to give them their proper name, called the Fengu their dogs and treated them abominably, as one would expect."

"Would one?" Andrew asked.

"The quality of mercy is not a recognised virtue in these parts," Abernethy said as he struck a match and began to puff smoke into the air. "Anyway, the Fengu came to the British for help and have proved valuable allies ever since."

"What's this current disturbance about?" Andrew asked.

"Drought, land and cattle," Abernethy told him. "Cattle is wealth for these people, and we've had years of drought here, leading to dry riverbeds and thirsty cattle." He looked up, holding his pipe between clenched teeth. "The trouble came to a head when some Fingoes brawled with a mob of Galekas at a wedding. So now you know."

"Now I know," Andrew agreed. "The usual reasons, clan warfare over resources and a drunken brawl. The same here as everywhere else." He sighed. "When will people learn to share what they have rather than grabbing everything for themselves?"

Abernethy raised his eyebrows. "That's a politician's question, not a policeman's," he said.

"Blame my father for that," Andrew said and quickly clamped his mouth shut.

"Hello, things are happening." Abernethy did not comment on Andrew's statement.

Inspector Chalmers and Ayliff conferred briefly, and Ayliff led his Fingo warriors up a nearby hill, where lone trees struggled up from the brown-ochre grass.

"That's Guadana Hill," Abernethy said. "The Fingoes are on this side and the Galekas on the other." He grinned. "Or rather, the Galekas have moved onto the Fingo side from the other."

Smith joined them. "It looks like the entire Galeka army has crossed into Fingo land," he said. "We have our work before us, however many Fingo warriors pretend to help."

"Come on, boys," Inspector Chalmers ordered. "Let's push the Galekas back where they belong." He posted the Fingoes onto the flanks, so they advanced along the hill slopes while the Mounted Police marched along on the road.

"Half a league, half a league, half a league onward
Into the valley of death rode the six hundred."[1]

No, this is not the place for Tennyson. Try something else.

Andrew changed Tennyson for *Blue Bonnets Over the Border* and closed his mouth.

"It's all right to be nervous," Smith told him. "We all are the first time. Just remember to aim low and watch your back." He winked. "You'll be all right, Bairdie. I'll keep my eye on you."

"Thanks, Sergeant," Andrew said. He felt some of his nerves ease at the thought of Smith looking out for him.

As the Fingoes began to shout and point ahead, the Mounted Police rounded a spur of the road, and Chalmers, leading from the front, held up a hand. The column halted, the dust slowly settled, and Andrew stared ahead.

"There they are, boys." Smith spoke as if offering a gift. Andrew stopped, taking a deep breath. He had grown up in a military family, hearing tales of military valour and bloody battles. His parents had met during the Indian Mutiny, and Andrew had watched his father's gradual rise through the officer's ranks. Now, he saw a hostile army for the first time.

Here we go. Welcome to the family business.

Andrew had expected the Galekas to be a formless mob carrying assegais. Instead, their commander had arranged them in three disciplined divisions, many carrying rifles. As soon as the Galekas saw the small force of police, they began to move forward.

"Now we'll have some sport," Abernethy said. He patted his horse's neck, added more tobacco to his pipe and checked his carbine was loaded.

"Sub-lieutenant Cochrane," Chalmers said softly to the artillery commander. "Does your seven-pounder have the range?"

"Yes, sir," Cochrane replied with a slight smile.

"Then fire," Chalmers ordered.

"Yes, sir," Cochrane said and gave a string of orders to his gunners. "Range! Elevation! Fire!"

Andrew started when Cochrane fired the mountain gun, with the report louder than he had expected. He saw the shell explode amongst the first division of the Galekas, knocking down a score of tribesmen and delaying their advance.

"Dismount!" Chalmers snapped. "Leave the horses and extend across the brow of the hill in skirmishing order!"

Andrew followed Smith's lead, waiting on the right of the gun as the Galekas continued their advance. The Fingoes were on the left, with their flank ending in an area of woodland known as the Guadana Forest.

Andrew felt a mixture of excitement and apprehension as the Galekas advanced, wavering every time a shell burst among them. He felt the sweat forming on his forehead, wiped it from his hands and gripped his carbine. His mouth felt dry, and he wondered how Smith and Fraser could look so calm.

"When we fought the Ashantis," Smith murmured, still holding his pipe between his teeth. "We hardly saw them. They hid in the forest and blasted us with their slug guns. These Galekas fight in the open, like men."

Andrew forced a grin and tried to make a joke, but the words caught in his throat.

"There's bloody thousands of them!" Hitchings' voice rose an octave.

"Which gives us more targets," Sergeant Duncan said. "Shut your mouth and fire low."

Andrew wriggled closer to the illusionary protection of a stunted thorn tree and pulled his carbine against his shoulder. A fly landed on a leaf beside his head, intent on its own world and unaware of the incipient violence humanity was about to create.

It is strange how humans and nature can co-exist side-by-side, yet each within its own orbit. Jesus, I am scared. Don't show it. Pretend you're as brave as Ashanti there, as immobile as Muckle Cheviot. Dear God, I hope I don't make a fool of myself. Concentrate on firing and forget what's coming your way, Andrew.

The three Galeka divisions gradually merged to form a single vast column, brandishing their weapons, and shouting to encourage each other. Cochrane's shells continued to pound them, tearing holes in their ranks, knocking warriors down and sending pieces of men high into the air.

How can they continue to attack through that? They must be brave men.

"They're nearly in range," Smith thundered. "Don't rush your shots, Bairdie; aim low and never mind their shooting. They always fire high and wild."

Andrew gave a weak smile. "There's a terrible lot of them."

"Every time the seven-pounder fires, there's less," Smith said.

Abernethy chewed on the stem of his pipe, puffed out smoke and hugged his Snider close to his cheek.

"Riflemen, fire!" Chalmers ordered.

Thank God! I can do something now rather than watch and wait.

Immediately Chalmers spoke, the police opened fire. Andrew took a deep breath, released it slowly, aimed into the mass of Galekas and fired. Without checking if he had hit his man, he ejected the spent round, thumbed in a brass cartridge, and fired again. He coughed as gun smoke caught at the back of his throat.

So, this is what it's like to be a soldier.

The combination of artillery and musketry stalled the Galekas' advance. They stopped, sought cover, and returned fire, with the muzzle flares stretching across the whole front. What sounded like a thousand bees buzzed and whined above the police's positions.

"Hold your ground," Chalmers ordered as the Fingoes also opened up. Gunsmoke wreathed the hillside, stinging Andrew's eyes and making him cough. He heard the whine of a bullet above his head and flinched when something scored the tree beside him. Splinters of bark and wood showered on his head.

"You couldn't hit a bull's arse with a banjo!" Hitchings sneered and laughed as he knocked back two tribesmen in two shots. "Keep bobbing up, boys, and I'll keep knocking you down!"

The mountain gun fired slowly, aiming for knots of the enemy to inflict more significant casualties, but the Galekas learned quickly, finding cover, and returning fire. For every shot the police and Fingoes fired, the Galekas fired four, adding to the noise with war cries, chants, and screams.

"Don't fire too fast," Smith warned Andrew. "Conserve your ammunition. We don't know how long this battle will last."

"The Xhosa don't like the seven-pounder," Abernethy said, still with the pipe between his teeth. "They don't understand where the explosions are coming from."

"Thank God for the guns," Hitchings said, thumbing in another cartridge.

He ducked as a bullet whined overhead, gave a lopsided smile, and glanced behind him.

"The enemy is over there." Duncan jerked a thumb towards the Galeka. "Face your front, Hitchings, and earn your pay!"

Andrew saw Simpson lying close to the ground, firing without aiming and whimpering whenever a shot passed overhead.

When a Galeka warrior stood up and ran a few paces forward, Andrew aimed, traversed his carbine as if he were pheasant shooting in Berwickshire, and squeezed the trigger. He saw the warrior leap in the air as the bullet hit and felt a surge of satisfaction, instantly followed by regret.

That is a human being, not a game bird. A moment later, Andrew heard a loud curse from the artillerymen.

"Something's up," Abernethy sounded worried. "The gun's stopped firing."

Andrew looked round to see the artillerymen clustered around the seven-pounder, talking animatedly. The artillery sergeant ran to Chalmers, who nodded.

"The gun will retire under Mr Cochrane and the escort!" Chalmers ordered.

"The bloody thing's broken!" Hitchings shouted. "The Xhosas will run right over us!"

"Riflemen, hold the line!" Chalmers ordered as the seven-pounder began a slow withdrawal, with its escort keeping close to ensure the Galekas did not charge to capture the weapon.

"Keep firing, Bairdie!" Smith said, as calm as ever. "Hitchings is right. Once the enemy realises we've no artillery support, they'll advance again."

"There go the Fingoes," Inspector Fraser said as their allies fled in sudden panic. Some dropped their weapons, and others merely turned and ran, leaving the few dozen police to face thousands of Galeka warriors.

The Galekas raised a loud shout, encouraging each other to charge.

"Time to go, boys," Smith said, glancing hopefully at Inspector Chalmers. "We can't hold this lot on our own."

Realising the gun no longer tormented them, the Galekas grew bolder, creeping closer and firing more accurately. Hitchings swore when a bullet buried into the ground at his feet, and another whined dangerously close to his head.

"Let's get out of here!"

Andrew reloaded, checked his ammunition pouch, and realised he had only a dozen cartridges left. "What happens now, Sergeant?" He tried to sound nonchalant even though his heart was pounding madly.

Smith ducked as a Galeka bullet whistled close overhead. "Whatever the officers say, Bairdie, when the Galekas come close enough to throw their assegais, old Ashanti leaves." He grinned. "Duty is all very well, but self-preservation is a wonderful thing. I already have an Ashanti slug in my leg, and I don't want any more African souvenirs, thank you kindly."

"We'll have to wait for orders." Andrew glanced over his shoulder, where

Inspector Chalmers was standing tall, sweeping the battlefield with his field glasses. Chalmers lowered his glasses to speak a few words to Fraser.

"Take some free advice, Bairdie," Smith said. "When it's a choice between saving your life and waiting for an officer to make up his mind, your life comes first every time."

A group of Galeka warriors rose and charged forward, screaming their battle cry. Andrew shot into them, saw one man fall and hastily reloaded, fumbling his cartridges as he controlled his nerves. Sergeant Duncan fired while Andrew closed the breech of his Snider. "Don't rush, Baird," Duncan said. "Treat a battle like a training exercise and follow the procedure we taught you."

"Yes, Sergeant," Andrew said.

"The Fingoes have scattered the horses," Hitchings yelled. "Look!"

Andrew glanced over his shoulder and saw several police horses had broken loose and were running in different directions. The retreating Fingoes were among them, with some grabbing mounts for themselves.

They'd better not take Lancelot.

"Get ready to run, boys," Smith said a second before Inspector Chalmers gave the order to retire.

"The Mounted Police will retire by numbers!"

"About bloody time," Smith said as Simpson turned and ran, losing his forage cap in the process.

Andrew heard a peculiar whizz and saw an assegai flick past him to thud into the tree at his side. The long blade embedded deeply into the trunk, with the shaft vibrating with the force of the throw.

"Come on, Bairdie!" Smith grabbed his arm. "This is no time to admire the view!"

The Galekas were advancing fast, encouraged by the diminished fire from the retreating allies. One warrior leapt in front of his comrades, carrying a traditional shield and a stabbing assegai and with a circlet of green feathers around his head. Smith turned and fired in the same movement, bringing the man down.

"And that's done for you, cully," Smith said. Dashing forward, he stooped, plucked two feathers from the warrior's head, and returned. Smiling, he attached the feathers to his forage cap. "I'll have these as souvenirs, my valiant Galeka friend."

"Form a firing line!" Chalmers ordered. "Inspector Fraser! Your troop will cover the retiral!"

"Yes, sir!" Fraser said. "Extended order, men. Fire at will, and don't let anybody fall behind."

"God help anybody the Galekas get hold of," Smith said.

Andrew rammed a cartridge into the breech of his Snider, knelt and aimed. The Galekas were about forty yards away, advancing at a run, with some firing and others throwing their assegais. Andrew fired and loaded without observing the effect of his shot. He heard the whizz-thud of another thrown assegai, fired again, and scrabbled for another cartridge in his ammunition pouch. "I'm running short," he said.

"We all are," Smith said.

"Mount and ride!" Fraser ordered. "Come on, lads. Time we were gone!"

Andrew saw that most of the police had already grabbed their horses and ridden down the slithering slope onto the road. He saw Lancelot running loose, seized the bridle and threw himself onto the saddle, thanking God that he was a good rider. When a Galeka warrior grabbed for the bridle, Andrew booted him away, glanced at a yelling face with wild eyes and kicked again, swearing. The tribesman fell back, and Andrew turned Lancelot and headed down the hill.

He heard somebody screaming and saw three Galekas repeatedly stabbing their assegais into the back of a dismounted policeman. He hesitated a second, saw the policeman lie still, decided he was already dead and thrust in his spurs.

More Galekas appeared, running alongside the retreating police. One warrior threw his assegai at Andrew, who ducked, swivelled in the saddle, and fired in the same movement. He did not see where the bullet landed but concentrated on controlling Lancelot.

"Rally here!" Inspector Chalmers stood in the middle of the road with a carbine in his hand and his forage cap missing. Half a dozen police rode to him, with Fraser on the road, counting his troop.

"Sergeant Duncan! Baird! Go to Inspector Chalmers!"

Andrew obeyed, panting, thankful for a return to disciplined normality. He noticed the seven-pounder was already half a mile away, with its escort ensuring no Galeka came close.

Smith reined up beside Andrew, panting, with sweat forming grooves through the dust on his sun-browned face. "That was a trifle hot," he said, loading his carbine. "I have three cartridges left."

Andrew nodded. "One less than me, Sergeant."

The Galekas hesitated when they saw a disciplined force waiting for them, but when they realised how few police there were, they began to work around the flanks.

"Pull back," Chalmers ordered. "One troop covering the other."

The police obeyed, keeping between the gun and the advancing Galekas until the tribesmen halted their pursuit and celebrated their victory with an impromptu dance.

"Listen to them celebrate," Hitchings said. "You'd think they'd won the Battle of Waterloo."

"Don't worry," Smith told him. "By the time they tell and retell the story of this little skirmish, they'll make it sound like they defeated the entire British Army rather than pushed back a handful of police."

Andrew said nothing; he was shaking with reaction after his first battle.

CHAPTER 3

"We lost six men and an officer," Smith said as they retired slowly towards Ibeka, "but I'd guess we accounted for at least two hundred of the enemy."

Andrew nodded and closed his eyes, seeing the sights and sounds of his first battle again.

I killed a man today, he thought. *Maybe more than one man. I do not know how many.*

Impressions of the battle returned to him. That unfortunate policeman, as the Galeka pounced on him, assegais stabbing. The tribesman he had shot and how the Snider bullet sent him spinning backwards. The spear that missed him by a couple of inches and thrummed into the tree.

"You're a veteran now." Smith broke into Andrew's thoughts.

"I don't feel like a veteran," Andrew said. He touched the gold signet ring on the index finger of his right hand, with his embossed initials intertwined. His mother had given him that on his seventeenth birthday as he left the family home for Sandhurst. "Do your best," she had said, with her white teeth gleaming in her dark face, "and remember who you are."

"I won't forget," Andrew had replied.

And now I am denying my identity every day. All I need is the crow of a cock, thrice repeated.

"Are you all right, Bairdie?" Abernethy asked, with his gaunt, haunted face a hint that he was also running from his past, and perhaps with more reason.

Everyone has a story.

"I am grand, thank you." Andrew mustered a smile.

"Who goes there?" Andrew heard the challenge when the weary police approached the Ibeka trenches.

"It's us, you stupid bugger!" Smith replied.

"Advance and be recognised." Andrew heard the tension in the sentry's voice. Two police rose from behind their entrenchments, with carbines ready to fire.

"Where did you lot come from?" a lanky corporal with a wispy beard asked. "We heard you were all dead!"

"Not yet, corporal," Smith snarled, "but if you don't take your finger off the trigger, we might soon be!"

"Sorry, Sergeant!" The corporal lifted the barrel of his carbine.

The garrison greeted the returning police as if they were heroes, more from relief than pleasure.

"We thought you were all dead." A dozen men repeated the sentry's statement.

"Not yet," Chalmers said tersely. "We'll have to get this place in condition to withstand an attack."

Andrew found the camp at Ibeka awash with rumours. A few frantic Fingoes had arrived with exaggerated reports of the skirmish, claiming the Galekas had massacred all the police and were advancing on the camp to finish the job. The police left in camp had heard the distant firing, believed the worst, and spent the night manning the defences and hourly expecting the entire Galeka army to arrive.

"How far behind you are the Fingoes?" a nervous constable asked.

"I have no idea," Abernethy replied coldly. "Why don't you go and find out? I'll hold the fort for you."

"Fill your ammunition pouches," Chalmers ordered tersely. "We don't know if the Galekas will follow us. Fraser, find a fresh horse, grab a bite, and take a patrol out to see what's happening."

"As you know, gentlemen," Inspector Fraser reminded his men. "We are right on the border of Galekaland, with the nearest European settlement, Butterworth, only seven miles distant. We are also on the best road, so if the Galekas want to invade the Cape, they'll have to pass us first."

Andrew looked at the small garrison of police and the shaken Fingoes and wondered at Fraser's confident tone.

The inspector continued. "That means we'll have to hold them here. Conversely, we can expect no help. As you know, the Butterworth road is badly rutted and marred by large boulders." He grinned. "We're on our own, fellows!"

Andrew glanced at Smith, who winked and adjusted the two green feathers in his forage cap. "Do you regret joining the Frontier Police now, Bairdie?"

Andrew pondered the question. *What would my father do, damn him? He would fight.*

"No, I don't regret a thing," Andrew said, fighting his fear.

"Good man!" Fraser clapped Andrew on the shoulder.

Apart from the police camp, Ibeka had a single European house-cum-store-cum-stable, with a man named John Barnett as the owner.

"Are the Galekas coming, Sergeant?" Barnett asked Smith.

"I'd expect so," Smith replied. "They'll be buoyant at their victory and imagine they can push us back to Cape Town."

"Then we're leaving," Barnett decided.

Loading his family and personal possessions onto a wagon, Barnett left Ibeka and chanced the rocky road to Butterworth. Within a few hours of Barnett's departure, a new commandant, Charles Griffiths, arrived to take command of the camp. Scorning the tents of the garrison, Griffiths requisitioned Barnett's house.

"This will do me," he said. "We'll have the store as a hospital. Inspector Chalmers! Move all the spare ammunition into the shop." He stalked around his new command, issuing orders to strengthen the defences.

"The commandant expects trouble," Hitchings said, eying the road to Butterworth.

"So do I," Smith said as the police sweated with spades on the hard ground, creating more rifle trenches around the encampment and filling and carrying sandbags for bastions for the three artillery pieces.

"Join the police and work up a sweat," Hitchings said as he dropped a sandbag in front of the central seven-pounder. "All this for five shillings a day, less expenses, which amounts to about ninepence in my pocket."

Andrew said nothing as he looked at the nearby hills. He guessed the Galekas would be there, spying on everything the police did. He could nearly taste the apprehension in the camp. These men were police, not trained regular soldiers. They had not signed up for a last stand against overwhelming numbers of warriors.

"I'm looking for volunteers," Griffiths shouted. "I want a party to return to the battlefield and recover the bodies of our men."

Andrew stepped forward, remembering the constable he had seen die. "I'll go, sir," he said and realised most of the police had volunteered. He saw Fraser watching him through narrowed eyes.

Smith put a hand on Andrew's arm. "Don't volunteer," he said quietly. "Take my advice, Bairdie and don't volunteer for anything. Keep your head below the parapet if you want to live longer. It's fourteen miles from here to Guadana, and that means you are marching for fourteen miles in hostile territory, with the Galekas watching you every foot of the way. Only a fool puts his head in a lion's mouth and expects it not to bite."

"I saw the Galekas killing one of our men," Andrew explained. "I wonder if I might have done more to help him."

"You couldn't," Smith told him. "It was every man for himself in that mad scramble down the hill."

"Baird," Chalmers said. "You come along too. Make sure you have ammunition and water."

"Yes, sir," Andrew said as Smith shook his head sorrowfully.

The patrol left half an hour later, with Chalmers leading twenty-five men towards the battlefield. Abernethy had also volunteered, riding alongside Andrew with his eyes dark and his mind evidently on something else.

"Back into your valley of death, eh, Baird?" Abernethy said. "Let's hope the Russians haven't loaded their cannon."

Andrew grinned, glad that Abernethy understood the literary associations.

Augmenting the police, a body of nervous Fingoes trotted at the side, carrying rifles and an assortment of assegais.

Chalmers nodded to Duncan. "Sergeant Duncan, take two experienced men and a dozen Fingoes as scouts. Watch for the Galekas."

Duncan nodded, selected a colonial and an ex-soldier and trotted ahead. The dust rose and slowly settled as Chalmers continued the slow advance. Riding three ranks back, Abernethy thrust an empty pipe into his mouth and hummed an unrecognisable tune.

Andrew felt as if he were venturing into hostile territory as the patrol advanced cautiously into Fingoland. Every man was on edge, with fingers curled around the triggers of their Sniders and their eyes constantly roving around the surrounding hills.

"I see two tribesmen," Abernethy said quietly. "They are beneath the crest of the hill, watching us."

Andrew stared without seeing anything.

"Don't look directly," Abernethy told him. "Look for things that don't belong, maybe a static shadow when others are moving or a solid block of one colour in a variegated bush. See that twisted tree beneath the skyline?"

"I see the tree," Andrew said.

"Good. Can you see the second tree close to the bole?"

Andrew nodded. "Yes."

"Well, that's a man watching us."

When Andrew concentrated, he could make out the figure of a man, partly concealed beneath a blanket. "I can barely see him," he admitted.

"You'll get your eye in," Abernethy reassured him.

"How do you know what to look for?" Andrew asked.

"I've knocked around a bit," Abernethy said.

About to ask more, Andrew saw the taut expression on Abernethy's face and closed his mouth. Some questions were best left unanswered.

The patrol continued, with Duncan and his scouts riding wide, inspecting isolated bushes, and swivelling to check the ground behind them. The watchers remained on the hill, following the police without descending.

"Here we are," Chalmers said when they reached the battle site. "Scouts, keep your eyes open."

"We will, sir," Duncan promised.

Andrew heard the buzz of flies before he realised they had been feasting on the bodies of the dead police. All the Galeka dead were gone, but the police remained beneath a black fur of insects.

"The Galeka have mutilated the bodies." Simpson sounded shocked.

"They always do," Abernethy told him. "It's their little way." He gave an entirely humourless smile. "Let's just pray the lads were dead before the Galeka began their butchery."

"Here's poor Evans." A man pointed to the man Andrew had seen killed. He stooped closer to inspect the body. "He's got seventeen assegai wounds, and the Galeka have ripped his stomach open."

"They rip open the stomach of everybody they kill," Abernethy said. "Such charming neighbours we have in this part of the world."

"Why?" Andrew asked. "Why tear the stomach open?"

"The Xhosa believe that if they don't, the ghost of those they kill will haunt them," Abernethy explained. "The Zulus do the same."

"Come on, lads," Chalmers ordered. "Sergeant Duncan, take twelve men and form a defensive perimeter. The rest of us will collect our dead."

Duncan selected the most experienced fighting men, leaving Andrew to help with the gruesome task of gathering the bodies.

The patrol recovered all the dead police, with men vowing vengeance when they saw the Galekas had stripped each man naked and mutilated the bodies. They had cut off one man's feet, scalped another and cut the fingers off two more.

"The witch doctors will use the knuckles for their potions," Abernethy said quietly as they rolled a man's remains into a blanket.

"These people live in the stone age." Andrew felt slightly sick at what he had witnessed.

"I think they've graduated to the iron age," Abernethy said grimly. "Certainly, no further."

"Gather them up, lads." Chalmers tied the ends of a blanket with his face taut. "Let's get back to camp and hope these bastards attack us at Ibeka."

Andrew could feel the alteration in the men's mood. In place of apprehension was a grimness. These men wanted to kill; they wanted vengeance for the mutilation of their friends and colleagues.

More Galeka warriors gathered to watch as the patrol returned to Ibeka. They moved parallel to the police, five hundred yards away on either flank, dodging in and out of cover with spears held horizontally above their heads. Occasionally they would shout a challenge, or a lone warrior ran towards the police but never approached sufficiently close to skirmish with the Fingoes.

"The Galekas seem confident," Andrew said.

Abernethy nodded. "They'll retell the story of the encounter at Guadana until they believe it's a major victory against us. By the time their grandchildren hear of it, they'll believe they conquered London and controlled the British Empire."

Andrew smiled. "A bit like our King Arthur conquering Rome," he said.

"Exactly so," Abernethy agreed. "Halloa! Something's happening!"

"What's that?" Andrew asked, lifting his carbine. He saw a swirl on the path a hundred yards away as some of the Fingoes ran back, shouting.

"It's the *IsiDawane*," one of the Fingoes said, immediately cowering behind Andrew.

"It's the what?"

"The *isiDawane,*" Abernethy explained. "I've heard of it in Zululand, but I didn't know it was also common in the Transkei. It's the Xhosa version of a werewolf or vampire, a mythical creature that hunts people to eat their brains."

"Whatever it is," Andrew said, staring ahead, "it's not alone. There are three of them."

Abernethy swore as the Fingo looked even more terrified. Three creatures emerged from behind a copse of thorn trees, with any remaining Fingoes taking one glance and running. "These things are worse than any *isiDawanes*," Abernethy said, altering the angle of his carbine so the muzzle pointed forward. "They're witch doctors."

"Witches?" Andrew remembered Smith's explanation of the power these people had and eyes them curiously. He lowered his carbine, despite seeing other police ready to fire.

The three women were of average height, very overweight and with animal entrails wrapped around their legs. What Andrew could see of their bodies was heavily tattooed and covered in what he hoped was red earth, while a variety of animal and human teeth and bones covered the short length of hide that passed for clothing around their waists.

"I was right," Andrew said. "These people are still in the stone age."

"Dear God," Simpson breathed.

"God's got little to do with these beauties," Abernethy said.

Simpson levelled his carbine, aiming at the women beside him. "I say we finish them off and do the world a favour."

Andrew shook his head, watching the nearest witch doctor with a snake-skin topping her matted hair. The snake's mouth gaped open, showing long teeth. For a second, Andrew thought the snake moved as if a spark of life still existed within the empty skin. He blinked, and the snake was static, although a necklace of human knucklebones rattled around the witch doctor's neck. She looked at him through dark, knowing eyes.

"Don't shoot them," Andrew said. "We don't understand their religion, but we should not interfere."

Andrew remembered his father taking him aside when they first discussed his proposed military career. "If you are ever at or beyond the fringes of Empire, my boy," Andrew's father had said. "The first and most important rules are never to interfere with the local women or religion. People will accept wars and a leadership change, but never that." He had given one of his rare smiles. "We are soldiers, and soldiers fight soldiers or warriors. We should always be merciful to women and children, whatever their station in life."

"They are terrible things," Simpson said, staring at the closest witch doctor. "They do horrible things."

"To our eyes, they are terrible," Andrew agreed. "Perhaps they are not terrible to the Xhosa. Let them go in peace."

Simpson lifted his carbine. "You can't tell me what to do!" He aimed directly at the closest woman until Andrew pushed down the barrel of his carbine.

"She's no threat to us," Andrew said.

Sergeant Duncan nodded. "Baird is right. Let them go in peace."

The witch doctor had not flinched when Simpson pointed his carbine. She stepped closer to Andrew and tapped him on the chest with a gnu's tail.

"You are not who you claim." Although she spoke in Xhosa, Andrew understood every word. "We shall meet twice more. The first time will be a disappointment, and by the second, you will know the truth." She bumped the gnu's tail off him twice more, with her dark eyes seeming to penetrate his soul.

"The truth, Mother?" Andrew asked in English. "What truth?"

"Beware of a foe who is a friend and take care of the friend who is a foe." The witch ignored Andrew's interruption. "Expect grief and loss. You have much blood in your future and a woman who will wait for you."

The witch tapped Andrew a final time with the gnu's tail and walked away unhurried. She spat on Simpson as she passed, and her two companions also touched Andrew. He found he was not afraid.

"What did she say? I didn't understand a word," Simpson said, wiping the spittle from his tunic with an expression of disgust.

"It was as clear as daylight," Andrew told him.

Sergeant Duncan shook his head. "Not to me; it wasn't." He looked curiously at Andrew. "You've hardly been in Africa long enough to get a suntan, yet you already understand Xhosa?"

"Only a few words," Andrew said and closed his mouth. He did not understand what had just happened, and it left him feeling unsettled. He did not look forward to the bloodshed in his future or the disappointment, sorrow, and loss, but the woman waiting for him was interesting.

"Beware of a foe who is a friend and take care of the friend who is a foe," Andrew repeated the witch's words to himself. *That makes no sense. "Expect grief and loss. You have much blood in your future and a woman who will wait for you." I'd expect grief and loss in a war, but which woman will wait for me? I don't know any women.*

CHAPTER 4

The camp at Ibeka was on high alert when they returned, with the outlying picket challenging them behind a loaded rifle.

"Returning patrol," Chalmers replied and led his patrol in.

"You should have brought in your new friends," Simpson said as Andrew dismounted. "You could have shown them round the defences and made them a nice cup of tea."

"Maybe next time," Andrew replied. He felt Simpson's eyes on him and knew he had made an enemy.

Simpson hawked and spat on the ground. Of average height and wiry, he had a nearly permanent sneer on his face and a jaundiced look on life. Andrew watched as Simpson stepped to Hitchings and pushed the incident out of his mind.

I wonder who the woman is who waits for me.

He allowed himself a smile, imagining a tall blonde with bright blue eyes.

I have never had any success with women. The witch was talking nonsense, like the rest of their kind.

As the Galekas grew bolder, pushing small parties of warriors close to the pickets, the garrison of Ibeka tightened their procedures. Griffiths ordered regular mounted patrols, with men sleeping in their clothes, wearing their ammunition belts and with their Sniders constantly at their sides.

"We're on permanent watch," Abernethy said. "Kreli hates us, and pushing our patrol back will have increased his warrior's confidence. Once the witches have doctored the warriors, they'll come at us."

Andrew nodded. His first experience of battle had not been favourable, and he was desperate to prove himself.

I don't want to live in my father's shadow.

"Come on, Bairdie; we're on outlying picket duty this morning."

Andrew saddled and mounted Lancelot and joined Fraser. The inspector led them half a mile into Fingoland and stopped at a small group of thorn trees.

"This will do, lads," Fraser said. "Our Fingoes tell us that the Galekas have been extremely active these last two days, dancing and singing, with a few parties probing into Fingo territory."

"Do we expect trouble, sir?" Andrew asked.

"Always," Fraser replied with a slight smile. "When the Galekas dance and sing, they are preparing for war."

The morning passed slowly, with a breeze ruffling dust from the track and a small herd of deer running past the picket. Fraser led a short patrol around the area, returning after an uneventful hour.

"It's quiet as the proverbial grave," he said.

"I can feel that something's going to happen, sir," Abernethy replied. "There's something in the atmosphere."

Andrew nodded. The witch doctor's words still reverberated around his head. *Who is this woman who is waiting for me? I hope I meet her soon.*

"Dust, Bairdie!" Abernethy said tersely. "Over there!"

"Have a look, Baird," Fraser ordered.

Andrew rode Lancelot to a slight rise a hundred yards ahead and peered into Galekaland. He returned at a fast trot.

"Sir! The Galekas are coming. Horsemen!"

Inspector Fraser cantered to the rise and lifted his field glasses. "A powerful force of mounted tribesmen under a flag of truce," he said and raised his voice. "Retire to the camp, men. I don't trust them to meet a small group of police, truce or not. The temptation to attack might be too much for them. You're the rear guard, Sergeant Duncan."

"Come on, Bairdie," Abernethy said cheerfully. "Things are happening again."

The police withdrew to Ibeka, with Duncan's rear guard constantly turning to watch the advancing tribesmen. A bugle sounded the alert, and the police ran to the entrenchments, carbines ready. They threw themselves into position, stared outward and waited for the Galekas.

Andrew glanced upward, where the Union flag fluttered fitfully against a bright sky.

"Trust to God," Abernethy murmured, "and keep your powder dry."

Andrew checked his carbine was loaded and murmured Tennyson's words. "Theirs not to make reply, Theirs not to reason why, Theirs but to do and die."[1]

Abernethy grinned. "Let's hope it's more doing than dying," he said. "Here come the Galekas."

"Not once or twice in our fair island story, the path of duty was the way to glory," [2]Andrew replied.

"If you must quote Tennyson," Abernethy said, "wait until after the fighting's over." He looked across at Andrew. "And sometimes through the mirror blue,

The knights come riding two and two."[3]

Andrew grinned. "Imagine meeting an educated man out here in Africa."

"This madness has come on us for our sins," [4]Abernethy said. "Here they come, Bairdie!"

Andrew nodded, aware that Abernethy had opened a gate into his soul. *What did Abernethy mean by that last quote? What sins has he committed?*

When the Galekas approached within three hundred yards of the camp, Captain Robertson and an escort of two men rode to meet them.

"That's far enough!" Robertson snapped, in English and Xhosa.

While the bulk of the Galekas halted, their leader and half a dozen men rode forward under the white flag. The remainder, which Andrew estimated at five hundred men, remained in a hostile clump.

Abernethy held his carbine close to his cheek, aiming at the leading Galeka. "They're just waiting for their chance to attack. Thank God for the guns."

Andrew glanced back at the camp, where the artillerymen were rapidly loading the seven-pounders.

"We are honoured today," Abernethy said. "That's Sidgow under the flag, one of Kreli's sons, the crown prince if you like."

"Does he speak English?" Andrew asked.

"Quite probably," Abernethy replied. "Captain Robertson knows Xhosa, so I'll translate the gist for you."

Andrew nodded. "I'll have to learn the local languages," he said. "I only know enough to say hello."

Yet I understood every word the witches said.

Sidgow greeted Captain Robertson with a wide grin that fooled nobody. "My father, Kreli, sent me to apologise for killing the white policemen." His words carried clearly to the forward positions, and Abernethy translated for Andrew.

"Now Sidgow says the Galekas only wanted to fight the Fingoes, who are terrible cattle thieves." Abernethy nodded. "That's possibly true. I suspect Kreli's men were surprised to see us in Fingoland but attacked when they saw how few we were."

Andrew grunted. A bead of sweat rolled from his forehead down his face.

Abernethy continued. "Sidgow says his father likes the police and has no desire to fight them, so he is sending some oxen for us to eat."

"That's very kind of him," Andrew murmured.

Abernethy smiled. "Now Sidgow is asking Captain Robertson to kindly march away with his police and allow him to attack the Fingoes. If the captain refuses, Sidgow says he'd return with a larger force and hammer the Fingoes anyway, police or no police."

"I can believe that." Andrew shifted his hand. The steel barrel of the carbine was hot to the touch.

Captain Robertson shook his head and told Sidgow the police were not moving and asked why Sidgow had brought a five-hundred-man escort on a friendly visit.

"We're going into Fingoland," Sidgow replied with a wide smile.

"No, you're not," Robertson denied and jerked a thumb towards the three artillery pieces. While he had been talking, the gunners had dragged the guns outside the encampment and aimed them toward the Galekas. "I have ordered these guns to point toward your men. Each gun contains case shot. That means there are sixty-three bullets in each gun." Robertson waited for the inference to sink in before he continued.

"Now take your men back to your own land, Sidgow, and tell your father Kreli that if he crosses into Fingoland, we will stop him. That is my word and the word of the government."

Robertson's speech seemed to hang in the air as the two parties faced each other. A breeze ruffled the Union flag, with the red, white, and blue opening for a moment and then closing again, as if Queen Victoria had peered out from Windsor to observe the fringes of her empire.

"What happens now?" Andrew asked.

"Wait and see," Abernethy replied and gave a twisted smile. "Pray to God and keep your powder dry."

"Warty Cromwell could not have said it better," Andrew said.

Sidgow returned to his men, with the wind flapping the white flag, and a few moments later, the entire Galeka force turned around and rode back to Galekaland.

Abernethy let out his breath. "That was interesting," he said.

Andrew heard the strain in his voice.

"They'll be back," Smith gave his opinion. "And next time, they won't be under a flag of truce." He produced a short clasp knife and began to clean the bowl of his pipe. "Don't relax yet, boys."

Rather than wait for the Galekas to attack, Captain Robertson sent another patrol into Fingoland.

"Fraser, take a dozen men and see what's happening. Check the frontier," Robertson ordered. "Don't get involved in anything you can't handle, and for God's sake, don't leave any wounded behind."

"Yes, sir," Inspector Fraser agreed as Andrew joined the volunteers filing behind him.

"You're an observation patrol, not a fighting patrol," Robertson reminded. He frowned when he saw Andrew. "Were you not with the last incursion, Baird?"

"Yes, sir," Baird agreed.

Robertson nodded. "Don't take too many chances, son. The good Lord only grants us a certain amount of luck."

Baird smiled. "Yes, sir. Thank you." He saw Smith shaking a disapproving head, ignored Simpson's poisonous glare, and trotted outside the camp and into Fingoland.

Fraser advanced cautiously, marching with a screen of Fingo scouts and halting whenever they saw movement. Twice the Fingoes ran back to report activity, and Robertson had to order them back in front.

"The Fingoes are nervous," Andrew said.

"The Fingoes know what the Galekas are capable of," Abernethy replied, glancing over his shoulder. "I'm a bit nervous that the enemy will get behind us and cut us off from Ibeka."

They moved slowly, holding their Sniders in capable hands, each man studying the ground all around until the Fingo scouts ran back, talking rapidly.

"Sergeant Duncan," Fraser said. "Take fine men to see what's happening up there. I can't understand the Fingoes gabbling!"

"Come on, Bairdie," Abernethy said. "The Fingoes say there are thousands of Galeka warriors ahead." He grinned. "I'd estimate about fifty men herding cattle."

"Into the valley of death," Andrew said as they passed the Fingoes and pushed on. "Come on, Lancelot!"

They had not gone a quarter of a mile before Duncan held up his hand. "That's far enough, boys. We'd better warn the camp that the Fingoes were correct."

Kreli had formed up his Galekas on either side of the road, three solid columns of warriors in fighting formation. Some waved their weapons in defiance when they saw the police.

"Kreli knew we would send a patrol," Abernethy said as Inspector Fraser ordered a rapid withdrawal to Ibeka. "He's waiting to ambush us."

As the police trotted back down the road, their hoofbeats echoing from the surrounding hills, the Fingoes ran ahead, outpacing the horses in their eagerness to find safety.

"Don't look now, Bairdie, but somebody's following us," Abernethy said.

The Galekas tramped behind Fraser's patrol, remaining in their formation, and slowly creeping closer. The proximity of the tribesmen unnerved some of the police, who kicked their horses into a trot.

"Don't run, boys!" Fraser shouted. "Keep a steady pace and watch the flanks."

The Galekas closed to within three hundred yards, shouting, waving their weapons and challenging the police to stand and fight.

"They want us to fire at them," Abernethy said. "Keep moving, Bairdie."

"I will," Andrew promised.

"We'd better hurry up a little," Fraser decided as the Galekas closed the distance, chanting rhythmically. The police increased their speed, so their withdrawal nearly turned into an inglorious retreat. Andrew heard the crack of a rifle and turned around in his saddle.

"Don't look back, Bairdie," Abernethy warned. "Concentrate on your riding."

More musketry followed, with the whine of a bullet passing far overhead and then the patrol turned the final corner and saw the outlying picket.

"What's the to-do, boys?" a corporal sentry asked.

"About three thousand Galekas is the to-do!" Fraser reined up. "Get your men back to the camp, Corporal."

"Jesus! I mean, yes, sir!" the corporal replied. "Mount up, lads! You heard the inspector!"

The sentries at Ibeka camp were on full alert when the patrol returned.

"The Fingoes told us what happened," Smith said as Andrew dismounted. "I warned you not to volunteer for anything." He grinned. "Isn't life on the frontier interesting?"

"That's two victories the Galekas can boast about now," Abernethy said. "Kreli will claim he chased away a full British army, infantry, cavalry, and guns, and he'll want the full hat trick. If I were Commandant Griffiths, I'd expect the Galekas to attack Ibeka soon."

When Andrew stared back into Fingoland, the road was empty except for drifting dust. Kreli's Galekas had not followed the patrol to the British camp.

There was no valley of death then, and what did that witch mean that a woman would wait for me?

Captain Robertson and Commandant Griffiths increased the police patrols and ensured the vedettes were alert, watching for movement along the frontier. A stream of eager Fingo spies informed them that the Galekas were gathering at Kreli's Great Kraal.

"That's the capital of Galekaland," Abernethy said. "Or the nearest thing Kreli can have as a capital." He chewed the end of his pipe. "I'd say Kreli is preparing some mischief on a larger scale than before."

Andrew cleaned his carbine for the fourth time that day. "Do you think he is preparing to attack us?"

"Kreli will either attack us or make a major incursion into Fingoland," Abernethy said. "Maybe both. If Kreli removes the British garrison at Ibeka – us – he can destroy the Fingoes and grab all their cattle."

Andrew looked along the barrel of his carbine. "We'll be fighting again, then."

"I'd say so," Abernethy agreed.

Andrew wondered if his father had felt so nervous before a battle. He glanced over the garrison, assessing the fighting capability of the men he was beginning to know. "How many men can Kreli field?"

Abernethy removed the pipe from his mouth. "Now that, Mr Baird, I could not tell you. Five thousand? Six thousand, maybe even seven thousand. A fair number against our little garrison."

Inspector Fraser joined them. "Discussing the situation, lads?"

"Yes, sir." Andrew scrambled to attention.

"Stand easy, Baird. If the Galekas come, we'll hold them," Fraser encouraged with a faint smile.

"Ibeka is not the best defensive site," Andrew said, looking around.

"Oh?" Fraser raised his eyebrows, semi-amused at such an observation from a junior constable. "What makes you say that Baird?"

"It's the position, sir," Andrew said. "We have a rising slope to the east, with a stony ridge at the top, so the Galekas can fire down on us, negating our protective wall."

Fraser nodded, checking Andrew's facts. "Carry on, Baird. Share your wisdom with us." He retained his tolerant smile.

Andrew pointed northwest and north. "Over there, the ground is level, with boulders and rocks to give cover to the Galekas. They can advance against us or snipe in safety. In the south, it's not too bad, a downward slope, but split by a stream and backed by a hill. The Galekas can use the bed of the stream for cover."

"We have artillery," Fraser said as his smile faded.

"The guns are only effective on the south side, sir," Andrew said. "Elsewhere, the low ground with plenty of cover favours the Galekas."

Fraser nodded. "Where did you get such tactical knowledge, Baird? You're fresh out of Britain, aren't you?"

"Yes, sir. A few months ago." Andrew hesitated for a moment. "I come from a military family, sir, and I must have picked it up somewhere."

I cannot tell the whole truth.

"A military family, eh?" Fraser said, with his eyes narrowed curiously. "You're from a long line of redcoats?"

"Something like that, sir," Baird said.

"Well, keep it up, and if you survive, you might make an officer someday," Fraser said. "How would you like that, eh, Baird? You could go home as a lieutenant or even a captain. Wouldn't that be a feather in your cap?"

"Yes, sir," Andrew agreed.

If only you knew!

"Aye." Smith hawked and spat on the ground when Fraser moved away. "All you have to do is survive, Bairdie-boy, and that might not be so easy if Kreli attacks."

Andrew nodded, wishing he had kept his mouth shut. He saw Fraser talking to Captain Robertson, both glancing in his direction. *I don't want them to ask too many questions about me.*

Three times that day, frightened Fingoes arrived at the camp with reports about Galekas appearing at various points on their border, and each time, Commandant Griffiths sent small parties of police to stiffen the Fingo defences.

"If Griffiths carries on as he's doing," Simpson said, "he'll leave us with three men and a one-legged dog to defend Ibeka."

"I'd rather have a one-legged dog than you, Simpson." Abernethy never concealed his dislike for Simpson. He lifted his tobacco pouch, realised it was empty and sighed. "You're right, though. We're already dangerously thin on the ground."

Augmenting the hundred and forty police, around two thousand Fingoes camped around and within the police base, with sub-inspector Allan Maclean, sub-inspector Veltman and a few local Europeans as officers.

"If I were Kreli," Abernethy said as they manned the trenches in the fading hour before dawn, "I'd attack now while we are undermanned."

"Kreli must agree with you," Smith said. "Look what's approaching."

A dozen terrified Fingoes ran toward Ibeka, keeping to their side of the narrow footpath that formed the boundary between Fingo and Galeka territory. The look on their faces was sufficient warning.

"Kreli is coming! Thousands of Galekas are coming!"

"From which direction?" Fraser stopped one of the refugees.

"That way!" The man pointed to the south, struggled free, and ran after his companions.

"Here we go," Hitchings said, smoothing a hand over the stock of his Snider. "This time tomorrow, we'll either be heroes or dead."

"Let's hope it's the former," Abernethy said. "I've always wanted to be a hero, feted by attractive women, drinking champagne and getting the best tables at London restaurants."

Smith shook his head. "It won't happen like that, Nethy. Nobody has heard of the Galekas, and I doubt one man in a hundred even knows where the Cape Frontier is, let alone that we're struggling to contain hostile tribes here. At the most, we'll get three lines in an inside page."

"Abernethy nodded. "You're probably right, Sergeant. The press is concentrating on the Russian-Turkish war or is over in Afghanistan. There's always trouble in Afghanistan. They'll send for General Roberts or Fighting Jack Windrush over there."

Andrew started at the name and quickly changed the subject. "Shall I ride forward and see if the Fingoes are exaggerating, sir?"

Fraser nodded. "Off you go, Baird. Take care."

Glad to be active, Andrew mounted Lancelot and pushed forward. Within half a mile, he realised the Fingoes were correct. Kreli had mustered the Galeka army on the hill south of Ibeka. He saw them form into columns of squares with a precision that told of long practice, halt and begin a deep sonorous chant. The bulk of the Galeka army was infantry, nearly equally divided between men with assegais and shields and others with rifles. The Galeka cavalry stood on the flanks, less disciplined than the infantry but still dangerous.

"Come on, boy," Andrew whispered to Lancelot. "Time we weren't here."

"They're coming," Andrew reported what he had seen.

"How many?" Fraser asked laconically.

"Between seven and eight thousand," Andrew estimated. "Riflemen, cavalry and spearmen."

"That must be the bulk of Kreli's army," Fraser said. "Sergeant Duncan, please inform the commandant that Kreli is coming with around seven thousand men, and we can expect him shortly."

"Very good, sir." Duncan saluted and headed for the main camp.

Simpson whistled and glanced over his shoulder. "We'll be hard-pressed to hold that lot off!"

Abernethy grunted. "At this moment, Kreli is telling his men that the witch doctors have made them invulnerable to our bullets. What a shock they'll get when we knock them down like skittles at a fairground."

Griffiths gave final orders to defend Ibeka. "Bring the horses inside the trenches," he said calmly. "Saddle and bridle them and secure them to the picket rope. Not you, Sergeant Duncan; I want you and three men to keep their mounts for scouting."

"Yes, sir," Duncan acknowledged.

The picket rope was in the house garden, stretched from tree to tree, with the confused horses attached. It would be the work of an instant to release them, ready for a hurried retreat or an equally rapid sally against the tribesmen.

Griffiths paced the defences, giving orders. "I want open ammunition boxes ready for use. Place them behind the walls and have water barrels nearby. Fighting is thirsty work."

The police ate a hasty breakfast, each man watching for the Galeka army approaching from the south. Andrew disguised his nervousness under false joviality that fooled nobody. The men shrugged off their coats, exchanged banter, lit their pipes, and readied themselves for the coming battle.

"Watch my back, Baird, and I'll watch yours," Abernethy said quietly.

"I'll do that," Andrew said. He watched a pair of vultures circling above, checked his rifle, counted his cartridges, and took a deep breath.

Here we go again.

CHAPTER 5

"Sergeant Duncan," Griffiths ordered. "Take three men and watch what Kreli does. Report back the minute he moves towards us."

Andrew watched Duncan canter forward into hostile territory.

They look very lonely out there.

"Don't stray far from the horses," Hitchings advised. "If the day goes against us, we can grab a horse and bolt."

Andrew listened, unsure if Hitchings was serious.

"You saw what the Galekas did to our dead after our last encounter," Hitchings continued. "I'm not waiting for Kreli to chop me up like that."

"You're damned right, Hitch," Simpson said. "If they bastards get too close, you won't see old Simmy for dust and small pebbles." He grinned as if he had said something clever.

Abernethy whistled a tune which Andrew recognised as Rossini's *Largo al Factotum.*

"That's a little out of place here." Andrew forced a smile.

"Nonsense," Abernethy said. "One can sing opera anywhere. It brings a little culture to the midst of barbarity, and there's nothing more barbaric than a battlefield."

"That's true," Andrew agreed.

Come on, Kreli! The waiting is worse than the fighting.

At half past nine that morning, Sergeant Duncan appeared with his men at his side. He trotted past the outer pickets, looking dusty but relaxed.

"What's happening, Sergeant?" Abernethy asked.

"A couple of thousand horsemen have joined Kreli," Duncan reported laconically. "They're approaching the ridge on the south."

"That's all we need," Hitchings said, glancing at the horse lines.

Abernethy returned to whistling Rossini, puffing out blue smoke with every note. He winked at Andrew. "Shouldn't be long now, Bairdie. Trust in

God and keep your powder dry." Andrew felt the vibration of thousands of feet on the ground before he heard the Galekas' war song rising from the ridge.

Smith peered ahead. "Here they come, boys. Look to your front."

Andrew took a deep breath, listening to the increasing chorus from ahead. He raised his carbine to his shoulder.

"Come on, Kreli," he said softly.

The Galekas emerged from a curtain of dust, with their mounted men concentrating on the ridge to the police left.

"There are thousands of them," Hitchings muttered.

"All the more targets, Hitchings," Fraser shouted with forced cheerfulness. "Even you can't miss."

Hitchings glared without replying. He had often boasted of his marksmanship.

The Galeka infantry advanced in three columns, shouting, and brandishing their weapons.

"They think they're bloody Frenchmen," Abernethy said. "And we're Wellington's army at Waterloo."

Andrew realised he was gripping his carbine so tightly his knuckles were white. He forced himself to relax.

The Galeka columns marched into a depression in the undulating ground, momentarily disappearing from view.

"Get ready, boys," Griffiths warned. "When they reappear, they'll only be twelve hundred yards away."

"Come, my Galeka friends," Andrew murmured and quoted Tennyson again. "It's not too late to seek a newer world." [1] He felt his heartbeat increase, wiped the sweat from his forehead, squinted down the barrel of his carbine and listened to Abernethy's singing.

When the Galekas reappeared, their skirmishers advanced to the front, moving with more discipline than Andrew expected, a whole host of lightly armed men trotting towards Ibeka.

Andrew aimed until Smith shook his head. "Don't waste your bullets, Bairdie. Let the Fingoes deal with the skirmishers."

Griffiths snapped an order, and Commander Veldtman led five hundred Fingoes outside the entrenchments on the British left flank. They faced the Galeka skirmishes in the rough, border-strewn ground beyond the British defences, exchanging taunts and bullets without causing many casualties. Allan Maclean did the same on the right, firing his revolver as he encouraged his hundreds of Fingo warriors to face the attackers.

"Advance, boys!" Griffiths ordered. "We're not waiting for Kreli to come to us. Extend into skirmishing order and meet them front and left."

Andrew took a deep breath and copied his colleagues. He held his Snider firmly and walked towards the Galeka mass. The noise was appalling as the Fingoes and Galeka skirmishers shouted, yelled, screamed, and fired at each other.

“Here comes the cavalry,” Smith said, nodding towards the ridge, where the mounted Galekas began to pour towards Ibeka.

Griffiths raised his field glasses to study the Galeka cavalry. “Artillery!” He raised his voice. “Target the horsemen!”

Two of the seven-pounders swivelled towards the ridge and fired, with both shells screaming over the horsemen without exploding.

“That was pointless,” Hitchings muttered. “What the hell are we doing?” He slowed down until Sergeant Duncan roared at him.

“Keep in line, Hitchings!”

The police tried a couple of rockets next, with greater success. The whoosh and fiery trail of the rockets terrified the Galeka horses, with some panicking and fleeing, carrying their riders to the rear.

“Artillery,” Griffiths shouted. “Switch your targets. Hit these columns!”

The Galeka infantry was within a thousand yards of the entrenchment, a mass of warriors moving forward steadily as their skirmishers sparred with the Fingoes and the police readied their carbines.

“Can we fire, sir?” Simpson asked.

“Not yet. We might hit the Fingoes,” Fraser replied.

“Bugger the Fingoes,” Simpson muttered.

“Common shell!” Lieutenant Cochrane shouted, and all three seven-pounders fired at once. Only nine hundred yards away, the columns were easy targets, and the shells exploded in their midst, each killing and maiming a dozen men. The column shivered, and the police stepped closer.

“Wait!” Griffiths ordered as the Galeka skirmished merged with the main columns. Veldtman and Maclean pulled their Fingoes back, giving the police a clear field of fire.

“Now! Volleys!” Griffiths ordered, and the police opened fire. The sharp crack of the Sniders added to the ear-splitting bang of the mountain guns while the rockets hissed and flared among the Galeka cavalry.

Andrew aimed and fired, feeling the comfortable jerk as the carbine rammed against his shoulder. His nerves eased as soon as he knew he was hitting back. He loaded, aimed, and fired again on the word of command, tasting the now familiar gun smoke.

“They’re firing at us!” Simpson howled, ducking.

“The dirty dogs! How dare they?” Smith mocked, laughing. “Keep firing, Simmy!”

Andrew saw men fall in the front line of the Galekas, toppling to the ground as bullets and shells hammered them.

“They’re slowing,” Smith shouted as the Galeka columns began to fragment.

“Fire!” Fraser ordered, and Andrew fired into the column, reloaded, and watched as the Galekas withdrew, still in good order despite their piled up dead and writhing wounded.

“One more volley!” Griffiths ordered, and the police fired again, reloaded, and waited for orders as gun smoke drifted in a grey-white haze.

The Galeka cavalry milled outside rifle range on the flanks, with the police rockets hissing amongst the horses, causing more panic than casualties.

"They're useless." Smith dismissed the mounted men in two words.

Andrew checked his Snider, counted his cartridges, and forced a smile. "We've pushed them back." He was no longer nervous.

"They'll return," Smith told him casually. "Say what you like about the Galekas, but they're not cowards."

Andrew looked ahead, where the Galeka dead lay individually, where the Sniders had got them, and in bloody heaps where the shells had landed. "No," he agreed. "No cowards would have run into musketry and artillery fire as they did."

"We showed them!" Hitchings shouted, suddenly brave. "I must have killed at least three."

"Did you see that last one I shot?" Simpson boasted. "I caught him right in the head. His skull exploded, with brains all over the place."

"Here they come again!" Abernethy shouted, slamming his Snider into his shoulder.

"Independent firing!" Griffiths ordered as the Galekas advanced a second time. No longer in mass columns, they had extended into skirmishing formation, presenting less of a target for the artillery.

"Case shot!" Cochrane decided, and each seven-pounder loaded with the canvas bags, each holding sixty-three bullets.

"Aim at the densest masses," Cochrane commanded. "Fire!"

The guns acted like giant shotguns, with each shot blasting a swathe into the advancing Galekas while the rocket men kept the enemy cavalry busy.

Andrew aimed, fired, and reloaded, feeling the acrid gun smoke nip his eyes and bite into his mouth and nostrils. He took a drink of smoke-tainted water and fired again, with the Galekas hardly seen through the smoke. It was impossible to target individual warriors, so Andrew fired where he hoped the enemy clustered most thickly.

"Keep firing, lads!" Fraser shouted. He walked the length of the police lines, firing and encouraging, exposing himself to the torrent of shots from the Galekas.

"They're firing high!" Andrew shouted as he heard a constant whine of bullets passing over his head.

"They always do," Smith told him. "And thank your God for that. We'll be in major trouble if the bastards ever learn to aim."

"They're slowing!" Fraser ordered, and Andrew realised he had been firing automatically. The steady firing of the police broke the Galeka attack, and they melted away, leaving their dead and wounded on the ground.

"Cease fire!" Fraser ordered. "Sergeants! Report any casualties to me!"

"Drink," Smith advised his section. "If you have anything to eat, take it now before the Galekas return. These lads won't give up yet."

Andrew realised he was ravenous and munched on a hard biscuit before drinking the smoke-tainted water.

"Check your ammunition," Fraser advised, pacing the ranks with encouragement and advice. He stopped at the newest members of his troop. "How are you doing, lads?"

"Killing them, sir." Simpson gave a greasy grin.

"Fine, sir," Hitchings said.

"Fine, sir," Andrew replied, replenishing his ammunition pouch from the chest. "Thank you."

"Good lads," Fraser continued his rounds.

"Here they come again," Abernethy shouted, his voice hoarse from smoke.

The Galekas had learned caution and advanced more slowly, hiding behind rocks and bushes and firing at the police, and Fingoes. They halted, rushed to the next piece of cover, and fired.

"When they get close," Smith advised. "Pick your man. Wait until he breaks cover and shoot him."

Andrew nodded, feeling the sweat trickling down his face. He blinked to clear his vision and sighted on a tall, athletic man who moved from rock to rock. For a moment, he was back on a Northumberland moor, shooting pheasants as a gentle rain cooled the sportsmen, and then his Galeka moved again, and Andree fired through instinct.

The warrior staggered but continued, still yelling. Andrew reloaded hastily, cursing as he nearly dropped the cartridge. He took a deep breath, slotted the cartridge home, and lifted the carbine to his shoulder.

The Galeka had found cover. Andrew swore softly and ducked when a bullet whined close above his head.

That fellow is a better shot than most.

He scanned the battlefield, ignoring the twitching wounded and the dead, searching for his man. Drifting smoke obscured his vision until Andrew saw the flash from a rifle muzzle, and something burrowed into the ground at his feet.

That fellow is aiming at me.

Andrew felt a peculiar sensation of vulnerability. He was no longer a cog in the official machinery fighting a faceless enemy but one man opposed to another. He instinctively knew that the Galeka firing at him was the same man he was attempting to shoot.

Suddenly the battle took on a new intensity. Andrew was aware of the men to his left and right, the harsh bark of the artillery, the hoarse shouts of the men and the sharp crackle of musketry, but only his personal duel mattered.

You and me, my Galeka foe. One of us must die today.

Andrew knelt with his carbine pressed into his shoulder and the barrel hot from use. He waited, focussing on the last position he had seen his enemy.

The following bullet was high, but the Galeka had momentarily exposed his arm. Andrew fired, with his shot crashing into the man's elbow. He reloaded feverishly, hoping to catch his opponent as he jerked upright, but the Galeka disappeared.

Where are you, my worthy foe?

"They're retreating!" Abernethy shouted as the Galekas, hammered by artillery and musketry, pulled back.

"Help them on their way," Fraser ordered.

"It doesn't seem fair to shoot men running away," Andrew said, looking for his wounded opponent.

"The more we kill now, the less there'll be to kill us next time," Smith said, loading, aiming, and firing without pause.

Andrew saw the logic and reluctantly fired at the retreating warriors.

"That's eight!" Hitchings exulted, loaded, aimed, and fired again. "And another one winged!" He grinned across at Andrew. "How many have you bagged, Bairdie?"

"I haven't kept a score," Andrew replied. He suddenly felt drained.

"They'll come again," Fraser predicted. "Get ready, lads."

Andrew refilled his ammunition pouch, listened to his comrades boasting, waved away a cluster of questing flies and sunk to the ground.

"You're a learned man, Andrew." Abernethy scraped the bowl of his pipe. "Have you ever read Darwin's *The Descent of Man*?"

Andrew licked dry lips and shook his head. "No," he said.

"You should," Abernethy told him, blowing through the pipe stem to ensure it was clear. "Darwin thinks that Europeans are a civilised race and Africans are primitive."

"Does he?" Andrew pretended interest.

"He does," Abernethy said and thumbed a quarter inch of tobacco into his pipe. "I can't quote directly, but Darwin says that what he calls the civilised races, us, will exterminate and replace what he calls the savage races."

"Is that what you think we are doing now?" Andrew asked.

Abernethy shrugged, scratched a match, and puffed life into his pipe. "No; we're fighting for our lives. I think Darwin equated civilisation with mechanical advances." He tapped his rifle. "He thinks we are more civilised because we can kill more of them than they can kill of us."

"Aren't we more civilised?" Andrew asked.

"God knows," Abernethy glanced at his watch. "It's five o'clock." He sounded surprised. "Doesn't time fly when you're having fun?" He raised his head. "I can hear them," he said. "They're coming again."

The Galekas emerged from the dip, twelve hundred yards from the police entrenchments. They advanced at a run, seemingly undeterred by their previous losses and the shells and rockets that exploded among them.

"They're not going to stop this time," Simpson shouted, glancing behind him at the horse lines. "They'll run right over us and kill us all!"

CHAPTER 6

Jama stood in the centre of his *imuzi* watching Yibanathi, his *iniKozikasi* - Great Wife - and Lerato, his second wife, preparing the mealies and milk curds – *amasi* – for the evening meal. Unlike most married Zulus, Jama's Great Wife was also his first wife, while prosperity had allowed him to afford three others. He was fortunate that all his wives got along well, with the younger women happy with their position. Yibanathi was his favourite, the companion of his youth and even now, she stirred a desire in him. Lerato was fifteen years younger, as shapely as a Zulu woman should be and obeyed Yibanathi's orders without demur.

Life was good, Jama thought as he walked around his *imuzi*, watching his people work and play with the elders sitting under the *umzimbeet* tree as the flowers splashed purple over the dark leaves. Two men were busy making assegai shafts from the hard wood, for the *umzimbeet* was the favoured tree for weapons.

Like many in Zululand, Jama's *imuzi* was east facing, built on sloping ground with easy access to a stream for fresh water, with woodland nearby for fuel, and only a short distance to grazing land for the cattle. In the centre of the *imuzi*, a circular fence of intertwined branches acted as a cattle pen. At midday, the herd boys escorted the cattle into the enclosure to be milked and again at night to keep them safe from wild animals.

It was a feature of Zulu culture that only males could tend the cattle. While women did most of the other work around the *imuzi*, including working with goats and lesser animals, dealing with cattle and fighting were left to the men.

Jama stopped at the cattle pen, wondering if the *amadlozi,* guardian ancestral spirits, were watching him. He knew they guarded the cattle pens and the winter grain reserve deep beneath the enclosure and hoped they approved of his actions.

Neat, bee-hive-shaped *izindlu* clustered around the cattle pen, where Jama's wives lived with their younger children. The *izindlu* were simple structures of a supple frame thatched with grass, with a central pole supporting the roof. The floor was of beaten clay and cow dung, with an open fire in a small hearth, over which earthenware pots hung for cooking. They were perfect for the climate, easy to build, provided shelter from the rain, cool on hot days and warm in winter. Jama knew the hazard of fire and ignored the cockroaches that infested the walls. They were as much part of life as road traffic was to city-dwelling Europeans.

Yibanathi lived in the central *izindlu,* where Jama ate his evening meal of *amasi* with boiled pumpkins and vegetables spiced with pumpkin leaves. The herd boys would drive the cattle to the central pen, and Jama would relax, watching the younger people dancing, telling stories, and playing board games by the light of reed torches. When he was ready, Jama would spend the night with whichever wife he fancied. They might make love, or not, as Jama decided, and slept on grass mats which hung on the wall during the day.

Life had always been thus and, in Jama's eyes, always would be. He did not consider changing his culture any more than he would consider flying to the moon.

Jama thought of his youth as a young warrior and the battles he had endured and enjoyed before the king had honoured his regiment by allowing them to marry. The *isicoco* [1] around his head proved his status as a married man. He smiled as he remembered fighting for his king, Cetshwayo, at the Battle of Ndondakusuka over twenty years ago. Cetshwayo's forces had defeated his rival, Mbuyazi, his brother, and gained the kingship.

Jama remembered hooking the edge of his shield under that of his opponent, thrusting his *iKlwa* into his body and shouting, "*Ngadla!* I have eaten!"

He had fought for the king since then, but that first kill was his favourite, and his *amabutho's* exploits had gained the king's favour and permission to take a wife. That was when he first met Yibanathi, the mother of two of his daughters and one of his sons. Jama caressed that memory and stopped to talk to the elders, enjoying their reminiscing and listening to their wisdom. He heard children's laughter from outside the circle of *izindlu* and smiled indulgently. If children were laughing, his *imuzi* was happy, and his world was complete.

Leaving the stout thorn barrier that protected the *imuzi* from prowling night-time predators, Jama trotted to the undulating grassy hills. Somebody had said that Zululand was the land of ten thousand hills, and Jama could not disagree. The land was the best in his knowledge of Africa, and under the benign rule of Cetshwayo, the people were healthy, free, and happy.

Within ten minutes, Jama was counting his cattle, talking to the youths who tended the herds, asking about predators and proving he had not forgotten them. Cattle were the pride and wealth of the Zulus, as of every tribe and people in southern Africa. Cattle formed the basis of the economy, with men measuring their wealth in the number of cattle they possessed. The animals were small by European standards, with long horns and only a vague regard for selective breeding. Jama had purchased all his wives with his cattle and was proud of the size of his herds.

Due to cattle's importance, herd boys had a vital place in Zulu society. In common with all Zulu males, Jama had spent his formative years with cattle and recognised each animal by its distinctive pattern, the shape of its horns or how it moved.

Two of the older boys were about to leave the herds and become warriors, so Jama sought them out.

"Funani and Kgabu. You will be leaving the cattle soon."

The boys looked at him, unsmiling. *No,* Jama thought, *they were youths now, no longer boys. Soon they would be men, carrying assegais and a shield with the Abanonya.*

"You will be taking your place with the men. Are you ready?"

The youths nodded. Both were as tall as men, with lithe, muscular bodies, hardened by spending years outdoors in all weathers.

"Good," Jama said. "Come to the *imuzi* in five days to start your training. Go now."

The youths left, running, and Jama watched them, hiding his pride, for both were his sons. Kgabu was his son by Yibanathi and Funani by Ulwazie.

A third boy approached Jama. Smaller and younger than Kgabu or Finani, he stretched himself to appear taller. "I want to be a warrior, too," he piped.

Jama tried to look stern. "You are too young, Jabulani," he said. "You'll have to wait for another year or two." He shook his head at Jabulani's disappointment. "The time will pass, Jabulani. Now get back to the cattle; that dun-and-black one with the twisted right horn was limping. Check its hooves." He watched as Jabulani, another of his sons, scampered away.

Smiling, Jama returned to the *imuzi*. His life had been a long succession of successes, and nothing should ever change.

"Keep firing, lads," Fraser stopped immediately behind Hitchings and fired his carbine a handbreadth from the constable's ear. "Push them back!"

The Galekas were yelling, firing as they ran, or brandishing their assegais and shields. The bravest of their cavalry had overcome their fear of the rockets and charged on the flanks, shaggy manes flying as the riders fired from the saddle. The infantry moved more slowly, with *indunas* in front and the warriors whooping and yelling as the rockets hissed among them.

Andrew looked for his wounded adversary, fired, aimed, and cursed as his carbine jammed. He hacked at the intractable cartridge with his clasp knife, cleared the jam, reloaded, and fired into the advancing mass.

"Here come the Fingoes!" Abernethy roared. "Come on, Maclean's boys!"

As the Galekas wavered, the Maclean brothers, Alan and John, led the Fingoes against the Galekas flanks, firing as they advanced. Caught in the crossfire, the Galekas lost their cohesion. They had hoped for a quick victory and believed the witch doctors had made them invulnerable. The truth lay around them in their colleagues screaming, shattered bodies.

"They're breaking!" Abernethy shouted.

Andrew nodded. That last charge had been the Galekas high tide. The concentrated fire of the police, plus the Fingoes' flank attack, had broken them. From a force of brave warriors intent on conquest, the Galekas became a mob of frightened men, scrambling to escape the bursting shells and vengeful assegais and firearms of the Fingoes.

Andrew suddenly felt exhausted as the day's excitement wore off. He slumped to the ground, watching as the artillery pumped shell after shell at the retreating Galekas and the Fingoes butchered the wounded.

"Well, Bairdie," Smith said, placing his pipe in his mouth, "you survived."

Andrew nodded, "I did," he agreed. All he wanted to do was close his eyes, but when he did, a thousand images of the battle returned. He looked upward as the rain began, destroying all hope of coffee or a hot meal.

"You did well, Baird," Fraser said. "I've got my eye on you. Come with me." He took Andrew aside and lowered his voice. "Where are you from, Baird?"

"I arrived in South Africa a few months ago, sir," Andrew tried to avoid a direct answer.

"I know that," Fraser said. "And I know you put your home as Berwick-upon-Tweed. That's not what I mean. You're not an ordinary trooper, not with an accent and attitude like yours, and you've picked up the basics of military discipline like an old soldier."

"Thank you, sir," Andrew replied.

"You're an enigma, Baird," Fraser said. "A man of mystery."

Andrew did not reply.

"What's your story?" Fraser asked as the rain increased, hammering down on the exhausted men.

"I come from a military family," Andrew admitted some of his past.

Fraser nodded. "That would help. Infantry or cavalry?"

"Infantry," Andrew said.

"What rank?" Fraser asked.

Andrew hesitated before he replied. "My father holds a field rank," he said.

"He holds the queen's commission?" Fraser sounded surprised but was determined not to let Andrew off the hook.

"Yes, sir." Andrew was equally determined not to give too much away.

"Colonel Baird?" Fraser was smiling, ignoring the rain dripping from his face onto the sodden ground.

"I haven't heard from him for a while, sir," Andrew tried to alter the direction of the conversation. "I honestly don't know what rank he will currently hold."

"Ah!" Fraser nodded, thinking he understood. "That's the way the wind blows, is it? A family dispute?"

"I'd rather not talk about it, sir," Andrew said.

"I see. Well, Baird, you evidently come from good stock, and you have the attitude and bearing of a gentleman. If you continue behaving the way you have so far, I'll recommend you for a commission."

Andrew felt a leap of elation. He often regretted leaving Sandhurst without obtaining his commission, yet knew he wanted to advance by his merits, not because of an accident of birth.

Fraser smiled. "You may have something to boast about to your estranged father, and that might help patch up your disagreement."

"Thank you, sir."

THEY SAT OUTSIDE THEIR TENTS WITH THE CAMPFIRE THROWING OUT A circle of heat and a million stars puncturing a sky of black velvet.

Smith stretched, took a long drink from a dark bottle, and passed it over to Andrew.

"Cape Smoke," he said. "It will either kill you or give you new life."

Andrew choked back a mouthful of the fiery spirits. "Thank you," he said, coughing.

"You know, Bairdie," Smith said, retrieving the brandy, "we're wasting our time here."

"What do you mean?" Andrew asked.

"I mean, we're risking our lives fighting a bunch of raggedy-arsed savages with no profit, but our pay, and that's little enough once they take off stoppages. Where's the benefit?"

"We're making the Frontier safer for farmers and settlers," Andrew gave the stock answer. "And advancing the flag and civilisation."

Smith grinned. "That's all very well if you believe that sort of thing, but what do we, you and I, benefit from it?"

"The knowledge that we're doing our duty, perhaps?" Andrew was unsure where Smith was heading. He did not mention the possibility of a commission.

"That won't pay the rent," Smith told him. "You're still green behind the ears, young Baird. In this world, we must take the opportunities that present themselves, whatever they are. And if they don't present themselves, we must make them ourselves."

"What sort of opportunities, Sergeant?"

Smith took another mouthful of Cape Smoke, passed the bottle to Andrew, and raised his eyebrows when Andrew refused. "No? Well, suit yourself. I met a trader the other day; you may have seen me talking to him."

"I saw you were talking to somebody, Sergeant," Andrew agreed. "I didn't pay much attention, though."

"No? Well, there was no reason why you should," Smith said. "His name was Johann de Vries, and he wanders all over Southern Africa from the High Veldt, where the backcountry Boers are, to the Great Karoo. He probably knows Africa as well as anybody and picks up all sorts of interesting information."

"Yes, Sergeant," Andrew threw more wood on the fire and watched the flames and sparks rise. He waited to see where Smith was heading.

"Well, Johann is just back from Zululand, up beyond Natal, and told me things about the Zulus that I did not know."

Andrew reached for the brandy, realising that Smith was about to share his new knowledge. "What were they, Sergeant?"

"We're off duty, Bairdie. There's no need to call me sergeant. Smith will do, or Ashanti. Most people know me as Ashanti."

"Yes, Sergeant. Ashanti." Andrew choked down some of the Cape Smoke. The taste was quite pleasant when he accustomed himself to the burn.

Smith's gaze was level. "You might know that Zululand is extremely rich in minerals, with deposits scattered everywhere."

"I didn't know that, Ashanti."

"Well, it's true. The only drawback is that the deposits are in penny packets. You'll have heard of Shaka; I presume?"

"Yes," Andrew said. "He was the king that made the Zulu nation into an empire by attacking and conquering all his neighbours."

"Exactly so, young Andrew. You don't mind if I call you Andrew, do you?"

"Not at all, Ashanti." Andrew tried more of the brandy.

"One of the tribes Shake eradicated was the Lala, from the Tugela Valley," Smith continued. "The Lala were miners and metalworkers, with other tribes calling them *izinyanga zokukhanda*, which apparently meant doctors for beating. They beat out the iron ore to fashion hoes, farming tools, battle axes and spearheads."

"Such things would always be in demand," Andrew agreed cautiously.

"They would," Smith said, "but the Lala also mined copper, silver, and gold, and from these precious metals made jewellery, particularly armbands. Shaka decided he should hold the monopoly for such articles so that he could gift them to his favourites."

Andrew nodded. "Such is the way of royalty," he murmured.

Smith swallowed more brandy. "Despite Shaka's best intentions, his plan failed. Maybe there was an impurity in the metal, or perhaps Zulus have more delicate skin than other peoples, but when they wore these armbands, people developed an unpleasant skin complaint."

"Shaka would not be pleased," Andrew said.

"No. He called in his witch doctors to find out the cause, and they said the Lala miners had poisoned each piece of jewellery to avenge themselves on the Zulus." Smith shrugged. "Maybe they did. After all, the Zulus had grabbed their land and massacred most of their tribe."

"What did Shaka do?" Andrew asked, remembering the three witch doctors he had met.

"This is where opinions differ," Smith said, smiling. "The popular theory is that Shaka gathered every item of jewellery in Zululand and sent it back to the Tugela Valley together with the Lala miners, smiths and all their relatives. The *indunas* – chiefs – threw the jewellery into one of the mines, and all the Lala people murdered and tossed on top of the jewellery so their spirits could stand guard."

"You said that was the popular theory," Andrew said. "What's the less popular one?"

Smith finished the brandy, casually tossed the bottle over his shoulder and grinned. "That's where things get interesting," he said. "According to Johann, Shaka did not send the jewellery to the Tugela Valley but kept it in a strong box bound with iron. He had the Lala people massacred and asked his witch-doctors to put a curse on the strongbox so nobody would touch it."

Andrew grinned. "That also sounds like the work of a king. I've never heard of a royal who willingly disposes of wealth."

Smith laughed. "I can't see it myself. Each successive king knows the secret of the treasure chest and carries it with them." He leaned forward, whispering confidentially. "Now all we have to do is wait for a war with Cetshwayo of the Zulus, get into his royal kraal of Ulundi and dig up the treasure."

Andrew nodded, half hoping the opportunity never arose and wondering if an officer could make his name fighting the ferocious Zulus. *That would make my father sit up and take notice.*

PART II

MEETING: JUNE 1878

CHAPTER 7

"We need you, Jama," Zuluhlenga, Chief Sihayo's brother, announced.

Zuluhlenga had summoned Jama to his *imuzi* and sat on a carved three-legged stool.

Jama stood before Zuluhlenga and his family in the centre of his *imuzi*. The people watched from a respectful distance, aware of what had happened and interested in how the chief's family would react.

"Yes, *inkosi*," Jama said. He noted that Mehlokazulu, Sihayo's eldest son was also present, looking restless as he shifted from foot to foot.

"Sihayo is absent at oNdini," Zuluhlenga reminded Jama. "While he is away, his Great Wife, Kaqwelebana and one of his lesser wives have been with other men."

Jama knew the story. The scandal of Kaqwelebana's adultery had spread around the area, with women speaking of it in hushed tones and men shaking their heads at the insult to Sihayo. Yibanathi had kept Jama fully informed as they sat together for their evening meal.

Jama remained mute until Zuluhlenga told him what his part should be. Mehlokazulu looked embarrassed, he thought. Maybe even ashamed of his mother's actions.

Zuluhlenga continued. "The family held a meeting in the absence of Sihayo and decided we should kill Kaqwelabana."

Jama acknowledged the justice of the decision. Yibanathi had told him what Sihayo's family would decide, for she was a font of knowledge on such matters. Jama wondered if Mehlokazulu had contributed to the decision to execute his mother.

"We surrounded her *izindlu* and attacked them as they lay together," Zuluhlenga said, with anger strong in his voice. "We wounded Kaqwelabana, but she evaded us, as did the lesser wife, and they fled across the Buffalo River."

Jama gave a brief nod, although he scorned a raiding party that allowed their target to escape. He would have placed a double ring around the *imuzi* so that Kaqwelabana and her lover could never break free. He waited to see what Mehlokazulu and Zuluhlenga intended to do. Would they allow the offenders to evade justice or follow them across the frontier?

"I will take a strong party to pursue them," Mehlokazulu announced.

"That is the correct decision," Jama replied. "Did you ask the king's permission to enter the white man's country?

Jama thought Zuluhlenga and his compatriots had bungled the attack badly. What should have been a routine execution had turned into an ugly drama, and evidently, Zuluhlenga and Mehlokazulu had no choice but to chance Cetshwayo's wrath.

"Others have crossed the frontier on similar missions," Mehlokazulu reminded. "We shall bring Kaqwelabana back to Zululand for execution and hurt nobody on the Natal side of the river."

Jama gave another brief nod. "What do you want me to do?" he asked, although he had already guessed the answer.

"Bring your warriors," Mehlokazulu said. "Bring the Abanonya."

"We are at your command," Jama said. He would show Zuluhlenga how to manage such an affair.

Lieutenant Andrew David Baird of the Cape Mounted Rifles reined up his horse and checked his men. He had a dozen riders behind him, all veterans of the Cape Frontier War with the Galekas, sun-browned, narrow-eyed, and dusty from hard campaigning and long hours in the saddle.

Andrew looked around the small settlement of Umtata with its handful of European houses and sprawl of African *izindlu*. "We'll outspan and camp here," he ordered. "Hitchings, go to the store and buy mealies for the horses."

"Yes, sir," Hitchings said.

"Kelly, attend to the horses. The rest of us will gather firewood and raise the tents, except Sinclair and Abernethy. You two are on picket duty."

Andrew watched for a moment as Kelly rung the horses. He fastened a *reim,* a length of rawhide, to the head collar of one horse, doubled it and secured it to the next until he had bound all the patrol's horses together. The horses were now in a circle, happy with each other's company and unable to stray, while a sentry ensured no wandering horse thief could take advantage of their position.

Once he was sure the horses were secure, Andrew rode to a nearby hillock to get a better view of his surroundings.

Brought up in the ancient towns of England and Scotland, Andrew had never been impressed with the settlements in South Africa, and Umtata was no exception. Twenty-five miles from the eastern coast, Umtata stood beside the Umtata River and looked raw. European settlers had recently founded the town, and the builders used galvanised iron as a building material. From his vantage point, Andrew could see the sun reflecting from the metal walls and the metal roof of the cathedral, although the Wesleyan chapel was brick-built, and the courthouse was solid stone.

Trust the authorities to ensure the court will endure.

Between the European-style houses, the local Tembu, Bomvana, Pondo, Pondomise, and Hala people had built their homes and moved around the town beside the British and Boer population.

"Why are we here?" Hitchings asked, adding a reluctant "sir" when Andrew stared at him.

"I don't know yet," Andrew admitted. "Brigadier Simonds wants to see me tomorrow."

Hitchings grunted and walked away, grumbling.

With the men settled and pickets on watch, Andrew lay in his tent that night, wondering why the brigadier had summoned him.

My men have performed all their duties. We've obeyed orders and fought a dozen skirmishes. He sighed, decided worrying was pointless and lay down to sleep. *Let the morning take care of itself.*

The neat triple row of tents beside the village gleamed white under the morning sun as Andrew rode across. He took a deep breath of the crisp air, decided that life could be much worse and approached the main British encampment.

"I'm looking for Brigadier Simonds," he announced to the erect, moustached private of the 24th Foot who acted as sentry.

"Old Smoulder is in the central tent, mate." The sentry jerked a thumb towards the camp. "Over that way."

"You call me sir, private!" Andrew snapped.

"Sir?" the sentry repeated and stiffened to attention. "Sorry, sir. I didn't recognise the uniform. I thought you were one of the irregular horsemen."

"I am a lieutenant in the Cape Mounted Rifles," Andrew told him. "Be more careful in future." He pushed Lancelot into the tented lines. The army was already awake, with scarlet-uniformed men bustling around and hard-eyed sergeants barking orders.

A tall sentry eyed Andrew as he approached.

"Lieutenant Baird to see Brigadier Simonds," Andrew announced himself.

"Ah, Lieutenant Baird." Simonds was thin faced with a moustache that concealed most of his mouth and extended below his chin. He leaned back in his cane chair and stuffed tobacco into the bowl of his pipe. "You'll know why I sent for you."

"No, sir," Andrew said.

"No?" Simonds raised his eyebrows in disbelief. "Don't you read the newspapers?"

"I haven't had much chance recently, sir," Andrew admitted. "I've been a little preoccupied with the Galekas and Gaikas."

"Yes, I suppose you have," Simonds allowed. "You've been through the Xhosa campaign from the beginning, haven't you?"

"Yes, sir."

"You started as a trooper with the Frontier Armed and Mounted Police, gained quick promotion to commissioned rank and remained with them when the unit was transferred to the army and became the Cape Mounted Rifles."

"That's correct, sir," Andrew was surprised that Simonds should know his history.

Simonds lifted a newspaper, passed it over, clamped his pipe between his teeth, struck a match and ignited the tobacco. "Third column, the second article," he said, puffing blue smoke into the already stuffy tent.

Andrew ignored the piece about Fighting Jack Windrush's exploits in Afghanistan and focussed on the second article.

Local vessel comes aground on East Coast. Amelia was bound from Cape Town to D'Urban in Natal when an unexpected squall drove her ashore north of the Great Kei. Despite valiant efforts to refloat her, Amelia broke her back and sank. Two of the crew and three passengers were lost, although some of the cargo was saved. Amelia was fully insured, so the owners may not have suffered a financial loss.

"It's about a shipwreck, sir." Andrew did not hide his confusion.

"That's correct, Baird," Simonds said, puffing aromatic smoke. "I want you to take the survivors from Umtata to St John's at the Umzinvubu River. They'll catch a ship to D'Urban in Natal from St John's."

Andrew nodded. He had learned that life in the army meant obeying any order. One day he could be holding a small garrison against Xhosa attack and the next herding cattle to a missionary station. Escorting civilians across country was all part of the job.

"Yes, sir. When do we start?"

Simonds smiled, with his smouldering pipe clenched between his teeth. "As soon as you can, Lieutenant. Ships regularly put into St John's, and I might need you back here." He puffed out more smoke. "Between you, me and every other soldier in Southern Africa, Baird, we're expecting trouble from the Zulus next and might need every rifle. The Zulus are a fearsome people, not to be taken lightly."

"I thought we were at peace with Zululand," Andrew said.

Simonds removed his pipe. "Peace is an illusion out here, Baird. It's only a breathing space for the tribes to gather their strength." He pointed the stem of his pipe to Andrew. "Mark my words, young man, if the Zulus mean war, you'll see something that takes your mind off the Galekas."

"I have heard they are formidable, sir," Baird said.

"They are the most aggressive, best-disciplined fighting force in black Africa," Simonds said soberly. "And we'll need every good man we have to defeat them, so get these civilians to St John's and return as soon as possible."

"Yes, sir." Andrew saluted and left the tent. Only when he returned to his riflemen did he realise that Simonds had paid him a compliment by calling him a good man.

Thank you, Brigadier. Andrew patted Lancelot as he mounted. "We're getting there, Lance. We don't need a family name and influence to make our way in this world."

The local authorities had placed *Amelia's* survivors in half a dozen locations throughout the town, and Andrew set Abernethy the task of finding them.

"You're a gentleman, Abernethy," Andrew said, "and you are better with people than I am."

Abernethy nodded. "I'll bring them to our camp, sir."

"I want to make you an NCO at least, Abernethy. You're far too good to languish in the ranks."

Abernethy shook his head. "No, thank you, sir. I'm happy in the ranks."

Andrew nodded. "As you wish. Off you go, then, and round up *Amelia's* people."

While Abernethy combed Umtata for the survivors, Andrew tried to find transport for the journey to St John's. With the Frontier wars flickering to an untidy end and rumours of an impending struggle with the Zulus, wagons were hard to come by.

"Hire a wagon?" The Boer dragged a hand down his shaggy beard and looked at Andrew through narrow brown eyes. "Why?"

"To take the civilian shipwreck survivors to St John's," Andrew explained.

The Boer, sun-browned and slow of speech, stroked his beard again. "That's a bad road," he said. "You might damage my wagons."

In Andrew's experience, all the roads in South Africa had proved to be bad.

"Bad or not, we'll be travelling that road," Andrew said. "I've twenty-five civilians to take to St John's."

The Boer shook his head and turned away. "You'll be going without me," he said. "Or my boys. You'll have to look elsewhere, *rooineck."*

Andrew knew that *rooineck* meant redneck and was a derogatory term the Boers used for the often-sunburned British soldiers. Boers were descendants of Dutch settlers who had been in South Africa for centuries.

Andrew found the same response wherever he asked in Umtata. Nobody was willing to hire out their wagons for the journey to St John's.

Ashanti Smith approached Andrew, smiling. "You're still too polite, Bairdie." He shook his head. "You're a British officer now; you don't ask these people. You have to command them. That's the trouble with you home-grown men; you've too many scruples and insufficient drive."

"Sir," Andrew suggested helpfully, smiling.

"What?"

"You say sir to an officer. Even a home-grown one," Andrew reminded.

Smith stiffened. "I'm damned if I will."

"You'll be on a charge if you don't," Andrew hardened his tone.

Smith glanced around, where other Riflemen waited to see the outcome. He grinned. "Quite right," he said. "You're learning!"

"You're learning, sir," Andrew prompted.

"You're learning, sir." Smith emphasised the final word.

"And now, Smith." Andrew pressed home his point. "If us home-grown officers are too polite, you can utilise your colonial skills to requisition us some wagons. No stealing, mind. I want everything done legally with no shame attached to the Cape Mounted Rifles." He turned away before Smith could protest. If forcing more experienced men to call him sir was part of being an officer, so was delegating responsibility.

What was Tennyson's closing line in Ulysses, *"to strive, to seek, to find, and not to yield?" That suits an officer's learning process.*

While Ashanti Smith was seeking and finding transport, Andrew spoke to the civilians he was to escort to St John's. Most were serious-looking people; some were men and women who had immigrated to Africa hoping for a better life. Others were the children of settlers from the Cape Colony, men and women who had been born and lived in Africa all their lives. Work-worn men stood beside their worried wives, holding children close by them as they listened to Andrew's words of hope. A young, plain-faced woman stood at the back, with a younger version of herself nervously fingering her coat.

"We'll be leaving Umtata soon." Andrew forced himself to sound cheerful, minimising the difficulties of the journey ahead. "We'll travel overland to St John's, where a ship will carry you to D'Urban. I'll be in charge of the escort in case the native tribes cause any trouble."

"You look very young to command an escort," one bearded settler observed. He tapped the long rifle at his side. "I'll rely on this."

"Thank you for the compliment," Andrew replied. "I have one of my men gathering wagons at present. As soon as we are ready, I'll contact you all again, and we'll move the following day, so be ready."

"We're ready now," the bearded settler said. "We've been ready for the last week."

Andrew nodded, marking the man down as a troublemaker. "I am Lieutenant Andrew Baird. I'd like to know all your names."

"Martin Hancock," the bearded man said.

The others gave their names, some boldly, others quietly, as Andrew wrote them on a small notepad. The two women were last.

"Elaine Maxwell," the older said. "And this is my younger sister, Mariana." Elaine was plain-faced and steady-eyed, a practical woman who could probably turn her hand to anything.

"Well, people," Andrew said. "I'll contact you again when we have transport. In the meantime, please don't stray too far from the town."

Smith proved as good as his word, rounding up nine wagons within two days, while Brigadier Simonds provided army rations for the journey, plus a small herd of slaughter beef.

"Beef on the hoof," Smith said. "That's always a good idea, except it's also a temptation for hungry tribesmen."

"You'll have your Cape Riflemen," Simonds said with his pipe smouldering between his teeth. "I'll lend you a section of the 24th as well. You probably won't need them, but you never know. If the tribes see what they think is a vulnerable convoy, they might forget we're at peace and decide to grab what they can."

"Thank you, sir," Andrew said.

"Best of luck, Baird," Simonds told him and moved away to other things.

Andrew had two types of wagons in his convoy. Two were what the army called General Service Wagons, weighing eighteen hundredweight and nine feet long. The remaining four were colonial ox wagons, twelve feet long and much heavier at nearly thirty hundredweight and with a correspondingly greater span of oxen to tow them.

"We should have twenty oxen for these colonial wagons," Smith said. "I could only find fourteen to sixteen for each, and they are not all best quality."

"You did well to find any," Andrew gave grudging praise.

"We'll have to use what we can find. I've whistled up a few native drivers; they're the best in the world with ox-wagons, sir, as you'll know."

"You did well, Ashanti," Andrew said.

Smith smiled and tipped his forage cap over his left eye. The green feathers were still in place, a reminder of past battles. He looked up. "It's hot today," he said. "I sense a storm coming, so we might not get on the road tomorrow."

"That's unseasonal," Andrew said as he sniffed the air. "We don't usually get storms this early in the year. They normally arrive in September or October."

Smith nodded. "If only we could regulate the seasons, eh?"

"Will it be bad?" Andrew trusted Smith with all things African.

"Can you hear that thunder, sir?" Smith asked.

"I can," Andrew said.

"That's coming our way," Smith told him. "Batten down the hatches."

Dust devils foretold the onslaught, miniature whirlwinds that lifted the dust on the road, followed by a surprisingly chill wind and then lightning that ripped across the sky accompanied by thunder like heavy artillery.

"Welcome to Africa," Abernethy said as the first rail fell in heavy splashes. "Land of sunshine, adventure and," he looked upwards, "this."

Andrew smiled as the civilians took shelter under the canvas covers of the wagons. He moved to Lancelot, who was agitated by the thunder.

"It's all right, Lance," he whispered in its ear. "It's only thunder. It won't hurt." He held a handful of mealies for his horse to eat.

"Did you call him Lancelot?" The younger of the two sisters emerged from inside the General Service wagon. Blonde-haired, with her sister's grey eyes, Andrew could not remember her name.

"I did," Andrew admitted. The girl was around seventeen, he estimated, sun-browned, with a plain dress to match her homely features.

"Lancelot was one of King Arthur's knights." The girl ignored the rain that flattened her hat and soaked her long dress.

"One of Arthur's best knights," Andrew agreed.

"Do you know about King Arthur and the Round Table?" the girl asked.

"A little," Andrew said. He noticed the older sister emerging from the wagon, looking concerned. "You'd better get back under cover. It's very wet out here."

"I don't mind the rain," the girl said.

"I mind the rain," the elder sister said sternly. "Get back inside before you catch a fever. Stop annoying that poor soldier!"

"I'm not annoyed," Andrew said with a smile. "But you are right; it's a bit wet for a young lady."

"In you come," the elder sister insisted.

"I'm Mariana," the younger sister reminded before a firm sisterly hand pulled her back inside the wagon.

"Good night, Mariana," Andrew called.

"Good night, Lancelot," Mariana replied. "A bowshot from her bower-eaves,

He rode between the barley-sheaves,
The sun came dazzling thro' the leaves,
And flamed upon the brazen greaves
Of bold Sir Lancelot."[1]

"That's from the Lady of Shalott!" Andrew said, surprised that somebody should quote Tennyson to him, but both sisters were back inside their wagon. Elaine had laced the flap tightly shut against the rain, and thunder was grumbling in the sky.

Andrew ensured the horses were secure, checked the pickets and retired to his tent. He lay on his bed, listened to the rain hammering at the canvas and considered where he was.

Umtata had been a wild place, home to all the drifters, the lawless and unsettled who made the frontier their home. Boers, British, Xhosa and men of uncertain colour, race and provenance had graduated to Umtata, making the town devoid of pity but rife in crime, prostitution, and casual murder. The last few years had seen massive improvement, yet Andrew swore, rose, and posted a sentry on the sisters' wagon.

"Abernethy, you and Ramsay watch these two women."

"Yes, sir," Abernethy replied at once. "I've seen some unsavoury people hovering around. And not only the locals." He glanced meaningfully at Hitchings, cowering under the lashing rain.

Andrew thought it best not to comment on his men. "Ensure the women are safe, would you?"

"We will, sir." Ramsay was an older man in whom the fires of lust should have long burned out. He stamped his feet and grimaced at the teeming rain. "Although it would be a brave man who'd venture out in this."

Andrew nodded in agreement and stepped away. He had done all he could and intended to start the journey the following day, whatever the weather. Until then, the world would take its course.

CHAPTER 8

The rain hammered for another three hours and then stopped as if somebody had turned off a tap. The sudden silence woke Andrew. He rose, rechecked the pickets, retired to bed and woke when bugles in the British camp sounded reveille.

"I'll have to arrange a soldier-servant," he scolded himself as he dressed, shaving by candlelight, and nicking his chin in the process. He swore quietly, dabbed at the tiny spot of blood, and stooped out of the tent.

"Hello, Lancelot." Mariana was with the horse before Andrew arrived and greeted him with a broad smile. "Then answered Lancelot, the chief of knights, as Tennyson wrote. [1]Good morning, Lieutenant Baird."

"Good morning, Mariana," Andrew replied. "I'm afraid I need Lancelot," Andrew told her. "We have a busy day ahead of us."

"I know. We're heading for St John's." Mariana gave Lancelot a final pat and glanced at her wagon, where Elaine was making the final preparations.

"We'll be moving in an hour," Andrew said.

"We'll be ready." Andrew judged Elaine to be nineteen or twenty, with the mannerisms of a woman of thirty. She raised her voice. "Come on, Mariana; I need a hand here!"

"Coming," Mariana said, with a final pat of Lancelot.

"You put a sentry on our wagon last night." Elaine sounded nearly accusing.

"I did," Andrew agreed.

"There was no need." Elaine patted the pistol at her belt. "But thank you." She gave a slight nod and began to check the fastenings of the wagon cover.

Andrew lifted his hat to Elaine and moved away, shouting to his men. He studied the map Brigadier Simonds had given him. The route to St John's seemed like a switchback, up and down a series of hills with little respite.

With the nine-wagon convoy lined up behind him, Andrew lifted his hand, patted Lancelot, and began the march. Although Brigadier Simonds had encouraged him to speed, he did not force the pace the first day, allowing the animals and drivers time to adjust to the conditions.

His riflemen, all veterans, rode as scouts a quarter of a mile from the wagons, with the infantry of the 24th Foot acting as close escort, ready to lend a hand when required. Andrew rode half a mile forward, checking the route, returning to supervise the wagons, and urging the men on.

Although Andrew had learned a lot about driving a wagon since he arrived in South Africa, he would not call himself an experienced driver. He watched the convoy struggle, noting the good drivers and the not-so-good. Some men required all their skill to drive up even the gentlest of the hills, while others worked with a nonchalance that spoke of hidden talents.

"Some of these lads are experts," Andrew said when Martin Hancock joined him.

"It depends on the team," Hancock told him. "If the oxen pull well together, this section of road isn't too bad." He removed his hat and scratched his tangled hair. "It's a lot worse further on."

Andrew viewed the road. Even the best sections were simply carved out of the side of the hills, with a rough, stony surface stretching forever and a steep drop to the left. The engineer, if there had been an engineer, had only left room for a single wagon, so the outside wheels were very close to the edge.

He watched as the infantrymen joked with the wagon drivers, black or white, and were always ready to lend a willing shoulder when the teams struggled. Private Miller, a cheerful Geordie, was constantly helping, with O'Donnell and Drummond close behind.

That first day they managed ten miles, and everybody was glad of the rest when Andrew called a halt. He posted three horsemen on mobile patrol as an outer line of pickets and three of the 24th as an inner defence pulled the wagons into a laager in case of attack and dismounted. Sitting on a fallen tree trunk, he lit his pipe, took off his forage cap and fanned his glowing face.

"Lieutenant Baird." Elaine approached him, smiling faintly. "You look exhausted."

Andrew lifted his head. "Good evening, Miss Maxwell," he said, standing up and taking the pipe from his mouth.

Elaine looked surprised at this small show of politeness. She bobbed in a brief curtsey. "Good evening, Lieutenant. I wondered if you would care to share our meal."

Andrew started. "That's very kind of you, but I have my duty to do."

"I'm sure you have, Lieutenant," Elaine replied quickly, "but even duty-bound officers must eat sometime."

Andrew could not stop his smile. "That is correct, Miss Maxwell."

"It's only stew," Elaine said, suddenly apprehensive in case Andrew did not like her cooking. "From the rations the army handed out, plus a few local vegetables I found."

"I haven't had anything except army cooking for over a year," Andrew admitted. "Stew would be most welcome." He smiled, blushed, and looked away. "My apologies, Miss Maxwell. I am unused to the company of a lady."

Elaine smiled. "I apologise if I seem forward," she said. "You were so kind to Mariana yesterday and this morning that I had to thank you." She pushed forward a bowl of steaming stew.

"Kind?" Andrew did not have to pretend confusion.

"When Mariana asked you about Lancelot and King Arthur."

Andrew shook his head. "I only spoke to her. It was nothing."

"It meant a lot to Mariana," Elaine said, looking away. "And to me."

Unsure what to say, Andrew tried the stew. "This is good," he told her. Andrew realised Elaine was not quite as plain-faced as he had thought. He studied her surreptitiously from the corner of his eyes, noting the firm line of her jaw, the high cheekbones, and the straight nose.

No, he told himself. *She is not plain at all. Elaine has a strong face.*

"Thank you." Elaine was watching him eat. She realised that Mariana was leaning out of the wagon, listening to everything she said. "We'd better get to work, Lieutenant, and you to your duty."

"We've finished work, Elaine," Mariana said, grinning.

"Come on, Mariana!" Elaine said. "Just leave the plate on the ground, Lieutenant," she said. "Mariana will wash it later."

Andrew began to protest, but Mariana had already lifted the plate. He walked away, aware that Elaine was watching every step he took.

They started before dawn the following day, with the road becoming progressively worse. As the hills grew steeper, Andrew took the advice of the experienced drivers and hooked one span of oxen onto another to haul one wagon at a time, yet they still made painfully slow progress.

"There should be a special kind of hell for the man who made these roads," Abernethy said. "They should have to lead a team of wagons up and down them for eternity."

"I feel that we're doing that already," Andrew said and raised his voice. "Get these beasts moving!" Brigadier Simond's instructions to hurry ran through his head. He rode beside each wagon, cajoling, threatening, and lending his strength by pushing at the back. "Get up this blasted road!"

"You'll hurt yourself." Elaine and Mariana had left their wagon to lighten it. "The oxen can only pull to their strength, Lieutenant Baird."

"Every little helps," Andrew said, hoping Elaine had not heard his strong language.

"We're making good time on these bad roads," Elaine told him.

"Maybe," Andrew conceded.

"Don't distress yourself so," Elaine said as Mariana nodded in agreement.

"You can't do the impossible, Lieutenant Baird," Mariana said and began to recite Tennyson.

"And up and down the people go,
Gazing where the lilies blow," [2]she smiled. "Except there are no lilies here."

"Not even one," Andrew agreed.

"Sorry to interrupt, sir, but somebody is watching us," Abernethy rode up. "If you look at the hill behind me and to the left, you'll see a body of natives."

Andrew was too experienced to look at once. The countryside was beautiful, with steep hills, fast-flowing rivers despite the recent drought, and well-wooded. It was also well populated, with the local tribe being the Amapondos.

"Who is the local chief?" Elaine asked, hushing Mariana with a raised hand.

"Umquiliso." Andrew had questioned the residents of Umtata about the local tribes. "He rules all the land between Umtata and the St John's River."

"Is he friendly, sir?" Abernethy asked, thumbing the lock of his Snider. "I don't know this area."

"I've been told that Umquiliso is friendly on the surface," Andrew said. "The Amapondos are not a warlike nation, but we'd be foolish to take chances." He warned the riflemen and infantry to stay alert and pushed on until the late afternoon. "Umquiliso pretends to be our friend, but we suspect he sent some warriors to help the Galekas. He's also attacked the Amsquesibes, who are undoubtedly friendly to us." Andrew realised he was talking too much. "Keep alert, boys."

"And girls," Elaine said, lifting her determined chin.

"And girls," Andrew amended with a smile.

They pushed on over hill country without a single level piece of ground. The distance to St John's was not great, but the road worsened hourly, with even the most experienced drivers muttering about the difficulties.

"We can usually carry nine thousand pounds weight in each wagon," one driver said. "I'm only carrying half that, and we're still struggling up these buggering inclines."

Andrew thought of the route ahead, Simond's warning about possible trouble with the Zulus, and studied the surrounding hills with his field glasses.

"Keep moving," he growled. "Use every trick you can but get these wagons to St John's."

"Yes, lieutenant," the driver said, hawked up phlegm from the back of his throat, saw Andrew glaring at him, and swallowed noisily. He stomped back to his wagon. Andrew watched him for a second, a weather-battered man in a broad-brimmed hat and faded brown corduroys, and turned away as Elaine pushed her wagon up the track with Mariana walking at the side. Elaine brushed a loose strand of hair from her face and spared a moment to smile at him before cracking her whip to encourage her oxen.

"Well done, Miss Maxwell," Andrew shouted.

The Amapondos followed the convoy, never coming close but always there as a potential threat. The male travellers carried their rifles and stayed close to their wives and families. With no men to look after them, the sisters looked more vulnerable, so Andrew frequently checked on them.

"Thank you for your concern, Lieutenant," Elaine said as Mariana smiled shyly and patted Lancelot.

"May I ask how you two ladies are alone?" Andrew asked.

"We lost our uncle in the shipwreck," Elaine said without visible emotion.

"Oh, I am sorry to hear that," Andrew was immediately contrite. "I didn't realise."

"We were in Cape Town on some legal business," Elaine said. "Settling the lease for more land for the farm." She smiled. "It's the first time we've been so far away from Natal."

"You are native to Natal?"

"Born and bred," Elaine told him with more than a hint of pride.

Andrew looked ahead, where the mountain of Quanyana presented a formidable obstacle. He knew the rest of the day would be challenging, and the Amapondos were still there, watching without approaching.

Andrew helped guide the leading oxen over a rough piece of track. "Is it not dangerous living close to Zululand?"

Elaine shook her head. "No more dangerous than anywhere else and less dangerous than the Cape frontier. From the stoep of our house, we can see across the Tugela into Zululand, and the herd boys water their cattle opposite our land. The Zulus have never given us any trouble."

Andrew raised his eyebrows. "People have told me the Zulus are Africa's most aggressive and dangerous nation."

When Elaine laughed, her hair bounced around her face, and the severe expression disappeared. "Their king, Cetshwayo, keeps them in order. I admit they have an interesting history, but they've never bothered us." She negotiated a turn with a skill any driver twice her age would have envied.

"What's your farm like?" Andrew asked as Mariana came closer, walking beside the front wheel of the wagon. Her skirt snapped against her legs with every stride.

"It's called Inglenook, and it's not very big," Elaine said. "Only a few hundred acres or so, but having the Tugela close ensures it's well watered, which is very important in this part of the world." She smiled as she spoke, with her eyes warm as she described her home. "We have a huge mopane tree only fifty yards from the house, and Mariana and I made that our own. We've climbed every branch, despite Mother's attempts to make us ladylike."

Andrew could not picture Elaine climbing a tree.

Mariana laughed. "Poor Mother! You should have heard the things she called us!"

"I can imagine," Andrew said. He could see Mariana scampering to the top, with her hair flying wild and her laughter sounding. "Your mother would have her work cut out with you two!"

Elaine glanced at Mariana and smiled. "Do you know the mopane tree, Lieutenant Baird?" She continued before Andrew had time to reply. "It has butterfly-shaped leaves that change colours in the autumn. We call it the kaleidoscope tree because of the different colours."

Andrew laughed, enjoying the play of emotions on Elaine's face as much as her words.

"Our tree is home to the mopane worm, the caterpillar of the mopane moth. The local people eat it either fresh from the tree or dried, and sometimes the Zulu herd boys cross the Tugela to find the worms." Elaine smiled. "We don't mind." She looked up, cracked her whip, and pushed the wagon over another rough stretch of road.

Andrew realised he was neglecting his duty and touched a hand to his hat. "If you'll excuse me, ladies, I must see to the convoy."

"Of course, Lieutenant," Elaine said as Mariana gave Lancelot a farewell pat.

"We'll tell you more about Inglenook later," Mariana shouted as Andrew pushed back down the convoy.

The soldiers of the 24th Foot were busy pushing the more heavily laden wagons, joking with the drivers. Veterans of the Border War, Andrew knew they would never pass muster on a British parade ground. The men had stained their once-white sun helmets brown with a mixture of mud and cow dung and mud. Battered by hard service, their serge uniforms, brilliant scarlet when they left Britain, were sweat-stained and faded to a dozen shades of pink and white. Their blue trousers were discoloured by red dust, patched, and darned above mud-caked black boots and gaiters.

Andrew watched them for a moment, wondering what an Aldershot sergeant would say about their tarnished brass buttons and general demeanour as they spoke to the native drivers in a language of their own devising.

"Come on, Sammy!" Private Miller said in broad Geordie. "Get these beasts up the hill!"

"Push, you booger," Drummond encouraged in his Yorkshire accent. "Coom on, lad, you can do it!"

Andrew wondered if the soldiers had ever been happier as they toiled in this unfamiliar landscape so far from their home. No landowners expecting deference, no cramped back-to-back brick houses rife with rats and damp, no factory chimneys belching filth into the atmosphere. These men looked healthy and fit.

"Sir." Abernethy rode up, saluting. "These Amapondos are a bit closer now."

"Let's have a word with them," Andrew said. He raised his voice. "Sergeant McBain!"

"Sir!" McBain was the senior infantryman present. A scarred-faced veteran of medium height and villainous appearance, he spoke with a Welsh accent.

"Take charge of the convoy while I look at these Amapondos."

"Very good, sir!" McBain saluted.

"Smith!" Andrew shouted. "You're with me!" If there were to be trouble, he'd rather have the experienced Ashanti Smith at his back than anybody else. He knew he could trust Abernethy not to let him down, and the men of the 24th Foot were steady veterans, but Smith had guile as well as experience.

"Sir!" Smith joined them, riding towards the Amapondos.

"Wait!" Andrew shouted as the tribesmen began to withdraw. Smith lifted his carbine, pointed it to one of the men and repeated the command.

When the Amapondos stopped, Andrew raised a hand to show he was in peace.

"I am Lieutenant Andrew Baird of the Cape Mounted Rifles," he said in Xhosa. "We mean you no harm."

The Amapondos were tall, muscular men but wary as Smith held his carbine in the crook of his arm with the muzzle pointing towards their leader. Behind the small group, Andrew saw men gathering, most carrying assegais and shields.

"Why are you watching us?" Andrew asked.

"We want to know why you are in the land of the Amapondos," the spokesmen said. "Our chief did not give you permission to come here."

"We don't need your permission," Smith began until Andrew stopped him with an upraised hand.

"Do you think we are trespassing?" Andrew asked.

"You are on Amapondo land," the spokesman insisted.

Andrew considered for a moment. From where he stood, he could see his convoy straggling along the road, a succession of slow-moving, heavily laden wagons, each pulled by a dozen or more oxen. The small infantry escort looked very thin on the ground, while the mounted men were mere dots in a vast landscape.

"Times have been bad here lately," Andrew commented. "You've had drought and famine."

The Amapondo agreed, watching Andrew intently.

"We have no desire to journey where we are not wanted," Andrew said. "We only wish to cross your land. To show our friendship to the Amapondo, we will give you four of our slaughter cattle." He knew he might be setting a dangerous precedent, but his duty was to get the convoy safely to St John's.

The spokesman's smile told Andrew he had made the correct decision.

"I will have my men herd the cattle to you," Andrew said. He nodded to the warriors in the distance. "If you take your men away and grant us safe passage."

The spokesman rose. "You have safe passage," he said.

When Andrew returned to the convoy, he wondered if he was an army officer or a diplomat and decided he had to be both. He glanced at the surrounding hills, saw there no Amapondo warriors were watching and knew he could concentrate on pushing the wagons through.

Time to do my duty, he thought and smiled as Elaine waved to him.

CHAPTER 9

They sat inside the laagered wagons with three campfires sending flames and smoke toward the star-bright sky. Outside the laager, the oxen stood within a thornbush barrier, with bored sentries marching on slow boots while outer pickets waited with ready rifles.

Andrew placed another log on the fire and watched as a ribbon of sparks spiralled upward. He smiled across at Elaine, who held a mug in both hands while sitting on a handy boulder. Mariana pushed back her broad-brimmed hat and returned Andrew's smile.

"This is the best part of the day," Andrew said. "When we've done the day's work, and we can relax for a little while." He nodded beyond the laager. "Except for the sentries, but that's part of the soldier's bargain."

That was my father's phrase. I hope I am not copying him.

Elaine pounced on Andrew's words. "Part of the soldier's bargain? What does that mean, Lieutenant?"

"I mean, soldiers have to accept the rough with the smooth without complaints. They accepted the Queen's Shilling and must abide by the consequences."

"Soldiering is a hard life," Mariana said.

"So is farming," Andrew replied. "Or working down a coal mine, or in a fishing boat or a Cape Horn clipper ship." He lifted his tea to his lips. "I doubt soldiering is any worse, and we meet some interesting people."

"Oh?" Elaine said. "Have you met some interesting people?"

"From time to time," Andrew said. He wondered if Elaine was fishing for a compliment, decided she was not and turned the conversation around. "You promised to tell me about your home."

"So we did," Mariana said.

"We did." Elaine quietened her sister with a look that could crack glass. "In the morning, we can sit on the stoep at Inglenook and watch dawn rise over

Zululand, tinting the Tugela pinky-red, and hear our cattle lowing to one another."

"Do you enjoy farming?" Andrew asked.

"It's the only thing to do," Elaine told him, with lights dancing behind her eyes.

Andrew nodded. "I can believe that." He listened as Elaine and Mariana took turns sharing their memories with him.

"We call it Inglenook," Elaine said. "The Zulus called it *Indawo Yokuthula* – the place of peace. Isn't that lovely? Zulu is the most beautiful language in the world. My grandfather came out with the Byrne Settlers in 1850 [1]and moved to our present land in 1858. We've carved a farm out of a wilderness."

"It sounds idyllic," Andrew said, watching the play of emotions on Elaine's face.

"Where do you come from, Lieutenant?" Mariana asked.

"A small town called Berwick-upon-Tweed, right on the Border between England and Scotland," Andrew said. "While you have the Tugela on your doorstep, I have the Tweed."

"Like Sir Walter Scott at Abbotsford," Mariana said.

"Yes, but without the towers and turrets," Andrew told her. "My house is a little more modest."

"Is it cold there?" Elaine asked.

"It can be cold in winter," Andrew admitted. "We get ice on the Tweed sometimes, clinking under the bridge and against the harbour walls, where the swans cluster."

"Do you live on a farm?" Mariana wanted to know.

"No." Andrew shook his head. "I live in a townhouse built right on the town wall." He saw their confused expressions and explained. "Berwick was a fortress town when England and Scotland were enemies, and Queen Elizabeth of England built a great wall to keep the Scots out. I used to run around the walls in the morning, watching the dawn on the North Sea and dodging the seagulls."

"What's your house called?" Elaine added wood to the fire, moving closer as the night-time chill began to bite.

"I changed the name to Joyous Gard," Andrew said, glancing at Mariana.

"That was Lancelot's castle!" Mariana exclaimed. "He took it from a robber baron and altered the name!"

"That's right," Andrew said. "Some Arthurian legends have him living close to Berwick, at Bamburgh Castle, so I borrowed the name."

"Did he really live near Berwick?" Mariana asked as Elaine smiled at Andrew.

"I'd like to think so," Andrew said. He glanced at his watch. "Well, ladies, I am afraid duty calls, and I must check the sentries." He stood up. "I'd advise that you retire soon; there's another hard day ahead of us tomorrow."

"Yes, lieutenant," Elaine said as Andrew straightened his forage cap and walked to the perimeter of the laager. When he glanced behind him, Andrew saw that the firelight was highlighting Elaine's face and reflecting from her fine grey eyes. He turned away before she saw him looking and did not see Mariana peering out from the half-closed wagon flap.

They crossed the Tugela in the darkness before dawn, with Mehlokazulu leading thirty mounted men and Jama with fifty of his Abanonya as insurance against any outside interference.

Jama heard the steady tramp of feet behind him. He knew Ndleleni and Bangizwe were at his back. They had been his constant companions since they were herd boys together, men he would trust to the death. Bhekizizwe and Bafana were nearly as close, veteran warriors, while his sons, Funani and Kgabu, were on the fringe. Jama expected Cetshwayo would soon call up his sons to place them in another *amabutho* of their age group but wanted to lead them on their first expedition himself.

Mehlokazulu stopped immediately after they crossed the Tugela, with moonlight reflected on the shifting water and the cry of a jackal eerie in the night. Jama hefted his shield, grinned across to Ndleleni and looked forward to the night's excitement. He was content with his wives and cattle but missed the excitement of fighting with his men.

"We have executed one of the errant women," Mehlokazulu told them. "And have found Kaqwelebana."

The warriors nodded their satisfaction.

"She is hurt and hiding in Maziyana's *imuzi*. Mazinyana is a border guard, paid by the British to stop any Zulus from crossing the Tugela into Natal." Mehlokazulu led the laughter.

"Cetshwayo does not want us to hurt anybody on the Natal side of the river." Mehlokazulu reminded. "Be careful with your assegais, for we don't want to anger the king."

Jama and the other warriors nodded. "We will take Kaqwelebana back to Zululand without killing anybody in Natal," Mehlokazulu ordered, mounted his horse, and led them into Natal.

Maziyana's *imuzi* was a short distance from the river and slept in the security that no Zulu would cross the Tugela. Jama's impi formed a guard around the *imuzi*, with half facing inwards and the remainder outwards. They held their assegais ready in case any of Maziyana's people resisted, but nobody did.

Mehlokazulu took only three men inside the *imuzi* and demanded his mother's return. Maziyana objected, knowing what the outcome would be. He ran outside his *indlu*, shouting for his warriors.

Jama saw Maziyana emerge and stepped inside the *imuzi*, holding his assegai ready to strike. Maziyana halted, hesitated, looked at the Abanonya warriors surrounding the *imuzi* and returned. He watched as Mehlokazulu grabbed Kaqwelebana and hauled the terrified woman away. Jama's Abanonya followed the mounted men across the drift to the Zulu side of the Tugela.

"Don't kill me!" Kaqwelebana pleaded. "I am your mother!"

"You shamed our family," Mehlokazulu replied. "Kill her."

The Zulus were merciful, shooting Kaqwelebana rather than subjecting her to a more lingering death.

The woman died immediately, and, according to Mehlokazulu, her demise closed the incident. Justice had been done, the Zulus had hurt nobody on the Natal side of the river, and life continued as before.

Jama returned to his *imuzi*, his wives, and his cattle. In his mind, Mehlokazulu had managed the whole affair poorly, but the outcome was satisfactory, although he hoped Cetshwayo did not object to the impi crossing the Tugela. Yibanathi was waiting for him with a meal, and after he had eaten, he trotted out to his cattle. One cow was due to calve, and Jama wanted to ensure the birth was trouble-free.

THE MOUNTAIN OF QUANYANA WAS THE FIRST MAJOR OBSTACLE IN THE DAY'S journey. The upward road was tricky but manageable, with a steady three-mile-long climb, while the downward slope swooped down at a fifty-degree angle for three-quarters of a mile.

Andrew noticed that the Amapondos had returned, with a handful of warriors standing on a neighbouring hill, silently watching.

"We might have to unload before we try this road," Hancock said, tugging at his beard. He spat on the ground and glared at Andrew as if he had created the mountain himself.

"Maybe so," Andrew glanced at his watch, "but I'd like to reach the bottom before dark, and it's already two in the afternoon."

"We can try it," a Hottentot driver known as Saul said with a sudden reckless smile. "I'll take the first wagon down."

"Take care," Andrew warned. He watched as Saul jumped onto his perch, released the brake, and cracked his whip. The wagon picked up speed, forcing the oxen to gallop down the hill, with Saul losing control before they were halfway to the bottom. The wagon lurched to the side, bounced on a protruding rock, balanced on two wheels, and turned over with a terrible crash, spilling the contents over the road.

"I warned you," Hancock said smugly.

Andrew swore softly. The journey was bad enough without careless delays. "Ramsay, ride down and check on Saul."

"Yes, sir." Before Ramsay was halfway, Saul appeared beside the wagon, limping but unhurt. He raised a hand in cheerful acknowledgement.

"It looks like we're not going much further today," Smith said, winking at Elaine.

"We'll get the wagons to the bottom of the hill," Andrew told him. He raised his voice. "Take the horses down with whatever loads they can carry. Abernethy, you and Sinclair are horse guards; watch for the Amapondos."

"They're watching us." Abernethy pointed to the warriors on the opposite hill.

"That's why you're on guard," Andrew told him. "Off-saddle the horses and let them graze. The rest of us will right the wagon and gather the goods." He was surprised when the Maxwell sisters joined the men at the stricken vehicle.

"We know how to work," Elaine explained as she lent her slight weight in attempting to right the heavy wagon. Fortunately, the accident had only superficially damaged the sturdy wagon, but it took half an hour to reload the contents.

"Right, Saul, on you get," Andrew ordered, and the chastened driver took his place in the driving seat.

"Drive slowly, Saul," Andrew ordered. "We can't afford to lose the wagon or the oxen." He paused for a significant second. "And we don't want to lose you."

He pretended not to notice Elaine's approving nod.

With the wagon and its contents safely at the bottom of the hill, Andrew wondered how to get the other wagons down safely. He called together the drivers for a conference.

"We need a more efficient brake," Andrew said. "Something to slow the wagons down without unbalancing them."

"I have an idea," Elaine said from outside the circle.

Nobody listened to her as they debated various plans. Andrew and Hancock were discussing locking the rear wheels together when he saw Elaine pulling Mariana to her side.

"Come on, Mariana," Elaine said, "we know what to do." Ten minutes later, Andrew saw Elaine take the reins of her wagon and head for the downward slope.

"Miss Maxwell," Andrew shouted, but Elaine was already on the move. As the wagon passed him, Andrew saw that the sisters had hacked down a couple of small trees and attached them to the back to act as drag. He could only hold his breath and watch as the wagon negotiated the slope, with Mariana leaning out of the back, laughing, and reached the bottom in perfect safety.

Andrew shook his head as Elaine leapt from her perch and gave him a cheerful wave. He lifted a hand in rueful acknowledgement.

"The rest of you, do the same," Andrew shouted. "Miss Maxwell has shown us the way!"

Grumbling that they should not have to copy a woman, the other drivers cut small trees from the surrounding countryside and tied them to the back of their wagons.

"This won't work," Hancock said. "It's a waste of time."

"Cut a second tree," Andrew told him. "You have a heavy wagon." He watched as the ever-helpful Miller hacked down a bush and fastened it to Hancock's wagon.

"There you go, chum," Miller said. "That should help." He stepped back, retrieved his Martini-Henry from O'Donnell, and stuck a stubby pipe between his teeth.

Andrew nodded to Hancock. "If you're scared, I'll ask Miss Maxwell to drive your wagon. I'm sure she'll oblige." He smiled at the expression on Hancock's face as he cracked his whip and guided the wagon down the hill.

Using the sister's braking technique, the wagons all reached the foot of the hill, but by then, the sun had set. Andrew ordered them to outspan for the night, set sentries and wondered what the next day would bring. The Amapondos were still watching without making any move to interfere.

"Watch for night-time raiders," Andrew warned the sentries. "They might try to sneak past you in the dark."

"Yes, sir." Miller patted his Martini. "We'll look for them."

"That was daring of you," Andrew said when Elaine was making her evening meal.

Elaine looked up and brushed the hair from her eyes. "I knew what I was doing."

"I noticed," Andrew said dryly. "How long have you been driving?"

"Since I was old enough to walk," Elaine told him.

Andrew nodded slowly. "You do it very well," he replied, stepped away and turned around. "Very well indeed." He took another step. "You do everything very well, Miss Maxwell."

"Elaine," she said without a smile. "My name is Elaine."

"Elaine," Andrew turned back to see her standing with a spoon in her hand, watching him with her head tilted to one side. She brushed another loose strand of hair from her face.

"Thank you for the compliment, Lieutenant Baird."

"Andrew."

"Andrew," Elaine repeated.

"Andrew," Mariana whispered from inside the wagon as Andrew walked away.

THE FOLLOWING DAY'S TERRAIN WAS THE WORST YET, WITH SLOPES SO STEEP that not even a double team of oxen could pull a loaded wagon.

"That must be a sixty, even sixty-two-degree slope," Smith said, pushing back his forage cap. "We'll never get up that with a full wagon." He shook his head. "I reckon we'll have to unload them and try that way."

Andrew sighed and glanced at Elaine, who nodded in agreement and made his decision.

"We'll lighten the loads," he said. "Try with half a load." He ignored Smith's headshaking and Elaine's raised eyebrows and gave the orders.

Even with a double team, the oxen failed to haul a half-loaded wagon up the incline. Exasperated, Andrew ordered the rest of the contents piled up beside the road.

"Sergeant McBain," Andrew snapped. "Set a guard on these goods. They'll be a temptation for the Amapondos."

"Very good, sir," McBain said.

It took the entire day for Andrew to ease the convoy up that single hill, with half the mounted men watching for the Amapondos and the rest helping the wagons. The infantry continued to mount close guard and toiled uphill with the contents.

“What is all this stuff for anyway, sir?” McBain asked.

“Most of it is material for the army garrison at St John’s,” Andrew explained. “The remainder is what the settlers salvaged from *Emilia’s* shipwreck.”

McBain nodded. “I see, sir.” He raised his voice to a bellow. “Bancroft! Be careful with that chest! It could be the young lady’s best china, damn your clumsiness!”

Andrew smiled and moved on. By the evening, he could look down on the steep slope, with his wagons formed into a laager and the sweet smoke of a campfire drifting over Amapondoland. He looked ahead, where a panorama of endless hills stretched before them.

“We’ll be another week at least,” Andrew said.

CHAPTER 10

While part of him was frustrated at the length of time the journey was taking, Andrew also felt his gaze settling on Elaine and hoped for more of her company.

"It will take us at least a week to reach St John's, sir," Smith agreed. "Unless we find some help." He indicated the riflemen and infantry slouched against the wagons. "The men are about out on their feet."

"Where will we get help?" Andrew asked.

"Dragoon the tribesmen," Smith replied at once.

"What do you mean?" Andrew guessed the answer.

"Round them up at gunpoint and force them to drag the wagons," Smith said. "Use them as forced labour."

Andrew did not have to consider. "No," he said. "We'll struggle on."

"Brigadier Simonds is waiting," Smith reminded.

"He'll have to wait," Andrew said.

"It was just an idea, sir," Smith said, grinning. He touched a finger to his hat and walked away, leaving Andrew wondering.

"I don't like that man." Elaine checked her oxen, removed a tick, and squashed it underfoot.

Andrew smiled. "He's all right," he told her. "He looked after me when I first arrived in Africa."

"Maybe there's some good in him," Elaine grudgingly acceded. "I still don't like him."

"He's one of the best soldiers I've ever met," Andrew said, "and we have a long journey ahead of us."

Elaine smiled.

"The way was long; the wind was cold,
The Minstrel was infirm and old."

Andrew joined in with the following lines.

"His wither'd cheek, and tresses grey,
Seem'd to have known a better day;
The harp, his sole remaining joy,
Was carried by an orphan boy.
The last of all the Bards was he,
Who sung of Border chivalry."[1]

Elaine laughed. "You know that poem, then?" She stepped away from the oxen.

"*The Lay of the Last Minstrel*, by Sir Walter Scott," Andrew replied. "My mother can quote it by heart. She loves Scott."

"She must be a very cultured lady," Elaine said. "You never talk about your family."

"No," Andrew said. "I never do."

"Why is that?"

Andrew looked away without replying.

"Come now, lieutenant," Elaine teased him. "You can't evade me with silence forever."

Andrew had resolved never to mention his family background. "I don't like to talk about it," he said.

"I sense a family squabble," Elaine said as Mariana edged closer.

Andrew shook his head.

Elaine raised her eyebrows and brushed a non-existent strand of hair from her face. "I see you don't trust me, Lieutenant Baird." Her voice was suddenly cold.

"Of course, I trust you," Andrew said, but Elaine was already walking away.

"Go after her, old man." Abernethy had been a silent witness. "Go on!" Forgetting their respective ranks, he gave Andrew a gentle push.

"Miss Maxwell! Elaine!" Andrew followed as Elaine stormed away, her skirt swaying and her head held high.

The sentries on picket duty looked, grinned, and sensibly said nothing as Andrew chased after Elaine. She did not look behind her, striding on until she was a quarter of a mile clear of the laager.

"Have you seen anything like this before?" Elaine spoke as if nothing had happened, catching Andrew entirely off balance.

"Like what?" Andrew wondered if Elaine was proffering an olive branch or asking an honest question.

"These." Elaine pointed to several paintings on the rocky side of the hill.

"No," Andrew said. "What are they?"

"Bushmen art." Elaine traced one with a stubby, work-hardened finger. "I don't know how long they've been here, but many years, I think."

"I've heard that Bushmen are dangerous," Andrew warned.

"Everybody's dangerous when somebody pushes them into a corner," Elaine said. "The Bantu, Xhosa, Zulu and all the rest have been hunting the Bushmen like animals for generations, maybe hundreds of years. The Bushmen hide in the mountains and deserts."

"Have they? How do you know that?" Andrew showed he was willing to be friendly.

"My Zulu friends told me," Elaine said.

"Do the Zulus speak English?"

"Not as well as I speak Zulu," Elaine said, saying a few Zulu phrases.

"You're a truly impressive lady," Andrew told her. "I've never met anybody like you."

"You must have a sweetheart back home in Berwick," Elaine probed hopefully. "Somebody you trust."

"No." Andrew shook his head, ignoring the barb. "I have no sweetheart," he told her.

"Oh, that's a shame. You must have somebody to go back for." Elaine probed again.

"Maybe," Andrew said, "but no sweetheart."

Elaine brushed another imaginary strand of hair from her face. "You don't say much about yourself."

"No, I don't," Andrew agreed. He knew they would reach St John's in a few days but did not want the journey to end, whatever Brigadier Simonds wished. Andrew did not want to say farewell to Elaine. Or to Mariana, who he was also beginning to like.

"Will you ever be posted to Natal?" Elaine asked.

"I don't think so. I am a Cape Mounted Rifleman, so my unit only operates on the Cape frontier."

"Oh." Elaine did not hide her disappointment. "If you ever are, would you like to come and visit us at Inglenook?"

"Yes," Andrew said and regretted his impulsive answer. He was afraid to reveal his feelings for this girl. *No*, he told himself, *she is not a girl; she's a full-grown woman.*

Is this the girl who will wait for me? Oh, God, I hope so.

That realisation brought a rush of blood to Andrew's face as he looked at Elaine from a new perspective. She was shapely, with finely curved hips and breasts that pushed against her top. He realised that she had lured him here so she could talk to him alone, without an audience of grinning soldiery or a curious sister.

I am a soldier; Elaine is my responsibility.

"Andrew?" Elaine noticed his discomfort. "Will you visit us even if the army doesn't post you to Natal?"

"I will," Andrew wondered why his voice had become a few octaves lower. "I'd like that." Why did he feel like a young boy rather than an experienced army officer?

Get a hold of yourself, Andrew. Take control.

"I'd like that, too," Elaine said quietly. "You can talk about King Arthur with Mariana and discuss horses with my father."

Andrew took a deep breath. "I'd rather talk with you," he said. "Unless you have your sweetheart with you."

"I don't have a sweetheart either," Elaine said quickly.

"That's good," Andrew said, feeling his heartbeat race, knowing what he wanted to do yet unsure what to say.

They were silent for a moment as the peace of the ancient Bushmen site washed over them. A pair of birds called, and a soft breeze carried cooled them.

"I like Tennyson and Scott," Elaine said. "*The Lady of Shalott* is my favourite, even though it's a sad story." She smiled and quoted the final stanza.

"They cross'd themselves, their stars they blest,
Knight, minstrel, abbot, squire, and guest.
There lay a parchment on her breast,
That puzzled more than all the rest,
The well fed wits at Camelot.
'The web was woven curiously,
The charm is broken utterly,
Draw near and fear not,—this is I,
The Lady of Shalott."

Andrew listened to her voice, knowing he would never forget this moment.

"I'm named Elaine after the Lady," Elaine said, suddenly eager to speak. "You'll like Inglenook." She stepped so close that Andrew could smell the perfume of her hair.

She's worn that, especially for me.

Andrew stretched his hand, brushed against Elaine's arm, and daringly slid down his hand until he gripped her fingers. Elaine gasped.

"Sorry!" Andrew said, immediately releasing her.

"No," Elaine felt for his hand. "It's all right. It's very all right."

Her hands were warm and hard as they gripped Andrew's fingers. He felt a thrill run through him and heard himself breathing. "Tell me about Inglenook."

Elaine squeezed his fingers. "In the morning, we can have a silver mist rising from the Tugela, so our cattle are like ethereal animals floating above the ground. I ride around them, checking the numbers while Father tends to the fences. Mornings are always the best times of day when the world is waking up, and the land is still."

"I like the mornings too." Andrew guided her to a couple of handy boulders, and both sat down. "I am up before dawn and walk around Berwick Walls, looking down on the town or out to sea, where the surf splinters silver on the beach, and the seagulls follow, hoping for food."

"Kiss me, Andrew," Elaine said.

Andrew hesitated. "I won't be very good, Elaine. I've never kissed anybody before."

"I've never been kissed," Elaine countered.

Suddenly, Andrew did not care. He was no longer nervous with Elaine. "We'll share a first time," he said and bent closer.

"The dark is falling," Elaine said a few moments later.

"Yes. I'd better get you back to the laager." Andrew did not want to leave this place. The Bushmen paintings seemed to glow as if the long-gone artists had left something of their spirit behind.

"Yes," Elaine said, clutching his sleeve. "Mariana will be worried."

"Elaine, take my signet ring." Andrew slipped it from his finger, held it for a second and pressed it into her hand. "It's the only thing of any value that I possess." He smiled, knowing she would take care of it. "Think of me every time you look at it."

Elaine closed her hand over the ring. "It will be like having you with me all the time," she said.

"That's the idea," Andrew agreed.

The ring was too large to fit on any of Elaine's fingers, so Andrew slid it onto the thumb of her left hand. "Wear this until I can buy a proper engagement ring."

"I will," Elaine promised. "Was that a proposal?"

Andrew was confused for a moment. "Yes," he said. "I thought," he hesitated. "It seems so obvious that we should be together; I didn't need to ask."

"I knew before you did," Elaine said, smiling. "When will you come for me?"

"As soon as I can," Andrew promised.

Elaine examined the ring. "These initials are not yours," she said. "It says ADW, and you are Andrew David Baird. Why is that?" She raised her eyebrows quizzically, with a slight smile on her face. "If you think you can trust me."

Andrew closed his eyes. "I don't tell anybody that," he said.

"Not even your fiancé?" Elaine teased. "Please? Unless it's some terrible scandal in which you were involved that you are scared to tell me? A passionate affair with an older woman, or a robbery that went wrong, and you had to shoot the burglar, and you are hiding from the police." She smiled with her mouth slightly open. "Mariana reads the most awful books, you see, but truly, you can tell me anything, but it's all right if you don't want to."

"There's no scandal," Andrew assured her. "But you might think I am silly when you hear my reason."

"You don't have to tell me," Elaine said, putting a finger to Andrew's lips. "It's quite all right."

"Have you heard of Major Jack Windrush?" Andrew asked.

"Fighting Jack Windrush? The soldier who tamed the Northwest Frontier and fought the Ashantis?" Elaine said. "Everybody's heard of him."

"The W on my ring stands for Windrush," Andrew said. "Major Jack Windrush is my father."

Elaine looked at him for a moment, evidently puzzled. "I don't understand," she said. "Why change your name?"

"If you lived in the shadow of a hero, you'd understand," Andrew told her.

"Everywhere I went, I was Fighting Jack's son. I was never me, and people expected me to be like my father."

"Aren't you?" Elaine asked.

"I want people to recognise me as myself," Andrew said. "I want to make my own way in life, rather than people praising me or helping me because of what my father did."

"Ah, I see," Elaine nodded. "Well, I didn't know anything about your family until five minutes ago." She smiled. "Although I knew Mariana likes you because you called your horse Lancelot and know about King Arthur!"

Andrew smiled. "Thank you, Elaine."

"Good. You can forget all that nonsense about your family with me." Elaine said sternly. "I notice you still joined the army, though, like your father."

Andrew shook his head. "I joined the police. I was at Sandhurst, the officer's training school, and every few minutes, somebody mentioned my father's exploits and told me how lucky I was to be a hero's son. When I realised, they all expected me to be my father, I walked out of Sandhurst and left the country."

"That was a bit drastic, wasn't it?" Elaine asked. "You must have felt very strongly about your name."

"I do," Andrew said. "I joined the Frontier Armed and Mounted Police as there was nothing else I could do; I mean, I have no other skills. A year or so later, the powers that be decided to transform the Armed and Mounted into an army unit, the Cape Mounted Rifles." [2]He shrugged. "So, my attempts to avoid the army came to nothing, and I ended up a soldier after all."

"But why did you choose South Africa?" Elaine asked, with a quizzical smile on her face.

"It was either South Africa, China, New Zealand or Australia," Andrew replied. "They're the only places my dear papa has never soldiered."

Elaine laughed. "Well, that's as good a reason as any, I suppose." She smiled at him. "I don't have such an interesting story. I was born in Natal, lived in Inglenook, and I'll probably die there." Her smile broadened. "I've been to Cape Town once, and the ship coming home ran aground."

"By the sound of Inglenook, you have made the right choice." Andrew did not mention his fear of war with the Zulus. He glanced at the sky. "I think we'd better be on our way, you'll need your sleep, and I have a convoy to get to St John's."

"Your men will think the Amapondos have got us," Elaine said.

Andrew saw the flicker of movement from the corner of his eye, decided it must have been an animal and guided Elaine away from the Bushmen's paintings. Strange, he thought, he had imagined a flicker of blue, like the uniform he wore, but he must have been mistaken.

CHAPTER 11

"And they came unto Camelot," Mariana said as they looked down on the small settlement of St John's.

"I didn't want that journey to end," Andrew admitted.

"Nor did I," Elaine said.

Mariana watched them, smiling. Although she petted Lancelot, her gaze never strayed from Andrew.

Andrew watched as the infantrymen of the 24th helped the civilians unload the wagons. As always, Miller was at the forefront, his voice loud and cheerful, with O'Donnell and Drummond at his back.

Andrew and Abernethy helped the Maxwell sisters, while Hitchings and Simpson managed to avoid manual labour.

"What are you doing now?" Elaine asked.

"Returning to Umtata," Andrew told her. "I'm taking the wagons back empty, which will make the journey easier. I'm afraid you'll have to wait for a boat to take you to D'Urban."

"We'll wait," Elaine said. She looked at the signet ring on her thumb. "I'll return your ring when you come to see us."

Andrew smiled, feeling sick at the thought of leaving her. "I have to go," he said.

"I know." Elaine put a small hand on his arm. "It's your duty. Take care until we meet again."

"I will," Andrew said. He saw Mariana watching from the opposite side of Lancelot. "You take care as well, Mariana, and we'll discuss Mallory and Tennyson's *Morte d'Arthur* in Inglenook."

Mariana smiled and intoned,

"To him replied the bold Sir Bedivere:

"It is not meet, Sir King, to leave thee thus."[1]

Andrew saw something shadow Mariana's eyes. "You know your Tennyson as well as I do, Mariana."

"Yes, Andrew," Mariana agreed and mouthed, "I love you," as Andrew turned away. She watched him march to the empty wagons, ignoring the single tear that seeped from her left eye.

The return journey to Umtata was faster than their outward trip, with the oxen pulling empty wagons and no civilians to nurse. Yet Andrew was unhappy, for every mile carried him further away from Elaine. He attended to his duties, driving the men harder than before and snarling at small matters he would have ignored a few days earlier.

"The men are noticing, sir," Abernethy said as they sat around a campfire in the evening of the third day.

"What are the men noticing?" Andrew asked, ramming tobacco into the bowl of his pipe.

"They're noticing your change of mood since we left Miss Maxwell."

"Nonsense!" Andrew snapped, grabbed a smouldering twig from the fire and thrust it onto his pipe.

"Sorry old boy," Abernethy drawled, throwing a log on the flames. "There's nothing nonsense about it. You were an efficient soldier before, and then you met the delightful Miss Maxwell. Now she's gone, and you're pining for her company." He stared into the distance. "You're turning into a bear without her, a veritable bear."

"I am nothing of the sort," Andrew said. "And you call me sir!"

"Yes, sir," Abernethy replied smoothly. "What's that in your hand?"

Andrew glared at him. "My pipe," he replied.

"Your other hand, sir," Abernethy said. "No, let me tell you. It's a button off Miss Maxwell's coat. You found it on the ground at the last campsite, where she must have lost it. You deliberately camped on the ground where she parked her wagon." Abernethy laughed. "Don't glare at me, sir. You're smitten, and the only cure is to scratch the itch."

Andrew opened his hand to look at the button. "How the devil can I do that if she's in Natal and I'm here?"

"Either find another woman," Abernethy said blandly, "or go to Miss Maxwell, depending on whether the itch is purely physical or something more serious." He stood up, humming opera music. "Plenty of women are willing to share their bodies with a British officer, sir. It's the uniform, you see, and the thrill of mating with a man of violence, a trained killer, added to the allure of position and money."

"I have no money except my wages, and I'm only a subaltern," Andrew reminded.

"I know that sir," Abernethy said. "But that sort of women see what they want to see and believe what their empty-headed little friends tell them. Take your opportunities when they arise, young sir, because you don't know if they'll ever come again."

Andrew lit his pipe and puffed furiously as Abernethy walked away, still humming.

Find another woman or go to Elaine.

Andrew considered his options. He thought of the women out here on the frontier, from the hardy wives of the settlers to their equally sturdy daughters or the gaudy drifters who haunted the bars. He discarded the wives out of hand. He had been brought up a gentleman and would never break the code; married women were sacrosanct. The daughters? If he used them in the way Abernethy hinted, he believed he would ruin them for life. That left the prostitutes, and Andrew had heard sufficient tales of the diseases they carried to give them a wide berth.

Neither of these options is viable to scratch this particular itch,

That left one option. Standing up, Andrew began to pace around the camp, nodding when men saluted him and looking outward as if watching for prowling tribesmen.

Damn it. I know what I am going to do. When I return to Umtata, I'll resign my commission and travel to Natal. I don't know what I can offer Elaine, but I want her. Maybe her father can employ me at Inglenook. I can ride, am strong and fit, and I've been around farms most of my life.

"We'll move before dawn tomorrow," Andrew decided. "I want everybody up, fed and ready to move before first light."

"Yes, sir." Sergeant Smith saluted, eyeing Andrew cynically.

With the decision made, Andrew relaxed a little, although he pushed his men as hard to return to Umtata. When small groups of Amapondo tribesmen watched their progress without attempting to hinder or communicate, Andrew ordered his mounted men to keep an eye on them.

"Get these blasted wagons moving! Double teams up the incline, damn it!"

"You're in a hurry, sir," Abernethy commented.

"Yes, Abernethy. I am in a hurry," Andrew agreed. The thought of seeing Elaine again spurred him, and the words of *Lady of Shalott* filled his head.

"DID YOU HEAR THE NEWS?" NEWLY PROMOTED CAPTAIN FRASER ASKED when they rode into the camp at Umtata. He ushered Andrew into his tent.

"What news, sir? We've been pushing wagons up and down hills for weeks," Andrew said. "The only news we've heard is what the Amapondos tell us, which was about crop failures and raiders on their borders."

Fraser shook his head. "It's a bit more serious than poor crops or border raiders, Baird. There is trouble brewing with the Zulus."

"What sort of trouble?" Andrew immediately thought of Elaine, with her farm so close to the Zulu border. He calmed down, telling himself that the frontiers between the European colonies and the native kingdoms were always rife with rumours of trouble and possible wars. Even the Boers, who had been in Africa for centuries, quarrelled with their neighbours.

"When Shepstone crowned Cetshwayo king of the Zulus, he warned him not to murder too many of his people," Fraser said, pouring them both a glass of brandy. "Here, Baird. You'll need this after your travels."

Andrew sipped the brandy, allowing the fire to spread through his body. He knew that Theophilus Shepstone, the Secretary for Native Affairs in Natal, had been alarmed when Cetshwayo succeeded to the Zulu throne in 1873. While a hostile Zulu nation would directly threaten the colony of Natal, Shepstone was more concerned that the Zulus might form an alliance with the Boers of the Transvaal and the Orange Free State. Such an alliance would allow the Boers, never pro-British, access to the sea, which Britain did not want. Accordingly, Shepstone made overtures of friendship to Cetshwayo, recognising him as king and crowning him with a gaudy tinsel crown in Queen Victoria's name.

However, British recognition came at a high price. Shepstone demanded that Cetshwayo obey certain British-orientated laws, including not killing his subjects at will and forbidding his warriors to pass into British territory.

"Do we have any right to tell the Zulu king how to reign in his country?" Andrew asked.

"Probably not," Fraser said with a grin, "no more than we have to tell the Czar of Russia how to reign, but that's not the point."

Andrew nodded, hoping Fraser could finish quickly so he could inform him of his decision to resign.

Fraser finished his brandy, looked at the bottle, and regretfully put it away. "When Shepstone warned the Zulus about their behaviour, Cetshwayo announced he would rule according to his laws, Zulu laws."

Andrew nodded again. "That's understandable."

As long as he doesn't bother Elaine.

"Perhaps so," Fraser did not argue. "In July, when you were pushing your convoy to St John's, matters deteriorated. A couple of chief Sihayo's wives fled from Zululand into Natal with their lovers."

"Love is like that," Andrew thought of Elaine.

"That was the beginning of the trouble. Some Zulus pursued the women into Natal, dragged them back to Zululand and executed them."

"That's a bit harsh," Andrew said.

Hurry up, Fraser. I have important news for you.

"Sir Henry Bulwer, the Lieutenant-governor of Natal, contacted Cetshwayo, demanding the men who crossed the border should be extradited for trial. Cetshwayo said he'd punish them for venturing onto Natal soil, but as the women had broken the law and the warriors had not killed them in Natal, he would not send them to Natal for trial."

Andrew nodded. "Cetshwayo has a point," he agreed. "As long as they don't attack people in Natal." He thought of Elaine again and shifted his feet in agitation.

"Bulwer was inclined to agree with Cetshwayo and let things go, but Sir Bartle Frere, the High Commissioner for Southern Africa and Bulwer's superior, disagreed." Fraser grinned. "If any of the accounts I heard were correct, he was spitting blood and feathers."

Andrew curbed his impatience until Fraser had finished. "What happened next, sir?"

"Frere stated that this border incident demonstrated the Zulus' savagery and thinks that Natal is in danger of a Zulu invasion."

Andrew shuddered, thinking again how close Inglenook was to the Zulu border. "God forbid that happens, sir." He took a deep breath. "That would mean war."

"You're damned right, it would," Fraser agreed, "but politics are behind our protests, of course. Sir Bartle plans to join all the scattered southern African colonies to create a confederation of South Africa. You know we are gradually reducing the danger by annexing the native tribes and civilising them with missionaries, schools, roads, hospitals and so on, and Zululand is on the list."

"Sir Bartle is merely looking for an excuse to start a war?" Andrew asked.

"I imagine so," Fraser agreed. "We've already annexed the Transvaal, and now we'll defeat the Zulus and later add Zululand to Natal."

"Is that fair on the Zulus, sir?" Andrew asked. "And how about the British settlers on the borders of Zululand?"

"It's for the Zulus' own good," Fraser said, "and to ensure the security of the settlers on the Zululand borders. Now, I'm not sure how things stand at present, but the Brigadier has cancelled all leave, and Frere has requested reinforcements from Great Britain."

"Yes, sir," Andrew said. He felt his heartbeat increase. *What does war with the Zulus mean to Elaine?*

Fraser fixed Andrew with a steady smile. "I know you've just returned from a rather arduous journey, Baird, but our company of the Mounted Rifles is moving to Natal soon, so get your men ready."

"Yes, sir." Andrew wondered what he should do.

We're moving to Natal to fight the Zulus! If I hand in my papers with war imminent, people will brand me a coward. If I remain, we'll be in Natal anyway, closer to Elaine.

Fraser smiled. "Now, we're the only company of the Cape Mounted Rifles moving to Natal. The others are remaining to guard Cape Colony. We're expecting trouble with the Basutos as well as the Zulus." He held Andrew's arm. "We're the chosen men, Baird, veterans of the Frontier War, and we'll show the redcoats how to defeat the Zulus!"

"Yes, sir," Andrew said, more confused than ever.

"Now, Baird, give your report to Brigadier Simonds, get some rest for you and your men, and prepare to face the Zulus." Fraser's eyes were bright. "We all knew we'd have to fight them, and the Cape Mounted Rifles, the CMR, will be in the forefront!"

As he marched away, Andrew told himself he could not resign on the eve of war. If he was bound for Natal, he would be closer to Elaine and could surely find an excuse to visit Inglenook.

I'm off to Natal at the government's expense. Once we defeat the Zulus, nobody can complain when I resign. He raised his head, with his life's path clear before him and Elaine waiting at the golden door of the future.

❄

"LIEUTENANT BAIRD!" FRASER THRUST A HEAD THROUGH THE OPEN FLAP OF Andrew's tent.

"Yes, sir?"

"I have some important news for our company," Fraser said without entering the tent.

"What's that, sir?"

"The powers-that-be have decided to issue our company with Martini-Henry rifles rather than Sniders. That way, we'll be in line with the rest of the army and have no trouble with ammunition." Fraser was smiling.

"That's good, sir," Andrew said. "I've heard the Martini is a more powerful rifle."

"Here you are, Baird," Fraser said, handing over a Martini-Henry and a training manual. "I expect you to be conversant with the Martini by tomorrow."

"Yes, sir."

"You'd better be," Fraser said, "because you're teaching the men how to use it immediately after the morning parade." He grinned and raised a hand. "Aren't you glad you're a commissioned officer now, Andrew, with all these responsibilities to earn your extra two shillings and sixpence a day?"

"I wouldn't swap it for the world, sir," Andrew said as Fraser withdrew.

Andrew had a busy evening. After penning a short but heartfelt note to Elaine, he opened the Martini manual, sighed, and began to read. He had not gone beyond the first three pages when somebody scratched on the outside of his tent.

"Come in!" Andrew said.

"Sir!" Abernethy poked his head into the tent. "I'm sorry to bother you, sir, but we have some men missing."

Andrew sighed again. "I'm coming. Who's missing?"

"Sergeant Smith, sir, and Riflemen Simpson and Hitchings."

"Ashanti Smith?" Andrew shook his head. "That's unexpected." He left his tent. "Sergeant Duncan!"

Duncan was in his late thirties, a red-faced, stocky man with a fine display of whiskers and eyes that had seen all the world's troubles. "Yes, sir."

"Sergeant Smith, Simpson and Hitchings appear to have mislaid themselves," Andrew said. "Do you have any idea where they might be?"

"Have you tried the local brothels, sir?" Duncan replied immediately. "Smith fancies himself as a lady's man, whether willing or not."

"I haven't tried anywhere yet," Andrew said. "That's your job, Sergeant."

"Yes, sir." Duncan mused for a moment. "I'll take half a dozen men, sir, with your permission."

"Granted," Andrew said, thought of the manual lying beside his bed and swore. "Damn the men. I'll come with you, Sergeant."

"Yes, sir." Duncan saluted and stepped back.

There was one recognised brothel in Umtata and a handful of lesser-known houses where willing ladies entertained sex-starved British soldiers. Sergeant Duncan knew them all and introduced Andrew to the gentle art of brothel raiding. Duncan's technique was to hide his men around the nearest corner, tap politely on the door and charge in when the inhabitants answered.

The evening taught Andrew a lot about the depravity of human nature and confirmed his belief that he'd avoid brothels in future. The search also failed to find Smith, Simpson, or Hitchings, although it confirmed that four horses were missing.

"They've gone," Andrew said. "Deserted."

"We'll miss Smith's experience," Duncan said. "Hitchings was a decent shot, but Simpson is no loss at all."

When Andrew reported the desertions, Captain Fraser sighed and leaned back in his cane chair. "I'm surprised about Ashanti Smith. I had him in mind for a commission once, but he is certainly no gentleman. The other two?" He shrugged. "Well, Baird, it's better we lose the dross now than when the fighting starts. The men must be able to rely on their comrades. Have you read that manual yet?"

"Not yet, sir," Andrew admitted.

"Best get down to it, then," Fraser advised, leaned back, set his hat over his face, and closed his eyes.

ANDREW RUBBED THE SLEEP FROM HIS EYES, STIFLED A YAWN AND FACED THE assembled riflemen.

"All right, gentlemen," he said. "You'll have heard that Sergeant Smith and Riflemen Simpson and Hitchings deserted last night. If anybody has any information, let me or Sergeant Duncan know."

Andrew did not expect an immediate flood of volunteers, but faced with utter silence, he moved quickly on.

"Today, we are looking at our new rifle, the Martini-Henry. We were promised a carbine, but unfortunately, we have the full-length rifle, but perhaps somebody will see fit to issue us with the carbine later."

Andrew waited until Sergeant Duncan handed out the Martini-Henry rifle to every man and gave them a few moments to get used to the length and weight.

"As you can see," Andrew said, "the Martini is forty-nine inches long, five inches shorter than the Snider, and weighs eight pounds twelve ounces, so it's lighter as well."

The men murmured their appreciation of the shorter, lighter rifle. Some pulled it into their shoulder, others held it at arm's length.

Andrew spoke again. "The Martini is sighted up to thirteen hundred yards, about three hundred longer than the Snider, and both are single-shot breech loaders."

The men grunted, with some hoping for a repeating rifle.

"The Martini is more powerful and more accurate at a longer distance," Andrew said. "You'll all have noticed the underlever. Pull it down to eject the spent cartridge and open the breech. Push in the cartridge and push up the underlever to close the breech, and you are ready to fire."

The men all tried the lever, nodding at the ease of loading.

"That little device will increase your rate of fire from ten to twelve rounds a minute," Andrew said. "And you'll see the calibre is different, a .45 bullet as opposed to the Snider's .577."

The men exchanged comments, with some nodding in appreciation.

"It's a man-stopper," Andrew said. "Most of you will have fought alongside regulars in the last war, so you'll have heard them praising and cursing the Martini. Now it's our chance to see how good it is. Sergeant Duncan has made up a rifle range specifically for the Martini, so we can spend all morning learning about our new friend." He grinned at the ironic cheer.

Andrew and the Cape Mounted Riflemen spent the next five hours with the Martini-Henry. They learned that the rifle had a powerful kick that surprised even experienced soldiers, so after a dozen shots, men were holding the weapon away from their shoulders. They also found the Martini overheated faster than the Snider, but the worst fault was the cartridge's dangerous tendency to stick in the breech when the soldier operated the underlever.

"We'll have to watch for jams," Andrew warned. "If your rifle jams in action, inform your NCO or officer, step out of the firing line, clear the jam and return. Don't panic."

The men nodded. The veterans of the Cape Frontier knew a cool head was essential when facing a thousand rampaging warriors.

Andrew liked the Martini. It felt like a soldier's rifle, robust and accurate. His men also liked it, yet at the back of Andrew's mind was the worry about losing three experienced men to desertion. Fraser brushed the affair aside, reminding Andrew that desertion was always a possibility, especially on the eve of a new campaign.

"It's not your fault, Baird," Fraser consoled him. "Desertion is a constant problem, especially in the colonies. Men look for adventure and find tedium and danger, or they cannot cope with the discipline, or they realise they can jump ship and carve out a better life for themselves here, away from the restrictions of Britain." He shrugged. "We might miss Smith and maybe Hitchings, but Simpson was a bad lot."

"Yes, sir," Andrew said. "Thank you, sir."

"Put them out of your mind, Baird, and concentrate on getting your men ready. We leave for D'Urban in two days."

"Yes, sir," Andrew threw a quick salute, turned, and left the tent. While part of him was unsure whether war with the Zulus was justified, another part sang with the prospect of seeing Elaine again.

When we beat the Zulus, we'll make it safer at Inglenook. That's sufficient motivation for anybody.

The riflemen saw Andrew's new enthusiasm as he organised them.

"God, Sandy, our Andy is keen to fight the Zulus," Kelly said.

"You'd think he had enough facing the bloody Galekas and Gaikas, but no, he wants more," Sinclair replied as he rubbed a cloth along the barrel of his rifle.

Kelly bit on a hunk of tobacco and ejected brown spittle onto the ground. "He's mustard keen, is Andy, a right firebrand. God help the Zulus when he gets at them."

"Aye," Sinclair said. "Afghanistan has Bobs Roberts and Fighting Jack Windrush. We have Gentleman Freddy Chelmsford and Up-and-at-em-Andy." He shook his head. "We don't have to go, Pat, Up-and-at-em, and the Gentleman will clear it up without our help."

Kelly laughed. "Oh, don't deprive me of all the fun, Sandy. I want my share of Cetshwayo's treasure."

Andrew walked away, smiling. When men gave him a nickname and unknowingly compared him to his father, he was making progress. Elaine would be proud of him.

CHAPTER 12

Natal was not what Andrew had expected. D'Urban impressed him as a growing, bustling port town with a mixed population and more positive energy than he had expected. The hinterland was green, fertile, and hot, with a beauty that surprised him.

I am not surprised people immigrate here.

When the troopship *Aberdare* landed the company of Cape Mounted Riflemen at Port D'Urban, Andrew hoped to visit Inglenook. He was disappointed when Captain Fraser marched them inland, past a mixture of settlers' farms and native kraals.

"The captain's pushing us hard," Sinclair grumbled.

Ramsay took off his forage hat to wipe the sweat from his forehead. "It's even hotter here than in Cape Colony." He took a swig from his water bottle. "He's pushing us hard because we're off to the Zulu frontier to make sure the Zulus don't invade."

"There are fifty of us," Sinclair said. "How many warriors does Cetshwayo have?"

Abernethy whistled his opera song, looking around at the scenery. "About forty thousand," he said cheerfully.

"Aye, but we've got Up-and-at- 'em Andy," Kelly reminded. "He's enough to scare anybody."

"He bloody scares me," Ramsay said gloomily.

"How good are these Zulus?" Sinclair asked. "They must be pretty ferocious if the Xhosa are all terrified of them."

"The Zulus are better than good," Abernethy assured them. "They are the bravest and best-disciplined soldiers in Africa."

"How the hell do you know?" Ramsay glared at Abernethy. "Have you met them?"

"I've seen them," Abernethy said and returned to whistling his opera airs.

After days of hard marching, the Cape Mounted Rifles camped on rising ground with a view northward over a broad river to rolling hills. Captain Fraser called the riflemen together, stood on a prominent rock and lifted a hand for silence.

"Right gentlemen, Riflemen and others," he said, smiling. "I've heard some of you wondering what the Zulus are like and what we might expect to face when and if we fight them."

The men nodded, with some voicing their opinion of the Zulus and others silent, content to listen. Andrew sat at the front, scanning the land with his newly purchased field glasses, wondering if any of the farms he saw was Inglenook.

"Well, light your pipes and pay attention," Fraser said. "Because I am going to educate you."

The men settled into silence as a pall of blue smoke rose above them.

"The Zulus have dominated this part of Africa for half a century, ever since their great king Shaka founded an empire by destroying all the other tribes and clans between the Drakensberg Mountains and the Indian Ocean. They are the most ferocious, bravest, and best disciplined native army in Africa, and we'd be foolish to think anything else."

Andrew realised that Fraser had captured the men's attention as he had intended. He saw Abernethy nod in agreement as Fraser continued.

"These Zulus are trained as warriors from early childhood and fight like fiends," Fraser said. "They are warriors from their teenage years until they are too old to carry weapons, which means that every man in Zululand is a trained fighter, able and willing to kill on his king's orders." He paused to allow his words to sink in.

"How many warriors does Cetshwayo have?" Ramsay's worried voice broke the silence.

"I am not sure," Fraser admitted. "Maybe forty thousand, maybe fifty thousand and maybe more. They are organised into regiments, each with its unique traditions, and, like our British regiments, some are antagonistic to others. Fights between regiments can be bloody and often fatal."

Sinclair laughed. "We were like that in the Cameronians,[1] sir," he said. "We were a Lowland Scottish infantry regiment and hated the Cameron Highlanders! We preferred to fight them than the enemy!"

"Exactly so," Fraser agreed. "Regiments with the darker shields are younger, those with lighter shields older and more experienced. Either will kill without compulsion. The Zulus have no idea of mercy or compassion. They kill the enemy wounded, and they expect us to treat them the same way."

When some of the men stirred restlessly, Andrew wondered if Fraser was lowering their morale by praising the Zulus to such an extent.

"I've lived in this continent all my life," Fraser said and hardened his voice, "as have many of you. We have lived alongside the native tribes and know their capabilities. We've fought and defeated them before, and we'll do it again."

Andrew noted the change in tone and direction and watched the men's reaction. They were paying close attention, some cradling their still new Martini-Henrys, others looking concerned.

Fraser lit his pipe, taking his time to heighten the tension. He shook the flame from his match, puffed blue smoke into the air and grinned. "You lads look scared," he said. "And with cause. The Zulus are a frightening enemy. They fight in a recognised formation, with a chest that hits their enemy head-on and two flanking attacks to surround them, the chest, and horns of the buffalo, as they call it, with a reserve they call the loins."

"Do they always attack, sir?" Andrew asked.

"They do," Fraser said. "They know nothing about defensive formations. They attack with shields and assegais. They know little about firearms and despise them, probably because the traders only sell them Brummagem rubbish or worn-out Tower muskets that Marlborough would have discarded."

The small piece of humour lightened the mood, and Abernethy led the laughter. Andrew saw some of the men looking puzzled, perhaps wondering who Marlborough was. He did not expect Frontier farmers to have a deep knowledge of eighteenth-century military history.

Andrew waited for a moment and asked the question that filled the men's heads. "How do we defeat such ferocious warriors, sir?"

"I was hoping somebody would ask that," Fraser said. He stepped to Abernethy. "May I borrow your rifle?"

"Of course, sir," Abernethy said.

"Thank you." Fraser lifted the Martini-Henry. "We stop them with this little lady," he said. "The British army is small, but it's one of the most professional in the world. We have fought in every climate and latitude, from Canadian snows to tropical jungles, from Egyptian sands to the bitter plains of Crimea." He grinned. "The Zulus may be good in their chosen environment, but we are good everywhere."

Andrew saw the men's mood lift as Fraser praised them.

"How do we defeat the Zulus? We keep our discipline, gentlemen; fire twelve rounds a minute and stop them before they get close."

Some of the men laughed nervously.

Fraser turned around. "Face that direction, Riflemen," he said. "Can you all see the river?"

The men nodded.

"That is the Tugela. On this side, we stand in Natal and across the river is Zululand."

While the men stared at the misty land of their potential enemy, Andrew swept his field glasses across the Natal side of the Tugela, wondering if Elaine had seen the same view.

"She'll wait for you," Abernethy whispered as the meeting broke up. "Have faith. Women, or most women, are more loyal than men."

"Is it that obvious?" Andrew asked.

Abernethy nodded. "I think it was Joseph Joubert who said a man should choose for a wife only a woman he would choose for a friend if she were a man."

"It is that obvious, then," Andrew said.

"Scratch the itch, sir," Abernethy advised. "Inglenook is only five miles to the southeast."

"How the hell do you know that?" Andrew asked.

"I used to be a trader in Zululand," Abernethy told him and nodded as Fraser dismissed his company, leaving Andrew alone. The Tugela slithered past, with the hills of Zululand beyond.

❄

As a pre-dawn mist slithered over the Tugela, Andrew fitted his saddle to Lancelot and left the camp. He was not orderly officer and had no duties until ten that day, so he rode away with a clear conscience.

"Keep a good lookout, boys," he shouted to the sentry, who lifted a hand in farewell.

"Give her our best, sir," the trooper replied, grinning.

Damn! Does everybody know my business?

Remembering Elaine's description of Inglenook, he rode towards the Tugela.

"Excuse me," Andrew tried his Xhosa on a group of men. "I'm looking for a farm called Inglenook." When the men looked blank, Andrew remembered the Zulu name. "You might know it as *Indawo Yokuthula*."

The men became animated, pointing southward, pleased that they were able to help.

"How far?" Andrew asked.

The men shook their heads. "Not far," the oldest told him at last.

Within fifteen minutes, Andrew saw the mopane tree thrusting skyward a spear cast from the river. He smiled, imagining Elaine and Mariana perched on the branches. Elaine would attempt the climb in deadly earnest, chiding Mariana for laughing and taking too many risks.

A hundred yards from the tree, Inglenook farmhouse was low and long, with a stoep facing the Tugela and a small fence defending a wrap-around garden from wildlife. Andrew lingered for a few minutes, enjoying his thoughts before he pushed Lancelot to the front gate. He dismounted, knee-hobbled the horse, straightened his uniform in a sudden bout of nervousness and walked to the front door.

"You took your time!" Mariana opened the door before he knocked. "We've been watching you dallying for the past seven minutes!"

"Seven minutes!" Andrew could not restrain his smile. "That's very precise!"

"Come in!" Mariana stepped aside, grinning. "Elaine is waiting for you." She lowered her voice. "She's pretending to be calm."

"Mariana!" That was Elaine's voice from an inner room as an older man and woman stepped behind Mariana.

"You must be Lieutenant Baird." The man was broad-shouldered, clean-shaven, and deeply tanned. "I am John Maxwell, and my wife is Linda."

Andrew took off his hat. "I am Andrew Baird," he said.

"My girls have told me all about you," Mrs Maxwell told him, with her shrewd eyes examining him from the cut of his hair to the scuffed toes of his boots. "In you come. Elaine is waiting for you."

Andrew felt something churning inside him at the words. *The witch told me a woman would wait for me.*

Elaine met him at the living room door, smiling nervously as she brushed a non-existent strand of hair from her face.

"Hello," Elaine said.

"I told you I'd come."

They looked at each other for a moment, unsure what to say.

"How long do you have?" Elaine asked.

Andrew glanced at his watch. "About an hour," he said. "I'm on duty at ten."

"So short a time!"

Andrew put out his hand. "It's good to see you."

Solid, serviceable, handmade furniture filled the room, while a packed bookcase occupied one wall.

"You, too," Elaine said.

They relapsed into silence, broken only by the ticking of a wall clock.

"Andrew!" Mariana burst into the room, laughing. "You must stay for dinner!"

"Mariana!" Mrs Maxwell cajoled. "Give them time alone together!" She poked her head through the open door. "Did you say only an hour, Lieutenant Baird?"

"Yes, Mrs Maxwell," Andrew replied. *She's been listening at the door.*

"We'll leave you alone, then," Mrs Maxwell said.

"No." Elaine shook her head. "I want you all to meet each other."

Andrew knew Elaine was correct, although he wanted her all to himself. He took a deep breath and prepared for an hour of dutiful self-sacrifice.

"Come on, Andrew." Mariana slipped a small arm inside his, smiling.

PART III
WAR

CHAPTER 13

DECEMBER 1878

The summons to oNdini took Jama by surprise. He had nearly forgotten about the incident with Sihayo's wives and travelled to the royal *imuzi* with as much curiosity as trepidation. His warriors trotted behind him, with each man aware he could face execution if Cetshwayo decided they had transgressed.

On his previous visit to oNdini, Jama had been excited to see the royal herds. Now only his meeting with the king mattered, and he led his Abanonya through the gate without hesitation. Ordering them to squat in the central space, where the king could see them, Jama approached Cetshwayo's *imuzi.*

Cetshwayo waited for him in the semi-darkness, an imposing presence with three or four veteran *indunas* inside the *isiGodlo* – the king's private enclosure.

"This man is Jama of the Abanonya," Ntshingwayo, one of the warriors announced in a deep voice.

Jama lay on the ground, hiding his fear.

Cetshwayo sat on a carved wooden stool, saying nothing as he contemplated Jama for what seemed like a long time. Jama remained still, knowing he would accept whatever judgement the king announced. The warrior who had spoken carried an axe and a knobkerry and watched Jama through dispassionate eyes.

"When you were last here," Cetshwayo said without preamble, "I ordered you never to cross the river into Natal. Why did you disobey my order?"

"My *inkosi* ordered me to," Jama knew he could never lie to the king.

"Jama's *inkosi* is Sihayo of the Quangebe," Ntshingwayo reminded.

"You disobeyed my order." Cetshwayo ignored the interruption.

"I did," Jama agreed.

"I could kill you, as you helped kill the disobedient wife," Cetshwayo mused without any apparent malice. He contemplated Jama for a few moments before arriving at a decision. "Sir Bartle Frere of the British has given me an ultimatum that includes disbanding the Zulu Army and accepting a British resident in our country to force us to live as they wish."

Jama lay still, awaiting the order for his execution.

"I will not agree to terms that mean we change our way of life to be under British control," Cetshwayo said. "There will be war between the British and us, and we will need every warrior we have to fight them."

Jama realised Cetshwayo was not going to order his execution that day. He felt a wave of relief.

"When the war comes," Cetshwayo said. "You and the Abanonya will be in the forefront. You will lead your warriors into every battle and wash your spears in British blood. If you survive the war or if you die, you will have atoned for your transgression against my orders. That is my judgement."

"Yes, *inkosi*," Jama said. He knew that Cetshwayo was treating him with leniency, for every warrior in the Zulu army would wish to be at the forefront of battle. He stood up and shouted the royal salute. "*Bayete*!"

"*Bayete*!" the men in the king's *indlu* echoed, and Jama trotted outside to give the news to his *amabutho*.

"Gentlemen, we're about to go to war," Captain Fraser told the Cape Mounted Riflemen. "We gave Cetshwayo an ultimatum, he'll refuse to agree to our terms, and then we'll be at war with the Zulus."

"The largest Empire in the world facing the most potent army in Black Africa," Abernethy said. He whistled a bar of Handel's *Hallelujah*. "This will be interesting."

"What was the ultimatum, sir?" Andrew asked.

"The ultimatum was a long, detailed document," Fraser said, "perhaps purposefully so, for Sir Bartle Frere intends to quell the Zulu threat. I can only paraphrase it. To the north of Cetshwayo's domain, a Swazi renegade called Mbilini has been raiding the Boers in Transvaal and the Swazis. Frere demanded that Cetshwayo hand Mbilini over to British justice."

Andrew nodded. "I see."

"Also, an induna called Sihayo had an unfaithful wife who fled into Natal. Sihayo's sons led a small impi across the Tugela and dragged her back to Zululand, where they executed her, according to Zulu law."

Andrew nodded again, glad that Elaine was not involved.

"Our ultimatum demanded that Cetshwayo hand over the Sihayo's sons and pay a fine of five hundred cattle." Fraser looked up. "I think these terms are pretty insulting to the ruler of a sovereign nation."

"Yes, sir," Andrew said.

"There was more. Frere demanded that Cetshwayo institute fair trials in Zululand, with only the king having the power to sentence anybody to death. He also ordered Cetshwayo to abandon his military system, disband the army, allow men to marry when they wished and accept a British resident to supervise these alterations. Finally, he must accept missionaries and only muster the army when Britain permits him."

"Dear God and all his angels," Andrew said. "How long did Cetshwayo have to comply?"

"He had thirty days," Fraser replied, tight-lipped.

"That's tantamount to a declaration of war," Andrew said. "No ruler, anywhere, would accept these terms."

"I agree with you," Fraser said. "We're pushing Cetshwayo into a war so we can smash him and annex Zululand."

Andrew sighed. He had imagined soldiering to be a noble profession of defending his country from foreign aggression, not being a pawn of deceitful politicians.

"Do you think there will be a peaceful resolution, sir?"

Fraser shook his head. "No," he said. "Prepare your men for war, Baird." He gave a crooked. "General Lord Chelmsford said he only hopes the Zulus fight. Oh, his Lordship defeated the Gakelas handily enough, but the lads over the river," he nodded to the Tugela, "are on a different level. Now is your chance to win your spurs, Baird, and impress your girl."

Andrew was unsure which of Tennyson's quotes was more relevant. Was it the last line of *Ulysses*, "to strive, to seek, to find, and not to yield", or "Theirs not to reason why, theirs but to do and die" from *The Charge of the Light Brigade?*

Both probably, Andrew decided, as he prepared his men for the forthcoming war. They all knew of the power and bravery of the Zulu army, which terrorised all its neighbours.

"Don't drop your guard," Andrew ordered. "Keep alert at all times, shoot low and ride hard."

As the thirty days of grace passed, Andrew knew he would be leading his men to war. He thought of Elaine, perched on the lip of the Zulu lion, wrote her a dozen letters advising her to leave before the war started and trained his men.

When the ultimatum expired, Lord Chelmsford allowed his invasion plans to filter to the junior officers, and Andrew gathered his men.

"We'll soon be crossing the Buffalo River into Zululand," Andrew informed the stern, weathered faces. "It is a land of rolling hills and red earth, dotted with kraals, as we call the *imizi*. I have spoken to traders and hunters, who tell me the countryside is not as open as it appears."

Andrew's troop listened.

"Have any of you ever been to Zululand?" Andrew asked, looking directly at Abernethy.

Abernethy lifted his hand. "I lived there for years," he admitted.

Andrew nodded. "Tell us what you know, Abernethy," Andrew said. "The more intelligence we have, the better."

"I was a hunter in Zululand," Abernethy said. "From a distance, the land may look like English parkland, but the ground is uneven, with rock-strewn *koppies* – hills – small streams that twist and turn, hidden gullies, isolated rocks and antbear hills."

The more intelligent of the men listened, realising that any scrap of information may save their lives.

"There are no roads in Zululand, just tracks connecting the kraals of beehive-shaped *izindlu* and the few hunting trails we left behind." Abernethy's face changed as if he were reliving his days of hunting beyond the Tugela.

"The coastal strip is low-lying, and the ground rises to the west, with two rivers, the Black Umfolozi and White Umfolozi, dissecting the land. In the north, the Zulus and the Boers dispute where the border should be." Abernethy stopped for a moment. "The king rules from oNdini, that you'll know better as Ulundi and the people are hardy, honest, loyal and bound by rules and laws as strict as any you'll find in Europe."

"Did you like them?" Andrew asked.

"I did, sir," Abernethy said. "They're a straightforward people, with a lot to admire."

Andrew listened to Abernethy's words, then unfolded a map from his saddlebag and spread it on his camp table, weighing down the corners with rocks.

"Here we are, gentlemen," Andrew said. "Our target is the royal kraal at Ulundi." He decided to use the more commonly understood names to avoid confusion. "We cannot defend two hundred miles of border with the small number of troops we have. We'd stretch ourselves too thin, and the Zulus, with their highly mobile impis, could punch through our defences at will. Therefore, we must invade, bring the Zulu army to battle, defeat it in the open, burn Ulundi and show all Africa that we are the masters."

Do I believe all that? Or am I merely saying what I have to say to justify our invasion of a nation that has not threatened us? We are going to war, and I am a British soldier; therefore, it is my duty to fight to the best of my ability.

"Ulundi is around seventy miles from the frontier," Andrew continued. "General Chelmsford has decided on a multi-pronged invasion; Colonel Pearson will lead Number One Column crossing the Lower Drift of the Tugela. Lieutenant-Colonel Durnford will lead Number Two Column at the Middle Drift. Number Three Column under Colonel Glyn will cross at Rorke's Drift, and Colonel Wood will lead Number Four Column in the north at Bemba's Kop."

The men listened, wondering which column they would join.

"There will be a fifth column held in reserve at Luneburg in the Transvaal to ensure the Boers don't take advantage when we're embroiled with the Zulus." Andrew had met a few Boers and found them resentful of British interference. He would not be surprised if they took the opportunity to rebel when the British troops were fighting in Zululand.

"We are with Number Three, or Central Column," Andrew said. "We'll be travelling with N Battery, Royal Field Artillery, plus the Royal Engineers, most of the 24th Regiment, a squadron each of the Imperial Mounted Infantry, Natal Mounted Police and Colonial Mounted Volunteers, the third regiment Natal Native Contingent and a company of Natal Native Pioneers."

The men gave their opinions of each unit, with everybody happy that the 24th Foot was with them.

"We fought with the 24th in Galekaland," Andrew said. "They're steady men with experience in Africa. The last thing we want is a regiment of raw *rooinecks* straight out from Britain."

The men laughed, with some making comments under their breath. After over a year in Africa, Andrew felt himself to be a veteran, an old soldier fit to stand alongside his peers.

"Right, men," Andrew was satisfied his men were ready to fight, and their morale was high. "Dismissed!"

"Sir." Andrew approached Captain Fraser, who was talking to the regimental farrier. "Could I have permission to leave the column for a day?"

"Why?" Fraser asked.

"To see a lady, sir," Andrew said. "Her farm is only a few miles away."

Fraser shook his head. "Sorry, Baird, Miss Maxwell will have to do without your amorous advances. We need all hands on deck, and there's too much to do to afford leave."

"Yes, sir," Andrew was too young to hide his disappointment.

"Cheer up, Baird," Fraser said. "It will be all the sweeter when you meet her again, and you can impress her with tales of your adventures in Zululand." He grinned. "Now you might have another opportunity to prove your nickname; Up-and-at- 'em Andy." He laughed at the expression on Andrew's face.

"Yes, sir," Andrew said, although Fraser's words were little consolation. *Is nothing secret in this army?*

Andrew wrote a long letter that afternoon, telling Elaine what he had been doing and how much he thought about her. He pondered over the final paragraph, started it three times, scratched out the words and sighed deeply before saying. "When we meet again, we can arrange a date for our wedding. Until then, please think of me fondly and be assured that I love you."

Andrew read and reread the final passage, afraid that he had said too much. Finally, he shook his head, decided he was only telling her what she already knew, folded the letter, and placed it inside an envelope.

Scribbling Elaine's address, *Elaine Maxwell, Inglenook, Tugela River*, on the front, he handed it over to be posted and walked away quickly before he lost his nerve.

Well, Elaine, now I've told you what I think. All I have to do is defeat the Zulus, survive the war, and return to you.

"It is war," Jama said solemnly, brandishing his knobkerrie. "The British have ordered the Zulus to give up our cattle, disband our army and allow the British to rule our lives. King Cetshwayo replied that the Zulus do not tell the British how to live and they have no right to tell us."

The Abanonya listened, nodding their agreement. One or two commented, with Bangizwe drumming the shaft of his assegai off his shield.

Ndleleni touched his *umzimbeet* necklace and took a pinch of snuff. "When do we march, Jama?"

"We have never fought the British," Jama spoke so even the least intelligent of his men understood. "They have soldiers in red uniforms who carry guns and obey a queen who lives across the ocean."

The Abanonya listened without comment. The warriors were mature married men with families and responsibilities rather than hot-headed young *amaqhawe* - untried warriors eager to prove their manhood.

"The British are known as fierce soldiers," Jama said, "but we are Zulus, and this is our land. Cetshwayo has ordered us to defeat the British and not to invade Natal."

Bhekizizwe led the Abanonya in drumming the shafts of their spears on their shields in response.

"*Usuthu!*" Kgabu shouted the war cry, and the others followed. "*Usuthu!*"

"I want larger shields to protect us," Jama said. "In the days of Shaka, we carried a war shield, the *isiHlangu*. I want every man of the Abanonya to carry such a shield."

The warriors drummed again.

"Although a shield will not stop a bullet," Jama said, "It will help conceal us until we are close and will give protection against a bayonet."

The warriors listened without drumming.

Jama continued. "We will also carry an extra throwing assegai. The red soldiers kill at a distance, and we will do the same. We'll break up their formations with the throwing spears, then close with the *iKlwa* or the knobkerry."

Nobody argued with their induna. They understood Jama's strategy.

"We have few guns," Jama said. "I want the men who have them to practise. When we meet the enemy, they will stand together and fire into the British ranks."

Jama stood up, saw Kgabu and Funani in the front rank and hid his pride. "Before our time, Shaka made the Zulus great, and we will not dishonour his memory." Raising his voice, he sang the first line of one of Shaka's favourite songs, with his men joining in, so the words rose to the free sky of Zululand.

"Thou hast finished off the tribes.
Where wilt thou wage war?
Yes, where wilt thou wage war?
Thou hast conquered the kings.
Where wilt thou wage war?
Thou hast finished off the tribes.
Where wilt thou wage war?

Yes, yes, yes! Where wilt thou wage war?

The Abanonya danced as they sang, preparing for the contest with the greatest colonial power the world had ever known.

THE DELICATE TRUMPET NOTES SOUNDED OVER THE WHITE RANKS OF British tents. Andrew woke from a fitful sleep, glanced at his watch, saw it was two in the morning and struggled from his camp bed. He shaved in cold water, scraping the razor across his chin and wincing as he nicked the skin.

Damn it. I always do that before a busy day.

He dressed, fastened the revolver around his waist, adjusted his forage cap and stooped out of his tent to greet the day. The camp was awake, with flaring torches giving a near-mediaeval atmosphere to the hurrying infantry, labouring bullocks and creaking carts.

"Ready, Baird?" Fraser appeared as fresh as if he'd been awake for hours.

"Ready, sir," Andrew replied.

"Check the horses and men are fed, strike the tents and let's be on our way," Fraser said. "We have a country to invade and a king to break."

"Yes, sir." Andrew saluted, glanced towards Zululand, and got to work, thinking that none of the books he had read as a boy prepared him for the hundreds of hours of administration and organisation that any military procedure demanded. In books, it was all battle and glory.

"I don't mind the killing part," Sinclair said as he stifled a yawn and buckled his equipment. "That's easy. It's just that on campaign, I'm so bloody tired all the time."

Andrew nodded. Tiredness, irritability, and hunger go hand-in-hand with war. Add dirt, boredom, and fear, and that was the life of a soldier. *Part of the soldier's bargain, as my father would say. I wonder what he's doing now in Afghanistan.* He grunted, *probably winning fresh laurels.*

A chilling mist sat heavily on the Buffalo River that morning of the 11th of January 1879. The river was fast flowing, a hundred yards wide and churned frothy brown around an islet in the centre.

"This crossing is known as Rorke's Drift," Andrew told his men. "The infantry will cross here. Our ford is five minutes ride upstream."

The Cape Riflemen watched as Colonel Harness unlimbered a battery of six seven-pounder guns on a rocky piece of rising ground to cover the landing.

"That's the stuff to give them!" Sinclair said.

"That's the give to stuff them," Napier agreed and laughed at his supposed cleverness.

Andrew said nothing as he wondered how many soldiers had cracked the same joke over the past thousand years. He could imagine the Roman legionnaires using similar humour as they prepared their catapults at the siege of Jerusalem.

"Come on, lads!" For some obscure reason, Lord Chelmsford had decided the mounted men should load their carbines onto the ponts at Rorke's Drift, ride upstream, plough through the ford and return for the weapons. Upstream of the ford, the Buffalo seethed white over dangerous rocks, negating any possibility of an easy passage. Andrew watched Lieutenant Chard of the Royal Engineers working on a pair of flat-bottomed iron ponts, ready to ferry the scarlet-coated 24th Foot to Zululand.

"Come on, Riflemen!" Andrew encouraged as the mounted men hesitated at the edge of the river. For a moment, he remembered the Common Ridings in the Scottish Borders, when scores of energetic riders forded the bright, shallow rivers in front of enthusiastic crowds. The Buffalo was neither bright nor shallow, and the only crowds here carried rifles or spears as the warriors of the Natal Native Contingent watched the horsemen test the water.

"Follow me, lads!" Andrew shouted, kicked in his heels, and plunged Lancelot into the river.

The water was colder than Andrew expected as the current pushed against him, but he was a skilled horseman and crossed without difficulty. His riflemen followed, with only one man struggling until Andrew rode back into the river to help him over the final few yards.

"Come on, Sinclair," Andrew said. "We can't lose an old Cameronian in an African river when we've fighting to do."

"Thank you, sir," Sinclair said, spitting out a mouthful of Buffalo water. "I think my horse slipped."

"That must be what happened," Andrew agreed.

"Push inland," Fraser ordered. "Hold the high ground and watch for any Zulu impis. I am sure Cetshwayo has men watching everything we do."

"Yes, sir." Andrew nodded and rode on, disturbing a lone bushbuck, which thundered through the long grass. He rode to a slight ridge, from where he could see into Zululand and over the river. The Royal Artillery battery still covered the crossing at Rorke's Drift, six guns eager for a target, while a battalion of the Natal Native Contingent waited to cross the Buffalo.

"They're a rum lot, sir," Abernethy said.

"I think they're from a mixture of tribes," Andrew said. "I wonder how many volunteered and how many we coerced." Most of the NNC carried assegais and shields, with only one in ten carrying a firearm.

"I doubt many volunteered," Abernethy said. "Hobson's Choice." He shook his head. "I didn't mean the men were a rum lot, sir; I meant the European officers and NCOs."

Andrew nodded. "You could be right, Abernethy. I think we scraped the bottom of a murky barrel for that lot."

Urged by their mounted officers, the NNC linked arms and rushed into the river, hoping to use the force of numbers to defeat the current. In mid-stream, the water reached their necks, and a few lost their grip, with the current sweeping them away. None of the NCOs or officers tried to help.

"Poor buggers," Abernethy said.

"Why don't they use the ponts like the 24th?" Andrew asked.

Abernethy whistled a few bars of Tchaikovsky's *1812 Overture*. "The army doesn't value the NNC," he said.

Andrew frowned without commenting. He understood.

Once across the river, the NNC lined the ridge to guard the crossing while the British infantry marched stoically onto the ponts. Each pont held eighty men, standing shoulder to shoulder with moisture beading on their bright scarlet uniforms.

The 24th, stoic and tanned, crossed without comment. Veteran soldiers, they would follow orders to invade Zululand, Afghanistan, or Russia. Some looked over to the opposite side of the river; others watched their allies, the Natal Native Contingent, the beleaguered NNC.

"Baird." Fraser joined them on the ridge. "Take a patrol inland and see what's happening. Don't get involved in any fighting."

"Yes, sir."

With the bulk of the NNC on the Zulu side of the river and the engineers gradually taking the 24th across, Andrew pushed further into Zululand. Although he expected an immediate Zulu counterattack, the only Zulus he saw was a group of herd boys with a small herd of cattle.

"It's as peaceful as a Sunday afternoon in Hyde Park," Abernethy said.

The rising sun burned away the mist, and then the heat grew, bringing sweat to Andrew's face and under his arms. He rode in increasing circles, learning the lie of the land, and feeling as if every eye in Zululand was fixed on him. He followed the track deeper into Zululand and found it plunged into a stretch of marshland.

Andrew dismounted and probed the mud while a flight of pigeons exploded from a nearby tree. "The engineers will have to strengthen the track here." He noted the area. "The wagons will sink axle deep into this filth."

"The Zulus are keeping out of our way," Abernethy said quietly.

"I wonder why?" Andrew replied. He stopped on a small hill and scanned the interior of Zululand with his field glasses. "I can see something over there beside that rocky hill. A native kraal." He consulted his map, ignoring the drops of sweat that fell from his face. "According to this map, that's Sihayo's kraal."

"Siyaho's the man who caused all the problems, sir," Abernethy said. "It was his wife who absconded and who his son killed."

"That's right," Andrew said. "More importantly, his kraal commands the track Lord Chelmsford must use to reach Ulundi, and he could give us all sorts of trouble." He raised his field glasses again, noting the *imuzi* was situated on a steep *kranz* above a deep valley. "The Zulus have a good eye for a strategic position."

"They are natural warriors," Abernethy said. "And Sihayo is one of Cetshwayo's favourites."

"I'll report the marsh and Siyaho's kraal to General Chelmsford," Andrew was satisfied with the reconnaissance.

When Andrew's patrol returned to the bridgehead, the British had completed crossing the Buffalo. Their camp spread along the bank in neat rows of white tents, with the cooks already busy preparing the next meal and the horses in neat lines.

"Haven't these men learned anything?" Andrew asked as he entered the camp. "The general's instructions were for every camp to be laagered, with the wagons drawn into a defensive circle."

"Relax, Lieutenant," Fraser said. "We haven't seen a sign of a hostile Zulu."

"That doesn't mean they haven't seen a sign of us, sir," Andrew said.

"Lord Chelmsford knows what he's doing." Fraser shook his head.

Chelmsford smiled benignly as he listened to Andrew's report. "Thank you, Lieutenant Baird," he said, speaking in short, crisp sentences. "I'll send Hamilton-Browne's battalion of the NNC to capture Sihayo's kraal."

Andrew had met George Hamilton-Browne, an articulate Ulsterman with much experience in the Maori Wars in New Zealand. Although Andrew was not impressed, he decided to reserve judgement until he had seen him in action.

"I'd better send you Cape Mounted Riflemen chaps with the cavalry, Baird. Captain Fraser can support the NNC," Chelmsford said casually. "You fought the Galekas, so you know how to handle these fellows."

"Yes, sir," Andrew said. He felt a leap of elation that he would be involved in the opening action of the Zulu War, with General Chelmsford as a witness.

The quicker we finish this war, the sooner I will see Elaine again, and when we defeat Cetshwayo's Zulus, Inglenook will be safe.

CHAPTER 14

Lieutenant-Colonel Russell commanded the cavalry that scouted ahead of the NNC. They rode well, as British cavalry always did, with the morning sun burning off Zululand's morning mist and the men tall in the saddle. The Cape Mounted Rifles were in the centre, with Lord Chelmsford and his gorgeously attired staff officers accompanying the striking force to Sihayo's kraal but remaining in the rear.

"Don't hurt any women or children," Chelmsford ordered. "And don't shoot unless the Zulus fire first."

"Yes, sir," Fraser agreed, winking at Andrew.

"We're at war with Cetshwayo," Chelmsford reminded. "Not with the Zulu people."

The riflemen listened, cast a jaundiced eye over the NNC with their heterogeneous collection of NCOs and wondered how they would fare against Zulu warriors.

Chelmsford smiled at Andrew. "How do you find Africa, Baird?"

Not used to a general addressing him, Andrew hesitated before replying. "I like it well enough, sir," he said at last.

Chelmsford beamed from under his low white helmet. With his long nose and black, bushy eyebrows, he looked like a professor rather than a victorious general.

"You've done rather well, Baird," Chelmsford said, "gaining a commission within a year. But you were at Sandhurst, I believe."

Andrew started. *How the devil did you know that?* "Yes, sir," he said, feeling Fraser's gaze fixed on him.

"You have the right background then," Chelmsford said, pleased he had surprised his most junior officer. "Good. Carry on, Baird."

Andrew could understand why everybody, officers and men, liked Lord Chelmsford. He cared for his men and treated his officers like individuals.

"Remember, gentlemen," Chelmsford said, "don't hurt the women and children. We are only here to fight the Zulu army."

"We won't forget, sir," Fraser said, turning away.

Andrew felt his heartbeat increase as they advanced toward Sihayo's kraal. The Martini was a comforting weight beside the saddle, and his revolver was reassuring in its holster, yet he knew the Zulus were more formidable than the Galekas had been.

"Extended formation, lads," Fraser ordered calmly. "Watch the flanks."

The riflemen spread out, each man two yards from his neighbour and the horses trotting over the uneven ground. A deer broke cover in front of them, jinking madly this way and that to escape the horsemen. A pair of white-backed vultures circled above.

"Trust the vultures to be here," Sinclair said. "I hate these bastards."

Andrew agreed. Vultures seemed to have a sixth sense where they could find fresh meat. They were a harbinger of death.

"There's the *kranz*, the rocky overhang." Andrew motioned ahead. "Sihayo's kraal is on the lower slope."

He spoke for the sake of talking, for Captain Fraser knew the location. *I'm showing my nerves,* he thought. *A good officer should be laconic and never reveal any weakness.*

When the riflemen came close, they heard cattle from the deep valley beside the *kranz*, and Andrew saw busy youngsters driving a herd before them. He lifted his voice.

"Sinclair and Kelly, check that valley in case there's an impi waiting to ambush us."

The two riflemen peeled away as Lord Chelmsford halted his staff, allowing the cavalry, NNC and Cape Mounted Rifles to advance.

Hamilton-Browne's NNC jogged behind the riflemen, easily keeping pace with the horses. Andrew watched them, wondering what they felt moving against the Zulus, warriors who had terrorised the local tribes for decades. The NNC looked no different from African civilians except for the strip of red rag tied around their foreheads. Although some waved their firearms threateningly, most seemed reluctant to advance, with the European NCOs and officers encouraging them with threats and kicks.

"That company seems better than the others." Andrew indicated one formation of the NNC.

"Number Eight Company is of Zulu stock." Abernethy was always a font of information. "Captain Duncombe leads them, and he chose the best men."

Andrew had never met Duncombe but respected his foresight. "Zulus fighting against their king?"

"They are the remains of a young regiment that defeated Cetshwayo's royal regiment in a stick fight," Abernethy explained. "The king was annoyed and had a fully armed regiment against them, spears against sticks. The survivors escaped to Natal and are back for revenge." Abernethy grinned. "Sihayo was the induna of the inGobamakhosi regiment who destroyed the youngsters, sir."

Andrew grunted. "Nothing is ever set in stone, is it, Abernethy?"

My father spoke of the Guides on India's northwest frontier, where Pashtun tribesmen were amongst the best soldiers Britain had. It seems that I am mirroring his experience in Zululand.

Sinclair and Kelly returned. "The Zulus hold the valley, sir! They've rolled boulders across the entrance and posted riflemen on the slopes."

"Thank you," Andrew said and reported the information to Fraser, who told Colonel Richard Glyn of the 24th Foot, commanding the assaulting party.

"Damned cheek," Glyn, a white-bearded, pipe-smoking veteran with dancing eyes, replied. "Shooting at British soldiers, eh? We can't allow that," he said and ordered Hamilton-Browne's NNC to make a flanking attack.

"Four companies of the 24th will support the NNC," Glyn ordered.

The NNC moved forward, shaking their weapons and shouting. Immediately they were in range, Zulu riflemen on the rocky slopes opened fire, with puffs of grey-white smoke revealing their position. Andrew heard the angry buzz as bullets passed overhead.

"They're firing high again," he said without ducking.

"Long may that continue, sir," Abernethy replied as they approached the gorge.

Sihayo's *imuzi* was on top of a steep hill, with the cattle in the gorge at the bottom and a profusion of rocks and thorn bushes littering the lower slopes. Fraser split the riflemen to the left and right while Hamilton-Browne charged forward with his infantry. The NNC had been shouting their war cries and brandishing their assegais while the riflemen were close, but when they realised they faced a Zulu *imuzi* alone, they fell silent.

"They know how dangerous the Zulus are," Abernethy said.

The NNC at the rear slowed down when they realised the British infantry were not accompanying them. They began to hang back, with one or two trying to retreat or hiding behind convenient rocks until the sergeants encouraged them with mighty kicks.

"Get up there, you cowardly bastards!"

"Fight! The Zulus are your enemies; now's your chance to get even!"

Abernethy watched, shaking his head. "The NNC volunteers don't seem eager to fight, sir."

"No, they're in a blue funk," Andrew agreed.

"No firing!" Hamilton-Brown ordered his men. Unlike many of his NCOs, he led from the front, with the Zulu-speaking Duncombe prominent. "Only use the assegai!"

As they approached the kraal, a man stepped in front of them. Tall, powerfully built and dignified, he wore the *isicoco,* the head-ring of a married man and carried a long shield, three assegais and a knobkerry. Andrew noted the leopard skin band around his head, the feathers around his knees and the pattern of his shield. While most of the cowhide was white, the outer border was black, and three black smudges sat in the lower half.

"Now there's a Zulu warrior," Abernethy said. "That's Jama, *induna* of the Abanonya."

Andrew reined up to study the first enemy warrior he had seen. "He looks very confident."

"He should be, sir," Abernethy told him. "He is one of the Children of Heaven."

The lone Zulu warrior seemed to paralyze the NNC, who hesitated despite the brutal urgings of their non-commissioned officers.

"By whose orders do you enter the land of the Zulus?" Jama demanded, facing the entire NNC without a flicker of fear.

Captain Duncombe answered after a slight pause. "By the orders of the Great White Queen!"

At Duncombe's words, the warrior withdrew, and a ragged volley of musketry sounded from the rocky slopes and Sihayo's kraal.

"They're sheltering in caves," Sinclair shouted. "Sir, can we shoot back?"

"Not until Colonel Glyn gives the order," Fraser replied.

Most of the shots were high, but a couple landed in the NNC ranks, which, combined with the challenge, was enough. The majority of the NNC either wavered or turned to flee, with only Dunscomb's Number Eight Company following Hamilton-Browne and the officers.

The firing continued for a few moments, joined by a rolling avalanche of boulders. One rock crashed into the backside of a Scottish officer, who swore loudly and long in Gaelic.

"Somebody's unhappy," Abernethy said, grinning. "When will Fraser let us play?"

"I don't know," Andrew said, fingering his rifle.

As they watched, the defending Zulus abandoned their firearms and resorted to more traditional weapons. They charged out of the kraal in a disciplined formation carrying long shields and stabbing assegais to crash into Number Eight Company with loud yells. Number Eight responded in kind, and Andrew saw the two Zulu forces fighting in the old, traditional manner with no holds barred and no quarter asked or expected.

Andrew looked for Jama and saw him leading a small *amabutho* into the NNC flank, scattering them in moments and striking with his knobkerry.

"I want to fight that man," Andrew said, glancing at Fraser.

"There he goes again," Kelly growled. "Go-get- 'em Andy, desperate to fight."

"Keep back, lads," Fraser ordered. "Let the Zulus deal with the Zulus. We'll remain out of this fight and mop up any who break through."

Despite his experiences against the Galeka, Andrew had never seen such ferocity as when the two rival Zulu regiments fought.

He heard the Zulu war cry "*Usuthu!*" and the oft-repeated, hissing "*ngadla*," – "I have eaten," - as a warrior thrust home with his assegai. Andrew saw the technique, the way the warrior used his shield to hook away that of his adversary, exposing his left side, then stabbed underhand with the short, broad-bladed assegai. The victor would thrust the assegai into the midriff and rip sideways with the same movement as he shouted the triumphant "*ngadla!*"

Andrew saw Jama carve a bloody path through Number Eight company, only to find more warriors opposing him. "It's a bloody business," Andrew said, controlling Lancelot as the noise and smell of raw blood unsettled him.

"No bloodier than the charge of case shot at close quarters or the battle of Flodden or Bannockburn," Abernethy replied. "We are just as bloody as the Zulus."

Andrew nodded. "That's for sure."

Jama's determined warriors broke through Number Eight Company, leaving a trail of dead and wounded men. They halted, panting and with blood dripping from their spears as they saw the riflemen waiting for them.

"Get ready, boys!" Andrew lifted his Martini-Henry, feeling a surge of apprehension and regret. Apprehension in case the Zulus should prove too much for him, and regret that he would have to kill such brave men defending their territory.

A dozen warriors grouped together, each man with a similar pattern on his shield, the black fringe around white cowhide. More Zulus joined them until twenty warriors faced the riflemen.

"Sihayo must have asked for help," Abernethy mused. "Jama's Abanonya are from the Batshe valley, but not this kraal. You'll notice their shields are different, sir."

Andrew nodded. Jama's men had more white on their shields, denoting an older, more experienced regiment. Jama lifted his spear, pointed to the Riflemen, and shouted, "*Usuthu!*"

His followers drummed the hafts of their spears on their shields, chanting, "*Usuthu!*" as they squared up to the Cape Mounted Rifles.

"Get ready, boys!" Fraser shouted. "Be careful if you fire in case you shoot our own men!"

The Zulus charged, with their shields held in their left hands and assegais in their right. They covered the ground faster than any human Andrew had ever seen, so he could only fire one shot before they reached him. Discarding the Martini, he drew his revolver and fired again, seeing his bullet slam into a shield. The Zulu staggered and continued, still shouting his war cry.

"*Usuthu!*"

"Usuthu!"

The Zulus crashed into the Riflemen, leapt into the air, and thrust with their assegais. Andrew heard a Rifleman scream as Jama stabbed him in the chest, and then he was too busy defending himself to notice anything else.

Two warriors leapt at him. He shot the first through the head, then swore as the second smashed his shield against Lancelot, nearly unbalancing horse and rider. Andrew fired, missed, and gasped as the assegai ripped through the leg of his trousers and opened a stinging wound in his calf. He swung his revolver sideways, felt the thrill of contact and fired again, with the bullet knocking the warrior backwards.

For a second, Andrew saw the man clearly. He was young, still a teenager, with a handsome face and his mouth wide open in surprise. *That could be me,* Andrew thought as the Zulu fell, and then he shot at the next man, hitting him in the leg. The warrior spun round, recovered, and threw his assegai.

Developed for thrusting rather than throwing, the assegai was clumsy in flight, and Andrew dodged sideways, thankful for his years of training on the Scottish Border rugby pitches.

The assegai whistled past, with the staff skiffing Andrew's back, and he lifted his revolver and fired again. The bullet hit the warrior in the chest, stopping him dead, and then Number Eight Company smashed into the Zulu flank, with a company of the 24th in close support.

Andrew saw Jama stop beside the men he had shot. The Zulu stooped over the young man with an expression of utter anguish on his face, and in a flash of insight, Andrew knew they were father and son.

"Oh, dear God," Andrew breathed. For the first time, he saw the enemy not as ferocious warriors but as people with wives and children, hopes and dreams. With two bullets, he had ruined that man's life.

Sorry, my Zulu enemy, but if I had not killed your son, he would have killed me.

Jama stood still amid the battlefield, and Andrew saw the pain in his eyes. Ignoring the battle that raged around him, the warrior lifted his assegai and pointed it directly at Andrew.

He's marked me down, Andrew said to himself. *He's telling me he's going to kill me for killing his son. No, his sons. Both these men I killed were his sons.*

Two men of Number Eight Company approached Jama, shouting. Andrew watched as Jama casually hooked away the leading man's shield and thrust his assegai into his chest, ducked the swing of the second man, smashed his shield into the man's face and killed him.

"That one's mine!" Sinclair yelled, aiming his Martini.

"No." Andrew pushed the barrel of the rifle down. "There's been enough killing for one day."

Lifting his bloody spear towards Andrew, Jama called on the remnants of his men and trotted away.

CHAPTER 15

"That was a success," Fraser said as the British set fire to Sihayo's *imuzi*, rounded up hundreds of cattle and counted the casualties.

"We lost two men," Andrew reminded, "and another was wounded." He did not mention the minor injury to his calf.

Fraser nodded. "I know about our casualties, Baird, but we captured a Zulu kraal and delivered a bloody nose to the induna who started the war by breaking the law. Now Cetshwayo knows we are in earnest he might agree to our terms."

"Maybe," Andrew said, although privately, he doubted Cetshwayo would back down.

"Now, Baird, while the engineers improve the track and move the transport forward, the infantry will consolidate our victory." Fraser smiled. "Colonel Russell wants us to scout forward into Zululand."

"Yes, sir," Andrew said.

"That means you, Up-and-at-em, Andy," Fraser said. He lowered his voice. "Be careful out there, Baird. We've won a border skirmish, that's all. I expect Cetshwayo is gathering his impis to send against us even as we speak."

"I expect he is, sir," Andrew replied. "If they are all as fierce as the men who defended Siyaho's kraal, we won't find this an easy campaign."

Fraser tapped his rifle. "Not even the fiercest and bravest warrior is proof against a Martini-Henry bullet."

"Yes, sir. You're right, of course. I'll get my men ready."

"Get your leg seen to first, Baird," Fraser said. "The surgeon will give you a couple of stitches."

"Yes, sir," Andrew agreed.

Lieutenant-Colonel John Cecil Russell of the 12th Lancers commanded Number Three Column's mounted men and sent forward strong patrols to explore the route towards Ulundi.

"Find us a credible route and camping places," Russell ordered. "And watch for any impis."

Andrew led his troop of Riflemen into Zululand, constantly wary in case of an ambush. He knew the establishment thought highly of Russell, who was a friend of Chelmsford, the Prince of Wales and General Wolseley, Britain's most notable soldier. However, although he had served in the Ashanti War, Russell had never led mounted men in action, and his promotion over the heads of veteran colonial troops did not enhance his popularity.

Andrew glanced over the other colonial mounted forces, for there was no British cavalry in the invading army. He saw the Natal Carabineers, the Natal Hussars, and the Buffalo Border Guard with the Natal Mounted Police. All were colonials, excellent on horseback and good shots, and many were experienced in frontier warfare.

This conflict is a colonial war as much as a British war. With all these mounted troops and the NNC, only the infantry, engineers and artillery are home-grown.

Despite the skirmish at Sihayo's kraal, Cetshwayo had not despatched an impi to deal with the straggling British column, and Chelmsford was free to consolidate his position on the Zulu side of the Buffalo River.

"Cetshwayo's dallying a bit," Fraser mused. "He's giving us time to settle in."

"That's kind of him," Andrew said. "By the time he acts, His Lordship will have us tucked up nice and snug behind a wagon laager with half a dozen guns, and Cetshwayo can whistle for his supper."

Fraser laughed. "Let's hope so, Baird. One decent battle should finish this war. We want the Zulu impis to smash themselves against a wall of our rifles."

Russell's mounted patrols pushed deeper into Zululand, probing towards the distinctive Isipezi Hill without molestation.

"Maybe they won't fight," Sergeant Duncan said, chewing his moustache as he peered into the misty distance. "Maybe Cetshwayo will prove a paper tiger."

"He'll fight," Abernethy said quietly. "Even if Cetshwayo doesn't want to fight, his indunas and young warriors will force the issue."

"Will they?" Andrew lifted his field glasses and scanned the land ahead, where a strangely shaped hill pushed out from a terminal spur of the Nqutu Range. "That looks like a suitable place for an initial camping ground. We're only ten miles from Rorke's Drift, an easy day's march for the infantry and wagons."

"Yes, sir," Abernethy agreed.

"That hill isn't named on my map," Andrew said and smiled. "It looks a bit like a crouching sphinx."

Abernethy looked more nervous than the other Riflemen, with his eyes constantly roving around the countryside. "The Zulus call it Isandhlwana," he said, "which is their word for a cow's second stomach."

"How evocative," Andrew said with a smile. "Trust the Zulus to involve cattle."

"This will do," Russell agreed with Andrew's location. "There is water for man and beast, fuel for fires and adequate grazing. Report to General Chelmsford, Baird, and tell him what we've found."

"Yes, sir," Andrew wheeled Lancelot around and returned to the camp at Rorke's Drift.

Chelmsford accepted Russell's recommendation with his habitual polite smile. "We'll form an advanced base at Isandhlwana," he said and ordered the army to begin its ponderous march.

Andrew helped guide the column to Isandlwana, pointing out the boggy areas of the track and watching for ambushes. The weather had been wet, making the ground soft, unsuitable for the heavy wagons, which rolled ponderously onward while the infantry marched like a scarlet snake.

"They're watching us," Abernethy warned.

"Where?" Andrew was too experienced to look around.

"A small group of Zulus are standing on the hill beyond your left shoulder," Abernethy said. "Five of them, from the Abanonya."

"That's the regiment that attacked us at Sihayo's kraal," Andrew said. "Jama's warriors."

"Yes, sir," Abernethy agreed.

"They were a handy bunch," Andrew turned casually, removed his forage cap, and looked around. "I see them."

"Maybe we'd best warn the captain, sir," Abernethy suggested.

"Do that," Andrew said. "Give Captain Fraser my compliments and tell him what you've seen." He watched as Abernethy trotted away, had a last glance at the Zulus and returned to his task of guiding the convoy along the track.

When they reached the campsite beneath the rocky hill, Fraser set out pickets.

Andrew found a small knoll on the slopes of Isandhlwana, dismounted and swept the landscape with his field glasses when a corporal and two privates of the 24th joined him.

"Here we go again, sir." Private Miller gave Andrew a gap-toothed grin. "You'll be missing your sweetheart."

Andrew was unsure how to respond to that. "Yes, Miller," he said. "I am."

Miller laughed, although he continued to watch his surroundings. "We used to leave you alone as much as possible, sir," he said. "Sergeant McBain sent us on picket duty to ensure nobody bothered Miss Maxwell's wagon when you were courting her."

Andrew had learned to accept his relationship with Elaine was common knowledge. "I'll have to thank the sergeant." The mention of Elaine made him smile and think of her mopane tree at Inglenook, and he jerked his mind back to the present.

The sooner we win this war, the sooner I will see her again. And her sister with that cheeky sense of humour.

Andrew lowered his field glasses for a moment and watched the infantrymen work in the camp. Sun-browned, with bristling moustaches or beards, they looked formidable in their single-breasted scarlet tunics and stained white, canvas-covered cork sun helmets. Dust and mud smeared their blue trousers, and their heavy ammunition boots thumped securely on the ground, although they were ponderous compared to the lightly clad Zulu warrior.

Fully equipped, each soldier suffered under fifty-seven pounds weight, including their Martini and bayonet, with greatcoat, mess-tin, seventy rounds of ammunition and a haversack. The infantry carried the Martini-Henry rifles and the triangular bayonet, which many soldiers called the lung or lunge bayonet. Unfortunately, not all the bayonets were well-made, and the cheap steel could bend or twist on contact.

Behind the infantry came the wagons, each pulled by an immense team of oxen with a driver managing them with the aid of a long whip. One by one, they rolled to the campsite in what seemed like ordered confusion.

"There are two hundred and twenty wagons in the column," Fraser said when Andrew returned to the camp, "each one with eight or nine pairs of oxen. No wonder the road's in such a mess." He looked up as thunder grumbled across the sky. "And that won't help any."

"A bloke in a pub told me that Africa was always warm and sunny," O'Donnell mumbled as he slouched past. "Wait till I meet him again! I'll tell him he's a bloody liar!"

Andrew looked up as the first of the fat raindrops wept from low, bruised clouds. "You're right, sir. The rain will make the roads even worse," he said.

"I'll be glad when this lot is safely laagered," Fraser said. "Half the wagons are still on the road to Rorke's Drift, with penny packets of infantry to guard them. If I were Cetshwayo, I'd send an impi to strike at the road and mop up the wagons when they're strung out."

Andrew nodded. "Yes, sir. Cetshwayo's missing a golden opportunity."

Fraser nodded. "Thank God. I know we haven't seen many Zulus yet, but that's when they're at their most dangerous."

"I agree, sir." Andrew lifted his collar as a meagre defence against the rain. "The Galekas were hard enough to defeat, and they were terrified of the Zulus."

"Everybody's scared of the Zulus," Fraser said. "That's why we're invading. We have to negate their threat."

Behind the campsite, the rocky hill of Isandhlwana reared skyward like a Southern African sphynx. It rose for hundreds of feet, dropped abruptly, and rose in a spur of the Nqutu plateau.

After an hour, the rain transformed every dry *spruit* – riverbed - on Isandhlwana into a waterfall, with rivulets cutting into the ground where the British camped.

"You look wet, Baird, and you're going to get wetter," Fraser said. "Check the Nqutu plateau. We don't want any more Zulus spying on us while we make camp."

Always hating to be idle, Andrew obeyed willingly. He rode Lancelot as far up the hill as he thought safe, dismounted, and scrambled to the summit on foot, holding his rifle but leaving his sword behind. When he reached the plateau, he found the rain had stopped, leaving everything clear and fresh. The tableland stretched into the hazy distance north and eastward, lovely under the watery sun. Andrew scanned the plain with his field glasses, checking every crevasse and bush for possible Zulus.

Empty, he told himself. *It's as if Cetshwayo doesn't care that we've invaded his land. What game is that man playing? We saw Jama's Abanonya, so the Zulus know we're here.*

Along the southern edge of the plateau, the ground dropped abruptly in an escarpment, broken here and there by *dongas*, wide ditches through which new streams gushed. From the head of the precipice, Andrew could see the four-mile-wide plateau east of Isandlwana, bisected by the rough track that eventually led to the royal kraal of oNdini. South of the plain were ranges of hills, blue in the distance, reminding Andrew of the Cheviot Hills along the English-Scottish border.

With his year of experience in Africa, Andrew scanned the position with a military eye. If the British kept Isandlwana behind them and formed a proper wagon laager, they would have a solid defensive position, should the Zulus choose to attack. They had an excellent field of fire to the east, as any attacking force must advance over the open, although they could use the *dongas* and a scattering of boulders. The only weakness Andrew could see was where he stood, where the northern spur linked to the plateau. A daring Zulu commander could descend from the spur and take the British in the rear.

Chelmsford's no fool. He'll post a strong picket on the spur to watch the plateau. If I can see the weakness, that vastly experienced man will have it covered. As long as we have a laager and decent defences, we can hold out against any number of Zulus.

"No sign of any Zulus, sir," Andrew reported when he returned.

"His Lordship is posting a picket on the spur," Fraser said. "You'd better get some rest, Baird. You've had a busy day."

"WHAT DO YOU MEAN, TREASURE?" ANDREW PAUSED AS HE OVERHEARD THE conversation outside his tent early the following morning.

"In Cetshwayo's palace," Miller said. "I'm telling you, man, Cetshwayo's been gathering gold for years, and he's got all the treasure from previous Zulu kings as well, from Shaka onward."

"What sort of treasure, Dusty?" Drummond was sceptical. "How would they get it?"

"All sorts," Miller said. "The Zulus robbed the shipwrecks and took everything from the Boers they killed, mined for gold, and taxed the ivory hunters for decades. I'm telling you, man, there's a whole kraal full of treasure at Ulundi."

Andrew listened for a moment, remembering Ashanti Smith's tales of treasure in Cetshwayo's kraal. These rumours, or shaves as the army called them, would be prevalent in any campaign and were usually without foundation.

Andrew dressed, buckled on his revolver, and left the tent. He was not interested in Cetshwayo's treasure. He only wanted to finish the war, escape from Zululand with its changeable weather and ferocious warriors and return to Inglenook. He smiled, quoting poetry as he walked.

> *"Elaine the fair, Elaine the loveable,*
> *Elaine, the lily maid of Astolat."*[1]

JAMA SMELLED THE SMOKE BEFORE HE REACHED HIS *IMUZI*. HE INCREASED his speed to a run, with his men following. They crested the final ridge and stopped as the flames and smoke rose in a funeral pyre over their homes.

"The British have been here," Ndleleni said quietly. He looked over the Batshe Valley, where smoke rose from the other *imizi*. "They have burned all our homes."

Jama grunted. "Spread out." Although his *imuzi* was in flames, Jama did not lose his warrior instinct or forget his training. He ordered scouts to check the neighbourhood for British patrols and advanced cautiously, ready for a trap, ready to fight and kill.

There were no traps. The raiders had struck the undefended *imuzi* and departed, leaving destruction in their wake.

Jama leapt over the burning thorn barricade and ran through the smoke to his *izindlu*. "Yibanathi! Lerate!"

Yibanathi's home was on fire, with the roof already collapsed and flames licking up the walls. Jama saw two bodies inside, one smouldering and the other ablaze. Jumping into the *izindlu*, he pulled both out, knowing he was too late to save them.

Both were dead, with Yibanathi nearly unrecognisable and Lerate's lower half on fire. Jama doused the flames with his hands, uncaring of the pain. He stared at both, momentarily unable to comprehend the magnitude of his loss. Lerate looked upwards with her fine brown eyes wide and a gash on her forehead where somebody had struck her.

"Jama." Ndleleni touched his shoulder. "You cannot help them, now." His voice was gruff with shared sorrow.

Jama stood up, hiding his emotions. "No," he said. "I cannot bring back the dead."

He knew the reality of war; the victor killed the vanquished without sympathy or mercy. Yet he would avenge the death of his wives and the destruction of his *imuzi*.

"They have taken all the cattle," Ndleleni reported, "and trampled or burned the crops. Our people will be hungry this winter."

Jama listened without expression. He could see his wives lying dead in their burning home. This war had barely started, and already it had taken everything except his life. Ndleleni guided Jama outside the *imuzi,* so they stood amid the swirling smoke.

"They killed all of the herd boys except two." Ndleleni waited for Jama to react.

"Where are they?" Jama asked.

"Here." Ndleleni pointed to a pair of young boys, the youngest barely nine years old, who stood a few yards away, staring at the burning *imuzi*. The older boy was Jabulani, Jama's youngest and sole surviving son.

"Bring them to me," Jama ordered, feeling sick relief that one member of his family survived.

The boys stood with their heads down until Jama spoke. "Lift your chin, Jabulani, and don't be afraid. You are a Zulu!"

Both boys obeyed, defiance sparking alongside the horror and fear in their eyes as he faced Jama.

"Tell me what happened," Jama ordered.

"The horse soldiers came," Jabulani said. "They surrounded the *imuzi*, killed everybody and set it alight. Then they trampled and burned the crops while others hunted for the cattle."

"How many horse soldiers?" Jama asked.

Jabulani did not know how many. "They were everywhere. White soldiers and black soldiers."

"Who led them?" Jama put a hand on Jabulani's shoulder.

"A white man with two green feathers in his hat," Jabulani said.

"Was he wearing a uniform?" Jama asked.

"No," Jabulani replied at once. "He wore dark clothes and boots, with a wide hat."

"A white man in dark clothes with two green feathers in his wide hat," Jama repeated. "I will find him. We are going to war, and I do not want you both with us."

"*Ubaba!* Father!" Jabulani said and closed his mouth.

"You." Jama touched the younger boy. "Go eastward and find an *imuzi* the white soldiers have not burned. Tell them who you are, and say I sent you. Go now." He watched as the boy trotted away.

"You must be a man now, Jabulani," Jama said. "You will come with us and carry our spears, fetch water and do as we tell you."

"Yes, *Ubaba,"* Jabulani agreed, happy to be with his father and the warriors.

"What will we do, Jama?" Ndleleni asked.

"Fight the invaders," Jama said. "Find the man with the green feathers and kill him, too." He lifted his assegais and knobkerrie and headed towards Lord Chelmsford's army.

CHAPTER 16

As the mounted men gradually extended their patrols to search for the elusive Zulu army, the central Number Three column settled in at Isandhlwana.

Rather than form a laager, the British set up their tents in a line from north to south, with the NNC on the north and the mounted men and the First Battalion of the 24th Foot on the extreme south. Even after his experience in the Frontier War, Andrew was surprised at the number of tents. As well as the bell tents, which held sixteen private soldiers each, there were hospital tents, headquarter tents, tents for officers and sergeants, mess tents and the adjutant's administration tent.

"We need scores of tents for even a simple camp," Andrew said. "How many do the Zulus need?"

"None, sir," Abernethy said. "They travel light."

Andrew grunted. "No wonder they can cover so much ground."

Andrew had read the orders for setting up the bell tents, although he had never seen an entire regiment erect them. He knew the men slept in a circle, with their heads on the outside and feet nearly touching the single central pole. With the guy ropes stretched outside the tents, even the most rigid sergeant major could not squeeze in more than thirty to the acre, so an entire regiment occupied a large area.

Andrew watched from a safe distance as officers supervised and sergeants shouted hoarse orders to the sweating privates.

Each NCO will be extended sixteen paces from the left by Officers Commanding, the instructions read.

Andrew had learned the theory at Sandhurst. *The senior Major will dress the NCOs of the first row of tents, along the front of the column, so that they will stand exactly on the line marked out as the front of the camp and the Captain of each Company will, from them, dress the NCOs of his squads who whilst being so dressed will stand to attention. After being dressed, No 7 of each squad will drive a peg in-between the heels of his NCO, who will, after turning about, take eighteen paces to the front where another peg will be driven in a similar manner.*

Andrew watched as the veteran 24th followed the procedure to the letter, and the tents rose like a row of giant white mushrooms in minutes.

These men know their job, Andrew thought. *The instructions sound cumbersome, but with good NCOs, they work.*

Dwarfed by the bulk of Isandhlwana, the regimental transport sat behind each regiment while Chelmsford placed the main wagon lines to the rear of the mounted camp and north of the tents of the 24th Foot.

"Why are the wagons not in a laager, sir?" Andrew asked when he reported to Captain Fraser.

"Ask His Lordship," Fraser replied. "Colonel Glyn, our esteemed column commander of the splendid beard, asked Lord Chelmsford for permission to form a laager, but our even more esteemed Lordship refused."

"It was Lord Chelmsford who gave standing orders for every camp to be within a laager!" Andrew reminded. He took a deep breath, remembering the tales of Zulu ferocity.

Fraser nodded. "I am aware of that, Baird. Many senior officers have raised similar objections, but his Lordship replied that forming a laager would take too long." Fraser poured two glasses of port and handed one to Andrew. "Especially with many of the wagons due to return to Rorke's Drift."

"Thank you, sir." Andrew sipped the port. "We could at least entrench the camp." He remembered his father's words about always building sangars – stone defences – along the Northwest Frontier. Zululand could prove equally perilous. *Damn! I am trying to escape the old man's influence, and here I am, looking for his advice.*

Fraser jerked a thumb outside the tent. "There are more stones than dirt here, Baird. It would take far too much effort for minimal reward." His grin was more crooked than Andrew liked. "We'll have to depend on the good old British infantry and volleys of musketry."

Andrew nodded. He wanted to put trust in Lord Chelmsford but remembered his father's tales of service on the fringes of the Empire. Not all British officers treated the opposition with respect. "We're trusting to luck," he said.

"We're trusting to the Martini-Henry," Fraser corrected, and Andrew thought it better not to argue with his superior officer.

Andrew kept two of his men on watch that night and was up before dawn to check the perimeter. He saw no sign of Zulus, and the men grumbled they had wasted their night.

"Better tired than assegaid." Andrew silenced their complaints and ordered his troop to build a breastwork around their section of the camp.

"More wasted effort!" Ramsay grumbled as a group of the 24th jeered at the sweating Riflemen.

"The Zulus know what's good for them," one heavily bearded Natal Hussar commented. "They won't attack a camp full of British regulars."

"I hope they do attack," his companion said. He was a teenage farmer with a sun-browned face and a bandolier of ammunition crossing his chest. "We'll give them pepper, won't we just?" He tapped his rifle, a long-barrelled German weapon that looked about thirty years old.

Andrew hoped the Hussars were correct and he was being overly cautious. He looked up at the great sphinx of Isandhlwana, wondering if any of the Abanonya was observing the lack of defences.

"Keep it up, lads," Andrew encouraged.

"Something's happening, sir." Abernethy looked up from his digging. "His Lordship looks agitated."

"He does," Andrew agreed as Lord Chelmsford rode past without his customary smile.

"He's concerned our supplies won't last," Abernethy said, "so he's going to push us on a bit toward Ulundi."

"How the devil do you know that?" Andrew asked.

"His soldier-servant told me," Abernethy replied with a casual shrug.

Andrew smiled. The rankers had diverse methods of discovering what was happening in the army. He resolved never to discount the intelligence of the other ranks.

"The enemy has camped at Isandhlwana, Ntshingwayo," Jama reported. He stood erect with his assegais and knobkerrie in his hand and his face immobile. He did not mention the pain that tore him apart or the images that ran through his head, hour after hour.

"How many?" Ntshingwayo kaMahole was one of Cetshwayo's senior commanders, a serious-faced man who dressed simply and held his staff of office in his left hand. He listened to Jama's report silently, with his quiet, intelligent eyes never straying from Jama's face.

"They have two *amabuthos* of red-coated infantry, some artillery and mounted men," Jama said. "The mounted men are all colonials, and they also have *amabuthos* of Africans."

Ntshingwayo kaMahole pondered the information. "Are the British behind entrenchments, Jama?"

"No," Jama said. "They have not dug themselves in like ant bears."

Ntshingwayo digested the information for a few moments before asking the next question.

"Have they formed their wagons into a fortification as the Boers do?"

"No," Jama said again. "Their tents are spread across the hillside, and their wagons are behind them. Many of the wagons go back and forward to *kwaJimu*.[1]"

Ntshingwayo contemplated Jama's answer before deciding what to do. "We'll split the British and defeat them in detail," he decided. "Without fortifications, they are vulnerable to our impis. I want you to lure some of them away from the camp, Jama, and we'll attack."

"Yes, *induna*," Jama agreed.

Jama knew that with his wives and two of his sons dead, war was the only thing left to him, and if he died in battle, he would see Yibanathi again and all his ancestors. He trotted away; his mind busy on the task Ntshingwayo had set him. He did not care about the possibility of death.

"We have work to do, Abanonya," he told his men. "We'll show ourselves to the enemy and lure some away from their camp."

"Then what?" Ndleleni asked.

Jama smiled and ran a finger up the blade of his *iKlwa.*

RUMOURS OF A ZULU IMPI RAN AROUND THE BRITISH CAMP, WITH THE sentries reporting bodies of warriors in the distance, trotting purposefully in different directions.

"They're planning something," Captain Fraser said.

"It looks like it, sir," Andrew agreed.

On the 20th of January 1879, Lord Chelmsford and a strong escort patrolled to the east of the British camp and returned without sighting any Zulus.

"What the devil is Cetshwayo playing at?" Fraser asked. "I wonder if he's going to fight at all."

Andrew caught Abernethy raising his eyebrows. "I think he will, sir."

"So do I," Fraser said, frowning. "I don't like doing nothing." He packed tobacco into his pipe. "This war is too quiet for my liking. I don't believe Cetshwayo is just sitting on his thumb waiting for us to pay him a visit or sending small impis to run around without reason." He stood up. "No, Baird. Cetshwayo is planning something. Take your men back to the Nqutu plateau. Keep out of trouble; there's a good chap."

Andrew had studied the track and found an easier route for his Riflemen. With a dozen men at his back, he rode on the windy plateau for an hour before he saw a flicker of movement.

"Over there, lads." Andrew indicated with his chin. "Extended order and take care."

Veterans all, the Riflemen did not need the extra orders and rode carefully with rifles placed across their saddles.

"I see them," Abernethy said quietly. "To our right and ahead, behind that stunted thorn tree."

"How many?" Andrew asked.

"Not sure, sir," Abernethy replied. "I'd estimate a dozen at least."

"Halt." Andrew lifted a hand, feeling the tension rise inside him. He rode to a slight knoll, took out his field glasses and swore when he saw half a dozen shields with the distinct black edging around the mainly white centre.

"Those are the Abanonya we fought at Sihayo's kraal," Andrew said. "Walk wide, lads. If there are some, there will likely be more."

"There are!" Sergeant Duncan said as a line of warriors emerged from a gulley to their right. They moved silently, with their shields on their left arms and assegais held ready to throw.

"Retire, boys," Andrew said and waited until the last of his men had turned before joining them in withdrawing across the plateau.

That's another of my father's maxims: an officer should be first in and last out of danger. Damn it! That man is with me everywhere.

The Zulus followed, running easily over the rocky ground as they carried their tall shields and spears. They kept pace with the horsemen, neither closing the gap nor falling behind. A brisk wind ruffled the feathers around their knees but carried no sound of their silent passage to Andrew.

"What will we do, sir?" Abernethy asked.

"Return to camp," Andrew decided. "We'll report their presence to the captain."

When the Riflemen descended to the camp, the Zulus lined the edge of the plateau, with their shields linked together and their assegais pointing upwards.

"Well, Cetshwayo knows where we are," Abernethy said.

"He does," Andrew agreed. "Now we'll see how he reacts."

While Andrew had been on the plateau, Chelmsford had sent Major John Dartnell of the Natal Mounted Police with most of the mounted men and a considerable number of the NNC in an extended patrol to the southeast. When he was ten miles from the camp, Dartnell encountered Zulus. Andrew heard the staccato rattle of musketry as darkness closed the day.

"Feed the horses, lads, and grab some food yourselves. Ensure your water bottles are full and snatch some sleep while you can. It sounds like Dartnell's found trouble."

"About time the Zulus fought," Sinclair said. "When they come, we can smash them and go home. This place is too wet for me."

Abernethy glanced at Sinclair, raised his eyebrows, and said nothing.

"Come on, lads, tend to the horses," Andrew ordered.

The Riflemen readied themselves and threw themselves into their tents with their rifles to hand. Within half an hour, those who were awake heard the drumbeat of hooves and the sentry's hoarse challenge.

"Halt! Identify yourself, or I'll fire! Who are you, you bastard?"

"Friend!" a lone horseman shouted breathlessly. "From Major Dartnell with a message for Lord Chelmsford!"

"Pass, friend!" The sentry lowered the rifle from his shoulder.

In common with half the officers present, Andrew walked to Lord Chelmsford's tent to discover what was happening, limping as his calf wound began to nip.

"Dartnell's brushed with two thousand Zulus near Isipezi Hill." The word spread around the camp. "He wants infantry reinforcements so he can attack them tomorrow."

"Dartnell's found the Zulu army!"

"Cetshwayo's main impi is at Isipezi Hill!"

"Thousands of Zulus have attacked Dartnell, and he needs help urgently!"

The rumours circulated, each one more impressive than the last. Andrew ensured the sentries were alert and lay in his tent, hoping to sleep.

Find the Zulus, defeat them, end the war, leave the army, and marry Elaine. Andrew planned his life. He closed his eyes, wished he had written to Elaine and woke to the sound of the bugle.

"Come on, lads! Let's be having you!" Barking sergeants roused the men with a mixture of threats and black humour; messengers ran around the camp, cooks worked feverishly at the fires, and farriers banged nails in horseshoes.

Andrew emerged, trying to appear calm as Fraser returned from a meeting with the staff officers.

"Dartnell's made contact with what he thinks is the main Zulu army," Fraser told him quickly. "His Lordship is marching out with Colonel Glyn, most of the second battalion 24th, the Mounted Infantry, four artillery pieces and the Natal Pioneers."

"Us?" Andrew asked hopefully.

Fraser shook his head. "Don't get excited, Baird. We're not required."

"Chelmsford has left the camp dangerously short of men," Andrew said. "We have a large perimeter to defend, and we know there are Zulus around."

Fraser watched as the second battalion of the 24th formed up. They were younger and less experienced than the first battalion, eager men with youthful faces. "Don't worry, Baird. His Lordship has ordered Colonel Durnford at Rorke's Drift to march here with every spare man he has. He'll leave a skeleton garrison at the drift, and until he arrives, Colonel Pulleine commands the camp."

Andrew nodded. He knew Henry Pulleine slightly, a forty-year-old brevet Lieutenant-Colonel who had no experience of active service but a talent for administration. He had only seen Anthony Durnford from a distance. One of the many able Irish officers in the British Army, Durnford was a Royal Engineer of thirty years' service. He had fought in one of the minor frontier wars, where his Natal Carbineers had abandoned him at a crucial juncture, but his Basuto horsemen remained by his side.

"Pulleine was on the staff during the last Galeka war without firing a shot or seeing an angry warrior," Fraser confirmed Andrew's thoughts.

"Let's hope Lord Chelmsford engages the Zulu Impi before it reaches us." Andrew did not hide his concerns as he looked around the camp. "We've got about eight hundred Europeans and about four hundred and thirty ill-armed Africans to guard two hundred wagons, fifteen hundred draught animals and nine hundred yards of tents."

"And no laager, entrenchments or defences," Fraser added. "Still, we do have the first battalion, 24th Foot, Praise the Lord, and thank God for a battalion of British infantry."

Andrew forced a smile, although he felt a terrible sense of foreboding. He watched General Chelmsford march his army eastward, ordered his men to build up their scanty defences and sniffed the wind.

"What are you doing, sir?" Abernethy asked curiously.

"It was something my father said," Andrew said unguardedly. "He told me you could smell the enemy if the wind's in the right quarter. You can smell fear, sweat and cooking."

"I can't smell anything, sir," Abernethy said.

Andrew grinned. "Nor can I, and long may that continue."

Why did I mention my father? And why am I so apprehensive? I've fought in a dozen skirmishes and battles already. Are the Zulus so ferocious? They are only a tribal army armed with primitive weapons, while we have trained professional soldiers with the most modern weapons man's ingenuity can devise.

Pulleine sent out strong infantry pickets, with Lieutenant Pope and G Company of the second battalion 24th fifteen hundred yards in front of the camp. The young soldiers stood in groups of fours along the crest of a rocky donga, looking very exposed against the vastness of Africa.

"We need more men or a laager," Abernethy said. "Maybe we can't smell anything, but we know something's going to happen."

Pulleine may have thought the same, for he extended two companies of the 24th and a nearly equal number of the NNC in an arc around the right front and the flank of the camp. A vedette of mounted men stood lonely guard further out on the high ground while one company of the 24th were busy improving the track.

"Listen to them." Fraser tamped tobacco into the bowl of his pipe. "Cursing and blinding like true British soldiers." He scratched a match and lit the tobacco, speaking between puffs of smoke. "If ever British soldiers stop grousing, then I'll begin to worry."

"There's nothing to worry about," a bearded Natal Hussar said. "It's not a good day for the Zulus to fight. It's the time of the dead moon, and the Zulus never fight then."

Andrew did not argue, knowing the Natal men understood the Zulus better than he did. He remembered the warriors on the plateau, the impi Dartnell had seen and wondered if the Zulu commander was forcing Chelmsford to split his army and said nothing.

My father always said to put oneself in the enemy's camp and think as he does. If the Zulu commander saw us from above, he may well wish to divide our forces and defeat us piecemeal.

"Even less cause to worry now," Fraser said as he saw dust rising on the road. "That's Durnford coming with our reinforcements."

CHAPTER 17

Andrew watched with relief as Lieutenant-Colonel Durnford of the Royal Engineers arrived from Rorke's Drift. One-armed and with an impressive moustache that drooped well below his chin, Durnford brought five troops of Natal Native Horse to reinforce the garrison. More men followed; two companies of the NNC and a rocket battery.

"I'd prefer more British infantry," Fraser admitted his apprehension. "Now that Colonel Durnford is here, I wonder if Pulleine is still in charge of the camp. Durnford has three years' seniority and more experience of actual battle."

Durnford made an immediate impact, sending Captain Shepstone and Lieutenant Raw's Sikali Native Horse to the plateau. These horsemen were from the local tribes and carried throwing spears and knobkerries as well as carbines.

"I heard there were groups of Zulus up there," Durnford informed Shepstone as the Sikali Horse mounted up. "A Lieutenant Baird found them yesterday. Clear them up."

"Yes, sir." Shepstone saluted and led his men up to the plateau. Some of the horsemen sang psalms as they ascended the path, and Andrew killed his envy.

Good luck, lads.

When the last of the Sikali Horse disappeared, Pulleine and Durnford sat down to lunch and called for a magnum of champagne.

"A toast, Pulleine." Durnford lifted his glass. "To a bloody war and a quick victory."

"I'll agree to the victory," Pulleine said and looked up in irritation as a gasping messenger arrived in a haze of dust.

"What is it, man?" Durnford asked, with the sun glittering from his crystal glass.

The messenger reigned up and caught his breath as the dust settled around him. "Five hundred Zulus to the northeast, sir," he reported. "They might be hoping to intercept Lord Chelmsford."

"Thank you," Durnford replied at once. He stood up and finished his champagne. "Call up my Basutos, will you, somebody? I'll take them and the Edendale men with the Rocket Battery. We'll stop these Zulu chaps from bothering His Lordship. He'll have quite enough to do as it is." He put down his glass. "I'll press you for a couple of companies of the 24th, Pulleine."

"I'll need all my infantry to guard the camp, Durnford," Pulleine said, visibly upset at the request.

Durnford pulled at his moustache. "Oh, come now, Pulleine. The 24th is sitting around doing nothing!"

"If I weaken the garrison any further," Pulleine said, "we'll be wide open to a Zulu attack."

"You'll still have the NNC," Durnford reminded.

"How reliable are they?"

"That depends on how well you've trained them," Durnford retorted.

Andrew was not the only officer listening as Pulleine capitulated until his adjutant, Lieutenant Teignmouth Melville, intervened, saying they had a large perimeter and a relatively weak garrison. "We'll need all the infantry, sir," he said firmly.

Durnford agreed reluctantly. "If I get into difficulties," he growled, "I'll expect you to support me!"

Andrew and the CMR watched Durnford ride away, leaving a rising ribbon of dust. A battalion of the NNC followed while a string of mules pulled the rocket tubes, bouncing over the rocky ground. When they departed, the camp seemed quiet, with an NCO bawling out a file of offenders, a few men guarding the spur and the last of the Sikali Horse vanishing on the plateau.

The dust settled, the NCO sent the offenders to double march around the camp perimeter, and Andrew spent a leisurely hour inspecting the horses until he saw a heliograph winking from the plateau.

A signaller read the flashing lights and reported to Colonel Pulleine, who immediately jumped to his feet.

"Captain Fraser!" Pulleine shouted. "Take your Riflemen to the plateau. Lieutenant Raw of the Sikali Horse reports some scattered bands of Zulus up there. Help him scatter them further."

"Yes, sir," Fraser saluted. "You heard the colonel, lads! Check your ammunition! Mount up! Come on, Baird, you young firebrand; you lead us; you know the way best!"

"Yes, sir!" Andrew responded, glad to be doing something. "Come on, men. Sergeant Duncan, you bring up the rear."

After his two previous trips, Andrew knew the route well and led his troop to the plateau with hardly a pause, with Fraser only a few yards behind. The final few steps were a scramble of loose stones and swearing troopers, and then the Cape Mounted Rifles were on top of the plateau with the vast dome of the sky above, and half of Zululand stretched before them.

Andrew lifted his field glasses and watched Raw leading his Native Horse to the east. He saw them disappearing behind the scattered boulders and then appearing again as they searched for the Zulus until one of the riders whooped.

"He's seen something, Baird!" Fraser said.

"Yes, sir," Andrew agreed and shouted for his men to get ready.

"What's that, sir?" Sergeant Duncan pointed ahead. "I saw movement!"

"Push forward," Fraser ordered. "Extended order."

Andrew allowed Lancelot to pick his way across the rough ground as he watched for Zulus. The wound in his calf throbbed, perhaps in anticipation of violence to come, and Andrew grunted, pushing away the irritation. Clouds gathered above, hazing the once-bright sky, and he heard nothing except the chink of equipment and the soft padding of horses' hooves.

"You were imagining things, Sergeant," Kelly grumbled.

Andrew glanced at Abernethy, who shook his head, holding his rifle ready.

"There!" a man shouted as a small herd of cattle broke cover in front of the Riflemen, twenty animals crashing over the undergrowth and around the rocks.

"Beef on the hoof!" Kelly shouted, pulling his horse to follow them.

"No." Andrew grabbed Kelly's bridle. "Cattle don't suddenly run without reason. Somebody's driving them."

"Round up these cattle, Baird," Fraser ordered. "The cooks will always welcome fresh meat."

"Yes, sir." Andrew raised his voice. "After me, lads! Keep your eyes open for the Zulus!" He kicked Lancelot forward with his men in extended order behind him. He heard the clatter of hooves on loose stones, a grunt as a horse stumbled, and the mutter as its rider regained control, and then they were ahead of the main body and heading off the small herd.

"There's a ravine ahead, sir," Abernethy shouted. "Be careful."

"I see it," Andrew said, thankful that Lancelot was sure-footed as he headed off a panicking cow. When he reached the edge of a ravine, Andrew pulled Lancelot up in disbelief. Below him, covering the foot of the gorge, extending up the sides and stretching as far as he could see, were Zulu warriors.

"Dear God in heaven!" Andrew shouted. "Zulus!" He hauled Lancelot back from the rim. "Halt, lads!" He signalled to Fraser and gestured urgently downwards.

Fraser hurried up, glanced over the edge, and made an instant decision.

"Bugler, sound the alert!"

"It's the entire Zulu army," Kelly yelled. "Thousands and thousands of the buggers."

"That's the uMcijo regiment." Abernethy halted on the lip of the ravine and looked down. He pointed to the massed warriors, speaking as calmly as if he were reading from a book, "with the uNokhenke and the uNodwengu on the right."

Andrew listened to the names without much interest as he counted his men.

"And the iNgobamakhosi and uMbonambi on the left," Abernethy continued as he scanned the static warriors. "This is the bulk of the Zulu army."

"Dismount!" Fraser ordered, and the Riflemen obeyed with a rustle of uniforms and a few muttered curses. Andrew saw Lieutenant Raw and the Sikali Horse line up beside the Cape Riflemen, stare into the ravine and load their carbines.

Raw looked to his Sikali Horse. "We'll try and thin them a little, boys!"

"Aim!" Fraser sounded surprisingly calm. Andrew looked at the mass of Zulu warriors, lifted his rifle and aimed at a stalwart man who stared up at the line of threatening horsemen.

"They're coming, boys!" Sinclair called as the uMcijo rose, humming like angry bees and began to climb from the ravine. Most of the other *amabuthos* followed, holding their shields in front of them and their assegais in their right hands.

"They'll form the horns of a bull," Abernethy said, aiming at a broad-shouldered induna. "The chest will come straight for us, with the horns overlapping to take us in the rear and flanks."

Andrew noticed two Zulu units, the uNdi and uDloko waiting in reserve. "How about them?"

"They're the loins," Abernethy said, still calm despite the vast array climbing towards him. "They'll reinforce wherever they're required."

"Fire!" Fraser ordered, with Raw echoing the command a second later.

Andrew fired, worked the underlever to eject the spent cartridge, inserted a bullet, closed the lever, aimed, and fired. He saw the Riflemen and the Sikali Horse firing into the advancing warriors, some snarling, others scared, yet all standing their ground.

Although warriors fell, dead or injured, the Zulus continued to push forward, with their losses not slowing their advance. When one warrior fell, more took their place, humming as they moved and with some rattling the butts of their spears on their shields.

"Keep firing, lads!" Andrew shouted. "Kelly, lower your muzzle! You're aiming too high."

Andrew was unsure how many rounds he had fired. He only saw the Zulus advancing, warriors with shields and spears, some with knobkerries and a few with rifles. He blinked away the gun smoke that nipped his eyes, reloaded, and fired again.

"They're getting close! Back, boys!" Fraser ordered. "Bugler! Sound the retire!" The Sikali Horse was already withdrawing, the men running to their horses without panic. The Riflemen fired a final volley, mounted, and retired, with the Zulus following, shouting, and rattling the butts of their assegais on their shields.

Andrew barely glanced up as tall Captain Shepstone assumed command of the Sikali Horse. He took in the situation at a glance. "Conduct a fighting retreat," he ordered.

"We are," Fraser said quietly and raised his voice. "Listen for the bugle calls, men!"

The Riflemen and Sikali Horse halted on a slight rise, loaded, and waited for the order to fire.

Andrew checked his watch. It was 11.45 AM. He glanced over his shoulder, where a company of the NNC had marched in support of the mounted men. The NNC took a single look at the thousands of Zulus spilling over the edge of the ravine, turned and ran without firing a shot or throwing a single spear.

The Sikali Horse watched them run, shouted abuse, and remained in the firing line.

"So much for our infantry support," Abernethy said cynically.

"Fire!" Fraser ordered.

The Riflemen fired, with more warriors falling. A small body of Zulus rushed ahead of the rest, ignoring the bullets that zipped and bounced around them. They stopped, threw their long assegais, and dropped into cover. One spear slammed into the ground a yard from Andrew and stuck there, vibrating.

"They're getting close," Sinclair shouted.

"Fire and withdraw!" Fraser ordered.

"There are warriors behind us!" Kelly yelled.

Are they friendly NNC or hostile Zulu? Andrew asked himself as he fired into the mass of advancing tribesmen. He loaded, feeling the Martini already hot in his hands.

The mounted troops, around a hundred strong, fired, reloaded, withdrew a hundred yards, and fired again, hitting their targets, bowling men over yet without delaying the Zulu advance in the slightest.

Andrew gaped at the approaching warriors, suddenly realising why all the other tribes in Southern Africa were afraid of the Zulus. They seemed unstoppable, a force of nature equipped with stabbing spears, incredible bravery, and a merciless desire to kill.

"They're pushing us off the plateau," Abernethy warned, glancing over his shoulder. "I hope the 24th are prepared to meet them."

As the horsemen withdrew, they merged with the infantry pickets, but even their combined firepower did not slow the Zulu impi. Andrew fired, reloaded, fired, and reloaded, seeing Zulu warriors fall, for their comrades to step over the bodies and continue. He blinked away the sweat from his forehead, felt the Martini-Henry grow hotter in his hands and wondered how many cartridges he had left. Reaching a rise, he glanced down at the plain and swore.

"The Zulus are everywhere!"

Out on the plain, Durnford was also in contact with a Zulu impi while more warriors surged over the escarpment to attack the scattered camp. The latter Zulu force could easily cut off Durnford, leaving him surrounded and hopelessly outnumbered.

"The Zulus have timed it well." Captain Fraser immediately took in the overall position. "We're spread out in penny packets, with no concentration of force anywhere."

Andrew nodded, loaded, fired, and ducked as a stray bullet whined overhead.

"Even our main camp is spread out," Fraser said. "Pulleine should pull everybody back and form a cohesive defence. Without a laager, he should form a square."

Andrew agreed. Masses of Zulus attacked each separate British force, with the individual companies of the 24th scarlet islands inside a Zulu sea. He saw the British artillery fire, with the smoke jetting out a couple of seconds before the sound reached him, and then the Zulus on the plateau charged again, and he had no time for anything except looking after his men.

"Sergeant Duncan! Watch your flank!" Andrew shouted and swore as a group of warriors broke ahead of the mass to close on the Riflemen.

The leading men of the group carried different shields from the others, and Andrew recognised the white shields within a black fringe.

"The Abanonya!" He aimed and squeezed the trigger, but his overheating Martini jammed. Swearing, Andrew opened the breech and worked at the offending cartridge with the ramrod. Old soldiers had warned him that the rifling in the Martini's barrel was cut deep and square, so they quickly fouled while the heat softened the thin brass case of the cartridges.

The Abanonya were frighteningly close, and Andrew could discern individual faces among the mass. The jammed cartridge seemed immobile, and in desperation, he resorted to his clasp knife, hacking at the brass and swearing in a long monotone.

Andrew heard the cries, "*Usuthu! Usuthu*!" as the Zulus advanced, a sea of leopard-skin headdresses, tossing feathers, broad shields and raised assegais.

"Thank God!" Andrew said when he finally yanked out the damaged cartridge, thumbed in another and closed the breech. As he raised the Martini to his shoulder, he saw Jama and another tall warrior approaching.

Kelly rose slightly from his saddle, aimed, and fired, with the bullet crashing into the second warrior's shield. The Zulu staggered, righted himself, poised an assegai and threw it from fifty yards distance. Andrew looked up and shouted another warning, but Kelly was too slow in responding. Andrew saw the spear hiss towards him with the tall Zulu still in the throwing posture. The point took Kelly in the side, burying itself deep between his third and fourth ribs. Kelly looked down in puzzlement as he saw the weapon protruding from his body.

Kelly stared at Andrew. "The bastards got me!" he screamed, dropped his rifle, and attempted to pluck out the spear. "Take it out! For God's sake, somebody take it out!"

"Get out of the firing line!" Andrew ordered, aimed, fired, and missed as his target ducked down. "Kelly!" He glanced up to see the Zulus only thirty yards away and Jama drumming the butt of his stabbing assegai on his shield.

Pushing Lancelot in front of Kelly, Andrew tried to shield him. He thumbed another cartridge into the breech of his rifle, lifted it to his shoulder, and searched for the Zulu who had thrown the spear.

The man was gone. Andrew fired into the mass, felt the thump as the

Martini recoiled and saw the Zulu right beneath him. He shouted, swung his rifle in a clumsy attempt to knock the man down and swore again when the warrior easily deflected the blow with his shield.

The Zulu jumped at Kelly, thrust in his iKlwa, shouted "*Ngadla!*" and dragged the assegai clear.

Kelly crumpled in the saddle with his eyes wide. His Martini clattered at his horse's feet.

The victorious warrior looked around at Andrew, shouted something, and plunged his assegai into Kelly again. Kelly slumped over the neck of his horse which bolted, carrying his rider's body away from the battle.

"Pull back towards the camp!" Shepstone roared. "For God's sake, pull back! They're all around us!"

Momentarily stunned by the death of Kelly, Andrew realised that Shepstone was correct. If the Sikali Horse and Cape Mounted Riflemen remained where they were, the Zulus would encircle and destroy them.

"Bugler! Sound the recall!" Fraser shouted. He had lost his hat somewhere, and his fair hair was tousled. "Get your men away, Baird!"

The horsemen's withdrawal became a hurried retreat. They fired when they could and avoided the more forward parties of Zulus.

Andrew tried to organise his men, saw Jama leap into the air and swing his knobkerrie at one of the Sikali Horse, heard another Native Horseman shout that he had no ammunition and then turn to flee.

"Keep together," Andrew shouted as some of the men began to panic. "Napier, don't dash ahead! Form up around me!" He fired, feeling the heat of his Martini-Henry, saw half a dozen warriors bounding up from the left and thumbed a cartridge into the breech.

Please, God, don't jam again!

Fraser was a hundred yards away with the bulk of the Cape Mounted Rifles. Andrew fired, reloaded, and called on his men. "Don't scatter, lads! Stay together." He saw one man panic, spur his horse, and run towards Fraser's unit.

"On me, lads!" Andrew shouted.

About half the men joined him; others dug in their spurs and ran. Andrew saw a strong force of Zulus break away and chase after them, throwing assegais and leaping over the rough terrain. He saw Ramsay struggling with a jammed rifle and Sinclair covering him. Sinclair shouted something obscene, fired, fumbled for another cartridge, and pushed closer to Ramsay.

Andrew swore again and concentrated on the men at his side.

"Fire and ride!" Andrew ordered. "If we stay together, we can form a more cohesive defence!"

"Here come the uNdi and uDloko," Abernethy sounded as calm as ever, although his eyes were wild, and blood seeped from a cut on his forehead. "The Zulu reserves have joined in the fun."

Andrew nodded. *Never panic,* his father had said. *Keep your men together, for ten rifles are better than one, and if the enemy is chasing you, they'll look for an easy target and avoid men who can fight back.*

Andrew grinned ruefully and entirely without humour. He wanted to avoid his father, and Fighting Jack was already inside him, giving advice. He checked his men; nine had remained with him. "Three men to fire," he ordered, "three to load and the rest as scouts. We'll move and fire together. Guard each other's backs!"

It was the best advice he could give. He ushed his men away, heading back towards the camp from where he could hear the regular volley fire of infantry augmenting the crash of artillery.

The Zulus have reached the camp then. It sounds as if they're not getting much change out of the 24th.

"If we get back to camp, we'll be fine, boys!" Andrew shouted. "Keep your nerve and hold together!"

Zulus surrounded them, running across the plateau, drumming their assegais on their shields, and shouting. Andrew saw one of his runaway men lying screaming on the ground with a Zulu ripping his belly open, turned and shot the warrior. The Zulu crumpled, and Andrew reloaded.

"Sir!" Ramsay pointed to a body of Zulus on their flank, running to head them off.

That's Jama's Abanonya again. These lads are good.

"Don't let them get in front of us!" Andrew shouted. "Volley fire, boys, on my word!" He waited a moment, took a deep breath, and aimed. "Fire!"

The Riflemen obeyed, with the crash of musketry nearly unheard among the triumphant shouts of the Zulus. Andrew saw his old adversaries' familiar, black-edged shields alongside, with Jama lifting another throwing spear.

"Sir!" Abernethy shouted, pointing.

"I see them!" Andrew said. He aimed at Jama, but more Zulus intervened. Sinclair yelled as a throwing spear sliced into his thigh.

"Take it out!" Sinclair screamed, and Ramsay leaned forward to help.

"Sir!" Abernethy roared and fired as a mass of Zulus erupted from behind a rock. He felled one and tried to pull away, swearing when two Zulus plunged assegais into his horse.

"Abernethy!" Andrew turned Lancelot towards Abernethy, who threw himself off the dying horse.

Abernethy rolled on the ground and lifted a hand to Andrew. "For God's sake, don't leave me!"

Andrew reined up and extended a hand. "Get behind me! Come on!"

Abernethy grabbed Andrew's hand, but before he climbed on Lancelot, a Zulu thrust an assegai into his kidneys. Abernethy screamed, twisting. Andrew saw his face contort in agony and shot the Zulu. Abernethy crumpled, writhing, and another warrior leapt on his body, stabbing downward into his back.

Andrew reloaded, aimed, and fired at the Zulu, knowing he was too late to save Abernethy. Another rush of warriors arrived, stabbing downwards at Abernethy's lifeless body before confronting Andrew. He saw the leopard skin headdresses, the tall shields, and upraised assegais, with Jama at the front. Without time to reload, Andrew jabbed in his spurs. In the short time he had spared to try and save Abernethy, his men had raced on, leaving him isolated.

The Zulus seemed to be everywhere, racing after the retreating British horsemen. Andrew paused to reload, pressed in his spurs, and headed for the track. He saw a trail of dead horsemen, European and Sikali, and a mass of Zulus in his path, running down towards the camp.

Where are my men? Where are the Cape Mounted Riflemen?

A spear whizzed past him, to thud into the ground at his side. Another followed, and a body of warriors charged at him. Without thinking, Andrew turned Lancelot and dug in his spurs. The horse responded, bounding away as Andrew leaned over its neck, aiming his rifle one-handed.

Ten Zulus were following, with their shields prominent and stabbing assegais ready.

This is where I die, in a pointless skirmish against an iron-age tribe in an obscure corner of Africa.

Andrew looked ahead, where a sea of warriors raced down to join the fight around the camp, and behind, where his pursuers were slowly gaining ground.

Damn it! I'm a good horseman; let's do what they don't expect.

"Come on, Lancelot! Come on, boy, let's show these Zulu lads what we can do!"

Spurring, Andrew pushed forward over the rough ground with a sudden spurt of devil-may-care bravado. He remembered a race he participated in on the Malvern Hills a few years previously when he took foolish chances, and now he was in a more important ride.

"Make way!" Andrew shouted and charged into the back of the Zulus. Lancelot's momentum and weight knocked aside the surprised warriors; Andrew parried a wildly swung assegai, smashed the barrel of his rifle against a warrior's head and powered through, shouting. He had already given himself up as dead, so he felt no fear. After a few moments of confused struggle, he powered clear, realised he was laughing hysterically and saw the camp at the foot of Isandhlwana.

The infantry was still formed in isolated companies, rather than a cohesive whole, with a mass of warriors attacking each unit. Gunsmoke wreathed the battlefield without concealing the piled-up Zulu dead as the 24th's volleys hammered into them.

This is a full-scale battle. I thought I knew war after the Galeka campaigns, but anything I experienced there was only a border skirmish compared to this.

Andrew guided Lancelot into a gulley, ducked as a spear whizzed past his head and heard the volley firing suddenly diminish. He pushed on with high rocks obscuring his view and emerged to see a terrible sight. The Zulus had overrun most of the 24th, with scarlet-uniformed bodies lying in neat lines and the survivors retreating to the wagons, firing all the way.

Dear God, the Zulus have defeated Chelmsford's army.

Andrew looked for the Cape Mounted Rifles and saw them at their old campsite, holding the line of trenches they had complained about creating.

Hold them off, boys! I'll be with you in a few moments.

Andrew saw the Zulus chasing after the remnants of the British infantry, with the 24th forming small groups and fighting back-to-back with bayonet and rifle-butt. He saw horsemen spurring to escape and a sergeant gathering men around him for a gallant stand. Mounted officers fled to safety, ignoring the frantic pleas of wounded men and the NNC.

Andrew guided Lancelot to the head of the path, avoiding the scattering of bodies as he rode down. He could hear nothing except the triumphant cries of the Zulus, the shouts of "*usuthu*!" and the sinister "*ngadla*!" as a warrior thrust his iKlwa into a cringing body.

Andrew spurred as a group of warriors emerged from the shelter of a rock and guided Lancelot down the path in a slither of loose stones and dust. Lancelot stumbled, recovered, and continued.

Thank God I chose a Kabul pony.

Andrew loaded desperately and fired at the foremost of his pursuers. He saw the man stagger, sawed at the reins, and pushed on, gasping.

The battlefield spread below him, with Zulus charging through the camp and knots of British soldiers continuing a hopeless defence.

"So, all day long the noise of Zulu battle rolled," Andrew gasped, misquoting Tennyson.

Two of the wagons were already ablaze, with flames and smoke obscuring what Andrew knew would be scenes of horror. Andrew saw Miller and Drummond standing back-to-back, parrying Zulu assegais with their bayonets, and then a warrior threw his assegai; Miller staggered, and the Zulus swarmed forward.

Andrew swore when he saw an impi leave the battlefield and run purposefully toward the Buffalo River and the Natal Border. The warriors were in a long column with the induna at its head.

They're going to invade Natal. Elaine's out there on Inglenook, and the Zulus have smashed our army. Cetshwayo will send his impis into Natal to kill and destroy, and we've nothing left to defend the Border.

CHAPTER 18

As Andrew descended the final hundred yards of the path, the Zulus overran the last organised resistance in the British camp. Andrew saw the First Battalion of the 24th Foot die, swamped by the sheer number of Zulus. He saw a thin trickle of men running for safety and knew he could not help; one rifle could not stem the Zulu flood.

The Cape Mounted Rifles were gone. Fraser and his men had died fighting, with a pile of Zulu bodies before them. Fraser lay in the forefront with two assegai wounds in his stomach and his head crushed. His company lay around him, most facing their front and only three where they had tried to run.

Andrew pulled Lancelot into the wagon park, watching the Zulus destroy what they could not loot and kill everybody they found. South African tribes did not take prisoners. He saw a group of Zulus surround a young drummer boy, who stood with his fists raised in an attitude of defiance. The Zulus closed in, lifted the boy, suspended him head down and ripped open his stomach.

Andrew fought nausea that rose in his throat. He could do no good here but must warn Elaine about that impi heading towards Natal. Deliberately aiming at the warrior who had sliced open the drummer boy, Andrew shot him in the back, reloaded without haste and joined the stream of refugees. A few moments before, he had not thought of survival. Now he had a purpose; he had to warn Elaine and get her away from Inglenook before the Zulus arrived. Saving Elaine was all that mattered. The death of the young drummer was an example of what the Zulus could do to Elaine and Mariana.

Andrew noticed that most of the fugitives ran in panic without looking right or left. He felt curiously detached, as if he were not here, not part of this massacre but a member of a theatre audience observing some play. Andrew was aware of the noise; he heard the screams of men and beasts, the war cries, and yells of triumph, yet they did not affect him. He rode with his rifle loaded, avoided any large groups of Zulus, and shot any who seemed threatening, immediately stopped to reload and rode on.

While others galloped, Andrew moved at a steady canter, aware that Lancelot must be tiring now. He saw warriors staring at him, but when they realised he was prepared to fight, they moved on to easier victims. A small impi jogged past, each man wearing bobbing plumes and green monkey caps.

A trail of dead men led to the drift across the Buffalo River, with men on foot pleading for help and small parties forming for self-defence. Andrew ignored them all, concentrating on survival to warn Elaine. After that, he knew it did not matter.

Andrew hardly noticed the others as he arrived at the drift. He heard the noise and saw Zulus, British and NNC, but they could be a thousand miles away for the little difference it made to him. Andrew slid his rifle into its holster and rode Lancelot into the river, where corpses and stray items of equipment bobbed, and bullets zipped and splashed in the water.

"*Usuthu!*" the warriors chanted.

A blue-coated officer stood on the bank, firing his revolver at a party of Zulus. He glanced at Andrew and lifted a hand.

"Get away, youngster," he said calmly. "I'm already dead." He pointed to the blood that bubbled from the gaping wound in his chest, reloaded and continued to fire.

When a Zulu spear hissed past, Andrew shrugged without any notion of danger and allowed the current to carry him downstream. By Andrew's reckoning, the greatest danger was at the drift, where both fugitives and Zulus gathered. The further he was from the main body, the safer he would be, and as Inglenook was also downstream, every hundred yards carried him closer to Elaine.

The river was rough, foaming past ragged rocks, and Andrew needed all his skill to keep Lancelot safe. He whispered encouragement into the horse's ear, prayed for Elaine and waited for an opportunity to get ashore on the Natal bank of the river.

A party of Zulus ran alongside on the Zulu bank of the river, but after a few moments, they lost interest and returned upstream to the main body. Andrew ignored them, patting Lancelot to keep him calm until the current eased and the river became smoother, although deep and fast flowing.

Get to Elaine, Andrew ordered himself as a strange lethargy set in. *I must warn Elaine.*

Everything seemed so peaceful that it was hard to believe thousands of men had died in great violence only a few miles away. There was no sound here except the soothing rush of the river, and Andrew barely looked when the body of a British soldier floated past, with an assegai protruding from his neck and his eyes wide with horror.

After another ten minutes, Andrew began to push Lancelot toward the Natal bank, gradually crossing the river and watching for rocks. He grunted when another body floated past, recognised a soldier of the NNC and pushed on.

Lancelot was flagging when Andrew saw a suitably low bank and eased onto dry land. He dismounted, dried his rifle, allowed Lancelot a precious half hour to rest and graze and remounted.

"I'm sorry, Lance. You'll get a decent rest when we reach Inglenook," Andrew promised. "Until then, we'll have to keep moving."

The sun beat down on them as Andrew pushed south, looking for familiar landmarks, hoping to meet anybody who could tell him how Elaine was. He saw no sign of any Zulus, only a few small farms and peaceful native kraals.

"Halloa!" Andrew stood outside a low, thatched farmhouse. The door was locked, and shutters covered the windows. "Is anybody there?"

"Who's that?" a suspicious voice called, and a rifle barrel poked through a hole in the shutters. "What do you want?"

"I'm Lieutenant Andrew Baird of the Cape Mounted Riflemen," Andrew replied. "I'm looking for Inglenook."

"This is Greenyards!" the reply came. "Don't you know there are Zulus about?"

"I know," Andrew said. "How far is Inglenook?"

"Three miles away. Follow the river!" The rifle barrel followed Andrew as he rode away. He sniffed the air, smelling smoke.

"Sorry, Lance," he said. "Just a little longer, and you can rest." Lancelot was slowing when Andrew recognised Inglenook's mopane tree nodding above a slight ridge. He smiled at the memories of Elaine's stories and patted the horse's neck. "Nearly there, Lance."

It was not how he had envisaged coming to Inglenook. Rather than arriving in triumph, he was a bedraggled fugitive running from defeat. For weeks he had imagined riding to the front door after a successful campaign, laden with honours and glory, to find Elaine waiting at the door.

The acrid smell of smoke alerted Andrew that all was not well. He raised his head and kicked Lancelot to one final effort. "Come on, Lance." He pushed the horse to the top of the ridge and stopped.

Inglenook was a smoking ruin, with the thatched roof collapsed onto the interior and the outbuildings still aflame.

Oh, dear God in heaven.

Dismounting in a rush, Andrew ran inside the house, shouting, "Elaine!"

He nearly tripped over the first body, an elderly servant who lay spreadeagled on the stoep with a gaping hole in her head and her stomach ripped open. He swore and pushed into the house. "Elaine! Mariana!"

Mr Maxwell was next, sitting against the wall with a bullet hole between his eyes. He was naked, with his entrails piled around him.

Andrew ran past. "Elaine!" he shouted, knowing he was wasting his time. "Elaine! For God's sake, where are you?"

Another servant lay on the ground, spreadeagled and obscene in death. Andrew covered her with a scorched blanket as his search became frantic. "Elaine! Mariana! Where are you?"

Flies rose in ugly clusters as Andrew ran from room to room. Mrs Maxwell's body lay under the kitchen table, with blood stains on the floor showing the family had put up a fight. Andrew glanced at Mrs Maxwell and looked away quickly.

"Dear God. What sort of creatures treat people like that? Elaine! Mariana!" He shouted the names, gagging at the sights in the house.

Andrew heard a slight movement in the next room and dashed in with his hopes rising, only to see a lizard scuttle across the floor and escape outside. "Elaine!" He pushed open her bedroom door and stopped.

Elaine lay on the bed with her eyes wide open, her skirt rucked up to her waist, and her throat cut from side to side. The killer had also slit her stomach, and a host of buzzing flies rose from the corpse.

"Oh, dear God." Andrew could only stare for a moment, and then he stepped forward, lowered her skirt, and closed her eyes. "Why? Why kill Elaine?" He stood still, too numb to react, unable to absorb the enormity of his loss.

"I'm sorry, Elaine," Andrew murmured. "I saw the impi move to the frontier. I should have come then."

Where is Mariana?

"Mariana!" Andrew shouted, knowing it was hopeless. When Mariana's room was empty, Andrew felt a slight lift of hope that she had hidden somewhere. He opened every cupboard and looked in all the corners as he searched the rest of the house without success. She was not in the dairy, barns, outhouses, or the surrounding fields.

Either Mariana escaped and is hiding somewhere, or the Zulus took her with them.

Andrew shuddered at the thought. He called Lancelot over, removed his rifle and held it tight, hoping for a Zulu raiding party.

Come now, you murdering bastards! Come here so I can kill you. Andrew felt himself shaking with silent sobs.

I'll have to find Mariana. I cannot leave her in Zululand with the savages that murdered Elaine and her family. Andrew raised his head to the sky and roared a wordless, formless cry of grief and anger.

He buried the dead underneath the mopane tree, hacking into the stony ground with garden tools and taking satisfaction from the physical work. He laid the bodies down and piled stones on the graves to protect them from wild beasts, all the time mouthing a combination of prayers and obscenities.

Andrew stood beside the grave, unable to stem the tears that slid from his eyes. He said a few words, choked and realised his mind was blank.

"I don't know what to say, Elaine," he admitted. "I hardly got to know you." He took a deep breath to control himself and intoned the final verse of *Lady of Shalott*.

"Who is this? And what is here?
And in the lighted palace near
Died the sound of royal cheer;
And they crossed themselves for fear,
All the knights at Camelot:
But Lancelot mused a little space;

He said, "She has a lovely face;
God in his mercy lend her grace,
The Lady of Shalott."

He stood, uncaring of the rain that suited his mood.

"Goodbye, Elaine," he said. "I'll finish this war, smash the Zulus and return to bury you properly," Andrew said. "And when I find Mariana, I'll look after her. I promise."

When he looked up at the mopane tree, he seemed to hear children's voices and see smiling faces among the branches.

CHAPTER 19

As Andrew approached the town of Helpmakaar, he saw the glow of campfires and the reflection on white sun helmets. The inhabitants had raised a wagon barricade around the settlement, and what was probably most of the male population waited nervously for a Zulu attack.

"Halloa!" Andrew shouted as he approached.

"Who's there?" a voice sounded from the dark, and somebody held up a flaming torch, the orange flame casting bouncing shadows across the ground.

"Lieutenant Andrew Baird of the Cape Mounted Riflemen," Andrew said.

"Come closer so I can identify you!" the voice ordered, and Andrew stepped into the circle of light. A line of men stared at him, some in ragged uniforms, others in civilian attire but all with rifles. "Where have you come from?"

"Isandlwana," Andrew replied curtly. "Who's in charge of the defences here?"

"I am." The speaker was a middle-aged sergeant with grey hair and a worried expression on his face. Torchlight reflected from his eyes and the barrel of his Martini. "Did you see any Zulus out there?"

"Thousands of them," Andrew said, "but none around this area. "Who's in charge of the town?"

"Nobody," the sergeant replied and added. "Maybe Lieutenant Smith-Dorrien or Spalding." His lips curled in a revealing sneer. "Smith-Dorrien returned from Isandhlwana, but Spalding fled from Rorke's Drift."

Andrew did not know either man. "What happened at Rorke's Drift?"

The sergeant shook his head. "I dunno, sir. Last I heard, the Zulus was attacking the mission station, so it's probably gone by now. Major Spalding led his men away when he heard the battle."

"Spalding ran from a fight?" Andrew asked without disguising his contempt. "Where's Smith-Dorrien?"

"In that house over there." The sergeant nodded to a simple house. "The one with the sentries outside. He's been awake for the last thirty-six hours."

Andrew grunted. He had lost count of time.

"Are any Zulus close by?" the sergeant asked.

"I hope so," Andrew said.

"You hope so?" the sergeant repeated. "Why?"

"So I can kill them," Andrew said and pushed past to Smith-Dorrien's house, where a pair of red-coated soldiers watched him approach.

"Is the lieutenant awake?" Andrew asked.

"I don't know, sir. You can't go in." The nearest sentry barred the door with his rifle.

"Don't try to stop me," Andrew advised, pushed the rifle aside and stepped inside.

Smith-Dorrien was sleeping on a camp bed when Andrew entered. He looked up and grabbed his revolver when Andrew lit the lantern on a side table.

"It's all right," Andrew said. "I'm not a Zulu."

Smith-Dorrien looked exhausted and unshaven, and his uniform was dirty and torn.

"Who are you, and what the devil do you want?"

"Lieutenant Andrew Baird of the Cape Mounted Rifles," Andrew said curtly. "Did any of the Cape Mounted Rifles make it back? We were separated on the plateau above Isandhlwana."

"What?" Smith-Dorrien put down his revolver. "I don't rightly know, Lieutenant."

Andrew looked around when a second man entered the room with his braces hanging over his hips. The man glowered at Andrew. "You have no right to barge in here disturbing our rest."

"Who are you?" Andrew already guessed the answer.

"Major Henry Spalding, and you call me sir!"

"Do I? You have no right resting after hundreds of good men died, and the Zulus are rampaging around the colony, murdering at will!" The words left Andrew's mouth before he considered them. "Do we have any men still in Zululand, Lieutenant Smith-Dorrien?"

"What?" Smith-Dorrien was still only half awake.

"In Zululand," Andrew persisted. "Are there any troops still fighting?" He leaned over the bed, glaring into Smith-Dorrien's eyes. He ignored Spalding, who stood beside the door.

Smith-Dorrien gathered his wits. "Yes, of course. Colonel Pearson crossed by the Lower Drift, and Brigadier Evelyn Wood is up north."

"Brigadier Wood!" Andrew repeated with satisfaction. "Unless I have orders to the contrary, sir, I'm heading north to join Brigadier Wood." Andrew knew Wood by reputation. He was a resolute soldier who had fought in the Crimea aged sixteen, won his Victoria Cross before his twentieth birthday and served in the Ashanti Campaign.

"The devil you will," Spalding blustered.

"If any Mounted Riflemen arrive, send them up to me," Andrew said. "I'll draw some stores and ammunition and grab a couple of hours' sleep before I leave."

"Good luck, lieutenant," Smith-Dorrien said.

Ignoring Spalding's protests, Andrew left the tent. Although Helpmakaar was not a garrison town, Andrew managed to scrounge seventy rounds of ammunition, and nobody objected when he helped himself to bread, cheese and salt pork from a mobile cookhouse. A private stable provided him with fodder and water for Lancelot, who ate with relish. Rather than enter one of the military tents, Andrew bedded down beneath a wagon with Lancelot knee-hobbled at his side.

"Enjoy the rest, Lancelot," Andrew said. "We're on our travels again tomorrow."

Images of Isandhlwana and Inglenook disturbed his dreams. He saw Abernethy dying again, a horde of yelling Zulu faces, that unknown, badly wounded officer in the Buffalo calmly firing at the Zulus and then Elaine's torn, ravaged body. Andrew woke with a start, mouthing Elaine's name, found he was damp with sweat and checked his rifle. The night was dark, with stars faint through a clouded sky and the sentries' muttered voices tense in the silence.

I'll find you, Mariana, Andrew promised and lay back down.

Andrew left before dawn the following day, acknowledging the sentries' greetings with a curt "good morning" and riding north before the day's heat became too oppressive. Andrew knew his behaviour could lead to serious disciplinary issues, including losing his commission, but he did not care. He had buried his girl, and the Zulus had kidnapped her young sister; nothing else mattered.

Where would the Zulus take Mariana? If Cetshwayo had sanctioned the raid, the attackers would carry her to oNdini. Therefore, Andrew would go there by the quickest route possible. With the central column shattered, that meant joining either the southern or northern invasion force, and Colonel Wood was the more dynamic of the two commanders.

What the army did to him after the war did not matter. With the decision made, Andrew settled his mind and rode north.

"I'm looking for Brigadier Wood." Andrew announced his arrival at the British camp.

"Over there." A morose-faced major jerked a thumb towards a man in the uniform and insignia of a colonel of the 90th Foot, the Perthshire Light Infantry. Wood was a balding man with a fierce moustache that contrasted with his mild eyes.

"Sir!" Andrew thought it best not to reveal too much. "Lieutenant Andrew Baird of the Cape Mounted Riflemen. I've come to join your column, sir."

"Are you alone, lieutenant?" Wood seemed amused.

"Yes, sir."

"Where are your men?"

"At Isandhlwana, sir," Andrew replied. "Dead."

Wood raised an inquisitive eyebrow. "You got away from that slaughterhouse?"

"Yes, sir."

"Well, Colonel Buller can always use an extra horseman. Do you have any battle experience apart from Isandhlwana, Baird?"

"I fought through the Galeka campaign, sir."

Wood frowned, searching Andrew's face.

He is wondering how I escaped, and my men died. I don't blame him.

"I see," Wood said at length. "Do you have a message for me, Baird?"

"The Zulus have murdered a family and kidnapped a white woman, sir," Andrew said.

"What?" Wood nearly stuttered. "Who and where?"

"They've massacred the Maxwell family and kidnapped the younger daughter." Andrew gave limited details without explaining how he happened to be at Inglenook.

"The current swept you far downstream." Wood was too experienced not to read between the lines.

"Yes, sir," Andrew gave a safe answer.

"We'll look for them," Wood said. "I'll give orders to Lieutenant-Colonel Buller."

Andrew knew Redvers Buller by name, as he had served with his father in the Ashanti War of 1873 and 1874. Buller had also fought in the late Galeka War, although Andrew had never met him. He was a big bluff man with a reputation for daring and one of General Garnet Wolseley's favourites.

"Do I know you?" Buller asked when Andrew made his introductions.

"No, sir. We've never met."

"You look familiar," Buller said and shrugged. "I know you served against the Galekas but never near me. The Ashanti campaign, perhaps?" He shook his head. "No, I must be mistaken; you're too young to have served in West Africa."

"I was fifteen at the time, sir." Andrew forced a smile. "Did you hear about the kidnapped woman, sir?"

"Brigadier Wood informed me," Buller said. "I've passed the news down the line, and all our patrols will be on the lookout."

"Do we have any spies among the Zulus, sir? People who could give us information?"

Buller frowned. "We may have," he said. "Can you speak Zulu?"

"A few words, sir. I learned some Xhosa during the Galeka war so I can make myself understood. I'll learn more Zulu during this campaign."

"I'm sure you will," Buller said. "I'll be sending out patrols to gather information about the Zulu movements, Baird, and we'll ask about this woman as well. Between you and me, if Cetshwayo sanctioned the raid, the woman will be in Ulundi. If he didn't, then she's already dead, if she's lucky."

Andrew said nothing. His hatred had partially masked his grief at Abernethy and then Elaine's death, but he hoped to salvage something by rescuing Mariana. If she were also dead, he would have nothing in his life.

"Sir, permission to take a fighting patrol to Ulundi to rescue the woman?"

"Denied," Buller said. "That would be suicide for you and cost me good men." He touched Andrew's shoulder. "Why the concern over a civilian, Baird?" He peered closer. "You know her, don't you?"

"Yes, sir," Andrew replied.

"I'm sorry to hear that." Buller sounded genuinely sympathetic. "We'll do our best to find her, Baird, and you can command one of the search parties, but riding directly to Cetshwayo is not on, you know."

"Yes, sir."

Buller pulled at his moustache and looked sideways at Andrew. "Are you sure we haven't met, Baird? There's something very familiar about you."

"Quite sure, sir."

"I know what the men called you," Buller said with a wry smile. "Up-and-at- 'em Andy. Well, Baird, I hope to give you the opportunity to earn your name."

How does Buller know that? The British Army is like a bunch of old women gossiping at a village well.

Andrew lifted his field glasses for the fifth time in half an hour and surveyed the land. Today was his fourth patrol in a week, and he was weary, with sweat blurring his vision as it seeped into his eyes. He coughed, trying to clear the dust of their passage from grating the back of his throat.

Andrew's initial hatred of everything Zulu after Abernethy's death and Elaine's murder had abated into a dull, ever-present ache and a desire to find Mariana.

The quicker we destroy Cetshwayo's empire, the sooner I can find Mariana. Now I've seen what the Zulus are like, I've no sympathy for them.

This northern section of Zululand was further from Cetshwayo's oNdini, and the chiefs were more independent than those further south. The terrain consisted of ranges of flat-topped mountains, where local indunas had held their warriors back to defend the locality rather than joining the royal army.

Andrew lowered his field glasses and considered the current situation in Zululand. When Wood's Number Four Column had crossed the Blood River, he made camp on the East -Zulu - side at a place named Bemba's Kop. Chelmsford ordered him to throw his weight about and ensure the local tribes did not reinforce Chelmsford's main invasion.

"We're only a diversion," Second Lieutenant Fletcher had groaned to Andrew. "While the Central Column grabbed the glory, we were forgotten away up here in the north."

Andrew grunted. "There was no glory at Isandhlwana," he said.

"What was it like, sir?" Fletcher asked with all the curiosity of an unblooded soldier. He was a young, freckle-faced youth with wide blue eyes.

Andrew swept his field glasses over the hill they were about to climb. "Confusion, chaos and slaughter," he replied at length.

"Why, sir?"

"Why?" Andrew lowered his field glasses and stared at Fletcher's red, peeling face. Although only a couple of years older, Andrew felt like an old man compared to this newly arrived subaltern. He considered the question. "Why were we defeated? It was a combination of bad generalship, poor organisation, laziness, and a refusal to treat the Zulus with the respect they deserved. They out-generalled us, Fletcher."

Fletcher looked shocked at the expression on Andrew's face. "Do you think we can defeat them?"

"Yes," Andrew said shortly. He hid his doubts, remembering how the Zulus had lured away half of Chelmsford's force before attacking the poorly organised camp. They had primitive weapons but used sophisticated tactics.

"They're good soldiers," Andrew said.

He remembered the superb discipline of the impis as they withstood the massed volleys of veteran British infantry, and he remembered Abernethy's dying scream.

"Are they as good as us?" Fletcher asked.

Andrew saw the nervousness in Fletcher's eyes. "No," he said. "We're better than them."

"That's a relief." Fletcher gave a weak smile.

"It all depends on the officers," Andrew said. "As far as I can see, we need to keep the infantry in a close formation. The Zulus are fast-moving, aggressive, and very dangerous at close quarters. If we want to defeat them, we'll have to use our best advantage, which is musketry and artillery."

"Yes, sir," Fletcher said.

Andrew looked at the hill ahead, searching for Zulus. His hand curled around the stock of his Martini as he imagined squeezing the trigger and the bullet smashing into a warrior's head.

I'll get them for you, Elaine, and I'll find Mariana.

After days of pouring rain, the sun had broken through to bake the mounted patrols Wood sent out. In command of the mounted men, Redvers Buller had demonstrated his skill by leading the Frontier Light Horse in recent South African campaigns. Not many British officers could lead the independently minded colonials, but Buller had the requisite combination of tact, strength, skill, and endurance. He won their trust and even admiration.

By the time Andrew joined Number Four Column, Wood had left his original base to establish a laagered camp at Tinta's kraal. A few days after Andrew arrived, Wood marched his force north-westward to a stronger position at Khambula Hill.

"What do you think, sir?" Fletcher asked as Andrew surveyed the camp.

Andrew nodded. "It's a good site," he approved. "We're between the settlement of Utrecht and the strongholds of the abaQulusi tribe. They can't attack Natal without passing us."

"Baird!" Wood called Andrew over as they stood on Khambula Ridge.

"How did His Lordship fortify the camp at Isandlwana? How did the Zulus manage to overcome the defences?"

Wood listened to Andrew's description of the battle without commenting on what Andrew saw as Chelmsford's failures.

"There was no wagon laager, sir," Andrew explained. "The wagons were constantly moving between Isandhlwana and Rorke's Drift, so Lord Chelmsford did not think it possible to laager them."

"Did Pulleine have the infantry in a square?"

"No, sir. Each company acted as an individual unit."

"Entrenched?" Wood asked.

Andrew shook his head. "No, sir."

Wood's mouth tautened. "Thank you, Baird. How did the Zulus attack? Describe their tactics." He listened to Andrew's reply, nodding at the right places. The brigadier was not as unfailingly polite as Chelmsford but still treated his junior officers with respect. "You can return to your patrolling work with Colonel Buller. Let me know if you have any success tracking this missing girl."

The tone of Wood's voice and the shadows in his eyes told Andrew the brigadier had already given up hope of finding Mariana alive.

"I will, sir," Andrew said. *I've not given up.*

While Andrew perfected the art of patrolling under Buller's expert guidance, Wood ensured the Zulus would not take his camp by surprise. He had two battalions of good quality infantry, the first battalion of the 13th Foot and the 90th Perthshire Light Infantry and used both to strengthen the camp.

Every time Andrew returned to Khambula from patrol, Khambula Hill was better prepared. Wood positioned his wagons in a hexagonal laager, with the boom of each wagon running under the body of the next. He ordered the pioneers to cut thorn bushes, and swearing infantry jammed them beneath the wagons to prevent any Zulus from ducking through to attack the defenders.

"I don't know about the Zulus," one ginger-haired private said, sucking blood from his hand. "But these wait-a-bit thorns would stop me."

"I haven't ordered you to stop, Sanderson," Corporal Peters growled. "So, no waiting a bit until I say so!"

Two hundred yards away, Wood ordered a second fortification for the beef cattle, with the toiling infantry hacking trenches from the stony ground and building stone barricades on the outside.

"Sangers, my father would call them," Andrew said in an unguarded moment.

"Would he indeed?" Brigadier Wood asked. "An old Indian hand, was he?"

"Yes, sir," Andrew confessed, cursing his wayward tongue.

Wood nodded. "I might have bumped into him," he said, "although I can't remember an officer named Baird."

Andrew kept quiet as the Brigadier continued.

"As you see, we also have a redoubt on that rise a little beyond the cattle kraal, with a palisade joining both. We've positioned four seven-pounders to cover the gap between the main laager and the redoubt, and a further two seven-pounders in the redoubt, facing north-east."

"Yes, sir."

"You're the only man here who's seen a Zulu attack, Baird." Wood revealed his professionalism by continuing to ask for advice. "Can you think of anything else that might assist in repelling them?"

"Maybe, sir." A few weeks back, Andrew would have hesitated to offer his opinion to a senior officer, but since Isandhlwana, he was less concerned with rank. "I'd put trip wires in front of the defences to slow the Zulus down."

Wood nodded. "I'll order that, Baird."

"And when the men have drunk their beer, sir, we can smash the empty bottles and strew them on the dead ground. I know the Zulus have hard feet, but nobody will enjoy treading on broken glass."

Wood narrowed his eyes. "You could be an asset, Baird. Now report to Colonel Buller and get back on patrol."

"Yes, sir." Andrew raised his chin. "Permission to take a patrol towards Ulundi, sir? If I get nearer to Cetshwayo's capital, I might learn about Miss Maxwell."

"You have already asked that Lieutenant Baird and Colonel Buller denied you permission," Wood said. "The AbaQulusi has been active these last few days. Buller has created a pattern of patrols without tempting the AbaQulusi to wipe one out. You're more useful here than lying dead with your men outside Ulundi."

Andrew swallowed his frustration. "Yes, sir."

I haven't forgotten you, Mariana. If you're still alive, I'll find you.

CHAPTER 20

"What do you see, sir?" Second Lieutenant Fletcher asked.

Andrew wiped the sweat from the eyepiece of his field glasses and raised them to the long ridge of Hlobane. He knew that Buller had already skirmished with the Zulus on the hill, and everybody expected another encounter. Even before Chelmsford's disaster at Isandlwana, Buller had led a patrol to this range of flat-topped mountains ten miles north of Tinta's Kraal in northern Zululand. The hills were named Zunguin. Hlobane and Ityentika, and Andrew winced as he remembered Elaine saying she thought the Zulu language was the most beautiful in the world. At that moment, he could not agree but ran the names over his tongue, savouring each syllable, and wishing Elaine was still here to speak them.

A thousand Zulus of the abaQulusi had chased Buller's small force away, but when Wood had returned the following day with infantry, the Zulus had withdrawn. British observers saw thousands of Zulus on top of Hlobane, and Wood had prepared for a full-scale attack when a messenger brought news of Isandhlwana.

Rather than hazarding one of the two remaining British forces in Zululand, Wood altered his plans and withdrew. Now, securely based at Khambula Hill, Wood sent mounted patrols to watch the Zulus at Hlobane and monitor the roads to the European settlements at Luneburg and Utrecht.

"What do you see, sir?" Fletcher repeated.

Andrew continued to survey the hills, looking for evidence of Zulu activity while always hoping to find some clue as to Mariana's whereabouts.

"I can see movement on Hlobane," he said. "Cattle and men." He glanced over his patrol of twenty-five men, a mixture of colonials and British Mounted Infantry. "We'll go closer." Ordering two colonials to ride wide on each flank, he told Fletcher to take command while he scouted towards the hills.

"Be careful, sir!" Fletcher advised while Andrew pushed Lancelot ahead.

Holding his Martini across the front of his saddle, Andrew headed for a small *imuzi* on the lower edge of Hlobane. He approached cautiously, ignoring the boys who ushered a small herd of cattle away at his approach. Women worked in the fields, backs bowed as they toiled with simple tools. One looked up when Andrew rode up and shouted a warning to her companions. The other women joined her, with all running back to the *imuzi*.

"You're in no danger from me," Andrew shouted.

A simple thorn barrier shielded a dozen neat beehive *izindlu*, with one slightly larger than the others.

The man here is not wealthy, Andrew told himself. *He has two or three wives and about twenty cattle.*

"You lads, wait here," Andrew ordered. "Allow any women or children to enter and keep watch for warriors."

"Yes, sir," Fletcher said as Andrew rode through the open gate.

"Who is the headman here?" He spoke in Xhosa, hoping the people understood him.

The interior of the *imuzi* was similar to a score of others Andrew had visited over the past year. He remained on horseback with his Martini-Henry across his saddle, ready for instant use, and his revolver loose in its holster.

The *izindlu* were neat, with women working outside or peering at him through the doorways while small children played happily or stared at Andrew in wonder. As was the custom in Zululand, the young, unmarried women wore nothing except a belt of woven grass around their waists. They looked at this stranger in their midst through wide eyes, some smiling and one, evidently the village flirt, thrusting a hip towards Andrew. Dogs lazed in the dirt, with a couple of thin goats wandering in their perennial search for food.

An old man rested in the shade of a tree and eventually lifted a frail arm to point in the direction of the slightly larger *indlu*. He gave a gummy smile and settled back down, watching Andrew with unafraid curiosity.

"Thank you," Andrew said to the old man. He shook away the image of Elaine's bloody, violated body, dismounted, and stepped to the larger *indlu*. It was unlikely that anybody from this far north had participated in Elaine's murder, yet Andrew still had to force away his twist of dislike.

"Come out!" Andrew ordered, pushing aside the door with the barrel of his rifle.

An elderly man emerged, with the *isicoco* only emphasising the silver hair on his head. He stood proudly in the sunlight, holding Andrew's gaze without fear.

"My name is Lieutenant Andrew Baird," Andrew said. "I am searching for a white woman."

The headman frowned as he translated Andrew's Xhosa into Zulu. "There is no white woman here," he said in a surprisingly deep voice.

"Have you heard of a white woman held captive in Zululand?" Andrew asked.

The headman frowned again. "If Cetshwayo ordered a white woman captured, he would have her in oNdini," the headman confirmed Andrew's suspicions.

"Have you heard of any white women in Zululand?" Andrew asked.

The headman denied any knowledge of white women. Andrew heard movement behind him and guessed the women and children were gathering their courage to inspect this strange white man.

"We are at war with King Cetshwayo," Andrew reminded. "Yet we have no quarrel with the people in this part of the country."

The headman eyed Andrew's Martini and said nothing.

"My chief, Brigadier Wood, wants to make an alliance with Uhamu, who rules this area of Zululand so that we can have peace with the Zulus. Do you know where Uhamu is?"

The headman denied any knowledge of Uhamu. Most of the population of the *imuzi* were now surrounding Andrew, keeping a respectful distance as they stared at him.

"If you hear of Uhamu or the white woman, let us know," Andrew said. "We will reward you with gifts of cattle."

Andrew hoped that bribery would prove more effective than threats to such a warlike people. Realising that the headman either knew nothing or would say nothing, Andrew withdrew from the *imuzi* with the crowd parting before him.

"Any luck, sir?" Fletcher asked.

"Not this time," Andrew replied.

"They won't tell you anything," Giles, one of the colonials, a heavily bearded man with bright blue eyes, said. "You'll have to force it out of them."

Kerr, his companion, younger and with a mobile face and well-groomed side whiskers, listened without speaking.

"Come on, lads," Andrew said as a gaggle of children followed, pointing at these strangers as their mothers called them back.

Andrew led his patrol around the area, asking about Mariana and Uhamu, for Brigadier Wood hoped to tear the northern region from Cetshwayo's authority, either by force or persuasion.

Apart from differences in size, the *imizi* were all similar, with the same barrier, the same circular *izindlu* and women performing much of the work except on the cattle. Very few contained adult males, which Andrew thought ominous, and nobody had heard of a white woman prisoner or Uhamu.

"You are too gentle, Baird," Buller echoed Giles' words when Andrew returned. "Force is the only thing these people understand."

"Yes, sir," Andrew said. "Are we not trying to teach them about civilisation?"

Buller's eyes narrowed as he looked at Andrew. "You say we haven't met before, Baird, yet you remind me of somebody. I am damned if I know who, but it will come to me."

As the infantry strengthened Khambula's defences, Buller's mounted men spent all of February patrolling in an ever-increasing radius. They raided any *imuzi* that seemed hostile, rounded up the cattle and penned them in the kraal at Khambula. They asked about the missing white woman, sought Uhamu and had an occasional skirmish with small parties of Zulu warriors. Andrew's patrol had one minor encounter when an impi of young abaQulusi warriors, eager to prove their manhood, ambushed them.

The abaQulusi exploded from a patch of woodland, drumming their assegais on their shields as they ran.

"Fire and withdraw," Andrew said, with bloodlust hot on him as he thought of Elaine.

The Zulus charged forward on a broad front, holding the shields in their left hand and assegais in their right. Andrew waited until they closed to a hundred yards, with the hatred washing over him.

"Fire!"

He selected a warrior in the central front, aimed and fired.

"Withdraw a hundred yards and reload."

His men obeyed, reining up to find the Zulus had nearly kept pace with the horses. "Fire!" Andrew ordered again, watched as more young warriors fell, and withdrew two hundred yards. The ground was uneven, broken by rocks and isolated trees, and he chose a slight rise to halt his men.

"Two volleys, lads," he ordered and picked his target.

The rifles cracked out, more warriors fell, and the Zulus stopped and retreated. Andrew watched them go.

"We could follow them and kill more," Giles suggested.

"No," Andrew said. "The Zulus led Chelmsford into an ambush and destroyed his camp. I am not falling for their wiles."

Giles grunted. "We're better to kill as many as we can," he said.

When he heard of Zulus raiding into the recently annexed Transvaal, Buller led a strong patrol of mounted men to scatter them. The patrol returned the next day with a couple of wounded men, and Andrew asked if they had heard anything about Mariana.

"Not a dicky bird, Baird," Buller reported. "Sorry, old man."

Lieutenant Peterson of the Mounted Infantry climbed down from his horse, shaking the dust from his clothes. "We bagged a few Zulus, but others are joining the fun now."

"Galekas?" Andrew asked.

"Swazis, ruffians, and God knows what else," Peterson said. "Some band of border renegades taking the opportunity to raid and despoil amidst the general chaos. I heard a shave there are white men amongst them, too."

Andrew nodded, remembering his father's tales of trouble along the Northwest Frontier when a minor incident would escalate, and half the tribes would rise. "Let's hope we end this war soon."

Peterson began to rub down his horse. "The way it's heading now, Cetshwayo will be the victor."

Andrew looked over the countryside, where the heat haze shimmered across the arid plain, and the distant hills were misty-blue. "No, he won't," he said softly. "We won't let that happen."

Peterson paused for a moment. "You were at Isandhlwana, Baird. You saw what the Zulus did to our men. Maybe this is a fight we can't win."

"I don't believe that," Andrew said. "The Zulus defeated us at Isandhlwana, but we often lose the first battle and win the war."

"I've heard a shave that we're going to make a negotiated peace with Cetshwayo," Peterson said. "We'll withdraw our army, and he'll pay the cattle fine. We'll let him keep his impis as long as he agrees not to invade Natal."

"No." Andrew shook his head. "That won't do."

Peterson stopped grooming. "Look at it this way, Baird, we're already embroiled in a major war in Afghanistan, and the Russians and Turks are still growling at each other. We can't afford to be diverted into a prolonged war with a backward native kingdom here as well."

Andrew looked away. If the British left Zululand, he would have virtually no chance of discovering what happened to Mariana. "I won't leave Zululand," he said.

"Oh, that missing woman," Peterson remembered.

"That missing woman," Andrew agreed.

"I forgot you were obsessed with finding her." Peterson shrugged. "You're wasting your time, Baird; the Zulus will have killed her weeks ago, or worse."

Andrew raised his chin. "If she's alive, I'll find her," he said. "And if she's dead, I'll give her a decent Christian burial."

"Maybe Chelmsford will include her in the peace settlement," Peterson said.

Andrew nodded. "Maybe so," he agreed, but he had already reached his decision. Whatever happened, he would continue his search for Mariana.

Jama crouched beneath the skyline of a long ridge, ignoring the rain that cascaded from low clouds as he surveyed the Intombi River half a mile away. He took a pinch of snuff as the clumsy British convoy splashed and jolted along the road.

"They won't cross the drift," Jama said.

"No," Ndleleni agreed, touching his *umzimbeet* seed necklace.

Jama looked over his shoulder, knowing his Abanonya were on the opposite side of the ridge, crouched out of sight and waiting for his command. They had been there for half a day in perfect silence and would remain for another day without complaint.

"Stay with the Abanonya," Jama ordered. "I'll follow the wagons."

Ndleleni moved at once, and Jama trotted down the slope. The small British convoy had outriders scouting for Zulus and infantry of the 80th Foot marching beside the wagons, but Jama knew he could avoid them without difficulty. The infantry slogged with heads bowed before the persistent rain, their heavy boots dragging and splashing through the mud.

Jama knew there was already a long wagon convoy stranded at a drift over the Intombi River, with the flooded river making crossing impossible. Now a second British convoy trudged over the muddy track, carrying planks, ropes, and other materials to build a raft. Jama followed at a distance, calculating the number of British soldiers in the escort, and planning how best to attack. He noted that the main convoy had split, with half a dozen wagons slogging ahead and the others a few miles away.

Didn't they learn from Ntshingwayo's victory? They are asking us to defeat them again.

Jama watched as the small convoy arrived at the drift, with hectoring sergeants supervising most of the infantry to build a raft to pass the wagons over the river.

"What shall we do?" Ndleleni asked.

Jama smiled. "Wagons without oxen are useless," he said and told the Abanonya his plan.

The British concentrated on driving the wagons, so their defences were down when Jama led the Abanonya in a sudden rush. The scattered infantry shouted a surprised challenge and fired a few shots as the Zulus drummed their assegais from their shields and shouted their war cry.

"Usuthu! Usuthu!"

Jama led from the front, thrust his *iKlwa* into the ribs of the first guard, shouted "*Ngadla*!" and finished his victim with a savage blow of his knobkerrie. He heard other warriors shouting behind him and pushed on. There were more soldiers and drivers, but today was not about killing.

As half the Abanonya fought the escort, Ndleleni led the others to cut the traces and drive the oxen away. The Zulus were accustomed to cattle since early childhood and captured the animals without difficulty, running through and past the convoy before the escort had time to gather their senses.

"How many oxen did we get?" Jama asked as he cleaned his *iKlwa.*

"Forty-six," Ndleleni replied, touching his necklace.

"That will bring more British," Jama said.

"Then what?" Ndleleni asked.

Jama's expression altered as he thought of Yibanathi, Lerato and his sons. "Then we kill them," he said.

Even Ndleleni turned away at the expression in Jama's eyes.

The following day, the scouts reported that another band of Zulus was approaching, and an hour later, they arrived.

"I am Mbilini." The leader was spare and intelligent. "More warriors are coming."

Jama eyed him sourly. "We don't need you," he said.

Mbilini touched his *iKlwa.* "Cetshwayo has appointed me to take command."

"As the king commands." Jama accepted the inevitable. He faced Mbilini. "Don't get in my way, Mbilini."

Mbilini saw Ndleleni slowly nod and guessed the temper of the Abanonya.

"You look after the Abanonya," Mbilini said. "I'll take the rest."

Jama agreed. "Together, we'll destroy them." He began to whet his *iKlwa* blade smoothing the stone in the same direction with intense concentration.

Ndleleni turned away to raise more reinforcements.

❄

THE ABANONYA WATCHED AS THE BRITISH INFANTRY OFFICER LOCATED THE stranded convoy. Jama noticed the officer was large, overweight, and slow-moving.

"We could kill them all now," Bafana said, raising his iKlwa.

"Wait," Jama ordered.

"One rush, and they'd be ours," Bangizwe insisted, whetting his assegai and humming Shaka's war song.

"Wait!" Jama repeated.

The British used their remaining oxen with more skill than Jama expected, with the officer in charge hitching the same animals to the wagons, one at a time. Despite the soft ground, the British dragged the wagons to the banks of the Intombi and formed them in a vee shape, with the open end closer to the river.

"We can kill them now," Bhekizizwe, always impatient, urged. "They'll cross the river and move to the British garrison at Luneburg."

"Wait!" Jama said, placing a hand on Bhekizizwe's bicep. He glanced upward. "The rain is coming."

Jama's prediction was correct. The rain began again, hammering down for two days, raising the river level and stranding the redcoats on the north bank. They pulled their helmets down, raised the collars of their tunics, and cursed the rain, the war, the Zulus, their NCOs, and everything else.

"Now?" Bhekizizwe urged.

"Wait," Jama replied and conferred with Mbilini. He continued to watch the British. The wagons remained in their Vee-shape, not close together and based at the river, with tents inside. Although dense bush covered the ground, the commanding officer in charge only posted a single sentry at each side of the laager and no outlying or mobile pickets.

"Why is he separate from his men?" Bhekizizwe asked as the commanding officer pitched his tent outside the laager.

"He's making it easy to kill him," Ndleleni told him.

"The rain will stop," Jama said, "and the river will fall. There will be a gap between the end wagons and the river."

That evening, more warriors joined Mbilini and Jama's Abanonya, so eight hundred Zulus waited within a short distance of the 80th Foot's laager. Mbilini sent another two hundred further up the river to attack the small British detachment on the south bank.

"Now?" Bhekizizwe asked.

"At dawn," Jama told him.

Jama gave orders to the assembled warriors, who circled the laager, moving silently into the familiar horns of the buffalo formation.

In the early morning, the rain began again, and the expected dense mist drifted across the river. Jama ordered his men to creep forward until a nervous young warrior fired his captured British rifle by mistake.

"Halt!" Jama commanded, and the attackers stopped and slid to the ground. They lay there, expecting the British to stand to their arms.

Nothing happened. Mbilini and Jama waited for an hour and gave the order for the slow advance to continue. The Zulus moved forward, inch by inch. They formed a vast horseshoe with the ends on the bank of the Intombi River. As the mist began to clear, a sentry with the small British detachment on the opposite side of the river spotted movement, shouted a warning, and fired.

"Zulus! Zulus attacking the laager!"

The sentries on the north bank, belatedly aware of the threat, also fired.

"Turn out! For God's sake, get up! The Zulus are all around us!"

Immediately the shots rang out; Jama stood up and charged forward, drumming his assegai on his shield.

"Come on, men! *Usuthu! Usuthu!*"

The Abanonya followed at once, with the other warriors joining them in a dense wave of shouting men, broad shields and stabbing *iKlwas*. Jama leapt through the gap between two wagons and thrust his *iKlwa* into a shouting sentry.

"Ngadla!"

Jama ripped the blade sideways, watched the light fade from the soldier's eyes and ran on. The Zulus were clambering over the wagons, disposing of the stumbling sentries as more soldiers emerged from the bell tents within the laager. Some of the 80th wore scarlet tunics, others wore shirt sleeves and blue trousers, with braces hanging loose over their hips. One man wore only a shirt, but all carried their rifles and attempted to repel these invaders.

The commanding officer emerged from his tent outside the laager, and rather than attempt to run, he climbed over a wagon to help his men. Jama ran forward, shield and assegai held ready.

"Captain Moriarty!" a young man shouted a second before Bhekizizwe attacked the officer.

Captain Moriarty stood on top of the wagon, firing a revolver. He shot Bafana and two more warriors before Jama launched his throwing assegai, catching the officer high in the chest.

"I'm done for!" Moriarty yelled, staggering back. "Fire away, boys! Death or glory!"

Leaping on the wagon, Jama thrust his *iKlwa* into Moriarty's stomach and finished him with the knobkerrie. As the captain fell, Jama turned to view the fight. The Zulus had won the battle with that single rush. Scores of British soldiers lay dead, with a scattering of Zulus, while another dozen British had jumped into the fast-flowing river to escape. The whole affair had taken only a few minutes.

Jama stood on the wagon beside Moriarty and watched as the rest of his plan unfolded. The two hundred men Mbilini had sent across the river descended on the British detachment on the opposite bank in a yelling rush of spears, feathers, and raw courage. Almost immediately, a British officer mounted his horse and galloped to safety while a tall, severe-faced NCO gathered a handful of survivors and made a fighting retreat.

Jama nodded with satisfaction, lifted his bloodied *iKlwa* and sang.

"Thou hast finished off the tribes.
Where wilt thou wage war?
Yes, where wilt thou wage war?
Thou hast conquered the kings.
Where wilt thou wage war?
Thou hast finished off the tribes.
Where wilt thou wage war?
Yes, yes, yes! Where wilt thou wage war?"

Yet even as he sang and the victorious Abanonya ripped open the stomachs of the dead and looted the wagons, Jama could only see Yibanathi. He knew he would swap all this triumph to have her back in his *imuzi*. He saw Jabulani watching him and felt a warm glow. Jabulani was all he had left of Yibanathi; as long as the boy was with him, he retained a part of his Great Wife.

CHAPTER 21

February eased into March, with Wood still pressing Buller and the mounted men into extended patrols. After a brief lull to lick their Isandhlwana wounds, the Zulus were also active. Small bands roamed the countryside, occasionally clashing with the British patrols and harassing the supply convoys.

"This period feels like the lull before the storm, sir," Fletcher said as they walked across the interior of the laager at Khambula.

"I agree, Fletcher," Andrew watched the 13th Foot pickets change, with the men hurrying under the driving rain, each footstep bringing a muddy splash.

The weather had deteriorated again, throwing down heavy rain that saturated the tents and turned roads into quagmires and every drift into a flood. The flooded roads delayed the supplies to Khambula, worried the quartermaster, and caused Wood to send extended patrols westward to escort the struggling wagons.

Andrew walked to a field forge to check on a shirt-sleeved farrier who was shoeing Lancelot when a sentry spied an urgent messenger panting towards the camp.

"Why don't people use the heliograph?" Andrew asked. "It's a damned good invention."

"Maybe they don't work in the rain," Fletcher suggested.

Andrew grunted and checked the farrier's work. "Make sure these nails are secure, farrier. I don't want Lancelot to shed a shoe when a hundred baying Zulus are chasing me across Africa."

"She won't, sir," the farrier said, double-checking his work to make sure, for Andrew already had a reputation as a firebrand.

"Sergeant Meek!" Andrew shouted. "Find out what that messenger said."

"Yes, sir." Sergeant Meek was a hard-headed, bitter-eyed veteran of the Mutiny and the Border Wars. He strode away, straight-backed, as Andrew continued to watch the farrier. He depended on Lancelot, and any message was less important than his horse.

"Sir!" Sergeant Meek returned a few moments later as the farrier was finishing the fourth shoe. "Another disaster, sir! The Zulus have wiped out a detachment of the 80th!"

Andrew felt the sudden chill as men looked around. All work stopped as one man crossed himself and muttered a prayer, and another checked his rifle was nearby.

"H Company of the 80th were camped beside the Intombi." The sergeant had to stop to take a deep breath. "Captain Moriarty didn't form a proper laager, only a vee-shaped defence, with no trenches and gaps between the wagons."

"Bloody idiot!" Andrew growled. He was aware it was bad form for one officer to criticise another in front of the men, but since the death of Elaine, he had little time for observing the niceties. "How many men did we lose, Meek?"

The sergeant paused for a moment and looked around as if expecting a Zulu impi to crash over the laager and assegai everybody inside. "Captain Moriarty posted a couple of sentries outside the laager and retired to bed."

"Did he have pickets?" Andrew asked sharply.

"No, sir," Meek replied crisply.

"What was the terrain like?"

"Thick bush, sir."

"Dear God," Andrew said. "Continue, Sergeant."

"There was a small detachment on the opposite side of the river, sir, under Lieutenant Harward and Colour Sergeant Booth. About five in the morning, with the usual morning mist clearing, the sentry there saw a Zulu impi around the laager. He fired at them and raised the alarm. The sentries at the laager also fired, and the men turned out of the tents." The sergeant took another breath. "The Zulus killed them all, sir. Everybody in the laager. Eighty men gone, just like that."

Andrew could picture the scene, with the Zulus' sudden rush and the sleepy, half-dressed soldiers staggering from the tents in shirt sleeves. He saw men grabbing for unloaded rifles and trying to fix bayonets in the dark and the bounding warriors stabbing and shouting and stabbing again.

"Captain Moriarty died well," the sergeant said. "He was in a tent outside the wagon laager and tried to get back inside when the Zulus speared him as he climbed over a wagon. He shouted, "I'm done for. Fire away, boys! Death or glory!"

He was a brave man but a poor officer not to take every precaution. Glory is no good when it gets good men killed.

"Did anybody survive?" Andrew asked.

"Some," the sergeant replied. "Eleven or twelve jumped into the river and managed to reach the other side, but the Zulus were there as well."

"They arranged an excellent ambush," Andrew gave grudging professional approval.

"Yes, sir. Lieutenant Harward ordered Colour Sergeant Booth to retreat to a farmhouse while he galloped away to get help."

An officer fled, leaving his men in danger? What is the army coming to? God, Harward was lucky my father was not there.

"Colour Sergeant Booth got the men to safety, sir, and Lieutenant Harward brought reinforcements."

Andrew nodded. "Thank you, Sergeant."

Another Zulu victory! If we don't show some success soon, the men will begin to doubt themselves. We'll need to do a lot better.

"So far," Colonel Wood said as he gathered his officers together, "Cetshwayo is winning this war. He's wiped out our central column, stopped the southern invasion in its tracks and destroyed eighty men of a good-quality regiment. Oh, I know the press and politicians will emphasise the defence of Rorke's Drift as an example of British pluck and all that, but that was merely a border skirmish. Colour Sergeant Booth did well at the Intombi, but his actions do not counteract the disaster. Or disasters, rather."

Although Wood did not elaborate, Andrew knew he was referring to Harward's desertion of his men. A few officers stirred uncomfortably as they listened, with Buller shaking his head in disbelief.

"Now, we must strive to overcome these difficulties by defeating Cetshwayo's army," Wood said. "You all know that we have been searching for Uhamu; some of you may not know he came into camp with some seven hundred of his people and a request for us to escort the others to safety. That's the first piece of good news we've had, gentlemen. It shows we have created a crack in Cetshwayo's kingdom."

Andrew wondered if Wood was attempting to raise morale after the recent reverse on the Intombi.

"Colonel Buller," Wood said, "I am sending you and a strong mounted force, together with two hundred of Uhamu's warriors, to the headwaters of the Black Umfolozi River. Bring back as many refugees as possible."

"Yes, sir," Buller said.

"In the meantime, I want the local patrols stepped up. Lieutenant Baird, I want you to guard the supply routes."

"Yes, sir," Andrew said.

"I know you won't find Miss Maxwell there, but you might help win this unfortunate war."

Some of the assembled officers murmured their sympathy, for all knew of Andrew's attachment to Mariana.

Andrew watched Buller ride away and concentrated on his routine patrols. After the disaster on the Intombi, the men were more alert, with some nervous but most angry, hoping for revenge on the Zulus.

"They've all gone," Fletcher said two days later as the patrol returned, weary, wet and without sighting a single enemy warrior.

"It seems so," Andrew agreed shortly.

The following day Buller returned after another successful mission that brought back a long column of refugees. Peterson approached Andrew as he checked his men's rifles.

"I might have something for you, Lieutenant Baird. Good news and bad, I'm afraid."

"What's that, Peterson?"

"A village headman told me about a white woman in a kraal three day's ride away to the east. Siyanda's Kraal, it's called. It might be nothing, just a crazy rumour, but the fellow said the villagers regarded her highly because she had magical properties."

"Where?"

Peterson gave the most accurate directions he could.

"I hope the magic properties help keep her safe," Andrew said, noting the details as he felt a flicker of hope for Mariana.

"That's the bad news," Peterson said. "Witch doctors and such like also think white women may have magic properties. My informant only heard about the white woman because a couple of witch doctors want to steal her and cut her up."

"Do they, by God?" Andrew felt his heartbeat increase. "Thank you, Peterson." He was on his feet in a second and ran to Brigadier Wood with the news.

"A white woman?" Wood looked up from behind his desk. "Are you sure it's her?"

"No, sir," Andrew said. "But how many white women will there be in Zululand? Whoever she is, we'll have to try and rescue her."

Wood grunted, nodding his head. "I suppose you'll want to lead the rescue mission?"

"Yes, sir," Andrew responded.

"I imagined you would. How many men do you want?"

"Twenty, sir," Andrew said after a moment's consideration. "Any more would be cumbersome, and twenty could fight off a small Zulu impi."

"Find twenty volunteers," Wood said. "Good luck, Baird."

"Thank you, sir." Andrew saluted and hurried from Wood's tent, full of conflicting emotions. Hope battled with sick dread as he thought of Mariana in the hands of a Zulu warrior and the horror of witch doctors using her for their medicine.

Andrew was surprised when more than forty men volunteered for what could be a dangerous mission, and he picked a score of experienced men, mostly older than him. He selected a mixture of colonials with knowledge of African conditions and steady regulars who could be relied on to obey orders and not panic in a crisis.

"Could I come, sir?" Kerr asked, stepping forward. "I speak Zulu and know the people."

"Do you know this part of the country?" Andrew asked.

"No, sir," Kerr said. "I know the south and east of Zululand better."

Andrew mused for a moment. "Yes, come along, Kerr."

Not wishing to waste time, Andrew left that same day, following Peterson's directions and the rough location of Siyanda's Kraal Peterson had marked on his map.

He made good time, pushing his men towards the east, so it was after dark when they camped on a piece of rising ground, with a group of Buffalo thorn threes offering shelter.

"No fire tonight, boys." Andrew consulted his map. "The Zulus probably already knew we are here, but we don't want to advertise the fact."

The men nodded, accepting Andrew's orders.

"I want five men on picket duty," Andrew said and spent half the night touring the sentries. Twice they heard animals prowling outside the camp, and all were glad to leave before dawn the following day. Despite his desire for speed, Andrew kept alert, with scouts out constantly.

"No Zulu warriors so far," Kerr said as they perused the terrain. "I've never seen the land so quiet. Even the last two *imizi* were empty of men."

"Not even a whisper of an impi," Andrew agreed. "It's as if a giant brush has swept them up, or they are gathering elsewhere for some major attack."

"Yes," Kerr agreed. "It's a bit worrying. The Zulus are not a people to cross with impunity. They're planning something."

"Maybe they're going to attack our camp at Khambula," Andrew guessed. "I think Brigadier Wood commands the only active British force left in Zululand." Andrew knew the southern invasion had bogged down, with the Zulus besieging the British in a fort at Eshowe. Only Wood's force was making aggressive moves against the Zulus.

"We'll have to return and inform the brigadier," Kerr said.

"Inform him of what?" Andrew asked. "Inform him we haven't seen anything? Keep moving."

They found spoor the following morning, beaten earth and the marks of humanity. Kerr crouched, inspecting the ground. "About thirty men," he said, "moving slowly to the east, with some women in the middle."

Andrew remained on horseback with his eyes never still as he surveyed the surrounding land. "Not warriors, then?"

"I'm not sure what they are, sir," Kerr admitted. "They're moving too slowly for an impi, yet if they were a family, they'd have livestock with them."

"Are they heading towards Siyanda's Kraal?"

"They may be, sir," Kerr said. "Or in that direction, at least."

"When will we overtake them?" Andrew asked.

Kerr screwed up his face, making calculations based on the relative speed and the difficulties of the terrain. "Maybe this evening, sir," he said at last.

"Before or after we reach the kraal?"

"About the same time, sir." Kerr sounded more confident.

Andrew raised his voice. "Increase the speed, boys!"

Rather than send out a scout, he left Sergeant Meek in charge and pushed in front, following the trail. With his rifle held ready and his hat shading him from the sun and the sudden showers, he moved quickly.

"They're making no effort to hide their spoor," Kerr said.

"All the better for us," Andrew replied.

In the early afternoon, Andrew pushed Lancelot to the summit of a rise and saw a straggling group of people a mile ahead. Glancing behind to check his men, he increased speed, so Lancelot cantered over the rough ground.

I see you, you bastards. You're not taking Mariana away for your filthy practices.

With a mixture of excitement and trepidation, Andrew moved in a wide arc around his quarry, not caring if any stray party of warriors tried to ambush him. When he overtook the column, he rode to them and reined up.

"Stop there!" he ordered.

The column halted immediately, thirty men carrying hunting spears and three women in the centre.

The witches.

"Lieutenant Baird." The leading witch recognised Andrew. "I told you we would meet three times."

"This is the second time." Andrew put his rifle in its sheath. "Where are you heading?"

"Siyanda's *imuzi*." The witch glowered at Andrew, flicking the gnu's tail in her right hand.

"Why?" Andrew's hand hovered over the butt of his rifle. His men arrived and surrounded the column with rifles ready to fire.

"We have somebody to see," the leading witch replied.

"We'll travel together," Andrew told her.

The witch flicked the gnu's tail, rattled the bones on her clothes and walked on with Andrew's men forming around the column of Zulus.

"Who do you have to see?" Andrew had resolved to be polite to the witches, although his insides were churning with apprehension.

"A woman," the leading witch replied.

"Is she a white woman?" Andrew asked.

"She is a woman without colour," the witch replied.

"Kerr!" Andrew snapped. "Scout ahead."

"Yes, sir." Kerr bounded forward, returning within fifteen minutes. "This way, sir." He led Andrew to a slight ridge.

"That's Siyanda's *imuzi*." Kerr pointed to the usual circle of *izindlu* within a protective screen of thorn bushes.

Andrew lifted his field glasses and peered ahead. Siyanda's *imuzi* looked similar to a hundred others he had seen. Smoke from cooking fires rose into the still air, and women moved around purposefully as children played and young boys herded scrawny cattle outside fields of mealies.

Is Mariana in there, waiting for me?

"Take over, Fletcher," Andrew ordered and spurred through the open gate and into the kraal. Hauling out his rifle, he dismounted and looked around.

"Mariana!"

The inhabitants of the *imuzi* stared at him, women, children, and old men. Nobody made a threatening move.

"I'm looking for a white woman," Andrew said in Xhosa. "Her name is Mariana Maxwell. Is she here?"

An elderly man approached, walking erect and proud despite his white hair and lined face. "The woman without colour died yesterday," he said. "The witches are coming to take her away."

Andrew felt despair grip him. "Mariana died?" he said and then shook his head. "Let me see her. I'll be damned if I allow the witches to take her!" When he realised he was speaking English, he took a deep breath and switched to Xhosa. "Where is she?"

The elderly man indicated the largest *indlu*, and Andrew stooped through the door. The interior was dark and smoky, with a group of women around a sleeping mat on the floor. Andrew stepped forward.

"Let me see, please," he said.

The woman lay nearly naked on the mat, with her arms crossed in front of her and her eyes closed. Andrew leaned closer and sighed with relief.

"That's not Mariana," he said. "Thank God, oh, thank you, God."

"Africans don't like albinos," Kerr explained when he stepped to Andrew's side. "They fear what they don't understand and call them *inkawu* – white baboons – or *isishawa*, people who are cursed."

"Poor woman," Andrew said. "I doubt she had a very happy life."

"Outsiders rarely do," Kerr murmured.

"I said you would be disappointed when we met again," the leading witch said as she stood behind Andrew. She looked down at the albino woman. "This *isishawa* has no colour, but she is not the one you seek."

"No, she is not," Andrew agreed. He stood back as four men from the witches' column entered the *indlu* and lifted the body.

"Should we stop them?" Kerr asked.

Andrew shook his head. "One thing my father imprinted on my mind was never to interfere with local religions. I'd say that these witches are part of Zulu religious life."

"They are," Kerr agreed.

"We might disapprove," Andrew said, "but I don't think we have any right to interfere." He watched as the witches' male assistants gently lifted the dead woman and carried her out of the *imuzi*. The horsemen stood back, some with expressions of disgust, others of concern or apprehension.

"Sir?" Kerr asked as Andrew stood in the *indlu*. "Orders, sir?"

"Orders?" Andrew repeated as he struggled with his feelings, relief mingling with disappointment. "We'll return to Khambula," he decided.

Maybe I am overly optimistic, and Mariana is already dead.

When Andrew returned from his abortive expedition, he found that reinforcements had reached Brigadier Wood. Lieutenant-Colonel Russell had ridden in with a squadron of Mounted Infantry plus the Edendale troop of Natal Native Horse. A few hours later, Commandant Pieter Raaf arrived with his professional-looking Transvaal Rangers, and then the Border Horse trotted in, bridles jingling, and horses lathered with sweat.

Andrew knew Raaf was a Boer and an experienced fighting man, while his Rangers included European and African riders.

"These Transvaal lads look quite a formidable force, sir," Andrew commented.

Buller nodded. "I'm not sure how far we can trust the Boers," he said. "I'll keep my eyes on Mister Pieter Raaf." He lit a cigarette and blew out a thin ribbon of smoke. "We seem to be collecting characters in this war. Commandant Weatherley of the Border Horse is also well known. He's a Canadian, a veteran of the Crimea and the Mutiny and a divorcee."

Andrew looked for the notorious Weatherley, for anybody who had gone through a divorce was subject to scandal.

"The frontiers attract the footloose and those who don't fit in elsewhere," Andrew said, remembering his father had told him the same thing.

Buller nodded. "The unconventional, the loners, the unwanted and the wild." He drew on his cigarette. "We also have a bunch of German settlers in the Kaffrarian Vanguard and, more importantly, five companies of the 80th Foot. They're at Luneburg."

"With that lot and Brigadier Wood in command, Cetshwayo can whistle for his supper," Andrew said.

Buller smiled, watching the Border Horse through critical eyes. "I hope you're right, Baird."

"Now we know the capabilities of the Zulus," Andrew said, "I doubt any semi-competent British officer will allow the Zulus to take his men by surprise. They'll laager in every camp and dig entrenchments every night."

Buller nodded. "Aye, Isandhlwana and the Intombi taught us a lesson, all right." He glanced at Andrew. "You didn't find your girl, then?"

"No, sir." Andrew shook his head. "All I found was a dead albino."

"Hard luck, Baird." Buller finished his cigarette, dropped the stub, and ground it into the dirt. "Don't give up hope, eh?" He stepped away. "I think that she'll be in oNdini if she's anywhere."

"Yes, sir," Andrew agreed. *I won't give up until I find Mariana or see her dead body.*

CHAPTER 22

"Gentlemen." Wood sounded pleased as he spoke to his assembled officers. "Lord Chelmsford has contacted us with good news. As you know, our southern column is under siege at Eshowe. His Lordship is going to drive through a relief column and wants us to create a diversion to draw off some of the Zulu army."

The officers nodded in satisfaction. They wanted revenge for Moriarty's reverse and the disaster at Isandhlwana. Buller's raids were morale-boosting but barely pinpricks against the forty-thousand-strong Zulu army.

"We know that British arms, properly led, can defeat the Zulus," Wood said, hardening his tone to drive the message home. "Our spies, while failing to locate the unfortunate woman captive, have given us some information that may prove invaluable."

The officers listened, with some lighting pipes and others with long cheroots. Andrew stirred impatiently. In his opinion, generals and brigadiers were very slow and ponderous.

Wood continued. "Our spies have informed us that Cetshwayo has sent an impi in our direction. We don't know whether it intends to launch them at Khambula or cross the border to attack Utrecht. If the former, we will be ready to receive them."

The officers stirred again, with some murmuring approval.

Wood waited until the hum died down. "We also know that a small impi has joined the abaQulusi on the heights of Hlobane." He nodded to the great flat-topped mountain ten miles to the east.

Buller lifted his head. "Maybe we should strike there, sir."

"My thoughts entirely, Buller," Wood said. "If we attack the abaQulusi on Hlobane and capture their cattle, we should draw Cetshwayo's impi toward us and not to Utrecht. So far, Cetshwayo has had things all his own way. His impis have found us unprepared. That will not happen here, gentlemen!"

The officers gave a subdued growl, unlike anything Andrew had heard before. He saw the determination on their faces, the set jaws, and clenched fists and some of his doubts about the outcome of this war dissipated.

"Colonel Russell and Colonel Buller," Wood said. "I leave it to you to prepare a striking force for Hlobane."

"Yes, sir," Buller said with satisfaction as Russell gave a brief nod.

Wood lifted his hand. "Infantry officers, you and I will ensure we adequately defend Khambula. I want the men trained to respond to an alarm within two minutes. Colonel Russell, organise your attack on Hlobane. That is all. Thank you, gentlemen."

Buller gathered his officers outside his tent and spread a map on the ground. "Gentlemen," he said. "You heard the Brigadier. I have drawn this map from my own observations, plus the information from spies and informers."

Andrew studied the map, memorising the main features. He pushed away his memories of the plateau above Isandhlwana as Buller, tall, commanding, and full of confidence, continued.

"I want you all to be familiar with the topography, so nobody gets lost when we're up there."

Hlobane was a high hill rather than a mountain, with a four-mile-long *nek* or pass connecting it to the Zunguin range. Hlobane consisted of two plateaux of different heights and sizes, with the lower plateau, 850 feet high, the smaller and closest to the nek. That plateau rose a rocky two hundred near-vertical feet to a narrow passage called the Devil's Pass, which led to the second and higher plateau. Andrew judged the higher plateau to be over three miles long and a mile and a half in width, with a nek at the east. This eastern nek, Ityentika nek, stretched to the mountain known as Ityentika.

"Now, gentlemen." Buller spoke softly, but nobody could mistake the intensity of his eyes. "You must remember that the abaQulusi is not a normal Zulu clan. Shaka himself sent them here, and they think of themselves as royalty, a cut above the normal Zulus. When they say they are children of heaven, they mean it."

Andrew fretted slightly, not caring what the abaQulusi thought of themselves.

Buller noticed Andrew's reaction. "That means the abaQulusi will be even more determined to defend their homes," he said. "They live in kraals across the area and withdraw to the plateaus when somebody threatens them. According to our spies, the abaQulusi also barricade the paths between each plateau with piles of rocks, so don't expect to gallop from place to place." Buller raised his voice. "This won't be a quiet stroll around Hyde Park, gentlemen. Prepare yourselves for some hard fighting."

Andrew studied the map again. "I see only two tracks up to the plateau." He jabbed down with his finger. "One at the western end and one at the eastern."

"That's correct, Baird," Buller said. "The one at the west is so steep that horses will find it nearly impossible, but we will use both paths. Once we reach the Hlobane plateaux, our informants tell us there are around two thousand cattle and maybe a thousand warriors."

"How will we proceed, sir?" Peterson asked.

"Colonel Wood has drawn up the plan," Buller said. "I will lead a force up the eastern track with the larger force of mounted men, plus a battalion of friendly Zulus and a rocket trough. We shall drive away the cattle. Colonel Russell will use the steeper western track and occupy the lower plateau with the Mounted Infantry, the remainder of the mounted men, a second rocket trough and the rest of the friendly Zulus. Colonel Russell is in overall charge of operations. There is a terrible road known as the Devil's Pass joining both plateaux, but we won't have to use that!" Buller looked up, smiling. "Are there any questions?"

"When do we start, sir?" Andrew asked, and Buller grinned.

THEY LEFT KHAMBULA BEFORE DAWN ON THE 27TH OF MARCH, RIDING across the country with scouts out and friendly Zulus marching alongside. Buller had given Andrew Second Lieutenant Fletcher, Sergeant Meek and twenty men to command, and he rode in the centre of the column. Most of the men were eager to avenge Moriarty and the dead at Isandhlwana, with others openly nervous.

"Can we trust these Zulus?" one man asked, jerking a thumb at Uhamu's men running beside the column.

"Yes," Andrew replied shortly. "If Cetshwayo or the abaQulusi capture them, God knows what their fate will be."

That first day was uneventful, and Buller set up camp in the early evening five miles southeast of Hlobane, with his tents mushrooming on the rough ground and the hill looming on the horizon. He sent out strong pickets and created a rough barricade in case of a Zulu attack.

"After Intombi," Buller said grimly, "we're taking no chances. If anybody hears or sees anything suspicious, wake me at once. Fire first, boys and ask questions later." He looked back towards Khambula. "And watch for the Border Horse; they seem to have got lost somewhere."

Andrew checked his rifle for the tenth time that day, brushed a speck of dust from the breech and stared across to where Russell's campfires winked through the dark. Russell had taken his force on a different route, heading for the opposite side of Hlobane.

"It's good to know we have company," Peterson said, lighting a thin cheroot.

"If you see their fires go out, sound the alarm," Andrew said. "I wonder how many Zulus are watching us now."

Peterson drew on his cheroot. "How ever many there are, there'll be less when we get among them."

Andrew did not smile. He could still hear the Zulu's triumphant yells as they plunged their assegais into the fugitives of Isandhlwana. "I hope you're right, Peterson." He thought of Elaine, caressed his rifle, and glanced over to Hlobane.

"Grab some sleep," Buller ordered. "We're only here for two hours rest."

Andrew dozed for an hour and then took over as duty officer. He was checking the pickets when Buller loomed out of the dark. "Where the devil is the Border Horse? Where are Weatherley's men?"

"They've not arrived yet, sir," Andrew said. "They must have taken the wrong route."

Buller shook his head. "I thought the colonials were better than that."

Andrew said nothing. *We'd have heard firing if Weatherley ran into trouble.*

"We can't wait for them," Buller decided. "Build up the fires so the Zulus think we're still here."

Leaving the fires blazing, Buller led his column toward the Ityentika Nek. They marched closer to Hlobane, halted for an hour, and moved again. At three in the morning, they reached the foot of the path.

Andrew looked upward at the looming mass of Hlobane to the left and Ityentika on the right, patted Lancelot and wondered what the day would bring.

"Somebody told me that it was always hot and sunny in Africa, sir," Meek said as the skies opened with heavy rain, punctuated by thunder and lightning.

"Maybe they've never been here," Andrew replied. He pulled his recently adopted broad-brimmed hat down and his collar up. "This weather is as bad as we have in Britain."

"Dismount!" Buller ordered. "Lead the horses up the path. They'll have enough work to do later."

The column filed onto the steep track, with the rain turning the ground into a torrent and the frequent flashes of lightning revealing where they were.

"Keep moving!" Buller ordered as Andrew trudged up with his head bowed.

"Come on, Lance!" Andrew said, with every footstep splashing and the hill rising, dark and ominous, before him. He held his rifle muzzle down to protect it from the rain and moved in utter misery.

Every step brings us nearer the top, and every fight helps us win the war. Keep moving; left, right, left, right, left.

Andrew heard the first crack of a rifle, far different from the deeper grumble of thunder and knew the Zulus had seen them.

"Here we go!" he shouted, suddenly uncomfortable at the thought of being shot at as he climbed a narrow path with a long drop below.

"The Zulus are in caves!" Kerr shouted, and a man screamed as a bullet tore into his chest.

"Fire at the muzzle flashes," Buller ordered, "and keep moving!"

When some of the men responded, a desultory firefight began between the slowly climbing column and the unseen defenders. Andrew peered into the slanting rain, decided he had little chance of hitting anything and plodded on.

The Zulus continued to fire, wounding a few men and more horses, but Buller pushed his column up.

"Don't stop," Buller ordered. "Keep moving. The allocated men will take care of the wounded."

Andrew swore as a bullet thumped the rock beside him. He saw the blue mark on the stone and pushed on, refusing to waste cartridges he might need later. He remembered Isandhlwana when the infantry ran out of ammunition. Twice he stepped over dead bodies on the track and once heard a terrible scream as a horse toppled over the edge.

"Keep moving, men!" Andrew repeated Buller's words and heard officers echo the order the length of the column, diminishing in volume as the command reached the men still near the foot of the path.

Buller forced their passage up step by stubborn step, and by dawn, the British formed up on the higher plateau. Piet Uys, who led the only force of Boers to join the British, spoke to his four sons and nodded to Buller, smiling. As the British formed up, the storm passed, leaving the ground slippery, with grey light reflecting from the wet rocks.

Andrew counted his men, thankful he had lost nobody from his squad, although they all looked bedraggled and downcast.

"Heads up, men," Andrew ordered. "Check your ammunition." He forced a wry smile. "At least we don't have to worry about filling the water bottles."

"Sir, look over there!" Kerr pointed to the right, where a powerful body of abaQulusi was trotting around the plateau's edge with shields held above their heads and the weak sunlight glittering from their spearheads.

Buller rode slowly in front of his men, tall and imperturbable.

"If we move into the plateau, sir, they'll cut us off from the path," Peterson said.

Buller smiled and gave a calm order. "I want a troop of the Frontier Light Horse to skirmish with these fellows. Stop them from blocking our retreat."

"Yes, sir," Lieutenant Carrington of the Frontier Light Horse said happily and led his men toward the abaQulusi. The Light Horse's sand-coloured uniforms, braided with black, bobbed away as their broad hats, sodden from the morning's rain, flopped over their heads.

Within a few minutes, Andrew heard the crackle of musketry as the Light Horse fired on the approaching abaQulusi.

"I want our Zulus and other African infantry to round up the cattle and drive them to the west," Buller said. "The Zulus are expert cattlemen."

Andrew watched the friendly Zulus trot over the plateau, covering the ground at a pace British light infantry would have envied.

"Baird!" Buller said. "You look eager. It's time you proved your nickname, Up-and-At- 'Em. Take your men and support the Frontier Horse."

"Yes, sir." Andrew pulled Lancelot out of the main formation. "Come on, lads! It's time to earn our magnificent pay!" He led his men after the Light Horse.

The tactics were simple. Approach close to the Zulus, keep out of range of the throwing assegais, fire, withdraw, reload, close, and fire again.

The abaQulusi trotted toward the Light Horse, dropping to the ground when the British fired to minimise their casualties, rising, and advancing. They never wavered despite the scattering of dead and wounded, held their shields at an angle and extended their ranks to outflank the British horsemen. Andrew led his men beside the Light Horsemen, firing and withdrawing, breathing in the gun smoke, reloading, and returning to the fight. They skirted the plateau's edge, with the rising sun rapidly drying the ground and the abaQulusi outflanking them and taking minimal casualties.

One of the Light Horsemen swore, pointed downward and shouted, "Look to the southeast!"

When Andrew looked down on the plain, he saw a long column of Zulu warriors in the far distance, with another further back. Ignoring the abaQulusi, he lifted his field glasses and studied the plain.

"Damnation!" Andrew saw another Zulu column a quarter of a mile to the right of the second and then a fourth and a fifth.

"That's the main Zulu army," Andrew shouted. "They must have left oNdini earlier than expected to get here so quickly."

Oh, dear God in heaven, here we go again.

CHAPTER 23

Andrew felt a chill run up his spine at the size of the Zulu army. Ever since he saw the thousands of Zulus smash into the 24th at Isandhlwana, he had dreaded witnessing such an impi again.

"Warn the Colonel, Fletcher," Andrew ordered and watched as Fletcher spurred across the plateau.

Andrew was aware of how dangerous their position could be. With the abaQulusi on Hlobane and a massive impi only a few miles away on the plain, the Zulus could easily cut off the British and destroy them piecemeal. Without Buller's mounted men and the African infantry, the British position at Khambula would be considerably weaker, and the Zulu impi might overrun the defences. Even worse, the impi could ignore the Khambula position and attack the town of Utrecht with its tiny garrison and civilian population. Andrew shivered, remembering the horror of Inglenook.

"Sir!" Fletcher returned at a gallop with his hat bouncing from his head and his face flushed. "Colonel Buller sends his compliments, sir, and requests that you join him."

"Very well," Andrew replied. "Take over here, Fletcher." He winked. "We're witnessing history, Paul!"

A group of officers surrounded Buller when Andrew arrived. "I saw the impi, Baird," Buller said. He looked along the plateau, assessing the situation. "We'll have to return to Khambula, but the impi is too close for us to chance the eastern track." He thought for a moment. "We'll have to take the Devil's Pass."

"How about the cattle, sir?" Peterson was a farmer from Cape Colony, and cattle were nearly as important to him as to the Zulus. "We can't abandon the herd to the Zulus." He pointed to a thin-faced ensign. "Go and warn the Frontier Light Horse and the Border Horse if you can find them. Tell them to retreat at once by the right."

"Yes, sir," the ensign shouted and galloped off.

"Well, gentlemen," Buller said, "here we are. We have the main Zulu impi advancing across the plain a few miles away and the abaQulusi approaching us with murderous intent." He grinned. "As soon as the last of the cattle is away, I think we should withdraw. Are there any dissenters?"

There were none.

"My men, sir," Andrew reminded. "My men are with the Border Light Horse."

"Fetch them, Baird," Buller replied. "You may withdraw by whichever route seems better."

"Yes, sir." Andrew kicked in his heels and galloped across the plateau.

"Come on, lads!" Andrew gestured from a hundred yards away. "Leave the abaQulusi! We're heading back to Khambula."

Andrew's men galloped across the rocky ground and formed behind him, still exchanging shots with the abaQulusi as Andrew led them towards the Devil's Pass.

"Fletcher," Andrew shouted. "Take the lead. You can see Buller's men ahead; ride for them." He dropped to the rear, where the abaQulusi followed at a steady trot. Encouraged by the British retreat, the Zulus redoubled their efforts and pressed hard on the heels of Andrew's men.

"No, you don't." Andrew saw one young warrior running ahead of the rest with his throwing assegai poised. He reined up, aimed his rifle at the man's midriff and fired. The Martini kicked back into his shoulder, and the bullet threw the shocked warrior backwards.

The short delay had enabled the abaQulusi to close, and three throwing assegais hissed toward Andrew. He pulled Lancelot aside, impressed by the distance the Zulus could throw their spears and gasped as an assegai ripped the arm of his tunic and opened a shallow wound.

That's my second wound in this campaign.

"Come on, sir!" Kerr had pulled back in support, fired at the nearest abaQulusi, and reined up beside Andrew. "You're hurt, sir!"

"Only a scratch," Andrew said, although the wound was stinging abominably. "Come on, Kerr!"

As they pushed on, more assegais whizzed past, some to impale themselves into the ground with the long shafts vibrating. Andrew saw his men ahead, with the most nervous crowding in advance of Fletcher and Buller ushering the mounted men towards the nek to the lower plateau.

"I asked Russell to cover this pass," Buller fumed. "Where the devil is he?"

"I'm damned if I know, sir," Lieutenant Browne, Russell's second-in-command, looked equally annoyed.

"Well, we'll have to do without him," Buller said. "I've sent the men down, Browne. You may command the rear guard."

"Yes, sir." Browne accepted the post of danger without hesitation.

Buller noticed Andrew approaching with his men. "Ready to meet the devil, Baird?" Buller asked, grinning.

"Not yet, sir," Andrew replied, glancing over his shoulder at the rapidly approaching abaQulusi. "I'll live to fight another day."

"That's the spirit," Buller said. He shook his head. "Are you sure we haven't met before? There is something very familiar about you."

"No, sir," Andrew said, ducking as a Zulu bullet whizzed over his head.

"I'm damned if I haven't seen you somewhere." Buller took no notice of the increasing Zulu fire or of the approaching abaQulusi. "We can discuss this later, young Baird." He lifted his revolver and fired at the abaQulusi. "Missed, damn it. The range is far too long. After you, my boy." Buller indicated the steep path, strewn with boulders, down which the raiding party struggled.

Andrew glanced down, seeing an almost perpendicular *kranz*, with boulders and rocks thrusting from the bottom of a path so narrow men would have to descend in single file.

Kerr, the last of Andrew's men, was already twenty yards down, riding his horse with supreme skill. Andrew watched Kerr, seeing horses and men all jammed together, with Piet Uys guiding his Boers down the steep, rock-strewn path.

"After you, my boy," Buller repeated.

"Thank you." Andrew gave a little bow. Buller's calm assurance gave him confidence. Although Andrew did not fear death, he wanted to live to burn down oNdini and rescue Mariana if she were still alive.

Dismounting, Andrew began the descent, leading Lancelot down the path. He holstered his Martini as being too unwieldy, grabbed his revolver instead and negotiated the rocks. The Devil's Pass was an accurate description, Andrew thought, as he braced himself to prevent Lancelot from sliding. He would have hesitated to use this descent even on a quiet day, and with an aggressive impi behind them, the British took appalling risks. Not for the first time, Andrew blessed Lancelot for being a sure-footed Kabul pony rather than a taller, showier thoroughbred that was less able to negotiate the precipitous slope.

A Zulu appeared behind Andrew, with his shield held high to his face and only his eyes and the upper half of his head visible. Feeling remarkably calm, Andrew judged where the warrior's body would be behind the shield and fired a single shot towards his chest. The hide shield was no protection against a pistol bullet, and the force knocked the warrior backwards. Even as he fell, he threw his *iKlwa*, but the weapon was designed for stabbing rather than throwing, and it was clumsy in flight. The *iKlwa* clattered against a smooth boulder and fell to the ground.

There was broken rock on either side of the path, loose scree with baboon paths, far too narrow and steep for horse riders to traverse, but lightly armed Zulus scrambled down to appear alongside the retreating British. They waited for an unwary man and lunged out, stabbed, and withdrew, or killed a horse, knowing the heavily encumbered British would be slow on the plain below.

Andrew stepped on, slid on a loose stone, and ducked as a throwing spear hissed past. He saw a man ahead stumble and fall, with a trooper saving him.

The rear guard was firing volleys, the sound reassuring on that hellish pass, and then the firing ceased.

"What the devil?" Buller looked upward, and for the first time since Andrew had met him, his calm façade cracked. "These idiots have stopped firing!"

"Yes, sir," Andrew agreed, ducking as a Zulu stood on top of a rock and threw an assegai, which whirred down and clattered against the rock beside Buller. Andrew fired back and reloaded before negotiating the next section of the pass. He saw a horse fall over the edge, legs kicking, to bounce on rocks and fall again. He saw a Mounted Infantry private crawling down the track, leaving a trail of blood.

This retreat is Isandhlwana all over again!

Scores of Zulus lined the edge of the plateau, throwing assegais or heaving rocks at the retreating column. More men and horses fell; some troopers returned fire, ducked, or tried to hurry down the crowded path.

"Don't rush!" Buller roared. "Everybody, keep calm. Every second man fire back, try to make the Zulus keep their heads down!"

The rifles and carbines cracked out, with bullets whizzing both ways. Andrew saw one of the Boers fall with old, heavily bearded Piet Uys dashing back to save him. Andrew lifted the wounded Mounted Infantryman and laid him across Lancelot's saddle, saw Piet Uys fall and gasped as a throwing spear sliced the outside of his thigh.

Three wounds, damnit. Andrew clasped a hand to his thigh in a vain attempt to ease the sting. Blood, warm and sticky, flowed over his hand.

"Baird?" Buller was at his side, concern in his eyes.

"I'm all right, sir," Andrew said. "It's only a nick." He felt the blood flowing down his leg, realised his arm was still aching and wondered if he would survive the day.

Things happen in threes, I believe. That's two wounds in this battle so far; maybe the third will be fatal.

Buller nodded and shouted encouragement to his men. "Keep moving, but don't panic. Help the wounded men!"

Andrew saw Buller lift an injured man onto a horse, stop to encourage the despairing, and fire at the Zulus above and on either side.

Does that man ever stop?

"Get down that hill, Baird!" Buller ordered. "You have a woman to rescue, remember!"

"Yes, sir," Andrew agreed. "I haven't forgotten." He was surprised that Buller could remember such a detail in the middle of a pressurised retreat. The Mounted Infantryman was moaning as he lay across Lancelot's saddle, writhing at the pain of a wound in his side. "Lie still, chum," Andrew said. "We'll get you home." He staggered as the pain in his thigh increased, took a deep breath, and continued.

They scrambled down that terrible pass, with Buller always at the rear, encouraging, helping the injured and shouting commands. Andrew guided Lancelot, limping as the wound in his leg throbbed. Every few moments, he heard the scream of a terrified horse or a wounded man. He shot at Zulus, reloaded, and moved on, unaware he was shouting Elaine's name, yet with an image of Mariana in his mind. When Zulus bounded at them from the baboon tracks at the side, Andrew crouched behind a boulder, fired, and reloaded. For a moment, he was unsure where he was, at Isandhlwana or Hlobane, until a heavy hand clamped on his shoulder.

"Don't stop, old boy. It's rather unhealthy here!" Buller grinned at him, as calm as if he were strolling around the parade ground at Aldershot.

"Yes, sir," Andrew said.

As they neared the foot of the pass, Andrew saw men streaming away across the plain, with many riding pillion and others wounded. A litter of dead and dying horses showed the appalling losses, and Andrew felt a twist of remorse that so many animals had died. Living on the Border between Scotland and England as much as the family home in Herefordshire, he had grown up with horses and developed a deep affinity with them.

"Come on, Lance." Andrew limped beside the horse, with his wounds stiffening and the wounded infantryman unconscious across the saddle. He knew it was a long walk back to Khambula, but he had survived the debacle on Hlobane, and tomorrow was a new day.

"Sir!" Fletcher shouted and rode toward him with the remainder of his men in a column of twos. "We thought we lost you in the melee!" He was hatless, with blood trickling down his face from a wound in his scalp. Sergeant Meek shared a horse with Kerr, and two men were injured.

"Not yet," Andrew said. "You did well, Fletcher," Andrew said, pleased his men had retained their discipline amidst such chaos.

"Get your men back to camp, Baird!" Buller ordered.

Andrew nodded, hesitating between obeying orders, and following his instinct to remain behind and help the stragglers. Buller took him by the shoulders. "Go, Baird! We need good officers, and you're carrying a wound."

"Yes, sir!" Andrew felt his strength draining away as the strain of the retreat told.

"Lead on, Fletcher; I'll take the rear."

He felt pride as his men headed back and lifted his head when he heard the war cry.

"Usuthu! Usuthu!"

"Dear God in heaven!" Andrew saw the small impi explode from a tangle of rocks where they had been waiting. Rather than attack the stragglers, the Zulus charged at a formed body of eight Mounted Infantrymen, spreading out into the horns of the buffalo. Andrew recognised the distinctive white shields with the black fringe and the leopard skin headbands as the Zulus ran with their stabbing assegais held high.

The Abanonya again.

Andrew was out of effective revolver range but fired, hoping to alert the Mounted Infantry of the threat. He did not see the effect of his shot as the Zulus smashed into the British. Assegais stabbed and slashed, the British fired a few rounds, and then the skirmish was over, with five British and three Zulus lying on the ground and riderless horses galloping away. The Abanonya raised a cry of triumph, and the three remaining Mounted Infantry were fleeing for their lives.

With the wounded man draped over Lancelot, Andrew could not ride closer, and he was reluctant to order his men into danger while he remained behind. As he hesitated, the affair ended. He unholstered his rifle as Jama stepped toward him with blood dripping from his *iKlwa.* The two men stared at one another across the plain, and the Zulu lifted his assegai. Andrew did not know if it was a salute, a threat, or a gesture of acknowledgement.

"Shall we attack, sir?" Fletcher asked.

Andrew glanced at his men; tired, with some wounded and riding wearied horses, they were in no condition to fight.

"Not today, Lieutenant," Andrew decided. He saw Jama form up the Abanonya and trot away.

"Come on, lads," Andrew turned Lancelot's head and limped towards Khambula, with his men following behind him.

29TH OF MARCH 1879

"That's another Zulu victory," Andrew said as he stood outside the wagon laager at Khambula, listening to the cattle lowing in the nearby kraal. The dawn was not far off, with the early morning chill keeping him awake. "How many did we lose?"

"Over two hundred, including the native troops," Peterson said. "The Zulus wiped out the Frontier Light Horse and the Border Horse. Both units went the wrong way and ran right smack into the Zulu army. We lost fifteen officers and seventy-nine white men."

Andrew shook his head and stuffed tobacco into the bowl of his pipe. "It seems that the Zulus have got our measure." He took a deep breath and looked around the laager. Everything appeared so ordered here, with a field kitchen making bread, butchers slaughtering cattle, a quartermaster checking the stores and a sergeant drilling an awkward squad of replacements. Andrew listened for a moment as the sergeant screamed, red-faced.

"Left foot, I said, Sanderson! Left foot! That's the one on your left leg, you useless bugger! Good God, when the Queen parted with a shilling for your services, she should have asked for ninepence change! Try again, you ham-footed, useless, ginger-haired bastard!"

Andrew looked away. He had seen the same scenes at Isandhlwana before the Zulus came, and then nothing except carnage. It did not seem possible that the Zulus could destroy so much regulated order in so short a time.

"They'll come here next," Andrew said quietly. He rubbed the wound on his leg. An army surgeon had cleaned and bandaged his wounds, but they still ached abominably.

"You were at Sandlwana, weren't you?" Peterson asked.

"I was," Andrew agreed.

"And now, Hlobane."

"And Hlobane," Andrew confirmed.

"The Zulus won them both. Maybe you're a Jonah," Peterson said pleasantly. "You were here when we learned about the Intombi massacre as well."

Andrew nodded. He did not feel inclined to discuss defeats.

I'm further away than ever from finding Mariana. Maybe I am foolish even to think she is alive. Nobody has heard of her, and the Zulus don't take prisoners.

"You lost your sweetheart as well," Peterson continued.

Andrew lit his pipe, feeling his hands tremble with anger. "Don't you have some duty to perform, Peterson?"

Peterson stepped back. "I'm keeping away from you, Baird," he said, only half joking. "You're bad luck."

"Thanks," Andrew said dryly. "Keep your distance if you wish; it's all one to me." He watched as Peterson walked away and joined a group of subalterns. As Peterson spoke to them, the subalterns glanced backwards, and Andrew knew he was the subject of their conversation. He shrugged. It did not matter. Once this war was over, he planned to hand in his papers and leave the army.

"What are you doing, Baird?" Buller strode over to him, frowning.

"Checking the men, sir." Andrew lowered his pipe and saluted, feeling untidy under the gaze of the imperturbable Redvers Buller.

Buller pulled at his moustache. "That won't do, Lieutenant Baird. That won't do at all. I don't like to see officers idling their time away when there's work to be done."

"Yes, sir." Andrew felt the colour rush to his face.

"You realise the Zulus could attack here any time," Buller said. "Or they could head for Utrecht." He held Andrew's eyes in a ferocious glare. "Which would you prefer, Baird?"

Andrew knew Buller was testing him. "It would be better if the Zulus attacked here, sir."

Buller lit a cigarette. "I didn't ask which would be better. I asked which you would prefer."

Andrew lifted his chin. "Yes, sir. I'd prefer them to attack here."

Buller puffed out smoke and nodded. "Why?"

"We are better prepared to meet them, sir," Andrew said. "It's time we faced the Zulus on our terms rather than theirs."

Buller moved away, then abruptly turned. "Are you not nervous about fighting them again after your experiences on Hlobane and Isandhlwana?"

Andrew stiffened, reading Buller's words to be an implication of cowardice. "No, sir."

"Are you sure?" Buller's eyes were like granite, unyielding as they bored into Andrew's head.

"Quite sure, sir," Andrew said.

"Good." Buller's expression softened. "I'd hate to have recommended a Victoria Cross to a man who would be too nervous about accepting it. Find another horse; yours will be done up and join Raaf's Transvaal Rangers; he's going out to find the impi."

"Yes, sir." Andrew saluted and stepped towards the horse lines. A few seconds later, Buller's words sank in, and he turned around. "The Victoria Cross, sir? Why?"

"For saving a wounded man under fire." Buller had not moved. "Now get out there and stop thinking about that blasted woman."

"Yes, sir."

Lancelot looked over when Andrew entered the horse lines, and Andrew fed him a handful of mealies. He selected a lively pony, introduced himself, mounted with difficulty as his wounded leg troubled him, and rode out to join the Transvaal Rangers.

Pieter Raaf looked younger than Andrew expected. He nodded when Andrew joined his force, grunted what could be a welcome and trotted out of the laager to search for the Zulu impi.

"Try to keep up, *rooineck*," Raaf said, speaking English with a thick accent.

"I'll do my best," Andrew told him. He had seen Raaf performing heroics on Hlobane and knew he was an excellent fighting man.

"I saw you at Hlobane," Raaf said. "You know how the Zulus fight."

"Yes," Andrew replied shortly.

Raaf nodded. "So do we," he said and spurred forward.

As they rode away from Khambula, Andrew noticed a couple of companies of the 13th Foot moving out to collect firewood for the field bakeries. Zulus or no Zulus, the daily routine of the camp had to continue. He also saw Uys's burghers ride away, disheartened after the death of Piet Uys at Hlobane.

We'll miss the experience and skill of the Boers.

"Come on, *rooineck*," Raaf shouted.

Raaf's Transvaal Rangers spread out, with Raaf at the head and the men in an extended formation. They moved quickly, allowing their horses to find the best route as they covered the ground with a minimum of fuss. Andrew had long known that colonials rode differently from the British, with longer stirrups, leaning back in their saddles and looking more relaxed, as if they and the horses were a single unit. He had learned from them and copied their stance, with his borrowed pony seemingly happy to carry him.

Within a couple of hours, Raaf lifted his hand. Andrew saw a lone man running across the stark countryside, raising a thin trail of dust. Set against the vast background, the runner seemed timeless, as if he could represent the spirit of Africa, jogging effortlessly and holding a shield and handful of assegais. The runner saw Raaf's patrol and altered direction towards them, neither increasing nor decreasing his speed.

Raaf kicked in his spurs and met the man, spoke for a few moments, and returned to the patrol.

"This man is one of Uhamu's warriors," Raaf announced. "The main Zulu impi is going to attack the camp at Khambula in about four hours. We had better warn Brigadier Wood."

The Rangers headed back, with the Zulu trotting at their side with the graceful ease that Andrew always admired. They arrived at Khambula at eleven, passing the pickets with a casual wave, and Raaf reported to Wood as men gathered to listen.

"According to Uhamu's man," Wood informed the officers, "Ntshingwayo commands the impi that is heading this way." He pushed back his hat. "To remind you, Ntshingwayo masterminded the attack on Isandhlwana when he split Lord Chelmsford's army."

Some of the officers stirred uncomfortably.

"How many men does Ntshingwayo have, sir?" Buller asked.

"Judging by what Uhamu's man told us, Ntshingwayo has around twenty-four thousand men."

"That's a fair number," Buller said.

Wood scratched his head. "Most of them are the regiments that fought at Isandhlwana; some were at Intombi, and the abaQulusi from yesterday's fight at Hlobane." He paused. "The Zulus will be high on confidence and expect to defeat us again."

Peterson looked at Andrew as if he were to blame for every Zulu victory.

Wood continued. "Some have rifles they took from the 24th at Isandhlwana, and some rifles from our dead at Intombi, so we are not only facing spears. The enemy has weapons as good as our own."

"Dust, sir!" One of the mounted patrols galloped in. "Dust approaching from the east."

"Go and check, Baird," Buller ordered. "No, hang it all," he said with a grin, "I'll come as well."

They rode to a ridge of high ground and focussed their field glasses. "Over there, sir." Andrew pointed. "Five columns." He tried to keep the tension from his voice. "I'd say about five miles away."

"Slightly closer than five miles, I'd guess." Buller gave his opinion. "We'd better warn the Brigadier."

CHAPTER 24

Wood nodded when Buller gave his report. "Shall we say the Zulus are four miles distant, gentlemen? They should arrive in about thirty minutes, by my reckoning. Well, we've trained the men so they can man the defences within ninety seconds of us sounding the alarm, so there's no rush." He smiled. "I don't like to fight on an empty stomach, and I see no reason to starve the men. Order them to have their dinner, drive the cattle into the kraal and call in the wood-gathering party."

The bugles trilled out across the laager; men hurried to and fro, frantic parties herded the cattle into the kraal, and sergeants bellowed the firewood parties from the plain outside.

Buller nodded to Andrew. "Baird, you have the twenty men you commanded at Hlobane. Act as a mobile reserve and support wherever you are most needed."

"Yes, sir," Andrew replied.

"Strike the tents!" Wood ordered and practised hands folded away the long ranks of weather-stained white canvas within half a minute.

"Bring out reserve ammunition!" Ever since Isandhlwana, officers had debated if a lack of ammunition had helped create the disaster, so NCOs removed the brass restraining bands and unscrewed the lids on the ammunition boxes. Sweating soldiers carried the heavy boxes around the laager and distributed them behind the men at the barricades.

Less-than-eager privates hauled more ammunition boxes to the redoubt, where a company of the 90th Perthshire and another of the 13th Foot waited, reinforced by two seven-pounder guns. Another company of the 13th shared the kraal with the draught oxen while the remainder of the infantry were in the main laager.

"Let them come," Sergeant Meek murmured. "They'll not face infantry in company strength this time, by God."

Andrew agreed. He knew that despite the mobility of the mounted men and the artillery's firepower, the infantry was the backbone of the army. Underpaid, often unglamorous, hard-drinking, hard-swearing and hard-used, the sweating men in scarlet tunics had the final say wherever the Union flag flew. Queen Victoria and all her government ministers may make the decisions and formulate policy, but it was the often-undersized men from the slums and the sodden country lanes who enforced British rule. Andrew looked at them now, the young, acid-eyed, jesting men who knew they might be dead within an hour and wondered from where they had come and what their futures might be.

The 90th Foot took up their stations at the north and west sides of the redoubt, with the 13th on the south and east. Andrew saw the lines of scarlet tunics and stained sun helmets, with the sun gleaming from rifle barrels. A sergeant stopped his shouting for a moment to encourage a nervous young soldier with a wink and then checked his platoon's rifles one by one.

"Make sure you fill your canteens from the regimental water butts," a long-faced corporal said. "Fighting is thirsty work. If you think I'm lying, just ask the missus; she always runs to the pub after she fights with me." He waited for the nervous laughter. "Not me, though; I get the drinks in before the fight to get me courage up to face her, see?"

Andrew could nearly taste the tension in the air. These men knew all about Isandhlwana; they had heard of the disaster at the Intombi and had seen the wounded survivors return from Hlobane. Now it was their turn, and twenty-four thousand highly trained warriors were about to attack them, ready to plunge their assegais into cringing bodies.

Augmenting the infantry, the Royal Artillery manned another four seven-pounders, standing between the laager and the redoubt. The guns were *en barbette*, sited on raised ground and therefore able to fire over the parapet at the Zulus. With a hundred and ninety yards between the guns and the laager, Andrew did not envy the gunners their position. Wood shared Andrew's thoughts as, with no infantry support or cover, he ordered the artillerymen to leave the guns and take refuge in the laager if the Zulus approached within throwing-spear distance.

"Throwing spear distance?" one of the 90th scoffed. "If these bastards came within two hundred yards of me and I hadn't got a bundook, [1] I'd be off like a bloody shot, so I would."

Andrew shared the private's concerns. He had seen Zulu warriors keeping pace with a cantering horse and knew the artillerymen were not trained in fast running.

The horse lines were in the centre of the laager with the irregular horsemen, mostly colonials who had long feared the Zulus and were eager to finally see the professional infantry destroying the impis with steady volleys.

"How many men do we have, sir?" Peterson asked Buller.

Buller did not hesitate. "Twelve hundred and thirty-eight infantrymen, a hundred and twenty-one artillerymen and nearly six hundred and forty mounted men, with ninety sick in the hospital tents."

"Just under two thousand men," Peterson said. "And the Zulus have twenty-four thousand veteran and blooded warriors." He glanced at Andrew. "Let's hope nothing goes wrong this time, sir. Let's hope we don't have a Jonah in the laager."

Wood frowned. "That's a strange thing to say, Peterson."

"Yes, sir. I wondered if there was a connection between our reverses at Isandhlwana and Hlobane, sir. Maybe one officer who was present on both occasions."

"The British Army does not believe in superstition, Lieutenant Peterson," Wood said coldly. "I'd thank you to attend to your duty."

Peterson coloured, saluted, and marched away, glowering at Andrew as he passed.

Andrew tried to control his nerves, fighting the worry that Peterson might be correct. He had returned the borrowed pony and reclaimed Lancelot, for he preferred to fight on a horse he knew.

Andrew checked his men had ammunition and water, torn between a terrible desire to grab Lancelot and flee or a thirst for vengeance. Strangely, he had no dislike of the Zulus for the dead at Isandhlwana or Hlobane, for that had been straightforward warfare. He even accepted the Zulus' custom of slicing open the bodies, but the murder and possible rape of Elaine and kidnapping of Mariana infuriated him. He disagreed with making war on women, especially when they were friends and more than friends.

Andrew sat upright on Lancelot, lifted his field glasses to his eyes and scanned the terrain outside the British position. The Zulus were close now, easily seen by the naked eye, and Andrew saw the two columns on the right altering direction to the north, just out of range of the seven-pounders as they circled the British position.

"Ntshingwayo knows his stuff," Buller murmured. "Not many savages could calculate the range of artillery like that. Give that fellow a frock coat and a top hat, and he'd pass top of his class in Sandhurst."

"He could probably lecture at Sandhurst, sir," Andrew said without irony. "Most of the lecturers are passed over officers and duffers."

"What makes you say that, Baird?" Buller asked. He gave Andrew a curious look. "Have you been to Sandhurst?"

Andrew swore silently, knowing his loose mouth had again betrayed more about himself than he liked.

"They're getting closer," Andrew tried to divert attention away from himself. Two Zulu columns had halted on the northwest, while the remaining three had positioned themselves south of Khambula Hill.

"They are no closer now than they were five minutes ago," Buller contradicted. "I don't think we should allow them to settle. Even Zulus must be weary after their marching." He smiled. "I think it's time to disrupt them before they're properly rested."

"Yes, sir," Andrew said, glad that Buller did not pursue his enquiries.

"Are you ready for some fresh air and exercise?" Buller asked, suddenly grinning.

"Yes, sir," Andrew said. He always felt it was better to act than to sit waiting for something to happen.

"Let's see if Brigadier Wood agrees with you," Buller said, wheeled his horse and approached the Brigadier.

Andrew surveyed the defences, with the waggon wheels chained together and the booms tied across the brief intervals between each vehicle.

"Come on, Baird!" Buller shouted as he called up the mounted men. "Let's goad these Zulus into attacking us! Bring your men!"

The mounted men followed Buller towards the Zulu force in the north. Andrew remained close to Buller with his men at his back. He noticed the colonial horsemen carried carbines, shorter and more manageable than the longer rifle he had.

"Here we go again." Sergeant Meek sounded tired. "Let's hope for a better outcome than we had yesterday!"

Yesterday? Was it only yesterday they had scrambled down the Devil's Pass from Hlobane?

They trotted out, with the horses' hooves drumming on the ground and the infantry watching from under tilted helmets.

"Good luck, lads!" a hard Perthshire accent called after them.

Buller led the mounted force around the laager and, within half a mile of the Zulus, lifted his hand and ordered them to dismount.

"Every fourth man, you are the horse holders!" Buller shouted.

Andrew patted Lancelot and stepped forward. After the previous day's debacle, he felt vulnerable as he saw the closest Zulu impi, maybe five thousand strong, with the regiments holding their long shields and the sun glittering from the points of thousands of spears. Yet he knew this day was very different, with hundreds of British regular infantry waiting in support only a short ride away.

All the same, Andrew knew that whatever else happened in his life, however long he lived, he would never forget the sight of a Zulu impi in full battle array.

Buller led by example, striding forward, and firing at extreme range. "We won't weaken them much," he said, ejecting the spent cartridge, "but we might irritate them into charging to clear us away, and the 90th can decimate them with volley fire."

Andrew agreed. He aimed toward the Zulu mass that spread across the landscape, tried to focus on an individual warrior and squeezed the trigger. The Martini-Henry kicked back into his shoulder, and he grunted. The mounted men had fired the first shots in the battle of Khambula.

This could be the decisive battle when the main Zulu impi meets a dug-in British force. We always fight best on the defensive, as at Waterloo or like Campbell's Highlanders at Balaclava.

"Keep firing," Buller ordered. "Move closer. Horse handlers, don't get too far behind." The dismounted men stepped closer, firing carefully. Those Zulus who had rifles tried to retaliate, with their shots whistling high.

Andrew saw the Zulu lines quiver as the shooting caused casualties, for the colonial troopers were nearly all excellent marksmen. The line inched forward, with some warriors shaking their spears in impotent rage.

"The UmBonambi don't like that," Kerr said casually. "I wonder which regiment will charge first."

"Which regiments are there?" Andrew looked for the Abanonya's familiar white shields with the black fringe.

Kerr fired, ejected his cartridge, and reloaded. "The UmBonambi, UNokhenke and uMcijo," he said, indicating each *amabutho* as he spoke. "I believe they were all at Isandhlwana, sir."

Andrew aimed and fired, worked the under-lever, aimed, and fired again. The Zulu line edged forward, drumming their spears on their shields.

"Back on horseback, gentlemen," Buller ordered, and the men thankfully remounted. Andrew felt safer knowing he might outrun the Zulus if they charged. "Now close with the enemy!"

The mounted men trotted closer until Andrew could make out the features of the individual warriors and see the pattern of the cow-hide shields. Buller spurred another ten yards, taunting the Zulus, so some warriors left their line and hurled their throwing spears. One spear thudded into the ground a few feet from Andrew, with the shaft nearly erect and the head deeply embedded.

"Fire!" Buller shouted and waited until his men obeyed before wheeling his horse and trotting away. That volley was one too many for the uNokhenke *amabutho*, which broke ranks and ran forward in pursuit. Andrew saw the sun glitter on hundreds of assegais and an array of cow-hide shields and bobbing plumes.

"*Uzitulele, kagali muntu*!" they sang. "He is quiet; he doesn't start the attack."

"Here they come!" Buller remained closest to the Zulus, holding his Martini one-handed. "Give them another volley, boys!"

The horsemen responded, then galloped back towards the laager with the uNokhenke in noisy pursuit. After four hundred yards, Buller halted again, ordered another volley, and repeated the manoeuvre.

"They're all coming now," Kerr said as he thumbed a cartridge into his carbine. He aimed and fired in a single movement and reloaded with a fluidity that told of long practice.

Other *amabuthos* had followed the uNokhenke, with the UmBonambi and uMcijo also charging toward the thin, galling line of horsemen.

"That's enough, lads," Buller shouted. "We've given them pepper; now let the infantry put salt on their tails! Head back to the laager!"

The mounted men turned and spurred for the sanctuary of the laager, except for the Natal Native Horse, who chose a different route.

"Where are the Native Horse going?" a deep voice asked.

"They're buggering off!"

Rather than ride into the wagon laager, the Native Horse galloped right past.

"They've had enough!" Fletcher shouted in disbelief. "Come back, you cowards!"

Andrew watched them flee with mixed feelings. He knew the defenders would miss the Native Horse's rifles but also knew they had fought at Isandhlwana. They had seen the business end of a Zulu impi and had no desire to repeat the experience.

I understand.

"Godspeed, lads," Andrew said.

A sergeant of the 90th roared orders to shift aside one of the wagons, and the riders galloped in. When the last of Buller's horsemen were safe, the sergeant supervised the privates to roll the defences back in place.

"Get these thornbushes back under the body, lads, and watch there's no gaps. I don't want an angry Zulu sticking a dirty great spear up my jacksie!"

"Yes, Sergeant!"

Andrew studied the terrain. To the north of the British defences, a gentle slope ran downward, forcing any attacker to run uphill to the waiting rifles of professional soldiers. On the south, the terrain favoured the Zulus as the British had a killing zone of only between a hundred and two hundred yards. Beyond that, a cliff descended into the ravine of the White Umfolozi River.

"If I were Ntshingwayo," Kerr said. "I'd mass my men in the Umfolozi Valley. They've only a couple of hundred yards to cover, and at the speed the Zulus move, our lads will only get in a couple of volleys before they're at the barricades."

Andrew nodded in agreement as his men gathered around him, breathing heavily from their exertions. Andrew's grasp of the Martini-Henry was greasy with sweat as he thought of the ferocity of the Zulu attacks. He heard the Zulus chant and saw the regiments advance, the line of long spears and glittering, deadly assegais and knew the decisive battle was about to begin.

"This is the first time a full Zulu impi has faced a British army in its chosen position, sir," Fletcher said. "If we lose here, we may as well pack up and go home."

"If we lose here," Andrew said, "you and I will be dead. I'm not retreating again."

How about Mariana? Will I condemn her to a lifetime of slavery in Zulu hands? I can't afford for us to lose. We must win here.

"Here they come!" Fletcher shouted. "God help us all."

CHAPTER 25

The 90th Foot was already firing volleys, the heavy crashes joined by the deep barks of the four seven-pounders. Jack saw the front rank of the Zulus ripple as hundreds of .45 bullets smashed into them, with shell bursts rising in columns of grey-white smoke. Unsure what the artillery fire was, some warriors paused in their charge and stabbed at the smoke, believing guns were firing soldiers at them.

"They're taking casualties and still coming on well," Fletcher said, focusing his field glasses.

"There's no doubting their bravery," Andrew said. He watched Lieutenant Arthur Bigge manage the seven-pounders, changing from common shell to case shot as the Zulus came closer. Each blast of case sliced a bloody swathe through the advancing warriors, slowing them without halting the charge. The artillerymen loaded, aimed, and fired, with Bigge giving crisp orders.

"The gunners are from garrison companies." Fletcher revealed a surprising depth of knowledge. "Not the top drawer, yet they're working like heroes."

"They are," Andrew agreed.

The gunners stood in the open, exposed to Zulu musketry, but fortunately, the warriors had not mastered modern rifles, and most shots whizzed overhead.

Despite their losses, the Zulus kept coming, shouting their war cry, "*Usuthu! Usuthu!*" that Andrew knew would haunt his dreams for years, provided he survived the day.

"Come on, lads, join the 90th!" Andrew ordered, hating being an impotent witness. "Fire when they reach three hundred yards."

"Yes, sir!" Fletcher replied as the men readied their carbines.

By now, the infantry in the redoubt had joined in, pouring in an enfilading fire that smashed into the Zulu flank. An induna charged in advance of his *amabutho,* holding his shield high and escaping the torrent of bullets.

Andrew sighed, lifted his Martini, and aimed at the *induna*, aware of the importance of good leadership. Sad to shoot a brave man, he fired and saw the *induna* spin as the heavy bullet smashed into his leg.

"That's you out, my man," Andrew said, feeling satisfaction he had hit his mark. "Fire, men!" He aimed into the mass, shooting, reloading, and shooting again, with little feeling except a desire to survive. The crash of infantry volley fire and the bark of orders, the yelling of the Zulus and the swearing and joking of the 90th all combined in such a cacophony that no single sound predominated.

Kerr was loading and firing slowly, aiming each shot, while Fletcher was racing.

"Slow down, Fletcher," Andrew advised. "Aim first and lower your sights; you're firing high."

"Yes, sir." Fletcher looked round, wild-eyed. "They're getting close."

"Look at the 90th," Andrew said. "Do you think they'll let the Zulus through?"

The 90th Foot was firing in disciplined volleys, waiting for the word of command, and exchanging dark humour.

"No, sir," Fletcher said, gasping for breath.

"Nor do I. Take a deep breath, mark your man, aim low, and you'll be fine."

Andrew moved on, giving encouragement and advice.

By the time the Zulus reached two hundred yards of the 90th, the heat had gone from the charge. Andrew saw two warriors helping the tall *induna,* and then the infantry fired another volley, and all three fell. A few warriors advanced to the British barricade, and some even leapt into the laager, but the 90th chased them out with the bayonet.

"Get back to Cetshwayo, you bastards!" the 90th jeered as the final Zulus retreated. "Or come back and try again!"

The NCOs shut the men up. "Enough! Save your energy! They'll be back!"

Andrew found he was gasping for breath, with his fresh wounds aching. He leaned against the timber wood of a wagon and counted his cartridges before checking on his men.

"Take the artillery horses back inside the laager," Wood ordered. "We're losing too many of them!"

Andrew realised the Zulus' plunging shot was landing among the horses, with half a dozen already dead or wounded. He ordered half a dozen of his men to help round them up. In South Africa, animal transport was vital. Without horses, mules and oxen, the British Army would be immobile.

As the attack on the 90th's position ended, Ntshingwayo ordered his men to charge the British right, advancing on the front and rear simultaneously.

"I told you they'd use that damned ditch, sir!" Kerr said.

The Zulus had crept along the ravine, safe from British musketry, emerged and threw themselves at the British positions. The defenders had expected this manoeuvre and retaliated with a blast of fire from both the south side of the laager and the men in the cattle kraal. The initial crossfire disposed of the initial assault, but the Zulus poured increasing numbers of men into the attack, forcing their way into the space between the cattle kraal and the main laager.

"Ntshingwayo knows his stuff," Buller said quietly. "He's buying space with his men's lives." He looked sideways at Andrew. "Even although he wasn't at Sandhurst." He nodded to the Zulus. "You'd better give the 13th a hand, Baird."

"Yes, sir."

Andrew led his men to the northeast side of the laager and fired into the mass of warriors attacking the cattle kraal. The company of the 13th fought the Zulus hand to hand, bayonets and rifle butts against assegais and shields, while British curses mingled with the more resounding chants of the warriors. They fought among the lowing cattle, with men leaning across the shaggy backs of oxen to strike at their enemies, but as more Zulu reinforcements poured in, the outnumbered 13th Foot withdrew. They backed away, step by step, to the redoubt that some called Fort Khambula.

"The Zulus won that round," Andrew said as Zulu riflemen lined up inside the cattle kraal to snipe at the British manning the defences.

A dozen *indunas* rose from the ravine and stood on the ridge, encouraging the inGobamakhosi *amabutho* to leave the shelter and charge the laager. Andrew noticed one *induna* carrying a red flag and wondered if that was Ntshingwayo. He aimed his Martini and fired to see the *induna* walking behind his men unharmed.

"Is that Ntshingwayo?" Andrew asked.

"I don't know, sir," Kerr replied. "I've never knowingly met him."

Wood countered Ntshingwayo by ordering Major Hacket to take two companies of the 90th Foot to support the 13th.

Andrew watched the move and counter move, seeing the warriors and infantrymen as pawns on the Khambula chessboard, with death and horrendous injuries the price for a failed manoeuvre.

It must be easier to command an army if one thinks of the soldiers as chess pieces rather than living men.

As the Zulus left the ravine, the warriors on the north side attacked again, this time in a screaming charge towards the exposed artillerymen and the east front of the laager.

"They're attacking both sides at once!" Fletcher shouted. "This Zulu general is no fool!"

"He's a master of manoeuvre," Andrew agreed, firing and reloading. He tasted the acrid gun smoke, blinked at the sting, and fired again. He grunted as the stitches in his arm parted, and the wound reopened.

Major Hacket marched his men out of the laager at the double and, rather than launch them immediately at the enemy surging from the ravine, ordered them to form a double line.

"Fix bayonets!" Hacket shouted.

Andrew heard the distinct click as the men fitted the long bayonets into place, and then Hacket led them forward. Lieutenant Strong, smiling, drew his sword and stepped to the front of his company. They advanced gradually, then broke into a charge that matched the Zulus in intensity and courage. Not many European regiments would stand against a British bayonet charge, but the Zulus held for a while until the Perthshire men won the battle and forced them back over the rim into the ravine.

"Fire on them!" Hacket ordered, and his two companies of the Ninetieth stood on the rim and fired volleys at the inGobamakhosi. Their bullets caused considerable casualties, but standing in the open, the British were also vulnerable. Ntshingwayo ordered his riflemen to crawl through the long grass of the British refuse tip and fire into the 90th's ranks.

Andrew heard the 90th's bugle sound the retire as Hacket and a few other men fell before the Zulu fire. Andrew wiped the sweat from his forehead, swore as his Martini jammed and worked furiously with the ramrod to clear the swollen cartridge. He saw Brigadier Wood fire and hit the induna with the red flag.

"Good shot, sir!" Captain Maude of the 90th shouted. "Was that Ntshingwayo?"

"No," Wood replied. "It was another brave Zulu *induna*." He grunted as he saw one of Hacket's men crumple, clutching his thigh. "Look at that poor fellow!" He darted towards the edge of the laager, shouting to the man to hold on.

Captain Maude of the 90th lunged forward and took the brigadier's arm. "Really, sir," he said. "It's not your place to pick up single men," and ran forward with Lieutenants Lyons and Smith of the 90th. They rescued the wounded man, but Smith returned with a Zulu bullet in the arm.

When Hacket's men withdrew, the Zulus in the ravine emerged again to find the 13th Foot waiting behind the wagons, with rifles loaded and ready. However courageous the Zulus were, they could not avail against the disciplined firepower of British regulars.

"Here they come, boys," the officers roared. "Aim low, never mind the shine and volley fire on my word!"

The infantry waited, cursing, joking, some with pipes in their mouths, and many hiding their fear. They sighted along the thirty-three-inch-long barrels of their Martinis, nursed bruised shoulders from the brutal recoil and blew on the fingertips of their left hands, blistered from the barrel's heat.

With memories of Isandhlwana fresh, the British officers were nervous about running out of ammunition and kept the men under a tight leash. They forbade independent firing, so the men only fired volleys. As the 13th Foot repulsed the latest Zulu charge, Brigadier Wood moved from the main laager into the open ground between the laager and the strongpoint of Fort Khambula. He watched the course of the battle from every angle, taking notes, issuing orders to his staff, and occasionally firing at the enemy.

On the left front of the laager, the Zulus continued to attack, wave after wave of determined men charging into massed musketry that killed them by the score and the hundred.

"Don't these lads ever learn?" Andrew asked as he led his men to the areas that seemed most hard-pressed.

"They're too stubborn," Buller said. "Keep firing, Baird. The more of the enemy we kill today, the less there is to kill us tomorrow."

"Yes, sir," Andrew said, watching his men take positions behind the wagons and fire into the enemy. They had learned not to waste ammunition and aimed before they fired, taking a terrible toll on the advancing Zulu warriors.

"Keep it up, lads!" Andrew encouraged. "Sergeant Meek, find us some ammunition. Ensure every man has at least seventy rounds."

"Yes, sir," Meek replied.

Gunsmoke lay heavy over the laager, reducing visibility so the Zulus were indistinct even under the glaring sun.

Brigadier Wood slipped back into the main laager and sent for Buller.

"You wanted me, sir?" Buller asked.

Wood smiled. "Yes, Colonel, because I think you are just going to have a rough and tumble."

"Do you want us to sally out, sir?" Buller asked hopefully.

"Soon," Wood replied. "Ensure your men are ready when I give the word."

"Yes, sir," Buller replied.

Wood raised his voice, ordering two companies of the 13th to remove the Zulus from the cattle kraal and another company to push the Zulus back from the right front of the laager. He watched as the infantry filed from cover with the sun glinting from their bayonets and their ammunition boots crunching on the hard ground.

Andrew spoke to his men as the 13th pushed back the Zulus.

"Only fire if you have a clear target," Andrew warned. "I don't want us to shoot any of the infantry; that's the men in scarlet tunics. They're on our side."

Andrew's men laughed. They seemed relaxed as Wood organised the defence, and the British quelled each successive Zulu attack. Andrew glanced at his watch and started when he saw how late it was. The battle had lasted over four hours, yet it seemed only minutes since the mounted men had fired the opening shots.

After charging into relentless musketry time after time, the Zulu attacks at last faltered. Andrew did not know whether they could not take any more or whether Ntshingwayo realised he could not win and ordered them to stop. Either way, the impis began to withdraw.

"Baird!" Buller shouted. "The Zulus are falling back, Baird. Stop fooling around and join us!"

Andrew lifted a hand in acknowledgement and raised his voice. "You heard the colonel, lads! Mount up!"

He ran to Lancelot in the horse lines, waited for his men to saddle and mount, and followed Buller as he led the mounted men in pursuit of the now retreating impi.

TROTTING OUT OF THE LAAGER TO CHASE DEFEATED ZULUS WAS A different proposition from running with a thousand warriors on his heels.

Andrew looked around, seeing the eagerness of his companions. They had lived in awe of Zulu power for the last few months, and after the massacre of Isandhlwana, they wanted revenge. The Natal colonists had lived on the lion's lip all their lives, while the Frontier Light Horse were hungry to destroy the abaQulusi for the killing of so many of their colleagues the previous day.

Was that only yesterday? It seemed like a different world.

Andrew felt as if he had spent his entire life fighting Zulus. If he closed his eyes, he could see screaming Zulu faces and raised assegais, and the sound of Zulu war cries rattled through his mind.

The Zulus had altered quickly from attack to rapid retreat, with few attempting to delay the pursuing horsemen. Buller's men pursued them, killing without mercy, shooting them from the saddle or picking up assegais from dead warriors and using them like lances. Andrew had little stomach for slaughter but joined the pursuit, if only because his duty was to kill.

I'm no soldier. I should be killing our enemy rather than making loud noises and galloping Lancelot across the plain. The Zulus would not hesitate to kill me if the position was reversed.

Andrew heard the whoops of delight as the horsemen hunted their quarry.

"That's another for the game bag!"

"Got you, you devil!"

"Shot him right through the head, by God! Good work, Carruthers!"

Andrew saw one slender Zulu trying to hide beneath a thorn bush and readied his rifle to fire. The man saw him, lifted his Abanonya shield and adopted a pose of defence, although he stood little chance against a mounted man with a rifle and revolver.

Andrew aimed, then hesitated when he realised how young the warrior was.

Good God, he's only a boy! He can't be more than twelve years old! The words of his father returned to Andrew.

"*We are soldiers, and soldiers fight soldiers or warriors. We should always be merciful to women and children, whatever their station in life.*"

"Put your assegai down," Andrew said in Xhosa. "I will take you prisoner."

The Zulu raised his shield higher. "You will torture me."

"No." Knowing he was taking a chance; Andrew lowered his rifle. "I won't torture you, and neither will anybody else. I will ask you some questions, and that's all."

"What questions?" The Zulu had a deep voice for a boy and a handsome, intelligent face that viewed Andrew with suspicion.

"Come back to the camp with me," Andrew said. "We can talk there. It's not safe here with all the soldiers."

The Zulu glanced around, where the horsemen were laughing, killing, and riding hard, chasing the fleeing Zulus as far as Hlobane. "I am your prisoner," he said, raising his shield above his head. "My name is Jabulani."

"Keep your spears, Jabulani," Andrew said.

They sat outside Andrew's tent with a small fire between them and the stars glittering in the black abyss above. Andrew passed a hunk of beef to Jabulani and bit into another.

"You are a brave people," Andrew said.

"We are the Zulus," Jabulani said as if that were a sufficient explanation.

"You attacked with great courage."

Jabulani smiled. "When we saw the soldiers take your tents down, we thought you were about to flee. We were dismayed when you began firing at us."

"I am looking for a white woman," Andrew said. "Some Zulus crossed the border into Natal, killed all the people on a farm and kidnapped the woman. Have you heard of such a thing happening?"

Jabulani chewed his beef for a few moments before he replied. "No," he said.

"Are you sure?" Andrew asked. "Think carefully, Jabulani."

"Cetshwayo ordered that no Zulu was to cross the border into Natal," Jabulani said. "Disobeying the king's command would mean death, and maybe death for the whole family."

Andrew frowned. "I saw the house," he said, frustrated. "I buried the people myself, and the younger girl was missing."

"The Zulus did not kill them or steal the woman," Jabulani repeated.

"There are renegade clans in the north who raid into the Transvaal," Andrew said. "Perhaps one of them moved south."

"If they crossed this land, the abaQulusi would have seen them," Jabulani told him. "They are loyal to Cetshwayo."

"What would the abaQulusi have done?" Andrew asked.

"Killed them," Jabulani replied with disarming simplicity.

"Ah." Andrew did not doubt Jabulani's sincerity. "You are of the Abanonya, I think?"

"I am." Jabulani lifted his head in pride.

"Thank you, Jabulani. If Cetshwayo had ordered a woman kidnapped, where would he keep her?"

Jabulani screwed up his face. "The ways of kings are not like the ways of other men," he said solemnly. "I cannot say what is in Cetshwayo's mind."

Andrew nodded. "I understand that," he said. "I have little understanding of what happens in our royal palaces as well. However, you are a Zulu and know the ways of your people better than I do. Tell me what you think."

Jabulani smiled. "If I had a woman prisoner, I would keep her close, or another man would steal her away."

"Do you mean she could be in oNdini?" Andrew asked.

"If she exists, and if the king ordered her captured," Jabulani said. "She will be in oNdini."

Andrew dug his heel into the ground and sighed. "That's what I thought, Jabulani. Then I'll go to oNdini."

Jabulani smiled. "Cetshwayo will welcome you," he said cryptically.

Andrew heard rapid hoofbeats and stood up hurriedly when he saw Buller approaching.

"Well, young Baird, I see you have a new friend." Buller dismounted and stepped beside Andrew.

"This is Jabulani, sir," Andrew said.

"Of Ntshingwayo's Zulus?" Buller asked.

"No, sir, he's of the Abanonya," Andrew said.

When Buller opened his mouth wide and reached for his pistol, Jabulani grabbed at the assegais at his feet.

"No, sir." Greatly daring, Andrew placed a hand on Buller's arm. "He's my prisoner, sir, and he won't attack us."

"Good God, Baird! The Abanonya are one of our most dangerous enemies!"

"I know, sir, but Jabulani and I jog along pretty well." Andrew put his free hand on Jabulani's shoulder.

Buller frowned, releasing his grip on the pistol butt. "I only knew one man with an attitude like that, Baird."

Andrew smiled. "I thought I was unique, sir."

"No. I have said I knew you, but I don't." Buller stepped back, still watching Jabulani. "You reminded me of somebody."

"Who is that, sir?" Andrew already guessed the answer.

"A man old enough to be your father, Baird. Fighting Jack Windrush."

Andrew could not help the blood rushing to his face. "Indeed, sir?"

"Indeed, sir," Buller said. "I know Fighting Jack well; we served together through the Ashanti campaign. I met his wife there as well, a handsome, charming lady."

"I am sure she is, sir," Andrew wished Buller would change the subject.

"Mrs Windrush had an Indian mother and a Scottish father." Buller was dragging the information from his mind. "Her father shared your name. He was Baird." The colonel stared at Andrew. "She spoke of her son, Andrew David Windrush."

Andrew looked away.

"By God, man, you're Jack Windrush's pup!"

CHAPTER 26

Andrew lifted his chin. "Yes, sir. Major Jack Windrush is my father."

"Well, my boy, why the devil didn't you say so?" Buller held out his hand. "Why hide who you are?"

"I want to make my own way in the world, sir," Andrew explained. "I don't want to live in my father's shadow."

"Good God, man, with a background like yours, you could have your pick of any regiment in the army and not be footling around in some ragamuffin colonial unit!" Buller pumped Andrew's arm as he was dragging water from far underground. "My God, Fighting Jack's pup out here in Zululand."

"That's just it, sir." Andrew rescued his hand and felt to see if any bones were broken, for Buller had a grip like an Irish navvy. "I want to rise on my own merits, not because of my father's achievements."

Buller eyed him. "I see. Well, we'll talk about this later, young Windrush."

"Baird, sir."

"Baird," Buller corrected himself. "In the meantime, what will you do with this Abanonya fellow? You can't leave him running loose around the camp. He might forget himself and start slaughtering people, and we can't have that, can we?"

Andrew smiled. "No, sir. I suppose not."

"Old Jack, I mean your respected pater, has a close friend among the Pathans, I recall. Is that your intention with this Zulu chap?" Buller nodded at Jabulani.

"I hadn't thought that far ahead, sir," Andrew admitted.

"Have you pumped him for information?" Buller asked.

"I've asked him about Miss Baxter, sir," Andrew replied.

"Ah, yes, the missing girl." Buller looked uncomfortable for a moment. "I'd forget about her if I were you, Baird. As your father would tell you, these savages aren't kind to their women. The Zulus probably killed her weeks ago, and she's better dead than a Zulu prisoner."

Andrew thought it best not to argue. "Yes, sir, but I'll keep searching until I know for sure."

"As you wish, Baird." Buller stepped back to his horse. "Well, if you've finished with this Zulu chap, either kill him or set him free, eh?" He faced Jabulani and spoke in a mixture of Xhosa and Zulu. "Before the fight at Isandhlwana, we had Zulu patients in our hospital, and when the Zulus invaded the camp, the patients rose and helped kill those who had been attending them."

Jabulani nodded without comment.

"Is there any reason we should not kill you?"

"Yes," Jabulani replied. "There is a very good reason you should not kill me. We kill you because it is the custom of the black men, but it isn't the white men's custom."

Buller grinned. "You are a plausible young rogue; I'll give you that." He faced Andrew. "What do you want to do with him, Baird? He's your prisoner."

"I'll set him free, sir."

"Very magnanimous of you. Kick his backside back to Hlobane, eh, so he can tell his little friends how powerful the white man is." Buller mounted and lifted a hand. "Fighting Jack's pup, eh? I should have guessed it." He frowned and pointed to Andrew's sleeve, stiff with dried blood. "Is that another wound?"

"No, sir," Andrew said. "The one I got yesterday opened up again."

"Get rid of young Shaka here and let the surgeon see it," Buller ordered.

"Yes, sir," Andrew said and watched as Buller rode away, shaking his head. "Come on then, Jabulani, let's get you back home."

THE CAMP EXPERIENCED ONE ALARM AT THREE IN THE MORNING OF THE 30th when an outpost fired a few shots at a lone Zulu, and the colonials within the laager immediately opened fire.

"Cease fire!" Wood jumped from his wagon as the colonials' bullets ripped through the canopy above his head. "What the hell do you think you're doing?"

A company of the 13th Foot echoed the Brigadier's sentiments with stronger language as the colonial's bullets zipped and whined past them.

"We're on the same side, you stupid bastards!"

As the colonials stopped firing, the alarm passed, and normality returned to the camp. When burial patrols found over seven hundred Zulu bodies within a few hundred yards of the laager, Wood ordered the men to shift location.

"There will be other bodies we can't see," Wood explained. "That will spread disease."

"What were our losses at Khambula?" Andrew asked.

"Twenty-nine killed and about seventy wounded," Buller replied, puffing at his cigarette. "We lost some good men, including Hacket, who had led the 90th advance."

"Did the Zulus kill him, sir?" Andrew asked.

"No, Baird. He is blinded," Buller told him. "He's an Irishmen and was a dedicated regimental officer, rather like your father."

Andrew did not reply.

"Hacket bought his promotion in the days when such things were normal." Buller watched Andrew closely for a reaction. "He was a good man."

Buller's use of the past tense was chillingly final. One day Hacket was a good officer, and the next, he was finished. Andrew nodded; only a fool thought that war was glorious. "Yes, sir."

"I hope his family look after him," Buller said. "At least they know who he is."

"I understand, sir," Andrew said.

Buller nodded. "Good. Did you hear about the white prisoner at Ulundi?"

Andrew lifted his head as his heart rate increased. "What white prisoner?"

Buller smiled. "I thought that might interest you. The Frenchman, Baird."

Andrew's hopes died. "Tell me more, sir."

"The Zulus captured a French fellow from the Border Horse at Hlobane, Baird. They took him to Ulundi and sent him somewhere else, but he killed his guard and escaped."

"Thank you, sir," Andrew said. "Is he in the camp now?"

"Try the hospital tent, Baird." Buller looked sympathetic. "Don't raise your hopes too high."

"I won't, sir. Thank you."

Ernest Grandier, late trooper of the Border Horse, was lying on a cot in the hospital tent, staring at the canvas ceiling, when Andrew stepped across to him.

"I didn't know there were Frenchmen fighting with us," Andrew said and introduced himself. "I am Lieutenant Andrew Baird. I believe the Zulus held you in Ulundi?"

"There are a few Frenchmen in Zululand," Grandier looked surprisingly healthy as he replied. "Some of us fought the Prussians and through the Commune."

Andrew showed polite interest. "What happened to you?"

"The Zulus captured me during the retreat from Hlobane," Grandier said. "They stripped me naked, lashed me to a pole and carried me to Ulundi."

Andrew listened, curbing his impatience.

"In Ulundi, women spat at me, and Cetshwayo interrogated me and sent me to Mbilini so that he could torture me to death. I killed one of the guards with an assegai and escaped during the first march."

"And you made your way here," Andrew said.

"Yes, sir," Grandier agreed.

"That was some adventure." Andrew doubted most of Grandier's story. "When you were in Ulundi," he said. "Did you see any other white captives?"

Grandier looked annoyed at the question. "I was the only prisoner of war the Zulus captured."

"Did you hear of any other captives?" Andrew persisted. "A woman? I am looking for Miss Maxwell, a woman the Zulus might have captured in the early days of the war."

"No," Grandier said. "I did not hear of any other prisoners."

"Thank you." Andrew left the hospital tent. Although he was no better informed, he felt that Grandier had confirmed Jabulani's story. The Zulus may not have captured Mariana, but if they had, she might still be alive. If Cetshwayo had not executed a prisoner-of-war, he was unlikely to kill a woman, who might be a useful hostage if the war turned against him.

Andrew held onto that tiny flicker of hope as Wood waited for Lord Chelmsford's orders to advance towards oNdini.

"Did you hear the news, Ginger?" Private Julian said as he passed Andrew's tent.

"What news?" Sanderson asked suspiciously.

"His lordship smashed the Zulus at a place called Gingindlovu," Julian told him. "Imagine that, a battle named after you."

"What do you mean, named after me?" Sanderson asked.

Julian smiled, knowing he had trapped Sanderson. "You're called Ginger, so the lads are calling the battle Ginger, I love you." He repeated the phrase. "Oh, Ginger, I love you!"

"If you say that again, Julian, I'll smash your teeth through the back of your head." Sanderson could imagine his peers tormenting him. "Anyway, you've got it wrong. It's not Ginger I love you; it's gin, gin, I love you!"

As their voices faded away, Andrew left the tent to confirm the rumour. Buller greeted him with a smile.

"It's true, Baird. We smashed the Zulus at Khambula, and Lord Chelmsford did the same at Gingindlovu," Buller said with satisfaction. We've turned the tide, and now all we need to do is capture Ulundi, and we'll break the Zulu power forever."

Andrew agreed. By winning his twenty-minute battle at Gingindlovu on the 2nd of April, Chelmsford had redeemed himself and lifted the siege of Eshowe. The Zulus tide had ebbed from the high-water mark at Isandlwana, Britain had endured the expected initial disasters, and retribution had begun.

Thousands of reinforcements left a Britain filled with nationalistic fervour. Bands played patriotic airs, and crowds of civilians cheered from the safety of the quayside as the scarlet-uniformed soldiers sailed to war. Union flags fluttered in the breeze, newspapers published glowing accounts of British valour, and politicians expended much rhetoric in praising or damning Britain's war effort, depending on their party allegiance. Meanwhile, in Zululand, Wood's garrison became part of the scenery as the horsemen mounted patrols that extended further afield.

"When are we going to advance, sir?" Andrew asked.

"When his Lordship decides we have sufficient manpower," Buller told him. "You know as well as I do, young Up-and-at- 'em, that Chelmsford wants a smashing victory before the government replaces him. He can't afford another reverse."

"Yes, sir. It seems that we've already broken the Zulus spirit if they only fought for twenty minutes at Gingindlovu. Khambula lasted over four hours."

"Cetshwayo still has over twenty-thousand men in his army," Buller reminded gently. "Lord Chelmsford will only move when he is confident he can defeat the Zulus in an open battle. Now take out another patrol and see what you can find."

"Yes, sir," Andrew said, saluted and left, hiding his frustration.

THE DAYS CRAWLED PAST, WITH ANDREW THINKING HIS PATROLS WERE without purpose and Lord Chelmsford slowly building up his army. As always, Andrew enquired about Mariana at every kraal, with the same replies. Nobody knew about a white woman held in Zululand.

Maybe Mariana is dead, but I won't give up. I may have to visit every imuzi in Zululand before I find the truth.

As the British eroded Cetshwayo's power, small groups of renegades began to raid the Boer lands and along the frontiers while rumours spread among the soldiers.

"Did you hear about the treasure in Ulundi, sir?" Fletcher asked.

"I've heard the shaves," Andrew replied cautiously.

"Cetshwayo's been storing gold and ivory for years," Fletcher said excitedly. "He's got thousands of pounds worth in his kraal."

"I doubt that, Fletcher." Andrew shook his head.

Fletcher continued as if Andrew had not spoken. "I heard a shave that Chelmsford's going to distribute the treasure among all the officers."

"How about the men?" Andrew asked, smiling. "They do as much fighting as we do."

"What would the men do with money?" Fletcher asked. "They'd only drink it away."

"The Zulus don't value gold and ivory," Andrew reminded. "Their wealth is in cattle."

Fletcher laughed. "Maybe Cetshwayo has a thousand prime breeding stock squirrelled away in a secret kraal, sir."

"That's more like it," Andrew said. "His Lordship will give two cattle to each officer. You can take them home to your parents."

Fletcher shook his head. "My parents would prefer the gold, sir. Cattle are not much good in a rectory in Wandsworth."

"Probably not, Fletcher," Andrew agreed.

Perhaps rumours of the treasure had spread, but Andrew noticed a steady influx of the more disreputable elements of colonial society and some from even further afield. Such men had made up the bulk of the NCOs in the NNC, but most left after the early disasters of the war. Now they eased back, some in rowdy bands on foot and others in groups of horsemen settling on the fringes of the British camp.

"Who are these people?" Wood asked as one group of wild riders made their camp close to his headquarters.

"I'm sure I don't know," Buller replied.

"Nor do I," Wood said. "Move them away in case they unsettle the men."

"With pleasure, sir," Buller said. "Come along, Baird." He glanced at Andrew and grinned. "Have you heard about the Natal Dragoons?"

Andrew frowned. "The Natal Dragoons? No, sir."

"I've noticed the same group follow you, Baird, and I decided to make you an official regiment of irregular horse. Congratulations, Lieutenant. You now lead the Natal Dragoons."

"Sir?" Andrew asked.

"Take over the Natal Dragoons, Lieutenant!" Buller said. "Join me outside the laager in an hour."

"Yes, sir." Andrew saluted, unable to hide his astonishment.

"You can create a uniform or not, as you wish," Buller told him.

The Natal Dragoons formed up before Andrew. Twenty strong, they were a mixture of hard-bitten colonials and a couple of newly arrived immigrants or New Chums as the colonials termed them, with a few strays from the Mounted Infantry. They viewed Andrew through suspicious eyes as he gathered them around him.

"Right, gentlemen." Andrew decided to make his speech short. "Colonel Buller has seen fit to make us a unit of irregular horsemen called the Natal Dragoons. You lads from the Mounted Infantry still belong to your parent units, but you'll be riding with me for the duration of this war or until you choose to leave."

The men did not comment. They were accustomed to military life with its long periods of routine followed by a sudden change.

"Everybody will retain their present rank and rate of pay."

That answered any immediate questions.

"Our first task together is to join Colonel Buller and remove these unruly civilians from their camp. Come on, Natal Dragoons!"

Andrew turned Lancelot without another word and headed away from the laager. He heard the rumble of hooves behind him and smiled. He was on his second campaign, a commissioned officer and had his own command, and then Andrew thought of Elaine and Mariana, and his good humour seeped away.

The civilians' camp was untidy, with no latrine discipline and a ragged collection of tents and wagons placed wherever the owner thought best.

Buller stood his horse on a slight incline, waiting until his officers gathered around him. "Let's clean this mess up, gentlemen!" He commanded a hundred and fifty men, divided equally between Mounted Infantry and irregular colonial units, and extended them in a line outside the civilians' camp.

"I am going to see who runs this shambles," Buller told the officers. "In fifteen minutes, ride slowly forward, taking down the tents and ordering the men back to Natal. If a Zulu impi finds them, there will be another massacre."

The officers nodded and returned to their units. Andrew checked his watch, counting the minutes.

"Are you ready, boys?"

One by one, the men nodded assent.

Andrew watched the minute hand of his watch slowly move, waited until the fifteen minutes passed and snapped the cover shut. "In we go, Natal Dragoons!"

He heard officers give similar orders along the line of horsemen, and they stepped forward into the civilians' camp, ordering the inhabitants to leave and tearing down tents.

"What are you doing?" a bearded man asked indignantly as Fletcher and Kerr cut the guy ropes from his much-patched tent.

"Saving your life," Andrew snarled. "If an impi comes, you won't last five minutes."

"They won't attack as long as the soldiers are near," the man said smugly.

"Pack up your belongings and get back to Natal," Andrew ordered. "I'm wasting time dealing with you when I could be defeating Cetshwayo."

All around the camp, Andrew saw similar conversations as the soldiers pushed out the civilians. He frowned when he heard a familiar voice.

"You've no bloody right to order us away!" the man said. "We've as much right in Zululand as you have."

"Hitchings!" Andrew remembered the man who had deserted from the Cape Mounted Rifles at the beginning of the war. He pulled Lancelot toward the voice.

"Hitchings! What the hell are you doing here?"

"Lieutenant Baird!" Hitchings gave a greasy grin and lifted his carbine in a threatening gesture. "I heard the Zulus killed you at Isandlwana."

"They didn't," Andrew said. "Nor at Hlobane. You're a deserting hound, Hitchings!"

Hitchings' grin broadened as his finger curled around the trigger. "I decided to seek alternative employment," he said. "Something that paid better without the risks."

Andrew realised two of his men had followed him. "Why are you here, Hitchings? Have you come to help fight the Zulus?"

Hitchings sneered. "Fight them? Chelmsford's got sufficient men to fight the bloody Prussians, let alone the Zulus!"

"Why are you here, Hitchings?" Andrew repeated.

"We're after the treasure," Hitchings grinned, holding his carbine, and glancing around. "Everybody knows that Cetshwayo has thousands of pounds of gold and ivory in Ulundi, and we want our share."

"You've got two minutes!" Buller shouted. "Then we'll set fire to your tents, impound your wagons, and arrest the lot of you. Two minutes!"

Hitchings lifted his carbine, realised that most of the Natal Dragoons had arrived to back up Andrew, and moved away, mouthing threats.

Should I arrest him? Andrew wondered.

"Sir?" Fletcher arrived at Andrew's side. "Orders, sir?"

"Kick them out," Andrew ordered and raised his voice. "And Hitchings, if I see you again on this side of the Buffalo, I'll arrest you for the deserting, cowardly swine you are."

CHAPTER 27

20TH OF MAY 1879

Jama looked over his Abanonya. They had taken many casualties at Hlobane and Khambula, and some of the survivors carried wounds. Ndleleni was still there, as staunch as ever, with his steady eyes and ready assegai. Bangizwe was wounded, with the long scar of a British bullet across his ribs, while Bhekizizwe had a bloody rag tied around his left arm.

"The British are winning this war," Jama told them bluntly. "They have defeated us in two battles and killed many of our warriors. Our people are losing heart."

The Abanonya listened without comment. They had all faced the massed rifles of British infantry and knew Jama was correct.

"We cannot get close enough in sufficient numbers to defeat them," Jama said.

The Abanonya stirred slightly, wondering where Jama was heading.

Jama allowed them to ponder for a moment. "The British are building up their forces to capture Cetshwayo and destroy oNdini. We will hunt for any British party we can destroy."

The Abanonya agreed. They had promised to fight and die for Cetshwayo, and they were Zulu warriors.

"We need rifles like the British," Jama told them. "Find some."

The Abanonya nodded, knowing the old ways were slipping away and unsure if they were ready to face the new.

Ndleleni rose from the long grass and watched the small British patrol ride towards them. He saw a Zulu guide, two officers and six men, well mounted and confident, nodded when he realised there was not a stronger escort and withdrew to inform Jama.

When the British patrol stopped on some high ground, the two officers scanned the country around the Tshotshosi River, and the younger of the two took a pad from his satchel and made a few sketches. Ndleleni noted that the younger officer wore a dark blue uniform rather than the normal scarlet. His trousers looked too tight, and his white cork helmet was slightly large above a smooth face. His companion wore a dark blue patrol jacket, while his thick moustache and mutton-chop whiskers appeared old-fashioned compared to other officers. The escort wore buff corduroy jackets and broad-brimmed hats and carried short Martini-Henry carbines.

Ndleleni noted all the details in case Jama found them important.

Jama gathered his men around him and told them what Ndleleni had observed.

"The six-man escort is well armed and moved like professionals, while the younger officer is fresh-faced and eager," Jama said. "The guide carries an assegai and may fight."

The Abanonya listened, rubbing hard hands along the shafts of their assegais.

"We will take them," Jama decided as he watched the British. "See how the older officer defers to the younger? The older man is of higher rank, a more experienced soldier, but the younger gives the orders."

"What does that mean, Jama?" Ndleleni asked.

"I think the young man is royal," Jama said. "Maybe if we kill him, the British queen will remove her army."

Ndleleni touched his *umzimbeet* necklace, tapped the blade of his *iKlwa* and smiled. They watched as the two officers led their escort from the high ground towards a deserted *imuzi* on the north bank of the Tshotshosi River.

"That's Sobhuza's *imuzi*," a local man who had joined them said.

"Come, Abanonya," Jama said and ran forward with his men at his back. When news of Jama's intended attack spread, remnants of other *amabuthos* joined them, men from the iNgobamakhosi, uMbonambi and uNokhenke. Mnukwa, a seasoned induna, shared the leadership of the combined force with Jama.

Tall fields of mealies surrounded three sides of the *imuzi,* descending to the river in a swaying, golden promise. Jama frowned to think that the harvest was going to waste since the British invasion had forced the villagers to flee. On the north side of the *imuzi*, the ground was open for two hundred paces before descending steeply into a dry donga deeper than a tall man.

Jama watched as the British escort warily approached the *imuzi*, dismounted and inspected each *indlu*, prodding their carbines into every corner and thatched roof. Three snarling dogs cowered away and ran as the troopers kicked at them with heavy boots.

"It's safe," the troopers said, and the officers joined them, with the younger smiling as he entered the *imuzi*.

The British knee-haltered their horses and allowed them to graze on the open ground to the north.

"They'll post a guard," Jama said, but the officers neglected even that simple precaution and the escort made a small fire and began to brew coffee. The smell made Jama's nostrils twitch.

The two officers began to talk while the guide wandered away on some mission of his own devising.

"What are they doing?" Bangizwe asked.

"I don't know," Jama replied. "Where has their guide gone?"

"There!" Bangizwe pointed to the Zulu guide, who stood on a small knoll, staring at them. "He'll warn the British."

"Follow," Jama said and led his mixed force into the tall mealies south of the *imuzi,* finding the British saddling their horses without urgency.

"Fire at them," Jama ordered his riflemen. The Zulus aimed and fired in a ragged volley.

The sudden sound panicked the British horses, which reared and plunged, but not a single shot hit its mark.

"Attack!" Mnukwa shouted.

"Attack!" Jama echoed and charged.

"*Usuthu!*" The Zulus shouted their war cry as they powered forward. "Usuthu!"

Caught unawares, the British fled, with the older officer the first to leave the *imuzi*. The other men ran towards the horses, some staring stupidly over their shoulders at the charging Zulus.

Jama was first into the *imuzi* and saw one gasping British soldier trying to run on foot. The man turned, lowered his carbine, and fired. Jama did not know where the bullet went. When the trooper turned to flee, Jama thrust his assegai into the man's back. "*Ngadla*!" he shouted, twisted the blade, and withdrew.

The Zulu guide and two of the British remained in Sobhuza's *imuzi.* Jama saw one drop his carbine and dismount to retrieve it, then throw himself awkwardly, face down, across his saddle. The young officer had not mounted and ran beside his panicking horse with one hand gripping the stirrup leather.

Ignoring the remaining men, Jama ran towards the young officer, with Ndleleni close behind and a mixture of warriors roaring at the back. The officer's grip slipped, and he fell, with the horse trampling him without stopping. Jama shouted in triumph, noted the other British riders fleeing towards the donga and chased after the officer.

As Jama closed, the young officer grabbed for his sword to find the belt had snapped, and a Zulu had lifted the weapon. The officer drew his revolver and fired, with the bullet whistling wide. Jama lifted his throwing spear, poised, and threw. The long weapon whizzed through the air to strike his target in the shoulder. The officer staggered, pulled the spear out and fired his revolver, missing again.

When a second spear thudded into him, the officer turned and fled into the donga. Ndleleni threw his spear, shouting in triumph, when it landed in the officer's thigh. The officer pulled it out, stumbled and fell.

A warrior named Xabanga overtook Jama and thrust his *iKlwa* into the officer's chest, with Jama next and others crowding around to stab the stricken man. A few moments later, the Zulus stopped, with the officer dead from a dozen wounds.

Mnukwa looked down at the dead officer. "He was a brave man," he said.

Jama agreed. "His men abandoned him. Their induna should execute them for cowardice."

Prince Louis Napoleon, twenty-three years old, great-nephew of Napoleon Bonaparte and one-time heir to the French imperial throne, lay broken and dead in the Zululand dust. It was another disaster for the British.

CHELMSFORD'S SECOND DIVISION AND WOOD'S FLYING COLUMN MET ON the second of June, with men waving to one another as they marched slowly towards oNdini.

"What's happening, sir?" Fletcher asked as the two columns marched side by side in a display of British power South Africa had never seen before.

"Lord Chelmsford is establishing a supply depot here," Andrew replied.

Fletcher nodded. "What will we do, sir?"

"The Natal Dragoons are remaining with Buller, scouting ahead of the Flying Column into the Mahlabathini Plain."

"I thought so, sir," Fletcher nodded sagely.

Buller, as usual, was in the van with a collection of mounted units that included Andrew's Natal Dragoons. They entered the Mahlabathini Plain with a thunder of hooves and jingle of equipment and rode cautiously onward.

Andrew looked around. "This should be ideal hunting country," he said, for the plain was an undulating basin of long waving grass and soft, sandy soil, where small groups of Zulus scattered before them.

"Yes, sir," Fletcher said. "I wonder who is hunting who. Are we hunting the Zulus, or are they hunting us?"

"Hopefully, we are hunting them," Andrew replied.

"Is it true that General Wolseley is going to take over the army, sir?" Fletcher asked.

Andrew nodded. "I believe so, Fletcher." The government in Britain, unhappy with British reverses and the death of the -pPrince -iImperial, sent General Garnet Wolseley to take command of the army in Zululand.

"Is that why His Lordship is finally pushing forward, sir?" Fletcher asked. "He wants to finish the war before his replacement arrives to steal the final glory."

"I am not privy to the mind of His Lordship." Andrew glanced at Fletcher. "You could be correct, or perhaps we're advancing because all the reinforcements have arrived. We'll do our duty as always."

"Yes, sir," Fletcher agreed.

Buller's cavalry probed deeper into Zululand, seeking a route to oNdini and a suitable spot for the decisive battle Chelmsford craved. Andrew's Natal Dragoons were in the van when Buller's force entered an area of long grass and scrubby bush. The men moved slowly, very aware that a Zulu warrior could easily conceal himself in such close country.

Andrew lifted his head. "There are Zulus here," he said.

"Are you sure?" Buller readied his revolver.

"Yes, sir," Andrew said. He was not sure how he knew. The grass was higher than a tall man, with the horsemen peering forward and around them.

Buller lifted his hand and ordered his men to halt. Silence closed around them, broken by the hum of insects and the gentle swish of grass, the pawing of horses' hooves on the ground and the harsh breathing of nervous men. Even though the cavalry knew the war was in its final stages, they were equally aware of how dangerous the Zulus could be.

"What's that?"

Andrew saw a flicker of movement among the grass ahead and heard the whirr of a thrown assegai. Moving instinctively, he pulled Lancelot aside as the spear whizzed past. A second later, hundreds of warriors rose from the grass, with scores of riflemen firing a volley. The sound was deafening after the previous hush while the muzzle flares sparkled amongst the greeny-brown grass.

"Zulus!" Buller shouted and fired his pistol.

Andrew fired without thought and heard shots whine above his head and hoarse screams as some of the Zulus' bullets found their mark. Three men were down, already dead, with others wounded or cursing as their horses lay, kicking and whinnying on the ground.

One Mounted Infantry sergeant lay under his dead horse, yelling, "Somebody get this bloody animal off me!" as the weight of his mount pinned him to the ground.

"Thank God you sensed something, Baird!" Buller shouted. "Another couple of hundred yards, and they'd have surrounded us!"

Exploding from the long grass, thousands of warriors charged towards the British patrol, rattling the butts of their assegais against their shields and shouting.

"Usuthu! Usuthu!"

"Dear God! These men have spirit!" an officer shouted. "We defeat them, and defeat them, and still they come on!"

Chief Zibhebhu led the Zulus, trying to prevent the British from advancing through the Mahlabathini Valley towards oNdini. The warriors charged forward, fighting a cause that was already lost, putting their bodies in the way of bullets with the courage of their race.

"Usuthu!"

The Zulu battle cry rose above the crackle of musketry and hoarse shouts of the surprised British soldiers.

"Shoot the buggers!"

"Bloody hell! Where did they spring from?"

"Let's get out of here, lads!"

"Usuthu!"

Andrew fired towards the rapidly approaching Zulus and saw a British officer dismount beside the trapped sergeant.

"Come on, man," the officer encouraged. Andrew saw it was Captain Lord William Beresford of the 9th Lancers. The sergeant, dazed by the fall, shook his head. He was too heavy for Beresford to lift, so the two stood, vulnerable as Zibhebhu's Zulus charged closer by the second.

"Frontier Light Horse!" Buller roared. "Natal Dragoons! Hold back the Zulus! Let Beresford rescue that trapped man!"

Andrew's men and the Frontier Light Horse turned around, rode towards the Zulus, and fired, knocking down half a dozen in the front rank. They retired, reloaded, and fired again, checking the advance for a few vital moments. In that time, Sergeant Edmund O'Toole rode beside Beresford, and both helped the stunned sergeant onto Beresford's horse.

Checked but not halted, Zibhebhu's Zulus swarmed around Beresford and O'Toole. Beresford thrust his sword into the nearest Zulu and, with O'Toole holding the injured sergeant secure in the saddle, they rode to safety.[1]

"Well now, gentlemen," Buller said, as calm as if he were in Hyde Park on a Sunday morning. "Now we know which direction not to go." He led them back to the vanguard of Chelmsford's army.

THE BRITISH LAAGER WAS NERVOUS THAT NIGHT. ANDREW COULD TASTE THE fear as the mainly young soldiers tried to sleep in their crowded tents while the moon shone coldly upon them.

"Can you hear something?" Private Julian asked.

Andrew had grabbed a few hours rest and was patrolling the interior of the laager, exchanging a few words with the sentries, and gauging their morale. As he expected, the younger men were apprehensive as the veterans regaled them with stories of the fierce Zulu warriors and the slaughter of Isandhlwana.

"I can't hear nothing," Sanderson replied.

"I can hear the Zulus. Listen, Ginger. I'm telling you, man. It's the Zulus coming for us!"

"They won't frighten me. I'm from Brummagem. We're tough stuff in Brum!"

Andrew stopped and raised his head. Julian was correct. He could also hear something drifting in the breeze. "Music," he said. "We can hear music."

"They're coming to get us!" Julian shouted.

"No, they're not," Andrew soothed the boy. "They're miles away. If they were attacking, they'd come in silence."

The Zulu singing continued, deep-voiced and distant. When the sound increased, a few officers ordered their men to stand to their arms, but then the noise faded.

"The wind is carrying it to us," Andrew said to the Natal Dragoons. He listened for a while, pushed aside the creeping melancholia that he was witnessing the end of a proud kingdom and retired to his tent. His men were either on picket duty or asleep, the horses well cared for, and there was nothing else he could do.

He thought of Elaine, shook his head, and slept to dream of the River Tweed rippling past Berwick Walls and skeins of geese passing overhead.

"Sir." A corporal shook Andrew awake. "Lord Chelmsford's orders, sir, and we've to get up."

"What time is it?"

"Nearly four o'clock, sir," the corporal reported.

"No bugles today," Andrew said, rubbing the sleep from his eyes. He could be up half the night but still hated an abrupt wakening in the morning.

"Lieutenant Baird?" A fresh-faced subaltern thrust his head into Andrew's tent.

"That's me," Andrew confessed.

"His Lordship sends his respects, sir, and could you take the Natal Dragoons to join Buller at the drift over the White Mfolozi."

"My compliments to His Lordship, and we'll be there forthwith," Andrew said, dressing quickly and buckling on his revolver.

As he left the laager, Andrew looked over Chelmsford's army, comparing it to the men who had fallen at Isandhlwana. Lord Chelmsford commanded over four thousand Europeans, mainly regular British infantry, with nearly a thousand African allies, two Gatlings and twelve pieces of artillery. Tall lances thrust upright in the ground marked the tents of the 17th Lancers, and sentries patrolled, watching for any sign of any Zulus.

The Zulus have taught His Lordship respect, Andrew thought.

Andrew had never seen a Gatling in action and viewed this killing machine with curiosity. He knew an American doctor had invented the hand-cranked, ten-barrelled weapon and wondered how it would perform in the arduous conditions of the field.

"It fires faster than ten men," a proud seaman told Andrew. "But it jams a lot. The extractor yanks the bases off the Boxer cartridges and fouls the barrels." He patted the artillery carriage on which the clumsy Gatling sat. "You're seeing the future of warfare, Lieutenant. In times to come, there will be ten men with Gatlings and no regiments of sweating Tommies." He winked. "Or even better, sir, wars will become so terrible that politicians will ban them and discuss their differences over a conference table."

Andrew raised cynical eyebrows. "I'd like to think you're right, but I doubt politicians have the humanity to stop wars. After all, they don't have to face a thousand screaming Zulu warriors." He shook his head. "And if that thing jams when the Zulus are charging, I'd prefer to be somewhere else."

The seaman laughed and touched the cutlass at his belt. "If all else fails, I've got this."

"So you have," Andrew said, smiling. "Good luck." He walked away, shaking his head.

"We're in the van again, Baird," Buller greeted him. "Where you want to be."

Andrew looked into the gradually lightening distance and wondered what Africa had in store for him next. "I'm not sure about that, sir."

Buller laughed. "I know differently, Baird. Make your father proud." He rode away before Andrew had time to reply.

As the main force marched away from the camp, the garrison they left behind watched through jealous eyes.

"Give them pepper, lads!" the Royal Engineers shouted while the five companies of the 24th Foot growled, wishing they could avenge the comrades they lost at Isandhlwana.

"Is Lord Chelmsford wise leaving the 24th to hold the laager, sir?" Fletcher asked. "The battalion is full of recruits, and they must be shaken."

Andrew nodded. "They'll fight all the harder after Isandhlwana." He rubbed his leg, where his wound was beginning to ache.

His Lordship is keeping the 24th out of trouble, he thought. *The regiment has suffered sufficient casualties.*

Chelmsford's army formed up, ready to march. Bugles trilled, boots thumped on the hard ground, horses neighed, and NCOs checked the men's ammunition and water. Mounted infantry, with bandoliers crossing their chests, rode alongside the infantry while Andrew's Natal Dragoons watched with the air of slight superiority mounted men felt for their foot-slogging companions.

In Andrew's mind, the battle of Khambula had been the decisive encounter of the war when a well-led British Army had repulsed a confident Zulu impi. However, the Zulus could claim the British could only fight behind a barricade and were afraid to fight in the open. By marching across country, Chelmsford was daring Cetshwayo to send his impis to attack and proving his confidence his men could defeat the Zulus in a straight battle.

"Will the Zulus fight, sir?" Fletcher asked, watching the British army form up.

"Cetshwayo doesn't want to fight," Andrew replied. "He's already sent peace envoys to Lord Chelmsford with elephant tusks, the Prince Imperial's sword, and gifts of cattle. He wants peace, but I can't see his warriors surrendering."

"Even after we defeated them at Khambula and Gingindlovu?" Fletcher asked.

"Even then," Andrew said. "They are a proud people."

Chelmsford formed his infantry into a hollow square, with the men four deep along the sides and the artillery and transport in the centre. They moved slowly, a scarlet uniformed fortress bristling with Martini-Henrys, crawling over the grassy plain of Zululand, challenging the amabuthos to attack.

"Come along, Baird, old man," Buller shouted. "Leave the Tommies to their marching. We have to guide them."

Andrew kicked in his heels and led his Natal Dragoons in front of the square. Lord Chelmsford marched his army with all the pomp of Victorian warfare. The regiments displayed their colours, the bands played martial airs, and the morning sun flashed from lance points, bayonets, and rifle barrels. Mounted men rode all around the infantry, ready to report any Zulus and slow their attack.

Come on, Cetshwayo; face us if you dare.

The British forded the White Umfolozi and tramped on; foot, horse and guns as the Zulus watched these invaders, whetted their assegais, and waited.

"Here we are, finally marching to Ulundi," Buller said, "after such a disastrous start to the campaign, we've been months on a journey that should only have taken days."

"Yes, sir," Andrew's thoughts divided between the campaign and Mariana.

Buller eyed him. "We'll have one last battle, Baird, and this war will end. You might find out about your missing girl, then."

"I hope so, sir," Andrew said.

Buller nodded. "Take your Dragoons to the right flank, Baird, and watch for the Zulus."

"Sir!" Glad to have an active task, Andrew called up his men and cantered away, leaving the slow-moving column behind.

The British passed two Zulu military kraals, kwaBulawayo and kwaNodwengu, and marched ponderously onto higher ground. The light was stronger now, and Andrew checked his watch, surprised that it was already half past seven. What had happened to the three and a half hours since the corporal woke him?

"Sir!" Kerr drew Andrew's attention to groups of Zulus in front. He raised his field glasses to study them, wondering which regiments they were. Sunlight flashed from assegais as a faint breeze rippled the decorative feathers each warrior wore.

"Come on then, lads," Andrew muttered. "Let's get this over with."

He swivelled to his right, the direction from where the British expected the Zulus to attack. Zululand's habitual early-morning river mist combined with smoke from Zulu campfires to obscure Andrew's vision.

"Are you down there, lads? Are you mustering to attack us?"

The British marched on, setting kwaBulawayo to the flames. Blue-grey smoke coiled behind them as Chelmsford's army left a trail of destruction through Cetshwayo's kingdom.

Welcome to our civilisation, lads.

Buller had already selected a site for Chelmsford to stand, and his horsemen led the infantry to his proposed battlefield. Andrew joined Buller, with his Dragoons extended across the country, watching for the anticipated Zulu attack.

"We'll fight them here, Baird." Buller lit a cigarette, took out a small telescope and scanned the surrounding plain. "An area of high ground with no cover for any approaching army. The Zulus will have to approach in the open if they approach at all." He grinned, nearly losing his cigarette. "Now we'll find the answers to our questions. Can His Lordship redeem himself with a victory over the main Zulu army? Will Cetshwayo send out his impis to attack us? And most important of all, will our soldiers stand without a laager to shelter behind?"

Andrew tried not to remember the carnage at Isandhlwana. He thought of Mariana, "We must win here, sir."

"Here comes the opposition," Buller said quietly as a Zulu impi emerged through the mist and smoke. The lines of long shields and spears moved steadily forward, gradually becoming clearer as the headdresses bounced in unison. Andrew wondered if anything could upset Buller's equanimity. He studied the left and left front of the square.

"They're advancing in good order," Buller said. "Regiment after regiment. They'll know what they're facing now."

Andrew nodded. "So do we," he said. "Look to the right."

More Zulus streamed from the thorn bushes off to the right, with *amabuthos* flowing around the square, spears held ready, and shields forming a continuous line of coloured cowhide. Andrew wondered if the world would ever see such a sight again, an Iron Age army preparing to fight; a truly independent African force defending its traditional way of life. He shook away the thoughts and watched the Zulus run around the British, dimly seen as the mist lifted.

"The horns of the buffalo," Buller said quietly. "They're performing their classic attack strategy, and we're in our traditional defensive formation, as we used at Waterloo."

Andrew nodded, remembering the nervous talk the previous night and how a Zulu attack had defeated even the experienced 24th Foot.

Here is the final encounter, Cetshwayo's last throw of the dice against a British army in the open.

CHAPTER 28

"How many are there, do you think, sir?" Fletcher had reined up beside them. He took a swig from his water bottle.

Andrew concentrated on one area, calculated the numbers, and multiplied by the length of the Zulu line. "Maybe twenty thousand," he said.

"That's what I reckoned," Buller agreed. He raised his telescope again, focussing on a hill in the middle distance. "Look over there, Baird. That's the Zulu commanders waiting to direct the battle." He shook his head. "I don't know their names."

"One of my men might, sir," Andrew said and sent Fletcher to bring Kerr across.

Kerr borrowed Andrew's field glasses. "There's Ziwedu, Cetshwayo's favourite son, sir and a clutch of senior indunas." He pointed them out, dim figures in the distance. "That's Ntshingwayo, who won at Isandhlwana; beside him is Zibhebhu, Mnyamana, and the last fellow is Sihayo."

"Sihayo," Baird said, "he was here at the beginning of the war, and he's here at the end."

"Sihayo's one of Cetshwayo's favourites," Kerr murmured.

"The Lancers are busy," Buller observed as a troop of 17th Lancers set fire to a small *imuzi* and withdrew amidst a pall of grey-brown smoke.

"That's started the ball rolling," Baird said as a group of Zulus left the disciplined ranks and rushed to attack the lancers.

"Tempt them, tease them, break their formation and defeat them piecemeal," Buller said happily. "There go the Basutos!"

Andrew saw the Basutos firing at the advancing Zulus, then withdrawing. Riding their small, shaggy ponies, the Basutos were fierce fighters, and Andrew thought them the only African people not overawed by the Zulu's reputation.

Buller lifted his voice. "Bugler! Sound the alert! Come on, men!"

Buller led his riders in support of the Basutos as the Zulu line menaced the Lancers. Andrew heard the drumming of assegai butts on shields, the stomping of feet on the ground and a constant low murmur, like bees in a flower garden, as the Zulus attacked. The Zulus had returned to their habitual discipline, *amabutho* lined up beside *amabutho*, each with their distinctive regalia, like the small details with which British units identified themselves.

"Fire a couple of rounds and retire," Buller ordered as the horsemen left the security of the infantry square. "Shepherd the Lancers back."

Having fired the *imuzi*, the Lancers were withdrawing, with Zulu skirmishers harassing the more laggard. Andrew looked for the white-and-black shields of the Abanonya, wondered if his old adversary was present, fired into the mass and withdrew. The Lancers rode past the defending screen, content with a job well done as the smoke from the burning *imuzi* spread across the plain. Andrew did not hear the order that saw the front and rear faces of the British square wheel out but rode thankfully past the infantry. He felt himself relax when the square closed again, presenting a solid scarlet wall to the oncoming Zulus.

"Look and remember," Buller murmured, indicating the Zulus. "For you'll never see the like again. A traditional African army in all its pride and courage."

Andrew nodded, feeling a twinge of sadness, for he realised the Zulus were advancing to a battle they could not win. If the British kept their discipline, mass rifle fire, backed by artillery and Gatling guns, would overcome the bravest of men armed with spears.

"Here they come." Private Sanderson licked dry lips and glanced behind him. "Just like at Isandhlwana!"

"It's nothing like Isandhlwana," Andrew whispered as images of that carnage burst into his mind. He checked his watch. It was two minutes short of nine in the morning.

The Zulu commanders had sent hordes of skirmishers ahead of the main battle lines, brave men who were first to test the British infantry's Martini-Henrys. Behind the skirmishers, the impi advanced four deep, with the morning sun glittering on their assegai blades and their feathers waving in a slight breeze. Andrew saw the white-and-black shields of the Abanonya, with their leopard-skin headbands and the feathers beneath their knees. He saw Jama in front and, strangely, hoped he would survive the battle.

Fight well, my brave enemy, and go home to your wife.

The British artillery fired first. Andrew heard the loud crack of the guns and saw the explosions among the Zulu ranks. Lifting his field glasses, he saw the results, the cloud of smoke, flame and dust and the mangled bodies of the warriors. Some of the men nearest the explosions prodded at the smoke with their assegais and then trotted on, ready to fight.

"It hardly seems fair, blasting them like that," a Geordie voice said.

"Let's hear you say that when they get among you with their assegais." A saturnine corporal snarled. "They won't show any mercy, son, and neither will we. Now face your front and do your duty!"

Andrew knew the corporal was right, although he also agreed with the Geordie. He hardened his heart, lifted his field glasses, and watched the Zulus advance. He thought they lacked the conviction of the impi at Isandhlwana and Khambula. They were every bit as brave but moved without the confidence of assured victory. Now a seasoned soldier, Andrew could sense the Zulus' hesitation.

"Get ready, lads!" a heavily whiskered officer ordered.

"They're getting awfully close!" Sanderson shouted, high-pitched, glancing over his shoulder until the saturnine corporal snarled at him.

"Face your front, Sanderson! You're here to fight, not squeal like a little girl!"

The two front ranks of infantry were kneeling, the rear ranks standing, and all presenting their rifles towards the advancing Zulus.

"Check your range," the whiskered officer shouted. "Wait for my word!"

The Zulus advanced through the smoke and fury of the shell fire, their shields held before them, and now Andrew could hear their battle cry.

"Usuthu! Usuthu!"

The sound raised the tiny hairs on the back of his neck as he recalled that same cry before the impis crashed into the luckless 24th Foot and as the warriors attacked at Hlobane. They had shown no mercy then, and there was no reason for the British to be merciful now.

"Usuthu!"

"Fire!"

The call echoed along the British ranks as officer after officer judged the distance, had a last glance at their men and issued the order.

"Fire!"

The infantry opened fire, with smoke jetting from the Martini-Henrys and hundreds of large calibre bullets smashing into the Zulu ranks. Andrew saw the warriors fall by the dozen and by the score. Bullets tossed men backwards, tore off arms and splintered skulls, raising a film of blood above the charging warriors so those at the back advanced through the blood and brains of their comrades.

"Fire," the officers ordered, and the remorseless volley fire of British infantry crashed out, rank after rank, section after section, company after company. The Zulus fell in rows, men leaping over the mangled bodies of their companions but still coming on, still chanting, still willing to fight.

"*Usuthu!*" the Zulus roared, deep-throated. "*Usuthu!*"

"They're not stopping!" Sanderson yelled.

"Then make them bloody stop!" the corporal snarled. "Fire!"

The volleys crashed out, jetting smoke in front of the British square, smoke that drifted back so men coughed and blinked. The Martini-Henrys slammed back against tender shoulders; men jerked the underlever and rammed in brass cartridges, firing automatically. Some shouted at the advancing Zulus; others hid their fear in obscenities.

"*Usuthu*!" The warrior's chants rose and fell, mingled with the yells and screams of the wounded.

Andrew recognised the veteran regiments who sprang up from the dead ground a hundred and thirty yards from the right rear corner of the square.

"Look at that!" Kerr marvelled, naming each Zulu *amabutho*. The uVe, uThulwana, iNdluyengwe and iNgobamakhosi rose to the attack, with the Abanonya in the middle. Experienced warriors who knew what British musketry could do, they still charged forward, screaming their war cry.

"Dismount and help the infantry!" Andrew ordered and led his Natal Dragoons to the firing line.

"Fire!" a calm voice ordered, and another volley crashed out.

A score of men fell, but the rest continued, assegais raised, shields held in front of them.

"Fire!" That was a west-coast Scottish voice as the 21st Foot aimed and fired. Although more Zulus crumpled, their advance never faltered. They were nearly within range of the throwing spears, chanting warriors trained to kill.

The 58th and 21st volleyed together, hundreds of rifles firing at thousand of warriors, with men blaspheming, praying, shouting defiance, laughing, or using dark humour to hide their fear.

The Zulus still came on, a hundred yards away, then only eighty, with Chelmsford riding over to encourage the infantry.

"Fire faster, men!"

Andrew thought Chelmsford sounded agitated, as if he envisaged the Zulus breaking through the four-deep ranks in a confused Donnybrook of assegais, bayonets, and rifle butts.

The nearest cannon, a nine-pounder, fired canister, but the range was too close, and the canister would not burst. Andrew raised his rifle and fired, watching the infantry prepare to receive the Zulus. Two or three privates of the 21st, the Royal Scots Fusiliers stepped forward to meet the challenge until outraged NCOs bellowed them back.

"Damn your eagerness, lads! Let them come to us!"

Gunsmoke lay thick in front of the infantry, obscuring their view. Standing in the fourth British rank, Andrew saw the Zulus advancing, closing ranks whenever a volley knocked over a dozen men and continuing to chant.

"Usuthu!"

Andrew fired, worked the underlever, loaded, and fired again. The Zulus were seventy yards away, then sixty, nearly in range of throwing spears, and they faltered. Another British volley crashed out, and the Zulu attack halted.

"We've stopped them!" Davidson yelled, and the 58th gave three cheers, joined by the 21st.

"Cavalry!" Chelmsford shouted. "Mount!"

The bugler sounded the order, and the cavalry sprang onto their horses, ready for the square to open so they could ride out among the Zulus.

"Mount up, lads!" Andrew ordered and clambered onto Lancelot. His Dragoons obeyed, checking reins and saddles, wiping sweat from their eyes, and looking over the infantry at the Zulu impi.

For the first time, Andrew realised that Zulu snipers were firing long-range shots at the square. He saw a man fall a few yards from him and another drop his rifle and swear, clutching at his arm.

"We make good targets, standing like this," Buller said, with a cigarette dangling from his lower lip. "Thank the Lord the Zulus are terrible shots."

Something whined past Andrew's head, and he knew some Zulu sharpshooter was targeting him. It felt strange that some unknown warrior, who he had never met and would never meet, was deliberately trying to kill him. Andrew straightened in the saddle, determined not to quail or show fear.

"Dismount!" Chelmsford shouted, and the bugle trilled out again. "They're coming again!"

"It's like bloody musical chairs," somebody grumbled. "Mount, dismount, mount; I wish his blasted Lordship would make up his mind!"

The Zulus altered their angle of attack, heading for the side of the square where the 21st abutted onto the 94th, the old Scotch Brigade. Simultaneously, the Zulu rifle fire increased, and Andrew saw some of the 94th fall, dead and wounded.

My father used to say that every battle had a crisis point, a hinge. We are at the hinge now.

The 21st and 94th fired steadily, meeting the Zulu charge with controlled volleys until the attack faltered.

"They're breaking!" Buller said and glanced towards Chelmsford.

The general agreed. "Lancers! Mount!" he ordered.

Andrew checked his watch. It was barely half past nine. The Zulus' attack had occupied only half an hour compared to the four-hour ordeal of Khambula, and only a few had come close to the British line.

"Lancers! Ride out!" Chelmsford ordered. "Go round to the left!"

"Stand to your horses," the Lancers officers shouted. "Mount!"

The lancers, the death or glory boys who sported the skull and crossbones as their cap badge, trotted out of the square chanting "Death! Death!" as they hefted their long lances.

Andrew thought the 17th Lancers made a fine show, with Colonel Drury Lowe leading them to the left as the Zulu sharpshooters altered their targets from the scarlet square to the tall horsemen. The Lancers dressed without haste as Drury Lowe led them at the main Zulu impi, with each troop deciding who they should charge. Immediately behind the Lancers, Captain Brewster led a troop of his King's Dragoon Guards out of the square.

"Heavy cavalry against agile infantry," Buller murmured as his colonial horsemen prepared to leave the square. "This could be interesting."

"You men, join the Lancers," Chelmsford ordered. "Buller, take your horsemen out!"

"Come on, lads!" Buller shouted. "Follow me!"

Already mounted, Andrew led his Dragoons as the 58th marched aside to give them passage. He saw the Lancers engaged with the now retreating Zulus, with men pinning the warriors to the ground while the Dragoon Guards wielded heavy swords that sliced through the Zulu shields.

Buller led his men forward, firing at any Zulu they saw and turning the Zulu withdrawal into a rout.

"Extended order, Dragoons!" Andrew shouted. "Work in pairs, guard each other's backs and don't wander off alone."

Very few Zulus turned to fight, preferring to flee once the battle was lost. Andrew shot one running man, saw him fall and stopped to reload. All around him, mounted men were chasing and hunting the retreating Zulus, shooting the wounded without mercy. The Lancers were experts at spearing their quarry, riding past, freeing their lances with a flick of the wrist, and seeking the next victim. Within minutes the lance pennons were scarlet with Zulu blood.

"Enough." Andrew pushed forward his rifle to lift a trooper's carbine as he aimed at a wounded Zulu. "That man's no threat to us."

"He'd kill us if the position were reversed," the trooper objected.

"We're meant to be the civilised ones here," Andrew said. He noticed another group of Zulus watching and saw the familiar shields of the Abanonya.

The retreating Zulus entered an area of broken ground, with bushes and rocks to provide cover. Colonel Drury Lowe and Buller arrived at the same conclusion and halted the cavalry as Zulu sharpshooters opened fire.

"This is not suitable country for mounted men," Drury Lowe said.

"Back to the square, boys," Buller ordered. "We've broken the Zulu army and chased them away. That's enough for the present."

We've won the battle of Ulundi, Andrew realised as he saw the infantry grounding their Martinis, lighting pipes, and chatting with one another. Such a short battle seemed surreal, an anti-climax after the tension and horrors of the previous few months.

Chelmsford greeted the mounted men with a brief nod. He ordered the square to march to a small stream, the Mbilane, and within half an hour, the cooks were busy making lunch.

"Buller," Chelmsford said. "You'd oblige me by taking your men to the royal kraal and burning the place to the ground."

"Very good, sir," Buller, ever restless, said.

"I've heard rumours of treasure in the king's palace," Chelmsford added. "If you find any, place a guard on it, will you? There's a good chap."

"Certainly, sir," Buller said. "Come on, lads! Let's visit Ulundi!"

CHAPTER 29

ONdini was by far the largest *imuzi* Andrew had seen, with a stout wooden palisade extending for what seemed like miles. He pulled Lancelot up a quarter of a mile outside the Zulu capital.

"I've never helped topple a royal dynasty before," Andrew said.

"It's something to tell your grandchildren," Buller told him. "Look long and hard, Baird, for it's something neither you nor anybody else will ever see again. The capital city of the Zulus, one of the last independent kingdoms in Africa."

Andrew knew that if Marina were not in oNdini, he would probably never find her, yet he hesitated before entering.

"I've heard there are over four thousand separate kraals within the palisade," Andrew said, "and Cetshwayo lives in the middle, in the *isigodlo,* in a house built in the European manner, with a thatched roof."

If Mariana is anywhere, she'll be there. The only reason Cetshwayo might have for taking her with her would be as a hostage.

Buller smiled. "You may be correct. We'll see in a few moments." He lit a cigarette and looked sideways at Andrew. "You'll have heard the shave about the treasure."

"I have, sir," Andrew said. "I've heard at least two different versions, one claiming it dated back to Shaka's day and the other saying it was a tax on the ivory hunters and traders."

"All sorts of rumours fly about in wartime," Buller said. "Come on, Baird. Let's get into Ulundi. There are some unsavoury chaps going around, and we don't want them to get there first."

"No, sir," Andrew agreed, thinking of Hitchings. He saw some stray horsemen heading for oNdini and guessed they were after Cetshwayo's alleged treasure.

"Come on, Baird!" Buller said. "Gallop in, man and see if your girl is there!"

At least a dozen horsemen were racing for oNdini, with Andrew and Buller near the back. All Andrew's competitive streak came to the fore in a horserace, and he urged Lancelot on, pushing for the open gate. For once, he wished he had a faster mount, for Kabul ponies were not renowned for speed.

By God, Mariana, I've strived for months to reach oNdini, and you'd better be inside, waiting for me.

oNdini seemed to stretch for miles, a proper city rather than a collection of *izindlu*, and Andrew wondered at the men who had created such a place without any of the accessories modern civilisation considered necessary. *The Zulus have put an immense amount of work into oNdini, and we're about to burn it to the ground.*

Andrew galloped through the gateway and into another world. He knew that Cetshwayo had ordered oNdini evacuated before Chelmsford's army grew close, but he had not expected such complete desertion. oNdini was a ghost city, with each family *imuzi* empty of everything. There were no people, cattle, goats, or possessions. The Zulus had left nothing for the British except memories and the sad ghosts of a defeated kingdom.

"Mariana!" Andrew roared, knowing his voice would be lost in the vastness of oNdini. "Mariana!"

He heard movement and saw other riders roaming around, some from units he recognised and others he guessed were searching for loot.

"Mariana!" Andrew's voice echoed among the eerily deserted *izindlu* as he made his way towards where he guessed the *isigodlo* should be, with more armed horsemen shouting around him.

"Where's the king's palace?" one London accent demanded.

"How the hell should I know?" a colonial voice replied and then came the crash of breaking glass as somebody threw a bottle on the ground.

"Where's the bloody treasure?" a coarse Liverpool voice sounded. "Where's Cetshwayo?"

Andrew pushed Lancelot on, past an outer row of *imizi* and into a vast inner ring where Cetshwayo had paraded his wealth. He could smell the homely scent of cattle and shouted again. "Mariana!"

"Who the hell's Mariana?" the Liverpudlian voice sounded. "I'll share her with you!" When the man laughed, Andrew loosened the revolver in its holster. He entered an area of small *imizi*, each containing one large and a few smaller *izindlu*. They were all empty.

A group of horsemen passed Andrew, with one man carrying a broken Zulu shield, another a throwing spear.

"Where's the treasure? There's no bloody treasure!"

"Hey, you," a large man with a sunburned face and the skin peeling from his nose shouted at Andrew. "Where's the king's palace?"

"I have no idea," Andrew replied and moved on, getting lost in the intricacies of oNdini. Every *imuzi* looked the same, deserted, sad and empty of life. Andrew knew he would never have the time to search every *indlu* for Mariana.

He smelled smoke and heard the tell-tale crackle of flames.

Somebody's set oNdini on fire.

"Mariana!" Andrew pushed Lancelot harder, poking into *imizi*, desperate to find Mariana. If she was a captive, she might be lying, bound, and gagged in any of these *izindlu*, or the Zulus could have taken her with them or killed her as an unnecessary burden. When a group of horsemen cantered past, Andrew looked around. They were mixed, Africans riding beside Europeans, but for a moment, Andrew thought he recognised the leading rider.

That was like Ashanti Smith. No, it couldn't be him. Andrew rode on until he saw the larger *indlu* above the pall of smoke and immediately knew it belonged to the king. If Cetshwayo held Mariana captive, she would be either in or near the royal home. He would have to try, however slim the chance of finding her.

The royal *indlu* was huge. Tethering Lancelot outside the door, Andrew pushed in, shouting Mariana's name.

"What the hell are you doing here?"

Andrew whirled around, recognising the voice. "Hitchings? You bastard! What the devil are you doing here?"

Hitchings was as untrustworthy as Andrew remembered, failing to meet Andrew's gaze as he gave a greasy smile. "The same as you, police boy."

"Soldier now, Hitchings, and with little time for a deserter such as you."

"Don't get all holier-than-thou with me, Baird," Hitchings sneered. "We're both after the same thing."

"What?" Andrew asked.

"Cetshwayo's treasure," Hitchings said. "Me and Ashanti and the boys are searching for it. We'll find it and divide it between us."

That was Ashanti Smith I saw!

Andrew coughed as smoke wafted into the *indlu*. He glanced behind him and saw an orange glow of flames. "I'm not interested in the treasure," he said. "You're welcome to any gold or ivory you find."

"Everybody's interested in gold," Hitchings contradicted him.

"I'm not," Andrew said. About to mention Mariana, he saw the firelight reflect on something on Hitchings' little finger. "What's that ring, Hitchings?"

"What?" Hitchings stepped away, tucking his left hand behind his back.

"Show me your hand!" Andrew unholstered his pistol. "Show me your hand, Hitchings, or I'll blow your bloody head off!"

Hitchings snarled, glaring at Andrew. "What's the matter, Bairdie? I'm not a Zulu!"

The crackle of flames increased, and smoke gushed into the *indlu* from outside. Andrew swore as Hitchings ducked and kicked upwards, aiming for Andrew's revolver. His boot cracked onto Andrew's wrist, causing him to gasp, but rather than drop the weapon, he involuntarily squeezed the trigger.

The bullet flew wide, puncturing a hole in the thatched roof.

"You fired at me!" Hitchings accused, bringing his rifle round. "You dirty bastard, Baird!"

Andrew fired again, with the bullet smashing into Hitchings' arm. Hitchings screamed shrilly, dropped his rifle, and grabbed for the wound. "What did you do that for?"

"Show me that ring, Hitchings, or by God, I'll put the next one between your eyes!"

"You wouldn't dare," Hitchings said, cradling his arm. He whimpered like a frightened puppy. "Come on, Bairdie, you and me are chums!"

"Are we?" Kicking Hitchings rifle into a corner of the *indlu*, Andrew thrust his revolver against the cowering man's forehead. "Let's see your hand, Hitchings."

When Hitchings held up his hand, Andrew saw the ring, now smeared with blood.

"Where did you get that?" He yanked the ring from Hitchings' finger. It was the signet ring his mother had given him, and which he had passed on to Elaine. Andrew pushed the muzzle of the revolver harder into Hitchings' forehead. "Tell me, you bastard!"

"Off a woman!" Hitchings screamed. "I got it off a woman!"

Andrew felt nausea rising in his throat. "Which woman?" he asked. "Where?" He relaxed the revolver, stepped back, and smiled. "Tell me, Hitchings."

The ring seemed to burn in Andrew's hand as he remembered Elaine's smile when he slipped the ring on her finger.

"Your woman," Hitchings whispered. "She gave it to me."

"When and why?" Andrew kept his voice mild, although the fear and worry tore him apart. "When did Miss Maxwell give you this ring, Hitchings?"

More smoke blew into the king's *indlu* as the sound of fire increased. Andrew looked outside, where an orange flicker revealed the *imuzi* was alight.

"At her house," Hitchings said as Andrew pressed the revolver muzzle against his forehead.

"How was she when you left her?"

"Very well," Hitchings gasped. "She was very well, I tell you."

"Who else was there?" The crackle became a roar as the thatch caught fire, with flames bright above their heads and sparks raining down.

"It was Ashanti's idea!" Hitchings said. "He heard you and the woman talking, and he wanted to visit her." He looked up. "We'll have to get out of here, or we'll get burned alive!"

"We'll get out when you tell me who else was there," Andrew promised.

"Ashanti Smith, Simmy and the boys," Hitchings nearly screamed. "Let me out!"

"Did you see the younger sister?" Andrew asked quietly, although he felt sick at the thought of Smith, Simpson, and Hitchings alone with Elaine.

A section of the roof collapsed, landing in a mass of flaming thatch three feet away. Andrew ignored it. "Did you see Mariana, the younger sister?"

"Yes!" Hitchings yelled, staring at the burning roof. "We took her with us!"

"What?" Andrew stepped back. "Took her where? Where is she, Hitchings?"

"Let me out!" Hitchings screamed as another section of the roof collapsed. Some of the thatch landed on top of him, and he pushed it off, yelling. A few sparks remained, quickly spreading on his dry clothes. He tried to beat out the flames.

"Took her where?" Andrew persisted. "Where is she now? Tell me!"

"Help me!" Hitchings screamed.

"Took her where?" Andrew asked. "Where?" He leaned closer until another section of the roof collapsed. Andrew jumped back, cursing, as the flaming thatch landed on top of Hitchings. The man's screams increased.

"Tell me!" Andrew began to haul the burning thatch from Hitchings.

"In the mountains!" Hitchings screamed. "Help me!"

As he spoke, one of the supports for the roof collapsed, bringing down half the thatch. Hitchings' screams intensified, then died away in the roar of flames. When the screaming stopped, Andrew left the royal *indlu.*

CHAPTER 30

Lancelot was outside, shivering with fear as the smoke and flames surrounded him. "Come on, Lance," Andrew said. He looked around oNdini, seeing nothing but dense smoke and burning buildings.

Have I left it too late? Am I trapped in here? No, damn it! There's always a way out!

Andrew tried to remember oNdini's layout, waved a hand in front of him in a futile attempt to clear away the smoke, chose a direction at random and pushed on. Smoke and sparks surrounded him, with the crackle of burning thatch and the whoosh of collapsing buildings loud in his ears.

After five minutes in Cetshwayo's burning capital, Andrew tried shouting, hoping that somebody could hear him, but the sound of the fire drowned his words.

Damn it! There must be a way out of here!

Andrew heard a distinct rattle above the other noises, and a shadowy shape appeared to his left.

"Halloa!" Andrew shouted. "Who are you?"

When the figure did not reply, Andrew saw it was a woman, covered in bones and furs, with a snakeskin around her neck. "Are you the witch doctor I've met before?"

In reply, the woman rattled her knuckle-bone necklace and stepped into the smoke.

Instinctively, Andrew knew the woman wanted him to follow her. He pushed Lancelot into the smoke, forcing the horse forward. "Where are you?"

Again, Andrew heard the rattle of bones. He headed for the sound, unable to see for the dense smoke while the sound of burning thatch filled the air.

"I hope you're not leading me astray!" Andrew croaked, coughing as the acrid smoke caught in his throat.

The bones rattled again, and Andrew saw the woman standing in a small clearing, watching him through familiar deep, dark eyes.

"I'm coming!" Andrew said, fighting to control Lancelot, who was nearly panicking in the heat and smoke. He kicked in his heels. "Come on, Lance! One more effort, and we are through!"

Lancelot whinnied, rolling his eyes backwards. Andrew patted the horse's head, leaned forward, whispered in Lancelot's ear, and pushed on. The witch backed off from him, and Andrew emerged into the clearing, with the palisade before him and oNdini burning at his back.

"Nearly there, Lancelot!" Andrew croaked. "A final effort, and we're out!" He looked around for the witch, but she had vanished.

Lancelot sensed fresh air, took as much of a run as he could and leapt over the barrier to land in a shower of dust outside. For a thoroughbred, the jump would have been easy, but a Kabul pony was not suited for such endeavours, and Lancelot staggered as he landed.

"Good boy!" Andrew patted him. "You got us out of there."

Riding a few hundred yards away, Andrew looked back. oNdini was a mass of orange, with the flames leaping to the sky beneath a pall of dark smoke.

What a sight. Camelot no more. A dynastic capital dying in a funeral pyre as a kingdom crashes to its end.

Andrew sighed. He lifted his water canteen, shook it to test the contents and lifted it to his lips.

"Here's to you, Cetshwayo, and the brave warriors of Zululand who are no more." He took a single sip, dismounted, and poured the remainder into Lancelot's mouth. "We'll find you a decent drink soon, boy."

Turning his back, Andrew walked away, leading Lancelot as a feeling of deep melancholia fell on him. He knew Britain had won the war but somehow felt dirty at the outcome.

JAMA VIEWED WHAT WAS LEFT OF THE ABANONYA AS THEY STOOD IN THE smoke of oNdini. Jabulani stood among them, a boy in years but a man who had faced the rifles of the British soldiers and survived. Jama allowed his gaze to linger on him for a moment, and then he returned to his duty.

"You fought like men," Jama told them. "You fought like Zulu warriors, but you could not prevail against the bullets and shellfire of the British."

The Abanonya agreed. About half carried wounds, and all were spent. They had fought in four major battles since the war began and a few more minor but still bloody skirmishes. All the warriors had charged into the wall of flames and lead that was a British position, and many had washed their spears in British blood. The Abanonya had done all that humans could do, fighting impossible odds with bare chests and spears against Gatling guns and case shot.

"It is enough," Jama said. "No man can expect more of you."

The Abanonya listened, leaning on their assegais.

"I am going to hunt for the men who murdered my wife and burned my *imuzi*," Jama said. "I do not expect any of you to follow me. Go home to your wives and whatever the white men have left for you."

Ndleleni fondled his necklace, looked at the ground and took a pinch of snuff. "The British killed my wives," he said. "The man with the green feathers in his hat is as much my enemy as yours, Jama."

Bangizwe stamped his feet. "We are the Abanonya," he said. "We will not leave you." He raised his voice in the song they sang before the war began, Chaka's favourite.

"Thou hast finished off the tribes.
Where wilt thou wage war?
Yes, where wilt thou wage war?
Thou hast conquered the kings.
Where wilt thou wage war?
Thou hast finished off the tribes.
Where wilt thou wage war?
Yes, yes, yes! Where wilt thou wage war?
Jama fought to keep his pride from showing.
"Very well. You are all fools to follow me."

Ndleleni grinned at him. "That is another matter, Jama. Where are you taking us?"

ONLY WHEN HE WAS CLEAR OF ONDINI DID ANDREW CONSIDER HITCHINGS' words.

I've been wrong all this time, blaming the Zulus for murdering Elaine and taking Mariana. If Hitchings was telling the truth, it was Ashanti Smith and his band of renegades that kidnapped her.

As Andrew rode towards the British camp, a score of images entered his mind. He saw Smith and his marauders advancing on Inglenook, laughing. He saw them passing under Elaine's mopane tree, surrounding the farmhouse, and breaking in. He saw them kicking in the door to Elaine's bedroom as she tried to fight back.

No. Andrew shook his head, forcing the images away. *Picturing such scenes is the path to madness. I must find Mariana if she is still alive. I can't leave her with these filthy creatures.*

Andrew stiffened as he remembered Elaine taking him to the Bushman's paintings on that terrible, magical wagon road. He had seen a flash of blue then. *That was a police uniform. Somebody was watching us, Smith, Simpson, or Hitchings, without a doubt. They planned this raid all along.*

Smoke from oNdini had drifted across the entire Mahlabathini Plain, hazing the landscape and polluting the sky. Andrew saw Lord Chelmsford and his staff officers standing on a small knoll, watching oNdini burn. They seemed satisfied with their days' work, examining the destruction through field glasses, and exchanging congratulations.

"Why the long face, fellow soldier?" Buller asked. "We won the battle, smashed the Zulus, and won the war. You look as though you found a sixpence and lost a guinea."

"I found out about Mariana Maxwell, sir," Andrew said.

"Tell me more, Baird." Buller's voice altered from joviality to sincerity.

Andrew explained, with Buller listening carefully. When Andrew finished, Buller nodded. "There is a chance she is still alive," he said and rode away.

Andrew worked mechanically for the remainder of that day, performing his duty, and speaking to his peers while his mind was elsewhere. He listened as Chelmsford paraded his army and congratulated them on their good conduct but said nothing. In the middle of the afternoon, Chelmsford marched his men back to the Mfolozi River, with the band of the 13th Foot playing *God Save the Queen* and *Rule Britannia*. When the band stopped, some of the men parodied themselves.

"Oh, the grand old Duke of York,
He had ten thousand men,
He marched them up to the top of the hill,
And he marched them down again."

Kerr grinned at Andrew as they rode on the infantry's left flank. "Cheer up, old Cock; sorry, sir. We'll be going home soon, wherever home is."

"I won't be coming," Andrew said.

"Whyever not, sir? Have you fallen in love with Zululand?" Kerr probed, with his eyes sharp. "Or are you still searching after that girl of yours?"

"Yes," Andrew said. "I'm still searching." He kicked Lancelot further ahead, desperate to torture himself with his dark thoughts.

The British infantry marched past, many laden with the assegais, shields, and knobkerries they had taken from the Zulu dead. Andrew wondered how many of these trophies would decorate walls the length and breadth of Britain in the years to come. He imagined the men boasting of their deeds, with the tales growing in the telling as the years dragged on.

"Well, Baird." Buller rode beside Andrew. "You'll be worried about Miss Maxwell," he said.

"Yes, sir."

Buller watched the marching army. "We don't know where Cetshwayo is," he said abruptly. "He's vanished completely."

"Yes, sir," Andrew said.

"I'm going to send patrols out to search for him." Buller seemed to be thinking as he spoke. "You speak Zulu, don't you?"

"I speak some Xhosa, sir. It's not the same, but I can generally make myself understood."

"That's good enough for me," Buller said. "I want you to take your ruffians to search for Cetshwayo. Try the hill country at the northern fringes of Zululand." He leaned across from his horse. "When you're out there, I have heard there is a renegade band who may have a woman prisoner. If you find them, Baird, do whatever is needful."

Andrew felt relief surge through him.

"Thank you, sir. When shall I leave?"

"As soon as you're ready, Baird. I don't expect to see you back until you either have Miss Maxwell or until you have definite news of her." Buller pulled Andrew's horse away from the column. "There will still be roaming Zulu bands out there, Baird, so be careful. Take as much ammunition, food, and water as you can carry."

"Thank you, sir."

"And, Baird." Buller extended his hand. "The best of luck. Your father is an expert with small mobile forces, and I can see he has passed his skills to you." He held Andrew's gaze for a long moment. "Now get out there."

Two hours before dawn the following day, Andrew led his Natal Dragoons away from the British camp on the Mfolozi. He had ensured all his men carried extra ammunition, food and water and borrowed twenty spare horses for the hard riding he expected.

"We're going to Ulundi first," Andrew told them.

"Why is that, sir?" Sergeant Meek asked.

"We have two missions," Andrew explained. "The first is to find Cetshwayo, and the second is to trace a certain band of desperados who have been attacking homes and native homesteads, murdering civilians."

"Is that the same bunch who kidnapped Miss Maxwell, sir?"

"The same bunch," Andrew confirmed.

Sergeant Meek nodded. "If I were you, sir, I'd make them my priority. Cetshwayo can do nothing without his impis, and this band of renegades sound unpleasant." He tapped the row of medal ribbons across his chest. "I don't like deserters, sir."

"I see." Andrew nodded. "How many others think like you?"

"We all know the story, sir. Nobody likes the idea of recreants kidnapping women, and some of our local lads," Meek jerked a thumb at the Dragoons, "have got families near the border."

Andrew nodded. "We all have our reasons to catch these men. Let's look at Ulundi."

The passage of thousands of feet had beaten the ground around oNdini stone-hard, but Andrew cast his men in a wide circle.

"Ashanti Smith's men were all mounted," he said. "They did not come with the British Army, so we are looking for a group of horsemen arriving from a different direction. They'd arrive after Cetshwayo evacuated Ulundi, so we know the prints will be fresh."

The Dragoons nodded. "We'll search for spoor," Kerr said. "It's unfortunate that there's been so much movement."

"Search," Andrew ordered. "We're not looking for Zulus or regular British cavalry. These men will be mounted and probably without any formation."

"Yes, sir," Kerr said.

Andrew split his men into pairs, one to check for any traces of Smith's renegades' trail and the other to watch for resentful Zulus. They started close to the smouldering remains of oNdini, worked in a circle, and gradually extended their search outwards. On three occasions, a man thought he had found traces of a band of irregular horsemen, only for the spoor to lead towards the British camp.

By evening Andrew was tired and downhearted yet determined to continue. They camped a mile from oNdini; Andrew set out sentries and started as soon as there was sufficient light the following morning.

"Sir!" Kerr shouted. "What's this?"

Andrew cantered across, more in hope than expectation.

"A body of horsemen have been here," Kerr said, crouching on the ground. "Around thirty men, coming and leaving the same way."

Andrew dismounted and joined Kerr. "When?"

Kerr pursed his lips. "They arrived and left about six hours apart. Yesterday."

Andrew felt his spark of hope grow to a miniature flame.

"Do you want us to follow them, sir?" Kerr asked.

Andrew considered. "Yes, damn it," he decided. "This is the best trail we've found."

The riders had not tried to hide their trail, so the Dragoons had no difficulty following them. Knowing how skilful Smith was, Andrew sent Kerr in front to watch for ambushes and followed with the remainder of his men.

"Where the hell are the Zulus?" Meek asked as they rode through a deserted countryside. "It feels as if somebody has taken a broom and swept the country clean."

"They'll be here," Andrew said. "They'll know exactly where we are, even if we can't see them."

They rode on, following the trail, ignoring the occasional deer that broke cover around them and the chattering of the birds. The trail was clear, as if the renegades had no fear of pursuit, or even dared anybody to follow them.

Is Ashanti luring us into a trap? Has he placed an ambush ahead of us? Andrew slowed his pace, checking ahead with his field glasses.

"Sir," Meek said quietly. "Kerr's returning."

Both men looked up as Kerr hurried towards them. "Zulus!" Kerr cantered towards Andrew. "There's a small impi three miles ahead, sir."

"How small?" Andrew asked, reaching for his Martini.

"Maybe thirty or forty men," Kerr said. "Large enough to be dangerous."

"Damn," Andrew swore as he made a rapid decision, glancing around. "We'll stay on that ridge," he nodded to an area of high ground on their left, "and you and I will have a closer look at the impi. If we're lucky, they'll pass on without stopping."

"They're Zulus," Kerr said. "And they're hurting after we've burned oNdini and defeated them in battle. They'll attack any small British column they come across."

Andrew knew Kerr was correct. "We'll have a look," he decided, "and more very circumspectly."

"With respect, sir," Kerr said. "I might be better than you at watching them unseen."

"I'm sure you are, Kerr," Andrew agreed. "You can ensure I don't stick my head above the skyline or blow a trumpet or anything. Come on!"

JAMA LED THE ABANONYA AT A FAST TROT THAT EFFORTLESSLY COVERED THE ground. He heard the rhythmic tread of his men's feet and knew they could keep up the pace for hours. Yet he felt that something was wrong.

"Do you feel it too, Ndleleni?" he asked.

"I can." Ndleleni carried a wound from the battle outside oNdini but still ran with the others. Blood had dried down his side where a British bullet had grazed him.

"What is it?" Jama asked.

"White men," Ndleleni replied at once. "I can smell them."

Jama agreed, still running. "There's a man on a horse ahead."

"Over beside that pile of rocks," Ndleleni agreed. "He's watching us."

"He won't be alone," Jama decided. "He'll be scouting for a mounted patrol, probably searching for Cetshwayo."

"I can kill him." Ndleleni lifted a throwing assegai.

"No. Let the scout see us, and he'll return to the others. We'll follow." Jama ordered. "We'll attack them when they camp for the night." He grinned. "Remember the Intombi River?"

Ndleleni smiled, running a thumb along the edge of his *iKlwa*. "That was a good day."

"We'll have another," Jama said. He altered his direction to pass in the sight of the lone scout, passing through an area of long grass onto open ground. He saw the horseman watching, allowed him a few moments to count his men and led the Abanonya into a patch of rocks.

"Stop!" Jama ordered. "Wait here. Ndleleni and I will follow the scout."

Jama waited until the horseman left his position to canter away, then followed, keeping out of sight and a quarter of a mile to his left. The horseman rendezvoused with a larger force of mounted men.

"You were right, Jama," Ndleleni said.

They watched as the scout made his report, and most of the mounted men rode to a rocky ridge.

"They'll camp there for the night," Jama said.

Ndleleni agreed. "The scout is leading another man towards us."

Jama took a deep breath. "That's their induna," he said. "He was at Sihayo's *imuzi* when they first invaded and at Isandhlwana and Hlobane."

Ndleleni knew that Jama was hiding his emotions. “Your son died at Sihayo’s *imuzi*,” he said.

“He did.” Jama agreed. He watched the two mounted men.

“We could kill these two now,” Ndleleni suggested.

“If we do, the others might take fright and run,” Jama said. “I want to kill them all, like at Intombi Drift.”

Ndleleni touched the blade of his *iKlwa*. “That is what we shall do,” he said.

CHAPTER 31

"They've gone." Kerr swept the horizon with his field glasses. "I can't see any Zulus anywhere."

"That may be a good thing," Andrew said, "although I don't like to think of an impi, even a small one, ranging near us."

"Do you want me to scout around, sir?" Kerr asked.

Andrew shook his head. "No. If we leave them alone, hopefully, they'll leave us alone, too." He patted Lancelot. "Come on, Kerr. Let's get back to the others. We'll pick up the trail again tomorrow." He nodded to the hills ahead. "Hitchings said the renegades were in the hills, and these lads are heading that direction."

"Yes, sir," Kerr said and stopped. "Something's wrong."

"What?" After two years in the bush, Andrew knew not to distrust a frontiersman's instincts. "What's the to-do, Kerr?"

"Did you hear that bark just now, sir?" Kerr did not move, but his eyes swivelled from side to side, searching for something.

"I did," Andrew said. "A wild dog, I think."

"No, sir. It sounded like a wild dog, but it was a nyala deer, sir, an antelope. That's their warning call."

"I've never seen a nyala deer." Andrew loosened the pistol in his holster and glanced down at his Martini-Henry. "Are they dangerous?"

"No, sir. They've very shy and well-camouflaged. They seldom come out of the forest and never in daylight, which is why something's the matter. We passed a patch of woodland half an hour ago, and if the nyala were anywhere, it would be there. Something must have alarmed it."

"A leopard, perhaps?"

"Maybe, sir, but leopards are night hunters. I'd say humans disturbed the nyala."

"Us?"

"We weren't close enough to the forest, sir."

"Zulus?"

"I'd say so, sir. I'd guess the impi I saw is following us."

Andrew felt a thrill of apprehension, knowing that a party of Zulus might be hunting him. After their defeat at Ulundi, the remnants of any impi would be resentful and desperate for revenge. A stray pair of British soldiers would be a perfect salve for wounded Zulu pride.

"Don't head for the others," Andrew said quietly. "Ride past the ridge without stopping."

"Yes, sir," Kerr said. "The lads will know something's up."

They increased their speed, never riding in a straight line in case the Zulus carried rifles, listened for any unusual sounds, and readied themselves to fight.

"Stop here," Andrew said when they reached a rise topped by a prominent tree. He thought of Elaine's mopane and took a deep breath. "We've no time to fight with Zulus," he said. "Finding Mariana and these renegades is more important."

"We have to be alive to do that, sir," Kerr pointed out.

"Zulu warrior!" Andrew shouted, speaking in Xhosa. "We know you are there. Show yourself so we can talk like men." He heard his voice echo across the undulating countryside as a flock of birds exploded from a nearby tree. "Can you hear me?"

"Why are you in Zululand?" the voice sounded from nearby.

"I am searching for the man who murdered my woman!" Andrew replied. "The war is over." He waited for a response.

"Do you seek Cetshwayo?" The voice seemed to come from right underneath them.

"No!" Andrew replied. "I seek the men who murdered my woman."

"Were they Zulus?" Those three words carried as much menace as any cry of "*Usuthu!*"

"No," Andrew replied, although shouting to an empty landscape was trying on the throat and the nerves. "White men." He saw the fast-closing dust coming towards him and wondered if that was a Zulu impi or his mounted men. "I am looking for a band of renegades that burned my woman's house and murdered her and her family. A white man with two green feathers in his hat led them."

"*Ingwenya*!" the Zulu replied. "The crocodile. A white man with two green feathers in his hat burned my *imuzi* and killed my wives."

"Are you looking for him?" Andrew asked. The dust cloud was closing fast.

"I will kill him," the Zulu replied.

"Then we are not enemies," Andrew said. "That man is Ashanti Smith, and he is my enemy. The enemy of my enemy is my friend."

"I am Jama." The Zulu appeared from three yards away. "This warrior is Ndleleni." Both men were lithe and muscular, with the *isicoco* of maturity. They carried spears and lifted shields from the ground.

"I am Lieutenant Andrew Baird," Andrew said. "This soldier is Mark Kerr."

The fighting men sized each other up warily.

"We fought each other at Isandhlwana," Andrew said. "And Hlobane and Khambula."

Jama nodded. "You killed my sons Kgabu and Funani."

"You killed forty of my men at Isandhlwana," Andrew countered.

Jama took a pinch of snuff. "We were enemies," he said. "I should kill you."

"That war is over. Now we're searching for the men who killed my woman."

Ndleleni was eyeing Kerr, holding his stabbing assegai underhanded as if ready to strike. "We're all searching for the same man," he said. "We could kill you here or join together to find him."

"Father." Jabulani ran to Jama's side. "This is the man who spared me."

Jama lifted his chin and looked at Andrew. "Why?" he asked curtly.

"He was too young to be a warrior," Andrew replied. "And the fighting was over."

Jama looked from Jabulani's open face to Andrew and nodded.

"Would you trust us to fight at your side?" Andrew asked. "We invaded your country and killed thousands of your people."

Jama smiled without humour. "If you betray us, we will kill you."

"That's fair enough," Andrew said. "But we might kill you first." He nodded to the mounted men who had arrived with rifles held ready.

Jama did not look surprised. "Look again, Lieutenant Baird."

As the horsemen reined up, thirty Zulu warriors trotted behind them, each with his assegai poised.

"Peace or war, Jama?" Andrew asked. "If it is war, we will both lose."

Jama felt Jabulani's hand on his shoulder. "It is peace until we find this man with the green feather in his hat."

Andrew nodded, realising how tense he had been. "Lower your rifles, boys. We have no quarrel with these Abanonya warriors."

Some of his men obeyed, while more were reluctant. Andrew lifted his revolver, reversed it, and handed it to Jama as a sign of trust. The Zulu accepted the weapon, studied it for a moment and returned it.

"We are at peace with these men," Jama said, and the Abanonya lowered their assegais.

Kerr breathed a long sigh of relief. "What now?"

"Now we find Ashanti Smith, rescue Mariana and get out of Zululand with a whole skin," Andrew said.

"If we can," Kerr said. "Our truce with Jama only lasts until we've dealt with Smith."

"We'll cross that bridge when we reach the river," Andrew said.

❄

Jama was a better tracker even than Kerr and found Smith's tracks without difficulty.

"This way, Lieutenant Baird." Jama set off at a trot, with his men at his heels and Andrew following. Twice they came to stony ground, and Jama cast around, searching.

"He's lost the spoor," Kerr said.

"Can you see it?" Andrew asked.

"Not a thing."

They watched the Zulus move back and forward, studying the ground, until Ndleleni pointed to a single blade of bent grass and summoned Jama.

"This way," Jama said and cantered away without another word.

"This way," Andrew repeated and followed, with his Dragoons at his heels.

I have lost command of this expedition, and we are in Jama's hands.

"How far ahead are they?" Andrew asked as the evening drew in.

Jama frowned at the question. "Maybe tomorrow," he replied. "We might catch them tomorrow."

"Then what?" Kerr asked.

"Then we kill them," Jama replied.

"I want the man with the green feathers," Andrew said.

"He is mine to kill," Jama told him.

Andrew felt the eyes of Jama's impi on him and knew if he argued, he'd precipitate a full-scale battle between his men and the Zulus.

"We'll have to find him first," Andrew said. *And when we do, Smith is mine.*

Jama eyed Andrew. "We'll find them," he promised.

"I don't know how much we can trust these people," Kerr murmured. "Remember what happened to the 80th Foot at the Intombi."

"I haven't forgotten," Andrew said. He raised a hand to Jama.

"We should camp for the night soon," Andrew said.

"There is sweet water ahead," Jama replied. "You camp on one side of the river and us on the other."

Andrew agreed. "You and I may trust each other, Jama, but our followers may be less controlled."

"How can we trust a nation that invaded our country?" Jama asked quickly.

Kerr stepped forward, gripping his rifle. "The Zulus invaded all their neighbours," he said until Andrew frowned at him.

"We're trying to establish friendly relations, Kerr," Andrew reminded. "You're not helping. Stand back!"

"You didn't grow up on the Zulu frontier, sir," Kerr said.

"No," Andrew said. "I lived on the Scottish-English frontier where we had a thousand years of warfare and slaughter. We managed to make peace, and so will Natal with the Zulus."

When Kerr opened his mouth to object, Andrew pushed him back. "Stand clear, Kerr!"

"Yes, sir," Kerr growled.

Jama watched the interaction, turned aside, and crossed the river with his Zulus at his back.

"Sergeant Meek," Andrew said. "Post three sentries tonight. One colonial and two British."

Meek had seen Kerr's reaction. "I'll take the first stag, sir."

"I'll take the second," Andrew decided.

Meek nodded. "Yes, sir." He lowered his voice, "We have to forgive the colonials for being a trifle volatile, sir. They've lived in fear of the Zulus all their lives."

"I understand, Sergeant," Andrew said quietly. "Things are changing rapidly."

"Yes, sir," Meek said diplomatically.

They camped for the night, with both parties keeping sentries in mutual distrust and keeping a fire alive. Kerr kept his rifle by his side, with his revolver under the saddle he used as a pillow.

Twice during the night, Andrew heard a lion roar and rose to grab his rifle. Each time he looked across the river, he saw Jama standing with his knobkerrie in his hand, watching him. When Andrew raised a hand in acknowledgement, Jama responded, unsmiling. Ndleleni sat under the shade of a tree, nursing his *iKlwa* and watching over Jama.

Jama's protecting his men, as I am looking after mine. We are not much different, he and I.

"WELL, WE SURVIVED THE NIGHT," ANDREW SAID AS THE MEN WOKE, yawned, scratched themselves and looked around. The Zulus squatted silently on their side of the river, waiting for the Natal Dragoons.

The combined party moved on, steadily heading north into the north and west of the country, an area disputed between the Boers and Zulus.

"Be careful here, Lieutenant Baird," Jama warned. "The Swazis infest this land, as well as European renegades. The Swazis are not warriors but can be treacherous."

"Thank you, Jama," Andrew replied. "We'll be careful."

They moved on, with the terrain becoming rougher and less cultivated with every mile. The hills were low but well-wooded, and they saw more wildlife, with leopard's harsh barks common and the terrifying roar of lions breaking the sultry heat.

"Here!" Jama pointed to the ground. He knelt with Ndleleni standing at his side, watching the Dragoons.

Andrew nodded to Kerr. "Take a look, Kerr."

"Yes, sir." Kerr dismounted and joined the Zulus while keeping one hand on his rifle.

"The renegades changed direction here," Kerr explained a moment later. "They're heading towards that mountain over there." He indicated a long, densely wooded hill ahead.

"That may be their lair." Andrew consulted his map. "From there, they can strike into Zululand, Swaziland or attack the Boer farms of the Transvaal."

Jama stood up, consulted with Ndleleni, and set off for the mountain. His men followed, showing no signs of weariness although they had been on the move for days.

"The trail is fresh," Kerr said. "It's not more than a couple of hours old. We are getting very close."

"Ride ahead and warn Jama to be careful, Kerr," Andrew ordered. "Smith is a wily man." *Kerr's the only Zulu speaker we have, but can I trust him not to restart the war?*

"Yes, sir," Kerr said and looked up as a rifle shot sounded sharp and clear, silencing the bird life. One of the Zulus staggered and crumpled, dead before he hit the ground.

"I think Smith knows we are here," Andrew said.

He stopped suddenly as the witch's words returned to him.

"Beware of a foe who is a friend and take care of the friend who is a foe." Jama was the foe who was now a friend, and Smith, the friend who had become a foe. *The witch was correct. "Expect grief and loss."* He had lost Elaine and Abernethy. *"You have much blood in your future and a woman who will wait for you."*

All the witch's prophesies have come true. Mariana must be waiting for me. Oh, please, God, let that be true.

CHAPTER 32

Andrew did not have to give an order as his men spread out and dismounted with their rifles held ready. Jama's Zulus had also scattered, with the warriors crouching behind trees or rocks, facing the direction from where the shot had come.

I should have known Ashanti would have guards posted. My carelessness cost that warrior his life.

"Can anybody see him?" Andrew peered forward, searching for tell-tale gun smoke.

"No," Kerr replied.

"Stevens, look after the horses," Andrew said. "Meek, take the right flank; I'll take the left. Now, ease forward and find that guard."

Andrew heard Jama talking to his men, with the Zulus creeping silently through the undergrowth.

After the cacophony of bird song, the silence was eerie. Andrew crouched, moving from cover to cover, hoping not to stand on a snake or scorpion. He ducked as the rifle sounded again, followed by a long scream. A deep voice rose, "*ngadla!* I have eaten!"

Ndleleni rose from behind a mopane tree, with blood dripping from his *iKlwa*. "A Swazi dog," he said casually and wiped the blade clean.

"Those shots will have alerted the others." Andrew fought the doubt that they had followed the wrong group.

"That is true, Lieutenant Baird," Jama said. "I'll send some scouts ahead."

Andrew nodded. "Your men are best for the job," he agreed. He wondered if he, as a British officer, should allow a Zulu induna to take command, then shrugged. Jama knew the local conditions better than he did, and his men moved faster and quieter in the bush.

"How did we ever beat these lads, sir?" Kerr asked as two Abanonya warriors seemed to disappear among the undergrowth.

“We nearly didn’t,” Andrew said dryly. “Move forward, boys, but be careful.” He checked behind him and saw Stevens had knee-haltered the horses to prevent them from straying.

“We’re on foot from now on,” Andrew ordered. He knew he was losing the better view on horseback, but he was also less of a target.

The trail divided a hundred yards further on, with individual horsemen choosing different routes, so even Jama’s men found it harder to follow the main force. The joint force moved slower, jinking left and right, although always heading towards the mountain.

When one of the Zulus hissed a warning, Andrew gestured to his men to halt. He crouched behind a tree, watching a procession of ants march across the trunk, lost in their world. When he heard a rustle ahead, Andrew eased his finger around the trigger of his rifle. Leaves shivered around him, a shadow moved, and Ndleleni appeared behind Kerr with his *iKlwa* in his right hand.

Andrew turned, rifle ready, but Ndleleni gestured ahead, where Jama slid from the shade of a mountain aloe.

“There was one sentry, Lieutenant Baird,” Jama said. “Ndleleni dealt with him. There are more ahead.”

Jama gave a quiet order, Andrew signalled to his Dragoons, and they moved forward, step by slow step. Andrew held his Martini ready, ignoring the insects that whined and buzzed around his head. He could no longer see a single Zulu or any of the enemy. Andrew felt as if he was alone in the dense undergrowth, a lone human among the insects.

He glanced up, where a pair of vultures circled, with others joining them, watching the ground below in the hope of fresh meat.

These birds know humans are predators, and where we go, death follows. They clean up our mess.

Andrew moved again, sliding towards a man-sized rock, half seen amidst a tangle of vegetation. He heard a shout from ahead and threw himself down.

“*Ngadla*!” a Zulu shouted and then came a fusillade of shots. Andrew stood, glaring ahead as a dozen men broke cover in front of him.

Kerr was only three feet away, although Andrew had not known he was close.

“What’s happening?” Trooper Grey asked and fell, choking, as a bullet smashed into his throat.

“Grey!” Andrew shouted. He saw the rising smoke where the shooter was, aimed and fired, with Kerr a fraction faster. They moved forward together, with the other Dragoons following.

As the Dragoons and Abanonya advanced, the defenders melted away, sometimes after firing a final, defiant shot.

What are these people guarding?

Andrew heard a long scream, followed by Jama’s voice, rising in triumph. “*Ngadla*!”

He shivered, knowing that sound would haunt him for years.

“Come, Lieutenant Baird,” Jama shouted. “The way is clear.”

As Andrew moved forward, with the Dragoons at his back, the Zulus appeared from cover, having removed any threat in their path.

"The horns of the buffalo," Kerr said with a wry smile. "We were the chest moving forward, and the Zulus went around the flanks, surrounded the enemy, and then bang! The end."

Andrew nodded. "I know," he said. "I've seen them in action before." He remembered Abernethy's death at Isandhlwana and that young drummer boy hanging upside down.

No, we're allies now. Think of Mariana and forget the past.

They moved on with Jama's Zulus scouting in front and on the flanks. The hill rose above, nameless on the rough map, rugged, with dense forest covering the lower slopes. Above them, half a dozen vultures circled, waiting for the men to provide them with a kill.

"There," Jama said, crouching behind a tree with his Abanonya spread out on either side. "Can you smell it?"

Andrew twitched his nose.

Kerr nodded. "People and cooking," he said. "People have a distinct smell."

Andrew lifted his field glasses and scanned the mountain. He looked for anything that should not be there, such as a drift of smoke or a flicker of an unusual colour. He stopped, frowned, and handed the glasses to Kerr.

"Under that spur; see what you think."

Kerr looked and slowly nodded while Jama watched.

"I see something," Kerr said. "The ground is worn away halfway up."

"Like a path," Andrew said. He told Jama and handed over the field glasses. Jama looked at them in suspicion and passed them back. He shouted for one of his men, pointed to the hill and ordered him to check.

"Thank you, Jama," Andrew said. He formed his Dragoons into a defensive circle, knowing that Smith was a very wily campaigner.

The Zulu scout returned within the hour, giving Jama a lengthy report.

"What's happening?" Andrew asked.

"The enemy has a camp at the base of the mountain," Jama reported. "Many men, Zulu, Swazi, Basuto and white."

Andrew listened, thinking of such a force of renegades invading Inglenook. He thought about how terrified Elaine and Mariana must have been and what they must have suffered.

"Did your scout see a white woman?" Andrew asked. "A white captive?"

"He did not," Jama replied.

Am I wasting my time and the lives of my men? Did Smith murder Mariana and dispose of her somewhere?

Andrew shook away his doubts. "We'll attack them," he said. "We'll use the horns of the buffalo again."

The Zulu tactics are similar to Wellington's at Badajoz. Put in a frontal attack as a diversion and hit them from the rear,

Jama considered for a moment. "Your men attack from the front, and we'll act as the horns."

"That's what I thought," Andrew said. He respected this tall Zulu with the haunted dark eyes and knew he could grow to like him. "Good luck, Jama."

"Fight well, Lieutenant Baird," Jama responded.

When Andrew held out his hand, Jama looked at him curiously until Andrew explained it was a gesture of trust and friendship.

Jama smiled uncertainly and took the hand, and then they parted.

"We're the chest of the buffalo," Andrew explained to his men. "Jama and his Zulus are the horns. We don't know how many of the enemy there are or what defences they have, but Ashanti Smith is a seasoned campaigner, and his men are desperados, outlaws, and they'll fight like fury."

The Dragoons nodded.

"I don't expect they will grant quarter," Andrew said. "Whatever the outcome, don't leave any wounded behind."

When Jama divided his Abanonya in two and set off through the bush, Andrew waited a few moments.

"We're going in fast and hard, boys," Andrew said. "Shoot first, aim low and guard your backs."

The Dragoons nodded, with some looking understandably nervous.

Andrew checked his watch, closed the cover, and tucked it away inside his tunic. He touched the signet ring he had replaced on his right hand, wondered why his twice wounded leg was beginning to trouble him again and forced a smile. "Right, men. I'll take point. Keep your heads down, shoot to kill and follow me."

Andrew moved forward, crouched low, dodging from cover to cover. He knew Smith would have sentries out and expected the challenge from a man perched high in a tree.

"Halt! Who are you?"

Andrew fired on the sentry's final word, with his bullet knocking the man back from his perch. The sentry hung perilously from the branch for a moment, then plunged, screaming to the ground.

"They'll know we're coming now," Kerr said laconically.

"Increase the speed, boys!" Andrew ordered, reloaded, and pushed on. He heard the crackle of musketry ahead and saw muzzle flares among the trees, with the hideous zip of bullets clipping the branches above. Andrew's men responded, firing at the flashes, and dodging between the trees as they moved on.

Andrew heard a yell behind him and knew the renegades had hit one of his men.

A ragged volley sounded from their front, with the bullets crashing past the Dragoons and thumping into trunks.

"God!" somebody said. "There's thousands of them!"

"Sergeant Meek!" Andrew shouted. "Your section will give covering fire! My section will advance!" It was a drill he had copied from the Mounted Infantry. They moved forward in short rushes, running from cover to cover and firing whenever they saw a target.

Another of his men fell, crumpling without a sound, and Andrew instinctively knew he was dead. A bullet screamed past Andrew's head, smashed into the tree behind him and sprayed him with wood splinters. He ducked and fired, reloading before he saw the result of his shot.

"Halt!" Andrew ordered. "Meek! Advance your section!"

Sergeant Meek moved forward as Andrew's men opened rapid fire ahead. Meek's men moved quickly, ducking behind cover, firing, reloading, and zigzagging forward until they were ahead of Andrew.

"My section!" Andrew yelled and moved again, gradually closing with the renegades' camp.

When a bullet ripped past Andrew's head to burrow into the ground beside his right foot, he flinched and looked upward. Smith had positioned men in the trees, from where they could shoot down at the attackers.

"Damn, but he's good," Andrew said and swarmed up the nearest tree. He heard another crack and saw a bullet slice a long splinter of bark from the trunk an inch from his face.

If they kill me now, who will rescue Mariana?

Andrew positioned himself on the fork of a branch, shuddered when he saw a snake coiling away and concentrated on the renegades. He lifted his Martini to his shoulder, aimed at an enemy sharpshooter and fired. He immediately knew he had hit his target, reloaded rapidly, and searched for more of the enemy.

Two further renegades crouched in the trees, one pointing a Snider towards Andrew. He slid further up the tree to put the man off his aim, brought the Martini to his shoulder and fired.

Andrew immediately knew he had rushed the shot, and splinters flew above the renegade. The man, heavily bearded and with the brim of his hat turned back, grinned, and deliberately aimed as Andrew frantically loaded.

Andrew winced as he heard the sharp crack, and then the renegade stiffened and fell to hang with his left foot trapped in the fork of the tree.

"There's another one, sir," Kerr shouted from below.

"I see him," Andrew replied and aimed at the same time.

The final sharpshooter was a Basuto and was already trying to descend when Andrew fired. The bullet caught him in the shoulder, tossing him backwards. He yelled, dropped his Snider, and began to whimper. Kerr finished him with a shot to the head.

"Come on, men," Fletcher shouted and ran forward. Andrew slid down from his tree, loaded rapidly and joined his men as Meek's section provided covering fire.

With their outer defences breached, the renegades clustered behind a thorn-tipped palisade, waiting for Andrew's men to show themselves in the open space before their camp.

"Wait!" Andrew said. "Keep under cover." The men crouched behind trees and rocks, firing at any defender bold enough to show himself. Smith had cleared the ground for two hundred yards in front of the palisade, making any frontal attack nearly suicidal for a small party of men.

"Keep their heads down," Andrew ordered, thankful his men carried spare ammunition in their bandoliers. He peered at the dense bush around the clearing, hoping Jama was ready to attack.

The defenders met fire with fire, laying down a barrage of shots that ripped through the trees around Andrew's position.

"How many are there, for God's sake?" Meek asked, firing, and ducking down as a bullet tore through the bushes at his side. "They outnumber us, that's for sure!"

"Too many," Kerr said. He lay prone, took careful aim, and fired. "That's one less."

Andrew grunted. *Can I trust the Zulus not to let us down? Jama is probably thinking the same thing about us.*

"I want half the men to lay down fire," Andrew said. "Sergeant Meek, you remain here and cover me. I only want volunteers to follow me."

He took a deep breath, knowing nobody would volunteer. *Sorry, Mariana. I might not live to save you.* "I'll count to five and charge forward."

Up-and-at-'em Andy indeed. I wonder what my father would have done.

He loaded his Martini, checked his revolver was loaded and loose in its holster and shouted. "Elaine!"

CHAPTER 33

The first shot lifted a fountain of grass and dirt a foot from Andrew's leg. The second shot ripped through his tunic, unsettling him, so he swayed to the side, which caused the third bullet to whine past his ear. At that instant, the wound in Andrew's thigh opened and he staggered, gasping.

"Sir!" Kerr shouted. "Are you all right, sir?"

Fighting the sudden weakness, Andrew nodded and ran on, limping heavily as bullets kicked up the dirt at his feet. His erratic progress might have helped as he saw heads bob up behind the palisade, barrels of rifles and the bright muzzle flares as men fired at him. He jinked from side to side, surprised he was still alive.

That wound might have saved my life.

"Nearly there, sir!" Kerr shouted, and then they were clambering up rising ground towards the base of the stockade. Bullets hissed past Andrew's head to knock splinters from the barrier. He felt blood flowing from his thigh, glanced down and saw his trousers already wet with blood.

I'll have to finish this quickly or I'll be too weak to stand, let alone fight.

"Meek is keeping their heads down," Kerr encouraged.

Andrew nodded, slammed against the palisade, gasping, saw half a dozen men had joined him and thought it miraculous they had crossed the open ground safely.

The stockade was composed of roughly hewn stakes, between eight and ten feet tall and topped with a barrier of thorns. Andrew knew that delay was fatal and threw himself up. Ignoring the thorns that ripped into his hand, he dragged his body over and vaulted to the interior, yelling as pain sliced through his leg. He lay dazed for a second, hearing other men thumping beside him.

A lithe Swazi gaped at him, pointing and shouting. Andrew shot him without compassion, ducked and reloaded, ramming in a cartridge with shaking fingers.

"Mariana!"

Inside the stockade was like any other *imuzi* in southern Africa, with a collection of grass *izindlu* and a couple of more solid-looking European-style buildings. Half a dozen renegades faced Andrew, some armed with assegais and two with rifles.

"Come on then, you bastards!" Andrew roared. "Where's Mariana?" He lifted his Martini, feeling a wave of dizziness wash over him. He staggered, recovered, and forced himself to concentrate as the world seemed to sway.

"*Usuthu*!" Jama yelled and appeared over the barrier at the left, with Ndleleni on the opposite side. The Abanonya cascaded into the encampment, shouting.

Thank God, Andrew breathed with relief, heard a thump behind him and then the sharp crack of a Martini.

"With you, sir," Kerr snarled, reloading.

Other Dragoons joined them, firing at the retreating renegades as the Zulus pushed in from the sides.

"Come on, Dragoons!" Andrew shouted. In such a confined space, his rifle was too cumbersome, so he dropped it, drew his revolver, and staggered forward, gasping at the pain in his thigh.

With the Zulus closing in on the flanks of the camp and the Dragoons in front, the renegades could either fight or run out the back.

"Fight them!" Ashanti Smith emerged from one of the European-style houses with a Martini-Henry in his hands and two holstered pistols at his waist. Two green feathers adorned his broad-brimmed hat. "Send the bastards to hell!"

"Ashanti!" Andrew roared, limping forward as his vision cleared. "Where's Mariana?"

Even above the cacophony of shots and yells, Smith heard Andrew's shout. He swivelled to face him, lifting his rifle. "It's you, is it? What are you doing here, young Baird?"

"Where's Mariana?" Andrew repeated, pointing his revolver. He saw Ndleleni disposing of a fleeing Basuto with a single thrust of his *iKlwa*, and then Simpson appeared from the door of an *indlu*, staring open-mouthed at Andrew. Simpson hesitated for a moment as a Swazi woman grabbed his arm, then pushed her to the ground and tried to run.

"Simpson!" Andrew shouted, aimed, and fired. He felt the kick of the revolver in his hand and saw the bullet strike Simpson high in the right thigh.

"Don't kill him!" Andrew said as Jama saw the writhing man. "I want to talk to him." Jama ignored the order and plunged his *iKlwa* into Simpson's stomach, ripped it sideways and moved on.

"Where's Mariana?" Andrew stood twenty yards from Smith, swaying as the blood drained from his leg.

"You've changed," Smith said, holding his rifle at hip level. "You were as green as a lettuce when I met you. Now you're a soldier." He ignored the fighting as the Dragoons and Zulus wiped out his renegades.

"Where's Mariana?" Andrew repeated his question, walking slowly towards Smith with the blood squelching in his boot. "You murdered my girl."

Smith smiled. "She fought back," he said. "You flaunted her, Bairdie. You shouldn't have done that. I'll make a bargain with you; let me ride away, and I'll tell you where the sister is."

Andrew felt hatred surge over him as he thought of Elaine and the Maxwell household. About to refuse, an image of Mariana came to him. She was laughing and talking to Lancelot, discussing Tennyson and King Arthur.

"Where is she?" Andrew asked, and lurched to his left as his leg gave way beneath him.

Andrew was a fraction too late to see the triumph in Smith's eyes. Smith raised his Martini and fired at the same instant. Andrew saw the muzzle flare the exact second as Jama's thrown assegai landed in Smith's shoulder, jerking him back so the bullet rose high in the air.

Andrew ducked instinctively as Jama strode forward. Wordless, Jama smashed Smith over the head with his knobkerrie, stunning him.

"You saved my life, Jama," Andrew said. "Don't kill that man. I want to ask him about the missing woman."

Jama plucked his throwing assegai from Smith's shoulder and cleaned the blade. "No, Lieutenant Baird. He murdered my wives and stole my cattle."

Ndleleni stood beside Jama, with the other Zulus gathering, some with blood dripping from the blades of their *iKlwas*.

"I think the strange truce is about to end." Kerr aimed his Martini at Jama as Sergeant Meek and the Dragoons lined up, ready to fight.

"Wait," a hoarse female voice sounded from the nearest *indlu*, and the witch appeared. "Stand back, Jama and the Abanonya!"

Andrew was shocked to see the sudden fear on the proud warrior's faces as all three witches stepped in front of them.

"Put your rifles up, boys," Andrew ordered.

"Sir?" Sergeant Meek sounded worried.

"Do as I say." Andrew holstered his pistol.

The three witches faced Jama.

"Go, Jama," the leading witch said, flicking her gnu-tail wand at him. "Take the cattle from the kraal and go to Cetshwayo. Your job here is complete."

"That man murdered my family." Jama pointed to Smith.

The witch flicked her gnu-tail wand at Smith. "I want him for his bones," she said. "I've been waiting for you, Jama. Go now."

Jama turned, with his Abanonya at his back, and trotted from the camp without another word.

"Witch," Andrew said. "I am looking for a white woman."

The leading witch faced him with her eyes full of age and wisdom. She touched Andrew's wound with her gnu's tail, then pointed at the *indlu* from where she had come.

"The woman has been waiting for you," the witch said. "You take the woman and I take him." She lashed Smith with her gnu-tail. "He has an *abaThakathis* within him and his bones will make strong medicine."

"I want to kill him," Andrew said, as Smith began to stir.

"I need him alive," the witch replied. "We will take his bones while he lives. Take the woman."

"Sergeant Meek," Andrew said. "Take over. Search the huts for renegades and stray Zulus."

"Sir," Meek said, glanced at the witch, saluted, and stepped away.

Ducking under the low door, Andrew entered the *indlu*. The interior was dark, with a small fire giving minimal light, and he heard shuffling in the corner.

"Halloa!" Andrew drew his revolver. "Who's there?"

"Andrew? Is that you?" Mariana crouched in a corner with a bloody bandage over her left hand and her eyes huge.

"It's me," Andrew confirmed, feeling a mixture of relief and worry. "I've been searching for you all over Africa." He holstered his pistol and held out a hand.

"I know," Mariana said.

"How do you know?"

"The witch told me. She told me to have patience and wait, and you would arrive."

Andrew had not heard the witch return, but she crouched in one corner of the *indlu*. She touched first Andrew and then Mariana with her gnu's tail.

"We won't meet again," the witch said.

"That woman looked after me," Mariana said. "She said my man saved her life, so she would save me for him. All the Africans are petrified of the witches and didn't allow Ashanti Smith to touch me."

"What happened to your hand?" Andrew pointed to the bandage.

Mariana lifted her hand. "I had to pay a price," she said quietly. "I paid one finger, which the witches use for their spells."

Mariana's words were so casual that Andrew knew she was hiding her true feelings.

"Come on, Mariana." Andrew put an arm around her. "You're safe now. You can tell me your story later."

Tears filled Mariana's eyes as she clung to Andrew. "Come friends," she whispered. "It's not too late to seek a newer world."[1]

Andrew held her tight. He had not quoted Tennyson since he had buried Elaine. *We are in a new world now, Mariana and me.* He looked at her fondly as she repeated the phrase while they walked out of the kraal.

"It's not too late to seek a newer world."

What was the newer world he was entering? And was Mariana a part of it? He looked into her dazed, vacant eyes and knew he would be there if she wanted him. He had tried to escape his father's influence, yet his father's advice had kept the witches alive, and they had held Mariana for him. Fighting Jack Windrush was still with him, whether he liked it or not. *One can't escape one's past.*

"Come on, Mariana, let's create our own Camelot."

Mariana looked at him as they limped into the sunlight.

"Where are your warriors, Jama?" Cetshwayo asked. "Where are the men of the Abanonya?"

Jama indicated the thirty men at his back. "We are the Abanonya, my king."

Cetshwayo eyed the Abanonya. All carried at least one wound. Their eyes sunk into tired faces, and they were gaunt from lack of food and rest, but all carried their weapons. They were still warriors. "Where are the others, Jama?"

"They lie on the field of Isandhlwana, at Hlobane and Khambula, Intombi and oNdini," Jama said, remembering the raw courage of his Abanonya charging into the smoke. He could name each man and how he fell.

"The witches will cleanse you, Jama, and then go home," Cetshwayo said. "You have given enough. Find a wife and build a new life for yourself. I free you from any obligation to me."

Jama stood up. "*Bayete,* Cetshwayo, *inkosi. Bayete*."

As Jama left the king, with Jabulani at his side, Cetshwayo signalled for a woman at the back of the *indlu* to follow him. Thadie smiled and obeyed.

GLOSSARY

abaThakathis - spirits that infest animate or inanimate things.
Amabutho –Zulu regiment
Amaqhawe – young warrior
Amadlozi- ancestral guardian spirits
Amasi – meal of milk curds, a staple Zulu food
Ashantis – tribe and nation in what is now Ghana, West Africa.
Assegai – spear
Bayete – a royal salute
Boer – Dutch speaking settler in South Africa. The name means farmer.
Bundook – rifle, British army slang
Donga – wide ditch, often dry except during heavy rain
IKlwa – Zulu stabbing spear
Imuzi – African homestead, often wrongly termed a kraal
Imizi – plural of African homestead
Indlu – African house, built of locally sourced materials
IniKozikasi- Zulu great wife, often chosen for dynastic or family reasons.
Inkosi – chief or king.
Isicoco - a band of fibre sewn into the hair, coated with gum, polished, and worn as a mark of a married man
IsiDawane - a werewolf or vampire
Isigodlo – king's or chief's private enclosure
isiHlangu – Zulu war shield
Izindlu- plural of African house
Kaffir – nonbeliever; an Arabic word
Kloof – deep ravine
Knobkerrie – Zulu fighting stick with heavy knob at one end
Kop – prominent hill
Koppie – small hill
Kraal – enclosure for cattle
Kranz/Krantz – cliff face or crag
Laager – defensive formation of wagons, perfected by the Boers.
Mealie – maize
Muckle Cheviot – hill on the Scottish – English border
Nek – mountain ridge between two hills
Paythan – British pronunciation of the Pashtun people of northern Pakistan and eastern Afghanistan
Pont – flat bottomed ferry boat pulled across river by means of ropes.
Rooineck – redneck, a term of abuse the Boers used against often sunburned British soldiers.
Spruit – riverbed
Stoep - veranda
Ubaba- father
UmuTsha - a cord around a man's waist from which hung lengths of fur or cowhide.
Umzimbeet – native South African tree
Xhosa – group of related Bantu peoples in Southern Africa

THE SOUND OF BOER RIFLES

THE SOLDIER'S SON BOOK 2

For Cathy

British officers make the grand mistake of thinking their opponents are as stupid as themselves.
General Petrus Jacobus Joubert (attributed)

Only the dead have seen the end of war.
Plato (attributed)

Freedom is a noble thing.
John Barbour

GLOSSARY

Afrikaans: The language of the Boers.

Boer: Farmer; a descendant of the original Dutch settlers in South Africa.

Bok-bok: Child's game where children climb on top of each other until the lowest boy can no longer take the weight and the human structure collapses.

Burgher: For the purposes of this novel, Boer and Burgher are interchangeable.

Commando: A collection of Boers gathered for war. They gather by area and can be of any size from a dozen to thousands.

Donga: Marsh.

Dorp: Village, settlement, town.

Drift: Ford of a river.

Floreat Eton: "May Eton Flourish."

Galekas: A numerous tribe of Southeastern Africa.

Heliograph: Signalling device much used by the British army in the late nineteenth century. It works by reflecting sunlight.

Kopje: Isolated hill that rises from the plateau of the veld; often flat-topped.

Koppie: A small kopje.

Laager: A circle or defensive encampment of wagons.

Landdrost: A local government official.

Mampoer: Home distilled brandy, made from peaches or other fruit.

Mealie: Maize; corn.

Meneer: Mister, sir.

Morgen: A unit of land roughly equivalent to two acres.

Oom: Uncle; a term of respect used for older men.

Public: Public house, a term since shortened to pub.

Rand: Ridge.

Rooineck: Redneck; Boer term of contempt for a British soldier or settler, so-called because of their sunburned features.

Sawnie: Slang word for a Scotsman, particularly a Highlander, from the pronunciation of the common name Sandy or Alexander. By the end of the Nineteenth century, the term Jock had superseded it.

Scoff, Skoff: Food; the term became more popular during the Second Boer War, 1899-1902.

Shave: Nineteenth-century army slang for a rumour.

Slim: Clever, cunning.

Spruit: Water course.

Staatscourant: Boer newspaper.

Stoep: Veranda of a house, often used as a gathering place.

Swaddie: Slang term for a British soldier; now more often pronounced squaddie.

Taal: Nineteenth-century word for Afrikaans, the language the Boers spoke.

Taibosch: Tough bush.

Tante: Aunty; a term of respect used for older women.

Tarry-arse: Soldier's slang for a Royal Naval seaman.

Terai hat: A type of slouch hat.

Trek: Journey; the Great Trek was a mass exodus of Boers from British controlled Cape Colony northward into what became the Orange Free State, Transvaal, and Natal.

Veld: The high plateau that makes up much of the landscape of the Transvaal.

Veldcornet: Junior officer of a commando.

Vingertrek: Game of strength where men or boys interlock fingers and pull.

Vrou: Woman or wife.

PRELUDE

CHURCH SQUARE, PRETORIA, TRANSVAAL, SOUTHERN AFRICA.

12TH OF APRIL 1877

A flock of pigeons fluttered over the small crowd in Pretoria's Church Square, circled and split into two groups. The smaller group landed on one of the wilting trees, and the larger landed on the corrugated roofs of the low buildings. A single dominant male perched itself on the bare flagpole above the most prominent building. Busy with their own affairs, the pigeons ignored the people who slouched across the square, talking, smoking, and waiting for events with little apparent emotion. The noise increased when an elegant man alighted from a carriage, stretched his legs, and mounted a raised platform in the flagpole's shadow.

Twenty yards from the carriage, a man on a slow brown horse entered the square, dismounted, nodded to a friend, and lit a huge pipe. The bandolier across his chest was half empty, although the rifle in its holster beside his saddle was oiled and well cared for.

As the crowd increased, a uniformed man slowly hoisted a flag up the flagpole, with a slight breeze momentarily ruffling the material, revealing the multi-crosses of the United Kingdom. When the breeze died, the flag hung limp, hugging the pole. The pigeon on top preened itself and cooed to attract a mate.

"That's not our flag," the man with the brown horse commented as he joined a small group standing in the shade of a broad *stoep*. He pushed the black hair back from his eyes.

"That's the British flag," a broad-shouldered teenager informed him. He stroked his smooth face, dreaming of the day he would feel a man's beard.

"What's it doing here?" the older man placed his thumbs in his braces and glared upwards. "We are not in Victoria's Britain."

"No," the youth agreed. "We are not."

"I am Theunis Steenekamp," the older man introduced himself.

"Jan van Collier," the younger man lifted his hat politely. "We farm Nuwe Hoop Plaas in the western Transvaal."

"Ja. That is a good name," Theunis said. "A farm of new hope." He nodded. "We all had hope until the British arrived."

Jan did not reply as he turned his attention to the head of the square where twenty-five uniformed police sat their horses. The police watched the gathering nervously, with some fingering the carbines in their bucket holsters. Jan thought they expected an outburst of emotion or perhaps violence from the crowd. He watched as the elegant man cleared his throat before talking.

"Is that Shepstone?" Jan asked, peering over the heads of the crowd.

"Ja," Theunis stuffed more tobacco into his pipe, puffed out smoke, and watched from under the brim of his broad hat. "That's the British diplomat who wants to take our land from us." He shuffled further back into the shade of the *stoep,* folded his arms, and watched through narrowed blue eyes.

Sir Theophilus Shepstone KCMG had spent fifty-seven of his sixty years living in South Africa and was an acknowledged expert in native affairs. Now he stood before the Free Burghers of Pretoria in the *Zuid-Afrikaanse Republiek,* the South African Republic or the Transvaal, intoning the proclamation that annexed their nation to the British Empire.

The crowd listened, occasionally speaking to one another, many smoking so a thick blue cloud rose from the array of large pipes, bearded faces, and broad hats.

"Why do they want our Republic?" Jan asked as he folded his arms in imitation of the older man.

"The British want everything," Theunis replied, slowly puffing smoke from his pipe. "They think the Lord has given them the right to own the world."

"Listen," a grey-bearded man spoke over his shoulder. "The *Rooineck* is still talking. Let him tell us how they can solve all our problems." He tilted back his terai hat, with the leopard skin band catching the light. Jan wondered how old he was, with his skin tanned mahogany-dark by the sun and a myriad of wrinkles half-hiding his faded eyes.

The crowd subsided into silence as Shepstone lifted his voice. The mounted police stiffened in their saddles, with some still resting their hands on the butts of their carbines. An officer in front scanned the crowd, with his gaze passing over Jan's smooth face before he studied the weather-browned features of Theunis.

Jan could nearly taste the tension in the atmosphere. He glanced up as the male pigeon left its perch on the flagpole and flapped above Shepstone, its slow wings audible in the near silence. Somewhere nearby, a dog barked, high-pitched, with others joining in. The sound died away, leaving only Shepstone's educated voice to fill the square.

"What's the *Rooineck* saying?" Theunis asked, puffing out smoke. He held the police officer's gaze, refusing to drop his eyes.

"He's saying the *Zuid-Afrikaanse Republiek,* the Transvaal, is in financial and political chaos, and Great Britain will annex us for our own good," Jan said.

"That's kind of Great Britain," Theunis puffed more smoke. "They are a very charitable nation, annexing half the world for its own good and Britain's profit."

The sun cast a shadow from the flag, which fell on the small group of watchers on the *stoep.* Theunis and Jan were Boers with generations of African-born ancestors. A third man stepped beside them. He was very tall, with the skin peeling from his nose from the unaccustomed strength of the sun. This man stood straight, unlike the farmers, and listened to Theunis and Jan as much as Shepstone's speech.

"Now the *Rooineck* is saying Britain will cure all our ills while also looking after our external affairs," Jan said.

"I thought that's what he said." Theunis continued to puff at his pipe. He eyed the tall, red-faced stranger standing at his side.

"Then Shepstone said the Transvaal needed help because of the threat of the Zulus and other tribes."

Theunis nodded. "The Zulus are a threat," he agreed. "But we have defeated them before and can push them back. When the British come, they think they have the right to all the land we tamed with our blood and our sweat."

The tall man turned around. "Forgive me for interrupting a private conversation," he said, removing his hat to reveal cropped blond hair. Although he spoke in the *Taal,* his accent marked him as foreign. "I am Konrad Bramigan, a visitor to your nation." The broad white scar down his left cheek seemed to glow in the sun.

Theunis replied politely while eyeing Konrad with the suspicion he reserved for any stranger.

Konrad replaced his hat. "Not only the *Zuid-Afrikaanse Republiek* distrusts the British," he said. "You have powerful friends in Europe."

Theunis puffed more smoke from his pipe as he watched Shepstone pack his carefully prepared speech away. "That may be true, *meneer,* but Europe is far from the Transvaal." He removed the pipe from his mouth and surveyed the tall man. "Warm words may look good on paper, but they cannot remove the British. When they stole our lands before, we took to the wagons and trekked into the wilderness. Now, the British have followed us with pretended friendship to grab what the good Lord gave us." He packed more tobacco into his pipe with a calloused thumb. "We shall have to fight them."

Konrad smiled. "We can help," he said.

Theunis struck another match to relight his pipe, dropped the match, and extinguished it under the heel of his boot. "Who do you mean by 'we'? Tell me more, Konrad," he said as Jan listened in the background.

The man with the leopard skin band on his hat patted the breech of his rifle, turned his horse's head, and rode from the square. He did not look back.

CHAPTER 1

FORT AMIEL, NEWCASTLE, NATAL, SOUTHERN AFRICA.

AUGUST 1880

"Where is she?" Andrew demanded.

"Where is who?" The army hospital orderly viewed Andrew with total disinterest.

"I am Lieutenant Andrew Baird of the Natal Dragoons," Andrew introduced himself. "I am looking for Miss Mariana Maxwell. Where is she?"

"Oh, the lunatic," the orderly said. "We got rid of her."

"Lunatic? What? What do you mean, lunatic?" Andrew looked away for a moment to control his temper. "I'll ask again," he said, breathing hard. "Where is Mariana Maxwell? I left her in the garrison's care while I was on duty in Zululand."

The orderly shrugged. "Not in my care, mate. I'm here to look after injured and sick soldiers, not stray lunatics."

Andrew grabbed the orderly by the throat and began to squeeze. "I've killed Galekas, Zulus, and renegades, my friend. Adding you won't bother my conscience."

When the orderly began to choke and turn red, Andrew released him, straightened his jacket, and smiled. "Where is Miss Maxwell?"

The orderly drew in a ragged breath. "She's locked up. We had to put her in the guardhouse." He rubbed his throat and backed away when Andrew lifted his fists. "It was for her own good, sir! She attacked Corporal Biden and was thrashing about, rambling in her sleep, and disturbing the other patients." He stopped when he realised that he was talking to himself. Andrew had already left.

The red-coated sentry at the guardhouse looked up as Andrew strode toward him. "Where do you think you're going, chum?"

"Inside the guardhouse. Step aside, private," Andrew ordered.

"I don't think so, mate," the private moved to block Andrew's way, hefting his Martini-Henry rifle. "This is a military fort, and civilians don't tell us what to do."

"I am Lieutenant Andrew Baird of the Natal Dragoons."

"Sorry, sir. I didn't realise you were an officer." The private snapped to attention.

"No reason why you should," Andrew glanced down at his civilian clothes. "I believe you have a young woman confined in the guardroom. A Miss Mariana Maxwell."

"Yes, sir, we have a woman. She's a colonial lunatic who attacked a corporal." The private smiled. "Not that I blame her for that, sir."

"Let her out," Andrew ordered. "I'll look after her."

"If you say so, sir," the private said doubtfully. "You should have a letter of authority or some such." He looked around for an NCO or officer for advice.

"If anybody enquires, tell them I have her," Andrew said.

"Yes, sir." The private stepped aside. "This way, sir." He hesitated for a moment. "Be careful, sir. She's a bit erratic. She shouts and screams in her sleep, and we had to restrain her."

Andrew took a deep breath. "Take me to Miss Maxwell, Private."

Knowing her history, Andrew felt responsible for Mariana. Her family had owned a farm on the border with Zululand, and Andrew had intended to marry Mariana's sister, Elaine. However, when the Zulu War started, a group of renegades murdered the Maxwell family and kidnapped Mariana, holding her prisoner for months. Andrew had been part of a mixed rescue party of British, colonists, and Zulus.[1]

"Yes, sir," the private said. "This way, sir."

Major Charles Amiel and the 80th Foot had built Fort Amiel only four years previously, and it still felt raw and unfinished. The guardhouse was solid, dark, and unpretentious, with small cells intended for drunken or insubordinate soldiers rather than traumatised women. Mariana sat hunched on the wooden shelf that served as bed and seat, with heavy handcuffs weighing her slim wrists and a gag in her mouth.

She looked up when the door opened, staring at the incomers through wide, red-rimmed eyes. Tears had streaked grime down her face.

"Good God! What have you done to her?" Andrew pushed past the private. "Mariana! It's me! Andrew!"

Mariana tried to cower away, hugging the cold wall as Andrew stepped closer and gently unfastened the gag.

"Don't touch me!" Mariana held her manacled wrists defensively in front of her.

"It's all right, Mariana," Andrew knelt before the bench. "You remember me. Andrew Baird."

Mariana gasped and tried to fend Andrew off with wild swings of her arms. He inched back to reassure her.

"I won't hurt you," Andrew promised.

"I told you we had to restrain her," the private tried to excuse the manacles. "She scratched the corporal's face. He ordered the restraints, sir, not me."

"Where's the key?" Andrew demanded. He took hold of Mariana's wrists, frowning at the ugly marks where the harsh steel manacles had rubbed off her skin. "Has she not been through enough with the renegades without the British Army treating her as a criminal?"

"I'll get the key, sir," the private said and hastily withdrew.

"It's all right, Mariana. I'm here now." Andrew put a hand on Mariana's shoulder. "You're safe with me. We'll soon have you out of these things."

Mariana's eyes were huge, but she did not resist when Andrew held her.

"Do you recognise me, Mariana?"

She nodded, holding up her hands in supplication.

"We'll have the manacles off you soon," Andrew promised.

The cell was tiny, stinking of urine and stale human sweat. Andrew heard a prisoner in the next cell bawling drunkenly, swearing with a long string of obscene oaths.

"Just a few moments," Andrew said reassuringly.

"What's all this?" A skull-faced corporal banged open the door and appeared in the doorway. "Who gave you authority to come into my guardroom?" He glared at Andrew suspiciously.

"The Queen did," Andrew replied tersely. "I hold Her Majesty's commission. Do you?"

"No, sir," the corporal said, coming to attention.

"Then release this woman." Andrew saw two long scratches on the corporal's left cheek and hoped they stung. "Now!"

"I'll need authority," the corporal said.

"You have mine. Set her free," Andrew demanded, "or I'll have your stripes and ensure you spend the next year cleaning out the latrines. If anybody asks who ordered her release, tell them it was Lieutenant Andrew Baird of the Natal Dragoons."

"Yes, sir!" the corporal reached for the keys at his belt, unlocked the handcuffs, and stepped back, watching Mariana warily.

Andrew placed an arm around Mariana's thin shoulder. "Come with me, Mariana." He eased her off the bed as she rubbed her weeping wrists.

"It's the moon," the corporal muttered, retaining his distance as if he expected Mariana to lunge at him. "She must have slept under the full moon, and it's sent her mad."

"It's nothing to do with the moon, and she's not mad!" Andrew guided Mariana out of the guardhouse and through the fort, with passing soldiers staring at her.

A heavily moustached officer approached, frowning. "What are you doing with that woman? Who the devil are you?"

"I'm Lieutenant Andrew Baird of the Natal Dragoons, and I'm taking this lady where she can be treated with care and attention, not shackled like a criminal!" Andrew recognised the insignia of a major and added a belated "sir" while lifting his chin challengingly.

"That's Up-and-at-'em!" a private pointed to Andrew. "He fought all through the Zulu War from Isandhlwana to Ulundi!"

A small group of privates joined the speaker, staring at Andrew as though he were an exhibit at a showground. A smooth-faced youngster lifted his hand to wave until an older soldier hissed in his ear.

"That woman is dangerous, Lieutenant," the major nodded to Mariana. "She attacked one of my corporals."

"I'll take care of her, sir," Andrew pulled Mariana closer as she stumbled.

"If it were up to me," the major spoke through his unruly moustache, "I'd send her to Robben Island. They know how to deal with lunatics there."

Robben Island treated people with mental health problems. At one time, conditions on the island had been notoriously poor, and although they had improved significantly, the name still made people shudder.

"That won't be necessary, sir," Andrew said. "She's not a lunatic, just a woman who has been through a terrible experience. Excuse me." He eased Mariana past the sentry at the gate.

"That's Up-and-at-'em, I tell you!" the first private repeated. "He rescued that woman from a thousand Zulus."

Andrew hurried away from the fort before the tales grew even more exaggerated.

Andrew had rented a small house on the outskirts of Newcastle with a surrounding garden and a single soldier-servant. The garden was small, with a lonely Natal Krantz ash tree and a couple of patches of flowers. Andrew had no pretensions of being a gardener, but he did like to see the surroundings tidy, and a splash of green reminded him of growing up in Herefordshire and Berwick-upon-Tweed in the far-off British Isles.

"In you come, Mariana," Andrew opened the front door. "I've got a room ready for you."

The house was basic, for Andrew had few requirements. The bungalow boasted a square hallway with four doors opening off it. One door led to Andrew's living quarters, one to his bedroom, and another to a kitchen. The fourth room had been empty until Andrew converted it into a bedroom for Mariana.

"Go straight in, Mariana," Andrew ushered her inside. "I'll give you a quick tour." He smiled. "It won't take long as there's not much to see."

Andrew had bought a basic bed for Mariana, with a chest of drawers, a stool, a dressing table, and a mirror. When he glanced inside, the room looked spartan. He regretted his lack of experience with women and wondered if she wanted more.

"We can go into Newcastle and see what else you need," Andrew suggested as Mariana stood awkwardly inside the house.

"I get nightmares," Mariana spoke for the first time since leaving Fort Amiel.

"That's not surprising after what you've been through," Andrew told her.

Mariana stood at the open door without entering her room. "I didn't mean to hurt the corporal. I thought he was attacking me."

"He's a corporal of British infantry," Andrew said. "He'll hardly notice a couple of scratches. Look inside your room and let me know if you need anything."

She'll need more clothes. I didn't think of clothes.

Both looked up as Andrew's soldier-servant appeared. "This lady is Mariana," Andrew said. "She'll be staying in the house for a while. Mariana, this man is Trooper Briggs. He keeps the place clean and tidy and does the cooking."

"Good afternoon, Miss," Briggs was in his late twenties, with quiet eyes. He nodded to Mariana and stood to attention in the hallway.

Mariana said a shy hello and dropped her gaze. She remained within the doorway, her hands twisting together and her head bowed.

"You'll be safe here," Andrew told her. "I'll come home as often as duty permits, and Briggs will ensure you want for nothing."

"I might talk in my sleep," Mariana said.

"Your talking won't bother anybody," Andrew said. "I'm in the room opposite, and Briggs sleeps in the barracks."

Mariana looked at her hands. "I had nice nails," she said. "When I scratched the corporal, some soldiers held me down and cut them."

Andrew lifted her right hand. A careless soldier had crudely hacked Mariana's nails, some into the quick. He drew in his breath. "They'll grow again."

"I might attack you," Mariana said.

Andrew put her hand gently down. "I'll understand," he told her. He gestured for Briggs to move away and guided Mariana into her room, where she sat on the bed.

"You've been through hell," Andrew said. "I am no doctor, but I can imagine how you must be feeling. It will take time, Mariana, but you will get better." He tried to smile. "I promise you will get better."

Mariana nodded, her hands twisting together. "Yes," she said with no feeling in her voice.

"I found you a book," Andrew said. "It's a bit battered, but better than nothing." Reaching across the table, he handed her a book of poetry.

"Tennyson," Mariana said, a flicker of light in her eyes. She leafed through the pages, stopping at her favourite poem.

"A bowshot from her bower-eaves,
He rode between the barley-sheaves,
The sun came dazzling thro' the leaves,
And flamed upon the brazen greaves
Of bold Sir Lancelot."

"The Lady of Shalott," Andrew said. "You always loved that poem." *So did Elaine.*

"Thank you," Mariana held the book to her chest.

"Briggs will make some breakfast for us," Andrew said. He looked up as somebody knocked on the front door.

"It's an officer for you, sir," Briggs reported.

A young subaltern, burned raw by the sun, threw a smart salute. "Lieutenant Baird, sir. I have orders to bring you to General Hook."

"Who?" Andrew asked. The name was vaguely familiar, but he could not recall the context.

"General Hook, sir," the subaltern said. "He's on the staff."

Andrew glanced at Mariana.

"I'll be all right," Mariana intercepted his thoughts.

"I'll look after her, sir," Briggs said. "Unless you want me to accompany you."

"No," Andrew decided. "Stay here with Mariana. Ensure she is safe and feed her well."

"I will, sir," Briggs said. He lowered his voice. "She'll be safe with me, sir."

Andrew nodded. "I know she will, Briggs." He nodded to the waiting subaltern. "Give me a minute to change into my uniform, Lieutenant, and you can take me to this General Hook fellow."

ELDERLY, GREY-HAIRED, AND WITH A NEATLY TRIMMED BEARD, LIEUTENANT General Hook leaned back in his chair and swirled the contents of his whisky tumbler.

"Tell me what you know about the Boers, Lieutenant Baird."

"I don't know much about them," Andrew admitted. "I fought beside a few in the Frontier War and Zululand, but they kept themselves to themselves."

"Tell me what you *do* know about them," Hook insisted. His eyes were as wise and knowledgeable as time. He poured a generous measure of whisky into another tumbler and pushed it towards Andrew.

"They're tough, hardy, good horsemen and excellent shots," Andrew said, remembering Piet Uys and his commando during the Zulu War. "They're also very religious and family-orientated."

Hook sipped at his whisky without his gaze leaving Andrew's face. "That's the Boers' positive traits. Do they have any weaknesses?"

Andrew cupped his tumbler in his hand. "I found them stubborn," he said slowly. "And a bit moody and argumentative." He recalled Uys's commando leaving the war when the Zulus killed Piet. "They're not very disciplined. They could ride away on a whim if they decided not to fight."

"That's a good start," Hook said, swirling the contents of his glass. "Do you know how the Boers came to be in Africa?"

"No," Andrew shook his head. "I haven't given it a moment's thought. I presume they just settled here, like the Americans in the United States or the Australians in Australia."

"Then sit back and listen," Hook said.

Andrew sat back in his chair, hoping that Mariana was alright and wondering why a general from the staff was questioning him about the Boers.

Hook poured himself another drink. "The Portuguese were the first Europeans to round the Cape of Good Hope, although they called it *Cabo das Tormentas*, the Cape of Storms. The Dutch passed by on their way to the Spice Islands of the East, and in 1652, the Dutch East India Company decided to build a fort at the Cape."

Andrew nodded. "The Dutch have been here for over two hundred years, then, sir."

"They have," Hook said. "With Cape Town fort as a base, the Dutch East India Company allowed discharged employees, soldiers, and sailors to settle. These people were known as Free Burghers and expanded eastward into lands the local tribes, the Khoikhoi, or Hottentots, claimed. It was inevitable that the Dutch and Hottentots would clash, with the first war in 1659. When that trouble ended, the Dutch bought lands from the Hottentots, but despite everything being ship-shape and legal, there was more trouble in 1673 and again from 1674 to 1677."

When Hook paused, Andrew nodded again, tasting his whisky. "I see, sir. So, the Dutch, or the Boers, have had to fight for everything."

"You get my point, Baird," Hook said. "The name Boer only means farmer. The Dutch were always a stubborn people, and they've had to battle for every square mile of land they own, which is one reason why they don't want us to annex their country. While the Boers continued to expand into the interior of Africa, their Dutch homeland also fought a series of wars with England. The constant threat of an English attack on their colony forced them to enlarge the fort at Cape Town."

"The Dutch were fighting on two fronts then," Andrew said.

"That's one of the downfalls of Empire. What you colonise, you must also defend," Hook said. "To return to our Boer friends. Around 1690, three hundred French Huguenots, or Protestants, arrived, including a parcel of women. They merged with the Dutch, adding new vitality and skills in wine-making." Hook smiled. "I find it hard to associate Boers with something as sophisticated and subtle as wine, but they are. South African wine is as good as French, in my opinion."

Andrew smiled. "I've never tried it, sir."

"You should," Hook recommended. "The Dutch colony continued to expand, with the Dutch East India Company very much in command. They rigidly controlled immigration, trade, the law, and what the Boers could grow. The Company could also press any Burgher into their service."

Andrew raised his eyebrows. "That's a bit draconian, isn't it?"

"Some of the settlers thought so, too," Hook agreed. "While most Free Burghers were law-abiding and stolid, others were not. As you'll be aware, every colony and every nation contain a wild element, the frontiersmen, Cossacks, bushrangers, or what have you. These wild men push the boundaries and see what's over the next hill. On the fringes of the South African colony were the Trekboers, the wandering or nomadic farmers. They farmed cattle and sheep, skirmished with the local tribes, and were arguably the toughest, most religious, and most bloody-minded colonists in the world. When they faced danger, they formed groups of fighting men called commandos to retaliate against the tribes or raid their cattle."

"Like the old riding families of the Scottish Borders," Andrew said.

"Very similar," Hook agreed, "except with a deeper religious base. Company restrictions irked the Trekboers, so they pushed further north into the unknown depths of Africa. However, while the Trekboers had been pushing north, the Bantu, another group of people, had been travelling south from Central Africa. Around 1780, the two cultures, or peoples if you will, met at the Great Fish River, to the consternation of both."

"The Bantu?" Andrew repeated. "The Black tribes?"

"You met some of them," Hook said. "The Xhosa, Galeka, Zulu, Matabele and all the rest."

"I met some of them," Andrew agreed soberly.

"In 1795, when Europe was in turmoil with the French Revolutionary War, the Boers kicked out the Dutch East India Company and became even more truculent. They lived according to their version of the Old Testament, put the local Africans into slavery and disliked all forms of authority save their own."

Andrew finished his whisky and placed the tumbler on Hook's desk. "Interesting people, sir," he said.

"They are a race apart," Hook said. "Their attitudes and ideas have barely progressed from the seventeenth century." He smiled at Andrew over the rim of his glass. "I'd say the frontier Boers make the American frontiersmen look like amiable businessmen, but again, they have spent upwards of two centuries dealing with floods, drought, storms, and various warlike tribes."

"And us," Andrew said sagely.

"And us," Hook agreed. "We arrived in 1795, acting for the Prince of Orange, whom the French had forcibly ejected from Holland. We took over South Africa, put down a Boer rising and held the colony until 1802. You'll remember we were at war with Revolutionary France and her satellites at that time. In 1803, we handed control of the Cape back to the Dutch Batavian Republic."

Andrew nodded. He remembered the basics from his school days when his history teacher had lauded Britain's military victories and glossed over the defeats.

"When the Napoleonic War started shortly after, we retook control of the Cape." Hook smiled. "The commanding general was a namesake of yours, General David Baird. Any relation?"

"I don't think so, sir," Andrew said. "Although I don't know much about the Baird side of the family. My mother barely mentions her forbears."

"No? Pity." Hook smiled. "When the Napoleonic Wars ended, Great Britain retained the Cape and imposed decent laws. When we prohibited slavery, thousands of Boers protested by leaving the colony in what is known as the Great Trek. They headed deeper into Africa; some clashed with the Zulus in Natal; others found what they termed the promised land in the high veld, empty of people and suitable for farming."

"Were there no native tribes there, sir?" Andrew asked.

"Not at that time. The rise of King Shaka of the Zulus led to some ugly wars that depopulated much of the veld. The Boers occupied it with little trouble. They formed a couple of republics up there, the Orange Free State and the Transvaal, both beyond British control."

Andrew nodded. "I can't agree with all the Boers believe, certainly not their keeping slaves," he said. "But I can't fault them for wanting independence. Or for their courage and determination."

"Perhaps," Hook said, giving Andrew a look that combined suspicion and doubt. "We had a couple of skirmishes with the Boers in the 1840s, and Sir Harry Smith annexed the lands between the Orange and Vaal rivers, renaming the area the Orange River Colony. With those lands safely under our belt, we signed the Bloemfontein Convention, declaring we had no interest in the Transvaal, the lands beyond the Vaal, which remained under Boer control."

"The Boers do the hard work, and we take over," Andrew murmured, wondering why a general was giving him a history lesson. He hoped that Mariana was all right.

"Careful, Baird, or I'll think you have divided loyalties," Hook warned.

"It's always best to see both sides of the argument, sir," Andrew said. "That way, we can determine what the opposition may do." *That is one lesson my father taught me.*

Hook raised a doubtful eyebrow. "I don't work like that," he said.

"As you wish, sir," Andrew thought it discreet to say no more.

"Naturally, there were complications between the British colonies and the Transvaal Boers," Hook said. "About eight or nine years ago, a prospector found diamonds in Griqualand West, where the Griquas live. They are another unique people with Boer and Khoekhoe ancestry. Harry Smith granted them some autonomy in 1848, but things change."

Andrew nodded. "Yes, sir."

"As Griqualand West is north of the Vaal, the Boers claimed it, but the Griquas sought British protection." Hook's eyes were level as he stared at Andrew. "The Boers' history of slavery and bad treatment of the natives counted against them, you see."

"I see, sir," Andrew thought it diplomatic to agree.

"An arbiter oversaw both positions and agreed with the Griquas, and in 1871, Britain annexed Griqualand West. We made it into a Crown Colony and bought the diamond rights from the Griquas for the princely sum of a thousand pounds a year."

Andrew grunted. "We cheated the Griquas, then." He glanced at the clock on the wall behind Hook's desk. *Mariana has been alone for nearly three hours now.*

"They had our protection against the Boers," Hook reminded him. "Both sides benefitted."

Andrew nodded. "Yes, sir."

"By 1877, the Transvaal was in difficulties," Hook said. "The state was bankrupt, the Boers were already fighting the Pedis and were on the verge of war with the Zulus, the most powerful tribe in South Africa," he looked up, "there's no need to tell you about the Zulus."

"No need at all, sir," Andrew agreed.

"Boers and Zulus argued about a parcel of land on their border," Hook explained. "A British boundary commission agreed with the Zulus, but added they wouldn't get the land back from the Boers until they disbanded their army."

"Yes, sir," Andrew nodded.

"The Zulus refused to lose their army, and the dispute continued. We annexed Transvaal, the so-called *Zuid Afrikaanse Republiek*, to save it from the Zulus and bankruptcy," Hook said. "Sir Theophilus Shepstone and twenty-five mounted police announced the annexation, and the Boers seemed to accept the fact. As you know, we hope to confederate all the disparate colonies in Southern Africa into one cohesive unit."

"Yes, sir," Andrew said.

"You might not be aware that there is an outside influence," Hook added steel to his voice. "We believe that Prussia, or the German Empire as it is now, is interested in grabbing the Transvaal for itself. The Germans and the Dutch are very similar people in many ways."

"I didn't know the Prussians were involved, sir," Andrew said. "That alters the situation."

"Over the last twenty years, the Prussians have defeated the Danes, the Austrian Empire, and the French," Hook reminded. "They are now the dominant military power in Europe and are looking to expand overseas. They want colonies, a place in the sun, and the only places remaining for them are in the Pacific and Africa."

Andrew nodded. "Their presence in Africa could complicate matters. We already have some friction with the Portuguese in southeast Africa, and God knows what will happen around the Suez Canal."

Hook grunted. "We're keeping a careful eye on Suez, but our attention is now on southern Africa." He poured himself more whisky. "Do you want another?"

"No, thank you," Andrew said.

"Very wise of you. It's a bad habit." Hook placed the decanter on the sideboard. "Now, to return to business. We have not helped our cause in the Transvaal by defeating the Zulus. The Boers needed our protection while the Zulus remained a threat, but now we have removed that menace."

"I see, sir." Andrew wondered where Hook was headed.

Hook's smile lacked humour. "With the Zulu menace gone, I fear the Transvaal Boers are again discussing independence." He swirled the whisky in his glass. "The situation has echoes of North America after we defeated the French. The colonies there no longer needed British protection and kicked us out."

Andrew nodded. "They did," he agreed. "With French, Dutch, and Spanish help."

"That's right," Hook said. "And Prussia may decide to help the Boers."

"Do you think the Boers will fight for independence?" Andrew asked.

"The Boers have already sent a delegation to London to ask for their lands back."

Andrew nodded. "I can't see the government agreeing to that."

"Nor can I," Hook agreed. "But I have heard the Prussians already have somebody in the Transvaal working with the Afrikander Bond." He waited to see Andrew's reaction.

"I've heard of them, sir," Andrew said. "The Afrikander Bond is a society of extreme Boers across South Africa. They want to unite all the South African colonies and lands under Boer control."

"That's correct," Hook sipped at his whisky. "Now imagine the Afrikander Bond with Prussia pulling the strings, and the diamonds of Griqualand, the gold of the Transvaal, and the strategic position of Cape Town under Bismarck's control." He leaned forward. "I don't care a twopenny damn if the Boers get their independent state on the opposite side of the Vaal. We can monitor them and control the worst of their excesses. I do care if the Prussians get control." He held Andrew's gaze with eyes that were suddenly basilisk-hard. "There's trouble in the wind, my boy, and I want you to tell me in which direction it's blowing."

CHAPTER 2

"Me, sir?" Andrew asked.

"You, sir," Hook said, with his gaze seeming to penetrate Andrew's mind. "You did good work in the Zulu War; you look like a colonial, ride like a colonial, and can talk like a colonial."

When Andrew said nothing, Hook continued. "I've known your father for years and discovered his talent for cloak-and-dagger missions. I hope his son has inherited the same skills."

That's how I recognised General Hook's name. He worked with my father, but I am my own man, not a copy of my father.

"I'm not even a proper soldier, sir," Andrew protested. "I was in the police, remember, and the army dragooned us into becoming soldiers."

"I believe you hold the Queen's Commission," Hook said.

"I do," Andrew agreed cautiously.

"Then you are as much a soldier as Lord Roberts, Sir Garnet Wolseley, or Fighting Jack Windrush."

Andrew grunted at Hook's use of his father's name.

General Hook grinned. "Now that that's cleared up, here's what I want you to do."

Andrew took a deep breath. "Yes, sir."

"I want you to enter the Transvaal as an observer, Captain."

"I'm a lieutenant, sir," Andrew reminded him.

Hook opened the top drawer of his desk, withdrew a thick envelope, and tossed it to Andrew. "Read the contents later. Her Majesty has seen fit to promote you to Captain. Congratulations."

Andrew stared at the envelope. "Thank you, sir." *I am now a captain.*

"No reason to thank me. Redvers Buller recommended your promotion."[1]

Hook continued. "In the Transvaal, you will wear civilian clothes and talk to the Burghers. I want to know how the people feel; I need to understand their mood. You speak the *Taal,* don't you?"

"A little, sir," Andrew admitted, stunned by his unexpected promotion.

"You'll need more than a little. Learn as much as you can." Hook tapped his fingers on his tumbler. "Do you know anybody who is fluent in the language?"

"I am sure someone from the Natal Dragoons will be fluent, sir," Andrew said.

"Find that someone," Hook ordered, "take him with you and bring me back intelligence about the Burghers across the Vaal."

"Yes, sir," Andrew said.

"You leave in two days," Hook said with a sudden grin. "Let's see if you can fill your father's boots, Captain Baird."

Briggs will have to cope with Mariana.

ANDREW PULLED LANCELOT TO A HALT, REMOVED HIS HAT, AND WIPED THE sweat from his forehead and face.

"Are you all right, Lance?" He patted the horse's neck and gave him a drink of water. He had known Lancelot since his first campaign against the Galekas, and the Kabul pony had never let him down. Lancelot was smaller than most British officers' horses and lacked speed. However, he possessed immense stamina, was as surefooted as a goat, and would continue when more spirited animals had long since given up.

Trooper Mark Kerr halted a respectful distance behind Lancelot.

Andrew looked around at the endless vista of the veld. In the nearly four years since he first arrived in South Africa, he had experienced many landscapes. He had seen the sunlit vineyards of the Cape, the hills of Transkei, the thousand grassy hills of Zululand, and the array of wildflowers of a Great Karoo spring. The austerity of the high veld was unlike any of these places.

Andrew felt a strange fascination for the veld. He found the idea of boundless space liberating, with the vast arc of the sky above and the long bare plateau stretching to a limitless horizon. He and Kerr could see a *kopje* chiselled against the sky in the early morning, ride towards it all day and feel no closer in the evening. The air was so clear it enhanced vision and confused men more accustomed to the misty atmosphere of the British Isles.

Yet Andrew knew there was more to the veld than mere space and freedom. There was some intangible magic in this landscape. Used to the grassy hills of the Borders, Andrew sought the solace of green in the sweeping array of dun, brown, and yellow. He felt relief when he saw the green line of mimosa trees marking a river valley, promising welcome coolness and water for horses and riders.

"How are you, Kerr?" Andrew asked.

"All right, sir, thank you," Kerr replied.

Andrew replaced his hat, lifted his field glasses, and examined the circle of the horizon. "We'll spend the night at that river course," he said. "And reach the next town tomorrow morning."

"Yes, sir," Kerr said.

They moved on, avoiding the conical red ant hills, four feet high and alive with insects. An ant bear watched them for a second from the security of its den and retired to await the cold of the night. A quarter of a mile further, they came to the communal circle of a meerkat family.

"Ride carefully here," Andrew warned, knowing the ground beneath the meerkats would be honeycombed with tunnels which a horse's hooves could easily collapse. Andrew was wary as Lancelot picked his way around the meerkats' domain and breathed more easily when they reached solid ground.

"The veld has hidden hazards, sir," Kerr said as they headed northwest. "Even the most charming animals can prove dangerous, and with *dongas* and *sluits* and stray predators, it's surprising that the Boers ever made this place their home."

They rode on slowly and steadily until Kerr sniffed the air. "I smell people, sir. We must be nearing a settlement."

Andrew nodded. The clear air of the veld had improved their sense of smell, so the distinctive scent of people carried to them on the wind. "Here we go again, Kerr. You know the drill."

"Yes, sir. We're horse traders and itinerant hunters."

Andrew's command of the *Taal* had improved over the last few weeks, but he knew he needed to be fluent. He allowed Kerr to do most of the talking as he listened and took mental notes. As they rode closer, they saw the *dorp* – the town – in the distance, with the details becoming clearer.

Andrew stopped at the outskirts of the *dorp*, allowed the dust to settle, and looked around. Used to the settlements of Cape Colony and Natal, he was no longer surprised by how basic everything looked.

"What's this place called, sir?" Kerr asked. "We've already been to Zwagershoek, Coetzeespos, Honingfontein, and Melkrivier." He reminded Andrew of the towns they had visited.

Andrew consulted his map. "This place is called Vryheidburg," he said. "It doesn't look much different from the others."

"Freedomburgh," Kerr translated. He looked around. "All these high veld towns look the same to me."

To Andrew, it seemed as if a blindfolded politician had jabbed a finger on a blank map and decided to place a village where his nail scored the parchment, for he could think of no other reason for Vryheidburg's existence. The village inhabited a barren stretch of veld no different from any other. The streets were rectangular, without any aspirations of architectural style, beauty, or grace, and held buildings that the owners might have erected in a day or two. The main roadway was broad, lined by small gum trees that wilted under the constant assault of an unrelenting sun, while the houses were single-storied and roofed with corrugated iron.

Andrew compared the settlement with the ancient villages of Northumberland, the Scottish Borders, or Herefordshire with their varied architecture, ancient churches, castles, and cobbled market squares. Vryheidburg did not gain by the comparison, although he admitted the British contrast between rich and poor did not exist in any of the *dorps* he had visited.

"It's easy to forget how new these places are," Andrew said as they rode into the town. "When the Boers rolled their wagons here only forty years ago, they found nothing except the empty veld. No villages, no roads, nothing. Not even a human being."

"No wonder the Boers thought it was the promised land," Kerr said.

Andrew patted Lancelot's neck. "Let's go and see what the people think," he said.

Kerr nodded. "Yes, sir. I doubt they'll be any different to the last lot."

"Nor do I," Andrew agreed with a wry smile. "Try to remember not to call me sir here. We're meant to be civilians."

"Yes, sir," Kerr agreed. "It's not easy calling you Andrew."

"Call me Baird," Andrew advised, "at least until we're back in uniform again."

"Yes, sir," Kerr agreed.

As usual in the Transvaal's *dorps*, Vryheidburg's stores had a stone frontage with the name above the door. The side roads met the central street at right angles, with orange and purple foliage covering the older houses and men lounging on long cane chairs on the *stoeps*, watching the two strangers.

Andrew and Kerr walked their horses slowly along the main street, with the hollow thud of the hoofbeats breaking the pressing silence. A lazy dog lifted its head from its paws, surveyed them briefly, slow-wagged its tail and returned to its daytime slumber.

"Not much happening here, sir," Kerr murmured. "Look, there's the weekly excitement."

An ox-wagon lumbered through the village, with the driver emitting a long, yodelling yell. Andrew watched the driver expertly handle his long whip, listened to him address each of his oxen by name and admired his skill at manoeuvring the wagon and team up one of the side streets.

"Is there any point in stopping here, sir?" Kerr asked.

"We'll talk to these men, Kerr."

Andrew pulled his horse past a couple of men deep in conversation on a shaded *stoep*. "Good evening, *meneers*," he said, lifting his hat.

Both men politely stopped talking to return Andrew's greeting. "Good evening, *meneer*," the older of the two indicated an empty chair on the *stoep*. "Join us." He clapped his hands to summon a servant and asked Andrew what he wanted to drink.

"Coffee, please," Andrew said. He had learned that the Boers were mainly temperate people.

When a servant brought the coffee, they drank silently as the men on the *stoep* appraised Andrew and Kerr. A pair of black-and-white birds flew past, with nothing else disturbing the peace of the *dorp*.

"*En wat over u, meneer?* And what surname do you bear, sir?" The older man eventually asked Kerr, the older of the two strangers.

"I am Mark Kerr, and this gentleman is Andrew Baird," Kerr introduced them both, and they shook hands, raising their hats politely.

"And your business in the *Zuid-Afrikaanse Republiek*, *meneer*?" the older Boer asked, courteously but with steel behind the words.

"A little bit looking for horses," Kerr said, "and maybe a touch of hunting thrown in."

The Boers glanced at the rifles both men carried beside their saddles. "Hunting?" the younger man smiled. "You're twenty years too late, *meneer*, if you want to hunt here. Maybe try the low veld." He sipped at his coffee, waiting patiently for a response.

"We might do that," Kerr told him solemnly.

Andrew had tried to follow the conversation. "We were a bit worried crossing the Vaal," he said slowly. "We were not sure what kind of reception British settlers would get here."

The older Boer removed his pipe from his mouth and contemplated Andrew before he replied. "That depends on what sort of British settler you are," he said at last. His smile was slow and genuine.

Kerr smiled in return. "This is good coffee, *meneer*. What do you mean?"

The older Boer nodded gravely. "Ja, we make good coffee in our land north of the Vaal. Our land." He paused to allow the words to sink in. "If the British come as friends, then we will be friends, but if they come to tell us what we can and cannot do in our land, then we will not be friends."

"The British come to help you," Andrew said.

"No," the younger Boer shook his head, smiling faintly. "The British come to help themselves." He placed his coffee cup on the faded wood of the *stoep*. "I do not mean you, *meneer*. I mean your government and your officials. Your settlers here are much like us, but your country wants to control everybody and everything. Attitudes like that are not welcome in our land." He glanced meaningfully at the rifle that leaned against the door.

Andrew nodded. He had heard the same sentiment expressed across the scattered *dorps* and farms of the Transvaal. The Boers mixed genuine hospitality with a stubborn refusal to accept British authority. "Thank you, *meneer*," he said. "I have heard others voice the same opinion."

The older Boer smiled again. "Visit Krugersdorp, *meneers*," he said. "You might learn something of interest there." He raised a hand. "Go with God, and I wish you success in buying the horses you have not mentioned again and hunting over land already cleared of much of its game." He raised his hat in a polite dismissal.

"Thank you, *meneer*," Kerr said. "And thank you for the coffee and your advice."

"These people are sharper than we believe," Andrew said as they rode away.

"Yes, sir. That old fellow worked us out in minutes. He told us everything we wanted to know."

Andrew nodded. "He told us the Boers' argument is not with individuals but with the British government trying to control them." He gave a rueful smile. "I would think that many people across the world would echo that."

"Probably, sir, even though we bring civilisation, order, and progress?" Kerr looked across to Andrew as they rode out of the dorp into the vast spaces of the veld.

"Even so," Andrew said. "In my experience, people wish to be left alone with their own culture. What we call progress, they call interference. Maybe we should leave people to their slavery and squalor."

"Maybe so, sir, but the slaves might disagree. Where are we going next?"

"Krugersdorp, as the old fellow suggested," Andrew said. "That seems to be an interesting town."

Krugersdorp, Transvaal, eighth of December 1880.

Andrew stood at the fringes of the crowd, trying to count the people. Most were farming men, the ordinarily taciturn, soberly dressed denizens of the veld, together with a scattering of women in their poke bonnets and a few better-dressed townsfolk. Andrew estimated at least eight thousand people were present, with the majority carrying long rifles and bandoliers of ammunition.

"There's an impressive number of people here, sir," Kerr murmured.

"There is," Andrew agreed. "The size of the crowd alone proves the Burghers' strength of feeling. We'd best keep quiet and listen to the Burghers' – the Boers' – point of view."

"Yes, sir," Kerr agreed.

The men gathered around a raised *stoep*, which acted as a stage for a procession of speakers, jostling for space, raising their hats politely yet arguing with fierce intensity. As with any gathering of Burghers, some men made long speeches, while others merely listened.

Most speakers argued for a return to independence, reminding the audience of the Great Trek, their struggles with the Zulus, Basutos, Matabele, and the land itself.

"We lived our choice of life until the British came," a neat-bearded man said. "They imposed their rules and followed us when we trekked away. We only want the British to leave us alone."

Most of the crowd agreed, with some voicing similar sentiments with much more detail. Andrew listened to the Burghers' complaints, and although he could never agree to their acceptance of slavery, he thought the British had been high-handed in incorporating them into the Empire. Man after man gave a passionate speech about returning Boer leadership to the Transvaal. Andrew listened, aware of the desire for independence yet surprised nobody voiced any hatred of the British.

As one passionate speaker followed another, Andrew knew he was witnessing the rebirth of a Boer republic.

"General Hook was correct," Andrew murmured to Kerr. "There is trouble in the wind."

Kerr puffed smoke from his pipe and surveyed the crowd from under the brim of his broad hat. "I can't argue with that, Baird. These men don't look the type to meekly allow us to take over their country."

Andrew ran his gaze over the thousands of men with grim, bearded faces and hard bodies. "No, they don't," he agreed.

A tall man slumped onto the stage, with dark hair spilling from underneath his hat to his neck and shoulders. "My name is Theunis Steenekamp," he thundered. "We need more than the *Zuid-Afrikaanse Republiek*. We should reclaim all the land the British have stolen from us from the Cape to the Limpopo River."

"There's one of the Afrikander Bond Boers now," Kerr said softly.

Andrew nodded. "I can't see even Gladstone agreeing to relinquish such a strategic location as the Cape."

Kerr smiled. "Not even Gladstone," he agreed.

William Gladstone was the British Prime Minister, a man notably averse to imperial adventures and wars.

Some of the gathering cheered at Theunis's words. Others stood in silence, smoking or waiting to hear more, while a few muttered their disagreement. Andrew noted one man standing at the edge of the crowd.

"That fellow there," Andrew murmured to Kerr. "Don't look now. He's a tall man, standing like a soldier. He's no more a Boer than we are, maybe a bit less."

"Less?" Kerr removed his pipe to add tobacco, dropped it, and scrabbled to pick it up, looking sideways at the man Andrew indicated. "I see the fellow you mean."

"What do you think?" Andrew asked while Theunis delivered a long speech. Andrew could understand about half the words, but the spirit was evident.

"He must be the only Boer in Africa to stand at attention like a Guardsman," Kerr said. "I'm not sure about that scar down his cheek either."

"That's what I thought," Andrew said. "It looks like a duelling scar; the Prussians have a tradition that gives them more honour if they have such a scar. Let's move a little closer."

As they inched through the crowd, Theunis closed his speech with a rousing call for unity. "We are one people!" He announced in language that even Andrew could understand. Theunis lifted his arms in a gesture that Andrew found vaguely disturbing. "First, we shall get freedom for the *Zuid-Afrikaanse Republiek* and then the Orange Free State. We shall unite the Boer people across the whole of Southern Africa!"

The tall, scarred man led the applause, clapping with his hands in the air.

"Speak to the tall fellow," Andrew urged Kerr. "Ask him his name."

Kerr walked towards the sunburned man. "*Meneer*," he said, raising his hat. "I think we share similar views about the unity of southern Africa."

The tall man inclined his head slightly. "Ja," he said. "The Boer people should unite."

"Unity is best," Kerr agreed. "We are from Natal. What surname do you bear?"

The man hesitated before he replied. "I am Konrad Bramigan," he announced. "A recent immigrant from the German Empire."

"I hope you settle well in the Republic," Kerr said solemnly, shaking the man's hand. He noticed Andrew gesturing to him. "Good day to you, *meneer*," Kerr lifted his hat politely and walked away.

"The Burghers are voting for political representatives," Andrew said. "We'd better back off a little, or somebody will count us as part of the Afrikander Bond." They stepped away while Konrad moved further into the crowd.

"The fellow calls himself Konrad Bramigan," Kerr said quietly. "He claims to have immigrated to the Transvaal from Germany."

"Well done, Kerr," Andrew said.

The candidates stood in a row, looking more like farmers at an agricultural fair than men hoping to recreate a nation against the wishes of an expanding empire.

An elderly man invited the people to vote, shouting the candidates' names one by one. Andrew was surprised at how orderly the crowd was as they selected three leaders. One was named Paul Kruger, and the others were Piet Joubert and Marthinus Pretorius.

"That's that, then," Andrew said. "The Transvaal has decided it wants independence."

"Yes, sir," Kerr replied.

"Let's see what Gladstone does next," Andrew said.

As the Burghers cheered, some waving their rifles and others their hats, Andrew decided he would be safer elsewhere and slid away. Two men stopped to shake his hand, smiling as if voting in new leaders had completed the business.

"What will Shepstone say to that?" one man asked as he raised his hat. "What will Shepstone say?"

"I don't know," Andrew replied honestly.

"He will say we are only backveld Boers who know nothing," the man had quiet blue eyes, with three mature sons standing at his back. "Then he will send the *Rooineck* soldiers to bring us back into the Empire." He nodded. "Ya, that is what he will do. And soon after, he will learn how Boers defend their land."

"The British Empire is very powerful, with tens of thousands of soldiers," Kerr reminded.

"Let them come," one of the man's sons said. He touched the rifle slung over his shoulder. "We shall send them back." He smiled as if he liked the sound of his words. "We shall send them back."

"Excuse us, *meneer*." Lifting his hat, Andrew ushered Kerr away.

When they left the crowd to their celebrations, Andrew mounted

Lancelot. "Come on, Kerr. We've seen and heard enough to deduce the Boers' mood."

"Yes, sir," Kerr replied. "If we stay much longer, the Burghers will recruit us into a commando or shoot us as British spies."

CHAPTER 3

General Hook placed Andrew's report on the desk. "Were you present at Krugersdorp?"

"Yes, sir," Andrew said.

"What was the mood of the people? Tell me verbally," Hook demanded.

Andrew replied immediately. "Determined, sir. They seemed angry that Britain interfered with their country."

Hook leaned back in his chair. "All the people I sent into the Transvaal found the same thing," he said. "The Transvaal Boers seek independence."

"That seems to be the prevailing mood," Andrew agreed. "Most just wanted us to leave them alone with their farms. A few seem to belong to the Afrikander Bond. The Bond men spoke loudly, but I am not sure they were the majority."

"This Prussian fellow you met, Konrad Bramigan," Hook tapped the paper. "What did you think of him?"

Andrew thought for a minute before replying. "I saw him supporting an Afrikander Bond candidate. He stood like a soldier, and when Kerr shook his hand, his palm was too soft to be a farmer."

"He admitted to being German?" Hook asked.

"He claimed to be a German immigrant," Andrew said. "I would say he emphasised his origins."

Hook grunted and shifted in his seat. "I'll pass his name to my people in the Transvaal. He could be the Prussian spy or a genuine immigrant trying to fit in." Hook's smile lacked humour. "You and I know recent converts are often the most enthusiastic."

Andrew nodded. "That's possible, sir."

"We'll keep an eye open for him," Hook said. "Now get back to your quarters, Baird. I may need you again. Dismissed."

❄

WHEN ANDREW RETURNED TO HIS BUNGALOW, MARIANA WAS SEWING THE hem on a skirt. She stood up, smiling. "Welcome home," she said. "I'm glad you're back."

"I'm glad to be back," Andrew said, sitting down. "I'll have to see how the Dragoons are getting on without me, but they can wait until tomorrow."

"Are you staying here tonight?" Mariana asked.

"Yes," Andrew said. "I'm staying here tonight." The house was familiar, but it was not home. *Maybe a soldier never has a home, only a place to sleep and eat. Perhaps that is why so many army officers retire to little villas in quiet British towns, tend their rose gardens, and sit outside, nodding benignly to everybody who passes. They have no other notion of a home life.*

"Good," Mariana remained on her feet, sewing in her hand.

"Sit down, Mariana," Andrew said. "How are you?" He saw Mariana's eyes were less vacant, with a renewed spark. "You seem a bit better. Has Briggs been looking after you?"

Mariana nodded. "Mr. Briggs is a good man," she said. "But very hard on his socks. I've darned three pairs since you went away." She sat down and recommenced work with her needle.

"He's meant to look after you, not vice versa," Andrew said.

"He does his best," Mariana said, concentrating on her sewing. She looked up suddenly. "Do you want me to go home?"

Andrew thought of Inglenook, the farm where Mariana grew up. "Do you want to go back?" he asked.

Mariana shook her head. "No," she whispered the word. "But I will if you think I'm in the way."

"I don't think you're in the way," Andrew said. "You can stay as long as you like."

"I don't want to return," Mariana admitted. "I get nightmares about Inglenook."

"Then you won't go back," Andrew reassured her. "Do you want to talk about the bad dreams?"

Mariana looked away, shaking her head.

"Can I help?"

"I want to see my parents' graves. And my sisters," Mariana said quickly. "Are they buried at the farm?"

"No," Andrew said. "When you were in hospital, I had them moved to a cemetery in Newcastle. I didn't think you'd want to return to Inglenook." *I think the sight would push you over the edge into total madness.*

Mariana shook her head. "I can't," she said. "I'm sorry, Andrew, but I can't return to Inglenook."

"Nobody will blame you for that," Andrew said. "I'll take you to your parents' graves tomorrow."

"Will you?" Mariana asked. "I thought you wanted to see your Dragoons."

"I doubt they'll miss me," Andrew said dryly. He could imagine his men smiling at their officer taking a young woman to a cemetery. "We'll go to the graveyard first thing tomorrow."

With trees for shade and the high arc of the sky as a canopy, the Maxwell family lay in Newcastle's peaceful cemetery. Andrew had ordered a separate headstone for each, a simple stone cross with their names and dates of their birth and death inscribed. The three crosses stood side by side, austere grey stone protruding from the verdant green of the grass.

Andrew stood back as Mariana stood beside the graves, holding a damp handkerchief. He watched her, wondering if he should place an arm around her shoulder.

"I don't know what to say," Mariana confessed. "There's so much in my head, yet so little in my mouth."

"Don't say anything," Andrew advised. "They'll know you're here." He kept close to Mariana without touching her. *I don't know what to say either, Mariana. I don't know how to help.* He looked at Elaine's grave, remembering their shared laughter and wondering how life would have been if she were still alive.

"Do you think they know I'm here?" Mariana asked.

"I'm sure they do," Andrew reassured her. *I'll look after your sister, Elaine. I promise you I will care for her.*

Mariana nodded. "I hope so. Oh, God, I hope so."

"They will," Andrew said. He stepped further back to allow her space. "Take your time, Mariana."

If Elaine's death still hurt him, how much worse would it be for Mariana, losing both her parents and her sister and then having the murderers kidnap her? Andrew watched as Mariana knelt beside the graves. She never spoke about her time in captivity.

Should I force her to talk? Would that help? Or would it make things worse?

Mariana ran her hand across the surface of her mother's grave as if seeking reassurance. Andrew saw her shoulders shake and yearned to offer comfort.

No. Mariana needs to cry. Crying is a catharsis to help her accept her family's deaths. The only thing I can do is be here if she needs me. Finding the nearest tree, Andrew checked for snakes and insects before settling down with the trunk at his back. He felt the ache of frustration, wishing he could ease Mariana's pain and clear her mind while knowing he could do nothing. He saw her shoulders shaking, half-rose to help, and forced himself back down. Mariana needed time alone with her family. Andrew thought of Elaine and, for a brief, betraying second, remembered her calm voice.

"I like Tennyson and Scott," Elaine had said. "The Lady of Shalott is my favourite, even though it's a sad story." She smiled and quoted the final stanza.

"They cross'd themselves, their stars they blest,
Knight, minstrel, abbot, squire, and guest.
There lay a parchment on her breast,
That puzzled more than all the rest,
The well-fed wits at Camelot.
'The web was woven curiously,

The charm is broken utterly,
Draw near and fear not, —this is I,
The Lady of Shalott.'"

The memory made Andrew smile. He knew that however long he lived, that poem would always be Elaine's rather than Mariana's. But Elaine was gone, and only Mariana remained of the pioneering Maxwell family. As he waited, Andrew watched Mariana, and, in his mind, he saw Elaine standing at her side, comforting her sister in her grief.

What should I do, Elaine? How can I help Mariana?

When nobody replied except the singing birds and the faint wind rustling the trees, Andrew knew he would have to find a solution without help.

I won't leave you, Mariana. I won't leave you alone.

It was nearly dusk by the time Mariana stepped away from the graves. Her face was puffy, and her eyes red-rimmed from weeping. She started when she saw Andrew under his tree.

"I'm sorry, Andrew," Mariana glanced at the gathering dark. "I didn't realise the time."

"It's not important," Andrew replied. "Don't leave until you are ready."

"I've said my goodbyes," Mariana said, brushing a tear from her eyes, and forced a smile. "I've cried myself dry."

"Let's get you home," Andrew said. "You'll be hungry."

Mariana looked at him. "Hungry?"

Andrew knew that food was not on Mariana's mind. "Come on, Mariana. You must eat."

They rode side by side, not speaking, with both lost in their thoughts. Andrew wondered anew what life would have been like if Elaine had survived. He would have treated Mariana like a younger sister. *Perhaps I already do*, Andrew told himself. Yet he sensed more within Mariana. He saw something in her eyes when she looked at him.

No, Mariana. I don't think of you that way. I can't think of you that way. You're Elaine's sister.

When they arrived at the bungalow, Briggs glanced at Mariana's tear-stained face and lifted an inquisitive eyebrow at Andrew. "Is Miss Maxwell all right, sir?"

"We've been at her parents' grave," Andrew knew he did not have to explain to a private soldier.

"Ah," Briggs nodded. "I wondered, sir. Shall I make coffee? Or would you prefer something stronger? A touch of brandy may help Miss Maxwell."

"Coffee, please," Andrew said. "And a decent meal." He raised his voice a little. "Bring warm water, soap and a towel to Mariana's room, Briggs. I am sure she wants to freshen up."

"Very good, sir," Briggs said.

Andrew ushered Mariana to the living room and poured them both a brandy.

"I don't drink," Mariana protested, staring at the glass.

"It's a bad habit," Andrew agreed, "but sometimes it helps." He watched as Mariana took a cautious sip of the brandy.

She coughed and screwed up her face. "That's horrible!"

"It is, isn't it?" Andrew agreed, finishing his drink in a single swallow. "And you thought people enjoyed drinking spirits!" He forced a smile, trying to cheer her up.

Mariana shook her head and placed the glass on the table at her side. "That is vile."

"Here comes the coffee," Andrew said as Briggs entered the room. "It will take away the taste."

"Thank you, Mr. Briggs," Marina said.

Briggs favoured her with a smile. "That's my duty, Miss Maxwell," he said.

Marina's smile froze as somebody shouted outside the house. The voice must have reminded her of one of her abductors as she stared into space, with her body present but her mind miles away in distance and months away in time.

"Mariana?" Andrew said gently. He made eye contact. "Are you with us?"

Mariana blinked, clearing the shadows. "Yes, sorry, Andrew. I drifted away for a moment."

"Try to stay with us," Andrew said, smiling.

I wish I were a doctor. Getting Mariana back to normal will take longer than I imagined.

ANDREW WAS IN HIS ROOM WHEN HE HEARD SOMEBODY OPEN THE GARDEN gate. He waited for Briggs to answer and looked up as somebody tapped on his door.

"Come in," he called.

"Excuse me, sir," Briggs said. "Lieutenant Fletcher is here for you."

"I'll see him in the living room," Andrew said. Fletcher was second in command of the Natal Dragoons, a young man who had rapidly matured during the Zulu War. He entered the room and snapped to attention.

"Sir," Fletcher threw a sketchy salute. "The Boers have done it, sir!"

"Sit down, Fletcher, and tell me what the Boers have done."

"Yes, sir," Fletcher sat straight-backed at the table. "The triumvirate who rule the Transvaal Boers have declared the Transvaal is a free nation known as the South African Republic, the *Zuid-Afrikaanse Republiek*."

Andrew grunted and poured Fletcher a brandy. "We expected no less," he said. "I'd better get back to the Dragoons and prepare us for war."

"Will there be war, sir?"

"Undoubtedly," Andrew said. "Not even Gladstone can see a British colony trying to break away." He saw Mariana listening at the door. "Tell me what happened, Fletcher."

"Yes, sir. On the 13th of December, sir, the Boers raised the *Vierkleur*; that's their flag, sir. It means 'four colours' because it's got a green vertical bar and red, white, and blue horizontal bars."

"Where did they raise it?" Andrew asked as Mariana sat down, looking pale under her tan. She began to twist her hands together.

"A place called Pardekraal, sir," Fletcher said.

"I don't know it," Andrew said.

"Nor do I, sir. Then, three days later, on Dingaan's Day, the 16th of December, at Heidelberg, the Boers declared a republic. Dingaan's Day is the anniversary of the Battle of Blood River, sir, when the Voortrekkers defeated the Zulu king Dingaan."

Andrew nodded. "Thank you, Fletcher." He wanted to reassure Mariana that everything would be all right.

"The Boers have reinstated the *Volksraad*, the legislative assembly," Fletcher said. "They're pushing on rapidly with their republic."

"I'll return to barracks with you," Andrew said. He raised his voice. "Briggs!"

"Sir!"

"I am going to the barracks."

"Your uniform is ready, sir. Shall I accompany you?"

Andrew shook his head. "No, Briggs. I have a far more important duty for you."

"What's that, sir?" Briggs stood impassive inside the doorway.

"I want you to remain with Miss Maxwell."

"Very good, sir," Briggs replied.

"Whatever happens, Briggs," Andrew said, "I want Miss Maxwell to stay here. Don't let anybody of any rank take her away."

Briggs glanced at Mariana. "I won't, sir."

"If anybody objects, tell them you're acting under my direct orders."

"I will, sir," Briggs said.

Andrew felt Mariana's gaze fixed on him and hoped she understood.

CHAPTER 4

As Newcastle possessed no official barracks, Andrew had based the Natal Dragoons in a group of farm buildings on the outskirts of the town. The farm owner had died at Hlobane in the Zulu War, leaving no heirs, but the buildings were solid and sufficiently spacious to house the entire unit.

Sergeant Meek was supervising the men grooming the horses and snarling good-naturedly at anything that failed to meet his high standards. He stopped at Trooper Ogden's horse and pointed to a single tangled hair. "I want that groomed, Ogden! Look at that! It's like an Irish blanket after a storm! Get that sorted!"

"Yes, sir!" Ogden flicked the hair back into place.

"Do you call that sorted? Groom your horse, Ogden!" Meek looked around as Andrew walked into the stables.

"I see you're busy, Sergeant," Andrew said.

"Welcome back, sir," Meek saluted. "How's Miss Maxwell?" Meek had helped rescue Mariana from the renegades.

"She's doing well, thank you," Andrew said. "How are the men?"

"Same as always, sir, a useless, lazy bunch who only joined for the *scoff*."

"No improvement since I crossed the Vaal then," Andrew said.

"No, sir," Meek said. "There's a message for you, sir. Some peacock left it soon after Mr Fletcher left."

"Thank you, Sergeant. Where is it?"

"In your office, sir."

Andrew could imagine the peacock. He would have been a young staff officer, well connected and just out of Sandhurst, with his boots shined to perfection, a chin smooth enough for a ski slope, and a disdainful attitude toward colonials and rankers.

The message sat on Andrew's desk beside a pile of letters he decided to ignore. He slid a knife under the seal and removed a single sheet of stiff paper.

The name at the top of the page read "General Hook", and the instructions were written in three clear paragraphs.

"Colonel Winsloe of the 21st Foot is constructing a fort at Potchefstroom to control any independence agitation among the local population. One of Winsloe's officers heard Germans among the town's inhabitants.

Report to Colonel Winsloe and see what assistance you can give. You have knowledge of the possible German threat and are the only officer under my command who may have seen the Prussian agent. Watch the inhabitants of the town for the agent. If the man is the individual you saw in Krugersdorp, detain him and hold him for questioning.

Currently, Colonel Winsloe does not need the Natal Dragoons. Inform Lieutenant Fletcher to remain in temporary command and keep them ready in case they are required.

Hook."

Andrew lowered the letter. *Potchefstroom is in the Transvaal; there's no rest for the wicked.*

POTCHEFSTROOM WAS LIKE OTHER TRANSVAAL TOWNS, WITH BROAD STREETS, solid public buildings, and slightly pretentious stores. A short distance from the settlement and set on rising ground, the unfinished British fort had low walls surrounding a collection of huts and tents.

That's hardly an impressive example of the Empire's might, Andrew thought.

"Halt! Who goes there?"

The sentry at the gate presented his bayonetted rifle as Andrew approached. Andrew saw a small, neatly made man with his cross belt and sun helmet brilliant white against a scarlet tunic.

"Friend!" Andrew announced. "Captain Andrew Baird of the Natal Dragoons!" He had worn his uniform especially for the occasion, for he knew that British infantry could have nervous trigger fingers when on sentry duty.

"Pass, friend," the sentry allowed, slamming to attention as his suspicious eyes watched the tall, sun-browned stranger in the unfamiliar uniform.

Andrew returned the man's salute. He knew the 21st Foot, the Royal Scots Fusiliers, were veterans of the Zulu War and, like all British infantry, could be relied on to fight if required.

When he entered the fort, Andrew was less impressed. The walls were only four and a half feet high, sufficiently thick to stop a rifle bullet, but no defence against artillery. Inside, a company of the 21st acted as the garrison, together with twenty-five mounted infantry and two nine-pounders of the Royal Artillery.

He looked around, noticing the relaxed way the men moved. *These lads don't expect trouble.*

"Sergeant!" Andrew shouted. "I am looking for Colonel Winsloe!"

A young sergeant glanced at Andrew's unfamiliar uniform. "Who are you?"

"Captain Baird of the Natal Dragoons," Andrew said.

"My apologies, sir." The sergeant stiffened to attention and threw a smart salute. "I didn't recognise the uniform. I can't see any badges of rank."

"You lads were at Ulundi, weren't you?" Andrew referred to the final battle of the Zulu War.

"We were, sir," the sergeant confirmed warily.

"So were the Natal Dragoons," Andrew said.

"Yes, sir," the sergeant allowed himself a grudging respect. "If you follow me, sir, I'll take you to the colonel."

Colonel Winsloe sat at his desk within the largest of the tents. He looked up when Andrew announced himself. "Captain Baird, come in."

The tent was stifling under the sun and crammed with Winsloe's furniture.

"General Hook sent me, sir."

"So I believe. Here's the situation, Baird," recently promoted to acting colonel, Winsloe had been wounded at Ulundi when the Zulus charged the 21st. Andrew knew his reputation as a steady regimental officer. "The Burghers of the Transvaal have declared themselves a republic against the wishes of Her Majesty's government."

"Yes, sir," Andrew saw the pain in Winsloe's face as he moved and wondered if he had completely recovered from his injury.

"One of my officers heard one of the Burghers speaking German," Winsloe said. "The man could be an innocent German settler, but with the powers-that-be in a jumpy mood, I thought I'd better pass on the information. The last thing we want is Prussian interference."

Andrew nodded. "Yes, sir. Could I speak to the officer concerned?"

Winsloe called for his servant. "Fetch Lieutenant Burke," he commanded.

Burke was old for a lieutenant, a saturnine man in his mid-thirties with a downward twist to his lips. "You wanted me, sir?"

"This gentleman is Captain Baird of the Natal Dragoons, an expert on the Prussians. Tell him what you heard, Burke."

Before Baird could protest that he was no expert, Burke began to talk. "I didn't hear very much, sir. It was more what I saw and how the fellow acted."

"What did you see, Burke?" Andrew wondered if he had wasted his time.

Burke screwed up his face in concentration. "A man who looked out of place, sir, as if he didn't belong. He spoke Dutch to some Boers, then switched to German when he addressed his horse."

Andrew nodded. "What did he look like?"

"He was well over six feet tall," Burke replied at once, "and he stood erect. The Boers don't often stand upright; they seem more relaxed, slope-shouldered even."

"I've noticed that," Andrew agreed. *The description fits the man I saw, but there could be hundreds of tall men in the Transvaal.*

"He was looking at the fort," Burke continued. "So was half the town's population, but there was something different about this man."

Andrew grunted. "You've had me ride over two hundred miles from Newcastle to tell me you saw a tall man looking at the fort?"

Burke looked uncomfortable. "It was more than that, sir. He just felt wrong. You know that feeling you get when something is not quite what it should be?"

Andrew relented. "I know it," he said.

"It was like that."

"Would you recognise this fellow again?" Andrew asked.

"Yes, sir," Burke replied.

"If Colonel Winsloe agrees, you and I will wander around Potchefstroom and the surrounding area. If we see this man, and I also recognise him, we'll arrest him."

Colonel Winsloe frowned. "On what grounds, Captain? We can't arrest a man simply because we don't like his looks. We're British, damn it, not some continental autocracy. We have the rule of law, innocent until proven guilty."

"Yes, sir," Andrew agreed. "We may also be at war."

Winsloe slowly shook his head. "We're not at war yet, Baird. So far, it's all been hot air and rhetoric." He stood up. "We're soldiers, not policemen. I will permit Lieutenant Burke to accompany you for two days to try and identify this man. After that, you can return to Newcastle."

"Yes, sir." Andrew recognised that Winsloe was balancing his sense of duty with a lifetime's experience as an honourable British gentleman. "Come on, Burke, if we change into civilian clothes, we'll be less conspicuous."

"You'll be riding away soon." Aletta van Collier spoke without apparent emotion. The Transvaal would soon be at war with the British Empire; therefore, the men would fight. There was neither argument nor question in her mind; the Boer men had always ridden to war when there was a threat from outside and always would. It was as inevitable as the seasons.

"Ja. We are going to war." At thirty-eight years old, Johannes knew the Commando Law. The Republic expected every Burgher between the ages of sixteen and sixty to fight on demand. Most of their wars had been against threatening tribes, although they had faced British redcoats more than once. It made little difference to Johannes if they fought the encroaching British Empire or an African tribe.

Aletta nodded stoically, hiding her anxiety as she continued to make bread. Making bread was her job this morning. The war was her man's business unless it threatened her farm.

When Johannes stepped outside to check his horses, Aletta watched him for a moment, sighed, and left the table with the bread half-made. She followed her husband, carefully readjusted her poke bonnet to shade her face from the sun and swept flour from her skirt. The hem brushed her ankles above many layers of petticoats.

"Are you taking Jan?" She pointed to their elder son, who was shaping a dozen new fenceposts.

Johannes nodded gravely. "Yes. He is seventeen now. Past time to learn the duties of a man," he said. He nodded to their younger son, who was whitewashing the dairy wall. "I will take Mannie as well."

"Mannie's only fourteen," Aletta's face fell at the thought of her baby riding to war. Her eyes softened when she looked at him, remembering the difficulty she had in labour. She would never admit that Mannie was her favourite.

"I was eleven when I first rode on commando," Johannes said. "Jan and I will be with him." He checked his horse's withers and patted its neck. "Mannie will be better learning young than never learning at all."

Aletta looked away briefly. "You are right, Johannes." She looked at her younger son, tall for his age, slim and handsome in her eyes. "You were fourteen when we met. Mannie looks like you at his age."

Johannes placed an empty pipe in his mouth and contemplated Mannie as if he had never seen the boy before. "He is taller and not as handsome."

Aletta smiled at the comparison and folded her arms. "He is taller than you were and more handsome."

"Yes," Johannes nodded. "That is what I said. Taller and more handsome."

They smiled simultaneously. After twenty years of marriage, they understood each other well.

"What will you take with you?" Aletta asked.

Johannes replied immediately. "The Commando Law demands we bring a riding horse, saddle, and bridle with thirty bullets, thirty caps, and half a pound of gunpowder." He looked at his two sons. "That's ninety between us. We will take double that. We must also carry sufficient provisions for eight days."

"A war with the *Rooinecks* will last longer than eight days," Aletta said. Boer women were as practical as their men. "They are not tribesmen on a cattle raid. You'd better bring sufficient provisions for fourteen days."

"Yes," Johannes said. "Fourteen will be better. Biltong, meat cut in strips, salted, peppered, and dried, with Boer biscuits."

Aletta knew Boer biscuits meant small loaves made with flour and fermented raisins rather than yeast, and baked twice. "I am already making the bread," she told him. "Make sure you take care of my sons."

Johannes smiled. "I will. And they will take care of me."

Aletta touched his arm. "I'll look after the farm until you return."

"I know you will," Johannes said. He stepped into the house, closed the door with his foot, and embraced his wife. They did not need words, for both knew the dangers of war and the hazards of leaving a woman alone on a farm in the high veld. Johannes could not rely on the servants to fight if any of the neighbouring tribes raided the farm. He knew he would worry until he returned, but that was the price of farming on the frontier. The alternative was to trek down to the Cape and suffer the oppressive laws of the British Empire.

Johannes shook his head. He could never live under British rule.

The van Collier men left Nuwe Hoop Plaas two days later as dawn coloured the eastern sky red like a harbinger of oncoming bloodshed. Johannes led, grim-faced, as he left his wife and his farm. Jan rode on his right, as eager as any youth when travelling to his first war, sure in his invulnerability and wishing his girl Engela could admire him. On Johannes' left, Mannie strove to emulate his older brother, although twice he looked back over his shoulder to see his mother, who stood outside the door of their house. She lifted a hand in farewell, hiding her fears and tears. Aletta took the part of generations of Boer women who had watched their men leave for war. She knew the truth behind their brave appearance and the reality that they were fragile humans who could return broken in mind or body or not return at all.

"God be with you," Aletta prayed, wringing a cloth between her hands, but she did not allow her men to see any signs of weakness. She knew they would need all their strength, as she knew her sons left her as boys but would return as men in everything but years.

"God be with you." Aletta watched them ride until they were only distant specks in the vastness of the veld, and then she returned inside. She had a farm to run, and the work would not do itself.

CHAPTER 5

POTCHEFSTROOM, ZUID-AFRIKAANSCHE REPUBLIEK

15TH OF DECEMBER 1880

"Dust, sir! Somebody's approaching the fort!" the sentry lifted his Martini-Henry as if readying himself to shoot the oncoming man. The fort's location afforded the sentry an extensive view.

"Keep me posted, McWilliam." Lieutenant Lindsell, the duty officer, ordered.

"Yes, sir," McWilliam replied. He lowered his rifle. "It's Major Thornhill in the postcart, sir, and he's in a hurry."

"Major Thornhill?" Lindsell repeated. "Open the gates! The major wouldn't return unless there was trouble!"

Andrew strode to the gates, more curious than alarmed. He and Burke had been on two abortive tours of Potchefstroom with no sign of Konrad Bramigan.

Major Thornhill, second in command of the fort, came at the gallop, his horses lathered with sweat and covered in dust. "Boers!" He shouted. "Hundreds of them!"

The postcart hammered inside the gate, turned in a tight circle, and came to a halt within a curtain of rising dust. The driver slid from his perch and looked around the fort's interior, as sweat-soaked as his horses.

"That's put the tabby cat among the pigeons," Lindsell murmured.

Andrew nodded. "It appears so."

"Sound the Assembly!" Colonel Winsloe ordered. "Close the gates! Man the walls!"

When the bugle gave its brassy blare, red-coated infantrymen ran to their posts, carrying their Martini-Henry rifles at the trail. Sergeants added their shouts to the din.

Andrew checked his revolver and strolled to his quarters to retrieve his rifle. *Never looked hurried in front of the men.* With no official duties in the garrison, he could only make himself as useful as possible. He watched the 21st Foot, trying to assess their capabilities. *They seem a handy bunch, with no panic.*

Colonel Winsloe gave rapid orders. "Major Clarke, take twenty men and garrison the Landdrost's office and the courthouse! Lieutenant Dalrymple-Hay, take a section to the flat roof of the jail."

The regulars obeyed without visible emotion, professional soldiers trusting their officers. Andrew joined the men on the wall, holding his Martini-Henry and waiting for an attack. He peered over the town, seeing only the quiet houses, with a few civilians moving around as if nothing unusual was happening.

"What are the Boers thinking of?" Fusilier Tosh asked. "They're a bunch of farmers! They won't have a hope against us!"

"People said that about the Zulus," a dapper corporal reminded, scratching an insect bite on his neck. "A bunch of naked savages, they called them, until they gave us the right about at Sandwala!"[1]

Andrew examined the interior of the fort. With its low walls containing a handful of recently erected huts and the usual bell tents of British infantry, it did not seem sufficiently strong to withstand an attack. The Royal Artillerymen waited at their guns, smart in their blue uniforms and reassuringly calm.

When Andrew returned his attention to the town, he realised that most of the civilians had disappeared. In their place, mounted Boers rode along the streets, holding their rifles ready. Most wore broad-brimmed hats and ordinary working clothes, while others wore suits but still carried a rifle.

We're on the verge of war, Andrew thought. *Let's hope both sides show some restraint and don't start firing.*

"I could knock that fellow off his horse, corporal," Tosh sighted along the barrel of his Martini at a Boer who rode into the open ground between the town and the fort.

"Hold your fire," Andrew pushed Tosh's rifle barrel down. "We don't know what the Boers intend and don't want to instigate any shooting."

Tosh nodded. "If you say so, sir."

"People coming, sir!" McWilliam warned as a rush of refugees headed for the fort. "They're civilians, sir, and they look scared."

Colonel Winsloe mounted the walls to assess any danger. "Open the gates," he ordered. "Let them in!"

When the gates opened, dozens of native drivers and British civilians from the surrounding area crammed into the fort as the Boers established control of Potchefstroom.

"Do you think they'll attack us, sir?" the dapper corporal asked Andrew.

"I couldn't say, Corporal," Andrew replied. He watched the sun swiftly set in an ominous red glow. "If I were the Boer commander, I'd come quickly while we are still disorganised. That's if he wants a fight and is not merely trying to scare us."

Darkness closed on the fort, with men listening for sounds and waiting for a possible attack. The duty officer lit watch lanterns, giving quiet advice to the sentries.

"Don't stand still for long, don't hover near the lights in case a Boer is waiting to shoot, and don't look at the light because that will damage your night vision."

"Yes, sir," the sentries said and continued their beats.

Andrew patrolled the walls, thankful that the defenders were veteran infantry, not young soldiers fresh from Britain's grim industrial streets. He stared at the town, where candles glowed in some windows while others were dark, hiding the secrets within. He heard the whinnying of horses, listened to the drumbeat of hooves on the ground, and, in the distance, he could see the glow of campfires outside the town.

"How many are there, do you reckon, sir?" Andrew asked Major Thornhill.

"Too many," Thornhill replied. "Hundreds if not thousands." He grinned, lighting a long cheroot. "If they'd come at once, they'd have a better chance of victory, though. As it is, we've nearly completed the fort and are ready and waiting. I'd put my money on a hundred British infantry against any number of rustics."

Andrew glanced around the low walls and the fort crowded with refugees. "I hope you're correct, sir."

Thornhill pulled at his cheroot. "You'll see, Baird. We're only facing armed civilians, not trained soldiers. A few volleys from Martini, and they'll run like scared rabbits."

"Yes, sir," Andrew remembered the quiet determination of the Burghers in Krugersdorp and hoped Thornhill was correct. The 21st Foot appeared professional enough as they stood behind the wall, exchanging black humour and grousing like the veterans they were. They remained at the walls all night, awaiting an attack that never came.

A spectacular dawn heralded what Andrew expected to be a dramatic day. He slumped against the parapet, Martini ready, rubbed a hand over his unshaven chin, and listened to the town wake up. Lights flickered in windows, voices sounded, and Andrew saw a small group of armed horsemen trotting close to the fort.

"Shall I fire, sir?" Fusilier Tosh asked.

"No," Thornhill replied. "They may just be curious to see the funny foreign soldiers. We must be a novelty to them."

"Yes, sir," Tosh lowered his rifle.

At nine o'clock that morning, a moustached corporal took over the guard at the gate. He had no sooner posted his section than he shouted, "A party of Boers is coming, sir!"

Colonel Winsloe stepped to the gate and raised his field glasses. He studied the approaching Boers for thirty seconds.

"Lieutenant Lindsell, take the mounted infantry and find out what they're after." He glanced at Andrew. "You go with them, Baird; you're supposed to be an expert on these people."

"Yes, sir." Pleased to be free from the fort's confines, Andrew and the mounted infantry clattered outside. The day was already uncomfortably hot, although Andrew felt a heaviness in the atmosphere as though rain was imminent.

"I know I outrank you, Lindsell," Andrew said, "but these are your men. I won't interfere in your leadership."

"Very good, sir," Lindsell agreed and raised his voice. "Open order," he shouted. "We'll see what these fellows want."

People in the town watched as Lindsell's mounted infantry approached the Boers. Andrew studied the faces, looking for Konrad Bramigan. He recognised the type of man, if not any individuals among the mass. As Major Thornhill had said, the Boers were farmers but also frontiersmen who leaned back in their saddles and carried their rifles as though they were part of their bodies, scrutinising the British as carefully as Andrew studied them.

> *The last real war we had with frontiersmen was back in the 1770s,* Andrew thought. *That began as a civil war over politics and spread across the globe when France, the Netherlands, and Spain got involved. I hope we can contain this dispute in the Transvaal rather than have the German Empire or any other Powers sticking in their long continental noses.*

"They're running, sir!" Sergeant Lennox reported calmly as the Boers turned and withdrew. Lennox wore a row of medal ribbons on his chest and had a finger missing from his left hand.

"I thought they might," Lindsell said. "Follow them up, boys, but don't get too close. I don't want them to panic and open fire."

The mounted infantry advanced, with some men smiling as they pushed the Boers back a few hundred yards. Andrew thought he heard a man cheer from the fort.

"And that's the end of the rebellion," Lennox said. "Close it down, get these lads back to their farms, and we can all go home."

As the British began to relax, one of the Boers turned in his saddle, lifted his rifle, and fired, with the muzzle flare distinct and a rush of blue-grey smoke clouding man and horse. The bullet whined well above the heads of the mounted infantry.

That's the first shot in this war, Andrew thought. *War? I hope there is no war.*

When another Boer fired, with the shot also passing high above the British heads, Lieutenant Lindsell frowned.

"The cheeky beggars," he sounded more surprised than alarmed. "Give them a volley, lads! Don't dismount; just show them we mean business."

Before the patrol returned fire, more Boers lifted their rifles with tell-tale jets of smoke and the sharp crack of musketry. The bullets passed overhead or screamed on either side of the mounted infantry. One trooper swore and fought the reins as his horse panicked.

"It's alright, Badger! It's only the Boers. Calm down, you stupid horse!"

Andrew unholstered his Martini and raised it to his shoulder.

"Fire!" Lindsell ordered.

The mounted infantry squeezed their triggers, with Andrew aiming for the Boer who fired the first shot. He saw his man jerk sideways and grab his arm, and then the Boers withdrew at speed.[2]

"That's enough, lads," Lindsell said cheerfully. "No need to follow. We've sent a message and chased them away. Return to the fort."

Andrew agreed with Lindsell's judgment. If he were the Boer commander, he'd draw the British away from the fort and ambush them inside Potchefstroom or in the countryside beyond.

"Keep the men extended," Andrew advised softly. "We don't want to present the Boers with a tempting target."

"Extended order!" Lindsell roared.

As the mounted infantry approached the fort, they heard more musketry from the Landdrost's office in Potchefstroom.

"Things are hotting up," Andrew observed. "It looks like we have a fight on our hands."

Lindsell nodded. "I hoped we had quelled this republican nonsense. It seems brother Boer needs a sterner lesson than a single volley."

The sound of Boer rifles increased as the mounted infantry neared the fort. The Boers were firing from three places in the town, aiming at the white sun helmets of the infantry at the walls. "Increase the speed," Lindsell ordered, "and let's hope the sentries open the gates for us." He barked a short laugh. "Ready boys! Canter now! I'd be obliged if you'd keep your head down, sir," he said to Andrew. "I can't have the colonel blaming me for losing a visiting officer."

Taking the rear, the post of most danger, Lindsell ushered his men to the fort, which was now the centre of a battle. Bullets were thudding against the wall, each raising a small spurt of dust, while others ripped through the bell tents in the fort's interior. The 21st retaliated with volleys, aiming at the gun smoke or any Boer sufficiently careless to reveal himself.

The gate was open, with a sentry at either side firing towards the Boers.

"Get inside!" Colonel Winsloe ordered as Boer bullets whined overhead. The mounted men ducked as they entered, swearing when some shots came close. "Take your positions on the wall and return fire, but be careful of the civilians!"

Andrew took his place behind the wall as the mounted infantry dismounted and ran to their stations. They slammed into their various positions, loaded, and waited for the officers' orders.

Andrew scanned his surroundings, noting the houses from where the Boers fired. Although the muzzle flares and spurts of smoke came from three directions, most came from a single house.

"Dr Poortman's house appears to be their main centre of resistance," Andrew pointed out when Colonel Winsloe walked around the wall.

“That’s what I thought, Captain,” Winsloe said. Ignoring the Boer fire, he approached Lieutenant Rundle of the Royal Artillery.

“Could you silence the men in that house, Lieutenant?”

Rundle grinned. “I thought you’d forgotten about us, sir! We’ll see what we can do.”

Andrew watched as the gunners made their preparations, ignoring the bullets that buzzed and whined overhead.

Rundle laid the nine-pounder himself, checked the aim, and stepped back. “Right, lads,” he said. “Fire!”

The nine-pounder roared, and Rundle’s first shell smashed through the front window of Dr Poortman’s house, exploding inside. The Boer firing ended abruptly.

“That sorted them out!” A Glasgow voice sounded.

The Boer musketry started again, with less intensity. The bullets kicked dust from the walls and perforated the tents, jerking the canvas with every shot.

“Good shooting, Rundle,” Winsloe studied Dr Poortman’s house through his field glasses. “There are still some inside. Give them another.”

“My pleasure, sir,” Rundle said as a bullet pinged off the barrel of the nearer nine-pounder.

The Boers are concentrating on the guns. “Protect the gunners, lads,” Andrew said, aiming at the smashed window of Dr Poortman’s house. “Make the Boers keep their heads down.”

“Volley fire!” Lindsell ordered. “Load! Aim! Fire!”

The infantry responded, firing at the doctor’s house, so ten Martinis cracked out simultaneously. Andrew saw puffs of dust all around the front of the building, with bullets smashing the remaining glass and thudding on the solid front door.

“Fire!” Rundle ordered, and the nine-pounder roared again. Andrew did not see the arc of the shell, only the explosion at Poortman’s front door. The return fire ended as the surviving Boers left hurriedly, spilling out the back to find a safer vantage point.

Rundle stood back to study Dr. Poortman’s house through his field glasses.

“Round two to us,” Colonel Winsloe said quietly. “Let’s see what Brother Boer tries next.”

After that flurry of activity, the day quietened down. The Boers and Fusiliers exchanged a few ineffective shots.

“I thought the Boers were all expert marksmen,” Lindsell said quietly. “They don’t seem any better than our lads.”

“Maybe these are town-based Burghers rather than the high veld farmers,” Andrew said quietly. “Or maybe they are holding back.” He looked up as Colonel Winsloe stepped closer.

“Any casualties?” Winsloe asked.

“No, sir,” Lindsell replied.

The colonel nodded. “Good. Did you see your Prussian, Baird?”

“Not yet, sir,” Andrew replied.

"Maybe you'd best return to Newcastle and report."

Andrew nodded. "I'd prefer to wait for confirmation, sir."

Winsloe pushed back his sun helmet and studied Andrew's face. "I know your reputation from the Zulu War, Baird. You're a fire-eater, but you have a duty to General Hook. My men can hold this fort against any number of Boers without your help."

"I realise that, sir," Andrew said.

Winsloe scratched his head. "I'll give you one more day, Baird, then return to General Hook with my blessing."

"Yes, sir," Andrew saluted, turned on his heel, and walked to the wall. He lifted his field glasses, hoping for a chance glimpse of Bramigan.

JAN RODE PROUDLY BESIDE HIS FATHER AND YOUNGER BROTHER AS THEY joined the Groenburg Commando, named after the village of Groenburg, where they assembled. The men greeted each other with handshakes and polite raising of hats. Most knew each other from farmers' gatherings, markets, weddings, and funerals, with many having ridden on commando against raiding native tribes.

"What happens now?" Jan asked, looking around for friends and neighbours. He had seldom seen so many men in one place and, suddenly nervous, edged back from the crowd. He had lived on the farm all his life, rarely venturing out of his familiar patch of veld, and knew only a close circle of people.

"Now we wait for Gideon, the area commandant," Johannes said, "and vote for two veldcornets for the commando."

Jan had expected to see some military men in splendid uniforms and cocked hats. Instead, everybody wore ordinary clothes, with bandoliers of ammunition draped across their chests. One man wore a bowler hat, and another a battered British-style sun helmet. Most of the men were talking, giving their views, and explaining how they would defeat the British if they commanded the republic's forces.

Jan waved to a youth from a neighbouring farm. "I'll speak to Abraham," he said, thankful to see his childhood friend.

"Ja," Johannes said. "You speak to Abraham Hertzog. Ask him how his sister will survive with both her men out on commando." Johannes laughed, for Jan had been courting Engela for two years. "And how you will survive without her."

Jan coloured and guided his horse through the crowd. Abraham greeted him with a grin.

"We're going on commando together, Jan," Abraham said. A freckled youth, he had a broad, cheerful face, long, untidy blond hair, and hands too large for his arms. Abraham was shorter than most Boer men but made up for his lack of inches with an erect stance, a bouncy walk, and a belligerent attitude. "We'll show the *Rooinecks*!"

"We will," Jan agreed with the supreme confidence of youth. "They wear red coats and think they're the lords of creation."

"They haven't met us yet," Abraham said. "Come on, Jan, there's fun over here." He pointed to a crowd of youths gathering a short distance from their elders.

With Jan and Abraham taking the lead, the boys enjoyed a quick game of *bok-bok,* with one reluctant youth standing against the wall of the house and the others jumping on top until the human tower collapsed in a laughing tangle. After they straightened themselves up, the youths played *vingertrek*, where two boys locked the middle fingers of their right hands and strove to break their opponent's grip. It was a trial of strength in which Jan delighted. As he had been engaged in strenuous physical work on the farm since he could walk, he was stronger than most grown men. Jan demolished a series of town-bred boys before realising Abraham was smiling without participating.

"Come on, Abe!" Jan challenged, and the two interlocked their fingers. Immediately, Jan knew the difference between Abraham and the urban boys. Abraham had also lived all his life with hard manual labour and matched Jan strength for strength.

The crowd watched; with the youths Jan had defeated all supporting Abraham.

"Go on, Abe!" one boy shouted. "Break his finger!"

"Beat him, Jan," Mannie countered. "Tear his arm off!"

Jan strained, enjoying the competition, feeling the strength in his finger drain as Abraham proved equally determined to win.

"Engela's not here," Abraham said to break Jan's concentration. "You don't have to show off, Jan!"

"I don't need to show off to defeat you," Jan responded. "You are as weak as a newborn calf!"

Mannie encouraged his brother until Jan and Abraham realised they were evenly matched. They released each other, stepped back, rubbed their aching arms, and smiled in unstated friendship.

"You should have won, Jan," Mannie sounded disappointed.

"I didn't want to embarrass him by showing his weakness," Jan replied.

As the youths played light-heartedly, their elders dismounted and gathered in a noisy group. Every man voiced his choice of veldcornets until an older man with a long beard fired a shot from his rifle.

"Silence!" he said. "You all know me. I am Gideon Coetzee, the commandant of the area. We will elect two veldcornets for the Groenburg Commando."

The men nodded, with Theunis pushing forward as if seeking the position. Johannes stepped back, looked over the crowd to ensure his sons were all right and returned his attention to the discussion.

"Which names are put forward?"

The men argued for a few moments until they chose four names. "Theunis Steenekamp, Johannes van Collier, Karl Cloete, and Hendrik Ackerman," Gideon Coetzee announced solemnly.

The men discussed the merits of the four, with anecdotes of their experience and character freely given. Although the Boers occupied a large area of southern Africa, the population was thinly spread, and everybody knew their neighbours from farmers' gatherings, weddings, and funerals.

"I select Johannes," a stocky man wearing a bowler hat announced. "He married my cousin Aletta. He is a steady man with a well-run farm."

Others nodded. "Johannes was on commando with me against the Basuto. He fought well."

"I have known the family for thirty years. His grandfather and mine were on the Great Trek together. They are a good family."

"Theunis is also a good man," a blond giant said. "He is of the Afrikander Bond and will stop the *Rooinecks* from taking our land." He nodded as if his opinion settled the matter.

"I know Karl Cloete," an elderly man said quietly. "He married my youngest daughter, thank the Lord. We had no peace in the house until she was gone."

The men laughed, and the conversation shifted from war and politics to wives and women.

"Stop!" Gideon commanded. "It's time to vote for the veldcornets."

The men quietened and looked to their front, where Gideon raised his hands.

"Who will vote for Hendrik Ackerman?" Gideon asked and counted the raised hands.

"And who for Karl Cloete?" Gideon asked. "He is my wife's nephew."

"Wife's nephew or not," the bowler-hatted man shouted. "I still will not vote for him."

Every Burgher present had the franchise, and when Jan voted for his father, he felt he had crossed a barrier to become a man. He looked at Abraham, knowing the Pedi had killed his father. "You are the man of the house, Abe," Jan said. "You might be the veldcornet in the next war."

Abraham grinned. "I'd do a better job than these old men."

Gideon gave his decision. "Johannes and Theunis are elected as veldcornets," he announced. "They will lead the Groenburg Commando in the republic's war against the British Empire. May the Lord guide them both."

Jan grinned as a dozen men crowded to shake his father's hand. Mannie was laughing while the grim-looking Theunis Steenekamp tried to recruit the Burghers into the Afrikander Bond.

"Good," Johannes said when the initial excitement died away. "Now we can remove the British and return to our farms. I have thirty cows in calf and want to be present when they give birth."

The men nodded in complete understanding. They would defend their land but were not natural soldiers. Their farms and family were more important than fighting, and going on commando was an inconvenient necessity in the business of life.

Jan grinned at Abraham. "We're going to war," he said.

"Ja," Abraham agreed. "And when we return, you still won't get my sister's hand. Engela is far too good for a rough farmer such as you. She will marry a rich man with a big house and ten thousand *morgen* of good pastureland, not the half-sandy desert of Nuwe Hoop Plaas."

Jan laughed. "She will marry me and help me farm Nuwe Hoop Plaas, bear me many sons and be very happy."

They walked off, leaving their elders to decide how a small nation with a scattered population and no army was to defeat the military forces of the largest empire in the world.

CHAPTER 6

Andrew scanned Potchefstroom through his field glasses. "Could I have permission to take another patrol outside the fort, sir? I want to assess the Boer numbers and see if Bramigan is among them."

Winsloe pondered for a moment. "Your chances of finding the German are slim, Captain."

"I realise that, sir, but I have to look."

Winslow gave a reluctant nod. "Only a short patrol, Baird. Take two of the mounted infantry, and don't get my men killed."

"I'll try not to, sir," Andrew promised.

With Fusiliers Mullan and Logan at his back, Andrew swept out of the gate and turned right, away from the town. He half-expected a flurry of shooting from the Boers, but they allowed him to move unmolested as he led his men at a fast trot around the fort.

"Spread out," Andrew said. "We're here to gather intelligence, not to engage in a battle."

The men nodded. Mullan was a broad-faced man with laughing eyes, while Logan was neat and dark-featured with a bitter twist to his mouth.

"We don't know how many Boers there are," Andrew said. "There might only be a few dozen, or there could be hundreds. Identify any large groups and estimate their numbers."

"If they fire, can we fire back, sir?" Mullan asked.

"Yes," Andrew replied and saw both men's faces brighten.

"Even if you don't give the order, sir?" Logan sought confirmation as he checked the breech of his Martini.

"Don't wait for my order," Andrew confirmed. "But only if the Boers fire first."

"Yes, sir," Logan replied.

"Keep your heads down, boys," Andrew said. "Follow me!"

With one of the spurts of madness that characterised him during the Zulu War, Andrew led his men into the town. He relied on the surprise of their sudden appearance and the speed of their horses to avoid Boer fire. Andrew knew how difficult it was to shoot accurately at a moving man, especially when they appeared unexpectedly.

Mullan gave a high-pitched yell, laughing as he spurred his horse, loosening the rifle in its bucket holster beside his saddle.

Varying his speed, Andrew rode through Potchefstroom, seeing the heads and occasionally startled faces of armed Boers. He kept a mental count as he rode, hoping he would survive to pass on the information, ignoring the occasional challenge and checking his men. Mullan was laughing, waving to both armed Boers and civilians, while Logan looked tense, riding with his carbine balanced over the saddle. The small British garrisons looked around in surprise as Andrew cantered past and burst out of the far side of town.

"Are you still with me, lads?" Andrew asked, looking over his shoulder. He had been so intent on assessing the Boer numbers he had ignored their intermittent musketry.

"Still here, sir," Mullan replied.

"Best not linger, sir," Logan said as a bullet kicked up a fountain of dirt a foot from Andrew's horse. "Brother Boer is awake and angry."

"Good advice, Logan," Andrew said, patting Lancelot and setting off in a mazy run to confuse the Boer riflemen. He heard the irregular crackle of musketry and the occasional hiss as a bullet whistled past.

Mullan laughed again, twisted in his saddle, and returned fire.

"Be careful, Mullan," Andrew ordered. "Make sure you don't hit a civilian."

"Yes, sir," Mullan said, reloading and placing the carbine on his saddle.

With the town behind them, Andrew pushed into the countryside. *The Boers are country-bred. They are bound to have a camp outside Potchefstroom.*

"Sir!" Logan shouted, spurring his horse to get level with Andrew. "Over there!"

Andrew followed the direction of Logan's pointing rifle. A group of Boer horsemen had emerged from a wooded ridge and headed towards the British patrol. Andrew estimated between twelve and fifteen riders.

Why the sudden interest in three horsemen? They're trying to scare us away from something.

"Split up!" Andrew ordered. "You two lads ride like the devil for the fort. Don't stop for anything and report what you've seen."

"Where are you going, sir?" Logan asked.

"I want to see where these fellows came from," Andrew said. "Go!"

The Boers were closer now, riding in an untidy group with a broad-hatted man a few lengths ahead.

That fellow is their leader.

Confident in his horsemanship, Andrew ducked down and kicked in his spurs. "Come on, Lancelot!" he whispered in his horse's ear. "We'll lead the Boers a dance."

Lancelot responded by lengthening his stride as Andrew slanted past the

Boers' left flank. Glancing over his shoulder, he saw the Boers split into smaller parties, most chasing the two mounted infantrymen but three riders following him.

Andrew already knew the Boers were nimble and enduring horsemen, but he was unsure if their ponies were fast.

Now is my opportunity to find out.

Andrew could not restrain his laugh, whether from nerves, excitement, or exhilaration, he did not know. He pushed Lancelot up the crest and stopped. On the opposite side, Andrew saw scores of wagons in laager, with knee-haltered horses and small groups of armed men riding to and fro. As he watched, more wagons appeared, and a small commando of armed men arrived within a curtain of dust.

Dear God, it's an army! Andrew said to himself. *No wonder the Boers tried to chase us away.* With his pursuers still safely distant, Andrew raised his field glasses to scan the encampment.

The Boers have hundreds of men here. No, thousands. Whoever leads this army must want Potchefstroom badly.

Andrew heard the double report of a rifle and glanced at his pursuers. The Boers had spread out to trap him, with one man firing from the saddle.

I've seen enough. Time to run. Andrew had sufficient experience to know a man on a trotting horse had little chance of hitting his target.

"Come on, Lancelot!" Andrew urged, put his head down and headed for the rider at the edge of the Boer flank. The Boer looked up, saw Andrew galloping directly towards him, and unholstered his rifle.

Are you trying to scare me? That won't work, my friend.

"Fire, then!" Andrew shouted, unable to restrain his crazed laughter. He rode directly at the Boer, saw the man aim, and heard the simultaneous crack of the rifle. He had no idea where the bullet went, except it was not near him.

"Missed!" Andrew yelled. "Come on, Lancelot!"

Seeing a yelling British officer charging directly at him, the Boer naturally pulled away. The riders passed within two yards of each other, and Andrew galloped on, leaving the Boer floundering in his wake. By the time the Boers recovered and altered direction, Andrew was fifty yards in front, with the distance increasing with every stride.

A lone house stood directly in Andrew's path. It was no different from a thousand other homes in the Transvaal, with a corrugated iron roof, a shaded *stoep*, a small garden with carefully tended flowers, and a plain gable. An elderly man slowly rose from his seat to close the green Venetian shutters, protecting his property from the flying bullets. By the time the man sat back down, Andrew was level with the house, with Lancelot's hooves kicking up dust and small pebbles. The elderly man scratched a light for his pipe and watched.

With Andrew's pursuers in a long line behind him, the remainder of the Boer riders were scattered between Andrew and the fort. He saw the fort gates open, and Logan and Mullan ride in, with a tall officer leading a substantial body of mounted infantry outside.

That's Lieutenant Lindsell.

Andrew jinked from left to right to put any hopeful Boers off their aim and heard the thrill of a bugle and the sharp barks of musketry. He saw the white sun helmets of men behind the fort wall and Lindsell pushing his mounted infantry towards him.

"Come on, Captain!" Lindsell shouted, leading his mounted infantry forward. "We'll cover you."

Andrew kicked Lancelot into a final effort, and the Boers veered away with some desultory shooting but no casualties on either side.

"In you come, Baird," Lindsell invited, firing his revolver at the withdrawing Boers. "You've had your outing for the day."

Andrew grinned. "Mother always told me to get home before the darkness came down," he said. He looked behind him at the retreating Boers and wondered at his stupidity as the madness drained away.

"That was sheer lunacy," Colonel Winsloe said, shaking his head. "Did you see your Prussian?"

"No, sir," Andrew shook his head.

"You saw a few Boers, though," Colonel Winsloe sat back in his chair. Above his head, Boer bullets had perforated the tent in three places.

"I estimate about five thousand Boers, sir," Andrew said.

"Five thousand!" Winsloe whistled and gave a rueful smile. "They far outnumber my hundred and seventy men."

"Yes, sir. Their main camp is beyond the town, and more were arriving as I watched." Andrew detailed what he had seen as Winsloe dipped his pen in an inkwell and carefully took notes.

"You say the Boers have taken over various houses in the town."

"Yes, sir. They're turning them into strongpoints."

Winsloe pressed a blotter over his notes and replaced his pen in its holder. "I had hoped they were only raiding. We are not in any position to withstand a long siege. However, we must make do with what we have." He looked up. "Thank you, Baird. Your Prussian spy is less important now."

Or, more important. If the Germans learn how few men we have in Transvaal, they may help the Boers. Andrew decided not to argue with his superior officer. "Perhaps so, sir."

"You are dismissed, Baird," Winsloe lifted his notes and reread them as Andrew left the tent.

As the sun dipped to the horizon, half a dozen artillerymen left the fort, looking to water their horses.

"Be careful, lads," Andrew cautioned.

"We will, sir," the leading artilleryman replied. The sentries let them pass and closed the gate.

The Boers must have been waiting for their opportunity, for they opened fire immediately after the gunners left the fort. One man, Driver Ross, fell, seriously wounded, and a bullet killed a horse outright.

"Open the gate!" Andrew roared. "Get these men back inside! Fire at the Boers! Make them keep their heads down!"

Two sentries dragged open the heavy gates while the remainder fired toward the Boer muzzle flashes.

"What's happened, sir?" Lieutenant Rundle asked.

"The Boers have ambushed your men, Lieutenant," Andrew replied. "Close the gate!" He shouted as the gunners drove their horses back inside the fort.

"Open the gate, close the gate," Fusilier McWilliam muttered. "I wish those bloody ossifers would make their minds up."

"That house there, sir," Sergeant Lennox pointed to a thatch-roofed building. "That's where the Boers are!"

As the artillerymen returned at a run, Rundle ordered his gunners to fire at the house Lennox identified.

"Come on, lads! They shot Rossie!"

With one of their own injured, the gunners worked even harder, and a brace of artillery shells blasted the house into rubble. The Boer musketry ended immediately.

"The Boers are tightening the siege," Andrew observed.

"You're correct, Baird," Winsloe agreed quietly. He gestured to Major Thornhill. "In the morning, we'll have the heliograph operator inform the nearest British garrison."

"Yes, sir," Major Thornhill replied. "If we had one."

"If we had one?" Winsloe repeated. "Are you telling me we don't have a heliograph?"

"That's right, sir," Thornhill confirmed. "It's due to arrive sometime next week."

Winsloe frowned. "Brother Boer won't allow that. We'll have to think of something else."

The desultory firing continued all night and into the next day, with the white helmets of the soldiers providing perfect targets for the Boer marksmen. "Dye the helmets brown," Andrew advised. "A darker colour won't show up so much at night."

Thornhill agreed, so the men gleefully rubbed mud on their helmets, much to the disgust of the NCOs.

"Sergeant Lennox doesn't like this much," McWilliam said.

"That's all the more reason to do a good job," Tosh laughed. "Lay it on thick!"

Whenever the Boer musketry became dangerous, the duty officer ordered a section of the defenders to fire a volley, so the noise of rifles kept the town awake. Ignoring the noise, Andrew slept in a borrowed tent for four hours until artillery fire woke him. He rolled over, rose, dressed, and strode to the wall. The defenders were keeping under shelter as Boer bullets hammered at them.

Lieutenant Rundle grinned as Andrew approached. "Welcome back, sir."

"Anything happened while I was gone?"

"Nothing of any moment," Rundle said. "We're inside the fort, the Boers are outside, and the bullets fly each way."

"I noticed that," Andrew said. "I'll have a look at the defences."

The 21st looked unconcerned at the Boer bullets, sitting behind the wall with their rifles held ready to retaliate. Mullan had propped his helmet on top of the wall and greeted Andrew with a grin.

"There you are, sir. Are we off for another wee jaunt around the town?"

"Not yet, Mullan," Andrew said. "Would you not be better wearing your hat?"

"It gives the Boers a mark to aim at," Mullan explained. "When a Boer bullet hits it, we pop up and fire back."

"Aim for the muzzle flare or the smoke," Andrew advised. "And aim low. The Boers are hunters, remember, they're used to lying prone for hours to kill meat for the pot."

"I wish they'd fight fair, like soldiers, or at least like men, not cowards skulking behind cover." Logan used a rag to polish the barrel of his rifle. "When we fought the Zulus, we knew we were facing real warriors."

Andrew remembered the Boers he met during the Zulu War. "The Boers are not cowards," he said quietly. "They don't fight the same way as us, but they're not cowards."

Logan opened his mouth, decided not to speak, and closed it again. A Boer bullet zipped over, whacked into Mullan's helmet, and knocked it off the wall.

Before the helmet hit the ground, Mullan jumped up, aimed at the smoke, fired, and ducked back down as two Boer bullets smashed into the top of the wall.

"They've learned your game, Mullan," Andrew warned. "They had two marksmen ready for you to appear. I'd not try that again."

Mullan gave his habitual wide grin. "I won't, sir!" Lifting his perforated helmet, he jammed it on his head. "I hope I got one of them."

"So do I," Andrew said. Lifting a couple of mealie bags from the ground, he placed them on top of the wall a few inches apart, placed a third on top and stared through the aperture with his field glasses. The town looked quiet except for the occasional spurt of smoke as the Boers fired.

Show yourself, Konrad Bramigan, Andrew thought. *I want confirmation you are here.*

A bullet whacked into the mealie bag above Andrew's head, releasing a small trickle of corn. He focussed on the smoke, hoping to see the face of his attacker. Another bullet followed, thumping into the bag to his right.

Andrew heard the crack of a rifle and Mullan's low chuckle. "I think I got that one!" he said as he ducked away. "They're targeting you now, sir!"

Andrew looked at the last spurt of smoke without seeing any Boer casualties, yet nobody shot at him when he lifted his field glasses.

❋

At half past ten on the morning of the 18th of December, smoke rose from the Landdrost's office. Andrew watched orange flames lick along the thatch, and acrid smoke discolour the clear air. He surveyed the rooftops, wondering at the vulnerability of the sun-dried thatch. Andrew was glad the houses were less closely packed as those in Berwick-upon-Tweed or Hereford, or the flames would race across the town.

Lieutenant Rundle shook his head. "The lads will have fun defending the Landdrost's office now."

Andrew grunted. "They'll have to pull out, but I doubt they can withdraw to the fort with thousands of Boers between us and them."

The flames rose, increasing in size and intensity through the morning.

"We could send a relief force to bring Major Clarke and his men back, sir," Rundle suggested to the colonel.

"The Boers would cut them to pieces in the streets," Colonel Winsloe said. "We'd lose more men than we saved. If Clarke wants to fight his way out, we'll help. Otherwise, we'll sit tight."

"Yes, sir," Rundle said, looking longingly over the wall as the flames consumed the thatch roof.

Just before noon that day, one of the sentries called out, "Major Clarke's lowering his flag!"

Andrew swore softly. The Union flag above the Landdrost's office jerked slowly down to the smouldering roof, with a white flag hauled up in its place. He could feel the disbelief inside the fort.

"Major Clarke's surrendering! To a bunch of bloody farmers!"

"They should have fought on," Fusilier McWilliam said.

"They'd have burned alive," Sergeant Lennox reminded.

"Well, have a fighting retreat here, then." McWilliam gripped his rifle, shaking his head. "We'd have supported him."

Andrew said nothing. He wondered if the men would have held on longer if they had faced Zulus rather than Boers, who took prisoners.

With the white flag hanging limp above the Landdrost's house, all firing ended as the British waited to see what happened next. A lone Boer rode to the fort with a white rag tied to the muzzle of his rifle.

"Let him approach," Colonel Winsloe ordered and strolled to the gate.

"Good afternoon, my man," Winsloe shouted. "Have you come to surrender?"

The Boer lifted his hat politely. "General Cronje asks for a truce until four this afternoon," he said in perfect English. "He wants to finalise the agreement between the general and Major Clarke."

Winsloe pursed his lips. "Tell your General Cronje that we agree," he said. "We'll grant his truce."

"Thank you, *meneer*," the Boer replied, lifted his hat again and withdrew.

Colonel Winsloe stepped back from the parapet. "Raise the walls," he ordered. "I don't care what you use. And how is our water?"

"Not great, sir," Major Thornhill replied. "We've been digging wells since we arrived without any success. Our first well sunk to twenty-four feet and hit rock. We're still hacking with the second."

"Keep digging," Winsloe ordered. "And raise these walls. The Boers can fire right over them."

"Do you know anything about civil engineering, Baird?" Thornhill asked.

"Not a thing, sir."

"As much as me, then," Thornhill said. "Let's get building while the truce lasts. One must make the most of whatever opportunities the Lord of War offers." He raised his voice. "All men not on duty on the well or wall report to me!"

The men ran up, some grumbling, others eager, a few adjusting their belts or helmets.

"I want these walls higher," Thornhill shouted. "Bring me cases of food, sacks of mealies, and anything else you can find. Keep Brother Boer out and us safe!"

Andrew helped Thornhill supervise the Fusiliers in strengthening the fort's defences. Men hurried to and fro with cases of food and bags of mealies, thumping them on top of the baked mud walls.

"Every sack keeps the civilians safe," Sergeant Lennox said. "Your sweat is helping win the war, so I want to see you dripping wet!"

"The lads at Rorke's Drift did the same," McWilliam staggered under the weight of two sacks.

"They were fighting Zulu warriors, not Boers," Tosh reminded him. "Savages with spears, not farmers with rifles."

"When I joined the army," McWilliam said, "I thought I'd be fighting the Russians or the French. Fight for your country, the recruiting sergeant said. Defend Britain from the grey Cossack hordes, he said. He never said I'd be a builder's labourer in the middle of bloody Africa."

Tosh lifted a wooden case and swore. "That proves what I've always said. Never trust a sergeant."

"You're too bloody late now!" Sergeant Lennox roared in Tosh's ear. "I've got you! You're mine! Get that wall built, or you'll feel the toe of my boot!"

"Yes, Sergeant!" Tosh replied, winking at McWilliam.

"Keep moving, lads," Andrew ordered. Although he knew officers should be above manual labour, he led by example, carrying boxes and sacks, knowing that each could stop a bullet and save a man's life.

"Keep one sack in three for supplies," Thornhill reminded. "We don't know how long the siege will last, and we'll have to eat."

Colonel Windroe toured the walls, pointing out weaknesses. "There are holes here and there. Fill them!"

"Spare clothes," Andrew said. "We can stuff them into any gaps in the walls."

"Will cloth stop a bullet?" Thornhill wondered.

"I don't know, sir, but it will stop the Boer marksman from seeing men on the inside," Andrew said.

Winslow rationed each man to one shirt and trousers, with the remainder of their clothes used to strengthen the defences.

"Every little helps," Thornhill said.

"How about a trench, sir," Andrew suggested. "Rather than raising the wall, lower the ground on this side."

"Maybe later," Thornhill said. "The men are already exhausted."

"Yes, sir," Andrew did not press the point.

At four in the evening, the Boer messenger returned to the fort bearing a flag of truce and a copy of Major Clarke's surrender agreement.

Colonel Winsloe met him at the gate. "Have you seen the error of your ways, *meneer*?" Winsloe asked. "We will accept your surrender on easy terms."

"We surround the town and the fort, Colonel," the messenger replied with a wry smile. "You and your men cannot get out, and nobody can relieve you. We will accept your surrender on the same terms as we did for Major Clarke."

Winsloe muttered something that Andrew could not catch before raising his voice. "Tell General Cronje that I have no intention of surrendering, and we can hold out for months as we lack for nothing in the fort."

Except water, food, shelter and ammunition, Andrew thought. He glanced at the civilian refugees crowded in the centre of the fort, listening hopefully to everything Colonel Winsloe said. The women looked nervous. *No wonder. A small fort does not have the facilities to look after women.*

When the official truce ended, the Boers still held their fire, and at nine that night, Colonel Winsloe looked for volunteers to recall the garrison from the town jail.

"Not you, Baird," Winsloe said. "You have other duties and a message to deliver to General Hook."

Andrew nodded. "Yes, sir."

The Boers did not interfere with the jail evacuation, and the garrison returned carrying one dead and two wounded men.

"We're pulling in our horns," Rundle said. "Brother Boer is pushing us back post by post." He lit a cheroot and winked at Andrew through a curtain of blue smoke. "It's not quite Lucknow, but I wonder what the people in Britain are saying about us."[1]

Andrew smiled. "Oh, we'll be pluckily defying the enemy hordes while saluting the flag and preparing to sacrifice our lives for Queen and country. Or some such nonsense."

Rundle drew on his cheroot. "We don't even have a flag," he said. "Major Clarke had our only flag, and it's gone now, probably a trophy in some back veld farm."

"We have to have a flag," Andrew said. "A beleaguered garrison needs a flag. It's a symbol of defiance."

As the fort settled down for another night under siege, Colonel Winsloe called his officers together. They gathered around him, some expecting Boer marksmen to open fire and others standing erect to prove their disdain.

"We're in a bit of a pickle, gentlemen," Winsloe said. "We have a hundred and seventy men in this fort, plus civilians and animals to look after."

The officers nodded in agreement. They knew the figures.

"Our walls are too low, and Captain Baird has estimated around five thousand Boers oppose us." Winsloe continued. "I intend sending a message to Colonel Bellairs in Pretoria, asking him to send a relief column."

The men nodded, some holding cigars and cheroots whose blue smoke coiled lazily into the still air. A subaltern started when a rifle cracked in the distance.

"I'll send two messengers in case the Boers capture or kill one," Winsloe was brutally frank. His mouth twisted into a smile. "Two messengers will double our chances of success. Passing through the Boer lines will be dangerous, so I'll need volunteers with experience in South African conditions."

Andrew lifted a hand. "I'll volunteer, sir," he said. "I'm not from the 21st, so the garrison won't miss me, and I've been upwards of three years in South Africa." He grinned. "I also have a message to pass to General Hook."

Winsloe nodded. "I knew you'd volunteer, Baird. Didn't your men call you Up-and-at-em?"

Andrew felt the blood rush to his face. "Yes, sir," he said.

"I'll go, sir," a tall officer held up his hand.

Andrew nodded to the second messenger, a young subaltern with the face of a schoolboy and the body of an athlete.

"Well done, Cunningham," Winsloe said. "You two volunteers remain here. The others are dismissed."

Andrew and Cunningham waited until the colonel's quarters were empty. They looked each other over, with the subaltern grinning as if everything were a great joke.

"Ride separately," Winsloe ordered. "Find Colonel Bellairs in Pretoria, inform him of our numbers and position, and tell him we are embarrassed by the presence of the ladies here, and we are using up ammunition at an alarming rate."

Andrew nodded as Cunningham jumped up. "Will do, sir!"

"We'll leave at night," Andrew decided. "Twenty minutes apart. Cunningham and I will study the maps and decide if we're going the same or alternate routes."

"One more thing," Winsloe said quietly. "Lt-Colonel Anstruther is also on his way from Middelburg to Pretoria with about two hundred and fifty men of the 94th Foot. If you meet him, let him know our situation. If you ride in uniform, the Boers won't shoot you as a spy, but you'll blend in better if you wear civilian clothes. The choice is yours. Oh, and remember, your duty is to pass your message along. Don't get involved in any situation that endangers you; the message matters above everything else."

Cunningham grinned. "We'll do our duty, sir!"

"I'll leave the fine details to you," Winsloe said. "Good luck, gentlemen."

CHAPTER 7

BRONKHORST SPRUIT, THIRTY-EIGHT MILES FROM PRETORIA

20TH OF DECEMBER 1880

Andrew lifted his head at the sound of jaunty music and recognised the tune "Kiss Me, Mother Darling."

That's a regimental band, not a Boer commando, but why the music? Don't they realise we're at war?

Andrew saw the rising dust next and pushed Lancelot forward, hoping it was Colonel Anstruther's 94th Foot. He felt a surge of reassurance, remembering the steady infantry of the Zulu Wars with their black humour and regular volleys that dissolved the charging impis. *It must be Anstruther. Nobody else would be out here.*

When Andrew heard the distinct jingle of a horse's harness closer at hand, he froze and leaned forward in his saddle. Experience from the Zulu and Frontier Wars made him pull into the shelter of a group of acacia trees. He heard a voice speaking in Afrikaans and the deep rumble of a man laughing.

Trouble. Keep still and assess the situation.

Andrew quietly dismounted. Forcing the horse to lie, he sank to the ground and crawled onto a small ridge, hoping not to disturb any snakes. He felt the ground vibrate and heard the regular tramp of boots and the distinctive bark of a sergeant.

"Heads up, boys, not long until we have a break!"

The 94th were marching in a rough column, many with their white sun helmets pushed to the back of their heads in search of a cool breeze. Some had their Martini-Henry rifles held at the trail or balanced on their shoulders, with the senior officers riding in front and the junior officers and NCOs marching with their men. Behind the main body of infantry, a long convoy of thirty-four wagons trundled across the rough track, with the drivers cracking their whips, shouting, and whistling to encourage the oxen. Andrew saw some civilians on the wagons and guessed they were the wives and families of the marching men.

A few mounted infantrymen rode four hundred yards ahead of the column, and Andrew saw one gallop back to speak to Anstruther. The colonel halted his horse and scanned a farmhouse with his field glasses before shaking his head and pushing on.

Listen to your scouts, Anstruther! That's why you have them. We're at war, for God's sake, not marching across Salisbury Plain!

Andrew looked ahead, where a small group of mounted Boers waited behind a rocky outcrop. He saw others, extended in a skirmish line hidden behind a ridge, with a thin screen of thorn bushes for cover.

Are these men watching the 94th? What's happening here?

It's an ambush, Andrew thought as he saw hundreds more Boers hiding among the rocks. *The 94th are in a peacetime formation, marching into a war situation.*

Andrew slowly unholstered his rifle. His orders were to deliver his message and avoid trouble, but the Boers would massacre the British column unless he warned the 94th.

A Boer spoke nearby, the words low but recognisable.

"Shall I fire?"

"Wait until Commandant Joubert gives the order."

Commandant Joubert? That must be Commandant Frans Joubert, who commands the Boers in this area.

Andrew slid further under the shelter of the trees and slid his finger over the trigger. He hoped that a single rifle shot would warn Colonel Anstruther.

Fire a single shot, mount, and ride like the devil.

Andrew tensed himself and stiffened when he felt something hard prod into his spine.

"What are you doing, *meneer?*"

Andrew froze and slowly looked around to see a young, bearded Boer. The Boer lifted his rifle, eyeing Andrew curiously.

"Who are you?" The Boer asked quietly. "I do not know your face." He prodded Andrew's stomach with the rifle.

"Who are you?" Andrew replied in his halting Afrikaans. "I don't know your face either."

"Jacobus Bester," the Boer replied. "Are you a *Rooineck?*"

"Do I look like a *Rooineck?*" Andrew tried to bluff his way free. He indicated his clothes, especially chosen to help him blend with the Burghers.

"You sound like a *Rooineck*," Jacobus sounded puzzled. He lifted his rifle so it pointed at Andrew's chest. "Stay there."

"I'm not going anywhere," Andrew said. He saw a bead of sweat form on Jacobus's forehead and knew the boy was nervous. *Sufficiently nervous to fire on the slightest provocation? I'll play this game by ear.*

A sudden movement from the British column diverted both men as the band stopped playing.

"Boers!" An officer's voice sounded.

Colonel Anstruther returned to the column, shouting orders. "Halt! Close up the wagons! Prepare the men for action!"

Andrew watched the bandsmen run to the wagons to find their rifles, and other men sought ammunition. In the meantime, a lone Boer rode towards the head of the column.

"That's Paul de Beer," Andrew's captor said, as casually as if discussing a neighbour. "Now we'll see the *Rooinecks* turn tail!"

Two officers accompanied Colonel Anstruther as he walked his horse toward de Beer.

"Colonel Anstruther," de Beer's voice carried clearly to Andrew. "You are in the free *Zuid Afrikaanse Republiek* of Transvaal. I insist that you and your men turn around and return from where you have come." He handed over a folded note. "This letter is from the leaders of the Republic in Heidelberg."

Anstruther opened the message. "This letter tells me to stop where I am," he reported to his officers. "It says that any further movement towards Pretoria will be seen as a declaration of war." He read the letter aloud, closing with "The responsibility whereof we put on your shoulders."

De Beer waited until Anstruther finished the letter, then added. "You have two minutes to respond."

"My orders are to proceed with all possible despatch to Pretoria," Anstruther snapped. "And to Pretoria, I am going, but tell the Commandant I have no wish to meet him in a hostile spirit."

"Do you wish war or peace, Colonel?" De Beer asked.

"I intend to continue my journey, sir," Anstruther replied.

"Is it war or peace, Colonel Anstruther?" De Beer repeated.

"I intend to continue my journey."

As Colonel Anstruther and de Beer spoke, Jacobus divided his attention between Andrew and the drama unfolding below. Despite the ongoing conversation, armed Boers advanced on the scarlet-uniformed officers. Unsuspecting British soldiers waited for the result, with many unarmed and the officers curious to see what transpired.

The Boers were about two hundred yards from the British when an angry Anstruther returned to his men. Andrew noticed an elderly Boer with a long white beard taking his position beneath a thorn bush. He lay on his stomach, loaded a hunting rifle, and pushed it forward, holding the butt against his cheek. For a moment, the sun highlighted the leopard skin band on the man's hat and reflected on his bright, aged eyes.

Andrew realised that Jacobus was watching the encounter. Slowly lifting his rifle, Andrew was about to fire a warning shot when a second Boer took hold of his arm.

"I'll have your Martini," the second Boer ordered in thickly accented English. With grey streaks in his beard and his hat pulled low over his eyes, he pressed his rifle against Andrew's chest. "Give it to me, *Rooineck*!"

Inwardly swearing, Andrew handed over his rifle without a word.

"Thank you, *meneer*," the Boer said. "What name do you have?"

Before Andrew could reply, movement from the British column distracted all three men.

De Beer had ridden back to the commando and searched for Frans Joubert even as Colonel Anstruther spoke to his officers. Only a few minutes had passed when an impatient Boer leader gave the order to attack.

Andrew saw the hundreds of Boers emerge from cover to open fire on the British column. From close range on an exposed enemy in column, the Boer musketry felled scores of the 94th before they knew they were at war. The Boer with the leopard skin band aimed at a tall officer, squeezed the trigger, and immediately reloaded. At such a close range, he did not need to check the result of his shot. The officer crumpled, dead before he hit the ground.

"Skirmish order!" Anstruther shouted as he galloped back to his men. "Open up to skirmish order! For God's sake, move!"

More Boers galloped closer to the column, dismounted, and lay behind every fold of ground, rock, and thorn bush. Andrew did not hear anybody giving orders, only the incessant hammer of musketry as the Burghers fired on the disorganised 94th Foot. Many of the British soldiers were still in columns of four and fell before they could level their rifles. The unarmed bandsmen died still holding their instruments.

It's a massacre. These lads don't know what's happening.

Andrew saw the long-bearded old Boer take careful aim at the officers and fell them, one by one. His leopard skin band hardly moved as he altered aim to Anstruther and fired, hitting the colonel in the left leg. Anstruther staggered but remained on his feet, shouting orders that were lost in the hellish din of musketry and wounded men. The old Boer aimed and fired again, knocking Anstruther to the ground.

Andrew could only watch in horror as the Boers formed a horseshoe around the British column, some firing from horseback but most from the cover of rocks and folds in the ground.

Those of the 94th who could retaliate stood in the open and fired back. Most of the shots flew high, and Andrew swore.

Adjust your sights! The Boers are close, and you're aiming for distance shooting.

Despite Colonel Anstruther falling with multiple wounds and nearly all the other officers being dead or wounded, the surviving 94th stood fast. Caught at a disadvantage in territory the enemy knew well, they refused to break or panic. Although their shooting was inaccurate, Andrew admired their courage.

Further down the column, scores of mounted Boers charged at the supply wagons. Andrew saw them fire from around four hundred yards, gallop through the smoke, shoot at the oxen, civilian drivers, and escort before wheeling their horses and returning. Some native drivers fell, dead or wounded, and the others fled, running before these merciless horsemen of the veld.

"Shoot them!" Jacobus shouted, firing towards the beleaguered British. "Shoot them all!"

With the second Boer holding him at rifle point, Andrew swore in frustration as the Boers massacred the British infantry. The 94th fired back, aiming at the hiding Boers or the mobile horsemen, but with the officers and non-commissioned officers gone, the men were leaderless and bewildered. Within ten minutes, over a hundred British soldiers had fallen, and five minutes later, Colonel Anstruther, badly wounded, ordered the cease-fire and surrendered.

"We won!" Jacobus began to cheer, with his friend joining in. They shook hands, yelling at their victory and nearly dancing as they watched Joubert approach the shattered British column.[1]

Now! Now's my time!

With his captors distracted, Andrew grabbed back his rifle, crashed the butt into the young Boer's shoulder, pushed his surprised companion away, and ran to his horse.

"Come on, Lancelot!"

Andrew had mounted before the Boers recovered, and spurred towards the south as the first shots screamed past his head.

You're too late, lads! You'll have to catch me now!

Jinking and turning, Andrew galloped away, not heading in any direction but determined to escape from the Boers. He gambled that Francois Joubert would be too busy with his prisoners to be concerned about a lone British horseman. Only a few Boers followed him, four riders on small Boer ponies and one with a larger horse. When Andrew looked over his shoulder, he recognised the horse as a thoroughbred, fine for European conditions but too delicate for the rough veld. Andrew frowned, easing Lancelot into an erratic run to disturb the aim of any potential marksman.

After a quarter of a mile, Lancelot had increased the distance over his pursuers. Andrew allowed him a few moments' rest while he lifted his field glasses to examine the Boers. Riding slightly behind his companions, the man on the thoroughbred was tall and straight. Andrew grunted.

That's Konrad Bramigan. That's the Prussian spy!

With Joubert blocking the route to Pretoria and the Boers having declared war on the British Empire, Andrew realised he was deep in a hostile country. Glancing behind him, he saw no signs of pursuit.

Joubert or no Joubert, I'll try to get to Bellairs in Pretoria.

CHAPTER 8

Andrew kicked in his heels, heading north, deeper into the Transvaal, to avoid Joubert's army. Watchful for parties of Boers, hostile or otherwise, he covered five miles before resting Lancelot at a *spruit*. He knew it was about thirty-two miles from Bronkhorst Spruit to Pretoria, a day's ride at most, but Lancelot was tired, and his route must be circuitous.

Twice, Andrew saw small bodies of armed Boers riding towards Pretoria, kicking up dust as they powered forward. He heard an occasional crack as somebody fired a rifle.

Well, Colonel Bellairs, I hope you are ready to launch a relief column. British arms aren't doing very well in this war, but we rarely do at the start of a campaign.

Andrew rode slowly until he realised something significant was happening outside Pretoria. He saw the Union Flag flying above a large walled encampment and dust rising from a concourse of people. Andrew pulled Lancelot to a halt and watched for a few moments. Men, women, and children moved slowly from the town, most on foot, some on horseback and others in wagons.

Exodus. I am watching an exodus of people; the Jews are leaving Egypt, but Bellairs is no Moses. What is happening here?

A group of mounted men escorted the civilians, wearing a uniform that Andrew did not recognise. He watched for a moment, wondering if the Boers had already captured Pretoria, and then rode forward. As he approached the refugees, he heard an officer snapping a command in abrupt English.

"Halloa!" Andrew shouted, keeping one hand on the butt of his rifle. "What's happening here?"

The uniformed officer turned to face Andrew. "Who the devil are you?"

"Captain Andrew Baird of the Natal Dragoons," Andrew introduced himself. "Who are you and what's happening here?"

"Captain? You don't look like a captain."

"What's happening?"

"I am Lieutenant Bryan of the Pretoria Carbineers, and Colonel Bellairs has declared martial law in Pretoria."

"Who are all these people, and where are they going?"

Bryan shouted a string of orders that saw his men urge the civilians to greater speed.

"These are the British citizens of Pretoria," Bryan explained.

"Sir," Andrew prompted, "you say 'sir' to a superior officer. What's happening here?"

Bryan stiffened in the saddle. "Yes, sir. Colonel Bellairs has established a camp half a mile southwest of Pretoria and a defended redoubt, the Convent Redoubt, near the Loreto Convent. We're commandeering all the food and moving the British civilians into the camp, sir."

Andrew saw the refugees hurry past, most carrying bundles of clothes and bedding, some with children in their arms, all confused, a few in tears. "Where's Colonel Bellairs?"

"He's in the camp, sir," Bryan said, pointing in the direction the civilians headed.

"Thank you." Andrew pushed on, watching for Boers as he passed the long column of refugees. It felt like the end of the world, or at least the end of British power in the Transvaal.

Did the British not play 'The World Turned Upside Down' when they surrendered Yorktown to Washington in 1781? This situation feels similar.

A veteran of the Crimean and Xhosa Wars, Colonel William Bellairs was slightly overweight, with a receding hairline and a fine moustache. He greeted Andrew with a nod and listened to his report from Potchefstroom.

"Thank you, Captain," Bellairs replied. "I cannot help Winsloe at present as I expect the Boers to invest me here in Pretoria."

"So I see, sir."

"Lieutenant Cunningham reached here hours ago, and I ordered him to inform Winsloe he'll have to wait for relief from Natal. I cannot afford men to help Potchefstroom when we are also under siege."

Andrew looked around the fortified enclosure with its bell tents and perimeter guards. A scattering of wooden huts and other buildings waited for the Pretoria refugees. "How many people will you have here, sir?"

"Around five thousand, mostly civilians," Bellairs replied. "Our garrison is five companies of infantry from the 21st and 94th Foot, with a troop of mounted infantry, and two nine-pounders of the Royal Artillery, maybe seven hundred regulars including support and medical staff."

"I saw some colonials as well, sir," Andrew said.

"I have over four hundred Pretoria Rifles and a couple of hundred mounted men, Nourse's Horse and the Pretoria Carbineers."

Andrew nodded. "That should be sufficient to stop the Boers," he said.

"I also have a couple of forts in the hills south of the town," Bellairs seemed desperate to detail his defence arrangements. "We'll need every man we can get. You confirmed the details of the dreadful affair at Bronkhorst Spruit, and I expect thousands of Boers to attack us any time."

Andrew looked at the haphazard array of tents, huts, and buildings within Bellairs' enclosure. "Will you be using this encampment as a base to attack the Boers, sir? The infantry could hold the fort, and the mounted men raid the enemy."

Never give unasked advice to a superior officer.

Bellairs' expression altered. "I'll attend to the strategy later, Captain. In the meantime, we'll hold the fort and await a relief column from Natal."

"I see, sir," Andrew said.

"You have delivered your message, Baird, and I have replied. Cunningham will be halfway back to Potchefstroom by now. You may return to Colonel Winsloe or not, as you please."

Andrew nodded, aware Bellairs had dismissed him. *I have a choice: find one of the British garrisons and sit tight until somebody relieves us, or ride for Natal. Well, I'm not sitting behind a wall to be sniped and starved by Brother Boer.* Andrew felt a surge of relief that he had made the decision.

"I'll ride to Natal, sir, and inform them of your desperate plight."

JOHANNES LOADED HIS RIFLE AND CHECKED HIS SONS. JAN LEANED AGAINST A tree, cleaning his rifle, while Mannie was pale beneath his tan, licking dry lips as he stared over the battlefield of Bronkhorst Spruit. Busy medical teams tended to the dead and wounded redcoats.

"That was your first battle," Johannes said. "And you both survived." He pushed away his guilt at putting his sons in danger. Jan was nearly a man, and Mannie also had to learn a Burgher's duties.

"Ja," Jan replied. He lifted his rifle and automatically pushed a cartridge into the breech. "We all survived." He looked up briefly and tried to ignore the pitiful groans of a wounded soldier. The smell of gun smoke and raw blood clung to the ground and his clothing. He had not realised that even such a short battle could smell so strongly.

Mannie continued to stare at the field of slaughter. "I killed a *Rooineck*," he said. "One minute, he was standing, and then I shot him, and he fell. He screamed. I heard him scream." Mannie's rifle lay on the ground at his feet.

"If you had not shot him, he would have killed you, Mannie," Johannes said. "That is his job. He is not a farmer like us or a storekeeper or a merchant. His job was to fight and kill for his country." He put a rough hand on his son's shoulder. "You did what you had to do."

"The good Lord said thou shalt not kill." Mannie refused to be consoled. He had only fired two shots. The first had missed, and the second killed the soldier.

"He also said an eye for an eye," Johannes reminded him. "The *Rooinecks* invaded our country."

"Yes," Mannie agreed, fighting the tears that threatened to unman him. "They invaded our land. We had to kill them." He pushed his rifle further away, reliving the instant his bullet hit the soldier, the expression on the man's face, the way his mouth gaped, and his body contorted as the bullet entered his chest. "I had to kill him."

Jan watched without saying anything. He shared some of Mannie's feelings but was older and hid them better. He remembered every detail of the battle, from de Beer challenging the British colonel to the men firing and falling and the final surrender. Although Jan had been on many hunting trips, killing men was different to shooting game. He had seen the bravery of the British soldiers, standing in the open as the Boers shot them down, but he also thought them foolish not to lie on the ground or find cover.

Ja, the Rooinecks are a foolish people to fight like that. The Lord made them act like targets so we could not miss. Jan smiled, trying to convince himself that God was on the Boer's side. He winked at Mannie and tried to forget the men he had shot.

"Engela will be glad you survived," Johannes tried to cheer his sons up. He remembered his first commando when he had ridden against a band of tribesmen who had murdered a neighbour and committed unspeakable atrocities on the man's wife.

When Jan looked up, a new light chased the dark shadows from his eyes. "I wonder if she ever thinks of me."

Johannes began to pack tobacco into the bowl of his pipe. "Ja, she will think of you more often than you think of her." He smiled as Jan coloured. "Why don't you write her, Jan? Tell her what you have been doing and how Abraham has been fighting harder than you."

"He has not!" Jan said.

Johannes scratched a match and applied the flame to his pipe. "I can guarantee he'll tell Engela about his heroic actions and how he defeated the British single-handedly."

"He did not!" Jan raised his voice.

"I know that, and you know that," Johannes said. "But Engela doesn't know. Maybe you'd better write and tell her what you've been doing. Women like men to talk to them." He stepped away and turned around as if to add an afterthought. "Ask how Engela is doing as well. Women also like you to be interested in their lives."

"Where can I find paper and a pen?"

"Didn't I say?" Johannes reached inside his jacket. "I found this in a British officer's saddlebag. He won't need it again." He pulled out a small leather case which contained a writing pad with pens, ink, and blotting paper. When Jan took the case, Johannes winked at Mannie. "Come on, Mannie, Jan will be busy for a while. We can talk in peace and then return to Potchefstroom."

ANDREW SAW THE HUMP OF MAJUBA HILL RISING AHEAD OF HIM AND EASED Lancelot to a halt at a cool spring. "Drink your fill, Lance," he said, "we might have a long day tomorrow."

For the previous three days, Andrew had avoided parties of Boers moving towards the border between the Transvaal and Natal. The Boers had ridden singly, in small groups or large commandos with ox-wagons driven by skilled Africans. As he waited beside the spring, Andrew heard the distinct crack of a wagon whip and the discordant rumbling of wheels on the ground.

How many Boers are there, for goodness' sake? The Transvaal seemed to have poured its entire Boer manhood to the border. *Will they invade Natal and invoke the Afrikander Bond to drive the British into the sea?*

Andrew pushed Lancelot harder, aware it would take a flight of imagination for a Boer to recognise him as British, as he wore similar clothes and rode in the same fashion. Wondering where the Boers were headed, Andrew followed one small commando, keeping half a mile in the rear and lifting a hand in acknowledgement when anybody passed nearby.

Within two hours, the commando rode into a large concourse of men and horses, with two large wagon laagers and scores of draft oxen.

That's far enough, Andrew decided. *I've found the Boers' main camp. Now, I must cross the pass into Natal and alert the British authorities.*

Potchefstroom, December and January 1881.

Jan loaded his rifle, checked the foresight, and winked at Mannie. "Are you all right, Mannie?"

The youngster nodded, brushed a fly away from his face and nodded. "Ja, I am all right." He forced a smile that lacked any humour.

They sheltered inside a large building with a view of the fort, avoiding the window, for it invited bullets when both sides exchanged gunfire. Hanging limply above the fort, the multi-crossed Union flag proclaimed British control. Other members of the Groenburg Commando occupied the other rooms, having commandeered the building as their base.

"We will soon remove that flag," Johannes joined them, passing out bread. "Keep your strength up, boys."

Lifting his rifle, Jan took a snapshot at a bobbing British helmet. "That made him jump."

"We are not here to make the British jump," Johannes reprimanded his son. "We are here to chase them back across the sea. Don't waste your ammunition."

Jan nodded, shamefaced, and reloaded, pressing home the brass cartridge. Mannie had not moved, holding the bread in his hand.

"Our artillery is arriving tomorrow," Johannes said. "Then we shall see how the British react."

"Artillery?" Mannie showed some interest. "I didn't know we had cannons."

Johannes sat beside his sons, leaned on the wall, and placed his rifle at his side. "We don't have parks of artillery like the *Rooinecks*, but we have a few cannons." Taking his pipe from his pocket, he stuffed tobacco into the bowl, scratched a match and applied it, puffing happily.

All three ducked when the British replied to Jan's single shot with a volley that crashed against the outside wall of the house. One bullet smashed the last remaining glass in the window, sending glittering shards into the room.

"That's another reason for not firing at the British," Johannes told Jan. "It makes them angry." He grinned, drawing on his pipe. "I was telling you about our artillery. When the British annexed our republic in April 1877, we knew their occupation would not last and prepared for war with them."

Jan and Mannie listened, with Karl, Abraham and a few others inside the house also paying attention. Jan flicked some loose glass from his bread and took a bite as Johannes continued.

"You may remember that when we fought the Zulus at Blood River in 1838, we had an old ship's gun for artillery, and we used another cannon at Boomplats."

Jan nodded, for the battle of Blood River was part of Boer folklore. He knew less about the Battle of Boomplats, probably because the British had won.[1]

"After Shepstone's announcement that the British had annexed our republic," Johannes continued, "we buried the barrels of the old cannon to prevent the *Rooinecks* from taking them." He puffed out smoke, removed the pipe from his mouth and prodded Jan with the stem. "One gun is called *Ou Greif* and comes from Carron in Scotland. It was made over a hundred years ago, in 1762."

"Does it still fire?" Mannie asked.

"We'll make it fire," Johannes replied solemnly. "We'll turn the British gun against them."

All three van Colliers looked over as Karl aimed and fired, with the British retaliating with a surprisingly quick volley. Bullets struck dust from the walls of the house and splintered wood from the window frame. Johannes looked up briefly, brushed dust from his shoulder and continued.

"The British navy used *Ou Greif* in the later eighteenth century," Johannes said. "It's not a big barrel, only twenty-four inches long, and was built for case, that's bags of small balls rather than cannonballs."

"It won't hurt the British fort then," Jan immediately understood. "We need something explosive or a heavy ball for that."

"No," Johannes said. "It won't hurt the walls, only the soldiers."

Mannie ducked as Theunis fired, but the British did not retaliate. "Shoot them!" Theunis shouted. "We won't defeat them by watching from a distance."

"We dug up *Ou Greif* and the other cannon," Johannes ignored Theunis's outburst. "Marthinus Ras of Bokfontein spent days mounting the barrel on a wagon axle and fitted a pair of wheels. Marthinus is a clever man who will use wagon wheel rims to make more cannon. He will help give the British a warm welcome to our republic."

"Or a hot farewell," Theunis said from the far corner of the room.

Jan wondered how even a skilled mechanic could create a cannon from wheel rims when an outbreak of firing brought all the Groenburg Commando to their stations. Johannes fired one shot, watched his sons, and nodded when he realised they were aiming rather than merely firing blindly.

"That's the way, boys," he encouraged. "Let the British waste their cartridges. Every bullet they fire costs Queen Victoria money and weakens their empire."

Karl fired and swore as a British bullet knocked a piece of stone from the wall against his forehead. He put a hand to the wound. "The damned British are learning how to shoot."

Johannes grunted. "They were probably aiming at the house next door," he said. "Let me see." He examined Karl's injury through critical eyes. "It is not even a scratch. It'll take more than a British bullet to damage your thick skull."

"My wife has done worse when she is in a bad mood," Karl said. "I pity the servants when she doesn't have me to shout at."

Jan laughed too loudly, a young man wishing to appear equal to his elders. He glanced sideways as Mannie coughed. "Are you all right?"

"Yes," Mannie said. "The smoke caught my throat."

Jan saw Johannes watching. "It's only gun smoke," he said. "It's because we're inside a room. You wouldn't even notice it outside." He thumbed a cartridge into the breech of his rifle and searched for a target in the fort. "The redcoats have learned how to take cover. We have taught them well."

"We had better not teach them anymore," Karl grumbled. "Or they will be as good as we are."

"Stop firing," Johannes ordered. "Unless you see a definite target." He thought of their limited supply of ammunition. "Don't waste bullets."

As the firing eased, Johannes heard the drumbeat of horses' hooves and a burst of wild cheers. "What's happening? Go and find out, Jan, but keep out of trouble."

Jan kept low as he left the house in case a British sharpshooter was watching, but soon straightened up and ran towards the sound of horsemen.

"What's all the noise?"

"Over there," an old man gestured with his hand. The leopard skin band on his hat seemed out of place in his drab clothing. "Another commando has just arrived in Potchefstroom."

Jan hurried to see the commando. "What's happened? You seem very excited."

A man of about Jan's age removed his hat and banged it against his leg, releasing clouds of dust. "We've been to Klerksdorp," he shouted, laughing. "We raided Leask's stores and got two thousand pounds of lead for bullets and took all the Martini-Henry cartridges he had."

"We don't have many Martinis," Jan said. "The rest will be useful though."

"We'll take out the lead and powder and make bullets for the rifles and round shot for the cannon," the rider explained.

"Could we have some for the Groenburg Commando?" Jan asked. "We are running short of ammunition."

"We'll distribute it fairly," the man said. "You'll get your due."

When Jan returned to the Groenburg Commando, he passed the news to his father.

"Now, can we fire at the British?" Karl asked.

"Not until we have the ammunition in our hands," Johannes replied. He looked up when a man entered the back of the house.

"Johannes van Collier?" The man glanced around.

"That's me," Johannes confirmed.

"You and Theunis are wanted, Johannes. There is a *kriegsraad* [2] in five minutes."

"I'm coming," Johannes replied. He glanced at his sons. "Keep your heads under cover," he said. "Don't let the British see you. They are terrible shots, but one might get lucky."

"I'll look after them," Karl promised. "I'll care for them like they were my own sons."

Johannes shook his head. "I've seen you with your sons, Karl. I expect better than that."

Jan laughed yet could not avoid his loneliness when his father left the house. He heard Mannie's heavy breathing and punched his arm playfully. "He's gone at last, Mannie! Now we can do as we like." Jan knew Mannie's smile was forced and pressed his last piece of bread into his brother's hand. "I can't eat this, Mannie. You'd better have it."

THE DARK CLOSED IN ON THEM, CRISP AND COLD. JAN HELD HIS RIFLE CLOSE to his cheek, sighted along the barrel, and wondered how his mother was coping at Nuwe Hoop Plaas. He felt Mannie trembling at his side.

"It will be all right, Mannie," Jan said. "The British only shoot when we do, and then they miss."

"It's the cold making me shiver," Mannie said. "I am not afraid."

"You are not afraid?" Karl spoke from across the room. "I am afraid. Your father is afraid; we are all afraid. You must control your fear, boy, and don't let it control you."

"It does not control me," Mannie said stubbornly. "I am not afraid."

"Is it time yet?" Jan diverted attention from his brother.

"Nearly," Johannes replied. "You will hear the signal at four o'clock." He resisted the temptation to put an arm around Mannie, knowing such an action would only embarrass the boy.

IN THE EVENING, THE BRITISH HAULED DOWN THEIR FLAG, LEAVING THE empty rope to snap against the flagpole in the breeze. The sound continued all night, a constant irregular crack that carried on the air, nagging at Jan's nerves. He had heard that the redcoats had to make a flag from soldiers' clothes.[3]

Jan did not care if the Union flag was handmade or straight from the queen's factory. He only cared that it was flying over his land.

"In a few minutes, we will wake them," Abraham nudged Jan with a sharp elbow. "You and me together, eh, Jan?"

"You and me together, Abe. And Mannie," Jan glanced at his brother.

Even though he had been expecting it, the sharp bang of a rifle made Jan start.

"Happy New Year, *Rooinecks*!" Karl shouted in heavily accented English.

"Fire!" Johannes ordered, squeezing the trigger. He was glad the recent raid had replenished the Groenburg Commando's ammunition.

Jan and Mannie aimed at the fort, hearing the fusillade from hundreds of Boers against the small British garrison.

"How many men do we have?" Jan asked.

"Over fifteen hundred!" Johannes told him. "And we have artillery!"

As Johannes spoke, *Ou Greif* fired a nine-pound cannonball at the British fort.

"Do you like our new toy, *Rooinecks*?" Theunis shouted. "Do you like it? We altered it to batter you into submission! Are you glad you came to conquer our republic?"

"Fire!" Johannes ordered. He could not see any soldiers on the wall, so he aimed for the tents, faintly white in the darkness of the fort.

Jan saw that the Burghers surrounded three sides of the British fort, with the constant flare from muzzles and the deep boom of the cannon adding to the confusion. After their initial surprise, the British replied, with the 21st Foot lining the wall and Lieutenant Rundle's artillery firing shrapnel wherever groups of Boers congregated.

Jan felt as if he were somebody else, watching events from above. In his mind's eye, he could see the British fort on its slight rise, with the Burghers in the houses and newly dug trenches and the little men firing amidst the orange flashes and thick smoke. He was not here in this foolish war but at home in Nuwe Hoop Plaas, tending his cattle, working with the servants, and dreaming of Engela. Jan could smell the homely cattle scent and hear the cows bellowing to be milked. Jan smiled, for as an experienced cattleman, he could tell what the herd wanted by the sounds they made.

"This time, we will chase them away," Theunis's grating voice brought Jan to reality. "Get back to London, *Rooinecks*!"

Konrad watched from the back of the room, nodding his head in encouragement.

"Aren't you going to fire, Konrad?" Jan asked him.

"I am a neutral observer," Konrad told him. "The German Empire is not at war with Queen Victoria."

"I thought you were here to help us," Theunis said.

"I can help in ways beyond a single rifle," Konrad replied.

Abraham grunted, brushed back his long hair and fired at the fort. "Watching is not helping," he said.

"Listen!" Jan reloaded his rifle. "The British are singing!" He lifted his head to listen. "I don't know that song."

The words came to the Boers, now distinct, now fading away as the sound of musketry drowned the words.

"By yon bonnie banks and by yon bonnie braes,
Where the sun shines bright on Loch Lomond,
Where me and my true love will never meet again,
On the bonnie, bonnie banks of Loch Lomond."

Jan heard the lighter tones of women as the first verse reached its chorus.

"Oh, you take the high road, and I'll take the low road,
And I'll be in Scotland afore ye,
But me and my true love will never meet again,
On the bonnie, bonnie banks of Loch Lomond."

"Why are they singing? Is that a war song to encourage them to battle?" Jan asked.

Abraham pushed back his hat. "It sounds like a love song."

"Fire, Jan!" Johannes pushed his son's shoulder. "Don't listen to their singing!"

Ou Griet roared again, the sound becoming as regular as the musketry.[4]

The British musketry died away after a few minutes, and only the artillery replied. Johannes borrowed a pair of field glasses and studied the fort. He saw the orange flashes of the nine-pounders and the white smear of tents jerking this way and that as Boer bullets ripped through the canvas.

"The *Rooinecks* are not showing themselves," Johannes said. "How can we shoot them unless they show themselves?"

Theunis fired another shot and reloaded quickly. "Perhaps they've had enough, or they've run out of ammunition."

Jan heard the brassy notes of a bugle sounding above the gunfire and the bark of a sergeant's voice.

"Are they going to storm us?" he asked, looking over his shoulder. Mannie was gasping for breath, holding his rifle in white-knuckled hands. Jan had not seen him fire a single shot.

"I do not know what they are going to do," Johannes said. "Maybe they think we are going to storm them." He focused his field glasses on the wall. "I can see the reflection of light on bayonets. They are waiting for us."

Jan shivered. "Bayonets are like spears. We do not fight like that."

"The *Rooinecks* do," Karl said. "I saw them charging the Zulus with their bayonets at Khambula. They enjoy stabbing their bayonets into people."

Jan put a hand on Mannie's trembling shoulder.

"Storm them!" Theunis shouted. "Come on, Burghers! Storm!"

"Stay where you are!" Johannes roared as Abraham and a couple of others rose to obey. "The British are waiting for us!"

Jan hugged the wall, fired, and reloaded, thinking of the horror of a British soldier charging at him with a long bayonet. He saw Mannie wipe a tear from his eye.

"It's the smoke," Mannie's voice shook. "The smoke got in my eye."

"Fire your rifle," Jan said urgently. "It will make you feel better." He pushed Mannie to the window, whispering in his ear. "Aim at the fort and fire!"

Sobbing, Mannie obeyed, firing without aiming. He reloaded clumsily, dropping a bullet so the brass cartridge clattered on the wooden floorboards.

"Pick it up!" Jan saw Theunis watching with a sneer on his face. "Come on, Mannie. The sooner we beat the *Rooinecks,* the quicker we can go home." He helped Mannie load his rifle. "Aim and fire; pretend we are hunting on the farm."

Mannie nodded, blinked away another tear, and obeyed.

"Now keep doing that," Jan dropped his voice. "It's all right, Mannie. This war will end soon, and we can go home."

"I want to go home now," Mannie sobbed.

"Soon," Jan said as he fired at the fort. The defenders were keeping under cover, so he aimed at the tents. He fancied he saw his bullet tear through the canvas, grunted, and loaded again. He saw his father crouch beside Mannie and concentrated on the fort, pushing away thoughts of Engela.

At seven in the morning, the Boers' firing stuttered to a halt.

"Have the British surrendered?" Mannie asked hopefully.

"Not yet, Mannie," Johannes replied. He heard the bugle playing defiantly and saw a man hoisting the Union flag back up the pole. "We haven't chased them away yet."

Gunsmoke drifted across Potchefstroom as the sun struggled to light up the scene of the battle.

"Will we ever shift these *Rooinecks*?" Jan asked, lowering his rifle. The barrel was hot to the touch.

"We will," Johannes said.

"When?" Mannie mumbled. "I want to go home."

"So do most of us," Karl said. "We only agreed to a few days away from the farm. I think I'll go back home tomorrow."

Mannie looked at his father hopefully. Johannes shook his head. "We stay here," he said. "Unless the British send an army to invade the republic."

"Then can we go home?" Mannie asked.

"No," Johannes said. "Then we will fight them." He tried to ignore the tears that Mannie dashed from his eyes. *Be brave, Mannie. Nothing lasts forever.*

CHAPTER 9

BRITISH ARMY HEADQUARTERS, NATAL, DECEMBER 1880

Major-General Sir George Pomeroy Colley, the British Governor and Commander in Chief of Natal, had a reputation as one of Britain's foremost soldiers. Like many of Britain's finest warriors, he was an Irishman, coming from Rathangan, County Kildare. Colley shone at Sandhurst, served in South Africa in 1857-58, and fought with the 2nd Foot in the Second Opium War. After spending time in the staff college, he travelled with Wolseley to West Africa, where he participated in the Ashanti War. He returned to South Africa as Wolseley's Chief of Staff, worked in an administrative role in the Second Afghan War, and recrossed the Indian Ocean to become High Commissioner for Southeastern Africa.

Colley occupied the latter role when he faced Andrew across the width of his desk. Tall, bearded, and balding, he looked down his long, straight nose, stroked his whiskers, and nodded.

"Thank you for your report, Captain Baird. I already know about the position in the Transvaal. We currently have less than three thousand men scattered in garrisons throughout a country larger than mainland Great Britain."

Andrew knew that Colley had doubted the Boers would rise against British rule. He drew in his breath. "That's a small number of men to hold down a country," he said.

"It is," Colley agreed. "We also have an unofficial base in Swartspruit far to the west, near the Kalahari Desert."

Andrew frowned. "I don't know that one, sir. I thought I knew the British garrisons in the Transvaal," he said.

Colley tapped delicate fingers on the desk. "Most of our positions, I'd hesitate to call them forts, are more than fifty miles from their neighbour. Some hold irregular colonials rather than regular soldiers and fewer than fifty defenders. Swartspruit has even fewer. Indeed, I doubt it has a dozen men." Colley looked up. "The Boers can isolate our posts and pick them off, one by one."

"I understand that, sir," Andrew agreed. "I know they are blockading Potchefstroom, and Colonel Winsloe hopes somebody will send a relief column. Colonel Bellairs in Pretoria is convinced the Boers will besiege him and also asks for help, sir."

Colley smiled gently. "I haven't forgotten your report, Baird. We have Wakkerstroom and Standerton in the south of the country, Marasastad in the north, and Rustenburg and Potchefstroom in the west." He stepped to a map on the wall and indicated each position. "You have informed me of the state of Potchefstroom and Pretoria. From what little information I can gather, I presume the other forts are similar."

"Yes, sir," Andrew said.

Colley stroked his whiskers again. "We hold our Empire with a skeleton force, Baird, and we can't let other powers call our bluff. To ensure we retain the world's greatest empire, we must maintain our reputation, which means winning all our wars." He paused to fix Andrew with a steady stare. "There are always hyenas baying around the Empire. Some are waiting for scraps we discard, and others hope to replace us as the world's foremost power." His fingers began tapping again. "Do you know who I mean, Baird?"

"Perhaps, sir," Andrew said cautiously. "The major powers are France, Russia, Austria, and now Prussia, although I think Italy may be hoping to join the club."

"France is interested in North and West Africa," Colley said. "Russia is our rival in Central Asia and hopes for a warm water port at the expense of Turkey. Italy is too young to be a threat, which leaves the German Empire."

"Yes, sir." Andrew did not know whether he should mention Konrad Bramigan and decided to keep quiet.

"We must show a bold face to hold them all at bay." Colley moved to the map. "I intend to muster an army, enter the Transvaal, and relieve the garrisons," he said. "If we are lucky, the Boers will stand to fight, and we can smash them in battle."

"They're a formidable people, sir," Andrew said. "I saw them at Potchefstroom and Bronkhorst Spruit when they defeated the 94th. They outmanoeuvred a column of good infantry."

"They vastly outnumber the garrison at Potchefstroom, while at Bronkhorst Spruit, they ambushed a column on the march," Colley countered. "They've declared war on us. Let's see how good they are." He smiled. "Now, Baird, you've witnessed the Boers at first-hand. Tell me everything you can about them."

"They are mobile mounted infantry, sir," Andrew said. "Excellent horsemen and fine shots."

"What weapons do they have?"

Andrew thought for a moment before he replied. "The men I saw carried a variety of rifles, sir. Some had Martinis, Sniders, or Snider-Enfields, and a few older farmers had muzzle-loaders that must be thirty years old."

Colley nodded.

Andrew thought back to the Boers' armaments. "However, most had the Wesley Richards breech-loaders, .45 calibre with percussion caps. I saw a handful with repeating rifles like the American Winchester or the Swiss Vetterli."

Colley scribbled notes. "Wesley Richards breech-loaders," he repeated. "Their weapons are as modern as ours."

"Yes, sir, for the most part," Andrew said.

"You told me that the Boer general, Piet Joubert, and around two thousand men have camped on the far side of the Drakensberg mountains at the pass of Laing's Nek."

"That is my estimate of his numbers, sir," Andrew said. "Boer numbers tend to fluctuate as men decide to join or leave the army."

Colley shook his head. "What a way to run a country. No wonder they needed us to rectify their economy."

"It's certainly not how we would do things," Andrew agreed.

"I intend to meet Joubert in battle," Colley said. "The Boers may be good at ambushing men before they know they're at war, but Joubert is a farmer, and I am a professional soldier. We'll see how the Boers fare against British soldiers with their tails up."

"I am sure you're correct, sir," Andrew said. "I neglected to mention the Boers are excellent at finding cover. At Bronkhorst Spruit, they lay behind boulders or in dead ground to shoot at our men, and most of our shots were too high."

"We found the Ashanti tribesmen were also skilled at hiding when they fired."

"Yes, sir," Andrew replied. "The Ashanti carried old-fashioned Danish muskets that fired slugs with little penetrating power. The Boers do not have that disadvantage."

"I am sure British soldiers can cope, Captain Baird," Colley said. "Thank you for your assistance and advice. You'll want to return to your unit now, Natal Rangers, isn't it?"

"Natal Dragoons, sir," Andrew said. "Before I return, I have another report to deliver."

"To whom?" Colley asked.

"General Hook, sir. It's a verbal report."

Colley gave Andrew a cold stare. "Very well. Do you know where General Hook is based?"

"I know his headquarters is in Newcastle, sir."

"Go to him," Colley allowed.

"Thank you, sir." Andrew left General Colley's office with a feeling of deep foreboding. *That man underestimates the Boers.*

Hook listened to Andrew's report without any change of expression. "You have no doubt it was Konrad Bramigan," he said quietly.

"No doubt at all, sir," Andrew said.

Hook sighed. "I sent to London for any intelligence on that fellow. He's a Prussian aristocrat named Von Bramigan, with large estates in East Prussia. He is close to the Prussian hierarchy and had a reputation as a fire-eater and skilled duellist at university."

Andrew nodded. "I thought the scar on his face was a souvenir of a duel. He's a brave man, then, and perhaps intelligent."

Hook grunted. "Perhaps so. The Prussians use swords with a large guard they call the soup plate of honour and wear protective head and body gear so any wounds will only be superficial. Then they allow the wound to remain open, making the scar more prominent."

Andrew smiled. "No false modesty with the Prussians, then."

"Evidently not," Hook said. "When Bramigan was young, he joined the army and fought in the Franco-Prussian War. He was a junior officer in the Prussian Guards and acquitted himself well, by all accounts. He won a medal or two and followed the rules and traditions of war, Prussian style."

"If he was a Prussian Guardsman, sir, why become a spy in Africa? Is that not beneath a member of the aristocracy?"

Hook nodded. "You hit the nail squarely on its proverbial head, Baird. I also asked myself that question and ordered my people in London and Berlin to investigate further. They discovered that Bramigan had a spectacular fall from grace and all over a woman."

"Ah," Andrew nodded. "The old story, was it?"

"The Prussian newspapers were alive with rumours and speculation," Hook said. "My people found out he seduced the daughter of one of the nobility, even though she was far younger than him and promised to another man. Bramigan challenged the girl's father and her fiancé to a duel, but both refused and instead had him kicked out of the Guards."

Andrew remembered Konrad's arrogant stance. "He wouldn't like that very much."

"Apparently not," Hook agreed. "Bismarck intervened and sent Bramigan to Africa. I don't know the details of his mission, but my people say he will be reinstated in his old regiment if he's successful. If he fails, he may as well not return to Prussia."

Andrew whistled. "He has a strong motivation to succeed."

"And we have a strong motivation to stop him," Hook said. He sighed. "All right, you've been busy and deserve some leave. Take two days to see that woman you rescued; what was her name again?"

"Mariana Maxwell," Andrew reminded.

"Yes, Mariana Maxwell. Take two days with her and then report to the Natal Dragoons. Have them in readiness for the fray."

"Will General Colley invade the Transvaal, sir?"

"The purely military is Colley's domain, Baird. I cannot interfere in his decisions." Hook sorted the papers on his desk with an air of finality. "However, Colley is an ambitious officer, and I am sure he won't allow the Boers to besiege British garrisons without attempting a relief." He paused for a significant moment. "Whatever the Prime Minister wishes. Her Majesty would not approve of inaction."

"No, sir. The Queen is more in touch with the nation's feelings than Gladstone seems to be."

"You'll be glad to return to real soldiering, Baird."

"Yes, sir."

"Your father was always thankful to return to his regiment," Hook said with a dry smile.

"It must be in the blood, sir," Andrew replied.

Andrew was thoughtful as he rode slowly home. It seemed that Konrad Bramigan had a weakness for women. *Is it any woman? Or was he only attracted to one woman in particular?* Andrew shook his head. *I doubt it will make any difference to this war.*

Mariana was hoeing the front garden when Andrew dismounted. "Andrew!" She dropped the hoe, lifted her skirt above her ankles and hurried to him. "Andrew! You're back!"

"I am!" It was instinct that made Andrew lift her and whirl her in a circle before placing her back on the ground. "How have you been?" He looked into her eyes, dreading to see the dark shadows that had dominated her since her kidnapping.

She smiled back, evidently happy to see him. "Mr Briggs has been looking after me," Mariana said. "He's been teaching me about the army, and I've been telling him about Natal and how to farm." She grabbed his arm. "Come on in, Andrew, and tell me what you've been doing."

The house looked immaculate, as Andrew had expected, with Briggs standing at attention outside the door. "Welcome home, sir," he said.

"Thank you, Briggs. Anything to report?"

Briggs slid his eyes towards Mariana before he replied. "All's well here, sir."

"Good. I think coffee is in order," Andrew said. "And whatever scoff [1] you can rustle up."

Briggs smiled. "Give me five minutes, sir."

Andrew was unsure what he thought when he looked at Mariana. On one hand, she reminded him of Elaine. On the other, he remembered the bubbly, laughing girl she had been before the renegades captured her and who still occasionally surfaced.

"How have you been, Mariana?" Andrew handed Lancelot's reins to a servant and entered the house.

"I've been well, thank you," Mariana replied.

The house's interior smelled of beeswax polish.

Briggs brought coffee for Andrew and Mariana before retiring to the kitchen, leaving them alone.

"Now," Andrew said. "Tell me all your news."

He listened, smiling, as Mariana related her catalogue of domestic triumphs and disasters, with Andrew watching the play of emotions on her face. Mariana looked up every few seconds, anxious in case Andrew's attention strayed. She smiled to please him whenever her flow of words slowed.

"Carry on," Andrew encouraged.

"I must be boring you," Mariana's words tailed off.

"You're not," Andrew replied, looking into her eyes for the recurring shadows. He grunted in satisfaction when her eyes remained clear. "You're looking a lot better."

"Mr Briggs has been looking after me," Mariana repeated.

"That's good," Andrew approved, unable to recognise the emotion twisting within him. "I am glad you two are friends." He thought for a moment of the impropriety of leaving Mariana alone with a man but dismissed the images that came to mind.

"How long are you here for?" Mariana asked.

"I have to return to the regiment in two days," Andrew told her. He saw the disappointment on her face. "We're in Newcastle," he said, "and I'll be able to see you often unless we're called to the war."

"I hope you're not sent to the war," Mariana said.

"So do I," Andrew replied truthfully.

POTCHEFSTROOM, JANUARY 1881

The church echoed to raised voices as hundreds of besiegers crammed inside. Jan stood at the back, with Mannie at his left. Both had their hats in their left hand as they sang the old familiar hymns.

"This reminds me of Sundays back home," Mannie whispered when the singing died away. "Do you think we'll ever see home again?"

"We'll be home soon," Jan told him. "Mother will be waiting for us at the door, and the table will be filled with food. You can tell her all our adventures."

"I've never been away for so long," Mannie said in a hush punctuated by half a dozen low voices.

"Neither have I," Jan admitted, caught the minister frowning at him, and concentrated on the service.

Silence descended save for the rustle of clothes and the shuffle of booted feet on the floorboards. Sunlight seeped through the plain windows, highlighting a face here and there, casting long shadows and revealing the motes of dust that floated in the air. One sunbeam glinted on the array of rifles beside the door, a reminder that peace was an illusion in this town at war.

Jan did not expect to have to use his rifle today, for both the British and Burghers kept an unofficial truce on the Lord's Day. However, Jan knew it was better to be ready to fight, however genuine his sentiments as he praised his Lord and thought of home and Engela.

They say that absence makes the heart grow fonder. I hope Engela feels the same. He glanced at Mannie and looked away, pretending not to notice the tears that glistened on his brother's cheeks.

As the siege entered its twentieth day, the weather changed. Jan looked up as the first drop of rain fell, heavy with portent. It landed on the street, where the dust soaked it up. A second drop followed, and a third, with a low growl of thunder in the distance.

"We're going to get wet," Jan predicted.

Karl nodded. "I have found that rain often gets men wet," he said solemnly.

"I thought you were returning to your farm, Karl," Johannes said.

Karl shrugged and pulled the collar of his jacket up as more rain followed the first few drops. "No. When Dolinde heard we were at war, she handed me my saddle and rifle. 'Go to war, Karl,' she said. 'I can always get a new husband, but I can never get another free republic.'"

Johannes smiled. He knew Karl's wife and believed the story. "It is the women who are the backbone of our nation. They were the strong ones during the Great Trek, and they will hold out against the *Rooinecks* when we have fired our last bullet."

"Ja. Anyway, I dare not go back until we have won. Dolinde will make my life a misery."

Jan listened with a smile. *Tante* Dolinde had always been kind to him, although he had heard her raging at Karl.

Johannes nodded. "If the women were here with us, we'd have captured this fort by now."

Karl laughed. "If Dolinde led us, we'd be flying our flag above Cape Coast Castle or Queen Victoria's palace in London."

"We'd better bring her, then," Mannie made a rare contribution to the conversation. "Then the war will finish soon." He shifted aside when Johannes ruffled his hair.

The rain increased, hammering on the Boers as they occupied the houses in Potchefstroom and the slowly expanding network of trenches.

"I shot another *Rooineck* today," Jan said. "He was crossing inside the fort, more concerned with avoiding the puddles than our rifles, and I shot him through the shoulder."

Johannes smiled. "You are a warrior, Jan," he said.

"I am not a warrior," Mannie looked at his rifle. "I never will be."

"You are young yet," Johannes reminded him. "Maybe you are too young to be on commando."

"*Oom* Gideon's grandson is younger than me," Mannie said. "He is only eleven, and he has shot three *Rooinecks*."

"*Oom* Gideon's grandson boasts of his deeds," Jan told him quietly, "but nobody ever sees him shooting soldiers. I do not believe he has shot anybody."

Mannie looked up. "I also hate the rain," he said.

"However wet we are," Karl reminded them. "The *Rooinecks* will be wetter."

Jan wondered how the British were coping inside the open fort, where they had even less shelter and knew any careless movement could bring down accurate Boer fire. He nudged Mannie with a brotherly elbow. "Cheer up, Mannie; maybe the rain will force the *Rooinecks* to surrender."

Mannie nodded miserably as the rain dripped from the brim of his hat. He coughed, covered his mouth, coughed again, and stifled a sneeze.

The Boers were no longer content to contain the British garrison within the fort, snipe at them and have an occasional shooting frenzy. They dug trenches from Dr. Poortman's house towards the town's magazine, partly to deny the contents to the British but mainly to increase their ammunition supply.

"It's our turn in the trenches today," Johannes told the Groenburg Commando as Jan watched the teeming rain.

"I'll come too," Mannie volunteered, desperate to be accepted in the company of men.

"No, Mannie. You're not well," Johannes said. Mannie had developed a hacking cough over the last few days. "Maybe later when you get better."

"I can dig," Mannie said. "I know how to dig."

"Not this time," Johannes repeated more sternly. "Stay under shelter until your cough gets better."

"Yes, Pa," Mannie lowered his eyes, hiding his relief as he sneezed.

"I've also got a cough," Karl said. "Listen!" He forced a dry rasp. "I'll stay behind as well."

"No," Johannes said. "The dampness in the trench will help lubricate your throat."

Jan found working in a wet trench miserable and tedious, but he hefted his spade and hacked at the sodden ground. "I didn't know that going on commando was like this."

Johannes grunted. "We do what we must do to defend our land. Keep down in case a British sentry decides to shoot you."

Jan shovelled wet earth to one side, where his father piled it on the parapet. He had imagined going on commando would be a short and glorious campaign of a week, perhaps two, with the *Rooinecks* running before them. After the victory, he would enjoy a triumphant return to Nuwe Hoop Plaas. Engela would come to greet him, holding her skirt up as she ran and with her bonnet only partially hiding her smile. Jan could smell her already, the homely, welcoming smell of fresh bread, with her blue eyes laughing in her broad, familiar face.

War was not as he imagined, but he would not complain. He was a man among equals, ready to share the hardships and shed his blood. He could endure. He would prove himself worthy to ride on commando with the other men and be a fitting man for Engela.

"Keep digging," Johannes said. "When we reach the magazine, we will ensure the British can't get more ammunition."

"We'll grind them down," Theunis said, grinning.

They worked on, gasping and panting with the effort of shifting wet soil under a constant downpour.

"That's our time finished," Johannes thrust his shovel into the sodden earth under the puddles. "Let's get somewhere dry, Jan, and find a fire, a mug of coffee, and something to eat."

With Engela still dominant in his mind, Jan smiled. "That is a good idea. I do not enjoy digging holes in the ground."

The coffee was hot, strong, and welcome. Jan leaned back, allowing the warmth to return to his body.

"Is that better?" Mannie asked and coughed. He sat with his back to the wall, watching his father and brother through huge eyes.

"Much better," Jan replied. "You make good coffee, Mannie." He closed his eyes, imagining the rain was pattering on the roof of Nuwe Hoop Plaas. If he concentrated, he could smell the crispness of the veld rather than gun smoke and unwashed male bodies and hear the lowing of cattle rather than grumbling men and *Rooinecks'* orders from the fort.

"Alarm!" Karl's roar woke Jan from his dream. "Alarm! The *Rooinecks* are coming!"

Jan heard an urgent spatter of musketry, with the blare of a bugle rising above the town. A distinctively British volley followed, then a rising cheer, with more gunshots.

"Groenburg Commando!" Johannes shouted. "Grab your rifles and follow me!"

Jan dropped his mug, reached for his rifle, and ran for the door to find his father in front of him and Karl disappearing to spread the word.

"Stay here, Mannie!" Johannes ordered. "You are not well."

"But Pa!" Mannie objected.

"That's an order!" Johannes said and dashed outside. Jan followed his father out of the door and into the teeming rain. "What's happened?"

"The British have made a sortie!" Karl spoke from under his dripping hat. "They have broken into the magazine and taken all the ammunition away."

Jan looked over to the magazine, still thirty yards from the edge of the Boer trench. "So, all our digging was for nothing?"

"Ja!" Karl stamped his foot in frustration. "We wasted time and effort, and the *Rooinecks* grabbed everything anyway."

"How much did they get?" Jan asked.

"I'll find out," Johannes strode away to return within half an hour, frowning.

"The British raid was successful," he told his commando. "Their Lieutenant Rundle led a strong patrol into the magazine. They took a ton of gunpowder, over twenty thousand Wesley Richards cartridges and about ten thousand Martini-Henry bullets."

Jan felt instant dismay. "They won't run out of ammunition for a while, then."

"No, but we might," Karl said. He glared at the fort as if he could defeat the defenders by the force of his dislike.

Jan flinched when they heard the explosion half an hour later. "The British are attacking us again!" He reached for his rifle.

"No," Johannes put his hand on Jan's arm. "That will be the British blowing up our ammunition."

Jan lifted his head to examine the fort, where grey smoke battled the falling rain. "Should we not attack them while they are distracted?"

"Stay put and trust in General Cronje," Johannes ordered curtly. "He won't waste lives advancing across open ground against British riflemen."

Konrad had arrived at the Groenburg Commando's house. He grunted. "Sometimes it is necessary to break eggs to make an omelette."

"Prussia may not care if it loses hundreds of men. The Transvaal does," Johannes said.

"The British are digging a trench to the magazine!" Abraham lifted his rifle and fired. "Stop them, everybody!"

Karl swore, following Abraham's lead as he fired, loaded, and fired again. Jan pushed a cartridge into the breech of his rifle and poked his head above the window frame. A bullet crashed into the wood an inch from his face, throwing a wooden splinter into his forehead. He pulled back, unsure what had happened.

"I'm hit!"

Mannie beat Johannes to Jan's side by half a second. "Let me see!"

Jan removed his hand, feeling a trickle of blood down his face.

"It's nothing," Johannes reassured him. "Barely a scratch."

Jan grinned. "I thought a *Rooinek* had killed me."

"They couldn't kill my brother," Mannie said.

"Wash away the blood and get back on duty," Johannes told him with false severity.

Jan felt sick when he realised the progress the garrison had made. The British had thrust a trench from the fort to the magazine, removed the building's roof and turned it into a strongpoint. With even a handful of riflemen in position, they could hamper the Boers' trench digging.

"Let's push them out!" Theunis shouted and pointed to the enemy trench. "Come on, boys!"

Jan stepped beside Theunis with the sting of his new wound encouraging him to finish the siege as quickly as possible.

"No," Johannes put a hand on Jan's shoulder. "We will not charge into British rifles."

"But," Jan said, "we have to push them out."

"It is not the way we fight," Johannes told him. "Watch and learn, Jan."

A dozen of the younger and more reckless Burghers followed Theunis in a wild charge towards the new British positions. When the men of the 21st opened fire, the Boers realised how exposed they were and quickly threw themselves to the ground.

"Covering fire!" Johannes ordered and aimed toward the British trenches. Jan joined him in an exchange of gunfire as the too-enthusiastic Burghers returned to their starting point. The skirmish ended without casualties but a slightly abashed Theunis.

"Stop firing," Johannes ordered. "We are wasting ammunition. You see?" he said to Jan. "You would have put yourself in danger for no purpose."

"What will we do?" Jan asked. "We are making no progress."

"We'll build more trenches around the fort," Johannes said. "We will fight a patient war." He tapped the butt of his rifle. "The British are an impatient people for whom speed is important. We are farmers and know that nature does things in her own sweet time. It is natural for every nation to be independent. The good Lord will not let us down."

"Amen," Jan replied as Mannie coughed again.

CHAPTER 10

BRITISH ARMY HEADQUARTERS, NATAL, 22ND JANUARY 1881.

Andrew stood at the back of the crowd as Colley spoke to the senior officers. He marvelled at the magnificent display of scarlet tunics and gold braid, with sunlight reflecting on arrays of medal ribbons that told of battles, glory, and hardship across the breadth and length of the Empire. His gaze roved over the faces, pondering the experiences and history of these distinguished officers.

"Who the devil are you?" a gaunt-faced Lieutenant Colonel demanded, staring at Andrew's badges of rank.

"Captain Andrew Baird, sir," Andrew replied evenly.

"This meeting is for senior officers. Good God, man, you're only a captain."

"I know, sir." Andrew did not explain that General Colley had asked him to attend the meeting because of his experience fighting the Boers. He ignored the colonel's frown and faced forward as Colley raised a hand for silence.

"You all know the situation in the Transvaal," Colley began quietly. "The Boers are blockading our garrisons and have set up camp near our border." He paused, allowing his words to sink in. "We must gather our men and defeat what is becoming a nation in arms."

"They don't have an army, sir," the gaunt-faced colonel interjected. "One regiment of British regulars will be sufficient to scatter them. They are only farmers."

Colley lifted his head towards Andrew. "What do you say to that, Baird? You've seen the Boer fighting men first-hand."

"I'd say every Boer is a born light horseman," Andrew replied. "They ride like centaurs and shoot like marksmen. They can vanish behind a rock or into dead ground, fire, and withdraw. We would be foolish to despise them." He felt the poisonous glare of the colonel.

"Forgive Captain Baird's hyperbole," Colley said, faintly smiling. "But he has fought the Boers at Potchefstroom and Bronkhorst Spruit, and his points are well made. Every Boer is a natural warrior. We must show them that even the best warrior will fail against a professional soldier."

"How, sir?" a staff major asked. "They tore us to ribbons at Bronkhorst Spruit."

"How, sir? We gather all our men and face them in open battle, sir," Colley replied. "I will send Piet Joubert an ultimatum, ordering him to disband his men, or he'll face the full force of the British Empire."

"We might raise fifteen hundred men, sir," Andrew's neighbour murmured, "if we strip every garrison to the bone. Let's hope the Basutos and Zulus don't take advantage of our men being tied down in the Transvaal."

Colley nodded. "We can't afford a long war. The Zulus will still be smarting after their recent defeat; the Basutos could strike at any time, and even the Galekas could take advantage of Europeans fighting among themselves."

Andrew said nothing, although he wondered if Colley also considered European powers watching Britain's discomfiture. The British military's reputation suffered considerably when the Zulus defeated Lord Chelmsford's army at Isandhlwana. Despite the press pushing the defence of Rorke's Drift as a counterweight, the sting remained. A recent reverse at Maiwand in Afghanistan only added to the hurt.[1]

"I'll send the message to Joubert tomorrow," Colley declared. "As well as my threat, I have written this piece for the Boer commander," he held up a sheet of notepaper and read to the silent officers.

"The men who follow you are, many of them, ignorant, and know and understand little of anything outside their own country. But you, who are well-educated and have travelled, cannot but be aware how hopeless is the struggle you have embarked upon, and how little any accidental success gained can affect the ultimate result."

Colley lowered his paper and looked around the officers. "I invite your comments, gentlemen."

The colonel nodded. "That's good, sir. We might tell them their fortunate achievements do not alarm us, and our outposts hold firm."

"Quite so," Colley agreed. "Now, I intend to relieve the closest of our beleaguered garrisons as quickly as possible. Every advance will lift our men, and the addition of even a couple of hundred soldiers will strengthen our force." He glanced at Andrew. "You're dismissed, Baird."

"Yes, sir," Andrew saluted and left the senior officers to discuss their strategy. He hurried to the makeshift barracks where his Natal Dragoons lived, aware he had neglected them for far too long.

WITH GENERAL COLLEY'S ARMY, NATAL-TRANSVAAL BORDER, SOUTH OF Laing's Nek.

27/28th January 1881.

"Keep up, lads!" Andrew called as his Natal Dragoons rode in file behind him. He surveyed the familiar faces of men he had fought beside through the Zulu War. Middle-aged and bright-eyed, Sergeant Meek wore his array of medals proudly, while Trooper Ogden was a wild drunkard but good in a fight. He carried a bugle at his saddle, looted from a British soldier after Ulundi. Spalding was an intelligent, thoughtful soldier, and Lieutenant Fletcher rode as straight-backed as if he were on parade. Briggs slotted into his place back in the ranks as if he had never left, although Andrew worried whether Mariana would be all right with only a couple of hired servants. He had asked the local doctor to call on her twice weekly and hoped his attentions were sufficient.

"It's not a great force to reconquer a country, sir," Fletcher observed, eyeing the British column that slogged doggedly towards the frontier.

"No, it's not," Andrew agreed.

General Colley's army of 1,200 men marched towards the Transvaal frontier, kicking up dust and grumbling in the manner of soldiers everywhere. Andrew halted to view the column, shaking his head at the general's overconfidence. Five companies of the 60th Rifles and five of the 58th Foot, the Rutlandshire Regiment, comprised the bulk of the column. Even beneath the covering of dust, the scarlet of the 58th's tunics stood out, with blue trousers and red piping moving rhythmically across the hard ground. Their long bayonets bounced on their hips, and the battered sun helmets gleamed like lanterns above each sweating, dusty face.

The Rifles wore their traditional green uniforms and marched with the jaunty swing that had characterised them since their formation.

"They're good fighting men," Andrew approved. *But far too few for the task at hand and insufficiently mobile to face the agile Boer horsemen.*

"The backbone of the army," Fletcher remarked. "If we had a few thousand more, I'd be happier."

Andrew nodded. "We'll work with what we have," he replied.

Augmenting the regular infantry was a squadron of cavalry, in Andrew's eyes, more fit to parade in London's Hyde Park than to fight the rough-riding Boers on their own territory. There were also mounted infantry, some of whom seemed more nervous of their horses than respectful of the enemy, and a Naval Brigade with two seven-pound guns. Andrew had served with seamen before and knew them to be brave, resourceful, and energetic. The Royal Artillery, true to their motto of *ubique*—everywhere—pulled their battery of nine-pounders. Lastly, Colley had recruited local horsemen and the Natal Mounted Police, the latter as tough as the Boers, veterans of wars with the Zulus and Basutos. Beside them, the Natal Dragoons rode in file rather than acting as scouts, which Andrew would have preferred.

Andrew noticed that many recruits rode Cape horses, notoriously hard to handle even when trained. Other horses included a few pensioned-off artillery mounts, quiet, inoffensive beasts that could barely muster a trot even when encouraged with bit, whip, and spurs. Although the horses were of poor quality, Andrew thought the riders were worse, men who would never have passed the most perfunctory medical examination.

"The Boers will laugh this lot to scorn," Fletcher commented. "Then they'll shoot them out of the saddle."

"I suspect you're correct," Andrew checked his men.

The road led from Durban on the Natal coast via Newcastle in Natal to eventually reach Pretoria in the Transvaal. Colley's initial destination was Standerton in the Transvaal, where Major Montague commanded a British garrison of under four hundred men, mainly of the 94th Foot. Although the distance from Newcastle to Standerton was only twenty-five miles, the road crossed the Drakensberg Mountains at a formidable pass known as Laing's Nek.

"If the Boers know their business, they'll have men at the pass," Fletcher said.

"They'll be waiting for us," Andrew replied grimly.

"Who the hell was Laing to have a pass named after him?" Fletcher asked.

Andrew shook his head and passed the question to his Dragoons.

"Henry Laing," Morrison, one of the newer men, replied immediately. "He farmed at the foot of the mountain."

"No," Kerr shook his head. "It was Willie Lang. He farmed the other side of the hill."

"Were they related?" Fletcher asked.

"I doubt it, sir," Kerr replied. "They spelled their names differently."

Leaving his men to bicker happily, Andrew studied the terrain. Laing's Nek was the lowest section of a ridge that extended from the Buffalo River to the prominent eminence of Majuba Hill. From his position, the hills looked steep and difficult to climb, especially for fully laden troops.

A sweating subaltern approached Andrew, gasping from the heat. "General Colley's compliments, sir, and could you join him?"

"Where is he?"

"On that little knoll, sir," the subaltern gestured to a small hill a quarter of a mile from the column's route.

"Take over here, Fletcher," Andrew said.

A knot of officers gathered around the general as he surveyed the hills through field glasses. "My scouts tell me that the Boers hold Laing's Nek," Colley said. "I hope so. If they stand, we will defeat them. Nothing is more certain."

The officers nodded, confident their men could defeat any number of ill-disciplined farmers.

"A solid victory here might be sufficient to convince the Boers they cannot win this war," Colley said. "Better a bloody battle at the outset than a long-drawn-out conflict that will eventually mean many more casualties."

Andrew could see the logic in Colley's strategy while hoping the general would outflank the Boers rather than chance a frontal attack.

"We'll camp here at Mount Prospect for the night and remove the Boers tomorrow," Colley ordered. "Form a wagon laager."

The British camped three miles short of the pass, with the hills looming like a brooding barrier to the Transvaal. Within half an hour, the wagons were in a circle, with the cooks lighting fires as officers and NCOs barked orders and set pickets.

"Water and feed the horses," Andrew ordered the Dragoons, "then grab some scoff yourselves. Kerr, you and Morrison take the first stag. Keep your rifles close by, knee-halter the horses and let them graze."

The Dragoons obeyed, most falling instinctively into the routine of active service after months of garrison duty. Leaving Fletcher and Meek to supervise the men, Andrew lifted his field glasses and studied Laing's Nek. When he saw a flash of sunlight on glass, he guessed that General Joubert would be scrutinising the British camp, making arrangements, working out what Colley intended and planning his counters. Andrew grunted, thinking that war was like chess, with move and countermove, except the pawns were fragile men of flesh, blood, and feelings.

Andrew glanced over the 58th Foot, who appeared relaxed as they raised rows of bell tents. The cooks were already toiling over their fires, with farriers shoeing two horses and sergeants fussing over their charges with hard words and concerned eyes.

Colley called another meeting that evening, sitting at his travelling desk with a map pinned to a wooden framework at his side and the officers grouped before him. Lifting a pointer, he indicated the road ahead. "This is not the easiest route over the Drakensberg," he said, "but it's the most direct to Standerton."

Lieutenant Alan Hill of the 58th nodded. "Yes, sir. We'll shift the Boers, never fear." He glanced at his companion, Lieutenant Lancelot Baillie, and winked. "We're the Steelbacks! The famous 58th!"

Andrew remained silent, wondering what part his Natal Dragoons would play.

Colley continued. "We'll leave two hundred and sixty men and both Gatling guns to defend the laager. The oxen will also stay here, with the Army Hospital Corps and the drivers." Colley indicated Andrew. "I want Lieutenant Fletcher and your Natal Dragoons to remain as a mobile screen, Baird, but I might need your knowledge so you come with the main force."

"Yes, sir," Andrew disliked leaving his men behind but had to obey orders.

Colley groomed his whiskers with an elegant hand and carried on. "We'll bombard the Boer positions with the artillery and rocket tubes to soften them up and then put in a two-pronged attack. The infantry will advance up Table Hill on the left, and the cavalry will take Brownlow's Kop, the hill on the right."

Andrew nodded. Colley had planned a classic attack. He only hoped the Boers would give a classic reaction or, better still, surrender without a fight. He looked up at the ominously steep hills, thought of the determined men waiting at the summit and was suddenly glad his Dragoons were not involved.

I should not think like that! I am a British officer; I should be leading my men forward to glorious victory.

The dawn broke in bands of silver and pink, throwing strange shadows over the terrain and altering the hills to sombre shapes against an ominous sky. Birds filled the air with song, competing with the harsh voices of NCOs berating the infantry. The British were already on the move, with Colley leading the attacking column, a commanding figure with squared shoulders and an air of outstanding confidence.

The men followed, stumbling in the dark, gripping their Martinis and either grumbling or silent. Andrew looked along the lines of young, determined faces under the white sun helmets and wondered what would occupy these men if they were back home. Most had fought the Zulus at Ulundi and knew the reality of war, the smell of raw blood and the courage and comradeship needed to stand in line and face a brave enemy.

"Halt!" Colley ordered. The men stopped, staring at the hills as the rising sun burned away the crisp cold of the night. They formed up on a ridge about two thousand yards from the hills, with the artillery in the centre and the blue-clad gunners fussing over their charges like mothers with newborn children.

The 60th Rifles were on the extreme left, with the bluejackets from HMS *Dido* and HMS *Boadicea* and the Natal Mounted Police at their side. The scarlet-clad 58th, with the mounted infantry, were on the right, stamping their feet, exchanging black humour, and pulling at their belts.

The ground rose steeply to the broad Table Hill, with a conical spur about fifteen hundred feet distant. Through his field glasses, Andrew could see a strong Boer picket waiting on the spur. He saw the Boers moving seemingly casually, some smoking large pipes, others cleaning their rifles and watching the movement of the colourful British army far below. They looked like men on a grouse shoot rather than warriors preparing to defend their republic.

"It's too nice a day for a battle," Lieutenant Hill said, lighting a cheroot. He looked young and very keen as he surveyed the hill.

Andrew smiled. "Amen to that," he thought. Hill was probably about his age but lacked his experience of hard campaigning.

"Let's hope the Boers stand," Lieutenant Baillie said. "One good victory will settle the issue."

"I doubt they'll fight," Hill said, drawing on his cheroot. "Not when they see we're in earnest."

Andrew recalled the Boers advancing at Bronkhorst Spruit. "They'll fight," he said quietly. "They're a stubborn breed, sure of their cause, and they've already defeated one British column. They won't run from a few hundred redcoats."

"How about green coats?" A Rifles captain asked with a faint smile. "My lads are in this affair as well."

"I served with the Rifles before," Andrew said. "They're a match for anybody."

The captain laughed. "We'll soon see, won't we?"

At half-past nine, all six British guns opened fire with common shell and shrapnel. Andrew saw dust and stones rising around the Boer positions while the orange-yellow flashes of the explosions contrasted with the dull grey-white smoke. Augmenting the artillery, the Navy unleashed their rockets, with the fiery missiles giving a thin hiss as they ripped through the air to land with a bright crash.

"Poor buggers under that," a bearded corporal of the 58th said. "There's nothing worse than being on the wrong end of an artillery barrage. All you can do is hug the ground and pray like hell."

"The Boers started it by rebelling," a thin-faced private replied. "It serves the buggers right."

After ten minutes of furious bombardment, Colley ordered the Naval Brigade and a company of the 60th forward.

"There go the Rifles and bluejackets!" the bearded corporal said. "We'll be next, lads, mark my words."

The Rifles and Naval Brigade moved in good order to a defensive wall, where the seamen again opened fire with their rockets. The hissing projectiles crashed onto the Nek and beyond, where Colley believed the Boer reserves waited.

The Boers retaliated, with riflemen in a patch of forestry targeting the Naval Brigade in an accurate fusillade. The Rifles fired back, with the crackle of musketry adding a background to the more resounding boom of artillery and whoosh of rockets.

"Get ready, lads," the bearded corporal shouted above the hammer of artillery. "Check your rifles. Watch each other's backs when the order comes."

After another twenty minutes of screaming shrapnel and high explosives, Colley gave the order for the main advance.

"Now, Major Hingeson," Colley ordered. "Take your 58th forward and capture the spur. The artillery will cover your advance."

"Here we go, lads!" the corporal said. "They're only farmers, but their bullets can still kill. Keep the line steady and aim low."

When Colley headed up the hill, Andrew followed, whispering encouragement in Lancelot's ear. "Ignore the shine, Lance; we've been through all this before."

The 58th moved slowly and in perfect formation as though they were on a field day at Aldershot. Lieutenant Hill carried the Queen's Colours in the centre of the line, with Lieutenant Baillie holding the Regimental Colours a few yards away. The regiment moved in column of companies up the steep slope, with men peering forward to find the still-invisible enemy.

Andrew watched for a moment, aware he was witnessing history, for British soldiers had advanced into battle in scarlet uniforms with the colours displayed for centuries.

Not for much longer, Andrew told himself. *The army is shifting away from scarlet to khaki now, and with rifles with longer range and better accuracy, regiments won't advance in this manner again.*[2]

On the right, the cavalry eased up Brownlow's Kop. Rather than move quickly, the raw colonials walked their horses, with the riders seemingly more concerned about retaining their seats than Boer musketry. As Andrew watched, a shell landed square in the centre of the bunched riders, fortunately without exploding, although the threat forced the horsemen to open their ranks and increase their speed.

"Our artillery better change their aim," Andrew told a grim-faced Major Hingeson. "They're hitting the colonial horse."

"It might be Boer artillery," Hingeson said, glancing casually at the horsemen.

"The Boers don't have any artillery," Andrew replied.

Hingeson frowned. "It's bad enough getting killed in battle," he said. "It's much worse when your own side fires on you!"

The ground was steeper than it had appeared from Mount Prospect, with men stumbling and gasping under the already hot sun. They slithered on loose stones and swore as they lost their footing, kicked at the long grass that tangled around their boots, and blinked to clear the sweat from their eyes.

"Push on, lads," the sergeants encouraged. "Follow the Colours!"

The 58th moved on, swearing and struggling with the steep hill. As they neared the three-quarters mark, they broke formation on the uneven, rock-strewn ground. At that moment, hidden Boer riflemen opened fire so fast and accurately that the hillside rippled with muzzle flares, and the bullets kicked up little fountains of dust and rattled from the rocks. Red-coated soldiers fell, with officers and NCOs shouting sharp orders. Some men pushed on towards the muzzle flares, others stopped to fire back, and always Hill and Baillie carried the silken Colours at the front.

Andrew suddenly felt conspicuous on Lancelot as bullets zipped past. He felt for his rifle and paused as the musketry ceased.

"They've stopped firing," Hingeson said. "What's happened? Have we chased them away?"

"I hope so," Andrew replied cautiously. "Come on, Lancelot," he urged his horse forward.

The spurt of Boer musketry had ended without a Burgher in sight. As the 58th approached the summit, nobody fired at them, although the horsemen on the neighbouring hill struggled to make any progress. Andrew glanced at Brownlow's Kop, willing the mounted men to advance. He saw a small bugle boy lift his instrument to his lips and sound the first note of the charge, then fall back as a Boer shot him through the head. After that initial shot, the musketry became general as the Boers sprung their ambush.

"They were waiting on the reverse slope!" Andrew said.

Major Hingeson nodded calmly. "The Boers were safe from our artillery. They've taken a leaf out of Wellington's book."

As at Bronkhorst Spruit, the Boers targeted the officers and NCOs, shooting them out of the saddles and killing and wounding the horses and the riders. Above the sound of Boer rifles, Andrew heard the trilling of a cavalry trumpet and the sharp bark of orders.

Andrew looked away; he could not help the cavalry but might be useful with the infantry.

"Where are the Boers?" the thin-faced private asked. "I can't see a single man."

"Maybe they've already run," the bearded corporal replied.

"They're keeping their heads down," another NCO said with great satisfaction. "They haven't faced artillery before."

The 58th Colours hung limp in the clear air, bright against the landscape of duns and browns. Andrew heard continuous firing from Brownlow's Kop and glanced over again. Tired, disorganised, and faced with a half-hidden enemy, the horsemen stood, taking casualties without being able to retaliate. After a few moments, they withdrew, slowly at first, and then faster as survival beckoned with sweetly crooked fingers. They left sixteen dead and wounded men on the rough ground.

"The Boers outmanoeuvred us," Andrew said. "Our artillery didn't even touch them."

That's something to add to my military knowledge, Andrew told himself. *If I ever command men defending a hill, I'll use the reverse slope.*

Despite the cavalry's repulse, Colley allowed the 58th to rest rather than pushing on to the summit of the pass. Some men pulled at water bottles, others exchanged bawdy jokes but most lay on the rough grass, gasping for breath as sweat soaked dark patches in their uniforms.

The thin-faced private wiped perspiration from his face. "Where's the Boers then? They must all be on Brownlow's Kop, facing the cavalry."

"They'll be here," the bearded corporal replied. "If I were General Colley, I'd keep in extended formation."

"You're not in charge here," the private told him, grinning.

"No, but if I were, I'd have the men extend into skirmishing order. Joubert seems to know his stuff." The corporal nodded towards the retiring cavalry on Brownlow's Kop. "He's given the horsey men the right about anyway."

The private grunted. "Since when did cavalry know anything about fighting? The Zulus smashed them at Hlobane, and it took us to finish the job at Ulundi."

Andrew dismounted, gave Lancelot a drink and listened without comment. He agreed with the corporal; Joubert knew what he was doing.

After half an hour's rest, the infantry moved off again, toiling to the summit.

"Extend the front," Major Hingeston ordered. "Watch for a Boer ambush. They're sneaky buggers."

The 58th marched cautiously over the skyline, with Lieutenants Hill and Baillie proudly carrying the Colours and the scarlet jackets and blue trousers of the men bright in the sunshine. When the British were only two hundred yards away and nearly impossible for a marksman to miss, the Boers opened fire. Andrew saw the spurts of smoke a millisecond before he heard the crash of the shots and then the bullets hammered into the advancing infantry. Men fell, some in silence, others with grunts or surprised yells. The thin-faced private grunted, staring at the spreading stain in his stomach and jerked back as a second bullet slammed into him.

"Return fire!" Andrew shouted, dismounting. He pushed Lancelot away, "Run, Lance!"

Once again, the Boers aimed at the officers. Those on horseback were easy targets, and Major Hingeston fell dead, hung from one stirrup for a few seconds before sliding to the ground. Boer bullets crashed into most of the other officers, killing or wounding them.

Andrew swore in frustration. He saw Major Essex from the 75th Foot, an Isandhlwana veteran, shouting orders that the men ignored.

"Push forward!" Andrew wished he had an official position with the regiment. He roared above the crackle of musketry and zip of passing bullets, "B Company! Find cover and fire back! Aim at the smoke! Keep the Boers' heads down! C Company, advance! Charge! The quicker you're there, the fewer casualties you'll take!"

Some privates of the 58th obeyed. Others stood in confusion, waiting for orders from officers of their own regiment.

Colley's aide-de-camp, Lieutenant Elwes of the Grenadier Guards, pushed to the front. Tall, slim, and debonair, he was an ex-Etonian with a loud voice. Noticing Monck, adjutant of the 58th and a fellow Etonian, standing beside his dead horse, he waved a cheerful hand.

"Come along, Monck! *Floreat Etona*! We must be in the front rank!" He pushed forward, only for a Boer rifleman to kill him outright.

Andrew swore again. *You were a brave man, Elwes, but bravery cannot stop a Boer bullet.*

The Boer musketry increased, with the near-invisible riflemen picking off the British infantry. Having repelled the cavalry attack, more Boers came on the flank, enfilading the 58th in a murderous crossfire.

None of the 58th charged forward, although many advanced slowly. Andrew responded to this new Boer threat. "With me, B Company," he shouted. "Move to the right flank and reply to the Boer fire!"

For the first time since the advance began, Andrew saw Colonel Deane of the 58th miraculously still astride his horse. The colonel spurred forward, yelling encouragement. When the Boers shot his horse, he struggled free and ran forward towards the now visible Boer trenches. Half a dozen bullets crashed into him, killing him instantly.

Andrew swore. *The Boers are slaughtering us.*

To the left of the 58th, two companies of the 60th Foot advanced, with the skirmishers firing at the Boers. They ducked, weaved, and fired, shouting encouragement to each other as they aimed at the Boer riflemen.

"We're getting murdered!" The bearded corporal shouted. He organised his section, returning the Boer fire on the flank, loading and firing with mechanical precision.

Andrew fired automatically and looked around. All he could see of the Boers was gun smoke, with the occasional muzzle flare or a bobbing hat. The 58th were falling fast, swearing as they tried to retaliate against men they barely saw. A dozen Boers advanced down the hill, the agile men in slouch hats shooting at the Naval Brigade, then dropped into cover, crouching in dead ground or behind rocks so only the muzzles of their rifles were exposed.

Major Essex had taken command of the rearguard, and together with Andrew's handful of men, they responded to the Boer fire.

"Hot stuff, Captain," Essex said.

"Yes, sir!" Andrew agreed.

The Boer musketry slackened as they rose from cover and advanced against the 58th, moving from cover to cover. With most of the officers and many men down, the British fired back, swearing in frustration.

Andrew did not see who ordered the retire, but when the bugles blared, the men withdrew, cursing as they stumbled back down the hill.

"We had them beat," a man complained. "I tell you, we had them on the run."

The bearded corporal grunted. "On the run? The only running the Boers were doing was chasing us!"

Andrew helped support a wounded man, saw Lieutenant Alan Richard of the 58th aiding another, and wondered how a bunch of farmers could repulse an attack by British regulars. The Boers followed, still firing.

A bullet caught Lieutenant Baillie, knocking him to the ground. He lay, writhing, with the Colours at his side.

"Baillie!" Still miraculously unscathed, Lieutenant Hill dismounted and tried to lift Baillie. "I've got you, man!"

With the Queen's and Regimental Colours in the crook of his right arm, Hill could not help Baillie into the saddle, so he wrapped his left arm around his friend's shoulder and stumbled down the steep hill. He ignored the Boer bullets that zipped past, kicking up small fountains of dirt.

Unable to leave his post, Andrew could only watch as another Boer bullet plunged into the wounded Baillie. He saw the anguish on Hill's face as he lowered Baillie to the ground, handed both the Regimental and Queen's Colour to Sergeant Budstock, and lifted a wounded private.[3]

The bugler repeatedly sounded the retire, blowing hard amidst the chaos of shouts, shots, and screams.

"Pull back, lads," Andrew ordered the men around him. "We're retiring."

"They beat us!" A shocked private said. "They beat us! How could they beat us?"

"We'll be back," Andrew told him. "It's only a temporary setback."

Andrew knew that many British soldiers would ask the same question that night. It was unheard of for untrained farmers armed only with rifles to defeat British regulars with infantry, cavalry, and artillery led by one of the most intellectual generals in the army.

The men staggered back to the foot of the hill with heads down and shoulders slumped. As the infantry counted their casualties and exchanged blasphemy and curses, local Africans helped carry the wounded and dead to the ambulances for the jolting, painful trip back to the hospital at the camp. Some of the less shocked soldiers acknowledged the African help.

"Good lads, these natives," one Geordie voice said. "We should recruit them against the Boers. They've got a score or two to settle."

"It's a white man's war," a Liverpool man replied. "Why should the Africans get involved? They can stand back and cheer as we and the Burghers shoot each other silly."

"That's a fact," a Bedfordshire man said. "After we kicked the blazes out of the Zulus, why should the natives help us anyway? The Boers are worse; they enslave them."

Andrew listened, watching the infantry retire, some helping the walking wounded, a few turning to shout insults at the Boers, but most were stunned by the defeat.

Lieutenant Richard and Andrew shepherded the last men down the hill, with an occasional defiant private firing at the pursuing Boers. A final bullet pinged off a rock beside Andrew, leaving a distinctive blue-grey smear. When he checked his watch, it was quarter past twelve.

"Reform," the surviving officers shouted, with the bugles reinforcing the order.

Andrew helped, getting the men back into ranks, sending the wounded to the waiting ambulances, and setting a rearguard in case the Boers tried to follow up their victory.

"I'll stay with you, lads," Andrew reassured the rearguard. "Retire slowly and fire if you see a Boer."

The 58th formed up, men straightening their uniforms as the non-commissioned officers roared them into orderly ranks.

"You're soldiers, not blasted scarecrows! Get that button fastened, Burrows! Jones! Stand straight! Just because the Boers repulsed us is no excuse for slouching! Stop bleeding on your tunic, Sinclair! You only bleed when I give you permission!"

The NCO's usual blandishments and a return to normality stiffened the 58th. They checked to see who had survived and marched back to Mount Prospect, three miles to the south. The rhythmic thump of boots on hard ground helped ease the hurt, and after a few moments, a man began to sing, with a few others joining in.

"Oh, a soldier and a sailor were talking one day.
Said the soldier to the sailor, 'Let us kneel down and pray,
And for each thing we pray for may we also have ten,
And at the end of every chorus, we will both sing, Amen!'
Now the first thing we'll pray for, we'll pray for some beer,
And if we only get some it will bring us good cheer,
And if we have one beer, may we also have ten?
'May we have a whole brewery,' said the sailor. 'Amen!'

Now, the next thing we'll pray for, we'll pray for our Queen,
To us, a bloody old bastard she's been,
And if she has one son, may she also have ten,
'May she have a bloody regiment,' said the sailor. 'Amen!'"

When the verses became more obscene, Andrew moved further away. The Boers may have won the battle, but if the British Army could laugh at itself and grumble at its leaders, Britain would survive.

Our army needs to improve, Andrew thought. *Survival alone is not sufficient. That's twice the Boers have defeated us, and this time, one of our best generals had planned the battle. Where are we going wrong?*

CHAPTER 11

BRITISH CAMP, MOUNT PROSPECT, JANUARY 1881.

"The enemy fought well," a plump staff major said. "The Boers are courageous and determined men who showed no fear of our troops."

Andrew nodded. "Our men were courageous, too," he said. "They pressed on as far as they could and fired back until they heard the bugle sound the retire."

The major looked up as if he had not given the other ranks another thought. "Of course, they were. They are British soldiers."

Don't take the men for granted, Major!

"Yes, sir," Andrew agreed.

"I was surprised how tenaciously the Boers acted," the major continued as he poured champagne for the senior officers. "They did not withdraw even when we were close upon them." He mused for a moment. "If we had more men, we could have shifted them."

"We can't allow the Boers to take control of the Transvaal," a burly staff captain announced. "It is a fact that they are too divided amongst themselves to rule a nation effectively. They divide and sub-divide into factions, like the Irish."

Andrew wondered what Irish-born General Colley thought of the major's words.

"Yet the Boers are easily led," the captain continued. "Given good British leaders, we can look forward to a combined South Africa under British rule." He sipped his champagne. "These backveld Boers cannot help their ignorance; they are the product of their environment and upbringing. Take away their archaic ministers and backward schoolteachers, cane them soundly on the battlefield, add powerful treason laws to teach them loyalty to us, and the next generation will be as British as the Canadians or Australians."

Andrew raised his eyebrows, saying nothing.

"Give it twenty years," the captain said smugly. "A good influx of British immigrants will drag the Boers out of the seventeenth century and into the nineteenth." He ordered another drink and sat back, pleased with his philosophy.

Irritated by the captain's words, Andrew had to reply. "We have to defeat them first," he said. "My duty as a soldier is to face the enemy on the field. I'll leave the aftermath to the politicians. I dare say they will make as big a shambles of the Transvaal as they have of Ireland or Britain." He paused to control his temper. "Between the rivalries of Tory and Whig, Disraeli and Gladstone, I don't think we can complain about faction fighting among the Burghers." He closed his mouth, aware that every officer in the Officers' Mess was staring at him.

"We shall defeat them, Baird," the staff captain said confidently.

"I am sure you are correct," Andrew retorted.

When the doctors reported the casualties, the British had lost eighty-three killed, with over seventy coming from the 58th Foot. Augmenting the dead were one hundred and eleven wounded, also mainly from the 58th. Although the British did not yet know it, the Boers had lost fourteen dead and twenty-seven wounded.

"That's another chastening day," a Rifles captain said, reading the casualty list. "We lost too many good men."

"The Boers seem to have our measure," a naval lieutenant replied. "What do you think, Baird?"

"I think we'll have to alter our tactics," Andrew said. "Advancing at a slow walk in broad daylight against concealed riflemen is just presenting our men as living targets."

"General Colley knows what he's doing," the burly staff captain said. "He's one of our best men. He's in the Wolseley ring[1], you know."

"I know," Andrew said. "But he's never faced the Boers before. Nobody in our generation has. Sir Harry Smith was the last British officer to defeat them."

"Ah," the captain said in a tone of triumph. "The Boers have never faced us either."

As evening approached, Colley addressed the men. "We suffered a reverse today, men," the general said. "You have not been beaten; you have simply been repulsed. There is no blame attached to you. You all behaved very well. Any fault lies with me." He waited for a moment. "With the number of troops at my disposal, it is impossible to renew operations, and I must wait for reinforcements. I hope the wounded will do well. I can say no more. I wish you all good night."

The men dispersed, some slope-shouldered and silent, others muttering incoherently, and a few talking loudly. Andrew joined his Dragoons, interested to hear their reactions.

"That was a fiasco," Fletcher said directly. "Did the general not think to scout the enemy positions?"

"Is that what you would have done?" Andrew asked.

"Yes, sir," Fletcher replied. "I'd have sent a couple of good men up first to see where the Boers were rather than advancing in daylight onto hidden positions."

Andrew grunted, thinking Fletcher would make a decent senior officer if he survived. "Learn everything you can, Fletcher. Make every campaign, every battle, every patrol a learning experience."

"Yes, sir," Fletcher said.

The camp at Mount Prospect was unhappy that night as the British licked their wounds and discussed their defeat. With over a hundred wounded crammed into the hospital tents, Andrew could smell blood wherever he went, despite the best attention of the surgeon and the seamen who acted as orderlies and nurses.

"We suffered a reverse today," Private Burrows repeated the general's words. "Well, Colley, you were in charge. If we suffered a reverse today, it was because you led us into the bloody reverse!"

Andrew sighed. Whatever the senior officers believed, the ordinary British soldier was no fool. He knew and understood what had happened.

POTCHEFSTROOM, JANUARY 1881.

"What's been happening here?" Jan asked as he placed his rifle in a corner of the room and slumped to the floor. Dust had stuck to the sweat on his face, and he smelled of rifle smoke and horses. "Or have you all been smoking quietly while we fought at Laing's Nek?"

Karl shook his head. "I would have been with you had it not been for my aching back. We were also fighting when you were away. Anyway, somebody had to care for your brother."

Jan glanced at the fort, where the makeshift Union flag still hung above the battered camp. "The British are still there, I see."

"Yes, and growing more aggressive," Karl said. "A British raiding party attacked one of our strongholds and fired three volleys at our men. We were not fast enough to catch them."[2]

"They should have surrendered by now," Johannes joined them, with the lines of responsibility etched deeply on his face. "They must be suffering from the rain." He knelt beside Mannie, lying on the floor in a cocoon of blankets.

"They are," Karl agreed. "They have dysentery in the fort, and we hear them digging at night. The *Rooinecks* are either strengthening their defences or burying their dead."

Johannes spoke to Mannie for a few moments, then lifted his field glasses, cleared raindrops from the lens, and surveyed the fort. "They have raised the walls a fraction," he said. "They are like ant bears, well dug in and refusing to move."

"The British work on the walls every night," Karl said. "We damage them during the day, and they add sandbags at night. It's a little game we play." He looked up as water began to drip through the roof. "Somebody will have to fix that hole before it spreads."

"We'll have to get the British out," Jan said. "We must clear the *Rooinecks* from our land." He hoped that Engela still remembered him.

"We will," Johannes reassured his son. "Be patient." He sat beside Mannie, concerned that the boy barely acknowledged his presence. "Once we win this war, we can all go home."

Theunis looked up. "I have a plan."

"You have a plan?" Johannes repeated.

"I'll see if the general will accept it," Theunis said with a smile.

"What is your plan?" Jan asked.

"To offer the British a way to defeat us," Theunis' smile broadened. He rose, placed his pipe in his mouth, and strode away.

"Theunis has a plan," Johannes said. "Now we shall see if he is as *slim* as he believes."

Jan began to clean his rifle, ignoring the steadily increasing drip of water from the leaking roof. He counted his cartridges, thought of the *Rooinecks* he had shot at Laing's Nek, and dismissed the images. War was war, and the British had invaded his country.

"How are you, Mannie?"

Mannie looked up and tried to smile through a coughing fit.

WITH HIS HAT PULLED LOW OVER HIS HEAD AND RAINWATER DRIPPING ONTO his face, Johannes raised the white flag and guided his horse to the fort's gate. He felt a curious tingling at the base of his spine, aware that at least half a dozen British soldiers would have their rifles pointed at him.

"Halt!" A British sentry poked a cautious head above the parapet. "I've got you covered, Piet! Who are you, and what do you want?"

Johannes saw more British soldiers appearing, with the constant rain causing the brown stains to run from their sun helmets. Their tunics were no longer scarlet but every shade from a rusty brown to faded pink. "I come under a flag of truce!" he said in his broken English.

"Aye, I see that!" Sergeant Lennox joined the sentry. "What do you want, Piet? Do you want to surrender?"

"No," Johannes shook his head, spraying water around his horse. "I have a message for Colonel Winsloe."

"Have you now?" the sergeant eyed Johannes suspiciously. "What sort of message, Piet?"

"I do not know," Johannes replied. "I have not read it." He lowered the flag and dismounted. "Could you bring him here so I can give him the message?"

"The colonel will not come at the whim of a Boer," Lennox said and relented with a wry smile. "Or at the request of a sergeant. If you give me the message, I'll ensure he gets it."

"No, Sergeant," Johannes shook his head. "The letter says, 'Private and Confidential.' It might be from his wife."

"What's all this?" Lieutenant Rundle bustled up and nodded to Johannes. "Who are you, sir?"

Johannes lifted his hat. "I am Veldcornet Johannes van Collier of the Groenburg Commando," he said. "What is your name, *meneer*?"

"Lieutenant Henry Leslie Rundle of the Royal Artillery at your service, sir," Rundle replied. "I heard you have a message for the colonel."

"I have," Johannes replaced his hat. "If I give it to you, do you promise on your honour as a British gentleman and officer to hand it to him unopened?"

"I do, sir," Rundle replied, smiling faintly.

Johannes nodded and removed a battered and sealed envelope from inside his jacket. "One of my men found this letter on the ground," he said. "We were going to keep it in case it was military information, but not even the British are foolish enough to lose that."

Rundle joined in Johannes's sardonic laughter. He glanced at the outside of the envelope. "It doesn't look like an official message," he said truthfully.

"It may be from the colonel's wife," Johannes said. "Maybe she is ill, or having a baby, or wants him to surrender to get him home quickly."

Rundle smiled again. "Two of your three ideas are possible," he said. "I shall hand this message to the colonel in person, Meneer van Collier."

"Thank you, Lieutenant Rundle," Johannes said. "I trust you not to shoot me as I retire."

"You are safe for five minutes, *meneer*." Rundle saluted. "And when you lose the war, I shall be honoured to meet you as a gentleman and a friend."

"You are also a gentleman, Lieutenant Rundle," Johannes replaced his hat and remounted with effortless grace. He rode away without looking back while Rundle strode inside the fort to Colonel Winsloe's tented headquarters.

"A message?" Winsloe looked at the envelope suspiciously.

"The Boer thought it might be a message from your wife, sir," Rundle suggested.

"Constance?" Winsloe shook his head. "Not her style and not her writing." Breaking the seal, he slit the letter open. "It's in code, damn it! It must be official. How's your Morse code, Rundle?"

"Fair to middling, sir," Rundle replied cautiously.

Winsloe handed over the message. "Read that, then. Just give me the gist of it, not every damned detail."

Rundle scanned the document, borrowed a pen, and scribbled down the message, letter by letter. "It purports to come from Colonel Bellairs in Pretoria, sir. He says he is sending a column to lift the siege."

"Does it, now?" Winsloe said enthusiastically. "That's good news. When can we expect them?"

"In three days' time, sir," Rundle said, frowning as he checked the Morse code. "Sir, there's a passage here that makes no sense. Listen. 'When you hear heavy firing, leave the fort with your party and attack the back."

"Attack the back?" Winsloe said immediately. "The back of what?"

"Precisely, sir. Maybe Bellairs means the rear," Rundle said.

"Then why the devil didn't he say so?" Winsloe took the letter from Rundle. "What do you think, Lieutenant?"

Rundle shook his head. "I'm not sure, sir, but I've never known a military message phrased like that."

Winsloe nodded. "Nor have I, Rundle. There's something wrong here." He scanned the lieutenant's translation, sighed, and listened to the rain hammering from the patched canvas above his head.

JOHANNES CHECKED THE WATCH HE HAD LOOTED FROM A DEAD BRITISH officer at Bronkhorst Spruit and nodded to the waiting commando. "It is time," he said. "Theunis, are the men ready?"

"My men are ready," Theunis confirmed. "Everybody knows what to do. Let's teach the *Rooinecks* how *slim* us stupid Boers can be." Some of his men laughed while others nodded in agreement.

"What if the British see us?" Karl asked. "That will spoil the whole plan."

"They will think we are going to fight the oncoming relief column," Theunis reassured him.

"Come on, Groenburg Commando," Johannes said. "Shoot low and keep under cover." He winked at Jan. "You too, Jan."

Thick clouds concealed any stars, forcing Johannes to ride by memory. He saw the gleam of light from the British fort and knew the British sentries would be sheltering from the constant downpour rather than looking for enemy activity. Sentries were the same the world over.

"No talking," Johannes reminded softly.

The commando plodded on, with the sound of their horses' hooves hollow in the dark. Mud and water splashed the horses' and men's legs while the rain wept onto their bowed shoulders, increasing as they entered the open countryside. When the commando was half a mile from the town, Jan inspected his rifle for the third time.

"Have you checked your rifle already?" Johannes asked quietly.

"Ja," Jan said.

"Was it all right?"

"It was all right," Jan replied.

"Has anybody taken it from you or touched it since then?" Johannes asked.

"No," Jan shook his head.

"Then leave it alone. It will not break in the space of two minutes," Johannes told him. "Concentrate on what will go right and let me think what may go wrong. That is the veldcornet's job." Johannes winked to remove any sting his words held. "You are a man now, Jan."

"Yes, Pa," Jan said, hiding his surge of pride. He straightened his back and rode beside Abraham, thinking of the task ahead.

"Halt here," Johannes stopped the commando. They formed a circle around him, with rainwater dripping from their hats and the horses' coats. Each man held his rifle in his right hand, with the barrel upended to protect the muzzle from the rain. "We gave the British a letter telling them Bellairs in Pretoria was sending a relief column. Our job is to pretend we are that column."

The men nodded and smiled, enjoying the idea of fooling the *Rooinecks*.

"When the British hear the noise we make, Colonel Winsloe will lead his men out of the fort to help the column, and we will have the *Rooinecks* out in the open," Johannes pushed his hands together. "When we hold Winsloe's *Rooinecks*, General Cronje will bring the Burghers out of Potchefstroom, and we'll have the British between two fires. Without their walls to guard them, the *Rooinecks* will be helpless."

Jan nodded. He could visualise the British falling before his rifle, dying like tin soldiers on a tabletop as he fired, with each shot helping cleanse the infestation from his land.

"It will be Bronkhorst Spruit all over again," Johannes said. He suddenly looked very old as the responsibility of command wore him down. "Theunis had the idea. You'll hear some loud explosions soon; that is Theunis." He smiled. "We must sound like British infantry, so we'll fire in volleys, as they do."

Jan looked at the other men in the commando. Individuals to a man, they were not used to firing on the word of command.

Karl nodded. "We will fire on your word," he said. "How will we know?"

Johannes nodded. "I will count to three and say 'fire'," he said. "Aim into the air so we don't shoot each other."

The men raised their rifles, some amused and others irritated at this novel method of fighting. Jan saw his father looking at him and smiled.

Even though he was expecting it, the explosion took Jan by surprise.

"That is Theunis simulating artillery fire," Johannes explained. "The British will believe the relief column is approaching. Ready? One, two, three: fire!"

Jan squeezed the trigger, with the Burghers firing a volley so ragged any self-respecting British sergeant would have turned purple with rage.

"Reload," Johannes ordered.

As Jan thumbed a cartridge into the breech of his rifle, he heard another explosion. To him, it sounded more like a charge of gunpowder than artillery.

"That's Theunis again," Johannes reassured them. "Is everybody loaded?" He waited for the men to nod. "All together this time. One, two, three," Johannes said. "Fire!"

The second volley was more controlled, with only two men later than the others.

"That's better," Johannes said. "Now we'll fire two more volleys and wait for Winsloe to lead his garrison out." He grinned. "If anybody wants to shout like a British sergeant, do so. I hope you can curse in English because their sergeants swear a lot." He waited for the laugh before ordering the next volley.

Jan fired with the rest and waited for any sound from the fort.

"Listen for the bugles," Johannes said as the minutes dragged on with only the steady hammer of the rain around them. The fort remained silent.

Abraham swore softly. "I hope Colonel Winsloe falls for Theunis's plan."

"Shall I go and check on the fort?" Jan volunteered.

"I'll go," Karl said. "An old head is better than youthful eagerness." He grinned. "You'll probably knock on the door and ask if the garrison is ready to come out yet."

Jan smiled, recognising that Karl's humour was not malicious. He saw Abraham laughing and nudged him. "You're not so clever, Abe!"

"Too clever to chase after Engela," Abraham replied. "I know how moody she can be!"

Karl laughed. "All women are moody," he said and rode towards the fort.

"Fire another volley," Johannes suggested. "That might entice the *Rooinecks* out."

Karl returned in ten minutes, shaking his head. "The British are not moving," he said. "Their sentries are in the same place, and they haven't opened the gate."

"The ruse failed," Johannes decided. "Ride to Theunis and tell him we're returning to Potchefstroom." He watched Karl trotting away, with his horse's hooves splashing up mud and water.

"Shall we fire another volley?" Jan asked, impatient to do something.

Johannes shook his head. "We will not waste any more ammunition," he said. "We have not fooled the British this time."

The commando was dejected as it returned to base. Jan was not alone as he glared at the fort, wondering if the *Rooinecks* were laughing at them. He could imagine them with their beery, drunken voices mocking the sodden Burghers riding back with their tails between their legs.

"The British must have found out," Theunis said when they slumped in their quarters. "Maybe somebody told them."

"Maybe they are more *slim* than we think," Johannes said, checking Mannie's condition. His younger son was shivering under his blankets, with his eyes deep sunk in his face.

"Maybe the rain will wash away the fort," Jan glared at the Union Flag, "and pour the *Rooinecks* back into the sea and back to London".

"Pray to the Lord for heavy rain," Abraham advised solemnly. "I am sure He will listen to you. More than Engela ever will."

The rain continued, hour after hour, day after day, with Jan watching the British soldiers working within the fort, dragging buckets through the flooded interior and emptying them over the walls. The Boers occasionally sniped the toiling men, but mostly, they kept under shelter and watched.

"*Suid Afrika* is drowning them," Theunis said. "The country is fighting for us."

Jan nodded. "It is also keeping Mannie sick," he nodded to his brother, who lay swathed in blankets, tossing and turning in a fever.

"Mannie is strong," Theunis said. "He will recover."

"I think he is getting worse, not better," Jan did not hide his concern.

"He'll get better," Theunis placed a sympathetic hand on Jan's shoulder.

"Look!" Johannes studied the fort through his field glasses. "The British are burning their wagons!"

Theunis took the field glasses. "They must have run out of fuel." He nodded in satisfaction. "Soon, they will want to surrender."

The garrison removed their wagons, one by one, broke them up, and burned the wood. They only kept five, which they added to the wall to strengthen the defences.

"They copied that idea from us," Abraham objected. "We taught them about wagon laagers."

"As long as we don't teach them how to shoot," Johannes said.

"Will they surrender soon?" Jan asked. "We have to get Mannie home."

"I hope so," Johannes replied so quickly that Jan knew he was equally worried about his son. "Maybe you should take Mannie back to Nuwe Hoop Plaas."

"I cannot leave the fight," Jan said. "People would think I am afraid."

"Nobody will think you are afraid," Johannes reassured him. "Everybody in the commando has seen you fighting."

Jan glanced at Konrad, who moved from the Groenburg Commando to General Cronje's staff when he was not seducing young townswomen. "*Meneer* Bramigan will think I ran away."

"Konrad will not believe you ran away," Johannes said. "He knows we are not the Prussian Guards."

"The Prussian Guards would have stormed that little fort weeks ago," Konrad stepped forward, running a finger down his scar.

"And lost many men in doing so," Jan retorted.

"Victory is more important than cost," Konrad replied with a shrug. "I hope to report a Boer victory here, not a prolonged siege with General Colley bringing in a relief column."

"They are holding out longer than I thought," Theunis admitted. "The British are eating raw mealies, and their cooks are only baking bread for the women and sick."

"I thought we allowed the women to leave the fort," Jan sat beneath the window with his loaded rifle in his hand.

"We asked the women to leave," Johannes reminded. "Those that remain are in a shelter in the centre of the fort. Or they hide in the dugout when the serious fighting starts. We wounded two when our artillery hit them, but they survived."

"I don't like making war on women," Jan said.

"Nor do I," Johannes replied. "We will not prevent the women from leaving the fort if they want to."

"Wait!" Theunis held up a hand. "Adriaan Coetzee is coming this way."

"Adriaan is Gideon's son and General Cronje's messenger," Jan reminded. "That might mean trouble."

"Maybe the British have surrendered, and we can go home," Karl sounded hopeful.

A young man with a wispy beard, Adriaan removed his hat when he approached Theunis and Johannes. "General Joubert wants you to know that the British are sending convoys to Mount Prospect," he said. "The general wants volunteers to disrupt their supply line."

"That's the Groenburg Commando," Theunis said immediately. "The *Rooinecks* fooled us last time. We won't let that happen again."

Johannes glanced at Mannie before he replied. "When are we going?"

CHAPTER 12

BRITISH CAMP, MOUNT PROSPECT, NATAL, 4TH FEBRUARY 188

"Well, Captain Baird," General Hook sat opposite Andrew in the tent, with a cigarette in a long holder curling blue smoke into the air. "I heard you've been busy fighting the Boers."

"We've all been busy, sir," Andrew replied.

"Indeed so." Hook drew on his cigarette and allowed the smoke to trickle from the side of his mouth. "You've been present at one siege and two battles so far. That makes you the most experienced Boer fighter in the army."

Andrew said nothing, wondering where Hook was leading. He allowed his eyes to stray to the map of Southern Africa on a wooden easel. Red pins marked the British garrisons, while blue pins marked the known Boer positions.

Hook let Andrew wait, scrutinising him through narrowed eyes. "The situation in the Transvaal is not as simple as you may imagine," the general said at last. "I have already told you about the German threat."

"Yes, sir," Andrew tried to hurry Hook along.

"Well, there is more to the story."

There always is, Andrew thought.

"You may be aware there is gold in the Transvaal," Hook seemed determined to test Andrew's patience by dragging out the interview.

Andrew nodded. "Yes, sir. People discovered gold a few years ago at the New Caledonian Gold Fields in the eastern Transvaal." He smiled. "Some people called them the Mac-Mac Fields because of all the Scottish diggers."

Hook smiled slowly. "That's correct, Baird, and then a digger named Alexander Patterson, Wheelbarrow Alex, found gold in Pilgrim's Creek, a few miles away."

"Yes, sir," Andrew curbed his impatience, for the story of the gold diggings was well known. "Does Britain want the gold, sir? We moved quickly enough to claim the Griqualand diamonds."

Hook shook his head slowly. "Mac-Mac and Pilgrims Creek are only alluvial gold, Baird. Useful but not necessarily commercial. We had geologists working in the country, and they believe a great amount of gold is sitting under the Witwatersrand, the Ridge of White Waters, and maybe elsewhere."

Andrew realised Hook expected him to say something. "Is there, sir?"

"We know it's there, but we don't want the knowledge to spread yet," Hook told him. "More specifically, we don't want the Germans to know."

"Yes, sir." *What the devil has this to do with me?*

"Naturally, having gold in the Transvaal will revitalise Prussian interest," Hook spoke so slowly that Andrew felt his impatience increasing.

"I understand that, sir," Andrew said.

Hook paused as if pondering how much information he should release. "The longer this war continues," he said at last, "the greater the possibility of Germany becoming involved and gaining a foothold in Southern Africa. We want a short war, whoever wins."

"Whoever wins?" Andrew stared at General Hook, hardly believing what he had heard. "Even if that means the Boers control the Transvaal, sir?"

"I thought that would surprise you, Baird," Hook gave a wry smile. "Sometimes, one must look at the big picture. We don't lose many wars, but occasionally, losing a little war is necessary to stabilise the world. Prussia is the dominant European military power at present, and we are the world's major naval power. Our army, however good the material, is modest compared to the continental powers and trained for small colonial warfare. If we ever war with the Germans, we'll need an ally with a large army, either France or Russia." Hook gave every point slowly, pressing a finger on his desk as he held Andrew's gaze. "We are hostile to Russia with this Afghan business and the last Ottoman nonsense. That leaves France, who has not recovered from its mauling in seventy-one and with whom we have difficulties over Suez."

"Yes, sir," Andrew followed Hook's logic.

"Given the geo-political situation, we must play our cards carefully," General Hook said. He leaned back in his chair. "We'll ensure Germany does not get a foothold in Africa for a few years yet." His eyes were like gimlets. "If that means losing a minor war against the Boers, then by God, we'll take our medicine and correct matters later."

"Yes, sir," Andrew said. "Do you mean we might allow the Boers to win and retake the Transvaal in the future?"

"What Gladstone and the Whigs believe and what the Tories want are two radically different things, Baird. Politicians are strange animals who alter foreign policy to suit their party."

"I don't want anything to do with politicians, sir, of whatever persuasion."

"We are soldiers, Baird. Ultimately, politicians decide our fate." Hook stood up, a tall, grey figure with great wisdom in his sad eyes. "In the meantime, watch out for Konrad Bramigan. If you find him in your sights, don't hesitate to pull the trigger."

"We're not at war with Prussia, sir."

"No," Hook agreed, "but one death now might stop thousands later."

"Yes, sir," Andrew agreed. "Politics is a dirty business."

Hook sighed. "So is life, Andrew, so is life."

Mount Prospect, Natal, 7th of February 1881

The horseman came at a gallop, kicking up dust as he rode. When he came closer, Andrew saw his hat was missing, and the horse was lathered with foam and sweat. *This lad's in a hurry.*

"Hold there!" The sentry stepped forward from the closed gate. He raised his hand. "What's your business, friend?"

"Behind me!" the man gasped. "The mail!" He indicated a distant plume of dust. "The convoy! The Boers are attacking the mail!"

Colonel Ashburnham of the Rifles hurried across. "Baird! Go and see what's happening!"

Andrew nodded and ran to the horse lines. "Briggs! Saddle my horse!"

"Yes, sir!" Briggs had anticipated the order and was already saddling Lancelot. "Take care, sir!"

Mounting Lancelot, Andrew shouted for the sentries to open the gate and trotted outside, increasing his speed as he came closer to the dust. Holding his Martini in his right hand, he guided Lancelot with his left, scanning the countryside as he rode, for the Burghers' horsemen could operate close to Mount Prospect.

The land seemed empty except for the rising ribbon of dust. Andrew stopped on a slight rise to check his surroundings. Behind him was the British camp, a sea of tents and temporary huts, where General Colley was waiting for reinforcements, ammunition, and stores. The tail of the Drakensberg mountains loomed ahead, a natural barrier between Natal and the Transvaal, and to Andrew's right was the curtain of dust raised by the mail coach.

Satisfied no Boers were waiting to ambush him, Andrew pushed on, encouraging Lancelot with soft words. He guided the horse towards the coach, slowing as he came closer. The dozen horsemen who acted as escort lifted their rifles as Andrew halted.

"Halloa there!" Andrew shouted.

The mail coach driver was wild-eyed as he headed toward Mount Prospect, driving his animals with the whip. The escort, a mixture of colonials and British, looked rattled, smeared with dust and sweat. A burly sergeant approached Andrew. "Who are you?"

"Captain Andrew Baird, Natal Dragoons," Andrew said quickly before a nervous trooper shot him. "What happened?"

The driver rattled past without stopping, barely glancing at Andrew.

"Boers!" The sergeant gasped, looking over his shoulder. "We were on our way to Newcastle, and they ambushed us. We barely escaped with our lives!"

"How many?" Andrew asked.

"Dozens of them," the sergeant replied. "They came from nowhere. Maybe fifty or more."

Andrew nodded. He saw a single bullet hole in the canvas cover of the wagon and wondered how many Boers had been present. He doubted it had been a full-scale ambush, or the clumsy wagon with its small escort would not have escaped. The men looked ready to flee or run from shadows.

"Best get into the camp," Andrew advised. The escorts were useless in their present nervous state.

"We will!" the sergeant said, spurring on with his men following in a ragged bunch. Even as Andrew watched, the escort overtook the mail wagon in their eagerness to reach sanctuary.

The Boers have unsettled us, Andrew thought. He remained with the mail wagon until it eased into Mount Prospect, and the sentries shut the gate.

Colley closed his eyes when he heard the news. "Boers ambushing our mail! We can't have that," he said. "We must keep the communications and supplies route open, whatever Brother Boer thinks!" He paced momentarily, pulling at his beard as he considered the situation.

"No, we can't allow this. There's a convoy due here tomorrow with ammunition and stores from Fort Amiel. The Boers are bound to attack."

Andrew knew that the general was not asking his opinion.

"I'll take an escort to guard it," the general decided. "Get your Dragoons ready, Baird," Colley said. "They might be useful."

Andrew nodded. "Yes, sir."

They left camp the following day, the eighth of February 1881, with dawn flushing the horizon pink. Despite their earlier setbacks, the infantry marched confidently from the camp with their heads up and hands gripping their rifles.

Colley had five weak companies of the 60th Rifles, two seven-pounders and two nine-pounders, with a platoon of mounted infantry and a few score colonial horsemen, including Andrew's Natal Dragoons. The mail wagon rumbled between the escort.

"Here we are again, sir," Fletcher glanced over the column. "Three hundred men as a wagon escort for Newcastle."

"Indeed, we are," Andrew replied. "Send out half a dozen scouts and change them every hour."

"Yes, sir," Fletcher said.

When the small convoy reached the Ingogo River drift, close to their objective, Colley ordered a company of the 60th, plus the seven-pounder mountain guns, onto a hill overlooking the river.

"Cover our crossing," he ordered. Colley waited until the infantry and artillery were in position before he sent the remainder of the force over the river. "I want vedettes in the front and on both flanks. Baird, take your Dragoons and the mounted infantry in front and scout for Boers."

"Yes, sir." Andrew lifted an arm. "Come on, lads!" As the Dragoons splashed over the shallow Ingogo, the sun caught the rising water droplets, creating a miniature rainbow that lasted a few seconds and vanished.

Even in war, there can be beauty.

"Extended order, men," Andrew ordered. The land was undulating on the opposite side of the Ingogo, slowly rising to a range of hills. Andrew rode to a prominent knoll, lifted his field glasses, and scanned the area. In the middle distance, the ground rose to a low plateau and then stretched in a sea of brown-dun grass interspersed with occasional trees and rocky outcrops under the high emptiness of the sky. He paused, refocused, and grunted. Over on the left, he saw a tell-tale ribbon of dust.

"Fletcher!"

"Sir!" Lieutenant Fletcher rode to him.

"Take a section to the northwest and investigate that dust cloud." Andrew watched Fletcher trot away and reported to General Colley. "Somebody's over there, sir, and I doubt they're friendly."

Colley lifted his binoculars to scan the area. "I see you've sent a patrol out."

"Yes, sir."

"When they return, report their findings to me."

"I will, sir," Andrew returned to the Dragoons. "Move out five hundred yards," he ordered. "Form a ring to cover the column as it crosses." He watched his men ride out and returned to his knoll.

Colley supervised his convoy, with the Rifles marching beside the wagons and the sun beating down on them, reflecting from rifle barrels and cap badges.

"Move on," Andrew ordered the Dragoons when the convoy was across, and Colley pushed onto the plateau.

"Wait here until we hear from the scouts," Colley ordered cautiously. The convoy halted, dust settling around the wagons and the men looking around.

Andrew pushed his Dragoons ahead of the column. "Keep your eyes open for signs of Boers. They'll have seen us coming."

Sergeant Meek nodded. "We can't hide a dozen wagons and hundreds of men."

"Not easily," Andrew agreed. He glanced over the column. The veterans were watchful yet relaxed, but some mounted infantry and recruits looked nervous. "Keep alert, boys, and guard each other's backs."

Fletcher returned, galloping the final two hundred yards with his hat bouncing from its chin strap and sweat glistening on his face. "The Boers are waiting ahead, sir!" he shouted.

"How many Boers?" Andrew calmed the lieutenant down. "Report properly; we don't want another Balaclava!"

"Sorry, sir," Fletcher took a deep breath to control his excitement. "The Boers are waiting six hundred yards distant, sir."

"Show me," Andrew ordered, leading Lancelot forward until he saw a long line of horsemen, most with distinctive slouch hats and using long stirrups so they appeared to be leaning back in their saddles.

"They may be friendly, sir," Fletcher said, ducking as the closest Boer lifted his rifle and fired. "No, they're not."

The bullet buzzed past, far over their heads.

Andrew and Fletcher fired back, with no noticeable effect on the enemy.

Andrew pressed another cartridge into his rifle, aimed, and fired. The Boers extended their line and moved forward, with further riders appearing on both flanks. At first, Andrew thought there were a hundred, then saw more in the rear, occupying a ridge slightly lower than their plateau.

"How many do you reckon, sir?" Fletcher asked.

"Hundreds," Andrew replied shortly. "Retire, lads. We can't do anything against these numbers, and we'd better let General Colley know."

"Keep the line, boys," Andrew ordered. "Fletcher, take a section and try to hold the Boers back if they get too close."

"Yes, sir," Fletcher moved forward with ten men as Andrew withdrew the bulk of the Dragoons, passing through the Rifles, who settled behind cover and readied for action.

"You're going the wrong way, Dragoons!" a Rifleman shouted.

Acknowledging the sally with a wave, Andrew approached the waiting general.

"How many Boers are there, do you reckon?" Colley asked.

"A few hundred," Andrew said. "Maybe three hundred." He nodded to the leading Boers, who sat in a loose formation a quarter of a mile from Fletcher's section. "Certainly, no more than four hundred."

"Greer," Colley said to the officer commanding the artillery. "Give them a couple of rounds with your nine-pounders."

Captain Greer grinned and issued a string of orders that saw his men unlimber the guns, train them onto the Boer positions, and hurriedly load. Greer strode across, checked the aim, and nodded.

"Fire!" he ordered quietly.

The guns roared with orange flame and spurts of white smoke. Andrew watched the Boer lines, but both shots passed over the horsemen and exploded in the rear.

Greer's mouth twitched. "Lower the elevation a notch," he said.

Watching through his field glasses, Andrew saw the Boers hastily dismount and run to shelter in a *donga*. As always in these long-distant battles, he found the fighting curiously impersonal. The Boers seemed very far away, the explosions only harmless puffs of smoke and the uniformed soldiers like toys on a tabletop. Men seemed to move in slow motion, speaking with a long drawl as they gave and accepted orders. Something hit the ground between Lancelot's hooves, raising a pretty little fountain of dust that hovered briefly and slowly drifted down.

"They're all around us," a Rifle lieutenant said as Boer bullets sang and whined onto the four-acre plateau.

The movement suddenly speeded up, with men moving quickly, officers giving staccato orders and men ducking and bobbing like fairground mannequins.

The Rifles were returning the Boer fire, and Greer ordered one of his guns to point right and the other left.

"Fire whenever you see a target," Greer commanded.

The gunners responded, aiming where the Boer gun smoke was thickest.

The explosions blasted dust and small stones into the air, adding their quota of smoke and noise to the day.

"Who said army life was boring?" the Rifles' lieutenant asked.

"Somebody who had never been to South Africa," Andrew replied. "I've been here less than four years, and this is my third campaign!"

"Lie down!" Colley ordered. "Send the convoy away, and we'll hold the Boers here."

The Riflemen and mounted infantry obeyed, but the gunners needed to stand to fire, making them more vulnerable to Boer musketry.

"Get the horses down," Andrew ordered, thanking Providence his men were well trained. The Natal Dragoons pulled down their mounts, but some of the lesser-trained mounted infantry could not comply, and Boer marksmen targeted their horses. The Riflemen also began to take casualties; although they wore green rather than scarlet, they were still conspicuous against the lighter ground of the plateau.

"Fire if you see a Boer," Andrew ordered. "Otherwise, conserve your bullets."

The Boers kept up a steady fire. Andrew saw one gunner fall and then another, with bullets pinging and whining from the rocks. Despite their casualties, the artillerymen continued to coolly work the guns. When a bullet hit Greer, spinning him around and knocking him to the ground, Lieutenant Charles Parsons, a veteran of the Zulu War, took charge.

"Case shot," Parsons ordered. "Brother Boer is only five hundred yards away. Let's see how he likes hot steel whirling around his head."

Another gunner grunted and crumpled as a Boer bullet smacked into his chest. Steam rose from the puddles of blood, and flies congregated, buzzing obscenely.

The artillery fired again as Boer bullets continued to hit horses and men. Andrew saw a wounded horse, maddened by pain, whinny, and rise to stagger around the plateau, trampling an injured man, whose screams joined that of the horse.

"Reverted shrapnel," Parsons decided. He did not flinch as a bullet ricocheted from the barrel of the nine-pounder at his side. Another horse screamed and fell as a Boer bullet slammed into it.

Overhead, thunder growled from horizon to horizon, with a heavy sky promising rain. Wounded men lay on the ground, some groaning, others suffering in courageous silence. Horses lay beside them, some still alive and bleeding, others already beginning to swell in the heat. Andrew offered water to one ashen-faced man who lay against the wheels of a gun limber.

"Thanks, mate," the man said, realised Andrew was an officer, and attempted to salute. He died with his hand halfway to his head.

"Rest easy, my friend," Andrew said. He glanced up as rain began slowly and then increased to a torrent that drenched the men on the plateau.

"Who said Africa was always hot and sunny?" the Rifles' lieutenant asked.

"I don't know," Andrew replied.

"If you ever find out," the lieutenant said, "send him to me, and I'll put a flea in his ear!" He ducked as a Boer bullet lifted the hat from his head. "That one was close!"

"Keep firing!" Parsons ordered as another of his men fell, hit simultaneously by two Boer bullets.

"This is getting ridiculous," the Rifles' lieutenant said as he toured his men with encouraging words and cheerful advice. "More Boers are joining all the time."

Andrew agreed. A steady trickle of reinforcements rode to help the Boers, some as individuals and others in small groups.

By half past two, so many gunners were down that Lieutenant Parsons asked for Riflemen to help service the artillery. Despite the obvious danger, there was no shortage of volunteers.

"Good lads, the Rifles," Andrew suggested. *If we lose this battle, it's not through a shortage of courage.*

As the Boers and British continued to exchange fire, the Boers once again proved superior in fighting from cover. The firing increased until about three in the afternoon when the musketry slackened.

"We're firing at ghosts," a Rifleman complained. "I can't see a blessed man."

"I bet they can see you, though, Deas! Keep your head down!"

"Cease fire," Colley ordered. "Conserve our ammunition."

Andrew passed the message on to his men. An eerie hush settled across the battlefield, punctuated by the groans of wounded men and the steady patter of rain.

The rain pressed the gun smoke to the plateau's surface and tormented the suffering wounded. Andrew saw a tearful mounted infantryman shoot his badly injured horse, then bury his head in the animal's neck.

Men peered towards the Boer lines, with the officers cautiously lifting their field glasses and private soldiers narrowing their eyes.

"I can't see anybody," a subaltern said.

"Maybe they've retired," the Rifles' lieutenant said. "We've chased them away."

Rifleman Deas began to cheer until an NCO snarled at him to be quiet.

"The Boers are having a lunch break," Andrew gave his opinion. "Either that or they're replenishing their ammunition. They've fired away plenty."

After ten minutes, the Boers began to fire again, hitting another gunner and a horse.[1]

The British retaliated, aiming at the gun smoke.

"Don't fire unless you see a definite target," Andrew ordered. He studied the Boer lines through his field glasses and, for a second, saw a familiar elderly, bearded man with a leopard skin band around his hat. The Boer fired; the bullet zipped past Andrew before he could move and slammed into the Rifles' lieutenant, blowing his brains out the back of his head.

Andrew dropped his field glasses and grabbed his carbine, but the Boer had vanished, leaving only a small cloud of grey-white smoke to mark his presence.

"Keep down, Lieutenant Parsons," Colley gave belated orders. "Only fire if you have a decent target."

A Rifleman raised a hoarse cry. "Look! The Boers are surrendering!"

Andrew saw a white flag rise above the Boer positions.

"Cease fire!" Colley ordered. "Maybe they want to parley."

As the British fire ceased, the Boers advanced, still firing on the artillery.

"So much for the white flag," Fletcher muttered. "Never trust a Boer."

"They're moving around our rear," Andrew reported to Colley. The plateau was roughly saucer-shaped, with a slight depression in the centre, so the men on the firing line on the rim were more exposed than those in the centre.

"Bring the wounded into the dip," Colley ordered. "They're safer there."

Cowering from the lashing rain, men dragged or carried their injured comrades away from the terrible rifle fire and into the depression.

"Another one, Doctor!" Deas supported a wounded colleague.

"Put him down there," Surgeon McGann pointed to a smooth area of ground. Two orderlies helped Deas lower the wounded man as bullets sighed and whined above their heads.

"I wonder what people will call this battle," Fletcher asked as he lay behind a rock, firing his carbine.

"I believe this place is called Schuinschoogte," Andrew replied, "so that will probably be the name." He looked toward the river, wondering if the other company of the 60th and the two seven-pounder mountain guns would come up in support.

Come on, lads. If you come now, you can catch the Boers when they're extended.

The Rifles fired whenever they thought they saw a Boer or the smoke from a Boer rifle, although the shooting eased as the afternoon ground on.

"Are these men deaf?" Fletcher indicated the Rifle company across the river. "They should be over here to roll the Boers up."

Andrew did not answer. He had never heard of a British officer failing to help men in trouble. *The Zulu War began with a defeat and ended in a resounding victory. This war lurches from defeat to disaster.*

Andrew checked his water bottle, had a sip, and allowed a wounded man to finish the final drop. Lifting his field glasses, he focussed on the camp without sighting the seven-pounders or any sign of a relief force. Down below, more Boers rode to join their companions.

"Half the blasted Transvaal is here now," Fletcher said.

"And the other half is probably on its way," Andrew agreed.

Shortly after five, the two seven-pounders beside the river finally opened fire on the Boers, with the rain distorting the sound of the explosions.

"Thank God for small mercies," Parsons said. "They've heard our gunfire at last."

"If they march now, they can still catch the Boers in the rear and roll them up," Fletcher said.

"Do the Boers have a rear?" Andrew asked. "They're all light horsemen and can alter their position in a heartbeat. Our infantry marches too slow to outflank them; we'll have to pin the Boers against a broad river or fight them with more horsemen."

One of Parsons' nine-pounder shells exploded in an area of thick vegetation on the right of the British position, scattering a dozen Boers.

"Oh, good shot, sir!" Surgeon McGann shouted as he looked up from operating on a wounded man.

"Good shot indeed!" Allan McLean of the Transvaal Light Horse echoed. He had been helping McGann treat the wounded, with both exposing themselves to Boer fire.

"Hold on until dark," Colley said. "We'll leave then!"

Andrew hugged a rock, firing at the puffs of smoke, all he could see of the encircling Boers. He heard a scream behind him as a Boer bullet smashed into a private's shoulder, while another man fell without a whisper, shot clean through the head.

As darkness fell, the desultory musketry ended, with men looking around, wondering that they were still alive and checking on their colleagues. Dead and wounded men littered the plateau.

"Collect all the wounded," Colley ordered. "Bring them to the surgeon."

As the darkness grew more intense, men carried their injured comrades to Surgeon McGann.

"Look after him, sir; he's hurt bad."

"Here's Nobby Clark, sir. The Boers put a bullet in his guts, but I don't think it's too serious."

"Could you look after Harry, sir? He's my backmarker."

Andrew stood up cautiously, expecting to hear the whine of a bullet. Peering through the dark, a rare glimpse of moonlight revealed scores of Boers retreating to their camp on Laing's Nek, avoiding the British on the other side of the river. Andrew heard a single rifle shot and saw a spurt of dust and rock splinters as the bullet struck nearby.

"I thought we had stopped fighting," Fletcher said.

"These are not disciplined professional soldiers," Andrew reasoned. "They are farmers, unused to taking orders from anybody."

Their individualism is both their strength and their weakness.

"Don't fire back!" Colley ordered.

The British held their fire, looking cautiously at the Boer positions and keeping low as they carried the wounded to the surgeon. Lieutenant Parsons walked to the nine-pounder on the right, gasped as a Boer bullet nicked his hand, shook off the excess blood and continued to his destination.

As the Boer musketry increased again, the infantry ignored Colley's orders and fired at the muzzle flashes. All the time, the surgeon and McLean tended the wounded as the chaplain, the Reverend Mr Ritchie, gave spiritual comfort to dying men.

The musketry intensified as the surgeon dressed Parsons' wound. Andrew saw little vignettes of the action. He saw the seven-pounders firing as the Boers retreated. He saw Major Brownlow of the mounted infantry moving from man to man, encouraging them. He saw Colonel Ashburnham standing beside the body of Captain MacGregor, the Assistant Military Secretary.

Too many men are dying for no real reason. War is humanity's most obscene creation.

As the wind rose to storm force, the rain hammered down on the plateau, increasing the soldiers' misery. Thunder grumbled and rolled above, split with intermittent lightning flashes that silhouetted the shapes of the hills in the crowding dark.

"The Boers have retreated," Colley said. "We can evacuate the position. Leave the wounded. Chaplain Ritchie will look after them. The Boers are decent chaps who won't abuse injured men, and we don't have sufficient horses to carry them away."

Andrew saw that the general was correct. The battle had left only two horses remaining for each gun and a pair for one of the ammunition limbers. Colley had to abandon the second limber along with the wounded. The most fortunate of the injured lay under blankets; the majority had nothing to shelter them from the teeming rain as the British withdrew. Andrew checked his watch: nine at night. The men moved in silence, unhappy at leaving their wounded behind and the dead unburied. They slogged back through the rain, frustrated and depressed yet aware they had done all they could.

Without using the bugle, Colley's men slipped away from the hill. They moved in a hollow square, watchful for a Boer ambush. Andrew swore when he realised the Boers had shot a third of the Dragoons' horses, although Lancelot was uninjured.

"Baird, use your men and the mounted infantry as a screen. Fend off any Boer attacks."

"Yes, sir." Andrew ordered the dismounted Dragoons to accompany the Rifles and gestured to the rest. "Come on, lads! We're the escorts and shepherds, rounding up stragglers and watching for the enemy."

The Dragoons rode outside the hollow square, plodding through the rain.

"Can you hear that sound, sir?" Fletcher asked. "What is it?"

Andrew was aware of something between a roar and a grumble coming from ahead. "That's the Ingogo River," he said.

The Dragoons stopped when they reached the Ingogo, staring at the rushing brown torrent. In the morning, the infantry waded across with dry knees, but the storm had swollen the river to four times its normal size, and now the water was chest high and powerful, worse because it was dark.

"How the hell are we going to cross that?" Morrison asked.

"God knows!" Ogden replied. "This blasted country is fighting for the Boers."

Andrew peered into the pelting rain. If the Boers had placed an ambush at the drift, the British would be hard-pressed to retaliate. As it was, crossing the Ingogo was as bad as anything else that day.

"Patrol the banks!" Andrew had to shout above the roaring water and the hammer of the rain. "Look for Boers!"

"They've got too much sense to be out on a night like this!" Sergeant Meek replied as he took his section to the right.

"Go to the left, Fletcher!" Andrew ordered. "My section, follow me!" He forced Lancelot into the surging water, gasping at the force of the current. Game as ever, Lancelot thrust his way across the surging river and emerged, dripping, on the far bank. Checking his men were all right, Andrew spread them out.

"You, three, take the right; the rest follow me. If you see any Boers, drive them off!"

The river was still rising, with the ground underfoot soft and slippery. Andrew guided Lancelot away from the treacherous bank, grunted as branches and other pieces of debris rushed past and hoped the Boers had decided to remain under shelter for the night.

"Any Boers?" Andrew shouted through the noise.

"Nothing here, sir!"

"All clear!"

"Nary a one, sir!"

The reports came to Andrew as the first infantry reached the river.

"It's safe to cross!" Andrew called. "Be careful of the current!"

Ordering his Dragoons to help the infantry, Andrew watched the Rifles tentatively step into the water. The first man stumbled and would have been swept downstream if Sergeant Meek had not planted his horse firmly in the way.

"Up you come, lad!" Meek said, hauling the Rifleman upright. "No lying down on the job! Her Majesty paid a good shilling for you, and she won't see her money tossed away in the river."

"Link arms!" Andrew remembered how the natives had forded the Buffalo during the invasion of Zululand. *Was that two years ago? Time has flown since I arrived in South Africa.* "Link arms and stay together!"

Pushing a reluctant Lancelot into the river, he tried to guide the infantry across, extending a helping hand to the weaker and offering encouragement to the rest. The night became a nightmare of roaring water, hammering rain and the hoarse cries of frightened men.

"Keep together!" Andrew shouted, blinking into the dark. "One step at a time!" He heard a despairing scream and saw one man's upraised hand as the river knocked him off his feet and carried him away. Andrew glimpsed the man's terrified face, and then the river rushed the soldier into the lonely night.[2]

"Get the stragglers over!" Officers shouted. Andrew knew the fording of the Ingogo River in the dark would remain in his memory for a long time, as vivid as leaving the despairing wounded on the bloody plateau.

"Back to camp, lads!" Andrew mustered his Dragoons and counted them anxiously, relieved everybody was present. He did not see General Colley. "We'll act as rearguard in case Brother Boer tries to harass us."

"Harass us?" Fletcher repeated. "The Boers have too much sense to come out in this weather."

"God help sailors, they say," Ogden shouted from the dark. "God help sailors on a night like this, they say. God help bloody dragoons in Africa, I say!"

Andrew rode around the infantry, shepherding them like a sodden collie dog with a flock of swearing sheep. The guns were in the centre of the reformed hollow square, rattling, jolting, and splashing over the uneven ground, with the remaining artillerymen urging their horses on, and Mount Prospect a distant dream. The world consisted of pelting rain, mud, the memory of Boer bullets, and the screams of stricken men and horses.

"March!" the officers ordered. "Keep in step!"

The men marched, stumbled, swore, and continued, an enduring, defiant, and angry army returning to their base.

"What next?" Fletcher asked.

"Try somebody else, for I'm sure I don't know," Andrew replied.

The column arrived back at Mount Prospect at seven the following morning. The skirmish had cost another hundred and thirty-nine officers and men from the already weak British force, and the morale of the survivors plummeted.

"How about the wounded?" a major of the Rifles asked. "We shouldn't have left them behind. They were our men."

"The Boers will look after them," Colley said. "The poor fellows will be all right." He nodded as if in satisfaction. "I think we can consider that operation a success, gentlemen. We pulled the Boers to us, enabled the convoy to get through to Newcastle, and inflicted God knows how many casualties on the enemy. They won't be so keen to face us again."

The major looked at Andrew in disbelief. "That's a quarter of the Field Force General Colley has lost within ten days," he murmured. "If we carry on like this, only you and I will remain to defeat them."

Andrew looked at his Dragoons as they groomed, fed, and watered the horses. In the turmoil of battle, he had nearly forgotten the convoy. "This war is not going according to plan," he said. "It's not finished yet, though."

"We need reinforcements," the major said. "Whenever we face the Boers, they pull men from all over the Transvaal, and we only have a diminishing force of a few hundred to fight them and garrison the country."

"We need more horsemen," Andrew agreed cautiously.

As the Dragoons cared for their horses and Andrew wrote a small letter to assure Mariana she had not been forgotten, General Colley sent a small convoy of wagons under a flag of truce to collect the wounded and dead.

The Rifles watched the wagons splash through the mud, cursed, and kept their rifles dry.

"I hope the bloody Boers don't think we're finished yet," one Rifleman growled. "I want another shot at them. I want them at the end of my sword."

His companion grunted. "You can have them, chum. I want to be in a public in Wandsworth with a pint in my hand and a woman on my knee. They can stick Africa where the sun don't shine and keep it there."

The first Rifleman laughed bitterly. "I'll join you in the public, mate. Bugger Africa. The Boers can keep it."

CHAPTER 13

POTCHEFSTROOM, JANUARY-FEBRUARY 1881

"Will this rain never stop?" Jan looked upwards. "The Lord is weeping to see his children fighting."

"The Lord is weeping to see the *Rooinecks* still in his people's land," Theunis corrected. "But we're wearing them down and forcing them out." He crouched beside Jan and peered over the trench parapet towards the fort.

"You won't see anybody," Jan said. "The British have learned to keep out of sight."

The Groenburg Commando was taking its turn in the trenches. They kept low to avoid any British marksmen, splashed through knee-deep mud, and crouched in misery as the rain continued to hammer down.

"I didn't think war would be like this," Jan removed his hat, shook off the excess water, and thrust it back, still sodden, on his head.

"Did you think it would be glorious?" Theunis asked. "Did you think we'd be wearing scarlet uniforms and charging behind a flag?"

Jan did not reply, aware that Theunis was mocking him.

"We don't see much of that Prussian fellow in the trenches," Karl said. "He prefers the company of pretty women to the grind of the front."

"I thought he was a soldier," Jan replied without much interest.

"He's the kind of soldier who likes the glory and not the hard work," Karl said. "I wonder if even half his stories are genuine."

"He won some medals," Jan said.

"He probably bought them in Cape Town," Karl replied.

"We are the closest Burghers to the British positions," Johannes interrupted their conversation. "We are the men in the front line, the most forward in all the Republic."

"It would be better if we could stop the rain," Karl said.

Jan raised his voice. "I saw movement in the fort," he said.

Theunis eased his head above the sandbagged parapet. The fort was three hundred yards away, sodden under the rain, and with the walls pock-marked with Boer bullets. "I can't see anything."

"Maybe it was just a careless sentry," Jan said. By the third week of January, the novelty of besieging the fort had worn off, and the Burghers no longer fired whenever they saw a British soldier. The cannon loosed an occasional shot, while General Cronje would urge a spasm of activity from time to time. Apart from that, the Boers and British observed a wary watchfulness, neither trusting the other.

"When do we return to the house?" Karl asked.

"We are on duty here until midnight," Johannes told him.

"I wish it were midnight now," Karl said.

Jan nodded silently. He thought of his warm bed in Nuwe Hoop Plaas and vowed never to leave home again. He looked around as Konrad slid into the trench.

"How are you doing?" the Prussian asked, crouching beneath the parapet.

"We are well," Johannes replied. "Have you completed your report to the Chancellor yet?"

Jan listened without interest. He had never taken to Konrad despite the German's friendliness and evident desire for people to admire him. Jan turned away so Konrad would not talk to him.

"General Cronje sent me to ask how you were," Konrad continued.

"Tell the general we are wet, cold, and hungry," Karl replied. "And ask him to come in person if he is interested."

Konrad shook his head. "The general is a busy man," he replied. "He has too much to do."

"And he'll stay nice and dry while he does it," Karl said.

"Movement!" Jan raised his voice. "The British are moving!" He lifted his rifle, ready for a British sortie.

"Where?" Johannes joined his son.

"Over there," Jan pointed to the left of the trench, where a battered group of houses stood between the Boers and the fort. "Something moved."

"I can't see anything," Johannes said. "Pass over the glasses, Theunis!" He scanned the buildings. "If the British are there, they are very still." He raised his voice. "Konrad! What do you think?"

"The German has gone," Abraham said. "He left when Jan told us the British were moving."

Karl gave a bitter laugh. "Maybe our hero is more sensible than I believed."

Johannes concentrated on the houses, reminded Jan to keep under cover, and moved further up the trench. He checked the time when the light died away, saw the watch-fires flicker to life on the fort's walls, and wished he was back with Aletta.

Why don't the British give up? Their infantry tactics consistently fail against us. Why don't they go back to London and leave us in peace?

"*Rooinecks*!" Jan yelled the warning as a British officer led a dozen infantrymen in a sudden charge on the trench. Jan levelled his rifle and fired as the British came closer. The officer was tall and slender, with a drooping moustache and a row of medal ribbons on his chest. Jan saw the soldiers' mouths open in yells and the glitter of their long bayonets, heard their savage battle cries and the officer's barked commands.

"Run!" Karl shouted, jumping from the back of the trench with another man joining him.

Jan hesitated; he knew Karl was no coward, but defending a position to a glorious death was not how the Burghers fought. They preferred to shoot, withdraw, and live to fight another day. Jan saw the first of the Fusiliersh arrive at the trench, plunging his bayonet into the cringing body of Daniel Eloff. He heard screams of pain and fear, saw the officer shoot a man in the chest, and his father fending off a bayonet with the barrel of his rifle.

"Pa!" Jan shouted.

Johannes stepped back as the British soldier withdrew a step and levelled his bayonet. "Run, Jan! Run!"

Jan shook his head and saw his father scramble out of the trench with the soldier five paces behind. He levelled his rifle but snatched at the trigger, causing the bullet to fly wide. The soldier raised his bayonet and leapt at Jan, snarling.

"Run!" Johannes grabbed Jan by the collar, hauled him bodily from the trench, and pushed him towards Potchefstroom. "Run, Jan! Run for your life!"

Jan ran, with his feet slithering and sliding in the mud and the sound of his breathing harsh in his ears. He heard musketry behind him and the sound of British cheers, the pounding of feet, and a man shouting.

The soldiers pursued the Boers for thirty yards until the officer called them back with some shouting taunts that Jan did not understand.

"Jan!" Johannes put a hand on his shoulder as he ran past the first buildings. "We're safe now. They've stopped chasing us."

Jan gulped in air, hearing the pounding of his heart. "I ran away," he said. "I ran away from the *Rooinecks*."

"So did I," Johannes said. "So did Karl. The men who did not run are still in the trench, dead or wounded."

"They fought with spears, like the Kaffirs," Jan found he was trembling. "That is not how civilised men fight."

"War is not civilised," Johannes replied.

Jan nodded as the truth hit him. The *Rooineck* bayonets had frightened his father, a man he had idolised all his life. Jan looked at him, suddenly understanding his father was as vulnerable as anybody else. War was a sordid, disgusting nightmare where men, women, and children were killed or maimed. "There is no glory in war," Jan said. "Do we need to fight?"

"If men did not fight," Johannes said. "The greedy, the evil and the power-hungry politician or king would always triumph."

"Maybe," Jan said. "But the price is high." He remembered Daniel Eloff's scream and knew he would never see him alive again. He farmed twenty miles east of Nuwe Hoop Plaas. How would his wife cope with two young children?

"Ja," Johannes agreed. "The price is always high, and the men who start the wars are seldom the ones to suffer."[1]

Jan looked around at the survivors of the commando. "Am I a coward for running?"

"No, Jan. You are not. Only an idiot stands still to be killed when he can run to fight another day."

"I feel like a coward," Jan said. He saw Mannie lying beneath his blankets, waxen-faced and shivering. Mannie had always looked up to him as a hero, but now Mannie would know he was scared.

"The *Rooinecks* have taken our forward trench," Johannes said. "We'll have to start over again."

Will this war ever end? Jan wondered. *Will Engela remember me?*

The reverse shook the Boers, and Johannes was quiet when the British sent an officer under a flag of truce with an offer to lend the Boers stretchers for the wounded.

"We'd care for them ourselves," the British officer explained, "but we've few facilities in the fort and less medical supplies."

Johannes nodded. "Thank you, *meneer*, we will accept your stretchers."

"I do have one question, sir," the officer said.

Johannes waited.

"Are you using explosive bullets? One of our lads, Private Colvin, was hit in the arm by what seems to be an explosive bullet. It's not the done thing, you know. Not in a civilised society."

Johannes shook his head. "We don't use such things, *meneer*."[2]

The officer nodded. "I didn't think you would. Well, good luck with your wounded." He shook Johannes's hand and returned to the fort.

Can any society be called civilised when it resorts to war to steal somebody else's land? Jan wondered. *And is an exploding bullet any worse than sticking an eighteen-inch bayonet into a man's stomach?*

Half a dozen British soldiers arrived ten minutes later, each man carrying a stretcher. Jan was one of the Boers who met the soldiers.

"Here we go, Piet," a tousle-haired man said with a grin. "It's not much, but better than a poke in the eye with a blunt stick."

"Yes," Jan's limited English could not follow the attempted humour. "Thank you, *meneer*."

The soldier held out his hand. "You take care, Piet. I'll try not to shoot you."

Jan took the man's hand. "I will try not to shoot you also," he said. "How are conditions inside the fort? Are you ready to surrender yet?"

The soldier laughed, shaking his head. "I'll tell you what it's like," he said.

"I spoke to one of the *Rooinecks*," Jan said after he had returned with the empty stretchers. "He was quite friendly and told me quite a lot, probably because he thought I was too young to take note."

"What did he tell you?" Johannes asked.

"He said the surgeons had hardly any supplies left," Jan said. "The men had been on short rations since the middle of December and will be eating mealies rather than biscuits soon."

"We're starving them out," Konrad said, smiling.

"They have bully beef only every third day," Jan continued. He ignored Konrad's gleeful smile, wondering where he had been when the British charged with their bayonets. "The garrison has no tea, sugar, or even tobacco, and the constant rain is making their sacks of corn rot and sprout."

Johannes nodded. "I'll pass that information to General Cronje," he said. "Now, let's get our wounded back."

Jan had never helped with the wounded before and was shocked at how quickly a single bullet or bayonet thrust could reduce strong men. He knew two of the surviving casualties and tried to reassure them they would get better, although it was plain that one would die. Daniel Eloff was already dead, curled into a foetal ball with an ugly bayonet wound in his stomach and congealed blood covering his clothes.

"I knew Daniel well," Abraham said. "He is my mother's cousin, and now he's dead."

"That's right," Theunis said. "He died to keep the Transvaal free."

Abraham stepped away from the house they used as a hospital. "I'd rather have Daniel alive than a free Transvaal."

"Then you are a traitor," Theunis said.

Jan felt sudden tension as Abraham faced Theunis with his fists clenched. Theunis was six inches taller, but Abraham was more pugnacious, standing erect and with his head tilted back so his long blond hair reached down his spine like the mane of an angry lion.

"I am not a traitor," Abraham denied. "If he were alive, Daniel would farm beside Dian, his wife. Now, she must farm alone or find another man. That is not a victory for the Burghers."

"We should all be willing to die for the Transvaal," Theunis said, glowering at the smaller, younger man.

"We'd all prefer to live for it," Johannes stepped between them as Jan clenched his fists, preparing to help Abraham.

"I meant Daniel's sacrifice is not in vain," Theunis said.

"Dian will be pleased to hear that," Abraham said, refusing to back down. He stepped closer to Theunis with his face raised to meet the taller man's gaze.

"That's enough," Johannes pushed Abraham back and watched Theunis walk away, muttering under his breath.

"I'll be glad when Theunis returns to Groenburg," Jan said, unclenching his fists. "I find him disturbing."

Abraham stared at Theunis's retreating figure. "You should have let me hit him, Oom Johannes."

"He is much bigger than you," Johannes pointed out. "And a noted fighter."

Abraham tapped the breech of his rifle. "If he had won, I'd have shot him," he admitted.

"Leave that to the *Rooinecks*," Jan said. "He's not worth hanging for."

When Johannes returned the British stretchers, General Cronje added fruit for the British wounded and carbolic acid for the medical supplies. "We are not savages," he said. "If we must kill each other, let's do it in a civilised manner."

"You are gentlemen," a Fusilier officer said. "You could be British."

"I'd prefer to be a free Burgher," Cronje replied with a smile.

The officer looked confused. In his eyes, telling a foreigner he could be British was the highest honour he could bestow. He did not understand why this farmer was not delighted with the compliment.

Mount Prospect, Natal, February 1881.

"What happens now?" a Rifles' lieutenant asked as he lit a long cheroot.

Andrew shrugged. "Don't ask me," he said. "We try again, I suppose. The Boers are a different kind of enemy from the Galeka or the Zulus, so we'll have to adapt our tactics to suit their style of warfare."

They sat in the large marquee that acted as an Officers' Mess with the rain pattering on the canvas above and the ground below churned into mud.

"Reinforcements are on their way," the lieutenant said. "Some fresh faces and veterans of Afghanistan too. They'll show the Boers what's what."

Andrew nodded. "More men might help. Trying to invade a country with a force of less than fifteen hundred is pointless, especially when every Boer seems to be a crack shot and a superb horseman."

The lieutenant blew smoke into the air. "We'll beat them, sir. We defeat everybody in time." He leaned back in his creaking cane chair and grinned across to Andrew. "That's how we own the largest empire in the world."

"That's reassuring," Andrew said dryly.

"Excuse me, sir," the lieutenant's soldier-servant interrupted. "There's a young lady to see Captain Baird."

"Show her in," Andrew said.

Mariana was dripping wet when she ducked inside the bell tent.

"Hello, Captain Baird."

"Good morning, Mariana," Andrew hid his surprise. "You look wet."

"That would be the rain," Mariana said.

"Well, Mariana," Andrew caught a few disapproving looks from the regular officers. "Ladies aren't allowed in the Mess except on guest nights, so we'd better go elsewhere. My tent is empty." He guided her outside, placed his tunic over her head as a makeshift umbrella, and escorted her to his tent.

"That's better," Andrew said as he opened the flap. "It's not much, but it's the only home I have. Take a pew."

"A pew?"

"A seat. Sit down." Andrew gestured to the only chair. "Tell me what I can do for you and how you got here."

"Thank you," Mariana perched on the edge of the chair. She looked at Andrew, smiled faintly, and then looked away. "When are you coming home?"

"I don't know," Andrew sat on his cot, hearing the structure creak under his weight. "When this campaign is over, I suppose."

"I don't like being alone," Mariana said quietly.

"You have the servants," Andrew spoke more brusquely than he realised.

"It's not the same," Mariana said. She twined her hands together. "It was all right when Mr Briggs was there. Can you send him back?"

"Briggs is a soldier; his duty is with the regiment," Andrew told her. "I'd be breaking all the rules if I posted him away during a war."

Mariana's hands twisted further. "I thought so," she said bravely. "I just wanted to ask."

"I'll be back as soon as possible," Andrew said. "Can you hold out?" He touched her shoulder. "I know it's not easy."

"I'll be alright." Mariana stood up.

"I'll send Briggs to escort you back home," Andrew said. "These roads are not safe with the Boers going about."

"The Boers don't bother me," Mariana said. "It's the nightmares."

Andrew understood. He knew nightmares troubled some Zulu War veterans, while his father, the famous Fighting Jack, often woke in the night with memories of the Indian Mutiny. *Not all war wounds are physical,* he thought. "Come with me. I'll take you to Dr McGann, the surgeon. He may have something to help."

"Yes, Andrew." Mariana hesitated for a moment. "I dream of what they did to Elaine," she said. "I was there when it happened."

Andrew rose and held her, unable to imagine the horror Mariana had experienced watching the renegades murdering her sister. Yet, he knew that recalling the memory was a step forward. "It's in the past now, Mariana," he said and listened as she told him what had happened.

"We were all in bed," Mariana said. "All sleeping when they came. We didn't have a chance. Father tried to fight, but there were too many of them. I was in Elaine's room when they arrived." She spoke slowly at first, then sped up as though attempting to unburden herself of the memory.

Andrew held her close as she spoke rapidly between the tears, allowing her time to recover.

"When they had killed everybody, they dragged me away." Mariana stopped there, gulping for breath. "They were laughing, boasting about their actions as though they were heroes for murdering unarmed women and men. They rode for days, shooting everybody they saw."

Andrew listened, aware it was cathartic for Mariana to speak about the horrors but sorry she had to relive the experiences. "I've got you," he murmured. "You're safe now."

Andrew did not know how long he held Mariana or how long she spoke of her time as a captive. He listened as she purged the memories while the life of the camp continued outside. He heard the trill of bugles and the crunch of marching boots, and then Fletcher scratched on the fly and poked his head inside the tent.

"Evening, Fletcher," Andrew said.

"It's morning, sir. That was the reveille."

Andrew started. Mariana had talked all night. "Very good. Could you take the parade this morning?"

Fletcher glanced at Mariana, who had continued to talk despite his interruption. "Of course, sir. I'll post a guard outside."

"Post Briggs," Andrew ordered. *Briggs will understand.*

Mariana spoke on, relieving herself of the burden that had haunted her for nearly two years. Andrew held her with his mind busy.

What am I to do with this woman? I wish I knew how to help.

POTCHEFSTROOM, FEBRUARY 1881.

"Here we are again," Jan said as he slumped in the bottom of the trench. The weeks of campaigning and fighting had hardened him. He had lost weight, and his face had altered, tightening the skin around his cheekbones and narrowing his eyes.

"Ja, back again," Abraham agreed. "We have defeated the *Rooinecks* in three battles, but we cannot dig them out of this damned fort."

"These are different *Rooinecks*," Jan said. "They refuse to surrender and won't understand that we have beaten them."

Theunis lifted his rifle and fired at the fort.

"Did you see a soldier?" Johannes asked.

"No. I was just letting them know we are here," Theunis replied. He also looked older, with a wild look in his eyes while his unkempt hair tangled across his face.

"What's happened here?" Jan checked his rifle, cleaned a speck of dust from the foresight and aimed at the fort without firing. "Nothing! We sit in the mud, and the British sit in the mud. We shoot at each other and make no progress."

Konrad stood in the deepest section of the trench, an observer rather than a participant. "The siege has progressed slowly. The Burghers captured some traitor Boers led by Pieter Raaf, who had fought with the British against the Zulus. The Burghers executed two of the Boers for treason, but Paul Kruger gave Raaf a reprieve and locked him up at Cronje's headquarters." Konrad shrugged. "I'd have shot them all, but Kruger is too soft to win a war."

"Oom Paul Kruger is a good man," Jan challenged Konrad's words.

"He is a good man," Konrad was placatory. "But not sufficiently severe. In Prussia, we would shoot traitors."

"Raaf had more than three men," Johannes said. "What happened to the others?"

"A court sentenced them to hard labour," Konrad replied. "They are working on the trenches now with some natives." He laughed. "A British shell killed one of them. The Burghers also hold Major Clarke under armed guard at the Royal Hotel."

Jan leaned against the wall. He was not concerned with Raaf, Clarke or any British prisoner. He closed his eyes and thought of Engela. *Konrad calls us the Burghers; he does not say 'we', so he does not see himself as a Boer.*

"Jan!" Abraham sunk beside him. "Are you awake?"

"I am now," Jan said with a faint smile.

"I have a letter from Engela," Abraham said. "I've never had a letter from anybody before." He showed Jan a battered and stained envelope with his name written in flowing script. "You see?"

"I see," Jan reached out, but Abraham pulled the letter away.

"She mentions you," Abraham teased, holding the letter at arm's length.

"What does she say?" Jan was immediately interested, forgetting the mud, the rain and even the British as he thought of Engela.

"Let me see," Abraham opened the envelope and extracted the letter. He read it slowly, mouthing each word as Jan waited impatiently. "Here we are," he said triumphantly. Abraham had never been skilled at reading; he was a man of the open veld, a practical farmer without any need for scholarship.

"Where?" Jan snatched the single sheet. He could see at once that Engela had taken great care creating the letter, with her copperplate writing filling the page without a single blot. Jan scanned the first two paragraphs, then slowed down when he came to his name. He lingered, smiling at the thought of Engela writing about him. If he could, he would have cut the word out and held it close, but Abraham was watching with faint mockery in his smile.

"Tell Jan that I am thinking of him." Jan read out, smiling, and looked up. "Your sister is thinking of me, Abe. May I keep this letter?"

"It's my letter," Abraham said.

"Yes, but my name is in it." Jan reread the passage where Engela mentioned him. He pictured her in his mind with her soft smile, snub nose, and winter blue eyes.

"I may let you have it later," Abraham retrieved his letter, folded it, and replaced it in the envelope. "She's only my sister, not a special woman."

About to say that Engela was special to him, Jan closed his mouth, knowing Abraham would laugh if he revealed his feelings. When Abraham walked away, keeping under the lip of the trench, Jan leaned against the wall and closed his eyes, wishing he was riding over the veld to see Engela.

How long will this war last? When will these Rooinecks surrender and let me go home?

The rain gradually eased away, but the siege continued. Jan was back in the Groenburg Commando's quarters when a rider from Pretoria arrived.

"I have news!" the messenger said as Burghers gathered around.

"What's happening?" Abraham asked.

The messenger explained that Kruger had offered Raaff and Major Clarke in exchange for Boers that the British had captured, but Colonel Bellairs, the British commander in Pretoria, turned him down flat.

"We do not negotiate with rebels," Bellairs said.

"A pity," Johannes said when they returned to their quarters. "Now we have the expense of holding prisoners. An exchange would benefit everybody."

"The British think differently from us," Theunis said, stroking the barrel of his rifle.

"Have you seen this?" Abraham entered the room with a newspaper in his hand. "It is the *Staatscourant,* and it talks about the battle of Laing's Nek." He waved the newspaper around his head. With a wispy blond beard and tired eyes, Jan thought Abraham looked like a dwarf from one of Grimm's fairy tales, except for the rifle slung over his shoulder.

"Does the article mention us?" Jan asked.

"Do you want to be mentioned?" Johannes sounded slightly worried.

"If the paper mentions us, I would let Engela see our names," Jan said.

Johannes smiled, shaking his head. "She will not forget you," he said. Taking the newspaper from Abraham, he handed it to Jan. "See if the paper says you were the man who defeated the British single-handedly."

Jan smiled and slowly read the account. "It does not mention the Groenburg Commando." He looked up. "We should give the British a copy of this paper. It might encourage them to surrender, knowing we defeated their relief column, and they are alone in our land."

"That is a good idea," Theunis approved. "I'll find some copies and hand them to Colonel Winsloe."

However, rather than lowering the garrison's morale, Colonel Winsloe was glad of news from the outside world and asked if the besiegers could supply newspapers on a regular basis.

Johannes shook his head. "Will that man never surrender?"

"You should storm the fort," Konrad said. "Charge down their guns and take it. There are enough of you to accept the casualties for the sake of victory. You are wasting time besieging a handful of the enemy when you could invade Natal and fight the British on their territory."

"How many casualties would you have us accept?" Jan asked. "How many men would we lose capturing a fort held by a hundred and fifty British soldiers? We'd have to cross hundreds of yards of open ground with their rifles and cannon firing at us, then face their bayonets."

Konrad shrugged. "As Bonaparte said, to make an omelette, one must break eggs."

"These eggs are farmers, husbands, sons, and brothers," Jan said. "We have to farm our land when this war is over, and we cannot do that if we are dead."

"A regiment of Prussian Guards would walk over this little fort in half an hour," Konrad boasted.

"There are no Prussian Guards here," Jan said. "We will fight our war our way." He saw Theunis listening intently to Konrad.

"Storming the fort could be the answer," Theunis agreed. "We might lose a few men, but the others would be free to push the British out of the Republic."

"I don't like Theunis," Jan said to his father when Theunis and Konrad left together.

"Theunis only wants what's best for the Transvaal," Johannes replied. "Maybe he's different from us, but he's a dedicated Burgher."

Jan sighed. "We are back in the trenches tomorrow."

"Let's pray for a quiet time," Johannes said. "And hope the British do not try any more bayonet charges."

"Let it please the Lord they remain behind their walls," Jan agreed.

The following day, the British artillery concentrated on *Ou Griet,* smashing the defences the Burghers had erected around the gun.

"Fire at the British guns," Johannes ordered the Groenburg Commando. "Defend *Ou Griet.*"

The British had expected the countermove and returned the Boer musketry with interest. Jan aimed at the gunners, fired, and ducked as a British volley hammered at the house, splintering what remained of the window frame and kicking up dust and plaster from the wall at his back.

"Won't these British ever give up?"

"You'll have to storm the fort," Konrad repeated his earlier statement. "It will be quicker than this long siege for a handful of men."

Jan rose to fire a single shot, and both men ducked when the defenders replied with another volley that knocked dust and chips of stone from the house.

"Best get your Prussian Guards, then," Jan said. "I'm not advancing into a Martini volley."

"Nor am I," Karl said. "You go first, Konrad."

The following day, the fort's garrison launched a lightning raid that shook the Burghers. The British grabbed five sheep to augment their rations, attacked the town jail and snatched a Boer prisoner. Before the Boers recovered, the British were back behind their walls, cheering. One man began to sing a bawdy song Jan did not know until an NCO barked for silence.

"These British are not going to surrender," Johannes spoke around the stem of his pipe. "They will be here until the Day of Judgement." He removed the pipe from his mouth and indicated the Union flag still hanging from the flagpole. "Will we ever clear them out of the Transvaal?"

Konrad threw a disdainful look at Johannes. "I have told you what to do."

When Mannie began to cough, Jan moved to his side. "I do not think Mannie should stay here."

Johannes knelt beside his younger son, placing a calloused hand on his forehead. "You are right, Jan. He should be at home. Will you take him?"

Jan thought for a minute, still aware some men would think him a coward for leaving the fighting. "I will take him," he said. He felt Mannie's eyes on him and knew he had made the correct decision.

"Thank you," Mannie whispered and coughed again.

Mount Prospect, Natal, February 1881.

A low hum of conversation filled the temporary Officers' Mess as Andrew ordered a whisky from a stony-faced mess waiter and searched for a chair. Most were occupied, but he found a cane recliner with a long-faced lieutenant sitting nearby, grooming his whiskers with an elegant hand.

"Who are you?" the languid lieutenant asked.

"Captain Andrew Baird, Natal Dragoons," Andrew said.

"Oh, colonial horse. I'm Primrose, 58th Foot. Did you hear the news?" Lieutenant Primrose selected a cheroot from his silver case.

Andrew shook his head. "Probably not. There are so many shaves going around that I've closed my ears to all of them!"

Primrose lit his cheroot, shook out the match, and puffed aromatic smoke into the air. "The Prime Minister has sent Sir Evelyn Wood to the Boers. He wants to seek an honourable peace."

Andrew sipped at his whisky, remembering the shattered dead on the battlefields and the sound of Boer rifles. *Was their sacrifice in vain? Or do men sign their lives away when they don the Queen's scarlet? Once we accept the fatal shilling, our destinies are in the hands of politicians and senior officers, and we become tools of an uncaring government.*

"An honourable peace? That's tantamount to surrender," a lean captain with a bristling moustache said. "It's a disgrace! We've lost nearly every battle. We can't have peace until we've defeated the Boers."

"The government did something similar during the Zulu War," Andrew remembered. "They sent out Sir Garnet Wolseley [3] to replace Chelmsford after Isandhlwana. And what did Chelmsford do? He launched another invasion and smashed the Zulus at Ulundi."

"Were you there?" Primrose looked over lazily. "I seem to remember mention of your unit."

"I was there," Andrew did not give details. "I'll wager Gladstone's news only spurs Colley to try again."

"With more success, hopefully," Primrose said. "Oh, God, how I'd like to get at these blasted farmers. We'd stop shilly-shallying around if I were there, I can tell you."

"Quite right, Primrose," the lean captain agreed, helping himself to a glass of champagne from the silver tray at his side.

Andrew kept quiet, remembering what General Hook had told him. Some things were more important than winning small wars. "Have you gentlemen seen much action?"

"Not much, old boy," the lanky captain agreed. "I was employed in staff duties mostly."

Primrose nodded. "A little in New Zealand and at Ulundi," he said languidly. "We saw off the Zulus, didn't we, Baird?"

"We did," Andrew agreed.

As Andrew had predicted, Colley decided to launch another attack on the Boer positions.

"Sir Evelyn Wood is coming, is he?" Colley growled to his staff. "I want this campaign all wrapped up before he arrives."

On February 12th, 1881, reinforcements marched into Mount Prospect. First to arrive were the 92nd Foot, the Gordon Highlanders, who had won renown in Afghanistan. Unlike most other British regiments in South Africa, the Gordons wore khaki tunics rather than scarlet, and the swing of their green tartan kilts reminded the watchers of their reputation. They swaggered into the British camp with a string of successes under their belts while the skirl of their pipes announced to the world that the Gordons, the Cocks of the North, had arrived, and God help any Boer who got in their way.

As well as veteran infantry, cavalry arrived to bolster Colley's force. The 15th King's Hussars had a history that stretched back to the Battle of Emsdorf in 1760, the Peninsula War, Waterloo, and the less glorious Peterloo Massacre in 1819.

"We're also expecting the 6th Inniskilling Dragoons and the 83rd County of Dublin Regiment, a unit which fought through the Peninsula and during the Indian Mutiny," Fletcher said.

"Colley has decided not to wait for the Inniskillings and the 83rd," Primrose contradicted, pulling at a cheroot. "Sir Evelyn Wood commands them, and our general wants to win the war himself."

Andrew looked around the Mess, crowded with officers from various regiments. "I suppose we'll try the passes again."

"Maybe so," Primrose shrugged. "I hope Colley makes a better job of it this time. Sending a few dozen men against entrenched Boers doesn't seem to be the answer." He stretched on his seat and blew a perfect smoke ring that hovered above his head for a few seconds before gradually dissolving. "Colley had better hurry up, though. Paul Kruger is pushing for a truce, and our government is too weak to disagree."

"The government's talking about withdrawing from the Transvaal." Lieutenant Hamilton of the Gordon Highlanders joined them. "We might have peace before we smash the Boers in battle."

"Colley will attack," Primrose said flatly. "He'll be smarting after his repulses and has to regain his reputation."

"A victory will give us a better position in the peace talks," Hamilton agreed. "If we negotiate without a victory, Kruger will hold all the cards. If we defeat him, we can name the terms."

"How many men will die to satisfy the politicians?" Andrew asked.

"That's a soldier's job," Primrose replied. "We're the final piece in the diplomat's chessboard. When the talking ends, send in the army."

Andrew grunted. "Or when the army fails, send in the diplomats."

CHAPTER 14

BOER CAMP, MAJUBA HILL, FEBRUARY 1881.

A breeze carried the bellowing of trek oxen from two hundred yards away and a distant murmur from the wagon laagers. General Joubert lit his pipe and surveyed the veldcornets who attended his *kriegsraad*, the tactical meeting before an impending battle.

Johannes and Theunis stood with the rest, listening to everybody's opinions. Theunis stroked the barrel of his rifle with almost sensual attention and checked the foresight while Johannes watched, waiting for Joubert to speak. At their side, Konrad studied the unmilitary ranks of the Free Burghers with partially disguised amusement.

"We have defeated the British in three encounters and have their garrisons under siege." Although Joubert spoke quietly, his words carried to every man present. "However, General Colley has gathered reinforcements and is preparing to attack again."

The commandants and veldcornets nodded in agreement. "Then we shall defeat them again," Theunis shouted. "And every time until we have sent them back over the Vaal and out of Africa!"

As some of the commandants and veldcornets voiced their assent, Joubert lifted a hand. Silence descended, broken only by the bellowing of an ox.

"I appreciate your sentiments, *meneer*," Joubert said, "but we'll take this campaign one battle at a time."

Most men laughed at the sally and waited for Joubert to continue.

"General Colley will be seeking revenge," Joubert said. "I know there are peace negotiations and talk of an end to the war, but Colley is an injured lion, and the British do not like to be defeated."

The commandants growled, shaking their heads. Theunis lifted his rifle in the air.

"Only the Lord knows what will happen," Joubert said. "We must pray for victory and peace, but we can help the Lord make up his mind."

A few of the Burghers shook their heads at Joubert's mild blasphemy. When a church minister began to pray, his congregation removed their hats and bowed their heads, begging God to grant them victory.

Joubert waited until the brief prayer finished. "Now, fellow Burghers, some of you are with me at the laager; others are in the various sieges throughout the republic. If General Colley tries to invade our land again to relieve one of our sieges, I will send a runner to call up men to fight. Be prepared to join us."

The men nodded.

"May the Lord bless our endeavours and our republic," Joubert ended and left the Burghers to return to their camps.

"General Colley is a British gentleman," Johannes offered his opinion as the veldcornets of the Groenburg Commando rode slowly back to Potchefstroom. "He will abide by the ceasefire."

Theunis smiled. "You are too trusting, my friend. The British have not won the greatest Empire in the world by being gentlemen but by deviousness, lies, underhanded diplomacy and sending their soldiers to die without thought for the suffering. British gentlemen are the worst of the lot."

Johannes looked away as Konrad barked his distinctive laugh. "British gentlemen live in the eighteenth century," Konrad said. "They hide behind their navy and play games with their little scarlet soldiers. If they cannot defeat a small nation of farmers, how will they fare against the Prussians?"

"The Prussians are not here," Johannes reminded. "We are."

MOUNT PROSPECT, NATAL, 25TH OF FEBRUARY 1881.

"Majuba, the Hill of Doves, is the key," Colley said. "I've been observing it since we arrived. The Boers keep a picket on the summit during the day but withdraw it at night."

The assembled officers nodded, with some smiling at the Boers' perceived amateurism.

"Majuba dominates Laing's Nek and overlooks both our position and the Boers' camp," Colley said. "I saw a working party of Boers on the summit today. If they entrench, they'll be better able to hold us at bay."

The officers waited for the general's next words.

"I plan to occupy Majuba, gentlemen," Colley said and treated them with a benign smile. "We'll take the hill and push off any Boers who attempt to take it from us."

Andrew looked upward, where three vultures circled the camp. *I hope that's not a portent of the future,* he thought. He watched the scavenger birds for a moment, chased away a shudder, and left to get his Dragoons ready to fight.

At half past nine on the evening of the 26th of February 1881, General Colley led his small army out of Mount Prospect. One hundred and eighty men were veterans from the Gordon Highlanders, with a hundred and forty-eight from the 58th, seventy seamen from the Naval Brigade, and a hundred Riflemen of the 60th. Captain Smith commanded the Rifles, Captain Morris the 58th, and Major Hay the Gordons, who brought along Ghazi, their Afghan hound.

"The Gordons look well," Fletcher said as the kilted infantry swung past. "They should give the Boers a fright."

"If they get close to them," Andrew said. "I doubt the Boers will stand still and wait for our bayonets."

Each man carried three days' rations, with seventy rounds of ammunition, a greatcoat, and a waterproof sheet. The Gordons looked confident as if they had no doubts about the outcome of any future battle. The other infantry looked grim-faced, with none of the usual black humour that carried British soldiers through difficult situations.

"How many of us will Colley kill today?" Private Burrows of the 58th asked.

"God knows," Private Jones replied. "If the Boers shoot me, you get my kit."

"And if they kill me," Burrows said. "Write a letter to the missus, will you?"

The Natal Dragoons rode on the flank of the 58th, with outriders scouting for any possible Boer ambush. Andrew recognised some of the 58th from their previous battles.

"How many of us are there?" Burrows asked.

Jones glanced over the column, hardly seen in the dark. "About five hundred," he replied. "Sawnies, Rifles, tarry-arses, and us."

"Has the general learned nothing?" Burrows grumbled. "He's leading a few hundred men to capture an entire country. The Boers will slaughter us! It'll be another Boer trap and another bloody reverse."

Andrew realised the grumbles were not the usual soldiers' grousing but came from men whom the general had led to two defeats within a few days. He glanced at Fletcher, who said nothing as they reached the foot of Majuba Hill, three and a half miles from Mount Prospect. Above, drifting clouds obscured the stars, with the wind whispering across the dark slopes. An unknown animal howled, raising the hairs on the back of Andrew's neck.

"That's a fair lump of a hill," Fletcher looked up at the massive bulk of Majuba.

"It is," Andrew felt a tight knot in his stomach. He sent the Dragoons to form a loose semi-circle on the flank of Colley's army. "Keep alert, but don't fire unless the Boers fire first. We're meant to be in a truce."

"The Boers don't know the meaning of a truce," Ogden said. "We've seen them firing when they fly a white flag."

"We'll keep our word, Ogden," Sergeant Meek said. "No firing unless the Boers fire first."

Colley left two companies of the Rifles and one of the Gordons at a low-level ridge to maintain communications with Mount Prospect Camp. "You're our insurance," Colley said. "If Joubert tries to outflank us, you will see him off."

Andrew grunted. *Joubert's mobile horsemen will ride rings around our slow-moving infantry.*

"We're only three hundred and fifty strong now," Burrows said as the remainder of the infantry began to slog up Majuba. "How many Boers are there?"

Jones shrugged. "I dunno. Thousands, I think. They seem to be everywhere when we fight them."

Burrows hawked and spat. "God, everything tastes of dust. If it's not dry and hot, it's bloody pissing with rain. What a bloody country." He stamped his boots on the ground. "If there are thousands of Boers, we'll have to pretend there are more of us."

"The noise you're bloody making, that won't be hard!" A corporal snarled. "Keep your mouth shut, you blasted idiots!"

"What happens when we get on top?" a diminutive man named Harris asked. "Do we throw stones at the Boers? We've only rifles, not even a seven-pounder mountain gun."

"You obey orders, Harris; that's what happens," the corporal fell back on the tried and trusted reply. "You obey orders."

Behind the 58th, the Gordons climbed slowly, kilts swinging, and Martinis held in brown-tanned fists. They exchanged low-voiced jokes, with a hard-faced sergeant cutting off one man's laughter.

"Keep your bloody voice down! We don't want the Boers to hear!"

"They're only farmers, Sergeant," the man replied. "We sorted the Afghans out; this lot will be easy."

"Easy or not, McGill, keep your voice down."

"Yes, Sergeant," McGill fondled Ghazi and returned his attention to climbing the hill.

Majuba stretched before them, dark, ominous, and steep. Andrew heard the harsh call of a bird and pushed Lancelot up the slope.

"Baird!" Colley ordered. "Leave Lieutenant Fletcher with your Dragoons down here. I want you with me on the summit."

"Yes, sir," Andrew replied as Colley stepped closer.

"You're the only man who can identify this Prussian fellow," Colley reminded.

"Yes, sir," Andrew had nearly forgotten about Konrad Bramigan.

Colley threw Andrew a sidelong look. "General Hook mentioned your expertise."

"I'll do my best, sir," Andrew said.

"Arrange your men, Baird and join us," Colley turned away and pushed uphill.

"You heard the general, Fletcher," Andrew said. "Take charge here." He dismounted and handed Lancelot's reins to Briggs. "Look after my horse, Briggs. I doubt I'll need him up there." Andrew lowered his voice. "If anything happens to me, look after Mariana as best you can."

"I will, sir," Briggs accepted the possibility of Andrew's death with as much composure as he did everything else.

With a final nod, Andrew left his Dragoons and headed for Majuba's summit.

"The Boers better not be waiting on top," Burrows said.

"It's the sort of thing Colley would do," Jones replied. "He'll lead us into another bloody trap."

"We'll have less talking and more climbing," a hard-voiced sergeant snapped. "Get up this blasted hill!"

The slope seemed to stretch forever into the gloom, with only a fading gleam of starlight to guide the infantry. Some parts of the hill were so steep the heavily encumbered men had to use their hands, while other stretches consisted of massive boulders or loose stones that slithered underfoot. Andrew heard the scrape of nailed boots on rock, muttered curses, and an occasional complaint as men fell on the uneven surface.

"Careful up there," a southern accent sounded from below, "you're causing an avalanche on us."

"I can't help it," the Midlands reply came. "These stones move if you just look at them."

"Well, stop looking then! It's too dark to see, anyway."

At four in the morning, the leading files of the 58th staggered to the top, with an ominously red dawn cracking open the sky to the east. Sweat dried in the early morning chill, men crouched on the ground, gasping for breath while NCOs counted their platoons and sections, rounded up stragglers, and put everything in disciplined order.

"Where's the bloody Boers, then?" Private Burrows asked. "No ambush today, Piet? You're slipping!"

It was well after five o'clock when the Gordons reached the summit, with the Naval Brigade last.

"Now let them come," a seaman said.

"Create a breastwork!" his petty officer growled. "Did you think you were finished?"

"No breastworks," a lieutenant said. "General Colley doesn't want breastworks or trenches."

"Yes, sir," the petty officer exchanged wondering looks with a kilted sergeant but did not argue.

Andrew looked around, wondering at the lack of resistance. The British occupied a gently sloping plateau with a circumference of around a thousand yards. In the centre sat a rocky ridge, hard-edged and dominant. Unseen except for their fires, the Boer positions on Laing's Nek were around two thousand feet below and two thousand yards away.

"If we had some artillery, we could spoil the Boers' morning," Lieutenant Hamilton of the Gordons said.

"We'll use what we have," Lieutenant MacDonald growled. Unusually in the British army, Hector MacDonald had risen from the Gordons' ranks after General Roberts had promoted him from sergeant in Afghanistan.

"Spread the men out," Colley ordered.

The Gordons obeyed, with the NCOs placing their men ten paces apart.

Andrew watched the kilted figures silhouetted on the lip of the hill with the wind playing around their sun helmets. They looked very martial, he thought, but also very thinly spread. Ghazi, the Afghan hound, moved from man to man, sniffed at a few rocks, and settled down behind McGill.

"If the Boers come up in force, we're in trouble," MacDonald said. "We're not strong enough anywhere to hold them."

Andrew nodded. "We'll need three times as many men to garrison this place effectively."

When the light strengthened, Andrew could see details of the Boers' camp far below, three separate wagon laagers, with tents and horses outside and the minuscule figures of men riding from laager to laager. A faint whiff of smoke from cooking fires drifted to him, reminding him he had not eaten that day. Regular darker lines told of defensive trenches around the laagers to repel any possible British attack, although the sentries seemed lackadaisical.

"A decent cavalry charge would scatter these men," MacDonald scanned the Boer positions through field glasses.

"Hamilton is right; artillery would be useful here," Andrew murmured. "I remember hearing how General Roberts carried mountain guns on the back of elephants in Afghanistan."

"Bobs Roberts is a good general," MacDonald replied without insulting Colley.

"I wish he were here now," Hamilton said.

I'd settle for Redvers Buller, Andrew thought and said nothing.

As the light strengthened, a small group of Gordons stood erect on the skyline, shouting insults at the Boers and waving their fists.

"Come and get us, Piet! Come and try the Gordons!"

"Enough of that!" a sergeant snapped. "Get back into position! You're soldiers, not wee laddies at school."

Andrew looked at the faces and realised that not all the Highlanders were Afghan veterans. The men who stood on the skyline were very young. They also looked very vulnerable as the edges of the plateau sloped down from the central north-south ridge, exposing the defenders to fire from all around.

Colley posted one weak company of the 92nd to cover the north, west, and most of the south, the most dangerous section of Majuba. A company of the 58th occupied the east. A company of each regiment, plus the hospital, sat between the 58th and the central ridge, where the reserve of the Naval Brigade and fifty of the 58th waited. Finally, Colley ordered the men to strengthen two points that overlooked a steep valley on the south.

"We're guarding a circuit of a mile with only three hundred and fifty men," MacDonald said. "Let's hope the Boers don't realise how thinly we're spread."

"What happens now?" Lieutenant Hamilton finished a cigarette and flicked the stub over the edge of the hill.

"Ask the general," MacDonald replied, "for I'm sure I don't know. The Boer camp is out of rifle range, and we've no artillery. I suppose we can join these young soldiers and shout at the Boers."

"Why did they do that?" Andrew asked.

Hamilton lit another cigarette. "Somebody ordered them to let the Boers know we are here."

"General Colley believes the Boers will see British soldiers on the hill and then withdraw," MacDonald told him. "He gave the order for the lads to make themselves known."

Andrew shook his head. "The Boers will not withdraw," he said. "They've defeated us in every encounter so far. They're filled with confidence while our boys doubt Colley's leadership."

"Look," Hamilton said, pointing to the Boer camp. "Maybe General Colley isn't as daft as we believe."

Andrew saw half a dozen Boers rounding up their trek oxen as if they intended to leave the camp. While some glanced backwards at the British soldiers on Majuba's skyline, others hurried to the wagons, preparing to inspan the oxen. One middle-aged man bundled his wife aboard a wagon and drove it slowly away.

"You're right, Hamilton. Some Boers are leaving." Andrew lifted his field glasses as a small group of men cantered into the laager and began to shout at the rest.

"Those lads must be in charge," Andrew said. "That could be Joubert himself." He shook his head. "If we had a battery of mountain guns here, a couple of rounds of shrapnel would solve a great many problems."

The arrival of Joubert and his veldcornets quelled the panic. The withdrawing wagon returned to the laager, and men stepped away from their oxen and horses.

"Damn it," MacDonald said. "We had them on the run for a few minutes. As you said, Baird, a few rounds from a seven-pounder could have broken their resolve."

Hamilton lit a cigarette and grinned. "It looks like General Colley will have his battle after all. Piet's coming to the front door."

With Joubert stopping their retreat, groups of Boer horsemen rode toward Majuba. Some moved in a semi-disciplined formation as though they were commandos; others approached as individuals, although all had the same objective. Within twenty minutes, they formed into three hundred-strong groups and began climbing the hill.

"That's not what the general intended," MacDonald said. "As you said, Hamilton, we're in for another battle. Best get the men ready."

The Gordons' officers strode to their men, shouting orders. "Watch your front, lads; the Boers are coming up the hill."

"Then we'll send them back down," a voice replied.

"That's the spirit, McGill," Hamilton replied cheerfully. He peered downhill. "I can't see a single Boer, but I know they're there. Number Three section, get down the slope and delay any Boer coming up. Skirmishing formation."

Andrew heard the first rifle crack just before nine in the morning, with the bullet pinging from a rock. Hamilton laughed. "Here they come, boys! Let's give them a Highland welcome."

The Gordons responded with a volley that crashed against the rocks, with bullets ricocheting and whining on the slopes.

"That's for you, Piet!" a man shouted. "There's plenty more if you've a mind to stay!"

Andrew moved to the shelter of a thornbush and stared downhill. He knew the Boers were there but could not see anybody. He jerked back as a bullet buzzed past his shoulder. More shots followed, and Andrew traversed his rifle, seeking a target.

These boys are experts at keeping under cover as they fire. The Gordons are retaliating, but I can't see any Boer bodies.

The Boer fire increased through the morning as they encircled the hill, firing at the desperately thin British line and gradually easing closer to the summit. The Gordons' skirmishers retaliated, only withdrawing when the overwhelming number of Boers outflanked them. Ghazi joined the skirmishers, barking whenever a Boer bullet came close.

"What was the point of climbing up here? It's Schuinschoogte all over again," a long-faced officer said, fired and moved on.

Andrew agreed, saw a flicker of movement beneath and squeezed the trigger of his carbine. Shooting downhill at elusive targets was never easy, especially when under fire. While the musketry continued, rising into crescendos and falling away, the Boers steadily advanced, concentrating on the area Lieutenant Hamilton and his twenty-strong platoon held. The Boers moved from cover to cover, firing whenever they saw an opportunity, so the Gordons were hard-pressed to hold them back.

"I cannae see them," a red-haired Aberdonian growled.

"Wait till they get closer," his rear rank man replied. "We'll give them the bayonet."

"We'll need to," the Aberdonian said. "I've used half my cartridges already."

At noon, after five hours of constant musketry, the Boers were slowly but relentlessly closing.

"Runner!" Andrew sought a subaltern. "Tell General Colley we need more men at this point."

"I can't, sir," the subaltern said. "General Colley is sleeping."

"He's what?" Andrew could not stop his reaction.

"He's sleeping," the subaltern repeated.

"We're in the middle of a bloody battle!" Hamilton strode across, loading his revolver. "Generals don't sleep during a battle!"

"This one does," the subaltern said smugly.

Hamilton rammed his revolver into its holster and strode to the central ridge. Ignoring the sleeping Colley, he raised his voice. "The Boers are massing beneath my position," he reported. "I believe they are going to rush us. Some reinforcements would be welcome."

The staff officers stared at Hamilton as if he were asking them for something unusual. With his message delivered, Hamilton returned to his men at the most dangerous spot on the plateau. Two hundred feet lower down, the half dozen Gordon skirmishers attempted to stem the Boer tide.

"Keep them back, lads!" Hamilton shouted. "Fire away, but be careful not to hit our men!"

Andrew loped towards Hamilton's position as the musketry increased. Hamilton's platoon remained in position, facing what Andrew estimated to be three hundred Boers. He fired towards the smoke, knowing his chances of hitting a Boer were minimal.

"Here's the general now," MacDonald shouted from further along the lip of the hill.

"I hope he enjoyed his wee nap!" a man said sourly.

"Reinforcements! Go and help Hamilton!" Colley ordered. "Move!" The staff officers gave sharp orders to the companies waiting behind the ridge.

Andrew glanced over his shoulder. For the first time in his experience, British soldiers were reluctant to face the enemy. Perhaps influenced by Colley's previous defeats, they moved slowly, looking at each other for support and reassurance.

"The general's sending us forward to get killed," Jones said.

"While he stands at the back," Burrows agreed.

The sergeants bellowed them forward, pushing the most hesitant to help the hard-pressed Highlanders.

"Come on, you laggards! The Gordons need our help!"

The tunics of the 58th shone scarlet under the sun as they slouched forward. "We done our bit," Burrows said. "Is the general going to send us into battle after battle until we're all dead?"

"You took the Queen's Shilling," a corporal snarled. "Now bloody earn it!"

"Come on, lads," Andrew encouraged. "Show the Boers what the 58th can do!"

Major Fraser, a Royal Engineers staff officer, raised his voice. "Men of the 92nd, don't forget your bayonets!"

"We won't, sir," a bearded private replied. "I'll gut the first Boer I see!"

The Boer musketry increased until the firing sounded like a single peal of thunder. *If you hear the shot, it hasn't killed you,* Andrew reassured himself. *A bullet travels faster than its sound.*

Andrew saw Lieutenant Hamilton encouraging his men, with Hector MacDonald striding from position to position. When a surge of Boers erupted over the lip, a handful of Gordons retired. Others fired, reloaded, and fired again as more Boers emerged, chasing the retiring skirmishers.

"There's hundreds of the bastards!" a man shouted. "Where's the bloody reinforcements?"

"Retire and reform!" another man stepped back.

"Permission to fix bayonets, sir? Sir?" A corporal asked. "Can we fix bayonets and charge them?"

One and then another, Gordon Highlander fell, shot at close range.

Hamilton strode to General Colley. "Sir! Excuse my presumption, sir, but may I have permission to charge with the bayonet? The men cannot stand the fire much longer."

Colley shook his head. "Wait until they come on, Hamilton. We will give them a volley, then charge."

"They can't come much closer, sir!"

More Highlanders echoed Hamilton's words, requesting permission to go forward with the bayonet.

"We're running out of bullets!" a man said, raking a dead man's pouches for ammunition. "Can we use the bayonet, sir?"

At his side, another private threw stones at the Boers, inviting them to come forward and fight like men.

"Come on! Stop skulking like cowards! Face us in the open!"

Andrew saw the Boers hesitate as though refusing to close with the handful of Highlanders.

If we fix bayonets, we could still turn this battle around.

"We're holding them!" MacDonald shouted. "Send them back!" Andrew saw dead and wounded Gordons all around him, with some men glancing over their shoulders towards the relative security of the central ridge.

"Oh, there they are," an anonymous officer shouted, "quite close."

Although Andrew was unsure if the officer was referring to the reinforcements or the Boers, his words affected the infantry, with the reinforcements, both 58th and Gordon Highlanders, turning away in sudden panic.

"Stand and fight!" Andrew roared.

"Fight!" MacDonald shouted, brandishing his revolver. "By God, I'll shoot any man who passes me!"

The fear spread to the Gordon skirmishers, who had contained the Boers for six hours of sniping and fighting. The survivors turned and ran with the rest, pushing each other in their eagerness to escape.

Dear God! I have never seen British veterans run like that. Andrew experienced a revelation that even the best troops could panic. He realised that underneath all the pomp and pageantry, despite the regimental pride and the years of training and hard discipline, soldiers were only men, subject to the same uncertainty and fears as the most softly-bred civilian.

As the British fled, the Boers leapt up and fired into their backs, killing and wounding more than they had in their initial assault. Andrew saw the Highlanders, bearded veterans of Afghanistan, and the red-coated 58th Foot running down the hill with the Boers firing, reloading, and firing again.

"That's the Gordon Highlanders!" An officer stared in disbelief. "The pride of the British army!"

Andrew refined his thoughts. *Men have a limited supply of courage, and when that ends, even the toughest are vulnerable.* He watched for a second, fighting his shock, for he had been brought up to believe that a British soldier never panicked and Highlanders were the cream of the army.

Not all the British ran. A mixture of Gordons, seamen, and men of the 58th gathered defiantly on the central ridge as Boer bullets felled them in ones and twos.

"Fight!" Lieutenant MacDonald roared at the running men. "Come back and fight, you cowards!"

MacDonald wasted his words. Panic is contagious, and men find it hard to rally once broken. The scramble to escape continued with men pushing each other as they fled and the Boers standing at the summit of Majuba, loading and firing at the retreating British.

Andrew fought the urge to join the retreating men. *Stay and fight.* It was not bravery, for he knew he was as scared as anybody else. *Why then? Pride perhaps? A sense of duty? I don't know. I only know I'd be damned if I'll run away; I could not face myself in the shaving mirror again. What would my father say? What would Mariana think?*

Mariana? Why did I think of her?

Climbing up on the central ridge beside the surviving defenders, Andrew began to return fire. The Boers were still elusive, hiding behind cover, appearing only to fire, and dropping away again. The British soldiers had not been trained to fight in such a fashion; they stood in the open to retaliate, and the Boers shot them for their bravery.

"Come on then! Show yourselves, you cowards!" a hard-faced sergeant shouted. Sunlight gleamed on his medal ribbons.

When the Boers appeared in front of the ridge, many defenders stepped forward for a better shot. Boer marksmen on the flanks killed them as they stood.

"Give them the bayonet!" Private McGill shouted.

"Give who the bayonet?" another man asked. "I can't see anybody!" His words ended in a gurgle as a Boer bullet smashed into his side, knocking him to the ground.

"They're on the flanks!" somebody shouted as Boer fire hammered the defenders from every direction. Andrew aimed and fired, trying to control his trembling hands. He heard Hamilton ordering independent fire. Then, a bullet smashed into Hamilton's arm, and he spun around and fell. *Order, counter-order, disorder. Where is General Colley? Why isn't he taking charge?*

As the bulk of the defenders retreated, the Boers followed, firing at the now defenceless men and leaving the ridge as a British island among a rippling ocean of Boers.

"Fight!" Lieutenant MacDonald roared, drawing his broadsword. "We're the Gordons!"

Andrew fired the last of his bullets and stood at MacDonald's side as the Boers surrounded them, pointing rifles from a few feet away.

"Hands up!" a Boer said, indicating the row of rifles aimed at the stubborn, frustrated survivors.

One by one, the British on the ridge threw down their rifles and glared at their captors. MacDonald was last to comply. "You'd better treat the wounded well," he growled. "And look after my men."

Reluctantly but inevitably, Andrew raised his hands. "You have captured me, *meneer*," he said to a young, freckled Boer with a shock of blond hair. "Now, what are you going to do with me?"

"I will take over now," a tall, prematurely aged Burgher said. "Collect the

British weapons and see to the wounded." He put a hand on Andrew's shoulder. "I saw you in previous battles, *Rooineck*. Who are you?"

"Captain Andrew Baird of the Natal Dragoons," Andrew said. "And you, sir?"

"I am Johannes van Collier of Nuwe Hoop Plaas and the Groenburg Commando," Johannes introduced himself.

They shook hands as if they were old friends meeting on a city street rather than enemies who had been trying to kill each other a few moments before.

"Will you *Rooinecks* leave our republic now?" Johannes shouldered his rifle and passed his water bottle to his prisoners.

"That's not our decision to make," Andrew said. "Ask the politicians." He saw a wild-eyed man join Johannes and recalled him from Krugersdorp.

"Theunis," Johannes spoke to the newcomer. "See if our prisoners need help. Give the wounded water and make them comfortable." He returned his attention to Andrew. "Come with me, Captain, in case you have any foolish notions of shooting us in the back."

Andrew complied, ignoring Theunis's baleful glare. He saw a Boer lifting the wounded and still smiling Hamilton and knew the Burghers would look after the injured. He looked up, suddenly tired, and saw a tall man at the back of a group of Boer leaders. The broad scar on the man's face was evident, and Andrew felt something lurch inside him.

That's Konrad Bramigan. That's the Prussian agent, and he's seen British soldiers run.

CHAPTER 15

NUWE HOOP PLAAS, WESTERN TRANSVAAL, FEBRUARY 1881.

"Mother!" Jan helped Mannie off his horse outside the familiar farmhouse. Nuwe Hoop Plaas looked smaller than he remembered but with the same smells and feeling of belonging. "Mother!"

Aletta appeared from the dairy, wiping her hands on her apron as she stared at her sons with a combination of elation and fear. "What's wrong, Jan? Where's your father? Is the war over?" She stepped towards her sons, quelling her panic. "Is Mannie hurt?"

"No, Mother," Jan tried to answer Aletta's barrage of questions. "No, the war is not over. Pa is well, but Mannie is sick. He needs you to nurse him."

Aletta enfolded Mannie in her arms. "I knew he was too young to go on commando! Where is your father? Why did he not come as well?"

"Pa is busy fighting the *Rooinecks*," Jan replied.

Aletta felt a mixture of relief her husband was alive, disappointment he had not come and pride that he was doing his duty. "Let me see you, Mannie," she held her younger son at arm's length. "Yes, you are thin and pale. I'll get you better. Are you staying home, Jan?"

"No," Jan shook his head. "I will head back tomorrow. I only brought Mannie home. The commando needs me."

Aletta closed her eyes to hide her pain at her son returning to the war. She looked at him, seeing the changes. Physically, he had lost weight, and his cheekbones were more pronounced, making him look more mature. He stood differently, too, Aletta saw, and his eyes were harder, yet it was his mouth that revealed more. Jan's mouth was firm, with new lines extending to the side of his nose. *I have a man for a son and a boy who still needs his mother.*

"Are you going to ride over to Engela?" Aletta asked, hoping to entice Jan to remain a little longer. "She will want to hear about her brother. She often mentions you and Abraham."

On the long journey from Potchefstroom to Nuwe Hoop Plaas, Jan had pondered visiting Engela. The temptation had been strong, the idea of seeing Engela's smile and regaling her with his adventures and experiences nearly overpowering. "No, Mother," he said, shaking his head. "I have wasted enough time. I must return to the commando and fight the *Rooinecks*." He pretended not to see the hurt in his mother's face.

Aletta turned away from this grown man who was her son. "Come, Mannie. We'll get you to bed. Jan: find some food. You have lost a lot of weight."

"I will," Jan said. "I will tell you what to say to Engela."

"She would prefer to hear it from you."

"I have to return to Potchefstroom." Jan touched his mother's shoulder. He felt her tremble and shift closer to him for an instant and saw the anguish in her eyes. "I cannot stay home, Mother."

"I know," Aletta replied. *It is a painful thing to raise a boy that turns into a man. It is a hard thing to be a mother.* She raised her chin, knowing that her life had altered forever. "There is food on the table, Jan."

Majuba, February 1881.

All over Majuba Hill, the Boers were helping the wounded British soldiers, with Dr Mahon giving orders in English and broken Dutch, performing simple operations in the open and moving from soldier to suffering soldier.

"Leave that man," Mahon ordered. "He's past help. Moving him will only increase his pain." He knelt beside a bearded Highlander who was moaning and holding his back. "Take this fellow down the hill. It's all right, my man; I'll soon have you patched up again."

Andrew moved to support an injured redcoat when Theunis jabbed him with his rifle.

"Back, *Rooineck*! You are a prisoner!"

"Back yourself, Burgher!" Andrew snarled. "This man needs help."

Theunis lifted his rifle until the barrel thrust into Andrew's throat.

"Back!"

"No," General Joubert stepped between them. "You are a good fighter, Theunis, but lack diplomacy."

"You two men," General Joubert pointed to Lieutenant MacDonald and Andrew. "You fought to the end. You, sir," he pointed to MacDonald, "may keep your sword." He handed back the weapon. MacDonald nodded his thanks and replaced the sword in its sheath.

"What happens now?" Andrew asked. He saw Konrad talking to Johannes van Collier and wondered what the Prussian was saying.

Joubert smiled. "You are both my prisoners," he said. "No doubt you shall remain so until the war is over."

Andrew sat on a rock, took his pipe from his pocket, and tamped tobacco into the bowl. *When you can do nothing,* he told himself, *have a smoke. It helps to clear the mind. I never wanted to be a soldier anyway.* He stared over the battlefield and wondered what the British public would say when they heard of another defeat.

"Come on, *Rooinecks*!" the freckled Boer guard seemed unsure what to do with his prisoners. "We will take you into the Republic until the war ends."

"Heads up, lads!" The hard-faced sergeant had survived. "Misfortune is part of a soldier's lot. You accept it and wait for better times. Let's be having you!"

"Has anybody seen Ghazi?" McGill asked. "I've not seen him for hours."[1]

The prisoners gathered in an untidy group, bewildered that ragged farmers could defeat professional soldiers. They looked at one another, unsure who to blame.

Andrew saw Johannes talking to Konrad. *How can I inform General Hook that the Prussian is still with the Boers?*

Johannes and the wild-eyed Theunis called out something, and a dozen men clustered around them. "Come on, Groenburg men!" Johannes shouted. "This battle is won. We'll return to Potchefstroom."

That's worth knowing. If one commando moves from place to place, others may do the same.

Andrew watched the Groenburg Commando ride away, a collection of shabby farmers and small-town Burghers who had defeated one of the finest infantry regiments in the world. *They will be proud of their victory,* Andrew thought, *but I'll wager most of them are more concerned about their farms than the war.*

"March," the Boer guards shouted, pushing the British prisoners into an untidy column. "March."

Unarmed and shocked, the British prisoners headed northwards. The British officers moved to the head of the column and tried to raise morale.

"Get your heads up! You're British soldiers!" Andrew snarled.

Twice, Boer guards approached Andrew to look at him curiously.

"Are you a *Rooineck*?" A broad-faced man asked in halting English. "Or are you a Burgher who has joined the enemy?"

"I am Captain Andrew Baird of the Natal Dragoons," Andrew replied.

The Boers poked at him. "You look like a Burgher. Why don't you wear a red coat? Other *Rooinecks* wear a red coat or look like soldiers."

Andrew agreed. The Gordon Highlanders wore khaki tunics above their green tartan kilts but were recognisably soldiers. "We don't all wear scarlet," Andrew said.

The Boer's words remained with Andrew as they marched north into the Transvaal with an escort of mounted Boers and frequent rain showers soaking them. They camped beside a small *spruit*, with now-familiar star formations sprinkling the great arc of the sky.

"We are here for the night, *Rooinecks*," the oldest of the guards told them. "If you try to escape, we will shoot you, or the lions and tigers will get you." He smiled, showing white teeth. "You'd be as well to remain prisoners because the war will be over soon, and you'll go home."

Some Highlanders responded with obscene comments, while most listened without interest. Typical British infantry, they would be mainly recruited from urban streets, and few would attempt to escape into the unknown veld.

Andrew scooped a hole for his hip and lay on his side, listening to the sounds of the night. He worked out the sentries' beats as they walked languidly around the prisoners. After a while, the sentries grew bored and sat on rocks to talk and smoke, with the perfume of their tobacco drifting over the camp. The prisoners settled down, most sleeping, a few stirring restlessly or muttering as memories of the day's events recurred in their dreams.

Andrew rolled over, keeping quiet. He examined the camp and noted the darkest areas where rocks and two thorn trees cast tangled shadows.

That will do.

Keeping low, Andrew crawled towards the thorn trees. The sentries were lax, laughing together and ignoring their charges. Like many countrymen, they would despise the town-bred soldiers for being helpless outdoors. Andrew exploited their prejudice as he eased into the nearest shadow.

When a sentry spoke loudly and stepped away from his companions, Andrew froze, thinking the man had spotted him, but the Boer was only finding some privacy to relieve himself. A jackal called in the dark, the sound a reminder of the dangers beyond the camp perimeter. Andrew waited in the bush's friendly shadow until the sentry rejoined his companions, then crawled beyond the sentinels' beat. He found a patch of dead ground, lay still for a moment, and snaked into the darkness. Andrew knew the Boers were expert trackers but doubted they would spare the manpower to search for a single escaped British prisoner. Lengthening his stride and using the stars as a guide, he headed south, knowing he had not far to travel before he found a British picket.

I must tell General Hook about the Prussian agent.

Potchefstroom, February 1881.

"We defeated you again!" Theunis roared to the British garrison. "We defeated your General Colley at Majuba!" His voice echoed from the battered walls. "You may as well surrender now and end your suffering! Why are you holding out?"

"We're the 21st Foot!" A lone voice replied. "The Royal Scots Fusiliers! Bugger off, Piet!"

"What does that mean?" Konrad asked. "The Royal Scots Fusiliers. Does that matter?"

"It means they are fighting for the honour of their regiment," Christiaan Niekerf replied. He caressed his rifle as rain dripped from the leopard skin band around his hat. "The British have great fondness for their regiments."

"But they're only an ordinary infantry regiment, not the Guards." Konrad sounded amused. "They are nothing, peasants with rifles, cannon fodder."

Johannes removed the pipe from his mouth. "You can tell them that if you wish, Konrad. I am sure it will persuade them to surrender." He replaced the pipe and watched Konrad for a moment before turning away.

"These *Rooinecks* are strange people, Johannes," Christiaan said. "I heard that while you and I were fighting at Majuba, some of them here at Potchefstroom carried a scarecrow, a model of a woman, near our lines, gave her an umbrella, and returned to the fort."

"Why?" Konrad asked. "How could that help their cause?"

Christiaan considered before replying. "To show us they could come into our lines at will," he said. "And to mock us."

"Mock us?" Konrad gestured towards the British fort. "We have them under siege. We have defeated their best general. How can they mock us?"

Christiaan removed his hat, scratched his head, and smiled. "I do not know, Konrad. I am not a *Rooineck*."

Johannes shook his head. "They are different from us."

"They are foolish," Konrad gave his opinion.

"They are stubborn," Johannes replied. He nodded to the Union Flag. "I will be happier when that flag is down."

"That strongpoint will help," Karl nodded to the Boer's new fortification northwest of the fort. They used native labour and reluctant prisoners of war for the heavy digging and completed the stronghold at the end of February, on the 75th day of the siege.

"Now we have the *Rooinecks* surrounded," Theunis said with satisfaction. "They can either starve or surrender."

"Whatever they choose," Jan said. "I hope they do it soon." He looked up as the fort's gate opened, and a lone officer emerged under a flag of truce. "Maybe they are surrendering now."

Adriaan Coetzee approached the officer, spoke briefly, and returned to Cronje with the news filtering to the Burghers.

"The British request a coffin and a truce," Johannes reported.

"Tell them to bury their dead inside the compound," Theunis said, tossing his hair from his eyes.

"Who has died?" Jan asked. He had missed the victory of Majuba while at Nuve Hoop Plaas and sought to restore himself at the centre of the commando.

"A lady," Johannes told him. "A Mrs Emily Sketchley died of enteric fever."

Jan looked away. "I don't like making war on women."

"Mrs Sketchley's brother also died of the fever," Johannes said. "And at least four of the soldiers." He cleaned out the bowl of his pipe with a knife. "I heard the garrison places patients in holes in the ground to prevent the disease from spreading."

"I hope it does spread," Konrad said, and Theunis nodded.

"The British have scurvy as well," Johannes said. "But they still refuse to surrender."

Konrad shook his head. "Are they crazy?"

"Maybe," Johannes said. "Colonel Windroe knows the British can't force a relief column past General Joubert, yet he still holds on. I don't know why." He glanced at his commando. "I hope Windroe gives up soon while we still have men left to fight."

By now, many of the besiegers had also drifted back to their homes, some because they considered they had done enough for the Republic.

"My wife will miss me," Karl said. "She'll need me on the farm."

"She'll manage better without you," Theunis replied. "We'll have no deserters in the Groenburg Commando."

"He went home!" Karl glared at Jan.

"Jan was escorting a sick man," Theunis said. "And he returned to the fighting. I am not sure you will."

Karl snorted. "Mannie could have ridden home alone."

"We stay here," Johannes gave his decision. "We will see this war to the end."

Jan sighed, thinking of Engela as he tried to ignore Karl's jealousy.

"Engela will wait for you," Abraham read Jan's thoughts. "I know my sister."

The Rooinecks are keeping me from Engela, Jan thought. *I hate the Rooinecks.* He stared at the low walls of the British fort, lifted his rifle, and fired. *I hate the Rooinecks.* He remained low, expecting the British to reply with a volley, but there was no return fire.

Fight us! Jan thought. *Come out and fight! You have made Mannie sick and keep me here.* Jan gave a high-pitched laugh, saw his father looking worried, and took a deep breath. *Things are worse since I've been home. I miss Nuve Hoop Plaas, Mother, and Engela. Once we win this war, I will never leave home and Engela again.*

MOUNT PROSPECT, MARCH 1881.

"Halt!" The British voice was welcome as Andrew walked through the dim. "Who goes there?"

"Friend!" Andrew shouted. "Captain Andrew Baird of the Natal Dragoons."

"The what? Never heard of them, chum," the cheerful reply came. "Advance and be recognised, or I'll shoot you."

Andrew stepped forward with his hands in the air. "Here I am!" He had walked for three days since escaping from the Boers, avoiding farmhouses and the isolated *dorps*, drinking from streams, and eating only the fragment of army-issue bread he had in his pouch.

"You look like something the dog spat out," the sentry said as he examined Andrew. "What did you say your unit was called?"

"The Natal Dragoons," Andrew repeated. The British outpost was half a mile from the main camp, with the sentries doubled and more nervous than usual.

"I know of them," a second voice sounded from the dim. "They was at Ulundi. In you come, sir."

Andrew could taste the tension in Mount Prospect, with men jumping at any unusual sound and NCOs barking at every fault. The sentries held their rifles in white-knuckled hands, with more men on guard than Andrew had seen since the aftermath of Isandhlwana. One young private swivelled and raised his rifle when Andrew passed.

"A Boer!" he said.

"He's an escaped prisoner!" A colonial pushed the private's rifle down. "Easy there!"

"Morning, Baird," General Hook greeted Andrew as calmly as if they had met in a London club. "Where did you spring from?"

"A hill called Majuba," Andrew said.

They stood in the middle of the camp, with dawn flushing away the dark and men hurrying about their duties. A bugler sounded reveille, with the silver notes ghosting across the camp.

"Majuba, the Hill of Doves," Hook said. "The Boers will be boasting of that little skirmish for years. You heard that General Colley died, I presume?"

"One of the Boers made sure we all knew," Andrew said.

Hook nodded. "Colley was a gentleman. I've requisitioned a tent here, so you'd better come in and tell me what happened." He shook his grey head. "You've as many lives as a black cat, Baird."

The bell tent was crowded with desks and three of Hook's staff. "Clear out," he ordered cheerfully. "See if the garrison needs some trenches dug or the wall repaired. Do something useful for a change."

Used to General Hook's style, the men left without complaint.

"That's better," Hook said. "I don't know why I have so many staff; they can't do anything I can't do myself. Now, sit ye down, Baird, and give me your version of events at Majuba." He listened as Andrew explained what he had seen and experienced, writing a few notes.

"The Boers outfought veteran British soldiers and one of our best generals," Hook confirmed Andrew's words.

"Yes, sir. The men were too thinly spread, and the Burghers used cover and marksmanship again. They outshot us once more."

"A recurring theme," Hook leaned back in his chair, watching Andrew through tired eyes. "You seem to have a knack for surviving battles."

"Yes, sir. What were the casualties at Majuba?" Andrew asked.

Hook did not have to consult any notes before he replied. "We lost ninety-two killed, a hundred and thirty-four wounded, and sixty men captured, including you. Some of the prisoners were wounded, and others had no ammunition or weapons." The general waited for a moment. "What is your opinion of General Colley?"

"Colley was a brave man," Andrew said. "I don't think he was a great general, however intelligent."

Hook did not respond.

"How about the Boers, sir? Did we kill many of them? God knows we tried hard enough."

"The Boers hardly had any casualties. They claim they lost one man killed and six wounded. From the moment they came over the summit, they pushed us off in about thirty minutes."

Andrew remembered the chaos and the carnage. "Yet the men were shooting well and tried to hold on at the ridge. Our marksmanship is terrible."

"What can we do about that?" Hook raised his eyebrows as if a general was seriously asking the opinion of a very junior officer. However, Andrew knew Hook would have an ulterior motive, so he considered his reply.

"Emphasise marksmanship rather than volley fire," Andrew said. "Volleys were fine eighty years ago when we fought Bonaparte and still useful against tribesmen such as the Zulus but useless against the Boers. When an officer orders the men to fire, the Boers dive into cover, and the volley is wasted. Then we stand in the open like scarlet targets. The Boers can't miss."

"Our infantrymen haven't got the brains to fire independently. We sweep them from the gutters of the slums." The general threw forward his hook and waited for Andrew to bite.

Andrew grunted and slammed shut his mouth on the bait. "Then our entire social system is wrong," he said. "Why does Britain, the greatest country in the world, have so many slums and such poverty? Why do we still, in the late nineteenth century, have so many men who can hardly read or write?"

Hook shrugged with his eyes sharp as he probed deeper into Andrew's psyche. "These men probably roamed the streets rather than attending school."

"We should make schools better then," Andrew responded. "Make education interesting rather than an ordeal where teachers use the stick more than the carrot. Our system lets far too many people down."

Hook shrugged again without taking his gaze off Andrew. "The men are immoral, drunken, foul-mouthed blackguards who would not join the army if they could find anything better."

That's one way of inspiring loyalty in the rank and file. "Maybe your men are," Andrew said. "I served with soldiers." He felt his temper rise as he faced General Hook across the width of the travelling desk. He wondered how such a man could profess to be an officer if he did not respect his men.

Hook's grin took Andrew by surprise. "You are more like your father than you know, Baird. He would have reacted in much the same manner, although with more subtlety. Relax, man, I was pushing to find out about you. I've worked with British soldiers all my life, and I know their strengths and weaknesses."

Andrew took a deep breath, still fighting to control his temper. "And what did you find out about me, sir?"

"That you are a man of deep beliefs, Baird, and genuine humanity," Hook leaned back in his chair. "Whether you can combine that successfully with a career as a soldier, I cannot say."

"Were you testing me, sir?"

"Yes," Hook said. "Your father cares for his men, and they respond with loyalty. I suspect you share that trait." His smile failed to conceal the intelligent eyes scrutinising Andrew from head to foot. "Loyalty is important in senior officers, but vital in small units on detached duties."

Andrew waited, wondering where Hook was leading.

"Have you anything else to tell me?" Hook asked.

"Yes, sir," Andrew said. "I saw the Prussian spy with the Groenburg Commando."

"Is he still there?" Hook looked surprised. "He'll have an interesting report to send to the Kaiser." He eyed Andrew for a moment. "I have another task for you, Andrew. Take a few days' leave to recover, and then ensure your men are ready to leave on short notice."

He called me Andrew; that's very informal. What unpleasant task has General Hook planned for the Dragoons?

❄

POTCHEFSTROOM, MARCH 1881.

"Their flag is still flying," Karl said gloomily.

"We should storm them," Konrad reiterated his earlier suggestion. Nobody replied. The besiegers were down to four hundred men, spread thinly around the perimeter. They occupied the trenches and strongpoints, keeping the British trapped by their presence and accurate musketry.

"How many days have the *Rooinecks* held out?" Theunis asked.

"Seventy-eight," Johannes replied. He saw a British sun helmet bobbing behind the parapet but did not fire. Few Boers bothered taking shots at stray sentries, while the defenders largely ignored single Burghers. The artillery continued a desultory duel, with both sides conserving their limited ammunition.

"They can't have many supplies left inside the fort," Karl said hopefully.

Johannes lifted his field glasses and scanned the fort. "I think they are eating rotten mealies," he said. "We will starve them into submission without losing any more lives."

"General Cronje has called for all the veldcornets," Adriaan Coetzee thrust a weary head inside the house. "You have fifteen minutes."

Johannes sighed. "That sounds like trouble," he glanced at Jan. "Don't take any risks until I get back."

Johannes returned within the hour. "General Cronje wants to storm the fort," he said. "He knows our morale is low and worries we may drift away and leave the fort in British hands."

"Good!" Konrad said with great satisfaction. "Cronje has seen sense at last! The British are weak with disease, and one firm push will defeat them."

"Jan," Johannes took Jan aside. "You have never had to charge a defended position."

"No, Pa," Jan agreed.

"When Cronje gives the order, we will obey, but it will not be like anything else you have done. Don't run forward in a straight line, or the defenders will shoot you. Move in irregular rushes, from cover to cover, and look for dead ground where the *Rooinecks* cannot see you."

"Yes, Pa," Jan wondered how often his father had attacked a fixed British position. He thought it best not to ask.

"The British will fire in volleys," Johannes said. "When you hear the officer shout 'Fire', throw yourself down. Don't care what others think of you; keep alive."

"I will, Pa," Jan said.

"Stand here," Johannes put his hands on Jan's shoulders as he called the Groenburg Commando to listen. "We are attacking that section of the wall." He pointed to the centre of the British fort. "Study the ground carefully and mark in your head where the cover is. When you run forward, head for these places."

Jan nodded, taking his father's advice.

"Don't bunch up," Johannes said. "You may feel more secure with your friends around you, but the British will aim for a group rather than an individual. Keep far apart, and your chance of survival is greater."

The men grunted or nodded, with some noting the best places to shelter from the British fire and others remaining silent as they contemplated advancing over open ground under fire. Only Theunis and Konrad were enthusiastic about the attack. Konrad walked from man to man, telling them how important their victory over the British would prove. "You can push the *Rooinecks* out of the Republic," he said. "It will be a victory to rank with Blood River."[2]

"Are you coming with us?" Abraham asked.

Konrad did not reply for a few moments. "No," he said. "I have a duty to the German Empire. I cannot get killed fighting your war."

"If you are not fighting," Abraham told him. "You have no right to encourage us to get killed."

Konrad glared at Abraham and stalked away.

Abraham scowled at his retreating back and spat on the ground.

As the Burghers waited for the order to go forward, Johannes and Karl wrote letters to their wives. Others did the same, slightly embarrassed. Nobody criticised them. Some men lit their pipes, watching the smoke coil upwards, and a few drank coffee or discussed their farms.

"Abe!" Jan said. "If the *Rooinecks* kill me, tell Engela," he trailed off, unable to complete his sentence.

"I'll tell her," Abraham said. He touched Jan on the arm. "You do the same for me."

Men were unable to share their feelings yet understood each other without speaking. One man tipped his hat forward over his face and fell asleep. Two others hummed hymns and silently prayed for help and guidance. Christiaan Niekerf cleaned his rifle and stared into the sky. He smiled and began to scrape out his pipe.

"I wonder if my dead wives are watching me," he said, lifting the bowl of his pipe in a silent salute before returning the stem to his mouth.

Jan could feel the tension as the Burghers checked their rifles, shook each other's hands, or simply stared towards the fort.

Johannes came close to Jan. "Remember what I told you. Don't be afraid to keep down. You're a farmer first and a soldier second."

"You too, Pa," Jan told him.

"Ten minutes," the word spread around the Burghers' positions. "Ten minutes. Move into the forward trenches."

"Ten minutes to live," Karl said without any humour.

Jan did not reply. He felt his heartbeat increase as he tried to force a smile.

The Groenburg Commando slogged forward, keeping beneath the parapet so the British could not see them. They took up their positions, with Jan crouched between Johannes and Abraham, humming a reassuring hymn.

The minutes ticked slowly past, each one an eternity as Jan thought of Engela and his home. *Thank the Lord Mannie is safely away from the war.*

"Five minutes," Theunis lifted his rifle, tossed the tangled hair back from his face, and glared at the fort. Jan thought he had never seen a man look so much like a wild animal.

Jan saw the strain in his father's face. He looked older, with deeper lines from his nose to his mouth and around his eyes.

"The Lord will look after you, Jan," Johannes said, touching his son's shoulder in unspoken affection.

"Go!" Theunis gave the order. "Storm, Groenburg Commando! Storm!"

The Burghers erupted from their trenches and houses, shouting to hide their fear.

"Now!" Jan heard the crisp command from the fort, and a line of sun helmets appeared above the wall, with a row of levelled Martini-Henry rifles.

"Fire!" the same British voice roared.

Jan dropped to the ground as the first volley crashed out, knocking down three Burghers.

"It's a trap!" Karl shouted. "They are waiting for us!"

Jan clambered to his feet. He felt strangely elated, as though he was not here but inhabited somebody else's body, a stranger advancing into the concentrated musketry of professional soldiers.

"Fire!" The same clipped, unemotional British voice repeated.

The Fusiliers fired again, with bullets crashing into the ground, hissing overhead, and wounding another two Burghers.

"Load!" the unseen officer commanded.

"Back! Get back!" Karl looked around in panic. "It's no good!"

Johannes grabbed Jan's arm. "Get back, Jan!"

Sudden panic enveloped the Burghers as they scrambled back to their positions with bullets kicking up dirt around their legs. Jan ran with the rest, panting in fear as the British fired another volley. He heard somebody screaming, felt the rush of a bullet zipping past his ear, and threw himself into the trench he had left only moments previously. He landed with a painful thump and lay in the trench, gasping, eyes wide open, and his heart hammering inside his chest. "Pa?"

"I'm here," Johannes said, his voice seeming to come from a long distance.

"Are you hurt?"

"No. Are you?"

"No." Johannes closed his eyes. "The British knew we were coming."

"Abe?" Jan said, seeing Abraham a few yards away, his mouth wide and his eyes darting from side to side.

"Get back to the house," Johannes ordered. "We won't be capturing the fort today."

"Load!" the unemotional British voice ordered.

A man was groaning, his voice the only sound between the Boer and British lines.

"They beat you," Konrad said when the shocked survivors returned to their quarters. "You ran away. If you had charged with more conviction, you would have captured the fort."

"I didn't see you advancing," Abraham retorted. "Why don't you return to Prussia and leave us in peace."

"You don't deserve Prussian help," Konrad told him.

Jan watched Konrad march away and looked over the land between the Boer and British lines, where dead and wounded Burghers lay in tattered bundles.

We'll never defeat these Rooinecks.

THE HARSH BARK OF ARTILLERY WOKE JAN FROM A CONFUSED DREAM. He lay still for a few seconds, thinking he was in his room at Nuwe Hoop Plaas, until he recognised the sound of the guns, and his heart dropped. *I'm still at Potchefstroom.* He struggled to his feet, shaking the sleep from his head.

"What's happening?"

"The *Rooinecks* are firing at *Ou Griet*!" Karl shouted. "All their guns!"

"Shoot them," Theunis ordered, "man the trenches and shoot the British gunners!"

Some Groenburg men rose to obey, but a controlled volley from the fort made the Burghers duck. The British artillery fired again, raising great clouds of mud from around the Boer cannon.

"They must be scared of our gun!" Theunis removed his hat and thrust a tangle of hair from his face. He lifted his rifle, aimed, and fired at the British artillery. "Come on, boys! Make them pay!"

Jan aimed at a now-badly stained British sun helmet, took a deep breath, and squeezed the trigger just as the soldier bobbed away. Jan swore at the waste of another bullet. "The devil is looking after these *Rooineck* soldiers!"

The British artillery barked again, with two shells landing squarely beside the Boer gun. Jan flinched as he saw the explosions lift tons of earth and rock and land them on top of *Ou Griet*.

"The *Rooinecks* have destroyed *Ou Griet*," he said. He heard the British give a thin cheer.

"Now we'll never capture the fort," Karl wailed.

With their task completed, the British artillery fell silent. A few Burghers revealed their frustration by firing at the fort, but the British remained below their parapet.

Jan watched as a breeze stirred the Union Flag, as if the Lord were mocking the Burghers' frustration. He slumped down, looked at Johannes, and shrugged.

"What next, Pa?"

"We put our faith in General Cronje and the Lord," Johannes said, but Jan saw doubt in his eyes.

POTCHEFSTROOM, 12TH OF MARCH 1881.

Jan stood at the back of the crowd, thinking of Engela. He pushed back his hat with a filthy thumb and watched his father and Theunis talking to General Cronje before they shook hands. The hum of conversation ended when the general stepped forward to speak to the Burghers.

"Fellow Burghers of the Zuid-Afrikaansche Republiek," Cronje smiled as he looked around at the besiegers. "Paul Kruger, the Vice-President of the Triumvirate, has contacted me with good news."

The Burghers remained silent, listening to the general. Karl was breathing heavily, leaning on his rifle. Johannes searched for Jan in the crowd and winked while Theunis stared ahead. Behind the leaders, Konrad stood erect, as pristine as if he were attending a ball in Berlin rather than observing a siege in an obscure Transvaal *dorp*.

Cronje lifted his voice. "*Meneer* Kruger has informed me that Commandant-General Joubert and General Sir Evelyn Wood have agreed to an armistice between us and the British." He waited for the crowd's murmur to subside. "I will read you one paragraph of Kruger's letter. Listen, my friends."

The men listened, some smoking, others holding their rifles in brown hands. Jan thought of his brother, white-faced and sick, lying in his bed at home, and of Engela, who would wonder why he had not visited when he was close.

"*Meneer* Kruger writes: 'It is your duty to notify Major Winsloe of the agreement between Wood and Joubert, but the armistice at Mooiriver is not to commence prior to the arrival of supplies, and the handing over thereof to you. Before such time, be free to continue warfare."

The veldcornets nodded. Any supplies would be welcome.

Cronje noted the approval. "We shall capture this fort, gentlemen, and then tell the British of the armistice."

The Burghers spoke together, some wondering how to capture the fort and others glad of the coming armistice. They had waited patiently and fought too hard to allow politicians to steal their victory.

Theunis smiled triumphantly. "We know the fort is running out of food, and disease is spreading through the garrison."

The Burghers nodded. "These things are well known," one man agreed.

"The British must surrender soon," Theunis continued. "I have a man inside the fort, a Burgher who pretends to be friendly with the British."

Jan inched closer, desperate for the siege to end.

Theunis continued, brushing the hair from his face. "The British colonel wants an honourable surrender before his rations are finished rather than have us make him surrender unconditionally."

"Any surrender would be better than sitting here while men are killed," Johannes said. "If it comes a week earlier, let the British have their honourable terms."

The Burghers agreed. "Let's finish this siege and return to our farms," Karl said. "I don't care if the British surrender honourably or dishonourably as long as it finishes this damned war."

Jan agreed. "We have been away from home too long," he said. "Speak to the *Rooinecks* and end the siege."

"Do we all agree?" the veldcornets asked their men.

After all the toil and suffering, Jan thought the siege ended with a whimper rather than a bang. *Maybe all wars end like this when men are too weary to continue fighting and lay down their arms through fatigue rather than in a glorious burst of victory.*

Jan acted as sentry as Colonel Winsloe and his officers met Cronje halfway between the town and the fort. He recognised Lieutenant Rundle among the British delegation and held his rifle ready in case the meeting was a British ruse. Fusilier McWilliam stood opposite him, stony-faced, until the officers disappeared inside the tent.

"All right, mate?" McWilliam asked Jan. "Let the ossifers work things out, and then we can all go home, eh?"

The man's accent and language baffled Jan, but he understood the message. "That would be best," he agreed.

He heard raised voices inside when Winsloe asked Cronje why he had not informed him about the armistice.

"The circumstances were beyond my control," Cronje replied.

McWilliam looked gaunt after months on short rations, but his uniform was impeccable, albeit threadbare, and he grinned and winked.

"Better them arguing than us firing at each other, eh?" McWilliam said.

Jan nodded, wondering if this man had shot at him in their late abortive attack. He smiled back, slightly nervous in case the soldier attacked him with his bayonet.

"We'll leave the ossifers to it, eh?" McWilliam said.

Jan smiled again, only understanding a few words. "Ja," he replied.

After an hour, Winsloe left the tent, leaving his junior officers behind.

"They'll be working out the final terms," McWilliam relaxed when his commanding officer stalked away. "You lads fought well, didn't you?"

"We fought well," Jan struggled over the words. "We thought you would surrender weeks ago."

"Not us, chum," McWilliam replied. "We're the Royal Scots Fusiliers, see? We hold on to the last." He grinned without any animosity.

"Don't you hate us?" Jan asked.

"Hate you?" McWilliam seemed confused by the question. "Bless you, no. Why should we hate you?"

"We are your enemy," Jan said slowly.

The Fusilier considered for a moment. "Aye, maybe, but we don't hate you. Fighting's our job, see. It's what we do. We'll try and kill you in the war, but once there's peace, it's all friends again."

"You live by fighting?" It was a concept Jan found strange.

"It's a job," McWilliam was suddenly serious. "It's better than starving on the streets or begging outside publics," he said.

Jan studied the man, seeing his small stature and pinched look of long-term poverty, and wondered that the richest and most powerful Empire in the world should raise such people.

"Anyway," McWilliam said. "You lads are pretty decent to the wounded and the prisoners."

"So are the British," Jan said slowly.

McWilliam grinned, showing discoloured teeth. "From what I've heard," he said, "the Paythans murdered their prisoners slowly. Bloody savages, them." He lifted his head as Jan wondered who the Paythans were. "Watch out, chum. The ossifers are coming out." The Fusilier stiffened to attention, facing his front and with his face expressionless. Jan watched as Lieutenants Rundle and Buskus left the tent.

"You can go now, Jan," Johannes said as the officers dismissed the Fusilier sentry.

"What's happening, Pa?" Jan asked.

"The garrison has surrendered," Johannes said. "We have won."

"Can we go home? Back to Nuwe Hoop Plaas?"

"We can go home," Johannes confirmed. "Engela will be glad to see you."

Jan had expected to feel elation when the Burghers won the war, but instead, it was relief that surged through him. He looked away. "That is good," he said. He did not know why he felt like crying rather than cheering.

Johannes put a hand on Jan's shoulder. "Go back to your quarters, Jan, and tell Abraham. Drink a cup of coffee together."

"Yes, Pa," Jan forced a smile. Abraham was always cheerful company.

POTCHEFSTROOM, 21ST MARCH 1881

Jan stood beside Abraham as the garrison left the fort. A tall officer held the Union Flag at the head of the column, and the red-coated soldiers, haggard and gaunt but still at attention, marched smartly out.

Theunis began to jeer but stopped when nobody joined him. Konrad stood beside General Cronjé with a slight sneer on his face.

"There are fewer *Rooinecks* than I thought," Abraham said.

Jan agreed. "We can go home now." He watched the women and children at the rear of the British column and wondered how he would feel if his mother or Engela were stuck in a besieged fort for months.

Abraham smiled. "I had cows ready to calve. The calves will be agile when I return."

"We had cows calving as well," Jan said. "It will be good to get back to farming." The fort was empty now, a slice of history that would never return.

I will tell my children of the day we forced the British from Potchefstroom. They will listen to my stories and believe I am a hero. They will not know I was cold, tired, muddy, and afraid. I can never tell them I was afraid.

CHAPTER 16

NEWCASTLE, NATAL, MARCH 1881

"You will remember I said I might have a job for the Natal Dragoons," Hook said, leaning back in his chair.

Andrew nodded. The series of defeats had been a chastening experience, shaking his confidence in British military expertise. "Yes, sir."

"You will also remember that we still have garrisons within the Transvaal."

"I do, sir," Andrew said.

"Swartspruit, in particular, concerns us," Hook said. "The smallest and most remote of all our Transvaal garrisons."

"Why are we concerned, sir?" Andrew asked.

Hook stepped to the large-scale map of Southern Africa on the wall. "Here is the Transvaal," he said. "And here is Swartspruit." He pointed to a point in the northwest, near the ill-defined border. "It is a hot, dry place, only a hundred miles from the Kalahari Desert."

Andrew nodded. "Yes, sir." He eyed the map. "That area looks very sparsely populated. Why do we have a garrison out there?"

Hook uncharacteristically hesitated before he replied. "We have been using Swartspruit to conduct geological surveys," he said. "You may know we preempted the Germans by taking over Walvis Bay a few years ago. It's the most convenient port on the southwest African coast and far better in our hands than in Bismarck's." Hook grimaced.

"Yes, sir," Andrew said.

"We want to ensure there are no more mineralogical surprises in the area," Hook explained. "Hence, we have a geologist working in the area. We must forestall the Germans, as the Prussian chancellor is continental Europe's most powerful and dangerous man."

"The Germans are becoming as troublesome as the French, sir," Andrew said.

"More so," Hook said dryly. "Their industrial strength is growing faster than ours, and their army is the best in the world." He glanced at the door and lowered his voice. "I'll give you a comparison, Baird. General Colley, one of our most intelligent generals, lost three battles to a rag-tag collection of African farmers. Over the last few years, the German Army has defeated both Austria and France, two major powers. Their victory over Austria took a few weeks and over France six months." Hook shook his head in wonder. "Only six months to defeat what was the foremost military nation in the world."

"Yes, sir," Andrew thought it best to change the subject. "I thought the truce with the Transvaal made provisions for the besieged garrisons, sir."

"You won't find Swartspruit mentioned in any document, Baird." Hook gave a wry smile and altered his tone. "We have a man in that little *dorp* that we want safely back. We don't want him to fall into Boer hands, and still less do we want the Boers to give him to the Germans."

"Would the Boers do that, sir?"

"Perhaps." Hook leaned forward. "You are an unconventional soldier, Baird, and the son of an equally unconventional soldier. You have campaigned in Africa for years, ride well, and shoot better than most. I want you to take a group of volunteers, say a dozen men from your Dragoons, break the Boer blockade of Swartspruit and bring this fellow back to British territory."

Andrew drew in his breath. "There are many colonials who know the Transvaal and are more experienced in that sort of warfare than I am, sir."

"I am aware of that," Hook said. "I also know you are very young for the task, but I have chosen you. Buller speaks highly of your abilities, and you have experience fighting the Boers." He held Andrew's gaze before continuing. "I have another order for you, Captain."

"What's that, sir?"

"I want you to ensure the Boers do not capture this man or get their hands on whatever documents he may be carrying."

"Sir?" Andrew did not hide his confusion.

"If it appears the Boers may capture this man, Baird, I want you to kill him." Hook's eyes did not waver.

Andrew was silent for a few moments. "I'm not an assassin, sir."

"Your duty is to the queen and country, Baird."

"Murdering people is not my duty," Andrew said quietly.

"Let's hope it does not come to that," Hook replied.

Andrew stirred restlessly. "Who is this man, sir, and why is he so important?"

Hook waited for a moment. "His name is Charles Abercrombie, but I can't tell you more than that, I'm afraid." He smiled without humour. "It's not as bad as you think, Captain. You won't be entirely alone in the Transvaal. You will lead a fast, very mobile force of horsemen to rescue Mr Abercrombie, but I'll also send a larger force complete with artillery to back you up."

"That's good, sir," Andrew said.

"You'll take a heliograph, and when you pick up Abercrombie and reach this spot," Hook jabbed his finger onto the map, "you'll send a message south and east. Our men will pick it up and meet you with horse, foot, and guns."

Andrew stepped closer to the map. "Why that spot, sir?"

"It is easily identifiable with two nearly identical *kopjes* standing side by side," Hook said. "Or so my informants tell me. I'll give you the coordinates and a marked map. I'll also send you a fellow named Turner, who could be useful."

Andrew studied the map. "Let me get this clear, sir. You wish me to take a small patrol, ride halfway across Africa to rescue a man I don't know, and be prepared to kill him rather than allow the Boers to capture him. There are an unknown number of angry Boers besieging their position and possibly some Germans, any of whom will kill us without warning or regret."

Hook gave his slow smile, with his eyes crinkling in his head. "Yes, that's about the size of it, Baird. When can you be ready to start?"

"I'll need to speak to my men first," Andrew said. "I'll explain the situation and see if there are any volunteers."

Volunteers? With the war all but over, who the devil will volunteer to go back into danger? And who is this Abercrombie fellow that everybody seems to want?

JAN STOPPED AT THE ENTRANCE TO NUWE HOOP PLAAS. "HOME AGAIN," HE pulled up his horse and looked around. "It seems like we've been away for years. I never want to leave the farm again."

"It's only been a few months," Johannes said. "And you returned with Mannie."

"I only stayed one night," Jan reminded him, smiling as they neared the farmhouse. He knew every tree, every fold of ground, and every rock of this land. Each square yard held memories of boyhood adventures and misadventures. He took a deep breath, savouring his home. His father and grandfather had broken this land from the wilderness, and he would farm it and raise his children here.

Aletta stood at the door with her arms folded and a small smile playing on the edges of her mouth. Mannie stood behind her, still pale and thin but looking better than he had for months.

Aletta held Johannes' gaze for a long moment before switching her attention to her son. "Engela is here, Jan," she said.

Jan tried to appear unconcerned as he dismounted and threw his horse's reins to a servant. Aletta stepped aside as Jan ran into the house.

"We are back, Aletta," Johannes said, "and I have brought guests."

"They are welcome," Aletta said.

"This is Konrad Bramigan, a friend from Prussia," Johannes said. "And this gentleman is Theunis Steenekamp, whose family have been merchants in Groenburg since the Great Trek."

Both men raised their hats to Aletta.

"I know the Steenekamps," Aletta said. "I know your sister Alice, *Meneer* Steenekamp. She often speaks of you."

Theunis raised his hat again.

"I do not know your family, *Meneer* Bramigan," Aletta eyed him. "But I am sure they are respectable people."

Konrad dismounted, clicked his heels together and gave a formal bow. "I assure you, madam, that my family is amongst the finest in Prussia."

Aletta nodded. "I believe you, *meneer*," she said. "Have we defeated the British, Johannes?"

"We have," Johannes replied. "Their Prime Minister has requested a cease-fire and promised they will leave our country."

Aletta nodded. "Dolinde, Karl's wife, will be pleased." She hugged Johannes briefly, aware the visitors were watching. "Coffee?" she asked, "or something stronger for men home from the war?"

"What do you have?" Konrad asked. "Schnapps? Brandy?"

"We have *mampoer*," Aletta told him.

"I shall try some of your *mampoer*," Konrad decided.

Engela met Jan in the kitchen, stepped towards him and stopped, slightly awkward in his company after so many weeks apart.

"Hello, Jan," she said quietly.

Jan echoed her shyness. "Hello, Engela," he replied. They looked at each other for a long moment. "It's good to see you again," Jan said.

"You too. How long are you back for?" Engela frowned as she examined him. "You're very thin."

"It's the war. I'll soon be back to normal," Jan said. "I'm back for good." He struggled for words. "I've missed you."

Engela nodded and stepped aside as Aletta ushered the others into the house.

"This way, gentlemen!"

Mampoer was home-distilled brandy, generally made from peaches, although the van Collier family made theirs from marula, a local wild fruit. The Nuwe Hoop Plaas *mampoer* was infamous across the western Transvaal for its potency, so even Karl, a man known for his drinking ability, called it lethal.

"However bad you feel," Karl had said after drinking a glass of Aletta's mampoer, "this stuff will make you feel worse."

"I am used to schnapps," Konrad said as Aletta poured him a generous measure. "And champagne and fine wine, of course."

"I have never tried schnapps," Aletta said. "We only drink here on special occasions."

Jan watched surreptitiously as Konrad tasted the mampoer. Rather than a cautious sip, he threw the contents back in a dramatic single swallow.

"That is good!" Konrad said and proffered his glass for more. He looked around the simple house. "I thought your farm would be larger," he said. "The house is small."

"It is sufficient for our needs," Aletta said defensively. Nobody had ever criticised her home before.

Jan frowned at Konrad's words. He had never thought of Nuwe Hoop Plaas as anything other than home. Now, he looked at the farmhouse through the eyes of a man who had seen more of the world. Oblong in shape, the house was built of plain, roughly baked bricks with a roof of mixed thatch and corrugated iron. Jan compared his home with some of the houses he had seen in Groenburg and Potchefstroom and realised Nuwe Hoop Plaas was functional without aesthetic beauty. The *stoep* provided shade and a place to sit in the evenings, while a prickly fence contained a handful of fruit trees.

Konrad nodded. "It is suitable for the Transvaal," he agreed. He placed his glass on the simple deal table and smiled at Engela, clicking his heels in a crisp bow. "And the women here are more beautiful than any in Prussia or elsewhere."

Jan looked at the home-made chairs and the shelf with the highly polished warming pans and brass candlesticks. Apart from the beds, a chest, and the leather-bound Bible, that was all the furniture the house possessed. *It is all we need,* Jan told himself. *Lord Jesus did not live in a mansion.* He looked at Konrad, suddenly aware of his home's simplicity.

He saw Engela smiling at Konrad's words and felt a surge of disquiet. Konrad was tall, elegant, wealthy, and refined, a gentleman who had seen half the world.

"I am going to visit Goeie Weiding," Jan announced. "I will take Engela with me." Goeie Weiding was the farm where Engela and Abraham lived with their widowed mother.

Aletta glanced at Johannes, who nodded. "Ja, that is good," Aletta said. Before the war, she would have trusted her son to behave with Engela, but he had returned a man with deep knowledge in his eyes. "Be careful."

"It is all right, *Tante* Aletta," Engela said, touching Aletta's sleeve. She understood Aletta's warning.

"Ja, it will be all right," Aletta agreed. "Take care of him, Engela."

Jan waited until Engela mounted her horse, and they rode over the familiar land. He glanced across to her, aware life was no longer as simple as it had once appeared.

"It is good to be home," Jan said.

Engela smiled. "It is good to have you back," she agreed. "What happened at the war? Did you shoot many *Rooinecks?*"

Jan thought of the things he had seen. "I shot some," he said, remembering the rain, the mud, the horror, and the sudden fear that had unmanned him during the abortive attack on the British fort.

"Tell me your adventures," Engela asked.

Jan rode in silence for a few moments, enjoying the openness of the veld. "We had some battles," he said. He had waited for his time alone with Engela, but now he could not find any words. The memories were too close and too intense to share. How could he talk to gentle Engela about shooting men and watching them die? Or feeling sick with fear when the British shot at him?

"Did you meet any other girls?" Engela asked coyly.

"No," Jan said. "I did not meet any other girls." He remembered the gaunt women who had survived the siege of Potchefstroom with their haunted eyes and sunken faces. He could not tell Engela about them or the desperate prostitute in Potchefstroom who offered her wasted body for bread. Engela would never understand.

"Were you at Majuba?" Engela asked. "I heard we won a great victory at Majuba."

"We won a great victory at Majuba," Jan confirmed. "I was not there."

"Oh?" Engela looked at him with raised eyebrows and a new heat in her eyes. "Where were you?"

Engela knows where I was. "I had to take Mannie home to Nuve Hoop Plaas," Jan said. "He was sick."

"Ah. You were at Nuve Hoop Plaas," Engela said with an increasingly tight voice. "Did you not think of coming over to see me? It is only an hour's ride."

"I had to return to the commando," Jan explained weakly.

"You did not think I might be worrying about Abraham and you?" Engela asked. "Or don't my feelings matter?"

"Of course, your feelings matter," Jan replied, not understanding why he was on the defensive.

"Not sufficiently, it seems," Engela retorted. Turning her head, she rode slowly away, with Jan half a length behind.

They were both silent when they arrived at Goeie Weiding. Abraham met them at the gate, smiled broadly, glanced at their faces, and withdrew. "I'll leave you two together," he said diplomatically.

Alizea Hertzog, Engela's mother, watched from an inside doorway, raised her eyebrows at the tension and forced a smile. "You are welcome, Jan."

"Thank you, *Tante*," Jan removed his hat and stood in awkward silence.

Alizea looked at her daughter's closed face. "I see you two have something to work out."

"Maybe, Mother," Engela replied stiffly without looking at Jan.

Alizea nodded slowly. "I will leave you with the *opsitker*. I am going to bed now."

The *opsitker* or sit-up-candle was a Boer tradition that regulated how much a young woman liked the man who courted her. The girl's parents retired to bed, leaving the young couple alone in the *voorkamer*, the front room. The girl brought a candle, with the couple left alone until it burned itself out. The better the girl liked the boy, the longer the candle she would provide.

Having dreamed of this moment through the long weeks of campaigning, Jan found his mind empty of everything. He felt he no longer belonged in this peaceful environment where nature regulated the day, and people slept in civilised beds. He should be sleeping in a muddy trench, with British bullets crackling past and desperately wounded men screaming for help.

"Here we are," Jan said at last, pushing away the raw memories.

"Ja," Engela replied. "Here we are."

They looked at each other across the table that seemed to stretch forever. Jan extended a hand, struggling to break through the horrors in his mind. "Engela," he said.

"Ja, I am Engela." Engela's hands remained folded neatly in her lap.

Jan looked away, noting the grain of the wood on the table and the hum of insects. He watched Engela leave the room and return with the stump of a small candle, which she placed firmly in the centre of the table.

"Sit, Jan," Engela lit the wick and the flame wavered.

Jan took a deep breath and sat down. The space between them seemed like a vast chasm, and he was more unhappy than he had ever been during the battles with the British. "It is a short candle."

"It is a short candle," Engela agreed. She held his gaze without helping. The candle flame guttered.

"Maybe I had better leave," Jan said. He could hear rifle fire in his head.

"Leave, then," Engela said and blew out the candle.

Jan stood in the darkened room, grabbed his hat, and left the room. He thought he heard Engela crying as he mounted his horse but could not be sure.

ANDREW STUFFED TOBACCO IN HIS PIPE, SAT ON HIS FAVOURITE KNOLL WITH a view to the south, and lit a match. He watched the flame for a second and applied it to the tobacco, puffing until he was satisfied the pipe drew.

"I thought I'd find you here," Mariana said from behind him. "What's happening?"

"I'm going back to the war," Andrew told her. He exhaled blue smoke as she digested his words.

"Oh." Mariana sat at his side, folding her skirt beneath her. "When?"

"Very soon," Andrew replied without looking at her. "And that leaves me with a problem."

"What's that, Andrew?" Mariana asked.

"My problem is what to do with you," Andrew said. "Last time I was away, you had servants to look after you. The time before, you had Briggs, and prior to that, you ended up in the guardhouse." He looked sideways at her through a cloud of smoke. "Next time, I might find you on Robben Island."

Mariana started. "That's a terrible place," she said.

"So I've heard," Andrew agreed.

They were silent for a while, with Mariana twisting her hands together.

"I can't help it," Mariana said at last. "I have nightmares, and sometimes the memories come to me during the day as well. They're so vivid that I feel I am back there, and I just stand and stare into space."

"I've seen you," Andrew reminded her. "I don't know what's best for you."

"I'll be all right," Mariana said bravely. "But I wish you weren't going."

Andrew nodded slowly. "I'd take you with me if it weren't so dangerous."

"I don't mind the danger," Mariana replied quickly. "Better danger than Robben Island."

"There might be fighting," Andrew added more tobacco to his pipe. He stared over the landscape without seeing the hills, farms, and forests as he wondered what to do with Mariana.

"I won't get in the way," Mariana promised. "Take me with you, Andrew. Please take me with you."

"If I get killed up there," Andrew said, "what will you do?"

"If you get killed up there," Mariana twisted the question, "and I'm down here, what will I do? The authorities will stick me in Robben Island until I rot away of old age or hang myself."

Andrew grunted. He knew Mariana was correct. She was a woman of the outdoors. Born and bred on a farm beside the Tugela River, she lived for the fresh air and sunshine. The few days shut up in Fort Amiel's guardroom had been bad enough; if the authorities locked her in the asylum at Robben Island indefinitely, Andrew doubted her mind could cope.

"Damn it all," Andrew said. "What a bloody, bloody mess everything is."

"I'm causing you complications," Mariana said.

"No," Andrew tried to reassure her. "It's not your fault, Mariana. We'll work something out."

"I'm not going to Robben Island," Mariana said desperately. "I'd rather join Elaine under the ground. Please don't send me there."

Andrew put a hand on her shoulder. "I won't send you to Robben Island," he said. He saw a small vein throbbing in her throat and heard her short, shallow breathing. "That's a promise."

"Where will I go?" Mariana asked. "I can't stay in your house forever; people are already talking."

"We'll work something out," Andrew said. *I have no idea what to do with you, Mariana.*

She edged closer, with the shadows flitting across her eyes as she remembered the horrors from her past. "I don't want you to go back to war."

"I know," Andrew said. He shook his head. "I don't want to go back either."

"Will you leave me with William again?" Mariana asked.

"William?" Andrew repeated the name.

"William Briggs," Mariana explained.

"Oh," Andrew had never considered Briggs having a Christian name. He was only Briggs, the self-contained, efficient servant. Andrew knew nothing about Briggs except his duties. "Yes, I'll probably leave you with William Briggs."

Leaving Mariana in Briggs' care will alleviate one temporary problem, Andrew thought. *It will not solve the long-term worry about what to do with her. I can't look after her forever, although I'll do what I can for Elaine's sake. And for Mariana's.*

"Thank you," Mariana said.

They sat side by side in miserable silence, each lost in their own thoughts.

"Let's go home," Mariana said. "It's getting cold here."

Andrew finished his pipe, tapped out the embers, and ground them beneath his heel. They walked home, with Mariana reaching for Andrew but dropping her hand before making contact. Deep in his worries, Andrew did not notice.

"How was Engela?" Aletta asked when Jan returned. "You were not long."

"No, I was not long," Jan agreed. He was aware of Konrad watching him, with a half-smile hovering on his lips.

"Was she unwell?" Aletta asked.

"She was well," Jan replied.

"Ah," Aletta understood. "You had a disagreement." She touched Jan's shoulder. "That is normal, Jan. You know that your father and I disagree from time to time. It means nothing."

"Yes, Mother," Jan moved away quickly. He did not want to talk about Engela with his mother. He did not want to talk about Engela at all. He wanted to curl up in a ball or ride across the veld or do anything except talk about Engela. He hoped the war would start again so he could forget his troubles by fighting the *Rooinecks*.

"Has she decided you are too young for her?" Konrad asked.

"No," Jan told him angrily. "She did not decide that I was too young." He wished people would leave him alone.

Konrad nodded in false sympathy. "Women are hard to understand, Jan," he said. "It takes years of experience. Some women need a firm hand, others gentleness and encouragement."

"I don't understand what Engela wants," Jan admitted.

Konrad patted his shoulder. "No young man understands what a woman wants." He smiled. "Would you like me to talk to her for you?"

"No," Jan said. "I do not want you to talk to her at all." Lifting his hat from the table, he threw open the door and stormed from the house. Nobody saw the tears he dashed from his eyes as he ran into the veld.

"I want volunteers for a dangerous mission," Andrew announced. The Natal Dragoons stood in a semi-circle around him with a faint breeze stirring the mimosa trees and a korhaan bird scolding them from a topmost branch.

He knew his men by name, character, and habit. They viewed him through cynical eyes in faces burned nut-brown by the sun and wind. Spalding, the most intellectual, listened intently; Morrison chewed a wad of tobacco while Trooper Kerr tamped down the bowl of his pipe. Ogden cleaned his rifle, half-smiling as Sergeant Meek stood at attention, immaculate in everything he did.

"How dangerous, sir?" Kerr asked.

"Suicidal," Andrew replied cheerfully.

"Where are you taking us?"

"I am not allowed to tell you," Andrew replied.

"Why are we going?"

"To relieve a beleaguered British garrison," Andrew told him.

"I thought there was a truce, sir," Sergeant Meek said. "Have the Boers broken their agreement already?"

"There is a truce," Andrew decided to release a little more information. "But some Afrikander Bond Boers are besieging an isolated garrison to capture an important person. We must ride across the Transvaal, relieve the garrison and the personage, and bring everybody back to British territory."

"How many men do you want, sir?" Meek asked.

"A dozen," Andrew said. "That's a handy figure, yet small enough to vanish in the veld."

"When do we leave, sir?" Meek asked.

Andrew smiled. "Are you volunteering, Sergeant?"

"Yes, sir. I think we all are."

"Thank you, gentlemen." The Dragoons' loyalty touched Andrew. "I need men who can ride in all conditions and outshoot the Boers. I also want men capable of shoeing a horse and navigating by the stars out in the bush."

"That's the Dragoons out then, sir," Meek said, "we'd get lost crossing the road on a sunny day," and the men laughed, knowing they were all capable frontiersmen.

"I thought as much," Andrew said. "That's why I'm going to the 15th Hussars next. I've heard they are at least half-decent horsemen." He expected the barrage of abuse and whistles from his loyal men. "We'll start some intensive training tomorrow, lads. You're looking soft and flabby." He grinned at the Dragoons' sudden expressions of dismay.

CHAPTER 17

FORT AMIEL, NEWCASTLE, NATAL

Major Fotheringham leaned back in his cane chair and surveyed Andrew over the rim of his champagne glass. "So, you're Lieutenant Baird of the Natal Dragoons, are you? Captain Baird, now, I hear."

"That's right, sir," Andrew said.

The officers' mess was busy as scarlet-coated men smoothed their whiskers, downed champagne and brandy, and read the newspapers. Mess waiters scurried around busily as the barman poured drinks as if the officers were celebrating a victory rather than living in the wake of a defeat.

Fotheringham nodded. "I've heard some of the men talking about you. They call you Up-and-at-'em because of your exploits against the Zulus."

Andrew did not reply. He had not sought a nickname and had no pleasure in hearing it.

"Well, Up-and-at-'em, let me tell you that I don't listen to the other ranks' gossip. They are only here to obey orders."

"Yes, sir," Andrew had met men like Fotheringham before, brave, sporting, probably an excellent shot and horseman but without any knowledge of the men he led.

"Were you at Sandhurst, Captain?"

"Briefly, sir," Andrew replied.

"The briefer the better," Fotheringham said. "All that theoretical nonsense is a waste of time. Now, listen to me. I've been serving the queen for thirty years, and I tell you this: Ignore what the other ranks say and ignore any officer who's only served in India. They only know how to fight Indian troops."

"I heard the Afghans and Pashtuns are excellent fighting men, sir," Andrew said.

"Nonsense," Fotheringham barked. "They are not. Now, take our infantry. They sign on for short service, six years, which is hardly long enough to break them in. Yet," Fotheringham lifted a finger as if he were about to reveal some infinite wisdom. "After six years, they can hardly return to civilian life. We have them, Baird. We have them here." He opened his left fist and closed it again. "Keep the men well in hand, Baird. If you give them too much leeway, they'll find a pub and drink themselves into insensibility. Ensure they fire in volleys on the word of command, or they'll fire wildly without aim or direction."

"I see, sir," Andrew said solemnly.

"They're brave enough when officers order them what to do," Fotheringham said, finishing his champagne. "Otherwise, they're emotional, irrational, and lazy." He stood up, hiccupped, and walked unsteadily away, leaving Andrew alone.

God help the army if that's the standard of leadership, Andrew thought. *In the world of the blind, a one-eyed man is king. In the world of British officers, even mediocrity may be seen as genius. No wonder the Boers ran rings around us.*

THE TROOPER APPROACHED ANDREW AS HE STEPPED OUTSIDE HIS QUARTERS. "Captain Baird?" He was middle-sized, with a square, sun-darkened face.

"That's me, trooper."

"General Hook sends his compliments sir, and says I have to hand this to you." The trooper passed over a sealed envelope.

"Thank you," Andrew accepted the envelope. "Did the general tell you to wait for a reply?"

"Yes, sir," the trooper said.

"Very well." Andrew broke the seal, opened the envelope, and read the letter.

"Captain Baird,

I suggest you include Trooper Turner, the bearer of this letter, in your expedition. You might find him a useful addition. Turner knows Abercrombie by sight and may help persuade him to accompany you.

Hook."

Andrew grunted. "Welcome to the Natal Dragoons, Turner." A suggestion from a general was tantamount to an order. Only a very foolish junior officer would refuse.

"Thank you, sir," Turner said.

"General Hook says you know Mr Abercrombie."

"Only by sight, sir," Turner said.

"General Hook also said that I might find you useful. What skills do you have?"

Turner was about thirty-three, with nothing distinctive about him except a light of intelligence in his steady eyes and an aura of self-confidence surprising for a typical British trooper. *Who are you? Hook would not send me an ordinary soldier.*

"I rode with Buller in Zululand, sir," Turner said.

"So did I, Turner," Andrew told him. "I can't remember your face."

"I remember yours, sir," Turner replied.

Andrew smiled faintly. "That war already seems long ago. If you rode with Buller, I'm sure you'll fit in."

"Thank you, sir."

"Go and report to Sergeant Meek at the Dragoons' barracks," Andrew ordered. "I am sure he'll find you something to do."

"Yes, sir." Turner gave a smart salute and marched away.

Andrew watched him for a moment, shook his head, and walked to the stables to check the horses. *Turner looks very regimental for one of Redvers' Bullers' boys.*

"A RIDER IS COMING TO THE FARM," ALETTA CALLED FROM THE EDGE OF THE field. "One of the native servants told me."

Jan had been working with the cattle, where a cow had a difficult birth. He had spent all morning helping the mother and had no interest in any visitor. He barely glanced up. "Pa can deal with him."

The horseman reined up in front of the house, with dust rising all around and froth and sweat covering the horse. He dismounted immediately, removed his hat to Aletta, and pounded off the dust against his leg.

"Is your husband at home, *vrou*?"

"Ja, *meneer*," Aletta nodded to the north. "You will find him out in the fields. My son Jan will take you."

Jan recognised the rider. "Adriaan Coetzee, wait a minute, *meneer*, and I will fetch my horse."

Adriaan carried himself with a grim self-assurance that he could face anything the world threw at him, and the rifle at his saddle looked well used.

"Why do you want my father, Adriaan?" Jan asked bluntly as they rode away from the farmhouse.

"It is about politics," Adriaan man said. "And war."

"The war is over," Jan replied. "There is my father with the dun cow."

Johannes straightened slowly to greet the visitor. "Many of my cows are calving," he said. "Good day, Adriaan. You are welcome to our farm."

"Thank you, Johannes," Adriaan took off his hat.

"And what is your business here, Adriaan?" Johannes asked, sweeping his hand around to indicate his cattle. "As you can see, I am busy here. My farm needs me."

"So does the republic, *meneer*," Adriaan told him. "The British have a spy in the western Transvaal."

Johannes wiped the blood from his hands on the seat of his trousers.

"What is there to spy on here? A few farms, a lot of empty veld, some native kraals, and too many rocks."

Adriaan ran a critical eye over Johannes' cattle. "Come, Johannes. We have been besieging a British garrison in the west for months without success. The spy is inside the *dorp*."

Johannes shook his head. "We have a truce with the British, Adriaan. There are no more sieges."

"This siege was left out of the truce," Adriaan replied. "We do not know why the British should send a spy, so we shall ask him."

"Then ask him, and don't bother honest men at their work." Johannes returned to his calving cow.

"To ask him first, we have to catch him," Adriaan explained. "He has holed himself into the *dorp* with other British around him."

"Which *dorp*?" Johannes asked with a feeling of resignation. "I do not want to return to war."

"Swartspruit," Adriaan told him. "You know it."

"I know it," Johannes confirmed. "There's nothing much there to besiege."

"I agree," Adriaan said. "That is also suspicious. The Groenburg Commando is closest, and with your help, we can end the siege and find out about this *Rooineck*. Will you come, Johannes?"

Johannes glanced at Jan, who stood nearby. "Did you hear that, Jan? This man wants us to ride to Swartspruit to catch a British spy."

"I heard," Jan replied briefly. "When do we leave?"

"Fetch my horse, Jan; she is knee-haltered a quarter of a mile away."

When Jan left, Johannes spoke to Adriaan. "Do you need me to help you find Swartspruit?"

Adriaan shook his head, smiling faintly. "We need all the local men we can raise, Johannes, and those of the Afrikander Bond who want to ride this far."

Jan brought Johannes' horse. "When are we leaving, Pa?"

"Are you ready to go back on commando so soon?" Johannes asked. "What about Engela?"

"Men go on commando, Pa," Jan said. "Engela is only a woman." *It is better to fight the Rooinecks than wait for a woman who no longer cares for me.*

Johannes nodded. "Do not disregard Engela so easily, Jan. She has not forgotten you."

"When are we leaving, Pa?" Jan repeated.

"We'll tell your mother first," Johannes said, knowing he would not enjoy that duty.

"Ah," Aletta looked at Jan without hiding her anxiety. "It is hard having two men in the house." Neither of them mentioned Mannie. She glanced at Konrad, who had been listening from the corner of the building. "You will be going as well, Konrad."

"In a day or two," Konrad said easily. "I have a report to write."

"To whom?" Aletta asked.

"To my superiors in Berlin," Konrad said. "I have to make a monthly report on my findings in the Zuid-Afrikaanse Republiek to justify my being here."

"I see," Aletta said. "How will you get it to them?"

"You will have heard of the Berlin Missionary Society?" Konrad said.

"I have," Aletta confirmed. "Alexander Merensky is a good man. He stays in Botshabelo, where he tries to Christianise the Sotho tribes."

"That is so," Konrad agreed. "Have you heard of the Wonderdorp Missionary Station?"

"Wonderdorp is in the Western Transvaal," Aletta said. "I know nothing about a missionary there."

"Wonderdorp is not a real missionary station, and the Berlin Missionary Society knows nothing about it," Konrad said. "It is the station where I send my reports, and they forward them to the coast and on to Berlin."

"Does that mean the Germans are already in the Republic?" Aletta asked.

Konrad smiled. "We are here. Soon, we will have colonies all over Africa to challenge the British and French."

"I see," Aletta stepped towards Johannes. "When will you men be riding away?"

"Very soon," Johannes replied.

"I'll make some bread for you," Aletta said.

ALETTA WAS IN THE DAIRY WHEN SHE SAW ENGELA ARRIVE.

"Good morning, Engela," Aletta called. "Come in."

"Abraham has gone back on commando," Engela entered the dairy. "Have your men gone to the wars?"

"Johannes and Jan have gone," Aletta was glad to recognise disappointment in Engela's face. *Good,* she thought. *She is angry with my son, but the true feeling also remains.* "Mannie wants to go, but he is still weak." She jerked her head backwards. "The Prussian is still here."

"Konrad?" Engela said.

"Ja, Konrad," Aletta confirmed.

"I rather liked Konrad," Engela said.

Do not play your games with me, Aletta thought. *I am not Jan.* "He can be very charming," she conceded.

"I thought so, too," Engela smiled as Konrad emerged from the house.

"Good morning, Engela," Konrad clicked his heels and gave a formal bow.

"Good morning, Konrad," Engela returned.

Aletta stepped between them. "Konrad had a very important report to complete," she said. "As soon as he finished, he will join the men." She smiled at the Prussian. "Is that not correct, Konrad?"

"That is correct," Konrad confirmed, his gaze roaming from Engela's head to her feet and back.

"That is good," Engela said. "A man must do his duty."

"If he does not," Aletta said softly. "He is less than a man." She felt Konrad stir behind her and knew her words had been successful. Konrad would leave the farm to join the Groenburg Commando.

❄

ANDREW VIEWED HIS MEN WITH GRIM SATISFACTION. EXCEPT FOR TURNER, all came from the Natal Dragoons, men whom he trusted with his life. He had sent Trooper Spalding for intensive training in the heliograph and knew his men would not let him down.

"All right, lads," Andrew said. "Most of you know me. We've fought together before, but I'll remind you of the rules. I am in charge, and the final decision and responsibility ends with me."

The Dragoons nodded, some smiling and others looking serious.

"This mission is a bit different," Andrew told them. Now, he had gathered his volunteers, he decided to tell them more. "We are riding to a place called Swartspruit in the Western Transvaal. Despite the ceasefire, a strong commando of Boers, members of the Afrikander Bond, are besieging a small British garrison, with some important fellow the Boers want to capture."

The men nodded again. They knew that wars never ended as tidily as politicians and newspapers claimed.

"We will relieve the garrison and bring them safely through the Transvaal to British territory," Andrew said. "Are there any questions?"

"How strong is the garrison, sir?" Sergeant Meek asked.

"We don't know," Andrew replied. "We know there are no regular British troops there, only local volunteers and civilians."

"If there are no soldiers there, sir, why are the Boers besieging it?" Meek asked. "Is it because of this important fellow?"

"I believe so, Sergeant," Andrew said. "But ours is not to reason why; ours is just to do or die."

"Yes, sir," Meek did not question further.

"Sir," Kerr asked, "How many Boers are there?"

"We don't know that either," Andrew replied. "The Boers don't have a command structure like ours. Their men seem to arrive and leave as they please or fight when they choose. They might have a hundred men one day and a thousand the next." He paused for a moment. "One thing is certain. If these are Afrikander Bond Boers, they will be hardy and determined."

"A thousand Afrikander Bond Boers, and how many of us, sir?" Lieutenant Fletcher asked. "Fourteen? That should be a fair match."

Andrew smiled. "I doubt there will be a thousand, Lieutenant. With the current truce, most Boers will be keen to return to their farms. There may be a couple of hundred or even less."

Fletcher gave an ironic smile. "Only about eight-to-one then, sir. That's much better."

Andrew laughed. "I'm glad you think so, Lieutenant! When we relieve the siege, we will head for this point," he showed them the twin kopjes on the map. "Once there, Spalding will heliograph to the east, where a larger British force will be waiting. We'll rendezvous with them and return together. Any questions?"

The men studied the map. "Memorise the details," Andrew said. "If I fall, any of you might have to take command. Whatever happens, the Boers must never capture the civilian we rescue."

Turner was not alone in nodding solemnly.

"Right, lads," Andrew altered his tone. "Before we begin, let's have a few reminders of the tricks of the trade. Check your horses; I don't want anybody riding a horse of a distinctive colour. That is an invitation to the Boers; some are phenomenal marksmen and will pick off a rider before he hears the shot."

The men agreed.

Andrew continued. "I know you are all aware of such basic details, but I thought I'd remind you."

"Always best, sir," Meek said. "Some of these lads don't have the brains of a turnip."

Andrew grinned. "That would be a small turnip at best. Secondly, don't bunch up if we get into action. Extended order presents a harder target."

The Dragoons nodded. The late war had reinforced their respect for the Boers' marksmanship.

"Thirdly," Andrew said, "if a long-range shot passes close, don't react. If you ignore the long-range shots, the Boer won't know how good he is and hopefully adjust his range to shoot short or over."

A few of the men nodded.

"All right," Andrew said. "Enough theory. Time for some practical training."

After long periods away from his men, Andrew decided to reacquaint himself with the intricacies of command. He had no intention of tormenting the Dragoons with all the formality of British cavalry drill but thought a return to some discipline might benefit them.

For the following two days, Andrew had his men advancing by sections and forming again, wheeling left and right, dismounting and remounting, firing at moving targets and changing front. After the initial sweat, toil, and frustration, Andrew eased the pressure. His men had lived most of their lives in the saddle, and he surmised that nothing would blunt their individuality more surely than repetitive manoeuvres.

"We all have Martini-Henry carbines," Andrew reminded his Dragoons. "We'll carry seventy rounds in our pouches and wear bandoliers with an extra seventy cartridges. If you want to carry a rifle with a longer range, that's entirely your choice. Likewise, if you wish to carry a revolver, then do so, but remember we're embarking on a long ride, and every ounce of extra weight will tell on the horse."

"Will we take spare horses, sir?" Kerr asked.

"Yes," Andrew replied. "We might need to ride hard." He ordered that each Dragoon carry a cloak, blanket, and rations for himself and his horses.

"We'll pick up food en route," Andrew told his men. "But not from farms. We aim to pass unseen if possible, so fishing and hunting are the order of the day, with packhorses carrying extra food, ammunition, and medical equipment. The Boer commandos travel light, and so will we."

"How about loot, sir?" Ogden asked with a villainous smile. "Are we allowed to relieve the Boers of their excess possessions?"

"No," Andrew shook his head. "We have a truce with the Transvaalers, so they are not our enemy. No looting." He paused for a moment's reflection. "That does not apply to anybody who attacks us. If a Boer fires on us and we kill him, his horse and any valuables on the man's body are ours. We don't touch personal letters and photographs, but we'll take any official documents back to Natal for the experts to analyse."

Andrew gave the Dragoons a moment to consider his words. "All right, gentlemen. Dismissed."

"I've heard that colonials were better irregular horsemen than British soldiers," Andrew said to Fletcher when the troopers had dispersed. "I disagree. Oh, the colonials are better than town-bred men whose experience of fieldcraft is limited to an annual camp on Salisbury Plain. However, Highland ghillies can stalk with the best of them, and given training or working with the colonials, the potential is still there."

"Even untrained colonials are better than the average Tommy," Fletcher disagreed. "They can read the stars and pick their way across trackless terrain, instinctively avoid the skyline and find dead ground and cover as well as any Boer."

Andrew grinned. "You've been watching the men, Fletcher. Good for you. Now, what we must do is train up our home-grown men to have the same skills."

Fletcher nodded. "Yes, sir. How do we do that?"

"We use the best men to teach the others, including you and me."

"We're officers, sir," Fletcher reminded him. "Should other ranks teach officers? Does that not blur the rank differences?"

"It will, and a damned good thing, too," Andrew said. "Any training will have to be hurried, unfortunately, but anything is better than nothing."

"Yes, sir, and a hell of a lot better than acting as baggage guard," Fletcher said.

Baggage guard was the least popular duty for mounted troops. The men rode in files of two beside a convoy of slow-moving wagons, with scouts posted further out to watch for the commandos. The outriders could get lost in the dark or even keep riding when the convoy stopped, while the men in files could fall asleep on the horse if they were working at night, leading to the horse wandering wherever it willed. If the Boers chose to attack, they would select the least defended section of the convoy, strike and vanish before the escort arrived.

"A lot better," Andrew agreed. "Let's get the men trained up."

However dangerous leading a small unit on a deep penetration mission may be, Andrew preferred the freedom of being in command to the stifling frustration of having some unimaginative senior officer in control. He wondered if he would ever fit into the real army, where strict routine reduced the flexibility of thought.

"A five-hour map reading exercise today," Andrew decided, "followed by some firing practice." He grinned. "Time to get to work, Fletcher."

❄

WITH EACH MAN LEADING A SPARE HORSE LOADED WITH EXTRA ammunition and supplies, Andrew's Natal Dragoons rode out of Newcastle for the north. Knowing that the Boers would watch the main passes, Andrew made a wide detour before he entered the Transvaal. The men quickly adapted to active service as Andrew rotated the outriders every two hours, kept them riding at a steady pace, and frequently stopped to water the horses.

Despite his worry for Mariana, Andrew could not deny his satisfaction at leading his Dragoons. He rode in front, glad to escape the back-aching foot soldier's pace and the perpetual grating dust of an infantry column.

Although the landscape did not alter, Andrew detected a subtle shift in the atmosphere immediately after crossing into the Transvaal. *Perhaps that is an instinct I inherited from my father.* He glanced over his shoulder where his men followed in column of twos, riding easily as the miles soothed past. Even with the ubiquitous film of dust over them, Andrew thought they looked professional, men who belonged in their environment rather than European intruders in Africa. He nodded, satisfied, guided Lancelot to a *koppie*, raised his field glasses, and scanned the surrounding terrain.

A small herd of antelope bounded to the east, presumably disturbed by the Dragoons' scouts. Andrew concentrated on the area until he was satisfied there were no Boers. Shifting his focus, he slowly traversed the land, searching for farms to avoid and watercourses for horses and men. Working with the most experienced Dragoon frontiersmen, he had already selected a route that avoided even the smallest *dorp*, but farms were not marked on the map.

Checking the flanks, Andrew looked to the rear and grunted when he saw two figures, distorted by heat and distance, and guessed who they were.

Andrew returned to the Dragoons. "Sergeant Meek!"

"Sir!" Meek rode closer. As dependable as always, he viewed Andrew from under the shade of his broad hat.

"Tell the scouts to extend their range, Sergeant. We're in the Transvaal now."

"Yes, sir," Meek replied.

"Extended order!" Andrew commanded, taking his men in a gliding walk under the glowing sun. He enjoyed the freedom of making the decisions, halting when it was best for his Dragoons, not for the slogging infantry or at the whim of a pedantic silver-haired general. Every half hour, he guided Lancelot to the nearest rise, lifted his field glasses, and surveyed the land.

He saw a ribbon of smoke from a lone farmhouse, the dust a herd of impala kicked up, and the endless yellow-brown plain of the veld.

"A man could get to like it here," Andrew said when he rejoined the Dragoons.

"Could he, sir?" Fletcher wrinkled his nose. "There's nothing here."

Andrew thought of the wind-cropped slopes of the Cheviot Hills, a place he considered home, and grinned. "Maybe that's why I like it," he said. He looked over his men, riding easily with their broad hats and bandoliers, looking as much like Boers as the Boers, sun-browned and confident. Even Turner looked competent in the saddle, although Andrew was not yet convinced that he fitted in.

As the Roman centurion in Matthew said, "I am a man under authority, having soldiers under me: and I say to this man, Go, and he goeth; and to another, Come, and he cometh; and to my servant, Do this, and he doeth it."

Do I like the power of command? Andrew asked himself. *Maybe I do. Maybe I am not the free thinker I believed I was, or perhaps the wars have changed me.*

At his next halt to survey the surroundings, Andrew checked behind them and again saw the two dots in the far distance, seemingly crawling across the vast landscape, yet he knew they were moving at the same speed as the Dragoons.

When they stopped to eat, Andrew ensured the pickets were alert.

"I know there's an armistice," he told his men, "But the Burghers may not take kindly to a unit of British soldiers crossing their land."

"We don't take kindly to some Boers besieging one of our outposts during a truce," Fletcher replied, and the men gave a deep-throated laugh.

When Andrew stopped to water the horses, he ensured the men filled their canteens upstream of the animals. The old rules applied: horses first, men second, officers last. Whenever Andrew checked the rear, the two figures were still there, retaining the same distance.

That first day in the Transvaal, the Dragoons camped in a small *sluit*, hidden from the never-ending plain above. The surrounding trees provided shade and shelter, as well as a plethora of birds and insects. Andrew saw a thoughtless Dragoon throw the reins of his horse over a thornbush, but before he spoke, Meek grabbed the unfortunate man.

"Does that bush look like a Dragoon, Ogden?"

"No, Sergeant," Ogden replied.

"We have three half-sections," Meek spoke in a forceful whisper. "Every fourth man is a horseholder. When we dismount, we give him the reins, either in action or when we camp. Is that clear?"

"Yes, Sergeant," Ogden agreed.

"It's basic drill," Meek drove his point home. "The horseholder looks after the mounts. If we were in action and you threw the reins over a bush, and the firing began, the horse would panic, and you'd have a hell of a job controlling it. The Boers would pick you off. Understand?"

"Yes, Sergeant," Ogden said.

"Right," Meek glowered at him. "You're on first picket duty tonight, Ogden."

Andrew hid his smile as he walked away. With Meek as his sergeant, sensible army discipline would continue wherever they were.

❄

Outside Swartspruit, Western Transvaal, June 1881.

Jan saw the dust from miles off. "A horseman is riding towards us," he said, sitting on the knoll with his rifle in his right hand, his eyes narrowed against the glare.

Johannes joined him, keeping low. He raised his field glasses. "A single rider," he said after a few minutes. "He rides like a Burgher but could be a British colonial. Here." Johannes passed the field glasses to Jan. "Keep an eye on him. When he gets close, let me know."

Jan raised the field glasses and watched, noting the easy way the man rode, the small, sturdy pony, and the long rifle in the bucket holster beside his saddle. "I think he is a Burgher," he said.

When the man was within a mile, Jan mounted his horse and rode to meet him. He lifted a hand in greeting.

"The Lord be with you," Jan recognised the man from the fighting around Potchefstroom.

The rider pulled up, watching Jan from beneath his terai hat. "And with you." He waited until Jan lifted his hat and did likewise. "What is your name?"

Jan noted the length of the man's beard and the leopard skin band around his terai hat. "I am Jan Van Collier of Nuve Hoop Plaas, *meneer*. I have seen you in various places where we fought the British, but we have never spoken. Nor do I know your name; you are?"

"Christiaan Niekerf." The man spoke without moving the pipe from his mouth. A lifetime of smoking had stained the beard around his mouth a dull yellow-brown while the rest was grey as it flowed to his chest. The leopard skin band around his hat was the only brightness in his attire.

"What do you seek, Oom Christiaan?"

Christiaan did not smile. "Johannes van Collier, the *veldcornet* of the Groenburg Commando," he said.

"My father," Jan explained. "Why do you want him?"

"He commands the only commando still fighting the *Rooinecks*," Christiaan explained. "I fought the *Rooinecks* at Boomplats, Laing's Nek, Ingogo River, and Majuba, and I will fight them until we drive them away. Take me to him."

"This way, *Oom* Christiaan," Jan turned his horse to return to the Boer positions. He could sense Christiaan following him and hear the steady plod of his pony's feet.

"Christiaan Niekerf," Johannes shook the elderly man's hand. "I remember you. You were a Voortrekker and fought with us at Potchefstroom."

"That is correct," Christian agreed.

"You are over sixty years old," Johannes said.

Christiaan nodded. "Ja," he said, "and over seventy. I have lived my allotted three score years and ten."

"The Republic does not require you to go on commando when you are over sixty," Johannes reminded him. "You can go home and live in peace."

"What would the Republic have me do? Waste away watching the grass grow?" Christiaan asked. "It is a man's part to defend his beliefs."

"Do you not have a family, Christiaan?" Johannes asked.

"I have buried three wives and two sons," Christiaan replied. "My daughters have their husbands and families to look after. All that remains is this," he tapped the stock of his rifle.

Johannes glanced at Jan, who was listening. "Then you are welcome, Christiaan. A man with your experience will always be useful."

"This may be my last commando," Christiaan said. "Let it be my best."

Jan thought Christiaan's old eyes were as keen as any hawk when he replaced his rifle in its homemade leather bucket.

❄

"Sir," Kerr rode up to Andrew. "There's somebody following us."

"Is there?" Andrew feigned surprise. "Best see who it is, Kerr."

"Yes, sir," Kerr said. "I think you already know, sir. It's Mariana Maxwell and Briggs, your servant."

"Mariana and Briggs!" Andrew repeated. "What the devil are they doing here?"

"Following us, sir, as far as I can make out," Kerr replied. "Do you want me to send them away?" He gave a crooked smile.

"No, Kerr," Andrew shook his head. "I'd better go myself. Lieutenant Fletcher! You're in command. I'll be back within the hour."

"Yes, sir," Fletcher replied.

As he rode back to fetch Mariana and Briggs, Andrew remembered his father telling him he had been campaigning during the Indian Mutiny, and his future wife, Andrew's mother, had joined them on campaign.

Maybe our family is destined to have spirited women, Andrew thought. *Except Mariana's not my woman,* he reminded himself. *I was going to marry her older sister, and I am only keeping a watchful eye on Mariana until she recovers.*

The two riders looked uncertain as Andrew drew closer. Although Briggs gave a nervous grin and saluted, Andrew ignored him to address the more pugnacious Mariana.

"What are you doing here, Mariana?" Andrew asked as he drew Lancelot to a halt.

"I'm coming with you," Mariana said calmly. "You knew I would."

"I told you not to," Andrew replied. "This is a dangerous mission."

"It's better than Robben Island," Mariana said. She smiled. "It would be noble to take me with you, Andrew. As Tennyson said, better not be at all than not be noble."[1]

Andrew hid his smile, for Mariana had been a prolific reader and quoter of Tennyson before the renegades raided Inglenook. Now, the quotes were few but welcome, a reminder of the bright personality bubbling behind her trauma.

"Come on, then," Andrew sighed.

I had sufficient responsibilities before Mariana appeared, but now she's here, I am happy to have her with me. The Boers won't shoot a woman, and I'll keep her well away from any fighting.

The Dragoons had helped rescue Mariana from her captivity at the end of the Zulu War and greeted her cheerfully.

"Welcome back, Miss Maxwell," Kerr said. "We've missed you."

"Thank you, Mark," Mariana replied.

Others waved and smiled as Mariana rode into the unit. Briggs remained at her back until Andrew ordered him to join the ranks.

"Congratulations, Briggs. You've volunteered to join a forlorn hope. [2] Report to Sergeant Meek, and he'll tell you what to do."

Briggs saluted. "Yes, sir."

WITH MARIANA RIDING IN THE MIDDLE OF THE DRAGOONS, ANDREW LED them deeper into the Transvaal, frequently consulting his map and checking on landmarks.

"Oh, look at that!" Mariana rode towards Andrew and pointed forward as a herd of a hundred springbok bounded before the dragoons. Andrew stopped to admire the deer he thought were the most beautiful of South African animals. Triple banded in white, brown, and fawn, the males boasted annulated horns for defence or show.

"This land has some truly noble animals, sir," Fletcher said. "It's a sportsman's paradise."

Andrew nodded. "We agree there."

The springbok caught the human scent, with their fluffy tails lifting straight in the air and white ruffs bristling on every sleek back. They bounced away, springing in the air as they crossed the veld in a display of grace and power. Even the most hardened Dragoon paused to watch the sight.

"Now that's something the people back in Britain will never see," Meek said. "It makes soldiering worthwhile, doesn't it, sir?"

Andrew nodded. "We are blessed sometimes," he agreed. "If we had shot one, we could all have feasted tonight." He saw no irony between his two statements.

"Shall I ride forward and bag one, sir?" Fletcher asked.

Andrew shook his head. "They're well away now, Lieutenant, but thank you for the offer."

They camped overnight with stars filling the high arc of the sky and frost crackling their blankets. Andrew listened to the eerie cries of a jackal and hoped such a notorious scavenger did not come near the camp.

With Mariana sleeping near the shaded fire, the safest place in the camp, Andrew was relatively content. He checked the knee-haltered horses and exchanged a few words with the pickets.

"All right, lads?"

"All right, sir," the pickets had chosen spots where they had a good view of the surrounding terrain as the bright stars illuminated the landscape. In the distance, a kopje showed darkly against the grey background.

If war were always this beautiful, I'd have no complaints. How can there be such serenity when we are carrying weapons to kill our fellow men?

Realising the stars had distracted him, Andrew nodded and moved on. He did not have to teach these veterans anything about watching by night. The jackal called again somewhere in the dark, a reminder that men were not the only predators in this land.

CHAPTER 18

BOER CAMP OUTSIDE SWARTSPRUIT, JUNE 1881

Konrad held his stomach and doubled up. "It's the fever," he said. He crouched on the ground, retching.

Behind the Boers, a small ridge overlooked the settlement of Swartspruit, with three sentinels lying behind bushes and examining the British positions beyond.

"Best rest until it passes," Johannes advised. He had seen many men sick with fever in the last few months. Most recovered and returned to duty. Others succumbed, died, and now filled sad graves on the veld.

"I think so," Konrad agreed. "I have an upset stomach, and my head is swimming, making me dizzy."

"That's not good," Johannes said.

Jan smiled as he walked away. He was on duty later that day, watching over Swartspruit. *I hope it's malaria.*

"Are you fit to continue with the siege?" Johannes asked.

"I cannot continue," Konrad said. "I would be a burden to the other men."

"It might pass in a day or two," Johannes told him solemnly.

"No," Konrad shook his head. "It feels more serious than that. I'd better get away in case I pass it on to everybody. It could be cholera."

"Cholera is a terrible thing," Johannes agreed. "It can kill a man in hours and spreads quickly. What will you do?"

"I will find a quiet place to recover or die without infecting anybody else," Konrad decided. "That is the honourable course as befits a Prussian officer."

Johannes did not object. "If you think that is best," he said. "I hope you get better and return to the commando." Johannes had long given up on Prussian help, and Konrad added nothing to the military power of the besiegers. He watched as Konrad saddled and mounted his horse, riding away without looking back.

We won't see you again, Johannes said to himself.

"Johannes," Karl slid down from his position on the ridge. "The British have added more men to the defences."

"How can they?" Johannes asked. "We have the place surrounded. Are they breeding them inside the *dorp*?" He scrambled up the ridge, lay down, and focused his field glasses. A row of men waited behind a stone-and-mud wall, with what looked like a disguised cannon in an emplacement further back.

"I don't know where they came from," Johannes said.

"We should attack now," Theunis suggested. "Before even more arrive."

"No," Johannes said. "Remember how many men we lost when we charged at Potchefstroom? The British have an open field of fire and a cannon. They will slaughter us."

"We have to capture this spy, this Charles Abercrombie," Theunis said.

"Why?" Johannes asked. "What good is he to us? Can we eat him?"

Theunis shook his head. "No; we can send him to the German Emperor, and then Germany will help us if the *Rooinecks* attack again."

Johannes nodded to the wisp of dust that marked Konrad's passage. "There goes the emperor's ambassador," he said. "I don't think the Germans will help us."

"I do," Theunis dragged hooked fingers through the tangle of dark hair across his face. "Konrad promised Germany's assistance."

"We'll see," Johannes said. He studied the tiny village again. "I don't know how the British could have passed reinforcements through our patrols without us noticing. I think they are only moving their men from place to place. We'll circle the *dorp* and count the defenders, Karl. You go left, I'll go right, and we'll meet back here to compare figures."

Karl nodded and headed left, dodging from cover to cover as he counted, while Johannes slid in the opposite direction. They met up half an hour later.

"I saw thirty-two," Karl reported.

"Thirty-one," Johannes said. "That's near enough. Did you see anybody at the gun?"

"No," Karl replied. "It's too well covered."

"The British might not always have men there," Johannes said. "We will say at least thirty British defenders. That's thirty rifles waiting for us if we attack, but thinly spread."

Karl nodded. "The *Rooinecks* have about a quarter of a mile of perimeter, but we'll have three hundred yards of open land to cover. The British could gather all their defenders to one spot in minutes."

"They'd knock down too many of our men if we attack," Johannes decided. "We'll remain as we are; keep them under observation and fire when we see a definite target."

"I agree," Karl said.

Theunis shook his head. "I think that will take too long."

"It will save lives," Johannes told him.

❄

ANDREW HALTED BESIDE A BLACK KAREE TREE, ADJUSTED HIS HAT TO FIND the maximum of shade, and looked around. The land seemed to stretch forever, limitless, flat, and featureless, save for the scattered *kopjes.* He could taste the Kalahari dust in his mouth as he lifted his field glasses and studied Swartspruit, baking under the eternal sun. The garrison had thrown up a five-foot-high wall with a ditch to defend a dozen flat-roofed houses with a central well.

"Why the devil would anybody want to settle here?" Andrew compared the fertile farms around Berwick-upon-Tweed to this arid, sun-tortured landscape.

"Why indeed?" Fletcher replied, waving his hand in a vain attempt to ward off a score of questing flies.

"Freedom," Mariana had followed them quietly. "These people want to escape civilisation with its boundaries and restrictions. They can live as they please out here on the edge of nowhere."

"It's a hard life they choose," Fletcher said.

"Freedom is sweet," Mariana replied. "That's why the Boers are prepared to fight so tenaciously to retain it."

Andrew traversed his field glasses to survey the Boer positions.

Between five and seven hundred yards outside the British perimeter, the Boers waited in three small wagon laagers, with horsemen riding to and fro and pickets watching Swartspruit. Andrew tried calculating the Boer numbers, checking each section of the besiegers' positions and counting the men he saw.

As Andrew lowered his field glasses, the sun set in a startling blaze of red, orange, and yellow. He watched without expression, aware that the very beauty of the sunset was a reminder that beyond the horizon lay the Kalahari Desert, a vast, thirsty land devoid of water or anything green or growing.

"How many Boers would you say?" Andrew handed the binoculars to Fletcher.

"Not a huge number," Fletcher said. "I doubt there are more than a hundred in total."

"We have fifteen men and one woman," Andrew said. "The Boers outnumber us seven to one, maybe less than that if there are any fighting men inside the British camp." He reclaimed the binoculars. "We'll also have the advantage of surprise, and our men are equal to any Boer." He grinned, remembering Major Fotheringham's advice to keep his men under control. "We're not red-coated infantry trained to march like marionettes and fire volleys at static targets."

"That's right, sir," Fletcher said. "Do you have a plan to get through the Boer defences?"

Andrew nodded. "Go for it bald-headed, like the Marquis of Granby."

"Who, sir?"

"He was a cavalry commander during the Seven Years War," Andrew explained. "He led a charge in a long-forgotten battle, and his wig fell off, giving us the phrase 'to go for it bald-headed.'"[1]

"I see, sir," Fletcher said diplomatically. "Do you mean we'll just charge them?"

"Yes," Andrew replied. "Keep together, hit them as one body, and not as a scatter of men, and we'll punch through their defences."

"What about Mariana, sir? She can't ride like us."

Andrew worried about Mariana. He had the choice to leave her out on the veld with Briggs and pick her up later, or bring her with the Dragoons. If he left her on the veld, the Boers might find her, and there was the danger of wild animals and food to consider. However, if Mariana rode with the main body, a stray bullet could hit her.

"Mariana grew up on a farm on the Natal-Zululand border," Andrew said. "She's been riding horses all her life, and if we place her in the centre of the men, they'll protect her."

"As you wish, sir," Fletcher said stiffly.

"I want two men with spare horses at the rear to pick up any casualties or men who fall from their mounts."

"I'll act as rearguard, sir, and take Kerr."

Andrew nodded. He would have preferred to be in the rear, the position of most danger, but he had to lead his men.

"We'll find where the Boers are weakest," Andrew said. "I want to hit hard, rescue the garrison, including this troublesome civilian, and return to Natal."

"Every Boer commando north of the Vaal will be after us."

"I know," Andrew said. "Thankfully, the truce will mean most men are back on their farms, so hopefully, by the time they've reassembled, we'll be well on our way." He considered for a moment. "All the same, we'll need more than pluck and determination. We'll need some cunning as well."

Fletcher nodded. "You and I must do the thinking," he said solemnly. "The men are decent enough fellows, but they are hardly suited to solving the intricate problems of command."

Andrew grunted. "Did you see some of the decisions the senior officers made in the late war with the Boers? Or with the Zulus?" *I should not criticise senior officers in front of a subaltern, but it's time Fletcher saw things as they are.*

When Fletcher looked uncomfortable, Andrew continued. "The British soldier will do his best. At Potchefstroom, we saw what he is capable of when well-led. The swaddies will do their duty."

Fletcher nodded.

"The British officer is as brave as he's always been, but many don't seem to understand that bravery is insufficient. The Boers have outfought and outgeneralled us. They fight to their strengths and our weaknesses."

"Yes, sir," Fletcher said.

"You and I had better prove the exception to a sad rule, Fletcher. Let's prepare the men to outthink and outmanoeuvre the wily Boer."

A handful of Dragoons and one woman against a veteran Boer commando. Let's see how good we are. Andrew took the men aside, explaining what he required.

"We hit them at night, shoot our way through and enter Swartspruit. I want everyone to make as much noise as possible. Try to sound like the entire Household Cavalry is breaking through their position. Shout, yell, sing songs, play the bugle, fire your rifle, anything you like."

Kerr grinned. "I have heard of people who try to sneak through the enemy positions, sir."

"So have I," Andrew said. "And another time, that would be the best policy. Tonight, I want speed and shock."

"I see, sir," Kerr said.

"We'll do our best, sir," Ogden promised.

"Keep silent until I give the word," Andrew said. "We'll get as close as possible and then make them think General Wood has led half the British army here, with Redvers Buller commanding the other half at his back."

Although some of the men smiled, most looked solemn. An advance through fixed positions held by expert Boer riflemen was not a pleasant prospect.

"Muffle your horse's shoes and ensure the equipment does not rattle," Andrew ordered. "We'll creep up slowly and quietly. I don't want them to hear us until we're close enough to unbutton their coats."

More Dragoons smiled at Andrew's attempted humour. "Will do, sir," Kerr replied.

"Cover anything that might reflect the moonlight," Andrew continued. "We're going to surprise Brother Boer and scare him senseless."

"How about me?" Mariana asked. "Can I have a rifle?"

"No," Andrew shook his head. "You are a civilian. I don't want to give the Boers any excuse to shoot at you. Stay in the middle of the men and concentrate on riding like the devil. Don't look to the left or right, just ride."

Mariana nodded. "Do you want me to make a noise as well?"

"Yes," Andrew decided. "Shout your head off!"

Mariana smiled. "I can do that," she said.

Andrew treasured that rare smile, although he was unsure if it was because Mariana looked more like Elaine when she smiled or for herself. He wrestled with the question for a moment, decided it was unimportant, and concentrated on the matter at hand.

For the remainder of that afternoon, Andrew studied the Boer positions, marking where their pickets were and the numbers of men. He noted the horse lines, their patrol routes, and what routine they adopted. Occasionally, he lifted his field glasses to inspect Swartspruit. Andrew noted the Union Flag hanging limply under the burning sun, the row of riflemen waiting patiently behind the wall, and the barrel of a piece of artillery pointing toward the Boer laagers.

"Swartspruit has a larger garrison than I expected," Andrew told Fletcher. "And artillery as well. At least a nine-pounder by the length of the barrel.

General Hook didn't mention that." He lowered his field glasses. "Swartspruit is well capable of defending itself without us."

We're not here to reinforce the garrison. We're here to get Charles Abercrombie to safety before the Boers or the Prussians capture him. That's our only objective.

When the sun set with its usual brilliant display of red and orange, the African night sounds began. Andrew waited an hour, allowing the Boer sentries to lapse into the boredom of watching nothing as the stars gradually filled the sky.

"Right, lads," Andrew whispered. "Follow my lead. Once we're close to Swartspruit, halt and shout who we are, or our own people will fire at us."

Fletcher passed on the order, and Sergeant Meek ensured everybody understood. When Andrew was sure his men were ready, he lifted a hand and pushed Lancelot forward.

Half a league, half a league, half a league onward,
Into the Valley of Death.

The Dragoons moved off in silence, with pads muffling the soft thud of hooves in sand and cloth shielding every item of equipment. The stars illuminated their road as Andrew felt his heart race. He remembered where the Boers had their outposts and guided his men to the least observed spot. He hoped Mariana kept her head down, wondered if he should have left her, knew it was too late to change his decision, and pushed on, listening for Boer voices.

Somewhere in the dark, a wild dog yapped while the howling of a pack of hyenas lifted the small hairs on the back of Andrew's neck. He smelled a drift of tobacco smoke and heard the low rumble of a man's voice, speaking the *Taal.*

Lancelot stumbled and recovered. Andrew patted his neck and walked on, fighting the urge to increase his speed. The closer the Dragoons came to the Boer positions without being detected, the safer they would be.

"*Wie is daar*? Who is there?"

Andrew heard the challenge from his left.

Here we go! They've seen us!

Lifting his carbine, Andrew fired towards the voice. "Come on the Household Brigade!" he shouted. "Give them hell!"

The Dragoons responded immediately, shouting and roaring, firing their rifles, and with Ogden blowing his bugle like a demented musician. Andrew heard the various slogans yelled behind him.

"Forward the Guards!"

"Blues forever!"

"Everything's Sir Garnet!"

"We're coming for you, Brother Boer!"

"God save the Queen!"

And the last, "Remember Majuba!" shouted out with the final syllable extended until it was like the howl of a wolf.

Andrew had never heard that slogan before but guessed it would resonate across the country. The British Army did not like defeats and used them to spur future success. Andrew wondered if the Boers would live to regret their victory on the steep slopes of the Hill of Doves.[2]

"Come on, lads!" Andrew encouraged, guiding Lancelot with his knees as he pushed his carbine into its bucket and drew his revolver. "Come on, the Natal Dragoons!"

A surprised Boer picket only fired two shots, and then Andrew was past and galloping towards Swartspruit. He holstered his revolver, took the reins in both hands, and spurred forward, enjoying the sensation of speeding through the night. He heard his men behind him, still shouting their slogans with Ogden's bugle blaring brassily. Some men fired their carbines, adding to the confusion. Lights flared ahead as the noise alerted Swartspruit's defenders.

"Halloa!" Andrew shouted. "British cavalry! British cavalry! Halloa there!"

He heard shouts, saw the sudden flare of watchfires and saw a low rampart with a couple of hats silhouetted against the light.

"British cavalry!"

The horses' hooves were hammering behind Andrew as the passage through the Boer positions had loosened or removed their coverings.

I hope Mariana is all right. I can't hear her shouting.

"Halt!" Andrew shouted, holding up a hand. "Halt!" he hoped his men would hear him before a nervous British sentry opened fire. One by one, the Dragoons pulled up, with only Ogden continuing the mad charge before he, too, stopped at the rampart and lowered his bugle.

"Who are you?" A man's voice demanded. Andrew saw his figure silhouetted beside a watch fire, rifle in hand.

"Captain Andrew Baird of the Natal Dragoons!" Andrew replied.

"Come to the light, Captain Andrew Baird," the defender told him. "We'll let you in. Any tricks, and there are a hundred rifles pointed at you."

"A hundred rifles be damned," Meek murmured. "If he had a hundred men, he'd chase the Boers back to Pretoria."

Andrew pushed toward the light to see two men waiting at a small gap in the wall. One was middle-aged, with the light reflecting from his bald head. The other was older, with a long hunting rifle in his hands, the muzzle aimed at Andrew's chest.

"How do we know you are British?" the bald man asked.

"If we were Boers, you'd be dead by now!" Andrew saw a long row of rifles on the wall, all pointing towards the Boer positions. The men behind remained still, dark shadows in the night.

"Come in," the bald man invited. "Slowly."

A rifle cracked behind them, a reminder that the Dragoons were caught between two fires. Andrew saw Fletcher and Kerr in the rear, making sure nobody straggled and felt relieved when he saw Mariana riding entirely composed amid the Dragoons.

"After me, boys!" Andrew led his Dragoons through the gap, stepped aside, and counted them all in. Immediately the Dragoons were inside the defences, the two sentries manoeuvred a gate back in position. Heavy with sandbags and topped with spikes, it appeared a formidable obstacle to any attacker.

"Who's in charge here?" Andrew asked. He frowned to see the other defenders had not moved when the Dragoons entered the compound. They remained at the low wall, facing the Boers, who had only fired a few desultory shots.

The two defenders glanced at each other before the older man spoke. "I suppose that must be me," he said. "Bernard Booth at your service, sir. Why are you here?"

"General Hook sent us when he heard the Boers still besieged you," Andrew did not mention Abercrombie. "How many men do you have?" He glanced at the static defenders.

"Seven," Booth said without emotion. "And two women."

Andrew jerked a finger at the dark shadows on the wall. "It looks a lot more than seven to me."

Booth shook his head, ignoring a sudden fusillade of shots from the besiegers. "They're dummies," he said. "To fool the Boers."

Dummies! No wonder they didn't react when we arrived. Booth is keeping back an entire Boer commando with a handful of men and a great deal of bluff.

"Return the Boer fire," Andrew shouted, and his Dragoons ran to the wall, threw themselves down and fired at the muzzle flashes.

"Sir!" Ogden shouted. "Half these men aren't men!"

"They're to fool the Boers!" Andrew said. "Fire!"

"Some of them haven't even got real rifles," Ogden said. "They're just bits of wood!"

Booth ran to a rope that ran through the trigger guards of the dummies' rifles. "Fire a volley!" he shouted, pulling the rope that operated the triggers. Six rifles fired at once.

"How about the nine-pounder?" Andrew asked as Booth grinned at him, and the bald man ran from rifle to rifle, reloading each from a box of cartridges. "It's made of wood," Booth said.

"That's clever," Andrew allowed. "Who thought of that?"

"Our pet geologist," Booth said. "He's a bundle of ideas, that man."

"Is that Charles Abercrombie?" Andrew asked. "Where is he?"

Booth jerked his head toward the main settlement. "I'll take you to him."

"Fletcher!" Andrew shouted. "Take command of the Dragoons." *At last, I'll meet the man who caused all the fuss.*

JAN HEARD THE SUDDEN ROAR FROM THE PICKET NEXT TO HIS, FOLLOWED BY the abrupt muzzle flare of a rifle. The noise rose, unmistakable British voices mingled with the blare of a bugle.

"Alert!" He shouted. "The British have arrived!" He fired his rifle towards what sounded like hundreds of British cavalrymen crashing through the outer picket line. The British roared as if they believed that noise alone could regain the Transvaal for Queen Victoria. "Alert!"

The racket brought other Boers from their tents and wagons. They ran toward the picket line, thrusting hats on their heads and holding their rifles ready.

"What is happening? Where are the British?"

"It is a major attack! General Wood must have brought his army!"

"Hundreds of them! Where did they come from?"

Some Boers fired towards the noise, while others looked over their shoulders as if preparing to ride away.

"Stand!" Johannes stilled the incipient panic. "We don't know what's happening!" He looked around. "Jan! Where are you?"

"Over here!" Jan ran to his father's side.

"See if there are any casualties!"

Jan nodded and ran towards the break-in point.

Theunis emerged from his tent, rifle in hand and his hair a tangled black mane down his back and across his face. "Send them back!" he shouted. He fired towards the noise, ejected the spent cartridge, and fired again. Before Theunis fired a third time, the noise had subsided, and the British had gone.

"Jan!" Johannes shouted as his son returned to his side.

"They moved fast," Jan said, thumbing a cartridge into the breech of his rifle. "We have no casualties."

"British cavalry," a stunned picket said. "I didn't hear them until they were close."

"They shouted 'The Guards' and 'Blues forever'," another Boer said.

"We are fighting the Brigade of Guards," the first man said.

"Ja," Theunis said. "They have sent their best against us!"

"Why send the Guards to Swartspruit?" Johannes asked. "There is nothing here for them." He shook his head. "That was not the Guards."

"Whoever they were, there were hundreds of them." Jan fired towards the British camp, reloaded, and fired again, ducking when the defenders replied with an ill-aimed volley. "They made as much noise as an army."

Johannes shook his head. "The British can be *slim* sometimes," he said. "Because they made a noise like an army does not mean they were an army. It may mean they want us to believe they are an army." He put a hand on Jan's rifle. "Stop wasting ammunition, Jan. In the morning, we shall see how many *Rooinecks* there were."

As the firing died away, Johannes reorganised the shaken besiegers, doubled the pickets, and ordered the mounted patrols to increase their vigilance.

"There might be more *Rooinecks*," Johannes warned. "If you hear anything, fire!"

"It might be our men," Karl said.

"Our men know to be quiet."

When dawn broke, Johannes accompanied Jan and Theunis to where the British had broken through. The closest sentry lifted his rifle until Johannes reassured him.

"See?" Johannes knelt on the ground, examining the hoofprints. "There were not hundreds of *Rooinecks*." He shook his head. "Look at the spoor, Jan. There are only thirty horses here, perhaps thirty-two or thirty-five." He measured the depth of the prints with an experienced eye. "Some prints are deeper than others, so maybe half the horses bore riders, and the others were spares. I'd say fifteen, sixteen men at most."

"It sounded like hundreds," Jan defended himself.

"The British wanted us to believe there were hundreds," Johannes said. "We are dealing with a *slim* man, Jan. This is a new type of *Rooineck* from the soldiers we defeated at Majuba." He ran a hand over his bearded face. "Who has General Wood sent against us?" He smiled. "Not the Brigade of Guards."

"I don't know," Jan said. "It is not the same redcoats General Colley led. These men are cunning."

"These men are dangerous," Johannes replied. "We've only held them under siege in Swartspruit. We should be more active now and push them harder."

Theunis stamped his feet. "Good," he said. "We'll destroy the *Rooineck* soldiers, capture the spy and hand him over to the Prussians." He tapped his rifle. "We can end this British occupation in a couple of days."

"ARE YOU THE GEOLOGIST?" ANDREW ASKED.

The man was about thirty, with a ready smile on a pleasant, clean-shaven face. "That's me," he extended his hand. "You've had a long ride from Natal to get here."

"That's correct," Andrew said, shaking the man's surprisingly strong hand. "Could you confirm your name, please?"

"Don't you know?" the geologist looked surprised. "I thought my name prompted Shepstone to send a rescue party. It certainly isn't because of my importance." He laughed self-deprecatingly.

"Who are you, sir?" Andrew asked.

"Charles Abercrombie," the geologist said and waited for Andrew's response. "Does that mean anything to you?"

"Not a thing," Andrew admitted cheerfully. "Except you are the fellow we are looking for."

Abercrombie looked disappointed for a moment. "Have you come to rescue us?"

"That's the plan," Andrew told him.

"Jolly good," Abercrombie replied. "How are you going to do that?"

"I'm not sure yet," Andrew confessed. "I'll have to look around the town first."

"I'll accompany you," Abercrombie said. "I could use the exercise and the diversion. There's nothing more tedious than sitting in a besieged village."

The circuit of Swartspruit took only twenty minutes, with Abercrombie pointing out the trenches, walls, and other defensive efforts the tiny garrison had constructed. "Boothie is a good man," he said cheerfully. "He does his best with limited resources, but if the Boers decided to attack in earnest, they'd walk right in. Dummies and bluff won't stop a determined Burgher forever."

Andrew smiled. "You've done splendidly so far." He scanned the Boer lines in the growing light, noting the waiting pickets and slow-riding patrols. "Unfortunately, our arrival has stirred them a little."

"You made enough noise about it," Abercrombie replied.

Andrew grunted. "That was the idea."

Returning to the Dragoons, Andrew drew up a plan of Swartspruit, sketching in the defences and the Boer positions and adding his estimation of the enemy's patrol routes. After consulting with Booth and Abercrombie, he finalised his plans.

"Here's my idea," Andrew addressed the entire garrison of Swartspruit, plus his Dragoons. "We're going to break out of here and head back to Natal, but the Boers will expect that, so we'll have to fool them."

"They're not easily fooled," Booth murmured. "They have a new man in charge, Johannes van Collier of the Groenburg Commando."

"Johannes van Collier?" Andrew said. "We met at Majuba. He's a decent man."

"And a good commander," Booth said.

Andrew nodded. "That's unfortunate. Do you have a farrier in the *dorp*? A blacksmith with a forge?"

Abercrombie shook his head. "We have a forge," he said, "but no farrier."

"It's the forge I want," Andrew confirmed. "All my men can shoe a horse. I want every horse shoed backwards. I want men to go on patrol tonight unseen but with sufficient noise to let the Boers know they were there."

"Shoe the horses backwards, sir?" Meek's tidy military mind objected to such an idea.

"It's an old Border trick," Andrew said. "I grew up partly on the Scottish-English Border, and the local reiving families were full of guile and trickery. If we shoe the horses back to front and the Boers find the spoor, as they will, they might believe even more reinforcements have arrived."

Abercrombie nodded. "You're a cunning man, Captain."

"I also want patrols day and night around the perimeter. I want the ground churned with so many hoofprints that the Boers won't be able to follow us for a while when we leave."

"That means a lot of work." Booth frowned.

"The Boers won't know if we're coming or going," Andrew explained. "Confusing the enemy is always a small victory."

Fletcher smiled. "Have you ever heard of a man named Fighting Jack Windrush, sir?"

"The name is slightly familiar," Andrew admitted.

"I've heard he was full of tricks, sir," Fletcher said. "I think you must be related."

Andrew did not tell Fletcher that he was Jack Windrush's son. "Right, gentlemen," he said. "I want to leave Swartspruit at night yet make the Boers believe we are still here. By the time they realise we are gone, I want to be miles away. Any ideas?"

"Keep the campfires burning," Fletcher replied immediately.

"That's a start," Andrew agreed. "And Mr Abercrombie's idea of dummy soldiers is also good. I wish we could make them move."

"That might be difficult," Abercrombie said. "Steam power, perhaps?"

"Do we have steam power here?" Andrew asked as some of his men laughed at the ridiculous proposal.

"Not even a little bit," Abercrombie admitted.

"If the dummies are too static," Andrew said, "the Boers will suspect we're up to something and come forward to have a look."

"We can discourage them with tripwires," Kerr said. "Tripwires and pits."

Andrew nodded. "We'll have to set them up at night. Boer marksmen will shoot anybody outside the perimeter during the day."

"How about a distraction, sir?" Sergeant Meek asked. "We can do something to take the Boer's attention from Swartspruit."

"What do you have in mind, Sergeant?"

"I'm not sure, sir, but I heard that the Boers tried to lure the 21st out of Potchefstroom with a false message and explosions like artillery. We could try something similar here."

Andrew nodded, with his mind working busily. "Do you have any gunpowder in Swartspruit?"

"A few pounds," Booth replied cautiously.

"How many pounds?" Andrew asked. "Five? Ten?"

"No, about seventy," Abercrombie told him. "I'm a geologist, remember. I use the gunpowder to blow up rocks to get samples to examine."

"I thought you people used a small hammer," Andrew said.

"Oh no, I can happily blow things up," Abercrombie told him. "We don't mind how large the rocks are. What's in your mind, Captain?"

"Playing brother Boer at his own game," Andrew said. "Now, I'm thinking on my feet here, so if anybody has any ideas or sees flaws in my plans, speak up."

The men nodded, with Fletcher still surprised at Andrew's democratic approach to leadership. The Sandhurst-educated officers of his acquaintance worked in a more authoritarian manner.

"We can use Sergeant Meek's suggestion," Andrew said. "At Potchefstroom, the Boers pretended that a British relief column was coming. We might be able to do the same."

"How, sir?" Fletcher asked.

"If we heliograph in the opposite direction from that we intend to leave, we might make the Boers think a relieving force is approaching."

"The Boers will see there's no answering flashes, sir," Meek said.

"We can try using very short messages at irregular intervals," Andrew replied. "We'll be on and off before the Boers have time to look." He grinned. "Hopefully. Then, if we can use Mr Abercrombie's gunpowder to make an explosion, we can add to the confusion."

The men nodded, with a low murmur of conversation revealing they were discussing Andrew's plan. He gave them a few moments before he continued.

"Are there any other suggestions?"

"I have one," Mariana lifted a hesitant hand.

"What's that, Mariana?" Andrew hid his pleasure that Mariana's mind was working again.

"Can we split the Boers' forces? Can we make some of them look for the relieving column, and the others remain outside the perimeter as if there are still men garrisoning Swartspruit?"

"How?" Fletcher asked.

"I liked the idea of having the dummies move," Mariana spoke slowly, gathering confidence as she realised most Dragoons were paying attention. "I was thinking about how to make that happen, and I thought of using sand or goats."

"Sand or goats?" Andrew silenced Fletcher's snort of contempt with a lift of his palm. "Could you explain further, Mariana?"

"When we had a leopard hunting our livestock at Inglenook," Mariana held Andrew's gaze as she concentrated on her explanation. "We tied up a goat as bait, and when the leopard came to get the goat, Father shot the leopard. Now, the goat was never still. It knew it was in danger and moved all the time." As she warmed to her subject, Mariana's speech quickened. "Maybe we can tie a goat to a couple of the dummies; give it just enough rope to move so it pulls the dummies around as if they were also moving."

Andrew nodded. "That might work," he said. "Would the Boers see them in the dark?"

"They would if you placed the dummies near the firelight," Mariana replied.

Andrew nodded. "We could try that if we had some goats."

"We can get goats," Abercrombie said cheerfully, looking at Mariana. "That's an imaginative idea."

"You also mentioned sand," Andrew reminded.

"It might not work," Mariana said. "But if we fill one of the dummies with sand and make a little hole so the sand leaks out, the dummy will slowly change shape as if it was moving."

"You have more in your mind," Andrew was beginning to understand Mariana's body language.

"Yes," Mariana said. "This is only an idea, but if some of the dummies fired their rifles, would that not make them more realistic?"

"It would," Andrew agreed as Fletcher shook a doubting head at the idea of a dummy firing its rifle.

"We could have a cable through two or three trigger guards," Mariana said, "and two buckets attached to each, with the top bucket full of sand and the lower bucket empty. We make holes in the top bucket, so the sand trickles into the lower bucket at different speeds, and the lower bucket attached to the trigger, so when the lower bucket is full, the weight pulls the trigger, and it fires."

"By God, that's clever," Andrew looked at Mariana with new respect.

"We could have different levels of sand so the rifles fire at different times to keep the Boers busy while we escape at the rear of the *dorp*," Mariana said and trailed away. "It's only an idea."

"And it's a good one!" Andrew said. "We've plenty of sand, but I've no idea about buckets."

"We can find something, surely," Abercrombie said, giving Mariana a hug. "You're a clever lass, aren't you?"

"Well, we have work to do," Andrew said. "Can anybody think how to distract the Boers with an explosion behind their lines? If you do, let me know."

"I could take a barrel into the bush and blow it up," Kerr said.

"That's a dangerous mission," Andrew reminded.

Kerr shrugged. "I've lived and worked in the bush all my life. When do you want me to go?"

"In two nights' time," Andrew knew Kerr was an excellent bushman. "See Mr Abercrombie for the gunpowder. Thank you, Kerr."

Kerr shrugged and lifted a hand to Abercrombie.

That's one problem sorted; now all I need is three or four spare rifles, a couple of goats, and half a dozen empty buckets.

CHAPTER 19

"We should raid them," Theunis said. "Go over at night and kill the British sentries."

Jan nodded. "That is a good idea," he agreed. "We need to take the fight to them." He thought of Engela and pushed her memory away. As she did not want him anymore, only war remained. "Let's attack them, Pa. Let's chase the *Rooinecks* back to London."

"That is not the way," Johannes eyed his son, worried about his new thirst for blood. "We have an armistice with the British except for their spy here at Swartspruit. Once we capture him, we will keep our word. We wanted our republic, and we have it."

"The British still have control over our foreign policy," Theunis said. "We want them gone completely from Africa."

"Ja! Completely!" Jan repeated Theunis's words. "This is our land."

"We have won the war," Johannes said. "Let's finish this last part and return to our farms."

They looked up at the explosion half a mile to the rear. "*Rooinecks!*" Jan shouted. "They are behind us!"

"Gather the commando," Theunis shouted. "The *Rooinecks* are attacking."

"Wait!" Johannes said. "Where are they?"

A second explosion followed the first, and then a third, all behind the Boer lines.

"There they are," Theunis pointed at the orange flashes. "They're firing cannon at us."

"Where are the shells landing? Nowhere! Not even the *Rooinecks* are that bad shots," Johannes said, but a dozen men had already rallied to Theunis, gripping their rifles and shouting that the British were attacking.

"Jan! Don't go!"

"I must go, Pa," Jan shouted. "We have to get rid of the *Rooinecks*!"

"Stay with me, Jan!"

Jan hesitated, looking from Johannes to Theunis and back. "Yes, Pa," he said reluctantly.

Only Karl and Jan remained with Johannes when Theunis led the Groenburg Commando towards the explosions.

"See what the British are doing at Swartspruit," Johannes ordered. "I think they're playing games."

Karl edged forward, ducking when one of the defenders fired.

"That was close," he said. "The *Rooinecks'* shooting has improved."

"We've taught them well," Johannes replied as another defender fired, with the bullet rising far above them. "That man didn't pay attention to the lessons."

Jan scanned the darkness behind them. "These explosions have stopped," he said. "But I can't hear any shooting. Theunis hasn't found the *Rooinecks*."

"Unless the British have bayonetted them all," Karl said.

Jan shivered as he remembered the glint of the sun on British bayonets at Potchefstroom. "The good Lord save us from that."

"We'll wait here," Johannes decided. "Things will be clearer in the morning."

Jan lay down and aimed his rifle at the British positions. "Yes, Pa. If I hear anything, I'll fire towards the sound."

"You do that," Johannes said.

THE DARKNESS EASED INTO AN ORANGE DAWN, WITH THE DRAGOONS AND the tiny Swartspruit garrison riding steadily towards the rising sun. Kerr's explosions had faded into memory, and the intermittent musketry behind them proved that Mariana's sand and goat idea had succeeded.

"Let's hope we've confused the Groenburg Commando," Fletcher said.

"Every hour gives us a better chance," Andrew replied. "If we reach the twin *koppies* and send our helio signal, we're home and dry. We'll rendezvous with the larger force and get back to Natal."

"Three days to the twin *koppies*," Fletcher said.

"Three days, and we have a decent head start and spare horses," Andrew agreed. "With luck, we should make it." He peered into the dark. "Let's hope that Kerr finds us."

Andrew pushed them hard, listened for pursuit, hearing nothing except the normal African night sounds. An hour after dawn, Andrew halted to feed the men and horses, then allowed them two hours' rest before starting again.

"Don't rush," Andrew warned. "We don't want to raise too much dust. Keep it slow and steady." He signalled to Fletcher. "Take over; head for the twin *koppies*."

"Yes, sir. Where are you going?"

"To look for Boers. Johannes van Collier is a capable commander."

Andrew rode to a small ridge and scanned the veld. He saw the smoke of a couple of farms but no Boer commando. Satisfied, he returned to the Dragoons to see Mariana talking to Abercrombie.

"Any sign of Kerr yet, Fletcher?"

"No, sir."

"Keep an eye open. I told him our route, but it's easy to get lost out here."

"Andrew," Mariana pushed her horse beside him as they moved slowly across the baking plain. "I was talking to Charles."

"I noticed," Andrew said. He tried to quell his pang of jealousy, knowing it was a sign of Mariana's recovery that she could talk to people.

"Do you know who he is?"

"He is a geologist," Andrew replied, more abruptly than he intended.

"That's *the* Charles Abercrombie," Mariana lowered her voice as if the veld were listening.

"*The* Charles Abercrombie? I don't know the significance of the name," Andrew admitted.

Mariana shook her head. "I presume you know who William Gladstone is?" She was vaguely mocking, with laughter a welcome addition in her eyes.

"I believe he's the prime minister," Andrew replied. "We haven't rescued him, too, have we?"

"No," Mariana shook her head. "We've rescued his nephew. Charles Abercrombie is the prime minister's nephew."

"Dear God in heaven!" Andrew glanced back at their cheerful companion. "Thank you, Mariana. That explains a lot."

Gladstone's nephew! No wonder General Hook wants him safe. And no wonder the Boers wish to capture him. With a relative of the Prime Minister as a hostage, Kruger could pressure the British government into giving the Transvaal complete independence, including control of their foreign affairs. That might allow the Germans a foothold in the area and threaten British dominance.

"We'd better get a move on," Andrew said, calculating the distance to the twin *kopjes*. *The sooner we rendezvous with the British column, the more secure I'll feel.* He raised his voice. "Pick up the pace a little, boys and girls. I want to make the twin *koppies* in two days."

"They've gone that way," Johannes examined the trail and stood up.

"No," Theunis shook his head. "They came from there. Read the hoofprints!" He pointed to the ground. "Another force of reinforcements made these marks."

"They reversed their horseshoes," Johannes explained. "This *Rooineck* is *slim*. Everything he does is intended to deceive us. How many men did you find when you chased the artillery fire?"

"We found the spoor of one man and lost him when he rode onto some rocky terrain."

"The *Rooineck* fooled us with a diversion, as we attempted at Potchefstroom," Johannes said. "He will not fool us again. Whatever you think you see, believe the opposite."

Theunis tapped his rifle. "This is my cure for the *Rooineck*." He tossed back the tangled hair from his face.

"His tricks have gained him a twenty-hour lead," Johannes said. "We'll need to ride hard to catch him." He looked at the Groenburg Commando as they sat astride their horses, waiting for his orders. "We follow this trail, men, and we ride hard. The *Rooinecks* are a day's ride ahead, but we are faster than them."

The Boers adjusted their hats, patted their horses, and prepared for a hard ride. Above them, two vultures circled, knowing that a gathering of armed horsemen invariably led to violence and fresh meat.

"Trek!" Johannes ordered and led the way.

Behind Johannes, Jan pushed the thought of Engela from his mind. Abraham's sister was not the only girl in the world. Africa was full of women equally as good as Engela, who would want to marry the heir to Nuwe Hoop Plaas.

"You are back early, *Meneer* Konrad," Aletta said.

"Your husband sent me back," Konrad dismounted stiffly, patting the dust from his clothes.

"Why did he do that?" Aletta asked. She stood outside her dairy, peering at Konrad from under the shade of her bonnet.

"He thought there might be a British patrol in the area," Konrad said. "And you might need a man on the farm to protect you."

Aletta nodded slowly. "Mannie is here," she indicated her younger son, who stood in the doorway, silently watching.

"Good," Konrad smiled at Mannie. "He and I will keep you safe."

"I am sure you will," Aletta said.

"Your husband said I should look after Goed Weiding as well, with Abraham on commando and his father dead."

Aletta nodded. "That was thoughtful of Johannes, *Meneer* Konrad. You will need coffee after your long ride."

"Coffee would be welcome," Konrad agreed.

Andrew had been watching the lone rider approach for half an hour before he was sure it was Kerr. Turning Lancelot, he rode to meet him.

"I'm glad you are safe, Kerr. I expected you yesterday."

Kerr reined up in a whirlwind of dust. "I had to make a few detours, sir. The Boers have picked up your trail, and van Collier has scouts everywhere."

"Damn!" Andrew scanned the veld through his field glasses. "That man is clever. How far back is he?"

"Ten hours, sir, at most." Kerr was travel weary, with dark shadows under his eyes and deep lines carved on either side of his mouth. "Whenever I thought I had a clear road, two or three of his riders appeared. He's set a wide net out for you."

"Well, he's not caught us yet," Andrew looked over his unit. Two days of constant movement had wearied the civilians, so they slumped in the saddle. He wondered how long they could continue without a rest. The women were not used to long-distance riding, but Andrew had refused to bring a wagon.

"We need a wagon," Mrs Murphy, red-faced and hollow-eyed, wailed.

"It will slow us down," Andrew replied firmly.

"The Boers don't make war on women," Mrs Murphy insisted. "If Murphy were here, he'd tell you that."

"The ordinary Boers don't," Andrew agreed. "I don't know about the Afrikander Bond, but the Groenburg Commando has a Prussian with them. They can be ruthless."

"I wish Murphy were here," Mrs Murphy had said. "He would not let you treat me like this."

Booth had told Andrew that Murphy had left his wife to try his hand at gold digging and never returned. That had been a full year ago.

"The twin *koppies* are only a few hours' ride," Kerr broke Andrew's train of thought.

Andrew nodded. "Join the men, Kerr, and we'll push on."

With scouts riding all around, Andrew forced the pace, discarding the civilians' complaints.

"Women can't ride as fast as men," Mrs Murphy wailed. "We can't keep this pace."

"Miss Maxwell is keeping up, Mrs Murphy!" Andrew replied sternly. "If she can ride on, then so can you."

I don't want the Army to remember me as the officer who allowed the Boers to capture the Prime Minister's nephew. We've already had too many disasters in South Africa with the defeats at Isandhlwana and Majuba, plus the death of the Prince Imperial of France.[1]

"Ride, boys and girls!" Andrew ordered, aware that the civilians and probably some Dragoons were cursing him. He reasoned they'd be safer once they sent their message from the twin *kopjes*, and he could hand Abercrombie over to a more senior officer.

Moving to the rear of the column, Andrew took the reins of one of the flagging women. "Come along, Mrs Murphy. You must keep going, you know."

"I'm trying!" Mrs Murphy said.

"I know you are," Andrew agreed. "I know it's hard for you, riding all night and half the day, but I am trying to keep you safe."

Mrs Murphy favoured Andrew with a weary smile that revealed something of the beauty she once possessed. "I know, dear," she said. "I only wish Murphy was here. He might never find me now."

"I'm sure he will," Andrew replied. "Only a fool would not search for a woman like you."

"Oh!" Mrs Murphy smiled again and redoubled her efforts.

The Natal Dragoons reached the base of the two *kopjes* in the early afternoon, with the sun high above and not a whisper of wind.

"Fletcher! Set up camp a hundred feet up the hill beside that *spruit*!" Andrew pointed to a stream that trickled down the hill. "Make a defensive perimeter, send out two-man pickets, water the horses and watch for the Boers. I'm going up with the helio."

"Yes, sir," Fletcher agreed.

"Look after Lancelot," Andrew ordered, passing the reins to Briggs.

The *kopje* was steeper than Andrew had anticipated, with hard-baked ground littered with boulders and cloaked in thorny scrub. He scrambled to the summit with Spalding at his side and Kerr and Ogden as porters.

"How far can that thing be seen?" Andrew asked as Spalding readied the heliograph's tripod.

"I'm not sure, sir," Spalding replied. "I've heard the Seaforth Highlanders used their helio over a distance of seventy-two miles in Afghanistan, but I've never used it over twenty."

Andrew nodded. "Well, I wonder if it can be seen over a hundred miles." From the summit, the veld stretched to a seemingly limitless extent, broken only by *kopjes* and the green curves of river valleys. Using his field glasses, Andrew could see a couple of lonely farms, dwarfed by the brown-yellow expanse of the high veld, but no sign of any British column.

Spalding pursed his lips. "It might, sir. The air is very clear out here."

"There's a British force to the southeast," Andrew said. He glanced at the neighbouring *kopje,* slightly smaller and about a mile distant. "I want you to signal in that direction."

"As you wish, sir," Spalding replied. "What shall I say?"

Andrew had considered his message for every mile since they left Swartspruit. "Signal: Natal Dragoons have secured the package. Require rendezvous coordinates."

Spalding raised his eyebrows. "Yes, sir." He wrote the message in a small notebook. "Thank you, sir. Give me a minute, and I'll set the helio. Give me a hand here, boys!"

Spalding erected the heliograph on its tripod, angling the mirror to catch the sunlight.

Kerr slid into the shelter of a thornbush. "I can see men on the other *kopje*, sir."

"Where?" Andrew turned around, lifted his field glasses, and swore. "You're right, Kerr." *You're too late, van Collier. Once Spalding gets his message away, there's nothing you can do.*

Andrew saw half a dozen Boers moving confidently across the hill. One climbed a slight elevation and lay down. "That fellow is going to fire at us."

Kerr nodded. "He's over a mile away, sir. Not even the Boers can fire at that range."

Andrew nodded. Although he did not want the Boers to see him, sending the message was more important. "Spalding, have you got that message away yet?"

"Not yet, sir," Spalding replied and bent to the heliograph.

"One of the Boers is aiming at us," Kerr said. "The silly bugger's ready to fire."

Nobody flinched, knowing the range was too far for even the most powerful rifle. They saw the puff of white smoke and half a second later heard the report of the rifle, with a corresponding echo slightly later.

"See?" Kerr said. "Nowhere near," and swore as the bullet burrowed into the ground between the legs of the heliograph. "Bloody hell!"

The Boer fired again, with the bullet smashing the lens of the heliograph, sending shards of glass over Spalding and Andrew.

"How the devil did he do that?" Kerr said as he threw himself to the ground.

"What sort of rifle does he have?" Andrew asked as the Boer fired a third time. The bullet kicked up dirt and rocks a foot from his elbow.

"A bloody good one, sir," Kerr replied. Lifting his Martini-Henry, he took quick aim and fired. "He's well out of range, but I may unsettle him."

"Did you get the message away, Spalding?" Andrew asked.

"Only the first part, sir," Spalding replied. "The part about the package." He ducked as the Boer fired again, with the bullet completing the destruction of the heliograph.

"Let's hope that was enough," Andrew said. *Van Collier must have guessed we were sending a message. He had his sharpshooter deliberately smash the heliograph. I'd like to meet that man.*

"Do you want the rifle, sir?" Ogden asked. "We can round him up." He grinned. "I'd like to see what kind of fancy weapon Brother Boer uses."

Andrew considered sending his men to the neighbouring *kopje*. It was tempting to capture the Burgher's rifle, but he knew the time and risk were not worth the prize. "No," he said. "That Boer has smashed the helio, our reason for climbing this hill. Best get back down."[2]

Andrew cursed as he scrambled down the hill. With the heliograph gone, he had no method of contacting the relieving column, and with an unknown number of Boers following him and many more in the country, Andrew knew his Dragoons were in a precarious position.

We'll get out of here, ride on, and hope the column saw our all-too-brief message. If not, we have a long ride to the Natal border and a dangerous enemy far too close behind.

"Thank you for coming to see I was safe, *meneer*," Engela said. "It was very kind of you."

"I must look after the most beautiful woman in Africa," Konrad said, bowing. He smiled and fingered the broad scar across his left cheek. "I can see you are curious about my scar."

Engela blushed. "It looks very romantic," she said.

"I got that in a duel," Konrad told her. "In Prussia, gentlemen prove their bravery and honour by fighting duels with swords."

"Do they?" Engela widened her eyes. "Why do they do that?"

"It is the mark of a gentleman to stand up to danger," Konrad told her proudly.

"Are you a gentleman, *meneer*?"

"I am," Konrad favoured her with a smile. "At home, I am Count Konrad von Bramigan, with an estate of thousands of acres in East Prussia."

Engela smiled, reached forward, and touched the broad scar. "Is a count very important in Prussia?"

"A count is fundamental to Prussian society," Konrad told her. "We are the nobility, with pedigrees that stretch back centuries." He smiled. "My ancestors were Teutonic Knights."

Engela did not ask who the Teutonic Knights were. "Why are you in Africa if you have lands to farm?"

Konrad sat beside her at the kitchen table. "The emperor asked me to come," he boasted. "Konrad, he said, Konrad, the German Empire needs your help."

"Did he say that?" Engela asked, widening her eyes.

"He did," Konrad continued. "He said: my friends, the Burghers of the Transvaal Republic are in danger. The British are trying to steal their land. I want you to go over, see what is happening and come back to tell me."

Engela looked at this tall man who was so different from the farmers she knew. "What will you tell the emperor when you see him again?"

"I will tell him that his friends in the Transvaal Republic are fighting hard against the British."

Engela smiled. "Tell him he can visit us whenever he likes," she said. "I've never met a lord before. Is a count the same as a lord?"

"I am of the Junkers class," Konrad told her. "That is higher than a British lord."

"You must feel strange coming to our little farm."

"Your presence would make even a hut feel like a palace," Konrad replied.

When Engela made food for him, sour milk and coffee, rusks, and quinces, he told her about his estate in Prussia and how he had fought in the Prussian Army against the French.

"My brother is also a soldier," Engela said. "You and he are alike."

"We both belong to the brotherhood of the sword," Konrad said. "We shall drink a toast!" Producing a silver flask from his inside pocket, he took a sip and passed it over to Engela. "Drink with me! This flask contains brandy."

"I don't drink," Engela said.

"In Prussia, noble ladies drink equal to the counts," Konrad said, shaking his flask and holding it out again. "Come, my sweet princess; when I take you to visit the palaces of Prussia, you must be able to act like Prussian nobility. Drink!"

Engela smiled and accepted the flask.

"Have you noticed all the wildlife out here?" Mariana asked.

Andrew shook his head. "I saw some antelope and a herd of springbok," he said. "I am a little more concerned about the wild Boers."

"We must have ridden past a hundred lizards," Mariana continued. "And an iguana, hiding in a willow tree. Plenty of bullfrogs, of course; you hear them croaking at night when the jackals are quiet. Sometimes, I hear the grasshoppers."

"Do you like the wildlife?"

"We used to hate it on the farm," Mariana said. "Father hunted the wild animals, partly for sport but mainly because they were rivals for our grazing, particularly in times of drought." She looked away, reliving happier times.

"Did you ever shoot?" Andrew asked, his eyes constantly moving as he scrutinised the landscape for any signs of Boer activity.

"Oh, yes," Mariana replied. "Father taught Elaine and me to shoot when we were quite young. We had to know in case a leopard or snake came." She smiled with memory. "We had a cobra in our tree once, hunting the sparrows. Father killed it because it was dangerous. Elaine wanted to shoot it, but Father said it was too wily an opponent for her."

"Not many women in Britain can shoot," he said. "The aristocracy probably can, and some farmers' wives and daughters." He negotiated an anthill, checked his men were still alert, and signalled to change the scouts. Above them, the great arc of the sky stretched to infinity, unbroken by a single cloud.

Andrew had increased the column's speed, moving steadily while trying to minimise the dust. He continually scanned the veld, searching over the yellow-brown landscape for the splashes of green trees surrounding a Boer's farm. The colours seldom varied; the grass was a dull yellow, as were the *kopjes* when the darting midday haze descended, yet the green of the British countryside was sadly lacking. The *kopje* flanks boasted the *taibosch* – tough bush – an attractive plant tinted in blue, while the aloe hedges that guarded the native kraals were coloured like steel.

"Do you like the veld?" Mariana seemed desperate for conversation.

"I find it fascinating," Andrew replied. "The sheer scale makes one realise how insignificant we are. We believe humans are the lords of creation, yet out here, we could be ants crawling across a playing field."

"Maybe this place is God's playing field, and we are his playthings," Mariana said. "He could be watching us now, deciding on his next move as we plot, scheme and plan our little dreams without real hope of achieving our ant-like ambitions."

Andrew smiled, glad that Mariana was thinking again and enjoying her twists of imagination. "Maybe that's God's idea of giving humanity the veld, to show us how small we are compared to the infinity of nature."

Mariana pointed ahead. "Look over there, Andrew, can you see that green slither? Like a snake coiling across space? It looks like nothing from here, a child's scrawl on a piece of paper, yet when we get close, we'll find a broad river, an obstacle we must cross."

Andrew studied the river through his field glasses. "You're right, Mariana. We'll camp on the bank tonight and cross when we are fresh tomorrow."

They pushed on, with the scouts searching for the searchers and seeking good water for the horses and men. They passed an acre of red conical anthills, three-foot-high mounds of grass and mud, teeming with minuscule life.

Andrew checked to ensure Abercrombie was still with them and thought life could be very pleasant riding with Mariana if the Boers left them alone. No sooner had the idea entered his mind than Sergeant Meek galloped towards him, and Andrew knew his few moments of relaxation had ended.

"Sir!" Meek said. "There might be trouble ahead."

CHAPTER 20

"What is it, Sergeant?"

"I saw a flash from that farmhouse, sir," Meek indicated a distant farm. "It might be innocent, or it might be a Boer watching us through a glass."

"Well done, Sergeant," Andrew said. He pondered for a moment. If he sent a man to scout, any hiding Boer could shoot the lone rider from a distance and gallop away before the Dragoons arrived. On the other hand, if he failed to investigate the farm, a Boer commando could ambush his Dragoons.

"Lieutenant Fletcher," Andrew said formally. "We'll advance in an open line, then split to take the farm in front and rear. You command the right flank, and I'll take the left."

"Yes, sir," Fletcher agreed.

"Sergeant Meek. You and Briggs remain with the civilians." He lowered his voice. "Whatever happens, Sergeant, ensure the Boers don't capture Abercrombie."

"Very good, sir," Meek was too old a soldier to show emotion.

"And Sergeant," Andrew glanced at Mariana.

"I'll look after her, sir," Meek promised. He grinned. "Or Briggs will; he's like a father to Miss Maxwell."

Andrew held Briggs' gaze for a moment. "Did you hear that, Briggs?"

"I did, sir," Briggs replied. "I'll make sure Miss Maxwell is all right."

With a final nod, Andrew turned Lancelot and rode away. The last thing he saw was Mariana waving goodbye.

"No shooting, boys," Andrew said when he joined his Dragoons. "Don't fire unless they fire first. This farmer may be completely innocent."

When Andrew gave the signal, the Dragoons advanced in a sinuous line. Andrew knew it was harder to shoot a moving rather than a stationary target and increased the speed to a canter.

"Sir!" Kerr pointed ahead, where a fold of ground concealed a *spruit* between the Dragoons and the farm.

Too late to stop; we'll have to chance it. "Ride through, boys!"

Willows surrounded the *spruit,* and a small herd of impala scattered in panicked flight as Andrew led from the front, encouraging his Dragoons to follow. Horses' hooves thudded and splashed through the water and up the short, steep slope at the other side. Andrew thrilled to the canter as he signalled for Fletcher to take his section to the right.

"Come on, lads!" Andrew increased his speed.

The Dragoons advanced, hooves pounding, men enjoying the exhilaration of the gallop despite the possible danger; one Dragoon's hat flew off to rise in the air and drop behind the horsemen, drifting in the falling dust.

Every man waited for the double crack of a rifle; every man lifted the Martini-Henry from its bucket and prepared to retaliate, yet they closed on the farmhouse without firing, slowing with as much disappointment as relief. Andrew dismounted first and ran into the steading to see a handful of hens and a middle-aged woman working in the dairy.

The woman looked up in surprise, holding a hand to her chest. "*Meneer?*" She stared at Andrew and spoke in a thick accent he could hardly understand. When more Dragoons burst into her dairy, rifles held ready, she stepped back in genuine alarm.

"It's all right, *tante*," Kerr reassured her. "We mean you no harm."

Andrew pointed to one of the hens that was scratching at the ground. "We would like to purchase some of your chickens," he said. "We'll give you sixpence for every hen."

The woman's eyes narrowed. "Ninepence," she replied.

"Sixpence," Andrew insisted with a smile. "And that's a thief's bargain."

With fresh oat straw for the horses and half a dozen freshly purchased hens to feed the men, Andrew felt the visit was worth the initial excitement as he led his Dragoons away.

The sound of the shot broke Andrew's mood as the bullet whistled past, burrowing into the dirt. "Extended order!" he shouted.

Andrew did not know if a lone Boer had fired the shot or if a commando had caught them. "Ride, boys; Kerr, take the right flank!"

The second double report sounded, with the bullet passing above Andrew's head. "Did anybody see the shooter?"

The Dragoons left the farmhouse at a trot, well spread out, with some men straining to see who was firing at them, while others were only determined to escape. Andrew glanced over his shoulder, counted his men, and saw a faint drift of smoke from the farmhouse, followed by an explosion of horsemen.

Damn! The Groenburg Commando has found us.

"Ride, boys! Ride for your lives!"

❄

"YOU MUST HAVE BEEN VERY BRAVE TO BE IN THE PRUSSIAN GUARD," Engela said.

Konrad tilted his head to one side, a trick he believed made him attractive to women. "No braver than anybody else," he said with mock modesty. "I did earn the Iron Cross at the Battle of Sedan."

"I thought you were brave. Was Sedan a big battle?" Engela did not admit her ignorance about the Iron Cross.

"We had about two hundred thousand men, and the French about a hundred and fifty thousand," Konrad exaggerated the French numbers. "I also fought at Gravelotte, an even larger battle, and the Siege of Paris."

"Oh," Engela could not envision a battle with so many men. She had never seen more than a couple of thousand people gathered at one time. "You have seen some huge battles."

"Battles are the culmination of a soldier's life," Konrad said.

"Were you not afraid?"

"No," Konrad shook his closely cropped head. "I was with the Prussian Guards, the best soldiers in the world."

"Better than the *Rooinecks?*" Engela asked.

"Much better." Konrad showed his teeth in a smile. "It was Blücher's Prussians who won the Battle of Waterloo. If we had not arrived, Bonaparte would have defeated Wellington."

"I see," Engela did not want to admit she had never heard of Waterloo or any battles Konrad had mentioned. She wondered how Konrad had felt when he fought. "It must have been terrible in these wars," she said.

"No," Konrad shook his head. "They were glorious victories, fighting for the Fatherland, defeating an ancient foe, and proving myself as a leader of the Guards."

"What is Prussia like?" Engela asked.

Konrad stepped closer. "It is the most magnificent country anywhere," he said. "We have the bravest soldiers and the best cities." He began to extoll the virtues of Berlin, leading Engela through the cultural delights of Prussia's capital.

Engela listened to Konrad's stories of elegant ladies, fine coaches, great opera houses, restaurants, and balls. Konrad's words transported her to a different world, where she imagined herself far from the farm and everything she knew. She looked down at herself, seeing a plain woman with short fingernails and clumsy shoes, wearing handmade clothes, and wondered what Konrad saw in her.

"I would never belong in Berlin," Engela said sadly.

"You would," Konrad assured her. "You are as beautiful as any woman I have ever seen."

"I am not!" Engela denied, hoping for a rebuttal.

"Oh, you are," Konrad said, smiling with his head on one side. "I can picture you in a silk and satin gown flowing to your ankles, a pearl necklace around your throat, diamond rings on your fingers, and your hair piled up. I would introduce you to the best hairdressers and dressmakers in Berlin, and you would look even more like a princess than you do now." He stood beside her, nearly a foot taller, slim, elegant, and more debonair than any man Engela had met. "Shall we step out of our coach?"

"What is the coach like?" Engela asked. "I've only ever seen a farm cart or the trek wagons."

"Oh, one of our family coaches has tall wheels of bright red," Konrad improvised, "with a dark green body and gold trimmings, deeply padded leather seats, and velvet curtains for the windows. We'll have a team of six matching white horses, a coachman and two servants in livery with my coat of arms – our coat of arms – and a man sounding a horn to clear everybody from the road."

"Do you have a coat of arms?" Engela asked.

"I have, and so will you," Konrad twisted the ring from his middle finger. "There it is."

"Oh," Engela examined the ring. "It's beautiful," she said. "Do you have a castle as well?"

"We have four castles. We live in the largest," Konrad told her, "with grounds and tenants and a host of servants."

"We have servants here," Engela defended her home.

"When I take you to Prussia," Konrad recovered his ring and replaced it on his finger, "I will show you wonders such as you would not believe."

"Will your family not mind that you bring a guest over? It must be very formal to live in a castle," Engela said. "I would not know what to say or how to act."

Konrad laughed. "Oh, you silly little princess," he said, putting his forefinger on her nose. "I would not be bringing you as a guest. I'd be bringing you home as my wife."

"What?" Engela stared at him. "I will probably marry Jan van Collier." She thought of Jan, the hard-working, determined boy she had known all her life, comparing him to Konrad with his elegant manners, wealth, and supreme confidence. Suddenly, Jan looked like a clumsy farm boy without knowledge of the outside world.

"I know Jan well," Konrad said. "He's a decent enough young boy. Honest and brave." He nodded. "Yes, Jan will make a good husband for an ordinary Burgher woman."

Engela frowned. "An ordinary Burgher woman?"

"Yes, but not for you," Konrad said. "You are far from ordinary."

"I am a Boer woman, sir," Engela shook her head. "Your words are weaving a spell around me, but I am no princess to sit on silk cushions and ride in a gold carriage. I have a farm to run."

"I will give you a far better life than anything out here in the wilderness," Konrad said. "I will give you palaces and furs, silks and satins, balls and opera houses, champagne, fine wines and intelligent, influential company."

"I am not suited to that life," Engela protested. "What do I have to give in return?"

When Konrad smiled, his scar puckered into a zigzag. "I am sure you already know what I want, Engela." He stepped towards her with his intentions visibly apparent.

"No!" Engela backed away, half laughing, half alarmed. "Get away!"

Konrad's laughter rose above Engela's sudden fear.

"THE BOERS ARE CLOSING, SIR," KERR WIPED THE SWEAT FROM HIS EYES. "The Groenburg Commando is two miles to our rear, and our scouts report dust in front, a great deal of dust, sir."

Andrew swore. *A great deal of dust means a large commando.* "Johannes van Collier is a good soldier." He looked around, wrestling with their situation. With no possibility of help, he had to rely on guile and determination to escape. "Keep the men moving. Where's Mr Fletcher?"

"Here I am, sir!" Fletcher rode up beside Andrew. His hat was perched on the back of his head, and sweat had created furrows on his dust-coated face. "What do you want me to do?"

"Take a good man and delay the Groenburg Commando. Try and act as though there are ten of you or a hundred. Hold them as long as possible and retire; you know the drill. Take spare horses and try not to get killed."

"Yes, sir," Fletcher said. "What will you do?"

Andrew forced the grin that had earned him his 'Up and at 'em' reputation in the Cape Frontier War. "I'm going to scatter the enemy in front."

"Yes, sir. May I have Kerr?"

Andrew glanced at Kerr, his best man but weary after days of scouting. "Are you fit, Kerr?"

"Yes, sir," Kerr replied immediately.

"Go with Fletcher."

"Yes, sir." Kerr and Fletcher trotted towards the Groenburg Commando.

Andrew returned to his men. Abercrombie was riding beside Mariana, with Sergeant Meek shepherding the Dragoons and civilians like an anxious father.

Meek moderated his habitual roar. "Come on, Mrs Murphy, try to keep up. Mrs Williams, there's no need to panic, even if the Boers catch us, they won't eat you. That's better."

"The Boers are in front and behind," Andrew informed his men. "I've sent Lieutenant Fletcher and Kerr to delay the Groenburg Commando so we can concentrate on the enemy in front."

The Dragoons listened, immediately understanding their position.

"We're going to show a bold front," Andrew said. "Rather than avoid them, we're going right for their throat."

Meek and Ogden grinned while others nodded grimly or lifted their rifles.

"What about the ladies, sir?" Briggs asked.

Andrew thought for a moment. "You and Booth look after the women and other civilians," Andrew said. "Keep them out of danger."

"Yes, sir." When Briggs hesitated, Andrew knew he would prefer to fight alongside his colleagues.

"That's an order, Briggs."

"Yes, sir," Briggs stiffened his back.

"Keep Abercrombie safe," Andrew lowered his voice. "And Miss Maxwell."

"I will, sir."

General Hook might consider Abercrombie more important than Mariana, but Briggs will put Mariana first, which suits me.

Andrew felt Mariana watching him, so he allowed her a reassuring nod and called the Dragoons together.

"We'll ride forward openly, and when we see the enemy, we charge," Andrew said. "There's a river ahead. If we can trap them between us and the river, we can do some damage and keep them away from the civilians." He thought on his feet, aware his knowledge of the local terrain was imperfect. He nodded to a small ridge where thornbushes crackled under the heat. "I want Brown and Spalding, the best two shots, to lie there and fire at the enemy. We all know a charging man will never hit his target, but a man lying can. If we charge and fire, and the two marksmen bring a Boer or two to the ground, the enemy might believe we're superb shots. Which we are, of course."

The expected ripple of laughter defused some of the tension.

"Are there any questions?" Andrew could see the dust ahead, concealing the second commando that closed the net on the British. They must have superior numbers to advance so openly.

Sergeant Meek shook his head. "No, sir. We'll just follow you."

Andrew hoped he appeared confident. "Keep your heads down, boys and the best of luck to us all."

Charging a more numerous force of expert shots was never easy. Andrew knew his chances of survival were slim.

I hope Briggs looks after Mariana. "Right, lads. Up and at 'em!"

The Dragoons moved forward, each horse kicking up a quota of dust, so they advanced through a choking haze toward the hidden enemy. Andrew heard his two marksmen firing, with the bullets hissing above the Dragoons' heads. Unable to see the Boers through the dust, Andrew could only advance, hoping his Swartspruit tactics worked a second time. He heard Ogden blow on his bugle and felt the shudder of scores of hooves on the hard ground.

"They're on the flanks, sir!" Sergeant Meek shouted.

Andrew glanced to his left, where half a dozen Boers surged from a shallow valley and charged toward them, while another group of riders appeared on their right.

"They'll cut us off from the civilians, sir," Fletcher said.

"Damn it," Andrew replied. "You're right." *Van Collier is after Abercrombie.* "Ogden! Sound the recall!"

Ordering cavalry to charge was one thing; halting them in full flow was completely different. Ogden blew his bugle while Andrew, Fletcher, and Meek roared their loudest, yet still the Dragoons galloped forward. Swearing, Andrew spurred on, turned Lancelot, and lifted his arms. "Retire! Get back to the ridge!"

One by one, the Dragoons halted and turned. Andrew saw angry, surprised faces and men pulling at excited horses.

Where are the Boers? Where are the men we were charging?

When a chance breeze cleared some of the dust, Andrew only saw two horsemen firing rifles in the air and dragging bushes behind them.

Only two men with bushes creating a dust cloud! Van Collier is using our deception tactics against us.

"Back to the ridge!" Andrew yelled. "Fletcher! Round up the civilians and get them to the ridge!" *Thank God Sergeant Meek saw the men on the flanks before it was too late.*

The Dragoons retired in a confused rush, each rider choosing what he considered the best route. Andrew counted his men, relieved none had fallen.

"Get these civilians onto the ridge," Andrew roared. "Horse holders, take the horses to the middle. The rest form a firing line and prepare to repel boarders." He looked over his men, knowing the Boer commander had outridden and outthought him. "We'll hold on here, lads, and hope the British relieving column finds us."

There is little chance of that in the vastness of the veld unless our gunfire attracts them.

The three groups of Boers merged until the Groenburg Commando came in a single wave of horsemen, shouting and firing as they advanced towards the ridge.

"Fire!" Andrew ordered. "Shoot them flat!" He aimed and fired, wondering which vague shape in the dust was Johannes van Collier. Although he wanted to shoot him for the sake of victory, a small part of him admired the Boer veldcornet.

The Natal Dragoons fired and reloaded, fired, and reloaded, trying to repel the Boers by the sheer volume of musketry. After five minutes of concentrated firing, Andrew saw the Boer line hesitate, with riders dismounting to seek cover and the dust slowly drifting away. The sun reflected from small piles of empty brass cartridge cases.

"Enough! We've stopped them! Don't waste ammunition, boys," Andrew saw Briggs usher the civilians into the safest section of the ridge. "We could be here for some time."

Here we go. How long can we hold out against the Groenburg Commando and whatever else van Collier throws at us? Unless the relieving column reaches us soon, the Boers will be able to boast of another victory.

"I WANT YOU, MY LITTLE MILKMAID," KONRAD SAID. "I'LL SHOW YOU WHAT a Prussian man is like." He slid off his jacket and advanced on Engela. "Once you've experienced me, you'll not want your peasant farm boy again."

"Get away!" Engela shouted, backing against the wall. She looked around frantically for help. Until recently, she had only met close friends and relatives and did not understand a predator like Konrad. "Leave me!"

"You don't mean that!" Konrad stood before Engela, blocking her escape as he removed his shirt. "You find me attractive, Engela, a sophisticated European man, rather than some clumsy boy from nowhere."

"No!" Engela looked for a weapon. "Get away!"

"Look!" Konrad lowered his trousers, grinning.

"No!" Engela shook her head.

"I'm looking," Mannie slid through the door behind Engela. "Leave her alone!"

Konrad hardened his voice. "Go away, boy; this has nothing to do with you."

"Leave her," Mannie stepped closer.

"Get out, boy!" Konrad snapped. "I am a Prussian officer, and I order you to leave. Engela wants me here."

Konrad's tone made Mannie flinch. He stopped, staring at Engela, who shook her head.

"Engela is my brother's girl," Mannie was younger, smaller, and slighter than Konrad and still weak from his recent illness. "Get away from her."

Konrad's backhanded slap knocked Mannie off his feet and slammed him against the wall. Engela screamed as Mannie slid to the floor, leaving a smear of blood down the rough stonework. He lay still, stunned.

"Now, my girl," Konrad said. "There are no more distractions." He grabbed hold of Engela's shoulder. "You're mine."

Engela tried to break free, but Konrad had a powerful grip. He squeezed cruelly, revelling in his strength. "Struggle if you wish, my little Boer milkmaid; I enjoy it when women try to fight back."

"What about the palaces, carriages and opera houses you promised?" Engela asked, wriggling. Konrad blocked her slap, twisted her wrist behind her, and began to rip off her clothes.

"Too good for the likes of a little milkmaid," Konrad responded.

"Leave her!" Mannie pushed himself up, blinking through the blood that covered half his face.

"Get away, boy," Konrad sneered. "Or I'll take a whip to you."

Mannie threw himself forward, using his anger as a weapon. With Konrad partially distracted by holding Engela, Mannie's rush forced him backwards. He swore, released Engela, and recovered.

"I'll take care of you first, boy," Konrad snarled, "and then show the little milkmaid what a Prussian is made of."

Mannie was slight but wiry and angry. His punch landed on Konrad's cheekbone, causing the Prussian to wince.

"I'll kill you for that," Konrad hissed.

Lifting a heavy milking pail, Engela swung it, catching Konrad on the side of his head. "You'll kill nobody!" she screamed. "Get him, Mannie!"

Konrad backed away, staggering as his trousers tangled around his ankles. When he bent down to unholster his pistol, Engela swung the pail again, knocking him onto his face. Konrad hauled out his gun, mouthing threats. He aimed at the advancing Mannie and curled his finger around the trigger.

The roar of the shot echoed around the dairy. The heavy bullet crashed into Konrad's head, smashed his skull, and sent fragments of bone, brain, and blood against the whitewashed wall.

Engela and Mannie stared as Konrad slumped to the floor with the pistol still gripped in his dead hand.

Aletta lowered the rifle. "I knew that Prussian was trouble," she said quietly, with the gun smoke curling around her poke bonnet.

ANDREW CHECKED HIS WATCH. THE SUN WOULD SET IN AN HOUR, WHICH meant the battle had raged for five hours. Now, the Boers were edging closer, keeping to the dead ground and shelter of rocks and ant hills, ready for a final rush in the dark. Three bodies lay in front of the Dragoons' position, the Boers' casualties from their first abortive advance, with a fur of flies feasting on each man. Two more lay beside rocks on the approach to the ridge. Andrew guessed that van Collier did not wish to risk further casualties from his commando, friends, and neighbours he had probably known all his life. The close-knit companionship was both a strength and a weakness of the commando system.

"They're closing in!" Turner said, aiming and firing. His bullet kicked up a fountain of dirt beside a rock as the empty cartridge added to the brassy pile at his side.

"They're coming for the kill this time," Ogden said. He touched the blood that had dried down the side of his face.

"They'll have to cross the open ground to reach us," Kerr reminded. "The Boers don't like that."

"We can hold them off," Andrew glanced at the civilians, where Mariana stood tall, watching him. "Keep your head down, Mariana! Even an Afrikander Bond Boer won't deliberately harm a woman, but a stray bullet might hit you."

Mariana lifted her chin and gave a brave smile. "I'll be all right," she said. "You look after yourself, Andrew." Her eyes were clear.

If Mariana survives this battle, I think she'll be fine.

Andrew rose to check on his men. The Dragoons were dug into shallow trenches or waiting behind rocks, firing at any Boer who showed himself. They had seen off one impetuous Boer attack and delayed the besiegers' slow advance, but at a prodigious cost in bullets.

My men could do no more. It's unfortunate that we're against such an innovative Boer commander. If only that marksman hadn't destroyed our heliograph, we could have rendezvoused with the relieving force. Now, Van Collier will capture Gladstone's nephew and hand him over to the Prussians. I have failed unless we have some miracle.

With the Dragoons as secure as possible, Andrew moved to the civilians, who huddled in a slight depression in the ridge, holding the horses and acting as bravely as any trained soldier. Booth greeted Andrew with a wave.

"How are we doing, Captain?"

"We're holding our own," Andrew replied. "The Boers can't advance without losing men."

"Good show," Abercrombie was on his hands and knees, examining the rocks. "Tell them to hold off, will you? I might find something interesting here, apart from ants and scorpions."

"You keep safe, Abercrombie," Andrew said. "Are you all right, Mrs Murphy? And you, Mrs Williams?"

"We're just grand," Mrs Murphy replied bravely. "Mr Briggs has been looking after us."

"Briggs is a very capable man," Andrew replied.

"Sir!" Meek shouted. "The Boers are advancing again!"

Andrew lifted his hat. "Excuse me, ladies. Duty calls!" He moved to the firing line, ducking as a Boer bullet hissed overhead.

"They seem serious this time, sir," Fletcher said. "They might charge us in the dark."

"Maybe so," Andrew agreed.

"What's happening?" Abercrombie emerged from the central depression.

"The bloody Boers are happening, you blasted idiot!" Andrew's response revealed the shredded state of his nerves. "Get under cover!"

"Oh, all right!" Abercrombie seemed unconscious of the bullets that zipped and pinged from the British positions.

Turner moved closer to Abercrombie. "You stay with me, Charlie boy. I'll do what's best."

What the devil does that mean? Andrew frowned and realised other matters demanded his attention. The Boers were closing in, firing from cover, and moving forward, nearly invisible against the dun and brown of the veld.

Andrew raised his voice. "How much ammunition do you have left, boys?"

"Five rounds, sir."

"Three rounds, sir."

"Seven rounds, sir."

"Seven? Haven't you been with us, McAlister?"

The laughter was forced but welcome as the Dragoons accepted any excuse to relieve the tension.

"Don't waste what you have," Andrew ordered. He tried to count the Boers, spotting them by a slight movement here, a bird's sudden flight or a puff of falling dust. A bullet plunged into the ground at his side, seemingly intent on hitting him but stopping three inches short of its target.

Half an hour until night, and then Van Collier's men will walk over us.

"Ogden! Blow your bugle! They might think reinforcements are coming."

The bugle sounded above the intermittent crackle of musketry, a defiant sound in the hot African air. When the liquid notes faded away, there was a moment of silence, as if the world waited for a reaction, then a single shot cracked the peace, and reality returned.

Half a dozen vultures circled above, waiting for their opportunity to feast.

Andrew saw the tip of a hat above a rounded rock and aimed his rifle. The man had to move slightly to fire. Andrew waited, saw a flicker of movement, the curve of a hip momentarily exposed and squeezed the trigger. The Boer reared up, reaching behind him, and rolled away, holding his wound. Andrew reloaded quickly, contemplated finishing the man off and decided he was already wounded and out of the fight.

Don't waste ammunition.

The Boer response came immediately, with bullets hammering around Andrew's position. He lay snug behind his rock until the fusillade ended and crawled to a new position.

"Hold on, Dragoons!"

"Sir!" Fletcher shouted. "They're showing a flag of truce."

"Hold your fire, boys!" Andrew shouted. Aware of the renewed hammer of his heart, he took a deep breath and stood up. When nobody fired at him, Andrew released his breath. Two Boers rode towards the ridge, one holding a white flag.

"Are you surrendering, *meneer*?" Andrew asked. He recognised the leading man. "You're Johannes Van Collier, aren't you?"

Johannes lifted his hat. "I am, Captain Baird. And this is my son, Jan."

"What can I do for you, Mr van Collier? I'm afraid I've no facilities to care for prisoners, but if you choose to return to your farm, we won't stop you." Andrew saw two men attending the Boer he had shot.

"We have a proposition for you, Captain," Johannes said.

"What is it, Mr van Collier?" Andrew asked.

"We have five hundred men," Johannes said. "You have about twenty soldiers and three women. We are in our own land, and you are lost in a foreign country. We have you surrounded, and you are short of food and ammunition."

Andrew listened without comment.

Johannes paused momentarily, with a faint breeze stirring the white flag. A fly buzzed around Jan's face, landed on his cheek, and began to drink his sweat. He brushed it away.

"Although we can kill or capture you all," Johannes said, "we will let you return to Natal unharmed, with all your horses, guns, and ammunition. On one condition."

"What is your condition?" Andrew asked.

"Hand over Mr Charles Abercrombie to us," Johannes said. "We will look after him; he will not be harmed."

Andrew held Johannes' gaze, knowing the veldcornet spoke the truth. He did not want any more bloodshed. Andrew shook his head. "Thank you for your offer, Mr van Collier, but we are fine as we are. You do not have five hundred men, although you may have a hundred at the most. We are not lost, but only a short distance from British territory; we expect a large relieving column any minute, and we have sufficient food and ammunition for an army ten times our size." He forced what he hoped was a confident smile. "As for Mr Abercrombie, he remains with us."

Johannes touched his hat. "Is that your last word, Captain?"

"It is, *meneer*," Andrew replied.

"As you wish, Captain," Johannes said. "I will allow you the night to consider my offer. If you have not agreed by the morning, I must regretfully attack and wipe out your handful of men. Good evening to you, Captain Baird." Raising his hat politely, Johannes turned his horse and withdrew. Jan lingered a moment longer, threw a poisonous glare at Andrew, and followed his father.

That lad will be trouble if this war flares up again.

"I could give myself up, Captain," Abercrombie volunteered when the Boers withdrew.

"No," Andrew replied shortly.

"It would end the killing," Abercrombie said. "I'm not really important, you know."

"You're the Prime Minister's nephew," Andrew snarled. "You've no business wandering off into the wilds."

"Would you have me wrap up in cotton wool because of my uncle's position?" Abercrombie asked.

Andrew calmed down. "No," he said. "Of course not. You have as much right to put yourself in danger as anybody has. Did you find gold?"

Abercrombie smiled. "I wasn't looking for gold," he said. "I was looking for diamonds and didn't find them either." His smile widened to a grin. "Either I am not a very good geologist, or there's nothing here except dust and space."

"If that's true," Andrew replied slowly, "it might be a blessing for all concerned. The earth's treasures seem to attract trouble."

"Captain Baird said there was a British column out here," Johannes said. "We had better end this stupidity before they arrive."

"We knew there were more *Rooinecks*," Theunis replied. "That's why Baird was signalling with the heliograph."

"He could have been trying to dupe us," Johannes said. "He is as full of tricks as a troop of monkeys."

"We should attack them now," Theunis looked over at the ridge, where the British campfires flickered through the night. "When they don't expect us."

"I gave my word to wait until morning," Johannes said.

"It was a foolish word to give. The *Rooinecks* think we have a hundred men. How many do we have left?" Theunis began to count, using both hands as he named the members of the commando. "Thirty-one men only."

"Thirty," Johannes corrected. "Karl is wounded and cannot ride."

"That's correct," Theunis said. "All the more reason to attack now. Come, Johannes, or we'll lose more men."

"No!" Johannes refused.

"At least we can take Abercrombie!" Theunis said. "If we capture him, the *Rooinecks* will have no reason to stay, and we can all go home."

Johannes looked at Theunis, thinking of Aletta and his farm. *Why does the Lord allow wars?*

❄

ANDREW HEARD THE MOVEMENT WHEN HE RETURNED FROM CHECKING THE pickets. *Have the Boers launched a night raid?* Holding his carbine, he sank low and listened to locate the source of the noise. His pickets were quiet, watching outward over the dark veld. Behind him, the two campfires crackled and hissed, sending aromatic smoke into the air. The civilians remained close to the heat, for the night on the veld was cold.

The noise came again, a definite rustle and the slight scrape of a boot on rock. Andrew remained still, quartering the camp with his eyes, examining each section before moving to the next. His practised eyes could distinguish the Dragoons by the hard edge of their bush hats or the faint glint of starlight on the barrels of their weapons.

"What?"

Andrew heard the single word, instantly stifled. *That's Charles Abercrombie's voice!* Andrew strode forward. He saw a shrouded figure beside Abercrombie with the glint of a blade.

What the devil? The Boers are trying to kidnap Abercrombie. So much for van Collier's word!

"Halt!" Andrew threw himself forward, crashed into the knifeman, and knocked him sprawling to the ground. "You oath-breaking bastard!" He swung his rifle, aiming for the man's head but hitting his shoulder. "Lie still, you Boer bugger!"

The noise had roused the Dragoons, who grabbed their rifles and glared around, searching for the enemy.

"What's happening?"

"Where are they?"

"I can't see anything."

"Bring a light!" Andrew snarled, and Sergeant Meek lifted a burning log from the Dragoons' fire and hurried across. "Right, my Burgher friend, let's be having you." He turned the attacker around so he lay face up. "Turner! What the hell?"

Meek lifted the makeshift torch with his left hand and jabbed the muzzle of his carbine into Turner's chest with his right. "What's it all about?"

Turner glared up at them, still holding a long-bladed knife.

Abercrombie was standing with his hair a tousled mess and his mouth open in shock. "Turner? Why?"

Andrew stood on Turner's arm and removed the knife. "Get up!"

Turner stood, holding his shoulder. "Orders, sir. I was obeying orders."

"Are you a Boer spy?" Meek asked as the Dragoons and civilians gathered around.

"No," Andrew shook his head. "He's acting for General Hook. Isn't that right, Turner?"

Turner shrugged with a faint smile on his face. "I was obeying orders," he repeated. "I was to ensure the Boers did not capture Abercrombie."

Andrew grunted. "Take this man away, Sergeant, tie him up and put him under armed guard."

"Very good, sir," Meek replied. "Come along, Turner."

Abercrombie dusted himself down. "All this fuss over a failed geologist. I didn't mean to cause any trouble."

"I'm sure you didn't, Abercrombie," Andrew said and raised his voice. "All right, everybody. Excitement over; get back to sleep if you can."

My father once warned me to avoid politicians. I'd add politicians' relatives to the list.

DAWN BURST ON THEM WITH A GLORIOUS SUNRISE AND NO MOVEMENT FROM the Boers.

"Do you think they'll attack, sir?" Fletcher asked.

"They might," Andrew replied. "Or van Collier could be bluffing. I doubt his commando is as strong as he wants us to believe."

The sun rose quickly, spreading light across the veld.

"Dust, sir," Kerr pointed to the horizon.

Andrew lifted his field glasses and studied the land in the direction Kerr pointed. "I see it," he said. "Now, we know a British column is out there somewhere, but there might also be another Boer commando."

"Yes, sir," Kerr said with a tight smile. "The question is, which force is creating that dust; us or the Boers."

The Boers already outnumber us by about six to one, but we're still holding them back. If more Boers arrive, we won't have a chance. However, if that's a British column, the Groenburg Commando will scatter, and we'll get home.

"What do we do, sir?" Fletcher was also studying the dust cloud.

"We continue as we are, Fletcher, and we pray." Andrew saw that Mariana was sitting beside Abercrombie in the centre of the civilians' position, with Turner lying at their side, bound hand and foot. Briggs was watching them, cradling his rifle, and his eyes unreadable. A single vulture flew overhead, circling as it waited for the inevitable casualties.

"GO TO YOUR MAN," ALETTA ORDERED STERNLY. "HE THINKS YOU NO longer want him."

Engela looked down at Konrad. "I nearly betrayed him with that thing there."

"It is a long step from nearly to reality," Aletta said. "Do you love my son?"

Engela nodded. "Ja," she said simply.

"Then go and tell him," Aletta advised. "Mannie will take you to the Groenburg Commando."

"Are you fit to ride, Mannie?" Engela asked.

"Ja. I am fit," Mannie ignored the blood drying on his face.

"Come then," Engela raised her chin. "I hope that Jan will take me back."

"That is between you and Jan," Aletta replied sternly. "Tell him how you feel, and let the Lord guide you both." She pushed Engela towards the door. "Go with Mannie." She watched as they rode away, smiling, for her younger son had also proved himself a man.

"That could be the British relief column, or it could be a Burgher commando," Johannes gestured to the rising dust.

"What do we do?" Theunis asked. He swept back his hair and smoothed a hand along the barrel of his rifle.

"Jan!" Johannes snapped. "Ride over and see who is making that dust. If it's the British, come and inform me. Don't do anything to alert them."

"Yes, Pa," Jan replied. Mounting his horse, he kicked in his heels and rode at a steady trot toward the dust. He knew it was some miles away, so there was no point in pushing too hard and tiring his horse. Jan loosened his rifle in its holster, adjusted his hat so it sheltered him from the worst of the sun and prepared for a steady ride.

More men had left the Groenburg Commando to return to their farms, leaving Johannes with less than twenty fighting Burghers. He held the Natal Dragoons by bluff and offensive action, but he would have to withdraw if a larger British force arrived.

"Watch the British positions," Johannes said to the remnants of his commando. "Baird will also have seen the dust. If he sends a rider, I want two men to hunt him down."

Theunis nodded. "I will go."

"Do that. Make sure the *Rooineck* does not hurt my son."

"The Boers have sent a man to greet the other column," Fletcher reported, watching through his field glasses.

Andrew nodded. "Either that or van Collier is checking to see who they are."

"That's possible, sir," Fletcher allowed. "Shall we send a man as well?"

"I can go, sir," Ogden volunteered.

Andrew scanned the Boer positions. Although he could not see them, he knew the Boers were there, remaining behind cover as they held the British on the parched ridge. "Do you think you'd get through their lines, Ogden, and then return with the information? Van Collier is an experienced commander. He'll expect us to try that."

Ogden nodded. "I can try, sir."

"No," Andrew decided. "Stay with us."

"What will we do?" Fletcher asked.

"We'll sit tight," Andrew said. "If that's a relief column, van Collier might try one last rush to capture Abercrombie, and if it's more Boers, well, we're already outnumbered."

Fletcher nodded. "It all depends on what that fellow discovers," he nodded to the thread of dust where the lone Boer rode towards the approaching force.

"It does," Andrew agreed. He glanced towards Abercrombie, but his gaze strayed to Mariana.

The Dragoons waited under the relentless lash of the sun. From their raised position on the ridge, they had a slight advantage over the Boers on the lower ground, watched for any movement and counted their cartridges.

"Fire if you have a definite target," Andrew said. "Make the Boers think we have plenty of ammunition, but don't waste bullets." He glanced upward, where the vultures circled in the vast arc of the sky. That morning, only one bird had watched them; now, half a dozen waited for death to feed them.

"I hate these birds," Fletcher said.

"Nature's cleansers," Andrew replied casually.

"When I die, I don't want one of these things to eat me," Fletcher stared upwards. "The idea of being inside their stomach is horrible."

"You'll be dead at the time," Andrew said. "You won't know anything about it."

"What if I'm only wounded, and they eat me alive," Fletcher said.

"Blow your brains out," Andrew told him. "Or even better, don't allow the Boers to shoot you."

Sergeant Meek raised his voice. "Dust from the west, sir. It looks like a lone rider, or maybe two."

Andrew focused his field glasses. "We know one thing," he said. "There are no British forces in that direction."

Kerr glanced at Meek, raised his eyebrows, and pressed a bullet into the breech of his carbine. He checked his bandoleer, found it empty and plunged a hand inside his ammunition pouch. His fingers scrabbled frantically until they closed on a couple of fat brass cartridges.

Three bullets left, and then it's butts, bayonets, boots, and fists. Kerr stamped his feet on the ground. *On you come, Brother Boers; we're ready.* His smile was self-mocking as he peered over the veld.

CHAPTER 21

Mannie felt his strength draining as he pushed his horse forward. Still not fully recovered from his illness, he found riding day after day across the veld tiring but knew he could not let Jan down. His brother had helped him during the siege of Potchefstroom and had taken him home, missing the victory of Majuba. Mannie wanted to return the kindness, whatever the physical cost. He slumped in the saddle, forcing himself to cover the miles. Whatever happened, Mannie knew he had to ride on. He stared ahead at the endless dun plain, listened to the remorseless hollow thump of his horse's hooves and continued.

I'm coming, Jan. I'm bringing Engela to you. Mannie repeated the exact words until they seemed to echo his horse's hoofprints on the hard ground.

Engela rode at his side, wondering what to say when she met Jan. She hoped he would understand when she told him about Konrad. She knew she would admit everything, for lying was not in her nature.

Oh, dear Lord, please let Jan forgive me. I don't want to lose my man.

"Over there!" Mannie smelled tobacco before he heard anything. He turned his horse and led Engela over the small ridge and down, where a man in a broad-brimmed hat stepped in front of them.

"Mannie!" Johannes lowered his rifle. "What are you doing here?"

"We are looking for Jan," Mannie explained. "Where is he?"

"He's out scouting," Johannes said. "I see you have brought Engela with you."

"Ja," Mannie said. "She wants to see Jan."

They all looked up as firing broke out to the west.

"A British column is coming!" Theunis roared. "Storm the Dragoons! Capture Abercrombie!"

❄

"The Boers are moving," Fletcher reported.

Andrew nodded. "I see them." He raised his voice. "Keep alert, boys, Piet is up to something."

The Dragoons checked their rifles and settled down. Few had more than three rounds of ammunition remaining, some less. Briggs looked from Andrew to Mariana.

"You keep your head down, Miss Maxwell," he advised. "Like the Captain told you, the Boers won't hurt you, but a stray bullet might."

"Thank you, William," Mariana said. "I'll look after myself. You take care of Mrs Murphy; she seems to favour you." She smiled at Briggs' startled expression.

Abercrombie lifted a tired hand. "I'm giving you all an awful lot of trouble," he said. "It might be better if I surrendered, and you could all go home."

"Now, now, Mr Abercrombie," Sergeant Meek rebuked. "We'll have none of that defeatist talk. You obey the captain's orders, and everything will turn out fine."

"Get back down, Mr Abercrombie!" Andrew snarled. "Kerr!"

"Sir!" Kerr hurried across with his carbine at the trail.

"If it looks like the Boers are about to overrun us, I want you to take Mr Abercrombie and break free. Ride like the devil for the border. Natal is only thirty miles or so to the south."

"I don't want to leave you, sir." Kerr protested.

"You'll do as you're damned well told," Andrew said. "You'll keep close to Abercrombie, ignore everybody else and get him to safety."

"What about Miss Maxwell, sir?" Briggs asked, "and the other ladies?"

Andrew realised that every Dragoon was listening to him. "Johannes van Collier is a gentleman," Andrew said. "He won't hurt any of the ladies."

"I wouldn't leave anyway," Mariana lifted her chin. "And you could not make me."

"That's another reason you're not taking Miss Maxwell," Andrew said. "She's as stubborn as a battery mule."

The men's laugh eased the tension. Mariana frowned for an instant, then smiled. "I am glad that's cleared up," she said.

"Keep your head down, Mariana!" Andrew snapped. "Or I'll have Briggs tie you hand and foot and carry you face down over a horse!" he closed his mouth as he realised the strain was affecting him.

Mariana looked sideways at him. "I'll keep my head down," she understood.

"Here they come!" Briggs said and unceremoniously shoved Mariana into her trench.

The Groenburg Commando advanced slowly, with some men firing and the others advancing from cover to cover. Theunis led them with his hair a dark tangle over his shoulders as he encouraged the men.

"Onwards, boys! Send the *Rooinecks* back to London!"

"Only fire when you have a definite target," Andrew reminded. He saw the dust cloud approaching and hoped it hid a British column. If he could hold out for another half hour, he might be safe. But half an hour was a long time when the Groenburg Commando was attacking.

The Dragoons fired slowly and carefully, conserving ammunition as Boer bullets hissed and cracked around them. Kerr shoved Abercrombie into a shallow depression beside a thorn bush, snarled at him to "keep out of the bloody way," and fired. The bullet caught a Boer in the shoulder, spinning him around. Andrew checked on Mariana, saw that Briggs was sheltering beside her trench and knew she was as safe as anybody could be in the middle of a skirmish. Andrew ducked as a Boer bullet knocked the hat from his head, aimed at a darting man and released his finger from the trigger as the man dived into cover.

Concentrate, Andrew. You can't look after everybody and shoot the Boers.

Fletcher gave a little grunt, opened his eyes wide, and rolled over, with blood spreading from his chest.

"The Boers got the lieutenant!" Ogden shouted. "Shoot the bastards!"

"Steady, lads!" Meek sounded as calm as if he were on exercise on Salisbury Plain. "Mark your targets!" He aimed and fired, hitting an advancing Boer in the stomach and doubling him up. "They can't take many more casualties!"

"Ammo!" Ogden shouted. "I've only one cartridge left!" He rolled towards the fallen Fletcher, scrabbled in his ammunition pouch, and removed two bullets. "Mr Fletcher has been hoarding them," he said.

"Throw one this way," McAlister shouted. "I'm out!"

"I've only one left," Morrison yelled. "I'm saving it until they get close."

Sergeant Meek fired again. "That's my last, sir." He lifted a fist-sized rock from the ground. "Boots and bayonets, lads, boots and bayonets!"

"Wait for them to come, now, boys. They don't like the bayonet!" Andrew ordered. He had surrendered at Majuba and was determined never to undergo that humiliation again. "Wait until they come close and attack them. Mariana! Are you all right?"

"Yes!" Mariana shouted.

"Keep down then," Andrew ordered. "Are you ready, Kerr?"

"Ready, sir," Kerr replied.

"When you see a gap, bundle Abercrombie onto a horse and run. Don't look back, and don't stop for anybody."

"Yes, sir," Kerr said.

"Here they come, sir," Meek warned.

JAN BLINKED AWAY THE DUST FROM HIS EYES AS HE GUIDED HIS HORSE INTO the shelter of a thorn bush. He saw the men approaching, riding in an untidy formation with dust obscuring them so he could not ascertain their identity. They might be Burghers, or they might be British Colonials.

I only have to identify them, and then I can outride any Rooineck soldier.

Jan watched them for a few moments without making up his mind.

I'll have to move closer.

Jan slid from the shelter of the thorn bush and guided his horse across the rough ground. He had missed the battle on Majuba Hill and hoped the Groenburg Commando would not engage the British without him. He hoped his father was not trying to keep him away from danger.

I am a man; I must fight to defend the Republic. There is nothing else in my life.

The riders were now closer, more easily seen even through the dust screen. Jan saw two men detach themselves from the mass and ride towards him. Both fired their rifles in the air to attract Jan's attention.

Briton or Boer? He would soon find out.

Jan loosened the rifle in its holster, remembered his father's words about not fighting and prepared to run.

"Who are you?" A further two men appeared behind Jan, both with rifles aimed directly at him. They spoke in English. "Give me your name and unit!"

ANDREW SAW THE BOERS HAD WITHDRAWN NEARLY ALL THEIR PICKETS TO concentrate on the attack, leaving a massive gap in the rear of the ridge. "Kerr!" Andrew roared. "Now!"

He only had time to shout the two words when the Boers were on them, yelling as they climbed the incline. *There are only sixteen of them. We have a chance.*

The British rose, some with clubbed rifles, others with fixed bayonets, and met the attackers face to face.

"Natal Dragoons!" Ogden roared. "Come on, you Boer bastards!"

"Send them back!" Andrew shouted, swinging his carbine at a hirsute man with a terai hat. "Come on, the Natal Dragoons!"

From the side of his eye, Andrew saw Kerr drag Abercrombie away and throw him on his horse. He saw Meek grappling with a young blond Boer, throw him to the ground, and thrust his bayonet into the man's arm. He saw Ogden falling as a Boer shot him from close range, and then the Boers were recoiling, withdrawing down the hill in a retreat that soon became a rout.

"They're running!" Meek shouted.

"They don't like the bayonet," McAlister strode forward. "Come on, lads!"

"Let them go!" Andrew ordered. "It could be an ambush! McAlister! Don't chase them! Are you all right, Mariana?"

Mariana emerged from her trench. "I'm all right." She stepped towards Fletcher. "Is he dead?"

"I think so," Andrew said.

Mariana knelt at Fletcher's side. "He's still breathing."

"Do what you can for him!" Andrew ordered. He saw Mrs. Murphy and Mrs. Williams emerge from shelter to check on Ogden and then concentrated on the battlefield.

Two dead Boers lay on the ground beside the youngster Meek had bayonetted. One dead man's hat had fallen off, revealing a mane of black hair around the bald crown of his head.

That's Theunis Steenekamp. I saw him talk at Krugersdorp. Andrew wondered anew at the terrible futility of war, where brave men and foolish men fought for ideas that would never benefit them and land they would never farm. Men who would be the best of friends in peacetime strove to kill each other because their political leaders disagreed.

"Send the wounded lad back," Andrew ordered. "He's no danger to us. Take his rifle and ammunition."

Andrew watched as the blond Boer limped down the slope, holding his wounded arm. Another Boer rode up under a flag of truce to help his colleague. Andrew recognised Johannes van Collier as the helper and was strangely glad the veldcornet had survived.

"Come, Abraham," Johannes murmured, deep-voiced.

"Good luck, Johannes," Andrew whispered.

As if he had heard, Johannes turned around, and for a moment, his eyes locked with Andrew's.

Andrew lifted a hand in greeting, saw Johannes respond, and turned away. A small ribbon of dust to the south showed where Kerr and Abercrombie were riding towards Natal.

The longer we hold the Boers here, the better chance we give Abercrombie and Kerr.

"Collect any discarded Boer rifles," Andrew ordered. "See what ammunition the dead Burghers had. Every single bullet helps."

"Sir!" Meek said. "Over there! Are they British or Boer?"

Andrew lifted his field glasses as a mass of men approached under the rising dust. "I don't know," he said. "They could be either."

JAN STOPPED AS THE TWO MEN HELD HIM AT GUNPOINT. "WHO ARE YOU?" the leading man asked again, then repeated the words in the Taal.

"I am Jan van Collier of Nuwe Hoop Plaas and the Groenburg Commando under my father, Johannes van Collier and Theunis Steenekamp," Jan replied proudly. He wondered if he could traverse his rifle, shoot both men and escape. "What are you *Rooinecks* doing in our land?"

"We are no *Rooinecks*," the leading man holstered his rifle. "I am Henrick van Renswick of Pretoria, and this is Piet Cloete, second cousin of Karl Cloete of the Groenburg Commando."

"You are Burghers?" Jan asked, unable to stop his smile.

"We are Burghers," Henrick replied. "We heard shooting."

"We have a British force trapped on a ridge," Jan said. "We didn't know if you were Burghers or British."

"That will be Captain Baird's Natal Dragoons," Henrick said. "Come with us and tell the commander."

All three men stopped as they heard renewed firing from the ridge.

"It seems that your father has ordered an attack on the ridge," Henrick said.

"It seems so," Jan replied.

"Here is our commander," Henrick said. "Tell him who you are and why you are here." He smiled faintly. "His name is Paul Kruger."

Jan gasped. "The Vice-President?"

Paul Kruger greeted Jan like an old friend and listened to his story. "Your father has done well, Jan. Lead us," he said, ordering his commando to follow. They were over five hundred men, all well-mounted and armed, veterans of siege and battle.

The ridge rose two hundred feet above the plain, marked by green thorn bushes and gun smoke. Kruger halted the commando as the British repulsed the Groenburg assault.

"Johannes van Collier?" Kruger approached Johannes, who helped a wounded man.

"That's me. Did my son bring you?" Johannes handed Abraham to Kruger's medical team.

"He is over there," Kruger pointed to Jan. "Where is Theunis Steenekamp?"

"Dead," Johannes said shortly. "He led a charge on the British."

Kruger showed no emotion over Theunis's death. He regretted the loss of any Burgher but had come to accept that war had its bitter price.

"We tried to capture the ridge before you arrived," Johannes said. "We thought you might be British."

Kruger looked towards the ridge, seemingly empty but still occupied by the enemy.

"I will talk to Captain Baird," Kruger said. He gave brisk orders that saw his commando surround the ridge, with each man disappearing behind cover. "Nobody will get past my commando."

"THEY'RE BOERS, SIR." MEEK SCANNED THE NEWCOMERS THROUGH Fletcher's field glasses. "Hundreds of them."

"They're Boers," Andrew confirmed. He felt sick when he saw the numbers arrayed against him.

The newcomers spread around the ridge, with the horsemen forming tight little groups at extreme rifle range.

"These lads know their stuff," Meek said. "They're tempting us to fire and waste ammunition while effectively blockading us."

"How many bullets do we have left?"

"Nine from the dead Boers, sir, but they're only suitable for their rifles. Three Martini cartridges. I took the liberty of borrowing Mr. Fletcher's revolver and all his ammunition, which will give us another seven shots, plus whatever you have."

"I've one Martini cartridge and six revolver bullets," Andrew said.

Meek lowered his field glasses. "Not enough to stop these boys. One more attack should be enough." He tapped his water bottle. "We're short of water and *scoff* as well."

Andrew looked around the ridge. Mariana and the two other women were tending to the badly wounded Fletcher while most Dragoons lay on the ground, seeking shade and cover. Ogden was dead. The sentries crouched behind rocks, watching the surrounding enemy.

"Sir!" Briggs said. "A group of Boers is approaching under a flag of truce."

"They do that a lot," Sergeant Meek said. "I've never known men to talk so much as the Boers."

Andrew forced a smile. "Let's see what they have to say."

A sad-faced, bearded man led the mounted group that rode carefully up the ridge. Andrew stepped forward to meet them. "That's far enough!" he cautioned when they came within two hundred yards of his perimeter. "Any closer, and I'll order my men to open fire!"

The Boers obediently halted. "Are you Captain Andrew Baird of the Natal Dragoons?"

"I am," Andrew confirmed. "Who are you, *meneer*?" He already knew the answer.

"Paul Kruger of the *Suid-Afrikaanse Republiek*," the sad-faced man remained on horseback, sitting easily as his companions studied the British positions. "You are outnumbered and surrounded, Captain."

Andrew affected nonchalance. "I see your men," he said. "We have them trapped around us, waiting for a British column to finish you off. We are the anvil, and the column is the hammer."

Kruger smiled. "You are no anvil, my friend. The British column returned to Natal days ago when we informed them we had captured your small party. You have about a dozen Natal Dragoons, six civilians, three women, and a British spy named Charles Abercrombie."

"We have nobody of that name here," Andrew said truthfully.

"Veldcornet Johannes van Collier has seen him," Kruger replied. "He was at Swartspruit when you arrived, and you took him with you."

"And now he is gone," Andrew replied.

Kruger sighed and looked up at the ridge, where the Dragoons waited with empty rifles. "Can you tell me on your honour that Charles Abercrombie is no longer with you?"

"I can tell you that on my honour as an officer and a gentleman," Andrew replied.

Kruger smiled sadly. "And what do you intend now, Captain?"

"That depends on you, *Meneer* Kruger. We could fight you here, or if you ride away, we will return to Natal," Andrew said honestly.

"We could storm the ridge," Kruger reminded.

"Perhaps," Andrew said. "But you would lose many men and make a lot of widows and orphans in the Republic."

Kruger nodded gravely. "Perhaps we would lose fewer men than you suggest," he said. "Why did you invade our land during a time of truce?"

"The Afrikander Bond Boers were blockading the garrison at Swartspruit, contrary to the truce," Andrew said. "I was sent to lift the siege and bring the garrison home."

"Including Mr Abercrombie," Kruger said.

"Including Mr Abercrombie, the geologist," Andrew agreed.

"Mr Abercrombie, the prime minister's nephew," Kruger amended. He stepped his horse closer to Andrew. "You will be aware that a mutual acquaintance of ours was also interested in Mr Abercrombie."

"Konrad Bramigan, the Prussian agent," Andrew said. "Is he with your commando?"

"He does not ride with us," Kruger replied. "Nor will we listen to his blandishments and exchange one foreign invader for another."

"Thank you for the information, sir," Andrew said.

"I take it you have no further reason to remain in our land?"

"I intend to leave as soon as my way is clear," Andrew replied.

"We shall not delay you," Kruger replied. "There has been enough killing in our Republic." He touched a hand to his hat. "I wish you a good day, Captain Baird."

"Thank you, sir," Andrew replied. "Please give my regards to Johannes van Collier."

Kruger nodded. "I shall," he said.

Andrew watched as the Boers withdrew from the ridge to form up half a mile away.

"Right, lads," Andrew said. "Mount up; we're going home! Column of twos, with the civilians in the rear." He heard Meek hector the Dragoons into formation, ensured Mariana was safe and led them towards Natal.

"JAN!" MANNIE SHOUTED. "JAN!"

"Mannie!" Jan felt a mixture of pleasure and apprehension when he saw his younger brother approach. "What are you doing here?"

"Engela wanted to see you," Mannie explained, stepping aside to reveal Engela standing nervously behind him.

"Hello, Jan," Engela did not smile. "How are you?"

"Engela?" Jan stared at her for a few seconds while all his doubts and anger faded.

Mannie smiled as Jan shouldered his rifle, extended his arms, and brought Engela close.

CHRISTIAAN NIEKERF WATCHED THE BRITISH RIDE TO THE SOUTH WITH THE women at the rear and their rifles in their bucket holsters.

"Are the *Rooinecks* returning to their own land?"

"Ja, Christiaan," Johannes replied.

"Is the war over?" Christiaan asked.

"It is over," Johannes said. "We have defeated the *Rooinecks*. They will leave us alone now."

Christian carefully placed his rifle in its holster and watched the retreating British column. Johannes could not read the expression on his face. "I do not trust the *Rooinecks*. I'll follow them as far as the border."

Johannes nodded. "That is a wise plan," he said. "Do not trust any foreign nation that says they are here to help us."

Christiaan patted his horse. "The Lord gave us Africa as the Promised Land. We tamed it from the wilderness, and we will hold it. It is our land." He tapped the butt of his rifle. "I will follow the *Rooinecks* back to Natal, and in time, we shall drive them over the sea."

Johannes smiled. "I hope we are both alive to see that day, Oom Christiaan."

Christiaan examined Johannes with his old, terrible eyes. "You are of good blood, Johannes van Collier. I hope to ride beside you again." Turning his horse, he followed the British, riding slowly.

"How old is that man?" Jan joined Johannes, with Engela and Abraham at his side. Abraham was pale, with his left arm in a sling.

"Christiaan was a Voortrekker back in the Great Trek of thirty-five," Johannes said. "The Zulus murdered his wife and children at Weenen,[1] so he was a grown man then, forty-three years ago. He must be in his eighties now." They watched Christiaan ride away, an indomitable old man who symbolised the spirit of the Voortrekkers.

"The Voortrekkers were men," Jan said.

Johannes looked at his son with a smile. "You are also a man," he said.

Cape Town, November 1881.

General Hook looked across the width of his desk at Andrew. "You got Abercrombie out safely and avoided a diplomatic spat, Baird. That was probably the only positive to come from this sorry affair, and we can't tell the papers."

"We lost some good men, sir," Andrew reminded.

"We always do," Hook agreed, pouring brandy into two glasses and handing one to Andrew. "And if you had killed Turner, we would have lost one more."

"Turner was a lucky man," Andrew said.

Hook nodded. "He was an insurance policy, nothing else." He changed the subject. "The peace treaty gives the Transvaal self-government in all internal matters, while Britain controls their foreign affairs."

"That should keep Germany out," Andrew said.

"That may be the idea," Hook agreed. "The treaty has not pleased everybody. There has been an exodus of British residents from the Transvaal. They've given up their homes and businesses rather than live under an oligarchical Boer government."

Andrew sipped at his Cape-distilled brandy and looked out of Hook's office window, where a crowd shouted their dislike of Gladstone and the government in London. One howling group set fire to Gladstone's effigy, while another mob mocked a model of the British lion, calling it a toothless remnant of the past. "Mr. Gladstone doesn't seem very popular here," Andrew said.

"He's not," Hook confirmed. "Many people see him as pusillanimous, refusing to perform his duty to the British. The British of Cape Colony and Natal think the Boers are a threat on their borders, much as they viewed the Zulus." The general shrugged. "Opinions are, as always, divided. Many others, particularly in Great Britain, see the treaty as the magnanimous action of a power that does not have to prove its strength by squashing a small nation. They believe Gladstone has shown that Britain is willing to aid a struggling country."

Andrew tried more brandy. "I doubt the Boers see things in that light."

"President Johannes Brand of the Orange Free State said the treaty was the noblest act England has ever done." Hook grunted. "He means Britain rather than England, but one must forgive these people their occasional lapses into ignorance."

"Yes, sir," Andrew agreed. "Miscalling Britain as England is a foolish mistake many people make."

Hook nodded. "Foolish indeed. However, the Boers of the Transvaal believe the treaty directly resulted from the skirmishes they won. They think Britain was scared to fight them."

"Gladstone has his own agenda," Andrew said.

"Don't all politicians? Many soldiers believe the government betrayed the army." He threw Andrew a sharp look. "You were present at Laing's Nek and Majuba. In fact, you saw most of our defeats."

"Yes, sir," Andrew agreed.

"How did it happen?" Hook asked. "How did a collection of semi-educated farmers defeat a modern European army? We already discussed your thoughts. Have you more to add?"

Andrew considered before he replied. "May I be frank, sir?"

"I wish somebody would be frank rather than soothing me with platitudes!" Hook said.

"Very well, sir. The trouble starts at the top. I think some officers are deficient in intelligence. The cleverest boys in school don't enter the army but find more lucrative employment in the professions or industry. We'll have to increase pay to attract a better-quality officer. At present, many Officers' Messes are little more than social clubs for gentlemen, with sport and hunting more important than soldiering. In the so-called smart regiments, only the rich and well-connected become officers. They are charming fellows, no doubt, but not always the most intelligent of leaders."

Hook nodded grimly. "Are you saying that many officers see the army as a glorified social club?"

"Yes, sir," Andrew said grimly. "If we hope to improve the army, we must end the system where money, titles, and old school connections ensure near-automatic selection and promotion."

"That would be a monumental alteration," Hook responded.

"Maybe every officer should serve at least a year in the ranks," Andrew continued. "Let them see what the men are like before they condemn them with brainless decisions."

"Anything else?" Hook asked.

"Training," Andrew said. "Standing men in line to fire volleys does not work against an enemy as wily as the Boers, who have weapons as good as ours. We must train our men to fire from behind cover and advance as the Boers do. We also need to improve our soldiers' marksmanship."

Hook scribbled notes. "You've given this some thought, Baird. Anything else?"

"Mobility," Andrew said. "The Boer commando could move from battle to siege and back at a speed we cannot emulate."

"Are you proposing we mount every British soldier on a horse?"

Andrew shook his head. "That would be ideal, if hardly practical, sir," he replied. "I would suggest more mounted infantry and less rigidity in drill."

"These are major proposals, Baird," Hook said.

"Yes, sir," Andrew agreed, "but in the eyes of the world, the Boers have defeated us, and it's a defeat that will rankle in the army."

"It's a defeat we may yet avenge," Hook said softly. "Although not if Gladstone is in office. Well, thank you, Captain. I have asked the opinion of several officers who served in the war. I'll add your ideas, create a file, and send it to the appropriate government minister."

"Thank you, sir," Andrew said. "Do you think he will listen?"

Hook shrugged weary shoulders. "That's in the lap of the Gods, Baird. Who knows the workings of a politician's mind?" He finished his brandy. "Now the fighting is over; what do you intend to do? Will you remain with the Natal Dragoons?"

"I don't know, sir," Andrew thought of Mariana. "I haven't decided yet."

"Keep in touch, Baird; I anticipate trouble in Suez next." Hook grinned. "Not your bailiwick, eh? You'd better get back to your Dragoons and that young lady of yours." He held out his hand.

"Yes, sir." Andrew shook the general's hand and left the office.

Mariana stood at the door of the house as Andrew dismounted. "What did the general say?"

"I don't think he's optimistic that our army will reform," Andrew patted Lancelot and handed him to Briggs. "How are you?"

"Fine," Mariana told him. She held out her arms. "Will the peace last?"

"For the time being," Andrew held her, looking into her eyes without seeing any shadows. "Many in the army will seek another round with Brother Boer, mainly men who have never met him. The papers will stir up discontent and print all sorts of nonsense."

"The papers often do," Mariana said. She slid her arms around his shoulders, examining him as minutely as he studied her. "You look tired."

"You look well," Andrew countered. "Better than you've done since..."

"Since the day the renegades came," Mariana said levelly.

"Since the day the renegades came," Andrew agreed, searching for the shadow's return. Mariana's eyes remained clear, with a sparkle he had not seen for over two years.

"I love you," Mariana said suddenly, with a slight lift of her chin. "I have always loved you."

Andrew felt his heartbeat increase. He instinctively held tighter.

"I know you always loved Elaine better than me," Mariana said without breaking eye contact. "But can you love me just a little bit?"

Andrew felt something twist inside him. He was unsure how he felt for this girl, no, this *woman* now; her experiences had altered Mariana, so her girlish years were behind her. He thought of the promise he had made at Elaine's grave to always look after her sister. "More than a little bit," Andrew said softly, unsure how much truth was in his words.

"More than a little bit?" For a moment, Mariana looked very vulnerable, and then she smiled. "For my sake or Elaine's?"

About to reply, "For both," Andrew changed his mind. "For yours," he said and saw Mariana's eyes widen.

"Will Elaine mind you loving me more than a little bit?" Mariana asked.

"No," Andrew told her. "Elaine won't mind in the slightest." He could picture Elaine standing in the room with her so-sensible smile as she watched them.

They entered the immaculate house, which smelled of beeswax polish and cleanliness. "You've got the place looking lovely," Andrew said.

"Elaine would like it this way."

Andrew shook his head. "This house is about Mariana and Andrew," he assured her.

When Mariana smiled, Andrew knew he had said the right thing. Mariana closed the door. "I've made coffee," she said and placed a possessive hand on his arm.

ALETTA LOOKED UP FROM THE TABLE WHERE SHE WAS MAKING BREAD. *JA*, she thought, *I have my men back. They have gone to war, and all have returned to me. Johannes has new grey hairs on his head, and the lines on his face have deepened. Working on the farm for a few weeks will not remove the grey, but it will smooth his face. Jan is a man now, with iron inside him. He will never tell me what he has seen and done, but he is now ready to take Engela to wife, and she is prepared for him.*

She kneaded the dough with her strong hands, allowing the rhythm of the work to ease some of her worries.

Mannie is the most affected. He left as a boy and returned as a boy, and then something happened, and he became a man. She nodded. *I could not have asked for more. A good man for a husband and two brave men for sons. The Lord has blessed me.*

"Aletta!" Johannes stepped into the room. He paused for a moment to wrap his arms around her. "I am going to check the cattle. I don't know how many we've lost to wild animals since the war started."

"You do that," Aletta agreed. "Take Jan with you. And Mannie, if he will go."

"They are both already outside," Johannes told her.

"That is good," Aletta said. She stepped to the door and watched her family ride away. *Life is as it should be,* she told herself as her men shrank with distance. *They'll be hungry when they return. My men are always hungry when they return from work.* Smiling, Aletta stepped back into the kitchen, humming a quiet song as the chickens scrabbled noisily outside.

THE CHILL OF THE IRRAWADDY

THE SOLDIER'S SON BOOK 3

For Cathy

The Burman give us Irrawaddy chills.
Rudyard Kipling

Come you back to Mandalay,
Where the old Flotilla lay:
Can't you 'ear their paddles chunkin' from Rangoon to Mandalay?
Rudyard Kipling

A large force of Dacoits attacked the Kyike Police Station, which was defended by Mr. Shaw, assistant commissioner, and Mr. Sladden, police inspector, very courageously. On the sound of the enemy's gongs and drums, their twenty Burmese policemen bolted, leaving them with twenty Sikhs and natives of India, with whom they defended the station for three days and nights, repulsing numerous attacks. When the ammunition was exhausted, they brought off their men safely by a long night march.

Newcastle Chronicle, 26 December 1885

PRELUDE

POLICE POST, BAN HTEIK CHAUNG, BURMA, JANUARY 1886

"Here they come again," Captain Andrew Baird looked around at the remaining defenders of the post. Of the original twenty Sikh policemen, only fifteen remained, while their commander, Lieutenant Hanley, lay in a corner of the building, bleeding from three wounds. Bo Thura sat under the window with a cheroot in his mouth, loading his Martini-Henry. He looked up when Andrew spoke, thumbed a cartridge into the breech, and nodded.

"They are coming," he agreed.

The Sikhs lifted their Snider rifles, waiting for the attack with their customary professionalism. Sukhbir Singh, closest to Andrew, grinned through his beard and stamped his boots on the ground. "*Unhāṁ nū ā'uṇa di'ō*," he said. "Let them come."

Another policeman slapped the butt of his rifle. "*Birdh ki Paij Panth ki jit*!" he shouted. "Rout of the Enemy and Victory of the Sikh Path!"

"I am not sure what you said, but it sounds good!" Andrew knew his father had always admired the Sikhs, and he now understood why. They were the most stolidly brave fighting men he had ever met.

Andrew lifted his head to peer out the window, ready to duck when he saw movement. Although the police had cut back the forest to a radius of a hundred yards, the dacoits haunted the fringes, watching everything the police did and sniping whenever they saw an opportunity. The dull green trees seemed sinister in the gloomy light, with the constant humming of insects a backdrop and the cries of unknown birds a distraction rather than a pleasure.

"How many are there, do you think?" Hanley asked, lifting himself to a more comfortable position. Blood had dried around the two bullet holes in his tunic and the *dha* gash on his thigh. He coughed, dribbling more blood from the corner of his mouth.

"I'm not sure," Andrew replied. "A couple of hundred, perhaps. Maybe more." He glimpsed the yellow umbrella through a gap in the trees and wondered if a snapshot might end the affair. Lifting his Martini-Henry, he aimed and cursed as the umbrella moved deeper into the forest. With limited ammunition, Andrew could not afford to waste a bullet.

"A couple of hundred," Hanley repeated. He coughed up more blood. "Was that an umbrella I saw out there?"

"It was," Andrew confirmed.

Hanley grinned, showing blood-stained teeth. "You remember what Wellington said when he saw a couple of Guards officers with umbrellas during the Peninsular War? He said, 'Lord Wellington does not approve of the use of umbrellas during the enemy's firing and will not allow the gentleman's sons to make themselves ridiculous in the eyes of the Army.'"

"Trust Wellington to have a quote for every occasion," Andrew replied. "There may be more than a couple of hundred. It's hard to tell when they move around all the time."

There are more than two hundred men out there. I'd estimate between four and five hundred, a mixture of raggedy-arsed dacoits and remnants of Thibaw's Army. It's best not to tell Hanley how bad the odds are.

The gongs began again, with their brassy clamour reverberating through the trees to bombard the post. Andrew glanced at the men. The stolid Sikhs appeared unmoved by the sound, but the local Burmese were uneasy, perhaps because they knew what the sound signified. One man spoke to Bo Thura, who replied with a short sentence. Hanley looked up, coughed again, and checked his revolver. Andrew noticed the butt was sticky with blood.

That poor lad hasn't got much time left to live. He'll fill another lonely grave thousands of miles from home in a squalid skirmish he had no part in starting.

The gongs continued, stopped for a moment, and started again.

One of the Sikhs grunted and spat on the ground. "Are they trying to scare us with their little gongs?" He grinned, showing white teeth behind his beard. "Maybe they think we are children, to be frightened by noise."

The sound increased all around the police post, and a drum added resonance to the racket. Andrew checked how many cartridges he had left in his pouch and stared at the surrounding forest.

"Here they come," Bo Thura said quietly as the dacoits slipped quietly from the trees. One second, the clearing was empty, and the next, a hundred dacoits were walking purposefully towards the post.

"There are more," Bo Thura said, and Andrew saw movement on the left. He lifted his Martini and aimed at the nearest, a squat man with the remains of a light red jacket uniform on his shoulders and a dha in his fist.

As the Sikhs prepared to fire, a volley came from the forest, with a second quickly following.

"How many rifles do these dacoits have?" Hanley asked. He struggled to the nearest window, gasping with pain. "I thought the Burmese Army had handed in all their weapons."

"Apparently not," Andrew said as bullets whistled and crackled around him. He swore as a group of dacoits stepped in front of the squat man. With only a few cartridges remaining, Andrew wanted to ensure he used them on leaders rather than followers.

"What the devil?" Andrew stared as the dacoit behind the squat man lifted a rifle. "That's a Winchester repeater, one of those fancy American rifles that can fire multiple rounds without reloading."

"These dacoits are better armed than we are," Hanley said.

The dacoits spread out to surround the police post, some with rifles, others with the wicked Burmese *dha*. The gongs continued their brassy clamour, a canopy of sound encompassing the handful of British and Sikhs.

"This will be their final assault," Sukhbir Singh said. "They're coming for the kill."

"And their leader has arrived," Andrew said. He pointed to a man on a hardy Burmese pony. The rider held a white flag surmounted by a blue peacock, the symbol of Burmese royalty. "These lads are still fighting for the Kingdom of Ava. Don't they know they've lost the war?"

At the sight of the peacock flag, the remaining Burmese policemen in the post shouted and ran to the door.

"Stop!" Hanley shouted and collapsed, coughing up blood.

Andrew shook his head. "Let them go," he advised. "They'd not be reliable."

Sukhbir grabbed one of the panicking men by the throat until Andrew intervened. "No, Sukhbir."

The Burmese policemen dragged away the barricades from the door and fled outside, leaving the post strangely hollow.

Sukhbir spat on the ground.

"Here they come," Bo Thura said as Andrew lifted his rifle. "And there are more." He pointed to the right, where another force of dacoits filtered through the trees. "Where the devil did these lads come from?"

CHAPTER 1

BERWICKSHIRE, SCOTLAND, SUMMER 1884

Andrew guided the dog cart to a twisted rowan tree at the side of the macadamised road and pulled Mariana's cape tighter across her shoulders. An easterly wind carried rain from the German Ocean to spatter on Mariana as she sheltered under the tree.

"It's lovely here," Mariana said, looking over the damp fields towards the River Tweed.

"Apart from the foul weather," Andrew replied.

"Oh, I don't mind the rain," Mariana said. "When we were young in Inglenook, Elaine and I always left the house when it was wet. We enjoyed the rain after all the dry weather."

Andrew smiled, thinking of Mariana back in her home in Natal. "I could imagine you two dancing in the rain," he said. He still thought of Mariana's sister, Elaine, from time to time, even though it was five years since a force of renegades had murdered her and her parents on their farm on the Natal-Zululand border.

"Elaine would love it here," Mariana looked over the green, fertile Border countryside, with the solid stone buildings nestling against swaying trees and cattle grazing in the fields. "It all looks so peaceful."

"It does," Andrew agreed. "It's hard to believe this was once the most contested frontier in Europe, with Scots and English having battles, raids and skirmishes for hundreds of years."

Mariana took a deep breath. "If you stand still and listen," she said. "You can hear the tension."

"Can you hear tension?" Andrew asked.

"Undoubtedly," Mariana smiled at him, brushing back a loose strand of hair that had escaped from her hat. "Can't you hear the voices of the old people?"

Andrew lifted his head. "All I hear is the wind in the trees and the rain pattering in the puddles!"

"Oh, Andrew!" Mariana tapped his arm. "You need to use your imagination! You can taste the tension in the wind and sense the old reivers and warriors." She surveyed the landscape, from the rippling Tweed to the broad fields and distant green Cheviot Hills. "There is poetry in this land, Andrew; can you not sense the romance?"

"Can you sense Sir Lancelot?" Andrew asked. "According to some legends, he lived at Bamborough Castle; that was his Joyous Gard."

"That's quite a few miles south of here," Mariana replied.

"He was a travelling man, a knight errant, and would go riding and hunting," Andrew said. "We don't know how extensive his lands would be, but I think he'd know this area well."

They stood two hundred yards from the River Tweed, five miles west of Berwick. A stone's throw away, a pair of stone buildings dominated a grassy knoll and sheltered behind a group of trees. One was a Georgian house, two storeys tall, with rain weeping from its grey slate roof and classically proportioned windows and doors. The other was much older, a crumbling ruin of a tower that had stood guard over a ford across the river for centuries.

"Can we look at the castle?" Mariana asked.

"We can," Andrew told her. "Come on!" Taking Mariana's hand, he helped her from the dog cart and guided her through the open five-barred gate and onto the rough track that curved upwards to the grey buildings.

"I hope the owner doesn't mind us nosing his property," Mariana said as they avoided the puddles and accidentally kicked loose stones up the path.

"He won't mind. I know him," Andrew replied.

Grass grew on the central ridge of the track, and a mouse scuttled in front of them. Andrew glanced sideways at Mariana, saw her genuine interest in the tower and nodded.

This idea might work. I have captured Mariana's attention; I hope I have set the scene for tomorrow's question. Andrew looked at her fondly, lifted a hand to touch her shoulder and dropped it again.

"What is the castle called?" Mariana hardly glanced at the Georgian farmhouse. Her eyes were busy on the grey-stoned tower, where a rowan tree clung precariously to the upper wall, and moss furred the lower layers. A bevy of pigeons exploded from the ruin, wings flapping noisily, with a single crow observing them from the topmost height.

"Corbiestane Tower," Andrew stopped at the apex of the curve, where a group of whins whispered in the breeze. "A corbie is a crow, so it means the Tower of the Crow's Stone."

"There's the corbie up there," Mariana nodded to the crow.

"The tower guards a ford across the Tweed," Andrew indicated the river. "On this bank, we are in Scotland, while the opposite side is England; this ford would be an important crossing point for both countries."

Miraculously, the rain stopped, and a shaft of sun landed on the tower's doorway, showing a carved stone above the entrance.

"What's the carving?" Mariana asked. She stepped closer, craning her neck to see. "It looks like," she turned away, facing Andrew with new colour flushing her cheeks. "It's not, Andrew! It can't be."

"It's a phallic symbol," Andrew hid his smile. "The Romans used it as a sign of good luck, which means either the original building here is very old, or the builder cannibalised a Roman ruin for his tower."

"So, this tower might have been here in King Arthur's time?" Mariana asked, glancing sideways at the symbol and then looking away.

"Not this particular tower, but I'd say there's been a building guarding the ford for centuries, perhaps back to Roman times. In that case, something would have been here in Arthurian times and perhaps owned by Sir Lancelot. He'd appoint one of his knights to watch for raiders, either Scots or English."

"Oh," Mariana lifted her skirt higher and walked to the tower, touching the stones as if to recapture the legends of King Arthur. "To think that Arthur, Guinevere or Lancelot might have been here." She looked over her shoulder at Andrew. "Do you think the present owner would mind if I went inside?"

"I am sure he wouldn't mind at all," Andrew replied. "But be careful; it's a bit tumbledown."

Avoiding looking at the carved stone, Mariana stepped through the battered doorway and looked up. The tower was a hollowed-out ruin, with bare walls reaching to the silver-grey sky, knee-high weeds sprouting on the ground and vegetation thrusting between the stonework. Birds had nested in the arrow-slit windows, and the wind moaned through the gaps.

"It's lovely," Mariana said. "To think Lancelot might have been here."

"This tower was built long after his time," Andrew reminded her. "He might have visited the site, though, if he ever existed."

"Of course, he existed," Mariana retorted.

Andrew smiled at her passion. "Of course he did," he agreed.

Mariana smoothed her hand over the rough stonework. "But Lancelot mused a little space; He said, "She has a lovely face; God in his mercy lend her grace, The Lady of Shalott."

"Indeed," Andrew recognised Tennyson's poetry.

"Maybe Tennyson visited here before he thought of the Lady," Mariana said. "He wasn't far away, was he?"

"I know he loves the Lake District," Andrew said. "I don't know about the Tweed." He changed the subject. "Would you like to see the house?"

"You know I love looking at other people's houses," Mariana replied. "Will the owner not object to two strangers dropping in unannounced?"

"The house is empty," Andrew replied. "And I have the key."

Mariana took his arm. "Oh, you clever thing! Come on then, Andrew! What are we waiting for?"

The key turned smoothly in the lock, and Andrew pushed the door open and stepped aside so Mariana could enter first.

"It's completely empty," Mariana said. She strode into the house, looking around her. "What a lovely place, and so fortunate being so close to Lancelot's tower."

Mariana has convinced herself that Lancelot lived on the tower, Andrew thought. *Maybe that's no bad thing.*

"What do you think of this house?" Andrew asked. He closed the door and stepped back to allow her a better view.

"It's beautiful," Mariana replied. Lifting the hem of her skirt, she raced to the landing upstairs, with the sound of her boots echoing in the hallway. "There are four rooms up here," she said.

Andrew followed her upstairs, checking the walls and ceilings for signs of dampness and black mould.

"What would you do with this house if it was yours?"

"Oh, that's easy," Mariana replied. "I'd have this room overlooking the tower, and your bedroom would be over there, with a view to the river." She hesitated for a moment. "I nearly said the Tugela River."

"I guessed that," Andrew said. "The house's situation is similar to Inglenook." He allowed Mariana a moment to recover from her memories. "Except for the possible Arthurian connection. Would you like to live here?"

"I'd love to," Mariana replied. "I'd see Lancelot and Arthur every day."

"Good," Andrew said. "That's why I bought it. Farming is currently going through a slump and prices have dropped, so it was dirt cheap."

"Oh," Mariana put a hand over her mouth, staring at him. "So it's yours?"

"Ours, if you want to share it," Andrew said. "Unless you have some secret sweetheart you want to run off with."

Mariana turned away. "You know very well that I do not have a sweetheart."

You used to think you loved me, Mariana. What happened?

"Indeed," Andrew said, hiding his disappointment. "When you've had your fill of Corbiestane, Mariana, we'll return to Berwick."

"When can we move in?" Mariana asked.

"When all the legal paperwork is completed, and I have the workmen install modern plumbing and lighting," Andrew said. "After that, you can do what you will to the house."

When Mariana smiled quietly, Andrew knew she was already planning her alterations.

"The stone," Mariana said. "Where is the Corbiestane?"

"At the back," Andrew led her outside, carefully locking the door behind him. The Corbiestane was a large lump of rock with the crudely carved figure of a bird inscribed on one side.

Mariana ran her hands over the carving. "What was it for?"

"Nobody knows," Andrew told her. "There are many legends, but nothing is certain."

"I think Lancelot's knight had a corbie on his shield, and he carved the stone to let everybody know he was guarding the ford," Mariana said.

"That's as good an explanation as any," Andrew agreed. "Now, shall we get away before the heavens open again? Tomorrow, I am taking you to Edinburgh to see Saint Margaret's Chapel." He saw Mariana looking at him but did not explain further. Mariana was studying Corbiestane farmhouse, deciding what type of wallpaper she wanted.

EDINBURGH CASTLE, SCOTLAND, SUMMER 1884

"It's very romantic," Mariana said, holding her hat against Edinburgh Castle's eternal wind. "Who was Saint Margaret?"

"She was Queen of Scotland in the eleventh century," Andrew said. "Married to Malcolm the Third, Malcolm Canmore. She brought the Roman Catholic faith to Scotland to replace the old Celtic Christianity."

"Oh," Mariana nodded. "Was this chapel named after her?"

They stood outside the small, stone-built chapel, recently restored after being used as a storeroom for years. Even Andrew could sense the history as he touched the ancient doorway and wondered how many people had been in this spot over the past seven hundred years. He thought of the long, long line of Scotland's kings and queens, the knights and nobles, and the thousands of soldiers who had garrisoned the castle.

"I said, was the chapel named after Saint Margaret?" Mariana raised her eyebrows.

"I think Margaret's son, King David, had it built," Andrew said, "so it's 12th century, about 750 years old." He saw that the age did not impress her. "It's also the oldest remaining building in Edinburgh Castle. King David was a very religious man who had half the abbeys in Scotland built."

Andrew realised that Mariana's attention had wandered. He allowed her to enjoy the vista of Edinburgh's New Town, with the Scott Monument arrowing skyward and the austerely regular streets contrasting with the blue Firth of Forth behind.

"It's a very nice chapel," Mariana agreed.

"I knew you'd like it with the Arthurian connection," Andrew watched as Mariana took the bait.

"What Arthurian connection?" Mariana lost all interest in Edinburgh's grey streets as she swivelled towards him.

"I thought you would already know," Andrew teased her. "One of the earliest mentions of Arthur might have been written here."

"In Edinburgh?"

"In Edinburgh Castle," Andrew replied. "Have you heard of the *Gododdin*?" He enjoyed Mariana's look of interested confusion.

"The what?" She shook her head. "What is it?"

"The *Gododdin* is a sixth or seventh-century poem about a band of warriors fighting against the invading Saxons," Andrew explained. "The warriors spent a year in the hall or fort of a king called Mynddog Mwynfawr before they rode south to fight the invaders."

Mariana persisted in her pet love. "Did Arthur lead them?"

"No," Andrew shook his head. "But the poet mentioned him. Listen."

Aware that a dozen garrison soldiers were watching him curiously, Andrew quoted from the *Gododdin*.

"He fed black ravens on the rampart of a fortress,
Though he was no Arthur
Among the powerful ones in battle
In the front rank, Gwawrddur was a palisade."

Mariana smiled. "Though he was no Arthur," she repeated. "That meant that Arthur was a greater warrior than Gwawrddur."

"That's how I interpret the words," Andrew agreed. "Somebody wrote the *Gododdin* here, in Edinburgh Castle, about five hundred years before King David built this chapel." He tapped his boot on the volcanic rock.

"Oh," Mariana's interest increased as she looked around.

Andrew placed both hands on Mariana's shoulders and gently guided her to the ramparts, where she had a better view. "Do you see that hill?" He asked, pointing to the great volcanic hill that overlooked Edinburgh's Old Town.

"Yes," Mariana said. "It's a very nice hill."

"That's called Arthur's Seat," Andrew told her. "Some say it was the site of Camelot, others that people just named it after King Arthur. Some identify this castle with the Castle of Maidens in Arthurian legend, and others that Lothian was named after King Lot, Arthur's brother."

Mariana's interest grew with each myth. "Is that why you brought me here, Andrew? To tell me Edinburgh's connections with Arthur?"

"That was one reason," Andrew said, taking a deep breath before continuing. "How would you like to get married in a site with such an Arthurian connection?" He put his right hand in his pocket, holding the small box he had carried for days.

Mariana was silent for a moment as she digested Andrew's question. "Was that a proposal?" she asked quietly.

"Yes," Andrew said. "Most people think we're already married."

"They do," Mariana said. "But we're not." She looked at him as the wind whipped her hair around her face. "You know I've loved you since we first met."

"You had a teenage crush on me," Andrew said.

"I loved you," Mariana corrected gently. "But you preferred my sister."

"I've got to know you better since then," Andrew said. "We've grown up together."

"Maybe," Mariana lifted her chin. "I wonder if you would have proposed if Elaine was still alive."

Mariana's sister Elaine had died at the beginning of the Zulu War of 1879 when a gang of renegades had attacked Inglenook. The raiders had kidnapped Mariana, holding her prisoner until Andrew had led a force to rescue her. The ordeal had traumatised Mariana, and Andrew had looked after her through a long recovery process.

"Have you proposed because you feel obliged to care for Elaine's little sister?" Mariana held Andrew's gaze.

"No," Andrew shook his head. "I proposed because I want you as my wife. I want to spend the rest of my life with you."

Mariana was silent for half a minute, then touched Andrew's arm. "Thank you, Andrew," she said quietly. "I wish I could believe that."

Andrew stepped back. He had planned his proposal for weeks, buying a house with spurious Arthurian connections, bringing Mariana to Edinburgh Castle, showing her Saint Margaret's Chapel, and unveiling the Arthurian legends. He had never anticipated her hesitation. "Are you turning me down?"

"It's not that, Andrew," Mariana said. "I don't want you to tie yourself to me for the wrong reasons."

Andrew nodded, deflated. "My intentions are honourable," he told her miserably.

"Of that, I have no doubt," Mariana replied gently. "You are the most honourable and kindest man I have ever met. I love you dearly, but I don't want you to marry me because of Elaine."

"I want to marry you because of you," Andrew felt his position was slipping away. He wished he had never asked. He wanted to run away and hide.

"You are a good man," Mariana told him, smiling. "I wish I could agree, Andrew, but, you see, I think you are just being kind."

And there is that shadow, Mariana thought. *That horror that waits at the back of my mind. I cannot release it, Andrew, and if I marry you, it will emerge.*

Andrew felt the small box as a weight in his pocket. "Will you think about my proposal?" He knew that half the castle garrison and the civilian visitors were staring at him, everyone amused at his embarrassment. He wanted to run away and hide.

"I will," Mariana told him solemnly. "Of course, I will think about it." She took hold of his arm. "Come on, now, Andrew. Let's just be friends as we have been for years. Show me the rest of this castle of yours." She favoured him with a bright smile. "Tell me tales of Arthur and the Scottish kings and queens." She held his arm like a younger sister. "Come on now, Andrew. No more long faces."

The journey back to Berwick-upon-Tweed was long, with Andrew brooding over the day's events and Mariana quiet. Both were glad when the train pulled up at the platform under the ruins of Berwick Castle, and they walked the few hundred yards to Andrew's house on the town walls.

Andrew opened his front door, and while Mariana removed her coat, he lifted the brown-paper-wrapped parcel from the side table, carried it to his desk, and placed it inside the bottom drawer, adding the small box from inside his coat. When he returned downstairs, Mariana stood before the slowly ticking longcase clock.

"Have you forgiven me?" Mariana asked quietly.

"There's nothing to forgive," Andrew forced a smile. "I asked a question, and you gave an honest answer."

"I hurt you," Mariana said. "I didn't want to hurt you."

Andrew looked at her. "I know," he replied. "My proposition stands, Mariana. I will not force the issue, I will not withdraw it, and I won't mention it again." He had been considering his response on the long, dismal journey home.

"Andrew," Mariana leaned forward and touched his hand.

Andrew never knew what Mariana was going to say, for at that moment, somebody knocked heavily on the door.

"Who the devil can that be?" Andrew asked, glancing at the clock. "It's past ten at night, far too late for visitors." Stepping to the door, he hauled it open and glared outside.

The man who stood there was gaunt and heavily tanned, huddled into a long greatcoat and with a bowler hat jammed on his head.

"Captain Baird?" he asked. "Are you Captain Andrew Baird?"

"I am," Andrew admitted. "I don't think I know you."

"You don't know me," the man said. "I am Captain Walter Kerr of the Royal Scots Fusiliers. I must talk to you."

CHAPTER 2

BERWICK-UPON-TWEED, ENGLAND, SUMMER 1884

"Who is it?" Mariana appeared behind Andrew, holding a poker and glowering at her visitor.

"It's a Captain Walter Kerr," Andrew said. "Of the Royal Scots Fusiliers."

Mariana lowered the poker, glanced outside where rain was beginning to fall, decided their visitor was harmless, and frowned. "Well, bring the poor fellow in. It's wet out there."

When Captain Kerr stepped inside the front room under the glare of the gas lights, Andrew thought he looked rather the worse for wear. He was even thinner than he had first appeared and had a yellowish tinge to his face that was decidedly unhealthy.

It looks like Captain Kerr has had malaria. He's probably been out East.

"Sit down, Captain," Andrew invited. "Would you like a drink? Whisky? Brandy?"

"Brandy, thank you," Kerr replied, trying to suppress a shiver.

"Sit down, Captain Kerr," Mariana ushered him to a seat. "You look cold. Shall we light the fire?"

"Don't go to any bother, Mrs. Baird," Kerr said, looking up.

"It's Miss Maxwell," Mariana corrected mildly. "And it's no bother."

"I do apologise, Miss Maxwell." Captain Kerr spoke with a strangely sing-song intonation that Andrew thought was Welsh.

"No need to apologise," Mariana said. "It's an easy mistake to make."

Andrew poured a generous glass of brandy for Kerr, then a whisky for himself and one for Mariana, adding water to the latter. "Now, Captain Kerr, what's it all about? Why do you wish to see me?"

"It may be rather a delicate matter, Captain Baird," Kerr glanced at Mariana.

"Miss Maxwell and I are old friends," Andrew said. "We met during the Frontier Wars in South Africa and have known each other ever since. Anything you say to me, you can say to Miss Maxwell." He felt Mariana's gaze on him and wondered what she was thinking.

"As you wish," Kerr said. "Can we drop the formality? Call me Kerr."

"Kerr, it is," Andrew agreed. "And I am Baird." He sipped at his whisky, waiting for Kerr to explain why he was there.

"How well do you know India?" Kerr asked.

"I don't know it at all," Andrew admitted. "All my travelling has been in Africa."

"I see," Kerr finished his brandy and glanced at the decanter. Andrew recognised a serious drinker and passed it over. He watched as Kerr half-filled his glass with a trembling hand, with a stump in place of his index finger.

"Some people call India the Jewel of the Empire," Kerr said at length, "but if so, it is a jewel with rough edges. On one side, we have the Northwest Frontier, the section facing Afghanistan, which has some of the wildest tribes in the world."

Andrew nodded. "So I believe," he agreed.

"On the other side, we have a jungly frontier with Burma. The southern part of Burma, Lower Burma, is British territory. The northern section, Upper Burma, or the Kingdom of Ava, is an independent nation ruled by a savage tyrant called King Thibaw."

Andrew sat opposite Kerr and noticed Mariana listening avidly.

"To get to the throne," Kerr continued, "Thibaw had to massacre scores of his relatives in a bloodbath that makes Nero look like a choirboy. That was in 1878. Before Thibaw swam to the throne in a wave of blood, one of his father's queens, a charming lady known as Hsinbyaumashin, had increased her influence. When Hsinbyaumashin's husband, King Mindon, was dying, she informed all the heirs, potential heirs, and possible rivals that Mindon wanted to say farewell. She gathered them together and killed the whole bunch, except Thibaw, whose main wife, Supayagi, is Hsinbyaumashin's daughter."

"Lovely people," Andrew murmured.

Kerr sipped more brandy. "England's Henry the Eighth would have recognised a fellow monster," he said.

"When the coronation occurred, Supayagi was due to be anointed, and her sister, Supayalat, barged in and also became queen."

"One king and two queens?" Mariana asked.

"And a royal mother-in-law," Kerr said. He failed to suppress a shiver. "The thought could put one off marriage forever."

"Are you cold, Captain Kerr?" Mariana interrupted. "You still look cold."

Kerr shook his head. "It's just the fever," he said. "I lived in the tropics for the past twenty years, and even a touch of cool damp wakes the blasted fever."

"Andrew will put a match to the fire," Mariana said, raising her eyebrows.

When the flames took hold and spread a modicum of warmth around the room, Kerr shifted closer to the fire and continued.

"Thank you, Baird and Miss Maxwell. King Thibaw, or perhaps Maung Thandar, one of his ministers, is creating havoc in Upper Burma, killing, robbing, and sending armed bands over the border into British-controlled Burma. There is hardly a week without these fellows committing some outrage or other in our territory."

Andrew watched as Kerr filled his glass again, replaced the decanter's stopper, and placed it at his side.

"King Thibaw has declared his intention to retake all the land that Britain conquered from his equally disreputable ancestors," Kerr said.

"How does all this concern me, Kerr?" Andrew asked.

"I'm coming to that." Kerr inched even closer to the fire. He glanced at Mariana before speaking again. "You may not be aware that a member of your family, Baird, a distant relative, married a Burmese woman."

Andrew remembered the array of family portraits on the wall of Wychwood Manor, his father's house in Herefordshire. Most were military men, salted with a few seamen, while one stood out as neither one nor the other. Andrew's grandmother had hidden the portrait behind a heavy curtain until her son, General Jack Windrush, had ripped the screen away.

When Andrew asked about the sitter's identity, his father had smiled.

"That's Uncle George," he said. "He went native in Burma and preferred to stay there rather than return home."

"Why?" Andrew had asked.

Jack Windrush's smile broadened. "The East can be an alluring place," he explained. "I know Uncle George had a Burmese wife and at least one son, but apart from that, who can say."

Andrew realised that Kerr was staring at him, awaiting a reply. He jerked himself away from his childhood past.

"I was aware of Great Uncle George," he said, "although I never met him."

"Very well," Kerr said, helping himself to more brandy. "Your great uncle had a son who is as Burmese as teak, without a trace of British in him except his blood."

"I've heard about him," Andrew admitted. He knew Mariana was watching him yet kept his gaze firmly on Kerr. He could discuss things with Mariana later, once they were alone.

The fire hissed as rain fell down the chimney. A spark shot from the coal, hit the inside of the fireguard, glimmered for a second and faded into darkness. Andrew heard a rising wind blow across the stone pavement at the front of the house. The sultry heat of Burma seemed a different world.

"This fellow, your distant relative, is called Bo Thura," Kerr shifted closer to the fire as the rain outside increased, hammering on the window as if determined to find shelter inside the house. Kerr looked over the rim of his glass at Andrew. "He is a notorious badmash, a horse thief and robber of repute and possibly a murderer as well." He glanced at Mariana again. "In fact, Bo Thura has the reputation of being the best horse thief in Burma. Are you certain you wish me to discuss such matters before a lady?"

"I've heard worse, Captain Kerr," Mariana said quietly. "I grew up beside the Tugela River on the border with Zululand."

Andrew nodded. "Carry on, Kerr. I've no secrets from Miss Maxwell." At such times, he valued Mariana's support.

"As you wish. Bo Thura, your distant relative, has now added kidnapping to his list of crimes. You may have heard of the kidnapping of young Mary MacConnacher."

"I have not," Andrew confessed.

Kerr looked surprised for a moment. "Have you not? It is the topic of conversation in India; perhaps not such an important event here, with all the furore over this trouble in the Balkans."*

"There's always trouble in the Balkans," Mariana murmured. "I try to ignore it." She lifted the poker, stirred the fire, and added two pieces of coal. "I read a little about Mary MacConnacher's kidnapping. She was five years old, I think."

"That's correct," Kerr was nearly huddled over the fire as the flames licked around the fresh coal. "A five-year-old little blonde girl and Bo Thura stole her and her *ayah* - her nurse - away. Two days later, we found the *ayah* unharmed but badly shaken, with a note addressed to Sir Charles Crossthwaite, the Chief Commissioner of British Burma, in Rangoon."

"That wasn't in the papers," Mariana said. "What was in the note?"

Again, Kerr glanced at Andrew as if for permission to speak. Andrew nodded.

"The note said that Bo Thura would hold young Mary MacConnacher hostage until General Jack Windrush or a member of his family came to speak to him."

"Why?" Andrew asked. "Why involve my father? As far as I am aware, he hasn't been in Burma since the war there in 1852."

Kerr shook his head. "We don't know why," he admitted.

"Who are we?" Mariana had been following the conversation closely. "When you arrived, Captain Kerr, you said you were from the Royal Scots Fusiliers. What have the Fusiliers to do with this situation?"

"I am presently with the Fusiliers," Kerr said. "I am also Sir Charles's aide-de-camp." He poured himself more brandy, looked at the decreasing level in the decanter, and sighed.

"Have you come from Burma to tell us about Mary MacConnacher?" Andrew asked. "A telegram would have been faster."

"It would," Kerr agreed, "but there are other factors." He faced Andrew directly. "When will you be ready to go to Burma to meet Bo Thura and rescue this little girl?"

---

* In the latter part of the nineteenth century, the Balkans were a hotbed of wars and rumours of wars as the Austrian, Ottoman and Russian Empires competed for power and influence. In 1884 and 1885, the trouble was between Bulgaria and Serbia, with the Bulgarians emerging as victors in 1885.

Andrew closed his eyes. *This day has been bad enough. Burma is on the other side of the world.*

"Would General Windrush not be a better choice?" Mariana asked. "He's been to Burma before, and a man of his rank has more power and influence."

"Yes," Kerr said. "But General Windrush may be needed in another part of the world soon." He nodded at Mariana once more. "I think ladies should withdraw."

"The lady is staying," Andrew said. "You have more to tell us, Captain Kerr."

"What I say must remain within these four walls," Kerr looked at Mariana. "You must not repeat any of it."

"We won't," Andrew promised.

"We believe the Russians have reawakened their interest in Afghanistan," Kerr said. "We want to retain some of our men with recent experience in that area, including General Windrush." He finished his brandy and placed the empty glass on the hearth.

"I see," Andrew said.

"Compared to the possible Russian threat to India through the passes," Kerr said, "King Thibaw's Burma is a bit of a backwater." He huddled even closer to the fire, extending his hands to the flames. "We won't be sending Sir Garnet, Bobs Roberts or Fighting Jack Windrush into the jungle when the Russian Bear is threatening."

"Of course not," Andrew agreed.

I see the logic, unfortunately. If Father is tied up in the middle of nowhere, it would be tricky to recall him if a Cossack horde threatens Peshawar.

"On the other hand, the British public will be upset if we allow little golden-haired Mary MacConnacher to languish unrescued in the hands of an unprincipled rogue like Bo Thura." Kerr stood up, paced to the window, and glanced at the hammering rain. "No familial offence intended, Captain Baird."

"None taken, Captain," Andrew replied.

"And I mean no offence when I say that having a lower-ranked officer stuck in Burma is less important than sending one of our most distinguished generals there."

Andrew smiled. "I have no illusions about my lack of importance in the Army, Captain."

Kerr smiled. "We share the same rank, Baird. As you'll know, the country is going to the voting booths shortly, and the public won't like a Prime Minister who allows a little English girl to remain a captive."

"Mary MacConnacher is Irish," Mariana murmured. "The daughter of an Army sergeant based in Rangoon."

Kerr shrugged. "A detail. According to the press, she's a golden-haired Anglo-Saxon angel, so that's what the public believes. Public perception is important when the elections come around, especially with this new craze for democracy." He shook his hand. "Damn Disraeli's leap in the dark. It's causing us all sorts of trouble." * He returned to his seat and controlled his shivering. "So, Baird, when can you leave for Burma?" There was little humour in his smile. "You can refuse, of course, but that would be damaging for your military career, as well as leaving poor little Mary a captive."

Andrew shook his head. "I don't care a twopenny damn about my military career," he said. "I never wanted to be a soldier in the first place. But I don't like to think of a little girl as a captive in Burma."

"Of course you don't," Kerr said. "Nobody with an ounce of humanity would want that. And we don't want the opposition to get into power, either."

"I care even less which political party is in power," Andrew replied. "I'll have to work out shipping times and prices."

"We'll arrange all that," Kerr told him. "And we'll find you a place to stay in Rangoon."

"How can I contact Bo Thura when I get to Rangoon?" Andrew asked.

"We will place you in a certain hotel, and Bo Thura will contact you there," Kerr said. "I don't know how."

Andrew grunted. "It seems that Bo Thura is in charge of this operation." He glanced at Mariana. "The move to Corbiestane will have to wait," he said. "Will you be all right on your own here?"

"You're not going to Burma and leaving me here," Mariana said.

Remembering Mariana's recent refusal in Edinburgh Castle, Andrew was about to ask why not but bit off the bitter retort. "This Bo Thura seems a dangerous man," he said. "I'm not putting you in danger."

"I'll be in less danger there than I was in Natal," Mariana replied.

"You'll go then," Kerr seemed relieved.

"Yes, I'll go," Andrew said. He glanced at Mariana, who lifted a defiant chin.

"I'll keep a journal of our adventures," Mariana said.

---

* Disraeli's "Leap in the Dark" – Disraeli was the Conservative Prime Minister, and his Second Reform Act of 1867 increased the franchise to include some working-class men. Disraeli believed working-class men would always vote Conservative. Many people believed the idea of allowing ordinary people to vote was a radical leap in the dark.

CHAPTER 3

RANGOON, BURMA, AUGUST 1884

The British India Steam Navigation Company flag hung limply from the stern, the white swallowtail boasting a red saltire that seemed vaguely out of place in the oppressive heat. Andrew wiped a film of sweat from his forehead and stared at his surroundings.

I'm used to heat after Africa, but the humidity here is terrific.

Andrew watched the anchor slide into the river with a dull splash that reverberated in the heavy air.

Now, we have officially arrived in Burma. That anchor sounded like the full stop for the story of the voyage.

"Where are we?" Mariana asked, adjusting her parasol to shade her face from the sun.

"We're in the Irrawaddy River," Andrew said. "A few miles downstream from Rangoon."

"We're certainly seeing the world," Mariana said. "It's only taken four days to get here from Calcutta." She twisted Andrew's wrist and glanced at his watch. "Four days to the minute. We cast off from Calcutta at ten minutes after three, and it's now three o'clock."

"I didn't realise you were taking notes," Andrew said.

"Oh, yes," Mariana said. "I write everything down in my journal. Everything."

"What have you written?"

"Do you want to hear?" Mariana looked pleased. "I haven't read it to anybody."

Andrew nodded. "Of course, I want to hear."

"I'll be back in a minute." Mariana disappeared to her cabin below decks and returned with a slightly battered blue notebook. "Here we are," she said. "Are you sure you want to hear?"

"Quite sure," Andrew replied.

Mariana opened the notebook, flicked through to her last entry, and read, looking up occasionally to ensure that Andrew was paying attention.

"We arrived at the mouth of a large river ten minutes since. The coastline has a very peculiar appearance, very much like what I've heard about a mirage in the desert. It appeared like a line of coconut trees, and palms were floating in the sky, a handsbreadth above the line of the horizon. The trees could have been growing in the air, without soil or land, and that was my first sight of the magical land of Burma."

Andrew nodded. "That is very poetic," he approved. "Let's hope that Burma continues to be a magical land for you."

"Thank you, Andrew." Mariana reclaimed her notebook and tucked it under her arm.

"It's only the truth," Andrew said.

"Mother used to say that my writing was too flowery and that I should only put down practical things. I stopped writing after that."

"You can start again," Andrew smiled. "There's nothing at all wrong with what you showed me." He watched as a pilot left the pilot ship, *The Guide*, and rowed towards them. The pilot, a local man with a distinct swagger, swarmed up a rope ladder to the deck, greeted the captain with a hearty handshake and issued orders to the helmsman.

"Do we need a pilot?" Andrew asked Ross, the second mate.

"We do, sir," Ross replied. "The Irrawaddy is a dangerous river, with the current constantly changing the safe deep-water channels." He pointed to the pilot boat. "There are sixty-four official river pilots, Captain Baird, most from Chittagong. Even the great Irrawaddy Flotilla vessels rely on Chittagong pilots, who each know one area of the river. Hence, the ships must use seventeen different pilots between Rangoon and Mandalay."

"I see," Andrew said, storing the information for future use. He knew that Rangoon was the capital of British Burma and Mandalay the capital of the Kingdom of Ava, or Upper Burma, where King Thibaw held sway.

"We're hoisting anchor again!" Mariana said.

Andrew saw the ship begin to move and glanced upstream as she steamed at increasing speed under the pilot's directions, with the muddy brown water surging against the hull. On either side was scrubby jungle, with the sun reflecting from something golden.

"What's that?" Mariana asked.

"That's the Shwedagon Pagoda or the Golden Pagoda," Andrew had been reading about Burma during the voyage from Britain. "I believe my father helped capture it back in fifty-two."

"Oh, did he?" Mariana answered dutifully.

"He did," Andrew watched as the ship passed a small flotilla of fishing boats. The boats had an open, double-winged stern, and a man that Andrew supposed to be the skipper was sheltering under a shade while the crew worked in the open. *Is that the Burmese version of democracy? There's little difference from ours, then.*

"Is the pagoda made of gold?" Mariana asked.

"I think it's gold leaf over timber," Andrew replied. "Burma is full of golden pagodas."

When Mariana opened her notebook and began to write, Andrew thought it best to leave her in peace. After what seemed only a few minutes, the ship moored at the port of Rangoon.

"We've arrived," Andrew said.

"It's busy here," Mariana wrote a few words and closed her notebook with a decisive snap.

Andrew agreed as he watched a score of ships moored or moving, most under steam but some with sail, both European and Oriental. Tall chimneys spoke of industry, but the giant Golden Pagoda dominated the city.

Religion is essential to this land, Andrew thought. *I wonder how Bo Thura will contact me.*

"A woman is coming aboard," Mariana said as one of the ubiquitous small Burmese boats drew alongside.

"That's Mary of Rangoon," Ross said as the elderly woman clambered easily onto the deck. "She comes to every ship that docks here and has been for a quarter of a century."

Mary of Rangoon approached Mariana and offered a selection of trinkets from a canvas bag.

"Could I have this, please?" Mariana selected a tiny carved Buddha.

Mary smiled as Mariana scooped a handful of mixed British and Indian coins from her pocket. "How much?"

Mary picked a single rupee, bowed, said "thank you," and presented Andrew with a rose before moving on to Ross and the other officers.

"That's a nice welcome to Burma," Mariana said, holding her purchase. "I wonder who carved this Buddha. Perhaps some dedicated monk in that golden temple over there, whittling away as he contemplated the meaning of life."

"Perhaps so," Andrew said. *Or a five-year-old child working in a gutter for a penny a day.* "Look, here's the boat to take us ashore, so get yourself ready, Mariana."

RANGOON WAS LOUD, BUSTLING, BUSY AND HECTIC, AS BEFITTED BURMA'S largest port. Andrew kept Mariana close by as he hailed a decorated bullock cart that seemed to do duty as a taxicab.

"Do you speak English?" he asked the driver.

"Yes, Sahib!" the man was a grinning Indian with betel-nut-stained teeth.

"Do you know the Wells Britannia Hotel?" Andrew asked.

"Yes, Sahib!" the driver nodded.

"Take us there, then. And give us a hand with the luggage."

The driver was helpful, piling in their bags with a smile as Mariana supervised.

"You're new to Rangoon?" A tall civilian stopped, lifted his hat to Mariana and watched Andrew and the driver loading the luggage.

"We are," Mariana answered. "We have just arrived."

"Trade? Or military?" the civilian asked.

"Personal business," Andrew replied, remembering that in some corners of the Empire, strangers spoke to each other without any formal introduction. He changed the subject before the man asked any more questions. "What are these vessels?" Andrew indicated the group of large, double-decked paddle steamers that lay in the river.

"Irrawaddy Flotilla Company ships," the civilian said. "It's a Scottish company managed by Henderson in Glasgow, although the operational head-quarters are here in Rangoon," he jerked a thumb to a light-coloured, colonnaded building.

"Interesting vessels," Andrew said.

"They are," the civilian seemed happy to talk, including Mariana in his answer. "The company builds them in Glasgow, dismantles them and sends them over here. They put them back together in the company's shipyard at Dalla, across the river."

"That's a clever system," Andrew said. He saw the driver place the final case in the back of the bullock cart. "Good day to you."

"And to you, sir," the man lifted his hat to Mariana again, smiled and strode away, straight-backed and swinging his cane.

"What a pleasant man," Mariana remarked.

"He was," Andrew said. "On we go, driver."

The Wells Britannia Hotel stood near the northern edge of Rangoon, with a Union Flag hanging from a pole in front and a smartly uniformed commissionaire standing at the entrance. The driver pulled the bullock cart to a stop on the street outside, allowing Andrew and Mariana time to view the building. Teak built and two storeys high, it had large windows with verandas facing the front, a garden extending around the sides and back, and three European civilians waiting outside.

"It looks all right," Mariana had wondered about the hotel since they left Berwick. "I rather thought it might be an Army barracks."

"I'm glad it's not," Andrew replied.

"I'll take your baggage," the commissionaire announced, snapped his fingers, and handed the luggage to two small boys who ran eagerly forward. They lifted the bags with a skill that told of long experience.

"Thank you," Mariana responded with a tired smile as Andrew fished in his pocket for a tip. Unsure of the local customs, he handed a British penny to each youngster and a silver threepenny bit to the commissionaire, which seemed to satisfy everybody.

The hotel interior was impressive, with a mixture of traditional Burmese and British architecture, palm trees in large pots and a fan spinning slowly from the ceiling. A teak pillar stretched to the ceiling, with the lower third beautifully carved into the figure of a long-eared Buddha. An elderly Burmese woman sat straight-backed on a teak chair beside the Buddha, watching everything and everybody.

"This is nice," Mariana commented, looking around.

Andrew thought of the punkah-wallah hidden in some corner, whose endless job was to pull the cord that rotated the fan. "It is nice," he agreed.

"Is Buddha their god?" Mariana asked.

"Burmese Buddhists are atheists," Andrew had studied all he could of the country while on the ship. "They don't worship Buddha, and the images represent a perfect being, with Buddhists aiming to enter Nirvana."

Mariana smiled at the elderly lady, who inclined her head gravely, inspected Andrew with bright eyes and resumed her placid scrutiny of the reception area.

Two or three military officers and a plump civilian sat at an array of cane tables and chairs. Only the civilian looked up as Andrew and Mariana walked to the reception desk while the officers read the newspapers and drank from long glasses. Andrew was surprised to see that the receptionist was female. She was also efficient and friendly.

I suspect Burma will be different from anywhere else I have visited.

"I believe we have reservations," Andrew said. "The names are Baird and Maxwell."

"Two separate and adjoining rooms," the receptionist confirmed. "Captain Andrew Baird and Miss Mariana Maxwell."

"That's correct," Andrew said.

"I have a message about you, Captain Baird," the receptionist said, reaching under the counter. She produced a slip of paper with Burmese writing on it. "I have orders to contact Mr Wells when you book in. Excuse me, please."

Perhaps Bo Thura already knows we have arrived. Andrew glanced around the reception area, searching for anybody who might look suspicious. Nobody caught his attention.

"Mr Wells?" Mariana repeated.

"Please wait here, Captain Baird and Miss Maxwell." When the receptionist rang a small brass handbell, a teenage boy dressed in a scarlet uniform appeared. The receptionist spoke sharply to him in Burmese, and he scampered away to a carved side door.

"I won't keep you a moment," the receptionist promised.

"Find a seat," Andrew said, guiding Mariana to one of the empty tables and pulling back a chair for her. They sat under the fan, with the palm trees giving the reception area a calm atmosphere. The civilian smiled and raised a hand in acknowledgement as the elderly lady watched everything.

After three minutes, the side door opened.

"Captain Baird!"

The man who approached had a face tanned by the sun and a military bearing despite his sixty or so years. He wore a European-style suit and extended his hand in greeting.

"That's correct," Andrew admitted.

"Edmund Wells," the man shook Andrew's hand with a powerful grip. His eyes were old and wise yet bright with life. Andrew realised he had underestimated the man's age by at least a decade. "I had a telegram telling me you were on your way."

"And Miss Maxwell," Edmund Wells bowed, took Mariana's hand, and held it gently.

"A telegram?" Mariana repeated. "Who sent a telegram?"

"General Windrush," Wells said. "I knew him when he was a lieutenant in the 113th Foot. We fought together back in '52." He grinned, showing surprisingly white teeth. "I was a sergeant then."

"What did the general say?" Andrew asked cautiously. He wondered what tales ex-Sergeant Wells had to tell.

Wells remained standing beside the table until Andrew gestured for him to sit down.

"General Windrush told me his son and his son's lady friend were coming to stay," Wells slid into one of the cane chairs with all the suppleness of youth. "He asked me to ensure you were comfortable and well looked after."

"That was kind of him," Andrew said.

"I have your room ready, Captain," Wells said.

"Two rooms," Andrew reminded as Mariana glanced at him.

"Two adjacent rooms," Wells agreed. "Please come with me, Captain and Miss Maxwell."

As Andrew passed the elderly lady, he saw her smile briefly at Wells before resuming her serene gaze over the reception area. Wells led them up the highly polished teak stairs to the upper floor, where a dozen numbered doors gleamed, and the scent of sandalwood lingered.

"This is lovely," Mariana approved.

"Mrs Wells ensures everything is to a high standard," Wells murmured as he walked, soft-footed, to the end of the corridor.

The rooms were clean and as well-appointed as any quality hotel in Britain. Both enjoyed views over the impressive Shwedagon Pagoda, with the sun reflecting from the gilding.

"That's beautiful," Mariana said.

"It is rather, isn't it?" Wells agreed. "Ask my wife about it; Myat knows far more about that sort of thing than I do."

"Is your wife Burmese?" Mariana did not hide her surprise.

"She is," Wells said. "Myat Lay Phyu's her name and she's the best businesswoman you'll ever meet. I may be the face of the hotel, but Myat makes all the decisions. You'll see her sitting beside the Buddha in the hallway, seeing everything without intruding."

Andrew nodded. "I read that Burmese women are skilled at business."

Wells smiled. "Britain could learn a lot from Burma," he said. "The societies for women's suffrage could come here and learn what potential women can have in the commercial world."*

Andrew watched as a couple of young porters deposited their luggage on the floor and left without expecting a gratuity. Wells waited until the porters had vacated the room.

"We don't want our customers to think they are obliged to pay extra," Wells said. "It's Myat's idea. That's one reason why businessmen return here time after time." He held Andrew's gaze and added meaningfully. "We are also the most discreet hotel in Rangoon. What happens in the Wells Britannia stays within these walls."

Wells knows about Bo Thura. "I understand, Mr Wells," Andrew said.

"You have a lovely hotel, Mr Wells," Mariana said.

"Thank you, Miss Maxwell," Wells replied with a smile and a slight bow.

"Now, Captain Baird, I doubt you are here as a tourist," Wells turned his bright eyes onto Andrew. "I followed your father's career as he advanced to his present position, and I suspect you are made in the same mould. After over thirty years of living in Burma, there's not much I don't know about the place, so if you have any questions, don't hesitate to ask." He smiled. "Nothing you say or ask will go any further, Captain. As I said, discretion is another reason this hotel is successful."

Wells extracted a small envelope from his inside pocket as he spoke, and pressed it into Andrew's hand. "This arrived for you, Captain."

"Thank you." Andrew had half-expected a message. He ripped open the envelope, with Mariana watching curiously.

"What is it, Andrew?" Mariana asked.

Andrew handed her the single slip of paper inside, with the name *Mandalay* written, together with *immediately*.

"Thank you, Mr Wells. I must get to Mandalay as soon as possible," Andrew said. "What is the best way?"

"The best way or the fastest way?" Wells asked. "The two are not the same."

"The fastest way. It may be a matter of life or death."

Wells only considered for a moment. "If you choose the fastest way, you are only twenty-four hours from the Frontier of Upper Burma," he said. "If you take the nine o'clock train from Rangoon in the evening, you'll reach the rail-head at Prome at six tomorrow morning. From Prome, you can catch the Flotilla steamer up the Irrawaddy at ten, giving you four hours to kick your heels in the town. The steamer reaches Thayetmyo at four in the evening, and you are about nine miles from the frontier. You can hire a boat from Thayetmyo to Mandalay. The alternative is to wait for the direct steamer from Rangoon to Mandalay. It takes days longer, but it's far more comfortable."

Andrew glanced at Mariana, who looked suddenly nervous. "How hard is it to hire a boat at Thayetmyo?"

---

* Societies for women's suffrage were founded in Edinburgh, Manchester, and London in 1867 following the 1866 Reform Bill, which failed to grant women the vote.

"That depends on how much money you have," Wells replied. "There's a man named Jamieson who runs a launch and doesn't ask questions."

"Jamieson," Andrew filed the name in his mind. "Are there border posts for inspections, customs and the like?"

Wells shook his head. "Nothing like that. Look for a line of white conoid pillars; that's all that marks the frontier. You might see a police post here and there if you are lucky. They are thin on the ground, as are the Army patrols. A couple of companies of the 21st Foot, the Royal Scots Fusiliers, guard the border with about one man for every hundred miles."

Andrew nodded. "Thank you, Mr Wells. I'll stay here for a day to ensure Mariana is settled in and then head for Mandalay."

Wells nodded. "Myat and I will keep an eye on Miss Maxwell," he said. "Be careful up there. King Thibaw does not love us."

"I'll do my best," Andrew felt Mariana's gaze.

I am not concerned about myself; I have been in wild and hostile territory before. I am worried about leaving Mariana alone in Rangoon. I am glad that Wells knew my father, although he is rather old to care for Mariana; he's more like a grandfather than a father figure.

"I hoped we might have more time in Rangoon before you left," Mariana said when Wells left the room.

"So did I," Andrew replied. "The sooner I leave, the sooner I return."

"Yes," Mariana said and retreated to her room.

CHAPTER 4

RANGOON, BURMA, SEPTEMBER 1884

They spent the next day unpacking Mariana's baggage and getting to know the hotel's immediate surroundings. Andrew felt guilty about leaving Mariana behind and kept close to her, wishing he had left her safely in Berwick yet paradoxically glad they had the few extra weeks together.

"I hope you are not away too long," Mariana said as they viewed the Golden Pagoda.

"I'll be as quick as possible," Andrew assured her.

"I'll be waiting for you," Mariana told him.

Andrew nodded. He hated partings but knew he had no choice. As Kerr had said, people in Rangoon discussed Mary MacConnacher's disappearance, expressing genuine concern about her welfare.

"I hear some terrible dacoit kidnapped her," a plump, red-faced man said. "By God, if I got my hands on him, he'd be sorry, I'll tell you!"

"Where's the Army? Why aren't they doing anything?" a thin-faced, malarial-yellow man complained. "We pay plenty of taxes for them. They are a waste of money, drunken scoundrels, the lot of them."

Andrew listened to the complaints without comment, advising Mariana never to be out at night and to remain in the safe parts of town.

"I'll be all right," Mariana assured him. "I grew up beside Zululand, remember? Rangoon is a civilised town, and Mr Wells will look after me."

In the evening, with Andrew ready for the morning's journey towards Mandalay, they ate in the hotel and settled in the lounge. Large windows afforded them a view overlooking the Golden Pagoda, where the setting sun reflected from the gold.

"That's a lovely building," Mariana said. "I imagined Burma would be like

Zululand, with savage tribes, but people who can create such architecture are to be admired."

"We often learn from the people of the Empire," Andrew said. He looked around the room, not sure what to say when leaving Mariana for an indefinite period. Most of the people present were British or European civilians, with three moustached military officers waiting to either travel up country or return to Britain on leave.

Andrew hoped to spend as much time as possible with Mariana before he left, but the tall civilian from the quayside joined them.

"Good evening to you both," the civilian said. "I didn't have time to introduce myself the other day." He held out his hand. "Jennings. Stephen Jennings of Jennings and Stanley. You may have heard the name."

"We have now," Andrew said, cursing Rangoon's informality but unwilling to appear churlish by ignoring the man. "I am Captain Andrew Baird; the lady is Miss Mariana Maxwell."

"Captain Baird and Miss Mariana Maxwell," Jennings repeated the names, slightly emphasising the word "Miss". "What a lovely name you have, Mariana."

"Why, thank you, sir," Mariana bobbed. "I was rather young to choose it myself, so I let my parents decide."

"They made a good choice," Jennings told her. "We don't often see such beauty as yours in Rangoon," he said as he sat on one of the padded cane chairs and signalled for a gin and tonic. "Oh, the Burman women are fine, up to a point."

"Up to a point?" Mariana asked, smiling at the compliment.

"Burman women are elegant, debonair, and intelligent," Jennings said. "But they lack that certain something that European women have." He sipped at his coffee and smiled at Andrew. "I am sure you agree, Captain Baird."

"I have not met many Burman women," Andrew said curtly. "Nor do I expect to meet any. I am here for one purpose, and once I have achieved that, we'll be on the next ship home."

Jennings nodded. "Perhaps," he said. "Perhaps. The East has a way of drawing one in, Captain Baird. It has a certain unexplained magnetism that holds one captive." He drank more of his coffee, smiling at Mariana. "There is a saying that one hates India for a month and then loves it forever. I can say Burma is the same; you will never forget your time here, and even if you leave, the memories, the colours, the sounds, and the atmosphere will remain with you."

Andrew saw Mariana listening intently. "Is that what happened to you, Mr Jennings?" she asked.

Jennings placed his drink on the table. "That's what happened to me," he agreed. "I came for a few weeks and can't see me ever leaving now." He smiled. "Burma has been good to me in some ways."

"In some ways? That is intriguing," Mariana said. "Do you live in Mr Wells' hotel all the time?"

"Good heavens, no!" Jennings smiled at the idea. "No. I'm meeting somebody here." He lowered his voice. "Trade is dull at present with all these dacoit raids, and King Thibaw no longer takes us seriously."

"Does he not?" Andrew thought of his impending visit to Mandalay. "What makes you say that, Jennings?"

"Our reputation is not as high as it used to be," Jennings signalled to a waiter and ordered a second cup of coffee. "Do you wish anything, Miss Maxwell? Captain Baird? No?"

"No, thank you," Mariana replied. "Excuse me, please. I must look out the window."

Jennings and Andrew rose as she swept away.

Jennings waited until Mariana was out of earshot before he spoke again. "We need a successful war to restore British prestige in Asia and Europe," he said. "It's been a bad few years for the British Army. The Zulus destroyed us at Isandlwana, the Boers humiliated us at Majuba, we withdrew from Afghanistan a few months after defeat at Maiwand, and when the Mahdi murdered Gordon, we retreated from the Sudan."

Andrew nodded. "All this is true," he said. "Up to a point." He used Jennings' terminology, remembering the slaughter and bravery in Southern Africa.

Jennings continued. "Our Army is a laughingstock among the powers. I've heard that when some European fellows saw a unit of rather bedraggled-looking Swiss artillery returning from a field exercise, they joked that it was the British retreating from Sudan."

"We'll get back our prestige," Andrew said. "We were unfortunate at Isandlwana but redeemed ourselves at Khambula and Ulundi."

"Did we?" Jennings asked. "I don't know these battles."

Andrew did not say he had been present at both. "They were hard fought," he said, "and victorious."

"Our glorious Gordons ran away at Majuba," Jennings said. "So much for the pride of the British Army."

"Some ran," Andrew admitted. "Others fought, and many died fighting. Have you ever been in uniform?"

Jennings smiled. "Not me, old boy. I am a merchant, not a fighter."

"I see," Andrew said. He looked up as Mariana entered the room.

Jennings rose at once and pulled back a chair with a flourish. "Welcome back, Miss Maxwell. The table felt desolate without you."

"Why, thank you, sir," Mariana gave a graceful curtsey before she sat down. "One can tell the measure of a man by the compliments he gives."

Jennings bowed and sat. "Which regiment do you honour, Captain Baird?"

"The Natal Dragoons," Andrew said. "That is a colonial regiment from Natal in Southern Africa."

"Ah," Jennings nodded. "You must have seen action in the late wars."

"Some," Andrew did not elaborate. He saw Mariana lean forward with her mouth open and guessed she was going to explain what had happened. "No more than anybody else."

"Andrew saved my life," Mariana began before Andrew put a restraining hand on her shoulder.

"That was a long time ago. If you'll excuse us, Jennings, we have had rather a long day, and I fear we must retire for the night."

Jennings stood politely. "Of course, Captain. Good night, Miss Maxwell. Good night, Captain Baird."

"Good night," they replied as Andrew guided Mariana past the carved teak pillar, nodded to the ever-present Myat Lay Phyu and negotiated the curved stairs to the upper floor.

"What a charming gentleman Mr Jennings is," Mariana said as they reached their rooms. She allowed Andrew to open her door, took her key, stepped inside, and lit the lantern. Warm light reflected from the mirror over the dressing table to the comfortable bed. "How fortunate to meet a friend so soon after arrival."

"Fortunate indeed," Andrew murmured. "Goodnight, Mariana."

"Goodnight." Mariana closed the door quietly, turned, leaned her back against it, and smiled, watching her reflection in the mirror.

We don't often see such beauty as yours in Rangoon. Mariana smoothed a hand over her hair. *What a charming man. And so handsome.*

ANDREW HEARD THE SHARP CRACK OF A FIREARM AND REACTED instinctively. He rolled from his bed, grabbed the revolver from its holster and glanced around the dark room. He lay on the floor for a moment with his pistol in his hand, thinking himself on the Zululand frontier or deep in the Transvaal.

Mariana!

"Mariana!" he shouted her name, and jerked himself upright, threw open the door, and dashed to Mariana's room. "Are you all right?" He heard quiet footsteps inside the room, and Mariana opened the door.

"Are you all right, Mariana?" Andrew repeated. He heard noises from within the other rooms on the landing.

Mariana stood, her nightgown reaching to her bare ankles and her hair an explosion. "Of course, I am all right. What else would I be?" She blinked at Andrew through tired eyes.

Andrew stepped inside the room and pushed the door closed as other guests peered into the corridor to see who was disturbing their peace. Jennings looked concerned as he hugged a quilted dressing gown over his broad shoulders.

I thought Jennings was only meeting somebody at the hotel. What's he up to?

Andrew stood with his back to the door. "Didn't you hear the shot?"

Mariana shook her head, causing further disarray to her hair. "I was fast asleep until you started banging on the door and shouting like a lunatic," she said irritably. "Now go back to your bed and let me get back to mine."

"As long as you are all right."

"Just go," Mariana pointed to the door.

Andrew left, feeling foolish. The revolver seemed out of place in this civilised hotel, and Jennings stood outside his door watching until Andrew returned to his room.

Was that a gunshot I heard? Or was I dreaming of past campaigns? Andrew lay on his bed, knowing he would not sleep again that night.

❄

The breakfast room was busy the following morning, with Andrew and Mariana finding the last vacant table.

"Are you still grumpy?" Andrew asked Mariana.

"No," she shook her head. "I was a bit alarmed when you hammered on the door, that's all."

"Did you hear a gunshot last night?" Andrew asked Wells as he supervised the breakfast orders.

"I did not hear anything," Wells replied, shaking his head. "It might have been trouble with one of the dacoit bands. They sometimes come into Rangoon itself and run before the police arrive. Excuse me, Captain." Wells strode to the kitchen to answer another query.

"Do you mind if I join you?" Jennings stood beside the table. "You appear to have the only space available in the room."

"You are welcome, Mr Jennings," Mariana replied before Andrew spoke.

"That's very civil of you," Jennings sat down gracefully. "One feels a bit out of it sometimes."

"You told us you were here on business," Mariana reminded. "Did your business last all night?"

Jennings raised his eyebrows as if surprised Mariana had remembered. "It does occasionally. As well as a director of Jennings and Stanley, I am the Oriental agent for the British, Burma and Chinese Shipping Company," he said.

"That sounds very important," Mariana told him.

Jennings laughed self-deprecatingly. "It's not as grand as it sounds," he said. "I saw you out of your room last night, Captain Baird. Was there something I missed?"

"I thought I heard a gunshot," Andrew said.

"You may have done, although I didn't hear anything," Jennings said. "It may have been the police or the Army dealing with a *loosewallah* or a gang of dacoits."*

"I have heard vague rumours about dacoits," Andrew probed for as much information as possible. "I am not sure what they are."

Jennings sat back, produced a cheroot, and raised his eyebrows to Mariana. "Do you mind?"

"Not at all, Mr Jennings," Mariana said. "I rather like the aroma."

* Loosewallah – bandit, thief or general lawbreaker

"A lady after my own heart," Jennings said, lit up and blew aromatic smoke into the air. "A dacoit can be many things," he said. "Most are ordinary villagers who have fallen on hard times, men forced to resort to stealing or brigandage to live. Once they can eat again, they may well return to the straight and narrow, at least until the next paddy failure." He smiled bleakly. "There is neither a Poor Law nor a workhouse in Burma for the desperately poor to seek sanctuary."

Mariana nodded. "Poverty is a terrible thing," she said. "If the dacoits are only desperate paupers, they can't be so bad."

Jennings drew on his cheroot. "I said that most were ordinary villagers. Others are quite the reverse. Some are professional thieves and bandits, the very scum of society. They may have been outlawed for some terrible crime, or perhaps they chose a life outside society for the love of plunder and," he hesitated, "forgive my language, please, rape."

Mariana looked away. "I have heard the word before, sir," she said.

Jennings glanced at Andrew before he continued. "You have a very understanding and intelligent lady there, Baird."

"I know," Andrew agreed.

"The professional or habit-and-repute dacoit is a much more dangerous fellow than his destitute companion," Jennings said. "He will gather a band of like-minded and equally desperate men around him and select a village to plunder."

"Rather like the old Border Reivers that Sir Walter Scott wrote about," Mariana said.

"Much in the same mould," Jennings agreed. "When he has selected his intended victim village, he will approach the headman and demand a ransom or blackmail payment. If the village refuses, then the dacoit band will fall upon it with fire and sword, looting, robbing, destroying, and murdering. They may also set it on fire, and Burmese villages burn exceedingly well." He paused. "They are built of timber and bamboo, you see."

Andrew saw the interest on Mariana's face and hoped she was not reliving the day when renegades raided and burned Inglenook.

"The dacoits won't live well if they burn everything to the ground," Mariana said.

Jennings nodded. "Quite so, Mariana, quite so. If they fail to find sufficient booty in the form of money, cattle, cloth, or valuables, they will choose some unfortunate victims and put them to the torture."

"Oh!" Mariana put a hand over her mouth.

"You may well say, oh," Jennings continued. "If they are pressed for time because, say, the police are approaching, or the villagers are reluctant to part with money, they will simply push a man's face against a tree. Once they have him secure, they'll lash his shoulders and back with a dha, their savage swords, until he has a crosscut down to the bone. After that, the unfortunate man tells all. If, however, they have time to spare, they will strip their victim of his clothes," again Jennings glanced at Mariana.

"It's all right, Mr Jennings," Mariana said quietly. "I am aware of the procedure of undressing."

"They will strip a man of his clothes, cover him from head to toe in earth oil – unrefined petroleum – and lay him in the sun. When he is cooked long enough, he will tell all he knows."

"Oh, how terrible," Mariana said. "What awful people."

"Terrible and awful indeed," Jennings agreed. He again glanced at Mariana and Andrew before continuing. "They do not restrict their endeavours to men, of course. They can also subject the gentle sex to terrible torments."

"I can only imagine," Mariana said.

"I don't want to imagine," Andrew said. "Perhaps you had better keep that intelligence to yourself."

"Pray continue, Mr Jennings," Mariana insisted, "I am not a child."

Now he was on the subject, Jennings seemed reluctant to stop. "The dacoits strip their victim quite naked and stretch her on a bamboo frame eighteen inches or so above the ground, then soak cotton in earth oil, place it beneath her and set light to it to slowly roast her."

"That's enough!" Andrew interjected roughly. "I don't wish Mariana to be subjected to any more horror stories of that kind."

Jennings leaned back. "I was merely educating the lady in the habits of the Burmese dacoits," he said. "On a less gruesome note, the dacoits also like to kidnap people and hold them to ransom, and sometimes they set fire to buildings. In fact, they are masters of every sort of crime known to man."

I know about the kidnapping. What sort of monster is Bo Thura? What sort of place have I brought Mariana to?

Mariana frowned. "What about the authorities?" she asked. "Does King Thibaw permit this sort of behaviour in his land? Do the British authorities not curb such barbarities?"

"Our police and soldiers do what they can," Jennings said. "And Thibaw sends out the occasional column to exert some sort of justice," he pulled on his cheroot, "When his soldiers capture the dacoits, they summarily execute them without the tedious process of a trial or any of that civilised nonsense."

"A good hanging works wonders," Andrew murmured. "Or so I am told."

"The poor devils would welcome the noose," Jennings said. "Thibaw's soldiers crucify them."

Andrew closed his eyes. "I should have guessed it would be something like that." He put a hand on Mariana's arm.

"I am all right," Mariana smiled at his concern. "You don't need to worry about me anymore, Andrew. I am perfectly fine now."

"You look perfectly perfect to me," Jennings said.

"Why, thank you, sir," Mariana replied with a broad smile. She turned a cold shoulder to Andrew. "You had better get ready for your train, Andrew."

"Your train? Whither are you bound, my good Captain?" Jennings asked.

"Northward to Mandalay," Andrew replied.

"Ah, the Kingdom of Ava, home of the Lord of the White Elephant, the

King of all Umbrella Bearing Chiefs and so on," Jennings said. "Well, the best of British luck to you."

"Thank you," Andrew said and walked away, bowing to Myat Lay Phyu beside the pillar. She watched him go and settled back down, lighting a long cheroot.

CHAPTER 5

LOWER BURMA, SEPTEMBER 1884

Mariana stood on the platform as Andrew boarded the train for the first leg of his journey to Upper Burma. She watched him store his travelling case in the rack above the seat, then roll down the window to talk to her.

"You be careful here on your own," Andrew said. "I don't like to leave you alone."

"I'll be all right with Mr Wells," Mariana consoled him. "You're the one going into dangerous Upper Burma, not me."

Andrew smiled. "There is a sizeable European community in Mandalay. It's a civilised city with strong trading links and a regular paddle steamer service to Rangoon. Remember that Bo Thura wants to see me, so I'm in no danger."

"I hope not." Mariana took hold of her hat and stepped back as the engine emitted a whistle and a great cloud of steam. A moment later, she emerged smiling. "I always get a fright when they do that."

"So, I see. Now get back to the hotel and keep safe," Andrew said. "I expect to be a couple of weeks. No more than three, and then we'll be together again and get back to Corbiestane Tower."

"Take care!" Mariana shouted as the guard made his way down the platform, banging shut the doors and checking the passengers. There was a mixture of Burmese and European, with most of the latter British businessmen sprinkled with soldiers in uniform. As Andrew was not on official military business and would soon enter Upper Burma, he wore a light civilian suit with a broad hat. He had packed his second-best uniform safely in his travelling case.

"You take care as well," Andrew said as the train began to pull away.

Mariana saw him lean out the window, waving as the train slowly gathered speed. Then clouding steam obscured him, and all she saw was his extended arm.

"Good luck, Andrew," Mariana whispered. "I'll miss you."

Standing on the platform in an alien town, she suddenly felt devastatingly lonely. Mariana watched the train disappear into the distance, heard a last whistle of steam, and knew she was all alone.

Oh, Elaine, I wish you were with me. Mariana looked around at the bustle of the station, folded her arms, closed her eyes, and talked quietly to herself. *It's all right, Mariana. I survived captivity and the aftermath. I am in a civilised city under British control. All I must do is wait for three weeks, and Andrew will be back.*

Mariana slowly returned to the hotel, wary of anybody coming too close to her. Men, Burmese, Chinese and European, looked at her, a lone woman walking the streets, and for a moment, she wished she had remained in Berwick rather than travelled halfway across the world.

"Miss Maxwell?"

Mariana started and lengthened her stride when somebody called her name.

"Miss Maxwell? It's me, Stephen Jennings."

Without slowing down, Mariana glanced over her shoulder. Jennings smiled at her from five yards away, lifting his cane in acknowledgement.

"Good evening, Miss Maxwell. What on earth are you doing out alone?"

Mariana smiled, slowing to allow Jennings to catch up with her. "I am returning to the hotel," she said.

"Alone?" Jennings asked, raising his broad-brimmed hat. "Is Captain Baird already away to Mandalay?"

"Yes, I am alone," Mariana replied. "Captain Baird left on the morning train." She decided not to provide more details.

"Then permit me to accompany you," Jennings said. "I am also returning to the hotel."

Mariana smiled, relieved to have some company. "Thank you, Mr Jennings," she said.

Jennings nodded, swinging his cane. "Ah, I see, and you were waving goodbye to the good captain."

"Just so," Mariana agreed.

Jennings stepped beside her, keeping a respectable couple of feet between them. "When do you expect him back?"

"Whenever he completes his business," Mariana said.

Jennings smiled. "Ah, you are unsure."

"That's correct," Mariana met the smile. She was beginning to like this man with his easy manners.

"You are also unsure about me," Jennings said. "I am quite harmless, you know. If you doubt me, ask Mr Wells."

"Do you know him well?" Mariana asked.

"I know Mr Wells very well," Jennings smiled at the coincidence of words. "Most people in Rangoon know each other, you see. It's not a huge European community, so we tend to bump into one another every few days."

"Oh," Mariana moved aside, allowing a hurrying man carrying a great load of sacks to pass. "In that case, I will undoubtedly see you from time to time, Mr Jennings."

"I hope you do not find the prospect too displeasing," Jennings said.

Mariana shook her head. "I do not," she replied.

"Here we are," Jennings said. "The Wells Britannia Hotel. If you are unsure, look for the pagoda. Wells is the closest hotel to the Golden Pagoda."

"I'll remember." Talking to the affable Jennings had made the journey shorter. "Thank you for your company, Mr Jennings," Mariana said with a slight curtsey.

"You are most welcome, ma'am," Jennings responded with a quick bow. "I hope we can meet at breakfast tomorrow."

"I am sure we will," Mariana said. "In fact, I rather look forward to it."

Jennings straightened up, smiling. "So do I, Miss Maxwell. So do I. Shall I accompany you to the door of your room?"

"Thank you," Mariana said. "I think I remember the way. Until tomorrow."

"Until tomorrow, then," Jennings replied.

Mariana withdrew to her room, closed the door, and sat on her bed. She drew a map from her case and traced the route to Mandalay.

Keep safe, Andrew, she prayed. *Don't have any adventures up there.* She remembered Jennings telling them he did not stay in the hotel, wondered why he had changed his mind and brushed the thought away. *It is unimportant.*

Pulling out her journal, she wrote the morning's events, made a three-week table, and prepared to score out each day. Twenty-one seemed a great many days.

After a long night-time journey by a less-than-comfortable train, followed by a voyage on a crowded boat, Andrew was tired when he arrived at Thayetmyo. A bustling port on the western bank of the Irrawaddy River, the town was strategically placed between the Arakan Mountains to the west and the Pegu Hills to the east. Andrew had already come to expect the local gold-covered pagoda and the busy market, but the size of the British population was reassuring. Merchants lived in comfortable houses, with carriages and buffalo carts in the streets, traders in teak and rice chatting in small groups, and people seemingly contented. The small garrison of British soldiers and Sikh and Burmese policemen moved around the streets without fuss, quietly keeping order without seeming to intrude in civilians' lives.

Leaving his luggage in the care of the red-faced harbour master, Andrew sought a reliable boatman to take him to Mandalay. As Wells had recommended a man named Jamieson, Andrew asked for him along the riverside.

The merchants seemed eager to help and equally willing to talk.

"Welcome to Thayetmyo," a cheerful rice merchant greeted Andrew. "The finest little town in the East."

"Is it fine?" Andrew asked. "Are you not afraid that Thibaw will invade?"

"Not a bit of it, my boy," the merchant replied. "If Thibaw comes, the Army will sort him out. The dacoits are a nuisance, but they'll fade away once we annex Upper Burma."

"Will we annex Upper Burma?" Andrew asked. He had heard other Europeans voice the same opinion.

"Eventually," the merchant said, "we can't allow such an unpleasant neighbour as Thibaw to remain on our borders, can we?"

Andrew had not responded, remembering similar statements about Cetshwayo of Zululand. Hiring a boat proved simple, with Burmese and British boatmen plying for custom.

"I'm looking for a Mr Jamieson," Andrew said as he stood at the riverside.

"Where are you bound?" a sandy-haired boatman asked.

"Mandalay," Andrew said. He expected a negative response, but the boatman didn't flinch.

"That's a fair journey. You'll need a decent vessel." The boatman glanced at his steam launch. "Like *Little Salamander* there. She'll take you anywhere you want to go."

"*Little Salamander*," Andrew examined the steam launch. Thirty-five feet long, she had a tall funnel in the stern, space for cargo and coal, and a couple of cabins. A canvas canopy shaded the deck from the sun. "She looks handy."

"She is," the boatman said, "named after HMS *Salamander*." He smiled. "She's a smaller version of the ship where I learned my trade."

"Are you Captain Jamieson?" Andrew asked.

"I am Captain Jamieson," the boatman said and pointed at a thin-faced man in his late fifties. "This gentleman is Sinclair, my mate and engineer."

Andrew nodded. He trusted Wells to give good advice. "Good afternoon to you both. I am Andrew Baird. How much would you charge to take me to Mandalay, Captain?"

Jamieson surveyed Andrew through calculating eyes. "When do you want to leave, Mr Baird?"

"As soon as possible," Andrew said.

"Tomorrow?" Jamieson sounded hopeful.

"Today would be better," Andrew said. "If you have sufficient fuel and supplies."

"We're fully loaded with both," Jamieson said. "We can leave in an hour." He looked Andrew up and down. "Do you have the readies?"

"How much?" Andrew liked Jamieson's direct approach.

"Shall we say five guineas?" Jamieson sat in the stern of *Little Salamander*, smiling. Broad-faced and bulky in body, his beard was more grey than black.

Andrew shook his head. "Shall we say two?"

Jamieson's smile widened. "How about four guineas, then?"

"Two guineas and ten shillings?" Andrew knew he had found his boatman.

They settled on three guineas, and Andrew carried his baggage to the steam launch. Years of campaigning had taught him to travel light, so he took up little space in the minuscule cabin.

"Welcome aboard, Mr Baird," Jamieson said. "Don't get underfoot, and we'll get along fine."

"I'll keep out of your way," Andrew promised.

He heard the brassy notes of a gong in the background, wondered what they meant, and took a last look at Thayetmyo. He saw a slender Burmese man watching him from the quay and lifted a hand in acknowledgement. The man did not respond but shouted something over his shoulder and stood beside a warehouse, gazing intently at *Little Salamander*.

"Ignore him," Jamieson advised. "Many of these Burmans have nothing better to do than sit in the sun, smoke and gamble. The women are their better workers." He raised his voice and shouted to a toiling labourer carrying a heavy box, speaking fluent Burmese. "We have a long journey ahead of us, and you'll be sleeping on board at night, Mr Baird."

"Do we travel at night?"

"No," Jamieson shook his head. "Nobody sails the Irrawaddy at night. The currents are too treacherous, and what was a deep-water channel on Monday could be a sandbank on Wednesday. I won't be running *Little Salamander* aground, Mr Baird, no matter how urgent your business in Mandalay."

"I understand, Captain Jamieson," Andrew said. "Mr Wells of Rangoon recommended you, and I trust you will get me to Mandalay faster than anybody else."

Jamieson grunted. "Edmund Wells, eh? He's a good man. I'll do my best, Mr Baird. Except it isn't Mister, is it? What's your rank, soldier?"

"Captain," Andrew replied.

"You have the look and the snap of a military man," Jamieson said. "If you want to pass as a civilian in Mandalay, Captain Baird, look less efficient."

Andrew found a space on the deck where the overhead canopy provided the most shade. "I'll do my best to look inefficient," he said, listening to the regular beat of the gong. The slender Burmese man remained on the quay, watching and puffing at a long cigar.

Little Salamander left an hour later with Jamieson in the bow. The minute the steam launch eased into the river, the slender man vanished, but the gong continued.

"What do the gongs mean?" Andrew asked.

Jamieson screwed up his face. "It's a message of some sort," he said. "Maybe telling somebody that we're on our way."

"Telling who?"

Jamieson shook his head. "I don't know," he said. "The Burmans live separate lives from us. We live, and they live; we are in the same country, in the same towns, and often in the same streets, yet we are apart. Except for the people we employ or the village officials, we hardly speak, let alone discuss our businesses."

"You don't seem to employ many people," Andrew nodded to the two silent Burmese who coiled the landing line and hoisted the anchor. "Don't you need a pilot?"

"I've been working the river for thirty years," Jamieson replied. "I know it as well as any Burmese."

"I see," Andrew said, turning away to allow Jamieson to concentrate on *Little Salamander.* The Irrawaddy was busy with boats, primarily small fishing craft but also a few larger vessels. Andrew saw Jamieson move to the stern and take over the helm from a middle-aged, serious Burmese man. Jamieson steered around patches of lighter-coloured water where sandbanks had appeared and avoided stray branches that twisted and turned a few feet from the launch.

"There must have been a storm up in the hills," Jamieson said casually, gesturing to a tree trunk swirling past them. "The Irrawaddy has a strong current, but often the deep-water channel is quite narrow, so we have to be careful not to run aground."

The sound of gongs continued as they chugged upriver, with the echoes of one clanging gong no sooner fading than another took its place.

Andrew found the riverbanks interesting, with patches of dense forest between extensive paddy fields. He saw men in broad hats working with water buffalo, ignoring the river traffic as they guided the giant beasts. *Little Salamander* passed villages of bamboo-built, palm-thatched houses that sat on long poles above the river, presumably to escape the flood season, with fishing boats busy on the water. Men either worked on the river, in the fields or sat smoking or gambling, while women constantly worked or tended to the children. The more prosperous women wore satin longyis, a ubiquitous garment resembling a long skirt that men also sported. The poorer or harder working wore less clothing, as in most cultures.

Andrew began to relax into the voyage. Sinclair was busy with the engine; Jamieson was skilled on the river, and the two Burmese boatmen were efficient and quiet. Monkeys chattered among the trees, brightly coloured birds fluttered overhead or squawked from the branches, and the thoughts of dacoits seemed like a different world from the somnolent life of the river.

I will be in Mandalay in a few days, and Bo Thura will contact me. I must try to free young Mary MacConnacher, but what does Bo Thura want in exchange? He shrugged. *Well, I'll find out in Mandalay. There's no sense fretting until I know the problem. That damned gong is still sounding, though.*

Andrew realised the regular beat of the gong had never stopped. Whether *Little Salamander* was moving or berthed, the single stroke had followed them along the river. *What the devil does that mean?*

Andrew lifted his head, sniffing. He smelled smoke drifting from ahead. Andrew knew immediately that it was not the smell of a cooking fire. He looked forward, seeing a few blue-grey trails across the water's surface. There were no fishing boats on this section of the river, only overhanging trees, the call of monkeys and the repetitive, single, sonorous boom of the gong.

The smoke smell increased as the boat rounded the bend of the river.

"What's happening?" Andrew felt for the pistol in the holster under his jacket.

"God knows," Jamieson replied, a cigar jammed between his teeth and his eyes focused on the water. "As I said, the Burmans have separate lives from us."

"I tell you what's happening. There's trouble ahead," Sinclair poked his head up from the engine compartment, wiping a dirty rag across his sooty forehead. "After a while out here in the East, you develop a sixth sense for trouble. The birds are quiet for a start, and the air feels heavier. Can't you feel it?"

"I can," Andrew agreed as Jamieson spat into the wind and steered *Little Salamander* around a patch of shoal water. "It was the same on the frontier in Africa. We felt the tension before anything happened."

"Aye, mebbe, aye." Jamieson slowed the steamer as a waft of smoke drifted from the bend, and Sinclair withdrew into the diminutive steer house to reappear, holding a Snider rifle. He glanced at the forest, deep green and tangled. "I don't like that gong," he said. "It's been with us since we left Thayetmyo, just the one gong passing on a message."

"What do you reckon?" Andrew asked.

"I reckon we'd better be careful," Sinclair said as he loaded the Snider, lifted it to his shoulder and aimed at the bank. "She'll do." He nodded to the revolver in Andrew's hand. "You'd better have that ready, Captain. The dacoits are not averse to attacking British boats if they think they can get away with it."

"Dacoits? Would they operate on the Irrawaddy?"

"They'd operate in the Chief Commissioner's mansion, Captain Baird," Sinclair replied. "Open a cupboard, and one could pop out, slice you open with his dha, and run off with your wallet and your wife. Except Bo Thura."

"Except Bo Thura? What's different about him?"

Sinclair grinned, holding the Snider in capable hands. "He'd prefer your horse to your wife. Bo Thura is Burma's greatest horse thief, although God knows what he does with them."

"Is that all he does?" The smoke was denser as they reached the apex of the bend, an acrid stink that nipped Andrew's eyes.

"God, no. He's like the rest; murder, rape, robbery," Sinclair nodded to the smoke. "And arson."

"Kidnapping?" Andrew asked.

"Not that I'm aware of," Sinclair replied.

Andrew shoved cartridges into his revolver as the steam launch rounded the bend. He heard chattering above and saw a troop of monkeys clinging to an overhanging branch.

"The monkeys don't look too concerned," he said.

"They're watching us too closely," Sinclair replied. "They want to see what we're up to."

"Ease up further, Sincs," Jamieson ordered. "Keep to the deep-water channel midstream."

"Aye, aye, sir," Sinclair replied formally, placed the Snider nearby and slowed the launch. The smoke grew thicker, wafting in billows across the water.

"Now you'll see what the dacoits are like," Jamieson murmured.

The village sat in smouldering ruin, with a scatter of dead bodies on the ground and the smoking remains of bamboo houses. Three fishing boats lay on the bank, one with a man's body inside it. All three were wrecked, with holes torn in the bottom. A small patrol of khaki-clad soldiers moved slowly between the buildings, with half a dozen Sikh policemen amongst them.

"You in the launch!" A slender officer waded into the river and gestured to them. "Come ashore! I want to talk to you!" He snapped an order, and the British soldiers splashed into the shallows, aiming their rifles at *Little Salamander*.

"Get in here!" the officer shouted.

CHAPTER 6

LOWER BURMA, SEPTEMBER 1884

"Here we go," Jamieson said, steering for the village. The soldiers kept their rifles trained on the launch until a worn-looking sergeant barked an order.

"Get that boat tied up."

"I'm Jamieson, captain of *Little Salamander*," Jamieson announced.

"They're British," the sergeant said. "Smith, stay with the launch. Corporal Rowan, take a patrol along the riverbank. Shoot anybody that looks suspicious."

"Yes, Sergeant." Rowan looked equally exhausted. He called up a section of eight men and headed north beside the Irrawaddy.

"Come ashore," the officer ordered. "I want to speak to you!"

"We're coming," Jamieson said. "That must mean you, too, Captain Baird."

Andrew was first in the village, followed by Sinclair and Jamieson.

The officer, a middle-aged major, eyed them sourly from behind his drooping moustache. "Who the devil are you, and where are you going?"

"Andrew Baird," Andrew said, then introduced Jamieson and Sinclair.

"Major Goudie, 21st Foot, Royal Scots Fusiliers. Can you vouch for the Burmans in your boat, Captain Jamieson?"

"I can, sir," Jamieson replied. "They've been with me for years."

"What happened here?" Andrew asked.

"Dacoits," Goudie replied laconically, glancing at the destruction. "They are getting bolder now, crossing from Upper Burma as if they can do as they like on our side of the frontier."

"What happened?" Andrew repeated.

Goudie pulled a face. "I don't know for certain," he said. "It looks as if they came last night, looted the place from Monday to Christmas, killed every man who resisted and escaped with the women." He faced Jamieson. "Did you see anything along the riverbank on your voyage upriver, Captain?"

"Nothing out of the ordinary," Jamieson replied.

"All right. They must have gone inland or upriver to Upper Burma. Be careful."

"We will," Jamieson replied.

"We never saw anything suspicious, sir," Sinclair said, "but we heard something strange."

"What was that, Sinclair?" Goudie asked. "Anything strange might signify some new trick these devils have up their sleeve."

"A gong, sir," Sinclair said. "I've been out East long enough to know that gongs are part of the culture, but I've never heard one quite like this before."

"What was it like?" the major asked.

"A single gong that followed us along the riverbank," Sinclair explained. "Just the one gong, as if it was passing a message, telling somebody where we were."

The major sighed. "I've never heard of that before. You'd better be careful out there."

"It's still sounding," Andrew lifted a hand. "Listen."

Goudie lifted his head and frowned as the gong sounded its single brassy note. "So it is, by God. However, there's nothing illegal about banging a gong. It might be completely unrelated to the dacoits." He looked at Andrew. "You haven't told me your reason for travelling to Mandalay, Baird."

"It's a personal matter, sir." Andrew had decided not to mention Bo Thura or Mary MacConnacher. He did not want his family history broadcast, nor did he want anybody to know the purpose of his mission until he had spoken to Bo Thura.

"Ah," Goudie was too much of a gentleman to pry. He smiled as a musket banged, followed by the sharper report of a rifle. "It sounds like my lads have contacted the dacoits."

Andrew instinctively slid behind one of the smouldering houses as a bullet zipped past, to thud into the ground. More musketry followed, with spurts of smoke in the surrounding forest and fountains of dust rising around the major.

The corporal returned with his patrol, his helmet awry and sweat streaking his face. He snapped orders that saw his men take cover, facing outward. "There must be a hundred of them, sir. They fired too soon, so I ordered the boys to fire a volley and retired on the village."

"Quite right, Corporal!" Goudie approved. He raised his voice. "Form up on the village, lads! Police as well!" He glanced at Jamieson. "We have an unknown number of dacoits along the riverbank, Jamieson, and the deep-water channel runs close to the bank for the next few miles. I'd advise you to remain where you are until we clear the dacoits."

Jamieson nodded. "Yes, sir." He glanced at Andrew. "The channel doesn't only pass close inshore here, Captain Baird; there's also a stronger than usual four-knot current. *Little Salamander* would only make a couple of knots at best, less than walking speed."

"We'd be a sitting target for the dacoits," Sinclair added. "Best wait until the swaddies have chased them away."*

"Captain?" The officer looked at Andrew.

"Captain Andrew Baird of the Natal Dragoons," Andrew explained.

"Natal Dragoons?" the officer repeated. "What the devil is a colonial African cavalryman doing up the Irrawaddy River? Never mind; you'd best keep your head down, Baird."

"I can help defeat these dacoits," Andrew decided. "I must get to Mandalay as quickly as possible. What's your plan?"

"Have you seen any action, Captain?" Goudie asked.

"Yes, sir. Three campaigns, including the Zulus and the Boers," Andrew replied.

"Were you at Rorke's Drift?"

"No, sir. Khambula, Isandhlwana and Ulundi," Andrew replied.

"Isandhlwana?" Goudie repeated. "You survived that?"

Andrew nodded. He had noticed that people looked at him strangely when he mentioned surviving Isandhlwana as if he had no right to be alive.

Maybe they are right. Far too many good men died that day.

"In that case, Captain Baird, a few dacoits shouldn't present a problem," Goudie said. "Take two sections of Fusiliers and a police platoon to hold the outer perimeter."

"Yes, sir," Andrew replied.

I started my career as a colonial policeman. My world has moved full circle.

Andrew counted the British soldiers and Sikh policemen as they formed up in the village. Twenty-two Royal Scots Fusiliers and twenty Sikhs.

The Sikhs looked like a stalwart bunch, tall men with red turbans and neat beards. The havildar in charge spoke English and eyed Andrew suspiciously, wondering what right a civilian had to give him orders.

"I am Captain Andrew Baird of the Natal Dragoons," Andrew introduced himself. "I want you in extended order around the edge of the village. Keep under cover, or the enemy will use you as targets."

The havildar frowned. "We are not cowards to hide from dacoits and badmashes," he said.†

"No, you are Sikh policemen," Andrew remembered his father's constant praise of the Sikhs. "You are too valuable to be killed by some dacoit's bullet." He saw the havildar's brown eyes widen as he digested his words.

"Yes, Sahib," the havildar replied, telling his men what Andrew had said.

The Sikhs found shelter, peering through the smoke into the surrounding forest. The Fusiliers were already in position, aiming their Martinis at the forest fringe. On the flank, the corporal's section was engaged in sporadic fighting, with the heavy crack of their rifles contrasting with the duller thud of muzzle-loading muskets and an occasional Dacoit's shout.

In the intervals between the gunfire, Andrew heard the regular beat of the

---

* Swaddies- soldiers. A slang term usually pronounced as squaddies in the 20th and 21st centuries.

† Badmash – rogue, thief, robber. Havildar: the equivalent of a sergeant.

gong. Invisible and unhurried, the brassy notes acted as a surreal backdrop to the skirmish.

"It's unusual for dacoits to face up to armed police, let alone the Army," Goudie said. "They're getting very bold. I'd say somebody up there is backing them." He jerked a thumb to the north.

"Somebody?" Andrew repeated. "Do you suspect King Thibaw?"

"A man who murdered all his relatives to secure his succession to the throne is capable of anything," Goudie said. "Can you hold the fort, Baird, while I lead a fighting patrol along the riverbank?"

"Yes, sir," Andrew said, looking along his defensive line. The men were steady, Fusiliers and Sikhs side by side, waiting and occasionally firing.

"What's your name, Havildar?" Andrew asked.

"Sukhbir Singh, sahib," the Havildar sounded surprised at the question.

"Well, Sukhbir, I want you to choose five of your best men and form a support unit ready to reinforce wherever you are required."

"Yes, sahib."

"I don't know how dacoits fight," Andrew confessed, "but we have a thinly protected firing line, and if they rush us and break through, you'll be our last line of defence."

"Yes, sahib." Sukhbir seemed pleased at the responsibility, as Andrew suspected he would.

Goudie led from the front, passing through Corporal Rowan's section and pressing on. The Fusiliers held their Martinis with the casual familiarity of veterans. A few looked at home in the forest, while most were clumsy, making too much noise for Andrew's liking.

With proper training, these Fusiliers could be good soldiers. Lift your feet, lads, and watch for dry twigs.

The sporadic firing ended, with the waiting British and Sikhs watching the forest.

"Is that something over there, on the right?" a Glasgow voice asked.

"Aye, it's a bloody tree, Wullie. And there's another on the left. Close your mouth and keep your finger on the trigger."

Andrew smiled, happy to hear the Royal Scots Fusiliers had the same dark humour as the other British regiments with whom he had served.

The Sikhs were silent, holding their Sniders, hoping to see the dacoits. Andrew could sense their eagerness.

The Sikhs are desperate to fight. They want to prove themselves, like the knights in King Arthur's Round Table. He grinned at the thought of Sir Lancelot wearing a turban, wondering what Mariana would think of that and if he was slightly mad.

I must be mad; no sane man would become a soldier.

The monkeys were back, chattering in the trees, and Andrew realised he could still hear the gong.

It's never been silent since we left Thayetmyo. What the devil is that all about?

"Sahib," Sukhbir Singh stepped to his side. "The badmashes are out there." He pointed with his bearded chin. "I can feel them."

Andrew looked beyond the small fields to the forest surrounding the village's small fields, trying to penetrate the trees with his eyes. He saw nothing but green vegetation until something moved.

Human or animal?

Damn it, I've fought Zulus, Boers and Galekas; surely I can see a handful of damned badmashes in a few trees.

Andrew slowly raised his revolver, wishing he had a rifle. With its rapid fire, a revolver was fine for close-quarter work but had no penetration at any range over thirty yards. He watched the movement in the trees, mentally calculating speed, size, and distance.

If a dacoit is aiming at me now, he has all the advantages. Is that damned gong still sounding? Yes, it is.

Andrew sensed Sukhbir Singh tensing at his side and saw two police aiming at the same part of the forest.

"Wait," he said softly.

Are these Burmans going to attack us? Or are they laying an ambush for Major Goudie's patrol when it returns? If they catch Goudie in the open fields, they could inflict considerable casualties.

"Who is the best shot of your men, Havildar?" Andrew asked.

"Ajit Singh, sahib," Sukhbir replied.

"Very well. I want him to target that man in the trees and fire a single shot."

Sukhbir nodded and passed on Andrew's message.

Andrew saw the smallest policeman take careful aim into the forest and fire. The Snider cracked, smoke spurted, and Andrew saw leaves jerk among the trees. He heard a startled cry and a commotion behind the forest fringe.

Well done, Ajit. Now we know they are dacoits.

"On my word, fire a volley," Andrew ordered, "but not parallel to the river-bank in case Major Goudie is leading the patrol back." He waited until Sukhbir passed on his message to the Sikhs and then did the same to the Fusiliers.

"We're ready, sir," an auburn-haired, steady-eyed corporal replied.

"What's your name, Corporal?"

"McGhee, sir," the corporal replied.

"On my word, McGhee."

Andrew gave his men a few more seconds.

"Fire!"

The Fusiliers fired together, as expected, and loaded without orders, waiting expectantly. Although the Sikhs were police rather than soldiers and were spread all around the perimeter of the village, the volley crashed out with near-military precision. Andrew saw leaves and twigs fly as the bullets crashed home and heard a long shriek as one found its mark.

"Another volley," Andrew ordered. "Fire!"

The Sikhs had also reloaded and fired another volley but without any sound from the dacoits.

They've either withdrawn or taken deep cover. Let's see if we can winkle them out.

"Cease fire!" Andrew ordered. "Corporal McGhee! Take a section into the trees, only a hundred yards, see what's there and return. Keep your men together, and don't leave any behind."

God knows what the dacoits would do to any British prisoners.

"Yes, sir!" McGhee led his men in open order, jinking and weaving across the fields in case the dacoits were waiting in ambush. Andrew heard them crashing around with hoarse shouts as they hunted through the thick bush.

I wish you were better trained in forest fighting, lads.

After ten minutes, Andrew heard a single shot, a coarse laugh, and McGhee returned with the patrol. They crossed the fields at a trot, with two men as rearguard, circling to scan the forest as they moved.

Corporal McGhee approached Andrew, saluted, and made his report.

"We found one dead dacoit, sir, and one shot through the stomach. The wounded man made a lunge at Private Halloran with his knife, and Halloran shot him."

"Very good, Corporal. Return to your post."

"Yes, sir," McGhee replied. "Come on, lads!"

Sukhbir watched the soldiers with what Andrew suspected was jealousy that his men were not involved.

You're policemen, Havildar, not soldiers.

Andrew toured the perimeter, trying to ignore the insects that tormented him and the insistent, regular beat of the gong.

"All right, lads?"

"All right, sir. All Sir Garnet."*

Andrew nodded. "Carry on, Fusiliers."

When Andrew returned to his central position, a volley sounded from along the riverbank, followed by a scatter of shots. Musket fire was mixed with the ear-splitting crack of Martinis, proving that both British and dacoits were firing. Andrew saw the Sikhs look towards the sound, with some men grinning and others lifting their Sniders as if to help.

These lads are natural soldiers.

The firing rose in intensity, then died away to an irregular spatter, followed by another two volleys in proximity. Andrew heard a cheer and then a few shots and then silence.

Major Goudie has met the dacoits.

Andrew listened; even the monkeys were silent, with only the rush and gurgle of the river as a backdrop and that incessant, frustrating, slow-banging gong.

"Shall I take a patrol along, sir?" McGhee asked. "The boys are wondering what's the to-do."

"No," Andrew shook his head. "You might be needed here if the dacoits double back."

"Yes, sir," McGhee replied.

---

* All Sir Garnet: a British Army phrase of the late Nineteenth Century, meaning everything was all right. It was a reference to General Sir Garnet Wolseley, who was reputed to be Britain's best general of the period.

Major Goudie was the first to return to the village with his men marching at his back. One Fusilier was limping, with blood on his thigh, and the others were in high spirits despite the sweat that soaked their uniforms and the insects clouding around their heads.

"Did you see that dacoit jump when I shot him? The bullet lifted him clean off his feet."

"You shot him, be buggered man! That was my shot. Right in the chest."

"If you line two up together, one bullet does for both."

"We heard shooting," Goudie said to Andrew.

"We chased off a group of dacoits," Andrew replied, "and Corporal McGhee took a patrol into the forest."

"We met your dacoits," Goudie said. "They ambushed us, and we retaliated and charged them with the bayonet."

That would be the cheer we heard.

"Did you catch many?" Andrew asked.

"Hunting dacoits is like catching smoke with a fishing net," Goudie said. "One minute they're there, and the next they're elsewhere. Occasionally, we get hold of one, but when we do, we can be sure it's only some benighted villager looking for a few handfuls of rice and not one of the professional robbers."

"Is it safe for us to continue?" Andrew asked.

Goudie nodded. "I'd say so," he said. "I doubt they linger along this stretch of the river. We inflicted a few casualties and scared them away for now, at least until Thibaw sends them back."

"Were they Thibaw's men?" Andrew asked.

"Probably," Goudie replied. "He sends them into British Burma to rob, murder, rape and generally commit mayhem. We shoot a few, capture others, and our judges release them on some pretext or other, and the whole thing starts again." He sighed. "I'd like to have captured the leader of that band, Baird. I glimpsed him through the trees, an ugly-looking devil with a gold-hilted dha. I'll keep my eyes open for him in the future."

"Yes, sir," Andrew added the information to his store. *I wonder if that was Bo Thura?*

"You'd better be on your way if you intend to reach Mandalay," Goudie said with a tired smile. "Thank you for your help."

"It was a pleasure, sir," Andrew said.

CHAPTER 7

LOWER BURMA, SEPTEMBER 1884

"Andrew?" Mariana stirred in her bed.

I heard somebody moving; I am sure I did.

Rising quickly, Mariana reached for the small revolver Andrew had given her on the voyage to India.

"You know how to fire a rifle," Andrew had said. "Can you fire a pistol?"

When Mariana replied in the negative, Andrew demonstrated the basics and made her practise every day, firing from the passenger deck at objects he threw in the sea. Mariana's first few efforts had been poor, with the bullets raising splashes yards from the target, but she had improved with practice and became an adequate pistol shot.

Now, Mariana blessed these forced sessions and held the revolver, peering into the dark. For one terrifying moment, her treacherous mind dragged her back to Inglenook, with the raiders breaking in and Elaine fighting and then screaming.

No, Mariana told herself. *That's past.* She took a deep breath, stepped away from the bed and strode to the window, revolver in hand. She dragged back the curtains, saw moonlight above the Golden Pagoda, and checked that the room was empty.

I am imagining things. Andrew's hardly been away, and my mind is playing tricks on me.

The sound of male laughter came to her, and she recognised Jennings' voice.

Don't go far, Mr Jennings. Stay close until Andrew returns. Mariana replaced the revolver under her pillow and lay on the bed, knowing she would not sleep. Memories of Inglenook returned, with every sound reminding her of the night the renegades came and that black hole in her memory, hinting at forgotten horrors.

❄

"HAVE YOU FINISHED SOLDIERING FOR THE DAY?" JAMIESON SPOKE AROUND A large Burmese cigar.

"I have," Andrew replied.

"We'll get going then," Jamieson said. "We'll get a few miles upriver before night and sleep on board tonight, mid-river."

Andrew nodded and stepped on board the launch. Sinclair had returned to *Little Salamander* to keep steam up, so they were back in the deep-water channel within ten minutes. The Fusiliers and police watched them leave without emotion.

"There's that gong," Jamieson said as they eased away from the still-smoking village.

The brassy clang followed them, a single stroke every fifteen seconds, sounding above the rush of the river and the engine's reassuring chug.

"It's following us," Andrew said, peering into the forest without seeing anybody. He took charge of the Snider and watched the riverbank as *Little Salamander* steamed only twenty yards from the trees.

"Maybe," Jamieson clamped his cigar between his teeth and concentrated on his steering, with his smoke adding to the smuts from the funnel. "Whoever's banging the gong can't be dangerous, though. If they meant us any harm, they'd have shot us when we were ashore."

Although Andrew nodded, he was relieved when the deep-water channel veered away from the bank to mid-channel, and they were further from potential danger. Even out here, with birds singing and the river much broader, he could still hear the sonorous beat of the gong.

"How far is the frontier?" Andrew asked. He heard the Burmese fireman shovelling coal down below.

"Not far," Jamieson replied. "There's a tricky bit of navigation ahead first, and then you'll see the Burman frontier posts."

Little Salamander steamed on, threading between a group of islands and sandbanks as the river broadened. Jamieson sent one of the crew into the bow to cast the lead and report the depth of water.

"The channels alter here," Jamieson explained. "They could be shallow one trip and deep the next. We must be careful and read the river."

This stretch of water would be a good place for an ambush, Andrew thought, watching the islands with his rifle ready. A flotilla of fishing boats hugged the western bank, with men watching the steam launch chug slowly past.

"General rule," Jamieson spoke around his cigar, expelling spurts of smoke with every word. "The broader the river, the shallower the water and the more likely large vessels will run aground. The narrower the river, the faster the current and more difficult to push against." He removed his cigar to glance at

Andrew. "The faster the current, the slower the ship travels and, therefore, the easier target for dacoits hiding in the forest."

When they passed the islands, Andrew unloaded the Snider and replaced it on its brackets in the wheelhouse. The deep-water channel was more central here as the river alternated between broad and narrow, with some gentle curves. He looked up as they rounded a bend, and a white fort glowered down at them.

"What's that place?" Andrew asked.

"We've just passed the frontier," Jamieson said. "That fort is Kulogon or Kuliyang, especially erected by Thibaw's pet Italian engineer. Take your pick of the name; the defensive work on the opposite bank is Minhla. These are King Thibaw's guardian posts."

Andrew lifted his binoculars and studied both fortifications with a soldier's eye. "If Thibaw puts in a couple of strong garrisons and adds some artillery, these redoubts could be tough to take." He grunted. "A couple of hundred Boer riflemen could hold them against anything except an ironclad ship and heavy artillery."

Jamieson nodded. "Maybe so," he said. "As far as I am aware, Thibaw doesn't have any Boer riflemen, although, as I mentioned, a couple of Italian engineers work for him. Nor do we have an ironclad ship or heavy artillery in Burma."

Andrew lowered his binoculars. "I hope we never need them."

"We might if we ever war with the Lords of the White Elephant, the King of all Umbrella Bearing Chiefs, the Lord of Earth and Air or whatever Thibaw calls himself these days."

"Will that happen?" Andrew asked.

"You've only been in Burma a few days," Jamieson said. "Yet you have already been involved with the dacoits. How much longer will Britain stand for a semi-barbarian king who deliberately sends bands of badmashes* into our territory?"

"That's the price we pay on every Imperial frontier," Andrew replied. "The Cape Colony, Natal, Egypt, Northwest India. We butt against the semi-civilised or uncivilised wherever we are."

"Why did we invade Zululand?" Jamieson asked. "To protect our frontier farms from such incursions. Why did we have so many wars along the Cape Colony border or the Northwest Frontier? The same reason: we wish to protect the people in lands we administer from the half-civilised folk next door." He issued a smart order that saw *Little Salamander* alter course to avoid a floating log. "War with the King of Ava is coming, mark my words. He's a nasty little piece, and his mother-in-law and that devil Maung Thandar, one of his ministers, have him under their grubby thumbs. The only way we can have peace is to have an open war and occupy the whole damned country."

"Or leave it," Andrew said. *I've seen enough of war.*

---

* Badmash: thief, robber, criminal.

Jamieson nodded. "Or leave it to its own devices. And what would happen then?"

"I really don't know," Andrew said.

"Either the French would move in, and they're already knocking at the side door over in Tonkin, or the Chinese would invade, or Thibaw would continue to send his dacoits." Jamieson drew deeply on his cigar. "He could do that until we decide the game's not worth the candle, as we did in the American colonies. If we pulled out of Burma, we'd lose a hell of a lot of trade, and our entire eastern frontier would be aflame with dacoits. Burma itself would be a nightmare for the people, with perpetual civil war and cruelty."

"Is that what would happen?" Andrew asked.

"I believe so," Jamieson said. "If we leave Burma, we'd have let the Burmese people, the folk we've sworn to protect and govern, very badly down by handing them to a monster."

"Is it that bad?" Andrew asked.

"It's that bad." Jamieson shook his head. "Gladstone has a point. Once we've started on this Imperial lark, we just get deeper and deeper embroiled in other people's troubles that we have to sort out. Take it from me, Baird; empire building is a mug's game, best avoided."

"I'll be sure to tell Her Majesty and Salisbury * that when next I meet them," Andrew said.

Jamieson smiled. "You're right, Captain Baird; people like you and I don't have much say in this world. We must just make the best of whatever hand the good Lord sees fit to deal us."

"We all have to do that, Captain Jamieson," Andrew said. He looked north, deeper into Thibaw's Kingdom of Ava, and wondered what lay ahead.

"You look stunning today," Jennings said as Mariana stood in the hotel's foyer after breakfast.

"Thank you," Mariana replied. "I thought you didn't stay in the hotel."

"I breakfast here sometimes," Jennings said. "I like the conversation, and my humble house can become lonely with only the servants for company. Have you recovered from yesterday's scare?"

"Quite recovered, thank you," Mariana replied.

"That is good," Jennings said. "What are your plans for today?"

"I don't have a plan," Mariana said. "I was going to look at Rangoon, maybe go inside the pagoda if the monks don't object."

"I have some free time from my work," Jennings said. "It might be better if a man accompanied you." He smiled. "I know I cannot match the gallant Captain Baird, but it can be daunting for an Englishwoman alone in a strange

* Robert Gascoyne-Cecil, 3rd Marquess of Salisbury, was the leader of the Conservative party and became Prime Minister in 1886.

city. Rangoon is not some quiet English market town, you see, or London, with a policeman at every street corner."

Mariana laughed. "I am quite used to strange places," she said. "I grew up in Natal, on the Zululand border, so I am not at all daunted by non-English people. Indeed," she widened her eyes. "Andrew and I have recently been to Scotland."

Jennings laughed, shaking his head. "Scotland! How exotic! That was daring of you moving amongst these primitive people."

Mariana smiled. "I can be a daring woman," she replied. "Sometimes I even talk to strange men in hotels."

"That is daring," Jennings agreed with a smile. "This strange man suggests he takes you to see the Golden Pagoda. It's quite an interesting place, Miss Maxwell."

"I am sure it is, Mr Jennings," Mariana said. "And you would be scintillating company. However, I will not accompany you today."

"As you wish, Miss Maxwell," Jennings bowed. "I wish you a very good day."

"Thank you, Mr Jennings," Mariana said. "I wish the same for you."

I don't think it is respectable to have another man accompany me so soon after Andrew has gone to Mandalay.

After a brief farewell to Wells, Mariana left the hotel and headed for the Golden Pagoda. She moved slowly, allowing herself time to absorb Rangoon's atmosphere. The streets were busy with traders, with an occasional farmer with his squeaking bullock cart, the ubiquitous array of laughing children, European, Burmese, and Chinese merchants, and dignified women.

The men were sturdy, mostly barefoot, often wearing the same simple longyi as the women, and seemed content to move without associating with the Europeans. Mariana noticed that women managed retail businesses with a freedom denied in most other countries. The trading women wore graceful clothes, and nearly all, prosperous or poor, wore large, hooped earrings, with some carrying cheroots in large holes in their ear lobes.

I won't be adopting many Burmese fashions, Mariana thought. *The dresses are too revealing, the way they cling to the women's bodies, the condition of their ear lobes is disgusting, and I don't like to see women smoking cheroots. I can't see myself smoking a cheroot as I walk around Berwick with gold-hooped earrings bouncing on my shoulders.*

Mariana stifled her laugh and realised that three Burmese men were watching her. She smiled at them without response and walked away, not picking any direction, yet hoping to reach the pagoda.

After a few moments, Mariana heard a high-pitched giggle behind her and looked over her shoulder. The three men were twenty yards away and following her.

Mariana quickened her pace, not yet alarmed but prepared to run. The street seemed to stretch forever, with the houses on either side becoming more ramshackle every ten steps. Men sat in the shade, smoking or gambling, watching her without interest.

I'm heading in the wrong direction. I want to return to the town centre.

Mariana turned around and saw the three Burmese only ten yards away, grinning. They looked dangerous, one with a long knife at his side and all three bare-chested and showing tattoos on their equally bare thighs.

What do they want with me? They would not dare follow if Andrew was here.

Mariana increased her speed again until she was nearly running, with the sound of her feet echoing from the buildings on either side of the street.

A crowd gathered on the street at Mariana's right, men and women who watched her and spoke together. A pack of dogs began to bark, showing their teeth, and a gaggle of children pointed to her and laughed, with one small boy jumping up and down.

What's so amusing about me? Is it laugh at the funny foreigner time?

The three men were closer now, ten yards away, with the central man holding the hilt of his knife. Mariana took a deep breath, wondering if she could outrun them or stand and fight. She knew she could not overpower three men but hoped the noise she made would attract some help.

Do they intend to rob me? Or worse?

I am not scared. Why am I not scared? What would Tennyson say?

"Though we are not now that strength which in old days moved earth and heaven, that which we are, we are; one equal temper of heroic heart."

I am not of heroic heart.

Standing with her back to the nearest building, Mariana faced the three men and raised her voice. "What do you want?"

They barely glanced at her as they walked past, laughing at some private joke.

Mariana let out her breath slowly as the children began to play a game, and one of the women smiled at her.

"Are you lost, Miss Maxwell?" Jennings strode towards her, smiling and swinging his Malacca walking cane.

"Not any longer, Mr Jennings," Mariana did not hide her relief. "For I am sure you will show me the way back to the hotel."

The pagoda will wait. I've had sufficient adventuring for one day.

"That will be my pleasure, Miss Maxwell." Jennings touched a hand to his hat. "It's easy to take a wrong turning in a strange city. You're only a short walk away." He stepped to Mariana's side. "I know Rangoon fairly well, as I have business with the Burmese, as well as the Europeans."

Mariana felt herself relaxing in Jennings' company. "You are a busy man, Mr Jennings."

"One should always keep oneself busy," Jennings replied seriously. "Do what one has to do with a full heart; that's my motto." He smiled across to her, revealing even white teeth behind his well-trimmed moustache. "You're an adventurous lady walking alone in a strange city. I do like a lady with spunk, I must say."

"Thank you, sir," Mariana bobbed in a curtsey. The street seemed less dark and not at all dangerous as Jennings smiled at her and tapped his cane on the ground.

"Now, let's get you back to your hotel. This way," Jennings turned up a side street and, within five minutes, showed her Wells Hotel. "There you are, Miss

Maxwell. I'd advise you not to wander too much in Burma, though, not with the dacoits going around."

"Are they dangerous?"

"I've never heard of them attacking a British woman, but there aren't many for them to attack." Jennings hesitated for a moment. "If you do choose to wander, please don't hesitate to tell me. I'd be delighted, more than delighted, to escort you. I am sure Captain Baird would not mind. He'd prefer to know you are safe with me than alone in Rangoon."

"Thank you, Mr Jennings," Mariana replied politely. "I will remember your kind offer." She smiled, pushing back a loose rogue strand of hair. "I was glad to see you in that street."

"I was glad to see you, too, Miss Maxwell," Jennings touched his cane to the brim of his hat. "Now, I must be off. Business, you understand."

"Of course." Mariana lifted the hem of her skirt and hurried to the hotel. When she turned at the door, Jennings was still watching. He lifted his cane in farewell, turned and strode away, with Mariana watching his tall, elegant figure in the light suit until he vanished around a corner.

She was smiling when she walked into the hotel and nearly bounced up to her room.

If I am a part of all I have met, as Tennyson says, then I must be a part of Mr Jennings. What a strange thought. How fortunate that he was there to look after me. Mariana closed the door, stepped to the long mirror, and looked at her reflection. She straightened her hair. *That's twice Mr Jennings has been on hand. He's like a guardian angel.*

I must get some clothes more suitable for Rangoon.

CHAPTER 8

KINGDOM OF AVA, UPPER BURMA, SEPTEMBER 1884

"What in God's name is that?" Andrew pointed to the riverbank.

A row of strange wooden frameworks lined the west bank of the river, each bearing the naked body of a man spreadeagled on top. Two men were still alive, groaning and writhing in agony as they slowly suffocated. The other eight were mercifully dead, leaning against their bonds as birds and flies feasted on their tortured flesh.

"Dacoits," Jamieson said casually. "King Thibaw, his first minister Kinwun Mingyi or Maung Thandar captured them and had them executed by crucifixion." He spat into the river. "We all know that he sends dacoits over the frontier to harass British Burma, but occasionally, he stirs his Army to catch them. When they operate on his side of the frontier, of course."

Andrew saw the suffering in the nearest victim's eyes. "Dear God in heaven," he breathed. "What sort of place is this?"

"It's Upper Burma," Jamieson said quietly. "The Kingdom of Ava. We carry passengers along the Irrawaddy and further afield for the right price, but apart from that, we don't have much to do with Thibaw's subjects or His Majesty himself." He gestured to the agonised men on the crosses. "You can see why."

Andrew nodded as *Little Salamander* eased past, with her wash creating waves that broke against the torture frameworks. "I can see why," he agreed soberly, wondering again what sort of reception Bo Thura would give him. "Can't we release these poor fellows?"

Jamieson shook his head. "How would you like some foreigner to release a condemned British man from the gallows? Or release a murderer from jail?"

Andrew considered for a moment. "No," he said. "I wouldn't."

"Nor would the Burmans like us to interfere with their justice techniques. We may disapprove, but it's their system." Jamieson drew on his cigar. "I've heard that Thibaw likes to tie his errant subjects to an elephant's foot and let them trample them to death. I don't know if that's true, but it seems more merciful than that monstrosity," he nodded towards the crucified men.

The gong continued its regular beat, as it had ever since *Little Salamander* had left Thayetmyo. Andrew had grown used to the sound, accepting it as part of the journey. Although he lifted his field glasses occasionally, scanning the forest hoping to find the man, or men, who beat the gong, he was unsuccessful.

"How far to Mandalay?" Andrew asked as they steamed past open paddy fields and small, prosperous villages.

"Not far now," Jamieson replied. He spun the wheel, holding the spokes with three fingers. "Mandalay is not a bad town, as long as you forget any British notions of how a town should look. It's cleaner than most in the east, but there again, the Burmans are a clean people."

Andrew nodded. "I have noticed that," he said.

"Thirty years ago, when I first came here," Jamieson said, "Mandalay did not exist. Nearly everything you'll see has been built since then, which shows how industrious the Burmans can be when they put their minds to it or when somebody stands behind them with a big stick."

"I think most people are like that," Andrew murmured. "Not just the Burmans."

Jamieson laughed. "There's a lot of truth in that," he said. "Don't expect another London or even Rangoon. The Burmans change their capital like we change our clothes. It's been at Ava two or three times, Amarapura at least twice and Mongyaw a couple of times, but Thibaw seems to like Mandalay, so there it stands."

Andrew looked up as he heard human voices ahead. Three boats were racing towards them, each high-prowed and packed with bare-chested men who paddled as if their lives depended on it. Jamieson held his arm as he reached for the revolver inside his jacket.

"It's all right, Captain Baird," Jamieson said. "They're racing each other. Boat racing and gambling are Burman obsessions, like cricket and horse racing in England."

Andrew released the handle of his revolver. He watched the boats surge towards them, turn at a distinctive tree, and race back, nearly neck and neck, with bare-chested paddlers grunting with every stroke.

"They're fast," Andrew said. "And agile on the water."

"In the first and second wars we had with Burma," Jamieson said. "The Burmans used their warboats. I don't think they have any now."

"That's reassuring," Andrew watched the boats disappear around a bend in the river. "They would have been formidable adversaries."

With the three racing boats out of sight, *Little Salamander* slowed down.

The gong sounded again, and its regular beat was even more sinister.

"There is the landing area for Mandalay," Jamieson said, allowing *Little Salamander* just sufficient steam to remain static on the river.

"Where's the town?" Andrew asked.

"Mandalay's a couple of miles inland," Jamieson replied.

Andrew nodded, took out his map and worked out the geography. He had travelled around four hundred and fifty miles from Rangoon, with the Irrawaddy running nearly north to south for most of the journey. For the last few miles, the river had run westward, and at the bend below Mandalay sat the terminus for the Irrawaddy Flotilla Company vessels. A dozen small craft sat alongside a Flotilla ship, with a group of naked laughing boys cavorting in the river.

"We'll tie up beside the Flotilla's terminus," Jamieson said. "What do you wish to do now?"

"I have to meet somebody in Mandalay," Andrew said.

"Mandalay has a large European community," Sinclair emerged from the minuscule engine room, wiping his hands on the ubiquitous oily rag. "Have you made arrangements to stay the night?"

"Not yet," Andrew said. He had slept rough on many occasions on campaign and was sure he could find somewhere in Mandalay's environs.

"Ma Gun runs a clean house," Sinclair said. "She's a decent woman with a modicum of English, although her establishment hasn't got the most pleasant of outlooks. Tell her that Robert Sinclair sent you."

"Thank you," Andrew replied. He looked up at the Flotilla paddle steamer *Panthay* beside them, dwarfing the tiny *Little Salamander*.

"Four guineas, Captain, I believe," Jamieson reminded, holding out his hand. "In case you don't come back."

"The fee was three guineas," Andrew corrected, handing over the money. "If you stay here overnight in case I want to return, I'll add another ten shillings plus the same fee to return to Rangoon."

Jamieson smoothed a hand over his jaw. "Make it an extra fifteen shillings, and it's a deal."

Andrew knew his man. "Call it twelve and six," he said, and they shook hands.

As Andrew left *Little Salamander*, a smaller, lighter draught Flotilla vessel left the terminus, heading north.

"She's steaming to Bhamo," Jamieson noticed Andrew's interest. "That's the head of navigation on the Irrawaddy and the last town before Yunnan in China. It's a troublesome spot, with the Burmans and Chinese not on friendly terms."

Andrew nodded. "I doubt I'll ever visit." He climbed the sandy bank on which the terminal was situated.

Andrew was unsure what to expect. The ground was level, with a broad road to the terminus and a group of chattering women carrying large earthen pots to fill at the river. Another woman stood with two ponies for hire.

Andrew thought of the two-mile journey ahead in the heat and quickly arranged to hire a pony.

"Shan ponies," the woman explained with a smile.

"Very good," Andrew recognised the quality of the horses.

After so long on foot and water, Andrew was pleased to ride again, yet within a few moments, he knew his pony was only partially broken. It was a high-spirited animal that needed all his skill to control, but once he had proved he was the master, it relaxed into a pleasant, if not speedy, walk. After a few moments, the track rose alongside a bund that kept the cultivated countryside safe when the Irrawaddy flooded. The pony negotiated the rise without difficulty, and Andrew came to a broader road than most in Britain, with houses on either side.

The houses were built of bamboo and matting, with poor-looking people watching the traffic passing by. Andrew guided his pony past a constant trickle of pigs and bullock carts, hordes of children, and tail-wagging dogs, with scores of people walking purposefully to or from Mandalay.

Andrew stopped when he neared the town. A wide moat encircled the city, with the road running straight over a sturdy bridge.

He heard the single clatter of the gong and glanced over his shoulder. A hundred yards down the road, a slender man held a brass gong in his left hand and struck it with a stick. When he caught Andrew watching him, he turned and ran, leaving the road to disappear in the houses lining the road.

I saw that man in Thayetmyo. Has he kept pace with us all the way?

Knowing he could not catch the man among the confusion of houses, Andrew turned his Shan pony and headed towards Mandalay.

A twenty-six-foot-high brick wall enclosed the town, with battlements at the top and a dozen gates allowing access. Above each entrance, a tall, pyramidal teak tower added dignity, while smaller watchtowers thrust out at various places around the walls.

What lies inside these walls? Andrew wondered. *And how will Bo Thura contact me? How will I let him know I have arrived? There are too many questions here.*

A group of soldiers stood or crouched beside the gate, watching the travellers. Two stared at Andrew and looked away without comment. Once through the gate, Andrew stepped onto a macadamised, hundred-foot-wide road, that arrowed through the town. He realised there was a network of roads from each gateway, with the houses ranged alongside. Most of the houses were of a familiar Burmese pattern: bamboo built, raised on bamboo piles, and thatched with leaves. A few houses were stone-built, with Chinese owners.

The gong began again.

Why the devil is that man following me? Andrew stopped beside an open space where a group of women traders had set up a bazaar for brightly coloured waistcloths and turbans. He could hear the gong sounding and slipped among the stalls. He suddenly ducked down behind a stall, surprising the Hindu owner.

Crouched on the ground, with a curious dog sniffing at him, Andrew listened for the gong and grunted in satisfaction. The sound had ended.

Whoever that man is, he's following me and bangs his gong when he knows where I am.

Andrew remained low, with the dog slowly wagging its tail and the stall keeper staring at him in stupefaction. He lay on the ground and watched as the gong-man peered around the bazaar and ran away, evidently desperate to find his quarry. Andrew allowed him a few minutes, rose, winked at the stall keeper, and slid away from the bazaar. A Burmese woman in a figure-hugging cobalt-blue longyi, a *htamein*, stepped back quickly when Andrew passed, and then he was back on a main street.

Dogs and pigs roamed freely among the fifty or sixty thousand inhabitants, and although they growled and bickered constantly, they also rid the streets of rubbish and discarded food.

Andrew wandered, trying to work out Mandalay's geography. In common with all eastern cities, Mandalay had its quota of bazaars, where people could purchase all the necessities of life and many of the luxuries. Andrew smiled to think of Mariana let loose in the Silk Bazaar as he looked around. Bo Thura's message was to arrive at Mandalay and wait to be contacted without any details.

Was that gong man Bo Thura's messenger? If so, he could have contacted me at any time.

Andrew heard the brassy clatter of the gong behind him. *You found me, then.* He turned around and saw only a bustling street. He sighed and decided to walk to the palace complex, wondering if he had wasted his time and money coming to Burma.

How about Mary MacConnacher? Somebody undoubtedly kidnapped her. Is somebody playing an elaborate hoax on me? If so, why?

Dominating the city, Thibaw's palace was the largest structure in Mandalay. It was situated in the centre, with all the other buildings radiating in a status-dominated organisation. Andrew thought the palace was among the most interesting buildings he had seen. Built of teak, it had richly carved upturned eaves, complete with gilding and vermilion. The outer walls were twenty feet high, red and crenellated, supported by earth embankments seventy feet wide at the base and tapering upwards.

Around the walls spread the moat, two hundred feet wide, filled with sparkling water and decorated with floating lotus plants. The royal barge floated on the water, looking like something from the Middle Ages.

Well, Bo Thura, here I am. Contact me.

Andrew stepped aside as a party of Burmese soldiers filed past. Stocky, unsmiling men in light jackets, they mostly carried old-fashioned muzzle-loading muskets and long, slightly curved dhas. They had broad-brimmed brass hats on their heads, which Andrew thought looked very uncomfortable, although the decorative griffins in front were attractive. Some wore red coats with green facings, similar to the old British redcoats; others were bare-chested. Unlike British soldiers, Thibaw's men did not wear trousers, with bare legs and feet.

Andrew watched the soldiers for a few moments, wondered how they would stand against British regulars, and saw a woman walking towards him.

That woman was at the silk bazaar.

"I know all the Europeans in Mandalay by sight," the slender Burmese woman in the blue longyi stepped up to Andrew. "You are new here."

"I am," Andrew admitted. "You speak good English."

"Thank you." She was in her late twenties, Andrew estimated, with a smiling face and a presence that stirred something inside him. "Are you interested in the palace?"

"I know nothing about it," Andrew admitted. He glanced around, searching for the man with the gong or anybody who might be from Bo Thura. *How does one recognise a dacoit?* People moved around, busy with their affairs, and although a few glanced at him as an interesting foreigner, they quickly moved away.

"The king's palace and gardens are within those walls," the woman spoke with near reverence. "As are the treasury, the royal courts, the mint, and the royal arsenal."

"That's impressive," Andrew said. The woman smelled fresh, scented lightly of flowers.

"Yes," the woman seemed pleased with Andrew's reaction. "We carried it from Amarapura."

Andrew shook his head. "I'm sorry, I don't understand. What do you mean, you carried it?"

"The former king thought that Amarapura was too restricted for a king of his stature, the Descendant of the Sun, so he moved here and built Mandalay," the woman explained. "He had his palace dismantled and carried here, piece by piece, and rebuilt."

Andrew looked at her. "I didn't know that was possible," he said as his respect for the Burmese people increased.

Who is this woman? She is beautiful, but that's not why I feel this immediate attraction.

Andrew heard the gong again, the single, regular stroke, slow and sonorous. *These people are different from us, but they are highly organised and very clever.*

"The king lives in the centre of his capital," the woman said, "with his chief officials around him in these houses." She indicated the larger buildings immediately outside the palace walls. "The next level of society lives beyond that," the woman waved a hand behind her. "The lesser officials, Army officers, and such like, while the merchants and common people live on the outskirts but are still within the city walls."

Andrew nodded. "Mandalay is very well organised," he said.

Keep talking. Ask her a question; get to know this woman. I must get to know her. Andrew smiled, looking the woman up and down from the top of her immaculately styled head to the painted toes of her bare feet. Her earrings were gold, nearly touching her shoulders, and Andrew knew she was aware of his interest.

"Do you like our pagodas?" the woman asked.

"I have admired Burma's pagodas ever since I arrived," Andrew said truthfully. "Could you tell me more about them?" He allowed his eyes to examine her face with her fine eyes and high cheekbones, that intelligent, nearly mocking twist to her lips and the slightly outthrust, defiant chin. *Who are you? What is your name? Can I ask her name in this country, or is that against their traditions? I wish I knew more.*

"That is the king's pagoda," the woman pointed to an impressive building towering above a surrounding wall. "What is your name, sir?"

"I am Andrew Baird," Andrew said, smiling. "And you are?"

"A messenger," the woman said, dropping her smile.

"A messenger? From whom?"

Who are you? Tell me your name!

The gong had stopped. Andrew could only hear the murmur of voices and the movement of bare or sandalled feet on the ground. He saw the slender man standing nearby with the gong in his hand. A second man joined him, short and stocky; he had a livid white scar running diagonally across his face and a long *dha* at his belt.

Andrew repeated his question.

"From whom are you a messenger?"

In response, the woman withdrew a piece of paper from inside her longyi and pressed it into Andrew's hand. She held Andrew's gaze for a long moment and winked surprisingly. "You'll have to read it," she advised.

"What's this?" Andrew glanced at the note, and when he looked up, the woman was gone. "What the devil? Come back!"

A few people glanced at him when he shouted, but he could not see the woman. The stocky, scarred man stood in his path, with one hand holding the hilt of his dha.

"I want to talk to you!" Andrew tried to push past the stocky man, who proved immovable as granite. The slender man still held the gong, watching Andrew as if unsure whether to fight or run.

A child pointed to Andrew and giggled until his mother scolded him into silence and threw an apologetic smile towards Andrew. The crowd seemed to thicken, with a couple of the king's soldiers threading through the civilians behind a group of yellow-clothed monks.

A man with a gold-hilted *dha* led the king's soldiers, and Andrew remembered Goudie mentioning such a man. The stocky man and the gong carrier drifted casually away as the soldiers marched past with a curious, high-stepping gait.

Andrew reread the note. It had two words, written in English and Burmese. *Yin Pauk.*

Yin Pauk? What the devil does that mean? Andrew stepped into the crowd, searching for the woman without success. *I'll ask Jamieson and Sinclair. I must see that woman again; is that her name? Or is it a place where I must meet Bo Thura?*

Sinclair was working on *Little Salamander's* engine when Andrew appeared. "Evening, Captain," he said. "Is your business concluded, and you all set to return?"

"I am not sure," Andrew said. He showed Sinclair the paper. "Does that name mean anything to you?"

Sinclair barely glanced at the paper. "Yin Pauk is a bit of a village about halfway between here and Bhamo," Sinclair replied at once. "It's well off the beaten track, on the border with the Shan and Kachin people and not too far from the Chinese frontier."

"Is it inside Burma?" The different names meant little to Andrew. He had only studied the map as far as Mandalay.

"Officially, yes. King Thibaw is the monarch," Sinclair said, "although his authority is a bit limited, especially since the Chinese are threatening Bhamo. Why do you ask?" He cleaned his hands on an oily rag, half-smiling as if he already knew Andrew's answer.

"I have to go there," Andrew decided what the short note meant.

Sinclair put his rag down. "How do you intend to do that?" He glanced at *Little Salamander.*

"Is Yin Pauk accessible by water?"

Sinclair nodded. "It is, but it's not on the Irrawaddy," he said. "It's on a tributary river."

"If it's on a river, could *Little Salamander* get there?"

Sinclair stood up and threw the rag to his fireman. "That depends on Captain Jamieson," he said. "You'll have to ask him."

"Ask me what?" Jamieson walked the fifteen paces from the bow.

"Could you take me to Yin Pauk?" Andrew asked.

Jamieson considered for a moment. "For a price," he replied. "A high price. Yin Pauk is a dacoit's stronghold."

"How high?" Andrew knew that Jamieson held all the aces.

"Eight guineas."

"That's a lot of money," Andrew said.

"No negotiations," Jamieson grinned. "Or you can try to hire a native boat in Mandalay."

"Eight guineas will nearly clean me out," Andrew said.

"You want me to take you to territory that the Shans, Karens and Burmans all claim, with the Chinese waiting in the background," Jamieson said. "It's a playground for the dacoits with some of the densest forest in one of the remotest parts of Burma."

"Eight guineas it is," Andrew knew he would not trust any Mandalay boatman to take him. "When can we leave?"

"Tomorrow," Jamieson told him. "Be here before dawn, and we'll catch the best of the daylight." He nodded to the town. "Be careful if you go back into Mandalay; there's trouble brewing."

"I'll be careful," Andrew said. "I saw a few of the king's soldiers in the city."

"Best keep out of their way," Sinclair advised. "They can be very charming or utterly ruthless." He shouted something to his fireman. "We'll have *Little Salamander* coaled up and ready to steam."

CHAPTER 9

KINGDOM OF AVA, SEPTEMBER 1884

Andrew estimated there were about a hundred Europeans in Mandalay, mostly traders but with others who looked decidedly shifty. The merchants greeted people with false bonhomie as they sought sales, while the others looked sideways at everybody as though assessing them as rivals or enemies.

Who are these fellows? Politicians? Ambassadors? Lawyers?

Although most of Mandalay's European residents were British, Andrew also heard French and Italian spoken in the streets. He remembered Jamieson mentioning that Thibaw had Italian engineers working for him.

"You're a stranger here," an overdressed and perspiring man said.

"I am," Andrew agreed. *This fellow is a merchant and prosperous by his appearance.*

"Where are you staying?" The man smiled and held out his hand. "Harding. Charles Harding, of Harding and Dowding."

"Andrew Baird." They shook hands. "And I am looking for accommodation for the night. I heard that Ma Gun's place is the best."

"Ma Gun is the most decent place to stay," Harding told him. "Come with me, and I'll take you there."

Andrew touched the revolver inside his tunic, wondering if he could trust this unknown man in a strange city. "Thank you, Harding," he decided.

Ma Gun's was a two-storey, timber-built house with a shaded veranda and a genial Burmese hostess.

Ma Gun greeted them with a broad smile. "Welcome, gentlemen. Now, would anybody like tea? Palm-toddy? Samshu perhaps, or Eagle Brandy?"

"Robert Sinclair recommended you, Mrs Gun," Andrew said.

"Robert! How is he?" Ma Gun asked, smiling.

"He's doing well," Andrew replied.

"You can have Robert's old room," Ma Gun said, ushering Andrew to a small upstairs room with a window offering a view of an ominously large building with high walls. Harding followed into the room, treading heavily on the teak floor.

Andrew nodded out of the window when Ma Gun left. "What's that building, Harding? It looks like a barrack block."

Harding grinned. "That's the jail, Baird. I hope you don't mind criminal neighbours."

"As long as I am outside and they're inside," Andrew replied.

Harding laughed. "Let's hope King Thibaw doesn't discover your past misdeeds."

"I'll keep them secret," Andrew promised. "Good night, Harding." He unpacked the case he had carried from *Little Salamander*, placed his revolver under the pillow and closed the matting blind. Mosquitoes whined around the room, and a line of red ants scurried across the floor. Andrew sighed, lay on the surprisingly comfortable bed, adjusted the mosquito net, and hoped for an undisturbed night.

Images from the past few days jumbled through his head, from the crucified dacoits to the skirmish around the village, the sound of *Little Salamander's* engine and the scent of that intriguing Burmese woman who had passed him the message. *I'll never see her again*, he thought. The gong ran through his memory, and he groaned, unsure if it was his imagination or reality. Andrew sat up, blinking. The gong sounded throughout the night, clanging every minute, sonorous, monotonous. He pulled the single threadbare blanket over his head, trying to deaden the noise.

That gong must mean something. I'll ask around tomorrow unless I leave the hotel tonight, find the blasted thing, and throw it in the Irrawaddy beside its skinny little owner. Wait, now. What's that noise?

The new sound was unmistakable, the regular tread of soldiers marching in step. A man, either an officer or NCO, shouted a command, and the soldiers increased their pace with the sound of bare feet slapping on the ground like hail on a November window.

Sinclair said there was trouble brewing.

Andrew reached for the revolver under his pillow and sat up, realising he could hear the gong even through the marching feet.

Something's happening out there. I'd recognise a military tread anywhere.

Struggling out of bed, Andrew dragged back the mosquito netting, wafted away a couple of whining mosquitoes, pulled on his trousers and jacket and jerked open the door.

"Is that you, Baird?" Harding emerged from the next room with a dressing gown flapping loosely over an embroidered nightshirt. He blinked at Andrew and fastened the cord of his dressing gown. "You're carrying a gun," he said.

"It's me," Andrew replied, sliding his boots onto his feet. "What's the to-do?" He smelled alcohol on Harding's breath.

"Thibaw has ordered the execution of some infamous dacoits, and the Army is toddling along to do the deed."

"Oh, I see." Having witnessed some of the dacoits' work, Andrew was ambivalent about their fate. "Well, it's nothing to do with us, Harding."

"Perhaps not," Harding agreed, still eyeing Andrew's revolver. "What-ho! Something else is happening out there!"

Andrew was first to the window and peered outside. He saw the soldiers running towards the jail and a group of men facing them at the gate. Some of the men held improvised weapons, lengths of wood, broken furniture, and a small knife.

"That doesn't look healthy," Harding said. "It looks like a jailbreak, by God."

"I'd try to escape if the king was going to crucify me," Andrew told him. "Here are more soldiers."

A company of Thibaw's soldiers appeared, with their light red jackets catching the rising sun and their muskets and rifles leaning against their shoulders. Seeing them arrive, the convicts attempted a desperate rush to break free.

The soldiers levelled their rifles and fired, with the sound of shots echoing from the high walls. Three of the escapees fell, one dead and the others writhing on the ground.

"No second chances there," Harding said. He seemed fascinated by the drama outside the jail.

"Better a quick death than crucifixion," Andrew replied. He watched the soldiers' movements, noting how the officers gave commands and how the men obeyed. *They are quick and responsive*, he thought. *These lads could give us trouble if we ever fight them.*

As the soldiers encircled the prisoners, firing at any who broke through the cordon, other prisoners pushed out of the jail. Some carried homemade weapons, lengths of wood or knives, and a few threw missiles towards the military.

"That's a bit of a mismatch," Andrew murmured.

Harding nodded, licking his lips.

An active man, obviously an officer, barked a command, and the soldiers knelt and fired a ragged volley that tore into the mass of escapees, hitting eight or nine. Another order saw the soldiers reload and present their rifles. Andrew noted that some carried modern weapons, French or British, while others had ancient muzzle-loading muskets.

"It's a massacre!" Harding called without tearing his attention from the scene.

"It is," Andrew agreed.

Realising the military was shooting anybody who tried to escape, the prisoners turned around and pushed back inside the jail, stamping over each other in their sudden desire for sanctuary. The soldiers fired again, with bullets thumping into unresisting bodies, causing blood to spray above the crowd and splatter the prison walls. When the officer snapped another order, the soldiers ceased firing. A stray shaft of sunlight glittered from the gold hilt on the officer's *dha*.

You again! Andrew thought. *You pop up wherever there is trouble.*

"This is terrible. I've seen enough now," Harding said as the officer stepped among the dead and wounded with a small group of men around him. He gave another brisk order, and his men began to shoot the wounded. After a few moments, only dead men and a few dead women sprawled on the ground.

"There is no mercy in Mandalay," Harding said. Despite his protestations of disgust, he remained at the window.

"Remember the Gordon Riots in London," Andrew reminded. "There was no mercy then, either. Or at Peterloo."*

Harding grunted and continued to stare at the drama outside.

With the prisoners trapped inside the jail, an official emerged from the royal palace and spoke to the officer commanding the troops.

"Who is that?" Andrew asked.

"I think that's Maung Thandar," Harding said. "He's one of Thibaw's ministers and a bad man to cross."

Andrew rummaged in his baggage, found his field glasses, and focused on the king's minister. He shivered as he saw the man's face.

If ever there was a study of pure evil, that's it standing there.

Maung Thandar spoke quietly to the officer and stepped back, smiling. The officer snapped an order, and a section of soldiers ran to the far side of the jail.

"What's he up to?" Harding asked, trying to stretch his neck to peer around the jail.

"Nothing pleasant, I'll be bound," Andrew replied. He lowered his field glasses as Maung Thandar withdrew another few steps. A woman joined him, with soldiers and interested civilians stepping out of her way in total respect.

"Good God! That's Hsinbyaumashin," Harding said. "That's the queen's mother."

"What's she doing here?" Andrew asked.

"Causing trouble," Harding replied. "I reckon she's the cause of half the palace murders and the instigator of the other half."

"I'll keep out of her way," Andrew promised. He lifted his head. "Smoke," he said. "And fire." He swivelled around to view the far end of the jail. "The Army has set fire to the jail."

"That must be what Thandar ordered," Harding sounded excited. "What is he trying to do?"

"He's forcing out the prisoners," Andrew said quietly. "They can either remain inside the jail and burn or leave and face the soldiers." He watched, aware of the futility of intervention, as the flames took hold of the building. The screaming began a few minutes later, and a horde of desperate people,

---

* The Gordon Riots of 1780 were a series of anti-Catholic riots in London. After days of trouble, the government called in the Army. Estimates of the dead vary between three hundred and seven hundred. The Peterloo Massacre of 1819 occurred when a body of cavalry attacked a rally for electoral reform at St Peter's Field in Manchester. The cavalry killed eighteen people and injured between 400 and 700.

men, women, and children burst out of the jail. They ran towards the waiting soldiers, who fired constantly, using their *dhas* on anybody who survived the bullets. The officer watched without apparent emotion, unlike Hsinbyaumashin, who nodded and smiled as the slaughter continued.

"Oh, good God in heaven," Harding said.

Andrew, war-hardened to horror, watched as prisoners, some on fire, ran out of the jail to be butchered, as the king's minister and mother-in-law watched.

"Time to leave," Andrew said. "Come on, Harding. We're getting out of Mandalay before this thing spreads." *I must reach Yin Pauk to rescue young Mary. I can't stay here.*

"Where will we go?" Harding asked.

"To the river. There's a boat there that will take us away."

Grabbing their baggage, Andrew and Harding left the hotel. The crackle of flames sounded behind the musketry and shouting of the soldiers. One sturdy soldier pointed his musket at Andrew, changed his mind, and ran towards the jail.

"Which way to the river?" Andrew asked, looking around him.

"This way!" Harding chose a road. "No! Wait!"

A section of soldiers appeared on the street. One shot a passing woman and laughed as his companion hacked off her head. The others looked around, with one man pointing towards Andrew and Harding.

"Try this way," Andrew suggested, choosing a street at random. Harding followed, glancing over his shoulder as he heard shouting behind them. A woman began to scream.

"More soldiers!" Harding warned.

"They've got the blood lust," Andrew said. He heard a loud noise ahead and saw another body of soldiers running, yelling, and shooting at anybody they saw. One man carried a woman's head by her hair, with blood trailing onto the street. "Back to the hotel!"

CHAPTER 10

MANDALAY, BURMA, SEPTEMBER 1884

"Is it safe there?" Harding asked.

"God knows," Andrew replied, "but safer than on the streets unless the soldiers set fire to the hotel." He saw the colour drain from Harding's face and shook his head. "We'll be safer inside," he said.

They hammered on the locked door, shouted who they were and dived inside when Ma Gun opened up.

"Come in, gentlemen," Ma Gun said, apparently unconcerned at the mayhem around her house. "Would you like tea? Palm-toddy? Samshu perhaps, or Eagle Brandy?"

"No, thank you, Ma Gun," Harding replied. "It's a bit early for that."

"Lock and bar the door," Andrew ordered. "Lock all the windows, pile furniture behind them, and have water ready in case of fire." He looked around at the guests: six frightened and confused European men, with Ma Gun smiling and apparently unconcerned. "If you have any weapons, I'd suggest you fetch them now."

"They won't attack us, though," one man said. "I'm English."

"I doubt they care what we are now their blood is up," Andrew replied. "In fact, they might consider foreigners as fair game."

The man frowned and smoothed a hand across his moustache. "But we're not foreign! We're English! Didn't you hear me?"

"I heard you. Do you have a revolver?"

"No." The man glared at Andrew. "I am Marmaduke Patchley of the Surrey Patchleys."

"Do you have any sort of weapon, Mr Patchley?" Andrew held the man's gaze.

"No."

Most of the men had left to strengthen their rooms or fetch whatever they had. They gathered inside the front door ten minutes later, brandishing a variety of revolvers, shotguns, and hunting rifles. One man carried a large Adams revolver.

"Good," Andrew said. "We don't have enough people to guard every room, so we'll barricade the upper floor and guard the ground level. Ma Gun and men without weapons can hold water in case of fire and look after any wounded. That means you, Mr Patchley."

"Tell them we're English, and they'll leave us alone," Patchley insisted.

"That won't work," Andrew told him tersely as Ma Gun offered everybody a selection of drinks.

"Who are you to tell us what to do?" Patchley asked.

"Captain Andrew Baird, Natal Dragoons," Andrew replied. He raised his voice. "Does anybody here have any military experience?"

"I was in the county militia once," a balding middle-aged man said. "I took part in a couple of field exercises."

"Good. Take charge of the back of the building and the left side. I'll take care of the front and right. Watch for incendiaries, men who want to burn the place down." Andrew glanced at Harding, who looked surprised at Andrew taking charge. "Mr Harding, go upstairs and keep an eye open for possible threats. You are our standing picket. Check to ensure the windows are secure."

"Yes, Captain Baird," Harding thumped upstairs.

With the upper storey as safe as possible, Andrew toured the ground floor, piling furniture behind the front and back doors and unguarded windows, working out fields of fire and listening to the increasing noise outside. He heard shooting, maniacal laughter, and the screams of terrified people, together with the constant crackle of flames from the blazing jail.

"Whatever is happening out there is not good," a man said, holding his rifle like a talisman.

Andrew nodded. "We can't do anything about it," he said. "All we can do is look after ourselves, keep out of the way and hope nobody attacks us."

"Trouble!" Harding called from above. "A mob of soldiers is approaching the house! Could you come up, Captain Baird?"

"Coming!" Andrew ran upstairs and joined Harding at the window.

Around a hundred soldiers marched down the smoke-filled street, singing and laughing. They balanced their rifles over their shoulders, and a man in front held a long bamboo pole with a human head thrust on the top. He laughed as blood dribbled the length of the pole and onto his hand.

Harding looked away. "Are they coming here?"

"It looks that way," Andrew said. "Stand by to repel boarders."

"Standing by," Harding forced a twisted smile. He held up his borrowed rifle as if for inspection.

Andrew took the rifle from him, checked it was loaded, slipped the safety catch on, and returned it. "Aim low," he said, "and don't jerk the trigger. Aim here," he patted his belly, "the broadest part of the body."

"Yes, Captain," Harding replied.

"You'll be fine," Andrew encouraged him.

The mob straggled closer, chanting loudly and bouncing the disembodied head up and down. More blood dribbled down the bamboo onto the holder's arm. He laughed again and lifted the head higher so that the man's head stared directly at the hotel through sightless eyes. The tongue protruded slightly, lolling from broken lips. In the centre of the men, three soldiers carried burning brands with the flames spitting and blue smoke coiling upwards.

"Keep a watch on them," Andrew ordered Harding. "For God's sake, don't fire unless they attack us first. We don't want to start a war."

"I won't," Harding said. He moved back slightly, enabling him to see outside without anybody noticing him.

"Good man," Andrew said and ran back downstairs.

"They're coming closer!" A sandy-haired merchant thumbed back the hammers on his shotgun.

Andrew pushed the barrels away. "They're no threat to us yet," he said. "They might only walk past. Keep your nerve."

Patchley peered out of the window. "Do you see what they have on that stake?" His voice rose, high-pitched.

"I see it," Andrew said. "Don't look if it bothers you." He felt the tension in the hotel as men glanced outside at the chanting mob parading the human head. "Keep calm, gentlemen and ladies," Andrew said. "They're not threatening us."

"I've got a charge of twelve-bore for the first man who comes too close," the sandy-haired merchant said.

"Don't fire unless they attack us," Andrew ordered. "We are in their city and their country. We may disapprove of their customs, but we've no right to interfere."

Father always insisted we should not interfere with anybody's religion, customs, or women. He emphasised that such interference was a sure way to create trouble. Damn! I am using his advice again.

One of the Burmese soldiers stepped closer to the hotel. He spoke to the man at his side, and both approached the front door with rifles slung over their shoulders and long *dhas* at their belts.

"They're coming closer!" the sandy-haired merchant levelled his shotgun.

"They're doing us no harm," Andrew said. "Keep your finger off that trigger!"

"One more step, and I'll shoot!" the merchant pulled the shotgun to his shoulder.

Andrew pushed him away. "You'll start a war!" He grabbed the shotgun and replaced the hammers. "I told you to wait for my order, damn it!"

"Tell them we're not foreigners! Tell them we're English!" Patchley yelled.

The two king's soldiers stopped five yards short of the front door and shouted something.

"What do they want?" Andrew asked Ma Gun, who remained in the centre of the room, smiling.

"They want to know if we're hiding any criminals in here," Ma Gun replied. "They say there's been a jailbreak."

"Tell them we know about the jailbreak, and we're keeping the door locked to ensure no dacoits come inside," Andrew said. He felt the comforting weight of his revolver but wished he had trained men with him rather than nervous merchants.

Ma Gun shouted what Andrew had told her. He watched the two soldiers hesitate. One unslung his rifle and slid a cartridge into the breech.

"I told you! I warned you we should shoot them!" the sandy-haired merchant said.

"We're English!" Patchley yelled. "English!"

"Shut up!" Andrew hissed. He watched the two soldiers talking outside the front door. The main body of soldiers halted and were watching, occasionally shouting to their colleagues.

If they decide to attack, I'll shoot the first two. After that, anything could happen.

Andrew held his revolver in a surprisingly steady hand. He could nearly taste the tension in the room. A man coughed behind him, and another gave a nervous giggle. The sandy-haired merchant regained his shotgun and thumbed back the hammers.

The next two minutes are crucial.

When the leading soldier shouted something, Andrew looked at Ma Gun.

"He said we had better send out any criminals, or they'll burn us down," Ma Gun translated, still smiling.

"Are you feeling courageous?" Andrew asked.

"I am a Buddhist," Ma Gun replied. "I have nothing to fear."

"That's a good answer," Andrew approved. "You and I will open the front door and assure these men we are not harbouring any escaped prisoners." He felt the horror within the hotel. "I'll look after you, Ma Gun."

Ma Gun smiled and began to move aside the furniture that barricaded the door.

"If you open the door, they'll all rush in!" the sandy-haired merchant said.

"I doubt it. They want a quick kill, not a fight against revolvers," Andrew held up his pistol, "and shotguns. Once they see we're ready to defend the place, they'll sheer off, sure as eggs."

"You'd better be right!"

Pulling back the last of the furniture from the front door, Andrew and Ma Gun stepped outside. The two soldiers were ten yards away, resting on their rifles with their colleagues thirty yards further back.

The two soldiers spoke together, addressing Ma Gun. She replied immediately, glancing at Andrew.

"They're asking who you are," she explained.

"Tell them I am Captain Andrew Baird of the Natal Dragoons," Andrew said.

"I did," Ma Gun said with her ready smile. "They want to know why you are here."

"I am meeting a personal friend," Andrew said.

The soldiers did not look interested. They asked another question, with one stepping closer. Andrew laid his revolver across his front, ensuring the royal soldiers saw he was armed.

"They're asking if we're hiding any escaped prisoners."

Andrew lifted the revolver. "Tell them we have no escaped prisoners, and I will shoot anybody who comes into the hotel without your permission." He smiled as Ma Gun repeated his words.

The two soldiers glanced at each other. One stepped towards Andrew until somebody shouted, and he looked over his shoulder.

The officer with the gold-hilted dha stood beside Maung Thandar at the rear of the troops. Maung Thandar spoke to the officer, who snarled another order, and the man carrying the disembodied head stopped. He ran to the front of the hotel and rammed the bamboo stake into the ground, with the head facing the hotel. The officer snapped something, and the soldiers marched on with Maung Thandar and the officer at the rear.

Maung Thandar examined Andrew as he passed, then turned his head and strode, long-legged, to join the soldiers. The officer lingered a few moments longer, examining Andrew up and down before marching away.

He'll know me next time.

"What now?" Harding asked when Andrew returned and locked the door.

"Now we sit it out until things quieten down," Andrew said, "and then we leave."

Ma Gun's smile returned when Andrew closed the door. "Good," she said. "Now, would anybody like tea? Palm-toddy? Samshu perhaps, or Eagle Brandy?"

Andrew nodded. "Ma Gun, you are a treasure. I'd love some tea. No, make that palm-toddy."

Ma Gun smiled as she poured Andrew a drink. "You are welcome, Captain Baird."

The day passed slowly, with a slight scare, when a handful of the king's soldiers passed the hotel. None of them looked, and the sandy-haired merchant lowered his shotgun with a look of regret.

"Maybe next time," Andrew sympathised.

"I rather enjoyed all the excitement," the merchant said. "I should have been a soldier."

They spent the night in the hotel, listening with gradually decreasing worry, and Andrew left before a glorious dawn burst over Mandalay. Keeping his revolver handy, he hurried through deserted streets, ignoring the occasional crumpled corpse and passed through an open gate where guards dozed carelessly.

Jamieson nodded when Andrew arrived. "You survived, then, Captain Baird. I'm glad we're heading upstream to Yin Pauk." He lit a large cigar and puffed aromatic blue smoke into the humid air. "Indeed, I doubt we'll be heading downstream for a while," he said. "Look down the river."

Andrew glanced past the Irrawaddy Flotilla terminus. Soldiers marched along the riverbank and manned small boats on the water, stopping all traffic from moving south. "Upstream it is then," he said, fingering the piece of paper the woman had given him. "Maung Thandar and Thibaw's mother-in-law have concreted our decision."

Jamieson removed his cigar. "Aye, maybe so, Captain Baird, but I'll still charge you full fare for the journey. I have fuel to pay for, and we're heading into dangerous waters."

Andrew smiled. "I would not expect anything else," he said.

He looked up as the gong began its sonorous beat. *I hope that the Burmese woman is in Yin Pauk. I must meet her again, whoever she is.*

"Are you ready, Captain?" Jamieson asked.

"I am," Andrew said. He had a last look at the landing stage and the road to Mandalay, where he had met the woman in the blue figure-hugging longyi.

"Cast off!" Jamieson shouted, repeating his words in Burmese and *Little Salamander* eased out against the current.

Ma Gun's words followed him. "Now, would anybody like tea? Palm-toddy? Samshu perhaps, or Eagle Brandy?"

CHAPTER 11

LOWER BURMA AND THE KINGDOM OF AVA, SEPTEMBER 1884

"We could go out on the river," Jennings said. "You and me."

"That would be nice," Mariana agreed. After growing up in the open country of Natal, she found the crowded streets of Rangoon confining. "Where would we go?"

They stood beside the quay, where the great paddle steamers of the Irrawaddy Flotilla lay, and ships came in from half the world. Mariana watched each vessel, hoping Andrew would alight from one, although she knew it was far too early for his return. She thought of her little chart where she marked off each day, with only half a week crossed out and the rest seeming to stretch forever.

"Just a little pleasure sail," Jennings said. "Nowhere in particular. Maybe watch a boat race; the Burmans are great racers and gamblers."

"That would be fun," Mariana replied. She tore her mind from thoughts of Andrew, knowing she only hurt herself. "You're fun, aren't you?"

"Thank you. So are you," Jennings said. "Life is about living, Miss Maxwell. My philosophy is to get as much enjoyment as possible."

"Oh," Mariana smiled at him. "I think Andrew's life is about duty more than enjoyment, although he does know Tennyson's poetry."

Jennings met the smile. "Tennyson, eh? The Light Brigade man. How about this one:

"If I had a flower for every time I thought of you,
I could walk through my garden forever."

"I like that one," Jennings said. "It suits you rather well, Miss Maxwell."

"Oh, do you think so?" Mariana replied. She altered the angle of her parasol to protect her face from the sun.

"Undoubtedly," Jennings replied. "How about this Tennyson quote: 'Tis better to have loved and lost than never to have loved at all.' That's also true."

Mariana waved away a questing insect. "I can't imagine a life without love in it," she said. "Tennyson is a very clever man."

"He understands human nature," Jennings agreed. "Now, let's find ourselves some transport and get afloat." He escorted her to the river's edge and searched for a suitable boat. "When you are back in Britain, and I remain here, sweltering under the Burman sun, I will sigh in happy memory of how your presence lightened the dull truth of my existence."

Mariana laughed. "Oh, Mr Jennings, you do talk nonsense. You'll forget me the minute I turn my back."

"And what a lovely back it is to turn," Jennings said. "No, Miss Maxwell," he lowered his voice. "I will never forget you. I think you are a special kind of girl, or lady rather, the kind of lady only the most fortunate of men meet, and then only once in a lifetime."

Mariana smiled at him. "I am not special." She handed a small coin to a persistent beggar and watched him run off, whooping in joy. "These poor people have nothing at all."

"That boy probably makes more in begging than most dock labourers do by the sweat of their brows," Jennings said.

Mariana pointed with her parasol. "Is that not a boat there? The man seems to know you."

"I can't think why," Jennings said. "I've never seen him before in my life. Now you wait here a moment, my dear, and I'll make the arrangements." He hurried ahead, lifting his hand to hold the boatman's attention.

Mariana watched them talk for a few moments while another of Tennyson's quotes rang in her ears. "Who are wise in love, love most, say least." She smiled, resolved to speak little when they were on the water, and allow Jennings to lead the conversation. *I believe that men like to be the dominant talkers,* she told herself. *I'll be quiet as a mouse or a demure lady and listen to Mr Jennings' words. After all, he is the most entertaining company.*

Jennings returned within five minutes, smiling as he extended a hand. "There we are, you see? I have arranged terms with the boatman, who has agreed to take us on a little trip on the Irrawaddy."

"Well done, Mr Jennings," Mariana replied, keeping pace with him along the quay to a small flight of wooden steps leading downward.

The boat had an upsweeping prow and stern, with three boatmen, the middle-aged man Jennings spoke to and a couple of supple youths in their late teens. Jennings descended the three steps to the boat first, turned, and held out a helping hand.

"Come along, Miss Maxwell."

Mariana took Jennings' hand and stepped into the boat, gasping slightly when it rocked. The middle-aged boatman shook his head, smiling as the youths grinned. One shifted from side to side, making the boat move violently.

Just like youths would do back home, Mariana thought. *People are not much different wherever one travels.*

The middle-aged boatman growled something and gave the nearest youth a cuff across the head.

That's a father and his sons, Mariana realised.

"It's all right, Miss Maxwell. The boat is stable," Jennings assured her. "You are perfectly safe with me. I won't let you fall in the river."

"I am glad to hear it, Mr Jennings," Mariana replied, slightly embarrassed by her recent display. She sat carefully, placing her parasol at her side.

The boat had two leather-padded passenger seats. Jennings helped Mariana sit and nodded to the father, who spoke to his sons and pushed off.

"Where are you taking me, Mr Jennings?" Mariana asked, holding her hat in place with her left hand as a gust of wind threatened to lift it from her head.

Jennings watched the boatmen take them past the Irrawaddy Flotilla steamer. "We'll have a little tour of the ships first, then maybe, if you are agreeable, paddle downstream to a little island I know. It's an idyllic spot with a most sublime beach where dear Adelie and I used to spend many a happy hour."

"Dear Adelie?" Mariana asked.

"My wife," Jennings said. "Or rather, my late wife."

"Oh, my dear Mr Jennings, I did not know," Mariana leaned forward to pat his arm. "I am terribly sorry to hear that. It must have been awful for you. When did you lose her?"

Jennings held the back of her hand. "Thank you, Miss Maxwell. It was two years ago now. The least said, the better, eh?" He spoke to the chief boatman, and they paddled around the ships, with Jennings telling Mariana their origin and cargo.

"She is *Calcutta Maid*, with rice for Sydney. That vessel is a teak carrier bound for London and that one, *Lord of the East*, has machinery parts from Glasgow. Am I boring you, Miss Maxwell?"

"Not in the slightest," Mariana said.

Jennings sat back. "As you see, Rangoon is a thriving port, Miss Maxwell, one of the finest in Southeast Asia."

"I see," Mariana tried to hide her disinterest.

"You are bored," Jennings said. "This subject does not interest you."

"It does not," Mariana agreed. "I am sorry, Mr Jennings."

"Then we shall discuss something else," Jennings decided with a quick smile. "Adelie's island is a fair distance off, or we can watch a boat race."

"The boat race," Mariana decided immediately. "The island was special to Adelie and you. I shouldn't disturb that memory."

It's best not to intrude where Mr Jennings has memories. That would not be fair.

"The boat race it is," Jennings said and spoke to the head boatman, who grinned, altered course, and steered them across the river. Mariana watched a sublime three-masted clipper ease in under the care of a Rangoon pilot, and then they were paddling up the far bank to a busy village.

"This place has a regular boat race with its neighbour," Jennings explained. "It's not quite as prestigious as the Oxford and Cambridge race but equally important to the people here. They gamble huge sums of money on it."

In a flash of insight, Mariana asked, "Have you gambled on the outcome of this race, Mr Jennings?"

"I have," Jennings admitted cheerfully. "One cannot live out East without adopting some local habits. It helps one fit in." He murmured something in Burmese, and the boatmen stopped. They sat in the middle of the river with the water gurgling on either side and the two young boatmen paddling occasionally to maintain their position.

A long, galley-type boat emerged from each village, both gilded and brightly painted, one in red and the other in yellow and gold. High-prowed and slender, they looked fast as they cut gracefully through the water. Crews of eager men in brief waistcloths wielded long paddles and shouted what Mariana took to be cheerful insults at their rivals.

"My money is on the boat with the red paintwork," Jennings said as their boatmen joined in the yelling.

"Then I will also cheer it on," Mariana said. "My father used to attend horse races. He always put a few pounds on his favourite."

"A man after my own heart," Jennings said. "If my boat wins, we'll crack open a bottle of champagne."

"I've never drunk champagne," Mariana admitted.

"Then you have never fully lived," Jennings told her solemnly. "I tell you what, Miss Maxwell, if my boat wins, I'll introduce you to my house, and we'll drink my success in a glass of champagne." He smiled at her. "I bought half a dozen bottles just for you. That is, if you trust me, of course."

"Of course I trust you!" Mariana pointed to the village. "Look! The boats are lining up!"

The boats manoeuvred side-by-side, with the paddlers glowering at each other and a man in each stern banging a large brass gong.

"That's our favourite," Mariana said, pointing to the red boat. "Come on, the red boat!"

"That's the fellow," Jennings agreed. He raised his voice in a shout, yelling something in Burmese that made the older boatman laugh.

"Faster, the red boat!" Mariana encouraged again. For a moment, the excitement of competition took control, and she forgot her loneliness without Andrew.

Mariana did not see who gave the order, but all the paddlers began to work furiously, thrashing the water into white fury. The men in the sterns kept the time, smashing their mallets against the gongs as the paddlers grunted or chanted.

"This is exciting," Mariana said, but Jennings was not listening; he stood with his legs balanced against the seat, waving his arms and shouting.

The two boats raced side-by-side as they passed Jennings's vessel, and then the red boat inched into the lead. Mariana cheered, standing up to show her support. As she did so, she knocked her parasol over the side, and the swift current quickly whisked it away.

"Oh, dear!" Mariana made a despairing clutch, nearly overbalanced, and righted herself with difficulty as the middle-aged boatman steadied her with a hard hand.

Jennings spoke to the chief boatman, who indicated the taller of his two sons. The youth stood up, glanced at Mariana, stripped off his waistcloth, poised naked for a second and jumped overboard.

"Oh, it's all right!" Mariana said, watching the youth's supple body as he kicked away from the boat and into the current. He reached the parasol in a few seconds, twisted in the water, and returned, hoisting himself onboard and handing the parasol to Mariana.

He grinned at her, dripping water and obviously pleased with himself.

"Thank you," Mariana was treated to a vibrant, naked young man standing a foot in front of her. She placed the parasol at her side and realised Jennings was watching her closely.

"Tell him to put his clothes back on," Mariana said quietly. "I grew up on the Zululand border where seeing naked Zulus was normal. You can neither shock nor impress me with a human body, Mr Jennings."

"That was not my intention, Miss Maxwell," Jennings said.

"Once this race is finished," Mariana said, "I think you had better take me back to Rangoon."

They all turned to see the red boat win by a clear margin. "Congratulations, Mr Jennings," Mariana said, but the magic of the day was gone. She could see the triumph in Jennings's face, yet she realised he was also disappointed, although she was unsure why.

ALL THE EXCITEMENT IN MANDALAY HAD PUSHED THE BURMESE WOMAN from Andrew's mind, but now he was safely aboard *Little Salamander*, her image returned. He found himself smiling at the memory. There had been something very satisfying about her presence as if he had known her all his life. He sat on deck, watching the riverbank drift by and wondered who she was.

Have you forgotten Mariana already? Andrew rebuked himself before answering his question. *Mariana turned me down, remember? I am not obliged to stay loyal to a woman who rejected me.*

He sat under the canvas canopy, watching the river drift by and the ever-changing scenery on the bank, with villages and paddy fields, patches of forest and an occasional man sitting on an elephant as they piled teak logs.

The gong has stopped. Andrew straightened up. *Have they lost me?*

Little Salamander pushed upriver, with Jamieson frequently glancing behind him as if expecting the king's soldiers to follow his launch.

"Is there anybody there?" Andrew asked.

"No. I'd be happier going downstream," Jamieson admitted. "If there is turmoil in Mandalay, God only knows what's happening in the rest of Upper Burma."

"The king's soldiers were a bit busy downstream," Andrew reminded him.

He paused for a moment, wondering how much information he should release. "By going upriver, you're helping to save a young girl's life."

"Who?" Jamieson asked.

"Young Mary MacConnacher," Andrew said and waited for the inevitable questions.

Jamieson did not ask anything. Decades in Burma had taught him not to pry. He grunted and spat into the river. "She'll be long dead by now," he said. "Or worse."

"Worse?"

"Her kidnappers may have sold her into slavery in China, Tonkin or somewhere else up that way." Jamieson nodded north. "The East can hold you in thrall, or it can repulse you. There is amazing beauty here and horrors the like you cannot conceive."

"Maybe I don't want to conceive them," Andrew said. He thought of a young child in the hands of dacoits and shivered. "Get me to Yin Pauk," he said quietly, touching the butt of his revolver.

"That's what you are paying me for," Jamieson agreed. He eyed Andrew up and down, opened his mouth to ask a question and clamped it shut again. Andrew let him wonder.

Little Salamander passed a village, with her wash gently rocking half a dozen fishing boats. The villagers watched them without interest and returned to their work. The wake subsided, *Little Salamander* moved on, and the villagers forgot her.

We are transitory here, Andrew thought. *We may change the face of the cities, but we are irrelevant in the countryside; these people live their lives as they have for a thousand years.*

"We'll leave the Irrawaddy tomorrow," Jamieson said. "You'll have to reconcile yourself to sleeping in your cabin for a couple of nights."

"Thank you, Captain," Andrew said.

THE FOREST SEEMED TO CLOSE IN ON ANDREW AS *LITTLE SALAMANDER* LEFT the Irrawaddy and chugged slowly up a narrow tributary. He heard the cry of bright birds and swatted vainly at the mosquitoes that clouded around his head.

"How far is this place?" Andrew asked. "We've been away for days."

"Not far, now," Jamieson said. "A few miles up this river, then we branch off again, and after that, it's only a few miles more."

Andrew curbed his impatience. His map did not mention the village of Yin Pauk, and he was entirely in Jamieson's hands. He thought of young Mary MacConnacher languishing in the hands of some savage dacoit.

The poor girl must be suffering agonies. God knows what horrors they are putting her through. He shivered, refusing to contemplate the possibilities, and wondered anew what sort of person Bo Thura was.

The river narrowed further, with an occasional village on the banks, frail bamboo huts built on stilts with near-naked men sitting smoking in the sun or venturing onto the water in their boats. Andrew saw a man staring at them, then lifting a stick to hammer on a brass gong. The sound reverberated along the river, to be repeated by unknown and unseen hands within the dense green curtain of the forest.

They've found me again.

"They're sending a message that we're coming," Andrew said. He unfastened his holster to get easier access to his revolver.

"I'd say so," Jamieson agreed. He gave a sharp order to Sinclair, and *Little Salamander* slowed, with the brown water surging on either side of the blunt bow.

"Why are we slowing down?" Andrew asked.

"Shallows ahead," Jamieson told him. "When we have heavy rain here, the river changes course, throwing up sandbanks where the previous week we had sufficient depth for a vessel of twice our draft. We must move carefully on this river, even more than on the Irrawaddy."

Andrew nodded. He did not want to run aground with strange messages sounding in the deep forest. *Little Salamander* slowed and Jamieson sent the deckhand forward to peer into the water.

"I don't know this tributary well," Jamieson explained. "But that lad does. He'll act as river pilot while I steer."

Andrew nodded, listening to the gongs sounding on both banks and the incessant chatter of birds.

Jamieson obeyed the pilot's orders, guiding *Little Salamander* past some dangerous sandbanks just underneath the surface. The pilot shouted something, and Jamieson translated for Andrew.

"Only a quarter of a mile of these, and then we're in clear water," Jamieson said.

The gongs continued to sound, echoing from the trees and competing with the birdcall, although the insects were unaffected.

The steamer eased around a bend into a stretch of water clear of sandbanks, where tall trees overhung the river. One tree had fallen into the water and remained there, thick with vegetation as the river churned creamy-white all around. A boy crouched on the trunk, watching *Little Salamander.* He did not respond when Andrew shouted a greeting.

Jamieson steered *Little Salamander* around the obstacle and smiled as the river widened. Andrew could see no sandbanks ahead, only another fallen tree extending into the water.

"That's better," Jamieson said and ordered increased speed.

Andrew looked up as the gongs suddenly stopped. Only birds and insects broke the silence, with the rhythmic grumble of the screw so constant that Andrew barely noticed it. "Something's happening," he said. He looked astern and saw half a dozen men on the fallen log, all carrying firearms.

The Burmese pilot looked alarmed, glancing from side to side as if expecting the trees to come alive. He shouted something, and the fireman emerged onto the deck.

Trained by serving through three campaigns, Andrew was first to notice the flicker of movement ahead. "Slow the boat," he said.

"Why?"

"Something's wrong," Andrew said. "Your crew knows. Slow the blasted boat!"

"Half speed," Jamieson said.

"That tree is moving!" Andrew said.

Jamieson turned the wheel, heading for the right bank to create some space and then heading hard to port to move *Little Salamander* in a U-turn.

Andrew watched as the tree pushed into the river, gradually shedding its greenery until he saw it was a paddle-powered Burmese warboat.

"What's happening?" Sinclair emerged from the engine room and saw the warboat paddling towards them. He reached inside the wheelhouse for the Snider rifle that hung on brackets above the door.

"There's no point in that, Sinclair," Andrew said. "Look behind you."

Three smaller boats paddled out from the riverbank, each with half a dozen armed men sitting inside, while the men on the fallen tree aimed their rifles at *Little Salamander*.

CHAPTER 12

KINGDOM OF AVA, OCTOBER 1884

"It's an ambush," Andrew said.

"Dacoits," Jamieson said. "We're dead men unless they're only after plunder."

"Your crew seem to agree," Andrew said as both Burmese crew members jumped overboard and swam towards the shore.

"Do we fight or surrender?" Sinclair loaded his Snider with practised hands.

Andrew realised that any man who chose to work in the Burmese backwater must have steady nerves. He tapped his revolver.

"I rather think they knew we were coming," Andrew said. "I suspect they want me rather than you."

"You?"

"I suspect so," Andrew said. "Remember that gong that followed us to Mandalay? It sounded outside Ma Gun's place when I stayed there. I think somebody was letting me know they were watching me."

"Why?" Sinclair checked the sights of his Snider. "We'll stand by you, Captain Baird."

"Thank you, Mr Sinclair." Andrew calculated the odds. With around thirty men in the warboat and another fifteen astern, resistance would end in all their deaths. *If that is Bo Thura, he only wants me, not Jamieson or Sinclair.*

"Put your rifle away, Mr Sinclair. One rifle won't be much use against so many."

"I'm damned if I'll surrender without a fight!" Sinclair growled as Jamieson lifted a boathook and stood in truculent defiance.

The warboat paddled swiftly towards them while the three smaller boats formed a line downstream, blocking the steamer's escape. Andrew fastened the button of his holster and stepped amidships to be clearly seen. He felt his heart beating faster, wondering what the next few moments would bring.

I came out here to meet a dacoit and now is my opportunity. I hope Mariana is all right in Rangoon.

"They're a wild-looking bunch," Andrew said as the warboat drew alongside and a dozen of her crew boarded the steamer. Most wore a simple waist cloth or something similar, with a long *dha* in their hands. A few dacoits carried firearms, and one held what looked like a large hatchet. All were tattooed, some from head to foot and others only from the waist down.

Andrew controlled the increasing hammer of his heart as he stepped forward. "My name is Captain Andrew Baird."

Should I have told them my rank? It may make things worse.

While the bulk of the dacoits stared at Andrew in incomprehension, one man stepped forward as the rest made space for him. He was short, stocky, and broad-shouldered, with a scar running diagonally across his face.

I met you in Mandalay, my scarred friend.

"Baird," the man grunted. "Windrush." He lifted his *dha* and ran a thumb along the blade.

Andrew felt the tension rise among the dacoits.

If I give the wrong answer here, these lads will skewer me, like as not.

"Captain Andrew Baird," he jabbed a finger at his chest, hoping his voice did not betray his nervousness. "My father is General Jack Windrush."

Andrew heard the water rushing past and the whisper of wind in the trees. The dacoits were utterly quiet as they listened to the conversation.

How the devil can I communicate with this brute? His English is as basic as my Burmese. Is this fellow Bo Thura?

The scarred man jabbed a finger on Andrew's chest. "Windrush?" He peered closer, his mouth slightly open and his eyes basilisk hard.

"Baird," Andrew repeated, much to the amusement of the other dacoits. A slender, heavily tattooed man leaning against the rail said something that made them roar with laughter. Andrew jabbed his finger again, "Andrew Baird!"

The scarred man turned to face his compatriots as though exasperated at Andrew's responses. He said something that made the dacoits laugh again, and the man leaning against the rail pushed himself forward, ruffled the scarred man's hair and shoved him to join the rest.

I hope to God these are the right dacoits and not a rival gang. I'll try again.

"My name is Captain Andrew Baird. Bo Thura sent for me. Do any of you know where Bo Thura is?" He spoke slowly and clearly, hoping somebody had a smattering of English. He pointed a finger at the scarred man. "Are you Bo Thura? Bo Thura?"

The man from the rail took another step forward. Even more heavily tattooed than his compatriots, the man wore only a waist cloth with a silver-hilted *dha* suspended from a simple leather belt. He looked to be about fifty, with the force of his personality shining through.

"I know Bo Thura," the tattooed man spoke in perfect English. "I asked you to come here, Cousin. I am Bo Thura."

Andrew was unsure whether to bow or hold out his hand, for despite his appearance, Bo Thura had the accent and bearing of a British gentleman. His smile was also familiar, although Andrew could not think from where. "Why?" Andrew asked and added. "How is Mary MacConnacher?"

"Bearing up," Bo Thura said, looking Andrew up and down. "His smile broadened. I haven't killed her, if that's what you're worried about, Cousin, but nor do I have her with me."

"Where is she?" Andrew tried to ignore the dozen dacoits who swarmed on board the steamer and began to lift everything portable while Jamieson and Sinclair tried to defend their vessel. "Could you stop your men stealing, Bo Thura? You asked me to come here. This man had the kindness to give me a ride, so you are in his debt."

Bo Thura didn't ask me to Burma to murder me, so I should be safe. I am not sure about Jamieson and Sinclair.

Bo Thura snapped something, and most of the dacoits returned to their warboat, although they did not return the stolen items. The scarred man remained. He held his *dha*, stood in the bows, and watched Andrew suspiciously.

"My men like to loot," Bo Thura explained. "That's why they became dacoits."

"British soldiers have also been known to loot," Andrew said. "I don't want my colleague harmed."

"He won't be," Bo Thura said. He snapped an order, and the scarred man and three others moved towards Andrew with *dhas* in their hands. "As long as you come with me."

"Are you kidnapping me as you did with Mary MacConnacher?" Andrew remained still.

"You are my honoured guest, Cousin Andrew," Bo Thura replied with that familiar wry smile. "Don't you want to meet your family?"

I didn't come all this way to baulk at the last minute. "Take me to young Mary," he said, stepping onto the Burmese warboat.

Bo Thura followed, with the scarred man last to leave *Little Salamander*.

"The handsome gentleman is Aung Thiha," Bo Thura explained. "He is my personal bodyguard."

Andrew nodded. "He looks a handy chap to have at one's side," he said.

"You'll get to appreciate his fine qualities," Bo Thura replied. "Find a space in the boat."

On a word from Bo Thura, the dacoits lifted their paddles and swept away, leaving the steamer abandoned in the middle of the river. Jamieson and Sinclair were unharmed and staring after them. The dacoits on the riverbank had vanished.

"Where are we going?" Andrew asked.

"To the border," Bo Thura replied as the paddlers shoved hard and the warboat sped upriver at an impressive speed, emphasising every stroke of the paddles with a grunt. The smell of male sweat was powerful in the boat. "Bhamo."

"How far is that?" Andrew asked. He saw a human head near the bow, rolling from side to side, and wondered who the unfortunate owner might have been.

"Two days," Bo Thura said. "If we are lucky. Settle back, cousin."

"Is young Mary in Bhamo?"

Bo Thura gave that wry smile that Andrew found so strangely familiar. "You'll see." He tilted his head to one side. "Tell me, Cousin Andrew, why you changed your name from Windrush to Baird. Are you ashamed of your father? I met him once, you know, when he was a raw lieutenant, and I was a boy."

"No," Andrew replied. "I am not ashamed of my father. I wanted to try and make my way without his influence."

"Ah," Bo Thura nodded. "Pride rather than shame. Why pick Baird?"

"Baird was my grandfather's name on my mother's side."

Bo Thura nodded. "You must tell me about your mother and that side of our family."

"I will," Andrew promised. "Once I am sure Mary MacConnacher is safe."

"She is safe," Bo Thura assured him. He raised his voice. "San Kyi!" A man rose from the paddlers' ranks, stepped to the stern, and began to beat time on a large brass gong.

"That fellow's followed me from British Burma," he said.

"San Kyi was keeping his eye on you," Bo Thura said. He relapsed into silence, looking sideways at Andrew as if unsure they were related.

I have mingled with frontiersmen, Zulus, and Boers, and now I am in the company of Burmese dacoits. Yet I only want a quiet life in the countryside. I hope I can get young Mary back safely and return home.

Andrew knew that the smaller, lighter ships of the Irrawaddy Flotilla steamed as far as Bhamo, but he was unsure what to expect so near to the Chinese frontier. He slept on board the warboat, huddled uncomfortably on a wooden seat, and watched the wooded hill country ease past.

"Nearly there, Cousin," Bo Thura encouraged.

"What's this all about, Bo Thura?" Andrew asked. "Why kidnap a child only to release her?"

Bo Thura smiled. "I will explain everything in time," he said.

Bo Thura eased the warboat to a berth on the riverbank as Andrew watched a small Irrawaddy Flotilla vessel steam downstream. They left the warboat and walked casually into Bhamo.

Andrew found Bhamo a compact town within a timber stockade, a defended gateway, and a mixed population of Shans, Chinese, and some Burmese officials, with the Burmese in the minority. Although there were only a few hundred houses, Bhamo was a bustling town with an excited atmosphere that reminded Andrew of the settlements on the Natal and Cape Colony frontier. The people were busy, agile and curious about the European stranger. Near the town centre, a large building stood secure behind formidable walls. Andrew knew Bhamo's Governor would live inside the luxurious palace.

Andrew sensed the tension in the town as if everybody expected something to happen, but nobody knew what.

"Welcome to Bhamo," Bo Thura said. "The departure point for caravans to Talifoo in Yunnan, if you are interested. It's a very convenient place, Cousin. If Maung Thandar sends a force against me, I slip into Chinese Yunnan. If the Chinese take a dislike, I move deeper into Burma, and if both want me, I can slide into Shan country."

Andrew remembered Maung Thandar during the killings in Mandalay. "Thandar is a violent man," he said. "Would he send men against you?"

"He may do," Bo Thura replied without giving details.

"And if the British want you for raiding in Lower Burma?"

Bo Thura smiled. "I am at the furthest point from British territory," he said. "No British expedition could reach this far without Thibaw's permission, and he won't give that."

"No, I don't suppose he would," Andrew agreed.

The houses were a mixture of Burmese and Chinese, mostly neat and clean, with a different feel to southern Burma. Bo Thura ushered Andrew into a small house, where two elderly women shifted aside to make room. Aung Thiha and San Kyi followed as Bo Thura sat on a low stool and invited Andrew to join him.

"As we're on the frontier, everything has two names. The local tribe between the Irrawaddy and Salween Rivers is the Kakhyen to the Burmans and Yeuh-jin to the Chinese; the British call them the Karen. Naturally, the tribesmen don't recognise either name and call themselves the Singphoos, which simply means human beings or just men."

"All things to all people," Andrew said.

"I rather like them, Cousin," Bo Thura said. "They are thieves and robbers; when thievery fails, they take to barter and trade." He smiled again, with bright humour in his eyes. "Rather like the English, really, a nation of pirates turned to trade. General Albert Fytche thought them 'dirty, unkempt barbarians armed with bows and arrows, lawless to the last degree,' and who are we to agree with a British general?"

"Fytche was the Chief Commissioner of Burma, wasn't he?" Andrew asked.

"He is also Lord Tennyson's cousin," Bo Thura said. He shook his head. "But times are changing. Being a Windrush, I can smell the wind."

Andrew started; his father had used the same expression and had the same wry humour around his mouth.

"What does the wind scent tell you?" Andrew asked.

"The wind tells me that my position is insecure," Bo Thura said. "The British are becoming unhappy with Thibaw, and the Chinese will soon move south to this town."

"Will they?" Andrew asked.

"Undoubtedly," Bo Thura told him. "And when that happens, my position here will deteriorate from insecure to untenable, and I will have to seek sanctuary with my father's people." That wry smile returned. "That's where you come in, Captain David Andrew Windrush, who now calls himself Andrew Baird."

Andrew met the smile with one of his own. "I won't come in anywhere until I know Mary MacConnacher is safe. Where is she?"

He felt the sudden tension in the room and leaned back, with his revolver a comforting pressure under his tunic.

"I'll ask again, Bo Thura. Where is Mary MacConnacher?"

CHAPTER 13

RANGOON AND BHAMO, OCTOBER 1884

"Do you like horses?" Jennings asked as they sat in the lounge of Well's Britannia Hotel.

Mariana put down her pen and closed her journal. "Everybody likes horses," she replied.

"Good," Jennings said. "If you come with me, I'll show you the finest horses in Burma, if not in all Southeast Asia."

Mariana glanced at her journal. She had hoped to finish the page. "Is it far?"

Jennings shook his head. "Not far at all."

Mariana nodded. "Let me put my journal away and freshen up, and I'll join you down here in ten minutes."

"All right," Jennings agreed. "Half an hour it is." He met her smile with a knowing grin, for he prided himself on understanding women.

Jennings' stables were on the outskirts of Rangoon, a quarter of a mile from the British Army Cantonments. A staff of half a dozen young Burmese women and men smiled as Jennings appeared.

"That's an impressive building," Mariana said. "Do you own it?"

"I and some others," Jennings said. "We have formed a syndicate to improve the breeding stock of horses in Rangoon and start a Turf Club here. * Do you know anything about horses?" He looked at Mariana sideways, finger-grooming his moustache.

"A little bit," Mariana admitted. "I grew up on a farm in Natal, remember? My father had two daughters and no sons, so he taught us how to ride, farm, and shoot."

---

* Rangoon Turf Club was founded in 1887.

"You'll know a good horse when you see one, then," Jennings observed.

"I should," Mariana replied. "My father bred them. Show me your horses, sir."

"This way, Miss Maxwell," Jennings opened the tall stable door and ushered Mariana inside.

Mariana breathed deeply of the familiar scent. "Horses are always such homely animals," she said. "Horses and cattle belong with people, while sheep and goats should be in the wilds."

Jennings fondled the nearest horse's ear. "Do you like my babies?"

Mariana walked the length of the stables, where ten horses extended their necks to nuzzle her as she passed. She stopped at each one, stroking their glossy hides and talking softly.

"They look like thoroughbreds," Mariana said.

"That's what they are," Jennings replied proudly. "These are the best horses from the best breeding stock in Southeast Asia. As I said, we plan to open a racecourse in Rangoon soon, this year, next year or shortly afterwards, and I intend to win every single race." He smiled across to Mariana. "I've invested nearly everything I own in this operation."

Mariana walked back along the stable, speaking to each horse in turn, fondling their ears and running her hands down their necks and flanks.

"These are adorable animals," she said. "Do you ride often?"

"Every opportunity I get," Jennings replied. "Rangoon is a bit limited normally, but things are looking up. I have my eyes on a tasty little filly to add to my collection."

"These beauties are mainly stallions," Mariana pointed out. "You could perhaps do with a couple of mares to balance things."

"Mares are always welcome in my stable," Jennings said. He caressed a powerful black. "When we establish the Rangoon Turf Club with regular races, you will be an honoured guest and Queen of the Course on Lady's Day."

"Like at Ascot during the Royal Meeting?" Mariana asked.

"Exactly like that," Jennings enthused. "Perhaps the queen, or rather the Empress, will grace us with her presence."

"I am sure Her Majesty would be proud to include Rangoon in her next visit," Mariana said.

They lingered in the stables, with Jennings extolling the qualities of each horse and Mariana listening. Her father had been a keen horseman, as had all the pioneer farmers in Natal, but out of necessity rather than desire for glory or profit. Maxwell's horses were noted for stamina and strength rather than for speed. After an hour in the cool stables, Mariana was reluctant to leave for the humid heat outside.

"You have lovely horses," she said. She thought of Lancelot, Andrew's Kabul pony, and wondered how he would compare with Jennings' pedigree bloodstock.

"Thank you," Jennings replied. "Will you come to my house for dinner, Miss Maxwell?"

Mariana hesitated. "That is a very kind invitation, Mr Jennings, and I am tempted."

"Does that mean no?" Jennings asked.

"I am afraid so, Mr Jennings," Mariana replied. "It means not on this occasion."

"I thought you enjoyed my company," Civilian exaggerated a pout.

"I do enjoy your company," Mariana told him. "But a lone woman meeting a man during the day is acceptable, but meeting a man in the evening?" She smiled. "People would talk. However innocent your intentions, and I am sure you are as innocent as a newborn lamb, people would still gossip."

"Which people?" Jennings asked. "Rangoon society is cliquish and close-knit, but any gossip will be confined to this little backwater of a town. Nobody either knows or cares what happens here."

"Andrew might," Mariana said quietly.

Jennings stepped back. "Andrew might," he repeated, "but Captain Baird will have no cause to be alarmed, Miss Maxwell."

"Thank you, Mr Jennings," Mariana said. "Perhaps next time."

"WOULD YOU LIKE A SMOKE, COUSIN?" BO THURA ASKED.

"I'd prefer to ensure young Mary is safe," Andrew replied.

"Smoking is a pastime in Burma," Bo Thura seemed in no hurry to move. "Everybody in the country, from Thibaw to the poorest farmer, smokes. Unless you understand our customs, you'll never understand the country."

I have no desire to understand the country.

"Will you smoke with me, Cousin?"

Bo Thura's mocking tone irritated Andrew. "Indeed, Cousin," he replied. "Tell me how you make these cigars of yours." He felt the atmosphere in the house alter as if he had taken a step towards acceptance.

"Aung Thiha will demonstrate," Bo Thura said.

Aung Thiha produced half a dozen large coarse leaves and filled them with a handful of woodchips.

"That's the start," Bo Thura said.

Aung Thiha added some raw sugar and a small amount of tobacco. He smiled at Andrew, rolled the leaf around the mixture, lit it, took a couple of puffs and handed it over.

"Thank you," Andrew said. The cigar was nearly five inches long. Aware that everyone was watching, he steeled himself and inhaled, held the smoke in his lungs and slowly exhaled.

They expected me to fall about, choking and coughing. That was their test. They won't realise that public schoolboys used to find quiet places and smoke everything from tarry ropes to crushed nettles.

"Not bad," Andrew said, passing the cigar to Bo Thura. "I've smoked a lot worse. Now, where is little Mary? Or will I catch the next steamer to Rangoon?"

Bo Thura grinned and stood up. "Follow me, Cousin. Now you've mastered the art of smoking a cheroot, we'll have to tattoo you!"

Andrew rose. "I can't see the Army allowing an officer to have tattoos." *What would Mariana think if I returned to Rangoon covered in Burmese tattoos? Or the good folk of Berwick?*

Bo Thura led them from the small house, with Aung Thiha walking between him and Andrew. People in the streets paid little attention as Bo Thura threaded through an area of poor-looking housing.

"Little Mary is in there," Bo Thura pointed to a bamboo hut like most of the others in the village. He stepped aside and smiled again.

Andrew took a deep breath, took hold of the handle of his revolver, and stepped inside the house, wondering what horrors he would find.

The house was cool and dim, with light easing through the windows and a pleasant scent of cooking and aromatic cigar smoke. Andrew heard a child laugh and a woman's low voice, followed by another laugh.

Three women looked around when Andrew entered. All had long Burmese cigars in their mouths while two children sat between them. One was a little Burmese boy; the other was undoubtedly European, a small girl with ginger hair who smoked her cheroot as adeptly as any Burmese.

The Burmese woman Andrew had met in Mandalay sat on the right, watching Andrew through musing, cynical eyes.

Andrew was unsure if he wanted to look at the little girl or the Burmese woman.

Rescue the girl! Rescue Mary and return to Rangoon.

"Mary?" Andrew asked. He felt his heartbeat increase and tried to ignore the woman.

The ginger-haired girl removed the cigar from her mouth and favoured Andrew with a broad smile. "I'm Mary," she said and spoke to her neighbours in fluent Burmese. The women laughed and looked at Andrew.

"You look surprised," Bo Thura said. "What did you expect?"

"I am not sure what I expected," Andrew admitted. "How have they treated you, Mary?"

"This is Than Than Aye, and this is Myat Phaya," Mary introduced the women. "Who are you?"

Than Than Aye. That's the Burmese woman's name.

"I am Andrew Baird," Andrew said. "I've come to take you home."

"I am home," Mary told him seriously. "I don't want to go back to that other place."

Bo Thura laughed. "Now you've seen young Mary, Cousin Andrew, and know she is safe and well cared for, we can talk."

"I'll come too," Than Than Aye said. She stood gracefully and walked beside them, with her hips an inch from Andrew's and her sandalwood perfume heady in his nostrils.

I must get to know this woman. Than Than Aye; that's an intriguing name.

How about Mariana?

Mariana turned me down.

Than Than Aye edged closer, with her hips lightly touching his. Andrew started, knew she was taunting him and abruptly looked away.

"You look nervous, Andrew Baird," Than Than Aye said softly. "Does a woman's company concern you?"

"I am not nervous," Andrew denied, shifting further away.

Than Than Aye laughed, "You may be the best soldier in the British Army, Captain Baird, but you have much to learn about women. We understand you." She looked at him through the corners of her eyes, smiling.

"I've come here for Mary," Andrew said.

"And you'll leave with her, Captain," Bo Thura promised. "Once we have reached an agreement."

Mary jumped up when Aung Thiha entered the room. "Aung!" She shouted, stretching out her arms. "*Kyawal! Kyawal!*"

Aung Thiha's scarred face puckered into a grin. He lifted Mary, swung her in the air and placed her across his back. Stooping to all fours, he thundered around the house with Mary on his back, shouting, "*Kyawal!*"

"*Kyawal* means buffalo," Than Than Aye explained. "As you see, we are treating the little girl abominably!"

"So, I see," Andrew agreed, trying not to smile at the spectacle of the scarred warrior acting as a buffalo for the laughing child.

Bo Thura touched Andrew's arm. "You have seen Mary, Cousin. It's time we talked business. Come to my house. This way."

Bo Thura's house was slightly larger than the others in the village, neat and clean. A woman smiled at Andrew as he arrived, offered him a cigar, and sat in a corner of the spacious room.

"I thought the house we visited was yours," Andrew said.

"That was Aung Thiha's house," Bo Thura said, smiling. "Sit down, Cousin."

Andrew sat on one of the backless stools and studied the house. He saw a faded red coat hanging in the corner of the room and wondered if his Great Uncle George had owned it.

"Yes," Bo Thura answered his unspoken question. "That uniform belonged to my father. Sit down, Cousin."

Bo Thura laughed at the expression on Andrew's face. "What did you expect, Cousin Andrew? Human heads on stakes? A cannibal feast?"

"Perhaps one of these," Andrew said. "You've gone to a lot of trouble with kidnapping that young girl and bringing me halfway across the world. Why did you want to see me?"

"I didn't want to see you," Bo Thura replied. "You are only a lowly colonial captain with no influence. I wanted to see your father, the general, the famous Fighting Jack Windrush, but as he's not available, you will be a perhaps adequate replacement."

"Thank you," Andrew replied ironically. "A replacement for what purpose? Why have you brought me thousands of miles across the world?"

"I need your help to get me safely into British Burma without your military hunting me down." Bo Thura laughed, with his eyes sparkling. "I am sure I could evade your clumsy khaki columns, but I don't want to. I want to settle in a quiet village without armed sentries and a bodyguard watching over me."

"You could still do that in Upper Burma," Andrew pointed out.

Bo Thura shook his head. "Unfortunately, Cousin, I can't. I have fallen out of favour with the authorities here, and do you know what they do to dacoits they capture?"

"They crucify them," Andrew answered brutally.

Bo Thura nodded. "Exactly so. It's rather a painful way to die."

Andrew remembered the crucified men he had seen. "I imagine so," he replied. "What did you do to annoy the king?"

"It wasn't the king," Bo Thura shook his head. "He's a weak sort of fellow, completely under the thumb of his mother-in-law and that savage Maung Thandar."

Andrew hid his surprise. "If not the king, then who have you annoyed?"

"Maung Thandar," Bo Thura said. "You may have heard of him?"

"I have heard of him," Andrew confirmed. *Maung Thandar was the evil-looking man involved in the massacre at Mandalay jail.*

"He is the devil," Bo Thura lit a cheroot and leaned back, holding Andrew's gaze. "He controls the dacoity, issuing licences and taking a percentage of all the dacoits gain. He sends bands into British Burma to disrupt your economy and weaken your prestige."

All the rumours are correct, except Maung Thandar takes a cut of the profits. "Does he, now?" Andrew expressed surprise. "I'll pass that information on when I return to Rangoon with Mary. Why did you kidnap her?"

"As bait," Bo Thura admitted. "I knew the British would not allow a little girl to be kidnapped, and I sent a note asking for your father."

"I see," Andrew said. "How did you cross Maung Thandar?"

"I refused to pay his tribute," Bo Thura said.

"That would annoy him," Andrew agreed.

Typical bloody-minded Windrush. This fellow may look like a Burmese dacoit, but the Windrush blood runs true. I should have known when I saw that wry smile: Father has the same look.

"Why don't you just cross the border into British Burma?"

"I have a certain reputation," Bo Thura said. "If the British caught me, they'd either hang or shoot me. Both are preferable to crucifixion, but I'd prefer to live a little longer."

"I can imagine," Andrew said dryly. "What do you want me to do?"

Bo Thura drew on his cigar. "It's quite simple, Cousin. I want you to return to Rangoon with little Mary, tell the Chief Commissioner that the reformed Bo Thura rescued her from a band of evil dacoits, and I wish to come into British Burma under your protection. Put in a good word for me."

"As you said yourself, Bo Thura," Andrew reminded, "I am only a lowly colonial captain. I have no influence."

"Use your father's name," Bo Thura said. "Everybody knows Fighting Jack Windrush."

Andrew pondered for a moment. "That might work," he admitted. *All my adult life, I have tried to break free from my father's influence and make my own way in life. Now, a distant relative from a far-off country is asking me to revoke my values to help him.*

Is the result worth the price?

Could I leave young Mary MacConnacher here with these people?

"I can talk for you, Bo Thura," Andrew did not give a direct answer, "but what can you offer the British in return? Returning Mary and telling the Chief Commissioner you will no longer rob and steal in British territory may not be enough for him to welcome you with open arms."

"I can offer more than that," Bo Thura said.

He's playing his hand one card at a time. "Tell me more," Andrew said. "I am not yet convinced I want to help you."

Bo Thura smiled again. "Even though we are related, and I could kill you at a whim?"

"That is not in question," Andrew said. "You are a powerful man with an array of dacoits at your back while I am a lone stranger. My life is in your hands."

"It is," Bo Thura agreed. He pondered for a moment. "You will be aware that the French are in Tonkin, just over the border."

Andrew nodded, sensing that Bo Thura was about to impart important information. "Our newspapers are full of the French activities in Tonkin."

Bo Thura drew on his cigar again, allowing the smoke to trickle from his nostrils before he resumed his conversation. "Were you aware the French have designs for Upper Burma?"

Andrew took a deep breath. "I did not know that," he said. "Are you sure?"

"I am sure," Bo Thura said, smiling. He waited for a moment. "Would that information prove useful to the Chief Commissioner?"

Andrew considered before replying. "It might be," he said. "Of course, he would need proof. The word of a known dacoit would not be sufficient."

"I have proof," Bo Thura said.

Andrew held Bo Thura's gaze. "What sort of proof?"

"I have a document that shows the French involvement and what they intend to do in Thibaw's kingdom, written in Burmese and French."

"Good God!" Andrew stood up and paced the length of the airy room. "Have you read it?"

"I have," Bo Thura said.

"What does it say? Give me the details so I can inform the Chief Commissioner."

Bo Thura smiled. "If I tell you too much, Cousin, I have given away my trump before the cards are even dealt."

Andrew thought of the consequences of the French moving into Thibaw's kingdom of Ava, controlling the upper reaches of the Irrawaddy. With the British and French sharing a common frontier in an already volatile region, disputes were inevitable, especially if the French tried to prove their strength.

"The French in Upper Burma would cause all sorts of problems," Andrew said. "We put the French noses out of joint a few years ago when we gained control of the Suez Canal and Egypt. Now, they are moving into our spheres of interest in Asia. Tit for tat, and they know we are already wary of trouble with Russia over Afghanistan."

Bo Thura leaned back, smiling. "Can Great Britain afford a dispute with two major powers, Russia and France, simultaneously?"

"Let's hope it never happens," Andrew said.

How does a dacoit in the Burmese backwaters know so much about European politics?

"Little Mary MacConnacher is my opening gambit, Cousin Andrew, and the French document is my trump. Do you believe Sir Charles Crossthwaite, the Chief Commissioner, may grant me a pardon and permission to live in British Burma?"

Andrew nodded slowly, with his mind exploring the ramifications of a French presence in Mandalay. "I believe he may," he said, "if I can get the information to him before he learns from other channels."

He realised Than Than Aye had been listening to their conversation, scrutinising him through her fine eyes.

"Good," Than Than Aye said. "That's one thing decided." She put a small hand on Andrew's arm. "It's my turn now, Andrew."

Andrew started, saw Bo Thura's amused smile, and followed Than Than Aye out the door.

"Now, Miss Maxwell," Jennings said. "I have invited you to my house on two occasions, and each time, you have made an excuse to refuse my hospitality. Now, I am formally requesting that you join me for dinner this evening."

"Not this evening," Mariana said. "Another time, perhaps."

They sat in the foyer of Wells Britannia Hotel, with the fan slowly revolving above and a pleasant hum of activity all around.

"Your Captain Andrew seems to have got himself lost," Jennings said. "He has left you alone for far too long."

"Something must have delayed him," Mariana said. She thought of the three weeks she had marked in her journal. She had marked off each carefully inscribed day, completed another three weeks and was already on the next. Her marks filled the lined page, and only she knew the stains came from her tears.

"That is correct," Jennings said. "Something or somebody." He smiled at his attempted humour. "Perhaps Captain Andrew has found himself an attractive Burmese lady."

"Andrew would not do that," Mariana said stoutly. She lifted her chin. "Andrew is a man of his word."

I rejected him in Edinburgh. Oh, why did I do that? Maybe he will never come back.

"Of course not," Jennings agreed. "I spoke in jest or perhaps in worry because the good Captain Andrew is so late."

These Burmese ladies are attractive. One captured Sergeant Wells, and Andrew's great Uncle George married another. Mariana shuddered. *Andrew's father, General Windrush, married an Indian woman; maybe it's a family trait. I wish we had never come East.*

"Are you all right, Miss Maxwell?" Jennings asked. "You look very pale suddenly. Sit down, please, and I'll fetch a glass of water." He raised his voice, calling for a waiter.

"I am all right," Mariana said as a waiter appeared with a glass of tepid water. She saw Wells watching from the corner of the room and mustered a smile.

"I've upset you, haven't I?" Jennings asked. "Unforgivable, and you such a lovely lady. I cannot apologise enough."

"There is no need to apologise, Mr Jennings," Mariana said. "Please excuse me." She rose, turned away and hurried upstairs to her room.

CHAPTER 14

BHAMO, KINGDOM OF AVA, DECEMBER 1884

"I like you, Andrew Baird," Than Than Aye said as they left the house. "And I know you like me." She led him to an open area, where women gossiped and children played.

"I do," Andrew agreed.

Than Than Aye laughed openly. "How much do you like me, Andrew Baird?"

I feel as if I've known you all my life, Andrew thought. "Why do you ask?"

Than Than Aye bumped her hip against Andrew's thigh. "In what way do you like me, Andrew Baird?"

Andrew thought of Mariana, but that feeling of having known Than Than Aye all his life returned. "You are a very attractive woman, Than Than Aye."

Than Than Aye laughed and bumped her hip against him again. "Do you think of me as a woman? Or as something else?"

"As a woman," Andrew replied immediately.

Than Than Aye's laugh was louder than ever. "You can't do that, Andrew. We share the same blood."

"What?" Andrew stared as Than Than Aye stepped back, with her eyes bright. "Say that again."

"You heard me the first time," Than Than Aye said. "I am Bo Thura's daughter, your cousin."

"Oh, dear Lord in Heaven!" Andrew shook his head. "I am sorry, Than Than Aye. I had no idea!" He stepped away as Than Than Aye continued to laugh.

"We can still be friends," Than Than Aye told him seriously. "But not the way you hoped. I told you I understand you, but you have much to learn about women."

When Andrew looked at her again, he realised that all desire had vanished. He saw her as a friend or a relative, but nothing else.

"Dear Lord in Heaven," Andrew repeated as Than Than Aye scrutinised him.

"Now you understand," Than Than Aye said. "You recognised something in me. It was blood. Blood calls to blood, Cousin."

Andrew grasped at that fragile straw. "I see," he said.

"Good," Than Than Aye nodded. "Now we can be friends. You'll want to take little Mary back to her mother." She grasped Andrew's arm in a sisterly fashion. "Bo Thura will need to hear."

"WE'LL LEAVE FOR RANGOON TOMORROW," ANDREW SAID AS THEY SAT IN Bo Thura's pleasant house. He held the Irrawaddy Flotilla timetable in his hand and consulted the lists. "The Flotilla steamer *Kaw Byoo*, under Captain Terndrup, will arrive in the morning, and she'll take me to Mandalay. From there, I'll catch the Flotilla steamer for Rangoon."

Bo Thura nodded. "You will take Mary with you," he said.

"I will," Andrew said. "That is why I came here." He looked out of the open door as the light faded. It already seemed normal to sit in a bamboo and teak house near the Irrawaddy River. When he returned to Berwick, he knew this episode would appear as a dream, as if he had never heard the tinkle of temple bells or smelled the sweet spices of Than Than Aye's cooking.

"Don't forget to ask the Chief Commissioner about me," Bo Thura gave his wry smile.

"I will tell him you rescued Mary from a band of very unpleasant dacoits and want nothing more than to return her to her mother," Andrew said solemnly. "I will praise you to the high heavens and remind Sir Charles that you also found details of the French plans to increase their influence in Thibaw's kingdom."

"Good," Bo Thura sat in the corner of the room. He drew on his cigar and passed it to Than Than Aye.

"I cannot guarantee Sir Charles' reaction," Andrew said. "I can only do my best." He accepted the cigar from Than Than Aye, drew deeply and passed it on to Bo Thura.

"Mary will be nervous about leaving us," Than Than Aye said. "I'll come with you to keep her calm."

"Will you be safe in Rangoon?" Andrew asked.

"Do you think the British will recognise who I am?" Than Than Aye asked. "To them, I'll just be another Burmese woman." She glanced at Andrew. "I'm better looking than most, though," she said and laughed.

Everyone looked up as Aung Thiha entered the room and whispered something to Bo Thura, who glanced at Andrew and shook his head.

"What's the to-do?" Andrew asked when Aung Thiha left as gracefully as a cat. "What's happening?"

"The Chinese are happening," Bo Thura replied. "Come with me."

"The Chinese?"

"I'll get the little one," Than Than Aye said and hurried away.

"This way, Cousin," Bo Thura guided Andrew through Bhamo. Groups of men and women gathered at doorways and in the streets, talking, smoking, and often laughing. They spoke casually to Bo Thura as to a long-standing acquaintance and stared curiously at Andrew.

Europeans must be a novelty here despite the Irrawaddy Flotilla's steamers.

"Look over there," Bo Thura said quietly, "but don't stare. One is never sure how the Chinese may react."

Andrew saw a small group of men drifting through the north gate, talking to each other while looking around them. Like many men at this frontier, they carried arms, either long, slightly curved swords or long muskets.

"They look a handy bunch of fellows," Andrew said. "Are they the Chinese you mentioned?"

"They are Chinese, from Yunnan province," Bo Thura agreed. "They've been sliding into Bhamo all night in twos, threes and small parties."

"I see," Andrew said.

Bo Thura watched the incomers for a few moments. "They are irregular Chinese military by the way they stand. I'd say there's trouble in the wind, Cousin. You're wise to get out of Bhamo tomorrow. I might take my people out as well."

Andrew glanced at him. "Are the Chinese any threat to you?"

Bo Thura attempted to look innocent. "There is one Yunnan official who thinks he has a grudge."

"What happened?" Andrew asked.

"He lost a prize horse once and blamed me for taking it," Bo Thura said.

"Did you take it?" Andrew asked directly.

"Yes," Bo Thura replied. "I didn't think he'd make such a fuss about it. He's threatened to execute me in various unpleasant ways unless I replace his horse."

"Maybe you'd best avoid him, then," Andrew advised. He watched as another group of men eased inside Bhamo. Their long, colourful jackets and tight headgear told him they were neither Burmese nor Chinese.

"Kachyeus," Bo Thura said quietly. "You'd call them Kachins. Sometimes, they ally themselves with the Chinese; sometimes, they act alone. They are wild tribesmen from the hills, often fighting with the Burmese, who claim their lands."

"What do they want here?" Andrew asked.

"Maybe to trade," Bo Thura said. "Maybe to rob, and maybe they are watching to see what happens, as we are."

Andrew glanced over his shoulder at the Governor's palace, thrusting above the mass of houses. "Should we warn the Governor?"

Bo Thura did not hesitate. "No. He would not trust the word of a British man and could arrest me. We'll sit tight tonight, and you'll leave on the steamer tomorrow."

"Does everyone want to arrest you, Bo Thura?" Andrew asked.

"Not everyone," Bo Thura replied. "But you can understand why I seek sanctuary in British Burma."

"I won't forget to tell Sir Charles," Andrew promised. He nodded as another group of Chinese slipped through the gate and moved purposefully into the town. "I think we should return to your house," he said. "We've left the women alone there."

Bo Thura locked his doors and windows and set two watchmen for the night, with Aung Thiha patrolling the streets.

"Keep Mary safe," Andrew ordered.

"I have her," Than Than Aye replied reassuringly.

Andrew slept uneasily with his pistol beside his bed. He remembered his recent experience in Mandalay and wakened every few moments, listening for the sound of gunfire or a shouting mob.

The trouble began before dawn. Bo Thura was already awake, and Than Than Aye had Mary dressed and fed. Andrew heard the deep notes of a gong, a single shot, and the rising cries of a crowd.

Here we go. Andrew had slept half-dressed and only had to slip on his tunic and boots before leaving the small cubicle where he slept.

"Trouble," Bo Thura reported with a calm smile. "San Kyi tells me there are about six hundred Chinese and Kachins inside Bhamo. That's about five hundred more than I'd like."

Andrew heard the gong again, with the sound bringing back memories of his voyage from Thayetmyo.

The shooting increased, accompanied by wild cries and screaming.

"Upper Burma is a wild place," Andrew said as Bo Thura sent his men to watch the windows.

"King Thibaw does not keep an orderly kingdom," Bo Thura said calmly.

Andrew glanced over his shoulder, where Than Than Aye was washing Mary's hair in a basin of warm water. Both sang a song in Burmese.

That child will find it hard to reassimilate into British culture. She is as well cared for with the dacoits as she would be back home. If I can even catch the Flotilla ship with this blasted trouble.

"Open the door," Andrew ordered. "I'm going to see what's happening."

"You're a fool if you do," Bo Thura told him.

"I can't make a decision without intelligence," Andrew replied. "Open the blasted door!"

Chinese and Kachins seemed to be everywhere, running through the streets in chaotic groups, firing at random, chasing women and slowly moving towards the Governor's palace where the small Burmese garrison lived.*

It's Mandalay all over again.

Andrew slid into the shelter of a bamboo and matting house as a party of

* The Chinese attack on Bhamo in December 1884 seems to have taken the Burmese by surprise. Hundreds of Chinese irregulars infiltrated the town and took control within a few hours, although sporadic fighting lasted a couple of days.

Chinese marched past. They headed directly for the eastern gate, casually shot the gatekeeper, and dragged the heavy teak doors open. A host of men, irregular Chinese soldiers and Burmese villagers poured inside and ran to the Chinese quarter. They shouted as they ran, with some brandishing weapons.

The Chinese are well organised; they've planned this operation in advance.

As the Chinese approached the palace, the gates banged open, and a lone horseman burst out. He was splendidly dressed and sleek with good living.

That's the Governor, Andrew realised.

The Governor's horse reared and whinnied at the sight of the crowd, nearly throwing the rider. He controlled the animal with difficulty, waving his left hand, and galloped away towards the Irrawaddy. A platoon of palace guards followed and fired a single ragged volley at the invaders before joining him in flight.

So much for Thibaw's soldiers, Andrew thought as the Chinese ran through the open gates into the palace and made free of the arsenal. About half the Burmese soldiers threw away their hats, ripped off their jackets and began to loot the town, breaking into houses and carrying away everything they fancied.

I've seen enough. Time to get back to Bo Thura's house. There won't be any Flotilla steamers in Bhamo today.

"Well?" Bo Thura waited behind the door with a rifle in his hand.

"Chinese and Kachins everywhere," Andrew reported. "The Governor and his guards have run, and half the garrison have joined the Chinese in stripping the place bare."

"As I thought," Bo Thura said. "We'll stay here until the dust settles." He smiled. "You'll just have to accept my hospitality." His smile faded. "Keep your revolver handy."

Andrew glanced at Mary, who was sitting quietly beside Than Than Aye, quite content to watch proceedings and share a cheroot. "The sooner I get her back to her parents, the better."

Bo Thura frowned. "Why? They'll probably pack her off to some maiden aunt in England, who'll restrict everything she does, or worse, her parents will send her to some terrible school with cold baths every morning. She'll be happier with us."

Andrew had a sudden memory of his school days in England. "That's probably true," he said. "All the same, she belongs with her parents." He looked around as a fresh burst of gunfire sounded.

"Shut and barricade the door," Bo Thura ordered.

They heard the fighting intensify and then fade away to sporadic shooting and an occasional burst of shouting and screaming. Bo Thura kept his doors locked, and his men took turns on guard. On one occasion, a group of Burmese soldiers approached until Bo Thura fired a warning shot in the air. He shouted to them, then translated for Andrew. "I told them that I'll blow the head off the first man to touch my property."

Andrew nodded. "I'll take the second man," he said, showing his revolver.

Bo Thura's laugh could have been a copy of Andrew's father. "That's the way, Cousin."

The soldiers replied with loud shouts, brandishing their weapons. One saw Andrew, recognised he was European, drew his *dha* and gestured to his throat.

"That man says he'll cut off your head," Bo Thura told Andrew.

"I'll shoot him first," Andrew said. He wondered how long these soldiers would stand before a Zulu charge. He held the knifeman's gaze, aimed his revolver and smiled.

"I know you will," Bo Thura said quietly.

The soldiers melted away as the sun rose, bringing oppressive heat to the barricaded house. Smoke from burning houses clouded the street, settling as a blue-grey layer close to the ground. It was noon before the soldiers returned, with a stout, swaggering man leading a yelling mob.

"They mean business this time," Andrew said.

"You can also read the wind," Bo Thura looked at him sideways.

"So, it seems," Andrew agreed. He checked his revolver was fully loaded, winked at Mary, and returned his full attention to the soldiers outside.

The mob's noise increased as they gathered their courage before attacking. Andrew saw firelight reflecting from their weapons and thought of the similar situation in Ma Gun's house in Mandalay. He glanced back, where Mary and Than Than Aye shared a small cheroot. Mary waved to him.

How ironic, to come to rescue the child just as trouble erupts.

"How many are there?" Bo Thura asked.

"Forty? Fifty?" Andrew hazarded. "It's hard to tell with the smoke drifting over them."

Bo Thura grinned, lifting a Martini-Henry from a dark corner of the room. "We'll see how they like this," he said.

"Where did you get that?" Andrew recognised the markings on the rifle. "That's a War Office issue!"

Bo Thura's grin widened. "I took it from one of your soldiers," he said. "He looked the other way at the wrong time."

"You're a rogue, Bo Thura," Andrew lifted his revolver as the soldiers moved closer. One fired a musket, with the bullet smacking into the wall without penetrating the teak.

"You know the locals, Bo Thura. Is it better to return fire or sit tight?"

"Return fire, Cousin Andrew," Bo Thura replied.

CHAPTER 15

BHAMO, KINGDOM OF AVA, DECEMBER 1884

Andrew fired on Bo Thura's word, with his bullet catching the soldier on the right leg. He fell without a sound, dropping his musket.

The other soldiers howled with anger and charged forward, waving their *dhas* or wildly firing their rifles. Andrew shot one, saw Bo Thura hit another, and they ceased fire as a second group appeared on the flank of the soldiers.

"That's Aung Thiha," Bo Thura said proudly. "He never lets me down."

Andrew saw the stocky man slice at a soldier with his *dha*, cutting the man's arm clean off, then thrust the point into another soldier's throat. Aung Thiha was laughing, enjoying the battle as he ran into the thickest of the soldiers. They scattered before him, with Andrew and Bo Thura firing at any who came close to the house.

"Your Aung Thiha is some fighter," Andrew said as the soldiers fled, and Aung Thiha shouted after them in triumph.

"He is," Bo Thura agreed proudly. "He'll remain outside until the danger is past."

If the Burmese Army has many like Aung Thiha, we'll be hard-pressed to defeat them.

They remained in Bo Thura's house all day, listening to the shouts, screams, and occasional shots from the streets outside. Twice more, parties of soldiers passed the house, one Burmese and one Chinese. Neither lingered, and Andrew began to relax. He hoped that Mariana was all right, thanked God that the Wellses were there to keep an eye on her, and wished he was back in Berwick.

I've been away from Mariana far longer than I expected. He had the crazy idea of introducing his new relatives to his father, wondered how they would get along and shook his head. *The strain must be affecting me if I am thinking like that. Let's hope the Irrawaddy Flotilla steamer arrives soon, and we can start the journey back to Rangoon. I can't allow Mary to remain in this dangerous environment.*

The night was tense, with Andrew expecting the rogue Burmese soldiers to return. He slept sitting upright in a chair with his revolver in his lap with the safety catch on. Twice, he woke to see Than Than Aye holding Mary. Each time, she smiled across at him.

That's my cousin. How could I have thought anything else?

The morning brought a sharp shower of rain that cooled the town but ended after half an hour, leaving water weeping from the roofs but nobody in the streets. Within ten minutes, the rainwater began to evaporate, creating a fine mist over the houses.

"The Flotilla steamer is overdue," Andrew said. "We'll see if she arrives and if we can get on board. I'll have another look around the town today."

Bo Thura looked up from his bowl of rice. "Why?"

"I want to see if it's safe to take Mary through the streets. I don't want to chance stray gunmen and mob rule."

"I'll come with you," Bo Thura decided.

They left the house half an hour later, wary of any sound as they threaded the streets towards the river. Andrew held his revolver, Bo Thura his rifle, and they moved from shadow to shadow without seeing a living human. Half a dozen bodies lay on the ground, men, women, and children, while packs of dogs and pigs roamed free.

"There's a ship in the river," Andrew said hopefully as they stopped at the wide-open town gate.

"That's a Burmese steamer," Bo Thura told him. "One of Thibaw's gunboats. Pass me your field glasses."

Andrew passed them over.

"The Governor's on board," Bo Thura said. "He's on the bridge, talking to the captain and drinking something."

A lone dog barked, joined by others in a cacophony of noise that echoed over the deserted streets.

Andrew retrieved his field glasses. "I see him. He doesn't seem concerned at the loss of his town and the death of his people." He peered down the river. "I can't see *Kaw Byoo* yet."

"She'll be here," Bo Thura said. "Captain Terndrup is a reliable man." He grinned. "I know the Flotilla steamer captains by name and reputation. In my occupation, such information is useful. Return to the house now before a Chinese patrol finds us."

Bo Thura was correct. Andrew saw *Kaw Byoo's* smoke in the middle of the morning, and she arrived in the early afternoon.

"Come on!" Andrew said. "Bring Mary, Than Than Aye. You'd better come too, Bo Thura. If we can get you on the steamer, you can be close to the border with British Burma when the Chief Commissioner grants you a pardon."

"If he grants me a pardon," Bo Thura said.

"He will," Andrew said.

"You have more faith in the British sense of fair play than I have," Bo Thura gave his wry smile.

"Come on, Cousins!" Andrew ordered. "We have an agreement!"

They left Bo Thura's house when they saw the smoke and hurried towards the riverbank, joining an increasing crowd of people anxious to escape Bhamo. Than Than Aye held Mary's hand, lifting her when the crowd grew denser.

Captain Terndrup approached the quay cautiously, pulled alongside and tied up as a nervous crowd of refugees waited to board. One of *Kaw Byoo's* crew stood on the upper deck with a Snider, watching the town through nervous eyes.

The second the crew put out the gangplank, the refugees rushed forward, clamouring to board, but Captain Terndrup stopped them by brandishing his revolver. He gave a sharp order, and the armed crewman fired a shot into the air.

"Ticket holders first!" Captain Terndrup shouted. "Show your tickets to the crew or stay on shore!"

"There might not be room for us," Andrew looked at the swelling crowd of anxious people trying to escape from the carnage in Bhamo.

"We can use my boat," Bo Thura said, avoiding the captain's gaze. "I'll take you as far as Mandalay."

"No, we can't," Andrew pointed to the quay, where Bo Thura's boat lay a smouldering wreck beside half a dozen others, ruined by Burmese or Chinese soldiers.

Bo Thura shrugged philosophically. "I'll get another," he said.

"I'm sure you will," Andrew said, "but that doesn't help young Mary or your cause with the Chief Commissioner."

As *Kaw Byoo's* crew checked the refugees' documentation, Captain Terndrup took a small boat over to the Burmese vessel. Watching through his field glasses, Andrew saw him speaking to the Governor. After a few moments of heated debate, Terndrup returned to his ship. He spoke to *Kaw Byoo's* officers first, climbed to her upper deck, and lifted a metal speaking trumpet.

"Silence!" Terndrup shouted and had one of his Burmese crew translate his words to the anxious refugees. "The Burmese Governor of Bhamo has granted me permission to take a party ashore and gather up all the European civilians who wish to leave. I will guarantee a place on the ship to any armed men who accompany me."

Andrew turned to Bo Thura, who shook his head and withdrew into the crowd.

"Bo Thura!" Andrew stretched out a hand.

"Let him go," Than Than Aye said quickly. "Captain Terndrup knows who he is."

Andrew nodded and pushed Than Than Aye and Mary towards the captain. "I'll come if you take this woman and child to safety."

Captain Terndrup frowned. "That is not what I said."

"This lady helped me rescue the little girl from her kidnappers," Andrew explained, finding it a strain to shout above the crowd's clamour. "I am Captain Andrew Baird of the Natal Dragoons."

"A soldier?" Terndrup replied. "I need all the experienced men I can get." He glanced at Than Than Aye and Mary. "Agreed, Captain Baird. Bring them on board."

Andrew expected the protests from the Europeans when Than Than Aye stepped forward. "But she's a Burman!" a red-faced merchant said. "The captain said he'd rescue the Europeans. I'm English, damn it!"

Terndrup ignored the howls as Andrew escorted Than Than Aye through the crowd and onto the gangplank.

"Don't stay on deck," Andrew hissed in Than Than Aye's ear. "Get inside where nobody can see you and keep safe. I'll find you later." He gave her a gentle push. "Go on! Ignore the shine." * He stepped to the captain's side.

"Mr Higgins!" Captain Terndrup shouted to the mate. "You take charge of the ship. Don't let anybody board until we return. Captain Baird, you are with me."

"Yes, sir," Andrew agreed.

Two more volunteers joined Terndrup's eight-strong force that trotted into Bhamo, with the Chinese and Burmese soldiers watching from a distance.

"We have a few American missionaries to rescue first," Captain Terndrup said. "Then I believe some Europeans have gathered in one house near the town centre." He looked around as a crowd of Burmese followed the landing party, with some howling abuse and others throwing stones and handfuls of mud.

"They don't seem to like us very much," Terndrup told Andrew.

"They were slaughtering each other and robbing the town blind yesterday," Andrew told him. "They don't like anybody very much."

A force of wild-looking irregular soldiers stood before the American missionary church, with a smartly dressed official in charge.

"Captain Terndrup?" the official stepped forward as the landing party halted, unsure what to expect.

"I am Terndrup," the captain stepped forward, with Andrew keeping his revolver ready.

"The Reverend Soltan is waiting for you with his people," the official said. "I am Kiugkwek-li, in command of the Chinese in Bhamo."

Terndrup bowed politely, then held out his hand. "Thank you for meeting me, Kiugkwek-li."

The two men examined each other with evident mutual respect.

"If there is anything I can do for you, Kiugkwek-li," Terndrup said. "I will be happy to oblige."

The Chinese official, tall, refined and elegant, nodded. "If you come across a Burmese dacoit called Bo Thura on your ship," he said. "Hold him for me."

"I'll do that," Terndrup nodded grimly. "Bo Thura. I know the name."

Kiugkwek-li is the Chinese official who has fallen out with Bo Thura. Is this attack

* Ignore the shine: ignore the noise.

part of Chinese policy? Or is it a personal hunt for my cousin? Either way, it's no wonder Bo Thura did not try to board Kaw Byoo.

The Americans came out slowly and noisily: a small group of missionaries, their wives, and a larger number of Karen followers and Christian converts.

The Reverend Soltan, a grave, dignified man with a long face and spectacles, bowed to Kiugkwek-li and formally thanked him for his assistance.

They spoke briefly as the Chinese soldiers helped the missionaries from the building, and then Kiugkwek-li spoke again to Captain Terndrup.

"We cannot endure Burmese oppression of our people any longer, Captain," Kiugkwek-li said. "When you return to Bhamo, China will be in charge. We will keep the country as far south as Mandalay and leave the British to hold the remainder."

"I look forward to seeing you again, sir," Captain Terndrup replied without committing himself to any political opinion.

"We will rid the area of the robbers and thieves," Kiugkwek-li said. "Especially the one known as Bo Thura!" He looked around as if expecting Bo Thura to spring from behind a building.

With the Americans safely beside Captain Terndrup, Kiugkwek-li's soldiers provided an escort to the second group of European refugees.

"Out you come!" Andrew shouted. "These Chinese lads are helping!"

The Europeans stared out fearfully, realised it was safe and emerged in a flood, some carrying cases and a few with Burmese or Karen servants laden with their possessions.

"The ship is waiting," Captain Terndrup said. "Form up in an orderly fashion!"

The civilians made a noisy mob, jostling for position as they followed Captain Terndrup. Some eyed the Chinese with disfavour, and a couple demanded priority treatment as they claimed to be important people.

"Get in line there!" Andrew snarled. "We are all in the same position."

When the Chinese escort left, the Burmese pressed closer, a mixture of soldiers and civilians taunting the European refugees. Andrew pushed one wiry youth back when he grabbed a woman's bags.

"Sir," Andrew approached Terndrup. "I think the armed men should be around the civilians to keep the rabble at bay."

"Do that, Captain Baird," Terndrup said. "I'll put you in charge of the escort."

Andrew nodded and snapped orders to the armed men.

"Two on each side, two in front and two in the rear! Keep a space between our people and the mob. Don't shoot anybody, and don't start trouble, but use a firm hand to show we mean business."

With the howling crowd in front and pressing on the sides, progress to the ship was slow.

"Push them aside!" Andrew hurried to the front of the European column when a surge of Burmese soldiers threatened them. He raised his voice to a roar. "Move aside there! Make way!" He pushed a snarling man out of the way, ducked as somebody swung a stick at him, felled the attacker with a right hook and gestured for the column to move forward.

"They're chanting 'kill the foreigners,'" a frightened merchant said. "They're baying for our blood."

"They can bay all they like," Andrew said, shoving a loud-voiced man aside. "They weren't so brave when the Chinese invaded." He raised his voice. "Push on, Captain Terndrup!"

Andrew circled the refugees, helping the inexperienced civilians and sailors with their unaccustomed duty. He grunted as a stone smashed into his head, opening a cut, looked for the thrower and saw only a mass of shouting faces.

"Get away!" Andrew grabbed a roaring Burmese by the arm and dragged him away. He kicked savagely at a gesticulating man who had grabbed a Karen woman by the hair and punched another in the face. "Keep moving, Captain!"

Andrew felt blood flowing down his face; he blocked a youth's flying kick and lifted one of the escort, whom three men had knocked down.

This escape is getting ugly. I hope there's not much further to the quay.

The crowd grew denser as more Burmans realised the Chinese escort had left, with rushes at the refugees and more missiles flying. Stones bounced off the road in front, women hurried their children away from the mob, and men tried to protect their wives.

"Push through!" Andrew said, encouraging the escort. He saw one of the sailors stagger as a stone cracked against his head and searched for the stone thrower without success. He knew that such people usually hid at the back of the mob, using others as shelter.

"You cowardly bastard!" Andrew roared, knowing his words were useless against the noise of the mob.

"Here's the quay!" a man shouted.

The mate had held *Kaw Byoo* secure and now ordered the crew to clear the gangplank. The crew pushed down, some with long staves, as they pushed the waiting crowd back.

"Make way! Make way, damn you!" The crew, British and Burmese, struggled against the press of civilians as missiles flew to clatter against *Kaw Byoo's* hull and bounce from her deck. Some hit the sailors or landed amidst the refugee column.

Captain Terndrup stood aside and ushered the refugees on board, with the crowd on the quay pressing forward to escape from Bhamo.

Andrew stood on the opposite side of the narrow gangplank to the captain, ensuring nobody fell into the water. He saw Than Than Aye on the ship, looking strained as she held Mary tight by the hand and watched the crowd clamour to get aboard.

"Get inside!" Andrew roared. "Than Than Aye! Get away from the deck! It's unsafe." He did not know if Than Than Aye heard him as the last refugees swarmed up the gangplank.

"That's them all on!" Terndrup shouted. "Is steam up, Mr Higgins?"

"All ready, sir!" the mate replied.

“Then let the others on board and stand by to depart!” Terndrup ordered. “Captain Baird! Get the escort on board as quickly as possible.”

“Yes, sir!” Andrew said no more as his men hurried onto the ship. The first of the crowd followed, kicking, punching, and pushing each other in their panic to escape Bhamo.

“Form an orderly queue!” Andrew shouted. He saw one overweight man shove a slender woman aside and thrust forward, with a young lad crawling between others’ legs and snaking on board. The slender woman fell into the water between *Kaw Byoo* and the shore. A man with two screaming children tried to rush the gangplank until a group of active young men elbowed them aside.

Terndrup looked up as gunshots sounded from the town.

“Get the last of these people on board!”

“We can’t take any more!” Higgins replied. “We’re already overcrowded.”

“All right! Cast off aft! Cast off forward! Let’s get away from here!”

Andrew saw one woman make a despairing leap from the quay to reach *Kaw Byoo* but fall short and land in the water. She began to swim to the ship until one of the sailors threw her a line. When she grabbed hold, the seamen pulled her in.

“There you are, darling, safe as the Bank of England, now!”

Andrew heard the shooting increase as he approached Than Than Aye and Mary.

That’s the first part over, but now we must pass through Upper Burma.

He patted the French documents in his inside pocket and wondered what Sir Charles Crossthwaite would say.

CHAPTER 16

IRRAWADDY RIVER, KINGDOM OF AVA, DECEMBER 1884

Andrew heard the first shots only an hour after *Kaw Byoo* left Bhamo. An unseen rifleman fired from the forest, with one bullet hissing over the steamer and the second boring a hole in the hull. One of the passengers screamed, and there was a minor stampede to get inside the frail protection of the interior.

"Is this normal?" Andrew asked Captain Terndrup.

The captain had not flinched. "It happens," he said. "Sometimes they shoot at us, sometimes they leave us alone." He shrugged. "They've never stopped us yet."

Andrew remembered his father's tales about tribesmen sniping at convoys passing through the Khyber Pass and wondered at the mentality of the snipers.

Perhaps they just don't like the British in their country, or are just natural predators.

Even with the current on their side, *Kaw Byoo* seemed to take an age to travel downriver. The steamer was overcrowded, with no space on board to stretch out. Food was limited, and the smell of human sweat and fear was overpowering.

After two days, another unidentified man shot at *Kaw Byoo.* Andrew saw him run along the riverbank, trying to keep pace with the steamer.

"Give me that Snider," Andrew asked. He took a packet of ammunition from behind the wheel, rammed in a cartridge and ran on deck. The shooter was a hundred yards in front of the steamer, using a tree bough as a rifle rest.

"Shoot him!" the overweight merchant shouted. "Kill him!"

Andrew aimed, took first pressure on the trigger, allowed for the speed of *Kaw Byoo* and fired an instant before the attacker. He saw his shot hit the ground an inch in front of the marksman and raise a fountain of dirt.

"You missed!" the overweight man accused bitterly.

"I know," Andrew said. "Look at the lad. He can't be more than fourteen years old." He felt Than Than Aye watching him, reloaded the Snider, and watched the marksman run across a flooded paddy field, leaving his musket behind. *Kaw Byoo* chugged on, keeping to the deep-water channel as Andrew appointed himself sentry.

"You could have killed that boy," Than Than Aye said.

"He was only a boy," Andrew replied. "A youth testing his masculinity. I gave him a fright, and no harm done."

Than Than Aye touched his arm, nodded thoughtfully and walked away.

ANDREW KEPT THAN THAN AYE AND MARY OUT OF SIGHT WHEN THEY berthed at Mandalay. "I don't know who might recognise you," he said.

"I'll keep out of the way," Than Than Aye promised.

Andrew watched as most of the Burmese and Karen refugees left the ship. As the crew loaded coal and supplies from the terminal's ample supplies, a few Europeans boarded. Three of the new arrivals noticed Than Than Aye with Mary and asked a hundred questions that Andrew was not keen to answer.

"Is that your child?" A bumptious man nudged Andrew and pointed to Mary. "I said, is that your child?"

"I'm looking after her," Andrew replied.

"You aren't doing a very good job, are you?" the man laughed at his pretended humour. "She looks rather, well, rather like a Burman, doesn't she? Tanned and ragged. You're not going native, are you?"

When Andrew gave a non-committal reply and turned away, the man shook his head and addressed his fellow Europeans.

"That fellow's a damned jungle wallah. That woman he's with is probably his mistress and the child; Good God! The child will be their offspring, like as not."

"That type gives us all a bad name," another man said. "It shouldn't be allowed."

When Andrew turned angrily Than Than Aye put a small hand on his arm. "Do they matter, Andrew?"

Andrew took a deep breath. "No," he said.

"Do their opinions matter?"

"No," Andrew replied.

Than Than Aye smiled. "They are small people with inflated opinions and, as such, are best ignored."

Andrew nodded. "You're a clever woman, Than Than Aye."

"I am not very clever," Than Than Aye replied. "I just understand people. There won't be any trouble if we keep out of their way."

"That's good advice," Andrew replied. "It will be a long journey to Rangoon."

"Every minute survived is a minute less," Than Than Aye said, smiling.

❄

Andrew stepped from *Kaw Byoo* at Rangoon with Than Than Aye at his side and Mary in his arms. He looked around, feeling strange in this urban environment, with European traders around him and English spoken as often as Burmese. The noise and bustle were slightly intimidating after his time in Upper Burma.

"I've never been to Rangoon before," Than Than Aye kept close to Andrew, staring around her. "I've never seen so many Europeans in one place."

"You're part European yourself," Andrew reminded her. "You have as much right here as they have. Probably more, as you're three-quarters Burmese in Burma and you're quarter British in a British possession." He grinned at her. "You belong to both worlds. Stay close to me, Than Than Aye."

"Where are you going?" Than Than Aye asked, holding his arm.

"We're going to hand Mary over to her mother," Andrew said.

"Shouldn't you give her to the authorities? Maybe to Sir Charles Crossthwaite?"

"Probably," Andrew said, "but if I know anything about officials, they'd make Mary's mother jump through hoops to get her back. They'd ignore Bo Thura's supposed part and claim all the credit for themselves. On the other hand, if Mary's mother has her child, she'll never let her go, and the Press will write columns about it. They love such a story."

"Is it good that the Press should write a story about Mary?" Than Than Aye pressed closer to Andrew as a dark blue Brougham carriage whirred past with two matching grey horses pulling hard. The man inside looked vaguely familiar as he stared out of the window at them.

"A newspaper column will give Bo Thura maximum publicity, so his name is known as the man who rescued Mary from the evil dacoits," Andrew explained. "Indeed, let's stop at the *Times of India's* offices and pass the word." He held Than Than Aye's arm reassuringly. "It's all right. Let me do the talking."

The clerk at the *Times* office looked up without interest as Andrew entered. "Yes?" he said with a look of disdain. Andrew realised the clerk would see him as a travel-stained, unkempt man with a Burmese woman and a rough-looking red-haired child.

The clerk spoke quickly. "Is it an advertisement you want to place? If you're seeking employment, you've come to the wrong place. We've no vacancies, and the coolies get all the labouring jobs anyway."

"Who is your chief reporter?" Andrew asked.

"Charles Mulhanney," the clerk replied. "Why? Do you want to report a missing bar of soap?" He smirked at his attempted humour.

"No," Andrew told him. "I want to report a found child. Tell him that Mary MacConnacher will soon be back with her mother, thanks to the help of a Burman called Bo Thura." Andrew leaned across the polished desk, took hold of the clerk's collar, and pulled him closer. "Will you pass that information on?"

"Yes, sir!" the clerk said, nodding violently.

"Good man," Andrew said, replacing him on his feet. Ignoring the clerk's astonishment, Andrew turned on his heel and stalked away with Than Than Aye at his side.

"He wasn't a pleasant man," Than Than Aye said, looking at Andrew with amused eyes.

"Men with a little authority often like to abuse what they think is their power," Andrew said. He led them towards the British Cantonment, shielding Mary from the worst of the noise and ignoring the curious glances of passers-by. With his ragged clothes and days-old beard, he knew he must look like the wild man of the woods, while Than Than Aye wore the clothes of an up-country villager rather than the more sophisticated clothing of the town.

The sentry at the cantonment gate stared as Andrew approached. "Who the hell are you, then, chum?"

"Captain Andrew Baird of the Natal Dragoons," Andrew said, "Stand aside and let me pass."

"Pull the other one, mate; it plays *My Grandfather's Clock*," the sentry held his Martini-Henry across his chest. "Off you go, now, and take your little winker with you."*

Andrew kept his patience, feeling Mary stirring in his arms. "Tell your sergeant I have arrived," Andrew said, putting an edge in his voice. "And be quick about it!"

The sentry stiffened, recognising the voice of authority. "Yes, sir." He stepped back and raised his voice. "Sergeant!"

"What's the to-do?" The sergeant was in his late thirties with a world-weary look in his eyes. He looked at Andrew. "Who are you?"

"Captain Andrew Baird of the Natal Dragoons, and this child," Andrew held up Mary, "is Mary MacConnacher."

The sergeant stared at Andrew, then at Mary and back at Andrew. "Good God in Heaven, sir. How did you manage to rescue her?"

"I didn't," Andrew said. "A Burmese gentleman named Bo Thura rescued her and contacted me. May we come in?"

"Yes, sir," the sergeant said. "Sanderson, tell Major Goudie what's happening. Come in, sir, and the lady, too."

The news had spread before Andrew reached the Royal Scots Fusiliers' quarters, and he saw a black-haired woman running across the maidan with her clothes loose around her and her bare feet flapping on the ground.

"My baby! Mary! My Mary!"

Mrs MacConnacher nearly threw herself at Andrew in her eagerness to regain her child, with scores of soldiers in all states of dress and undress hurrying across the maidan to witness the reunion.

"Oh, sir! How can I thank you?" Mrs MacConnacher asked, holding Mary tightly as tears flooded from her eyes. "Oh, Mary, what have they done to you?"

---

* Winker: a bright-eyed young woman, sometimes by association a prostitute, mistress or lover.

The familiar sight of Major Goudie stalked across to Andrew. "It's yourself, Captain Baird! Well done, sir, well done indeed! Let me shake your hand." He looked Andrew up and down.

"Captain Baird! Well, bless my soul! Well, Captain, whatever else you do in your life, you have performed a noble deed by rescuing this child from the grasp of the barbarians. Whatever else you might achieve in your career, you will never be forgotten, sir. Mark my words."

Andrew saw a smartly dressed civilian approaching and guessed it was the reporter from the *Times of India*. He waited until the reporter was within earshot.

"I did nothing," Andrew said. "All credit must go to Bo Thura, the Burmese gentleman who rescued the child and notified me."

"What was that name again?" the reporter asked. "Bo Thura? How do you spell that?"

"How the devil should I know how he spells his blasted name?" Andrew asked testily. "Spell it any way you like? You reporters usually do, anyway."

Than Than Aye stretched out a hand to Mary as Mrs MacConnacher took her confused and crying daughter away.

"No more *kyawal* for her," Andrew said quietly, remembering Aung Thiha laughing as he acted like a buffalo and carried Mary on his back. "Mary will never forget you," he said.

"Nor will I forget her," Than Than Aye said. "You'd better return to Mariana, Andrew, or she'll think you have forgotten her."

Andrew nodded. "Thank you," he said as Than Than Aye smiled, turned, and walked gracefully away, swinging her hips to tease him. He saw the blue Brougham coach again, with the curtains inside the windows twitching as if the occupant was watching him.

MARIANA STARED AS SHE OPENED HER DOOR, AND ANDREW SMILED AT HER. "I thought the Burmans had killed you," she said quietly. "I've had no news for ever so long."

"It was a bit hectic," Andrew slumped onto a chair. "And the telegraphic and postal system in Upper Burma leaves a lot to be desired."

Mariana nodded. "You look awful," she said.

"You don't," Andrew replied. He grinned. "I've been looking forward to this minute for a long time. Let me look at you."

Mariana stood within the door, with a beam of sunlight from the window highlighting her hair. Her eyes were busy on Andrew, and concern shadowed her pleasure. "Where have you been, Andrew? It's been months."

"It feels like years," Andrew told her.

Mariana took the sun well despite the bonnets that hung from pegs on the wall. An elegant blue dress hugged her curves as it extended to the ground. Andrew thought of another woman in a blue longyi and shivered. *How could I ever have looked at anybody else?*

"We can't have you walking around like that," Mariana said firmly. "Look at you! Even the cat wouldn't drag you in!"

Than Than Aye would say something like that. Mariana is growing more like Than Than Aye all the time.

Andrew caught himself in the oval mirror on the wall. He had lost about a stone, his cheekbones prominent above an unshaven face, while his eyes seemed huge and staring. His clothes were rumpled, faded, and roughly patched. "Give me a minute, and I'll tidy myself up," Andrew said.

"You'll do more than tidy yourself up," Mariana said. "It's a bath for you, Andrew, before anything else, and we'll get rid of these clothes! Have you been rolling in mud?"

"It's been an interesting time," Andrew replied. He looked Mariana up and down, enjoying her company, and reminded himself of her movements, manner of speech, and even the hidden smile in her eyes. "I've missed you."

Mariana started. "I've missed you, too," she said.

"We have much to catch up on," Andrew told her.

"I heard you brought little Mary MacConnacher home," Mariana said. "How was she?"

"She was fine," Andrew said. "As long as her mother doesn't mind her smoking cigars." He laughed at Mariana's expression. "I'll explain later."

"Why not explain now?" Mariana asked.

"I can't stay long," Andrew said. "Sir Charles Crossthwaite wants to see me."

"The Chief Commissioner?" Mariana looked impressed. "You'd better get ready, Andrew." She stepped closer. "Try not to be long."

"I'll try my best," Andrew promised.

"SIR!" ANDREW STOOD AT ATTENTION. EVEN AFTER MARIANA'S ministrations, he knew he looked shabby, with his Natal Dragoons uniform smelling of mothballs and unfamiliar in Rangoon, while he was underweight and drawn with hardship.

The Chief Commissioner's office was resplendent with polished teak and brass. His desk was tidy, and a map of Lower Burma dominated one wall.

"Captain Baird," Sir Charles eyed Andrew up and down. "You've been through the mill, I hear."

"It's been interesting, sir," Andrew agreed.

Sir Charles nodded. "You helped the Royal Scots Fusiliers repel a dacoit attack on a Burmese village."

"I played a small part, sir. Major Goudie was in command."

"And you were at the massacres in Mandalay."

"Yes, sir," Andrew said.

"And saw the Chinese invasion of Bhamo."

"I did, sir," Andrew said. "The Chinese were no threat to us, sir. They treated us well."

"Indeed," Sir Charles indicated that Andrew should sit down. "Yet you still managed to bring young Mary MacConnacher home."

"Than Than Aye helped, sir, and Bo Thura had her safe and well." Andrew did not mention that Bo Thura had kidnapped Mary. "Indeed, Bo Thura brought my attention to her plight."

"Why did this dacoit contact you, Baird? He could have handed the child to any British post."

Andrew had anticipated the question. "We have a slight family connection, sir. My father met Bo Thura's father in the last Burmese War, back in Fifty-two."

"Your father being Major-General Windrush," Sir Charles said.

"That's correct, sir," Andrew agreed.

When the Governor nodded, Andrew wondered how much he already knew or guessed.

"Very good," Sir Charles said. "However, this information far surpasses all the rest." He lifted the document that Andrew had carried back from Bhamo. "Do you know the contents, Baird?"

"No, sir. It was sealed when Bo Thura handed it to me, and I didn't break the seal."

Sir Charles grunted. "Very commendable. If it's genuine, and I have no reason to doubt its accuracy, this document is a copy of a secret treaty between King Thibaw and France. It gives railway concessions in Upper Burma to France with interest on profits going to Thibaw." Sir Charles looked up. "The Kingdom of Ava is quite cash-strapped, despite Thibaw taxing the gambling dens he encouraged."

"I noticed gambling dens in most of the towns in Upper Burma, sir," Andrew agreed.

"Yes." The Chief Commissioner returned his attention to the document. "This agreement allows France to establish a bank in Mandalay, with France securing the finances by controlling all the customs receipts on the Irrawaddy River." He looked at Andrew. "As we control most of the commercial river traffic, Baird, the French will be raking in tax money from us."

"Yes, sir." Andrew could understand how that would rankle among the British commercial world. "The Irrawaddy Flotilla Company or the Bombay and Burmah Trading Corporation would not appreciate paying money to French tax collectors."

"Indeed," the Governor said. "The French would also gain the revenue from the tea trade and the Burmese ruby mines."

Andrew took a deep breath. "It seems the French would control Upper Burma in all but name. I wonder what Thibaw gets out of this arrangement?"

Sir Charles gave a faint smile. "I have not finished yet. You may not have heard the latest while you were gallivanting around Upper Burma, rescuing children and battling stray dacoits."

"What has happened, sir?" Andrew asked.

"Thibaw's officials claim that the Bombay and Burmah Trading Company have been underreporting the volume of teak it fells and exports and has not been paying its employees."

Andrew remembered the men and elephants working the teak forests. "Are the allegations true, sir?"

"No!" Sir Charles snapped. "The Burman officials are corrupt."

"What was the result, sir?"

"The Burmans are demanding the company pays twenty-three lakhs of rupees to Thibaw, under pain of forfeiture of their forests."*

"I see," Andrew said.

"I suspect that some French company will move into Bombay and Burma's place the day they leave," the Governor said. He leaned back in his padded leather chair, put the document on his desk and pressed his hands together. "You have provided me with some interesting information, Captain."

"Yes, sir," Andrew said. "It was all from Bo Thura, sir. I was merely the carrier."

"Quite," Sir Charles replied. "I have heard a rumour, a shave as you military people call it, that the French consul in Rangoon boasts the British need French permission even to enter Mandalay."

Andrew shook his head. "That's inaccurate, sir. I would estimate that three-quarters of the Europeans in Mandalay are British."

Sir Charles nodded again. "I'd rather believe that than the word of some Frenchman. Remind me, Baird; who is this fellow who found this document?"

"A man named Bo Thura, sir. The same gentleman who showed me where Mary was."

"What did he want in return?"

"A free pardon for past misdeeds and permission to live in British Burma," Andrew said. "He asked me to request a written pardon and a safe conduct from you before he arrives."

The Chief Commissioner pressed his fingers harder together. "Why doesn't he just cross the frontier, Captain?"

"He's afraid the British will hold his past misdeeds against him, sir," Andrew replied. "He has been a dacoit in the past but is now a reformed character."

"I'll look into it," Sir Charles promised. "If this fellow is wanted for a serious crime, such as murder or rape, any pardon is out of the question."

Andrew touched the French document. "Even though he found us evidence of this treaty, sir? And helped restore Mary to her family?"

"As I said, Captain Baird, I will investigate it. The fate of one dacoit, reformed or not, pales into insignificance beside our international obligations and difficulties. I'll contact the Secretary of State for India with details of this treaty and release the main facts to the press." He grinned. "That should alarm the French."

"Yes, sir. And Bo Thura?"

---

* A lakh is a hundred thousand, so twenty-three lakhs is two million, three hundred thousand.

"I told you I'd investigate his case. When I've made my decision, I'll let you know. Good day, sir."

"Good day, sir," Andrew replied.

He breathed deeply when he left the government building, for dealing with officialdom always drained him. The bustle of Rangoon's streets was almost a relief.

"Andrew?" Mariana hurried to meet him. "How did it go?"

"How is it always with government officials?" Andrew said. "One-sided and vague. We'll have to wait and see."

Mariana opened her parasol to shade her face from the sun. "It's good to have you back," she said. "Now you can tell me your adventures."

"And you can tell me yours," Andrew said. He ignored the dark blue Brougham that whirred past.

CHAPTER 17

RANGOON, LOWER BURMA, 1885

When the press published what they knew of the treaty between France and Upper Burma, the British merchants in Rangoon were outraged, which, Andrew suspected, was what Sir Charles had intended.

"Allow the French to inspect our ships on the Irrawaddy?" Jennings said as he read the *Times of India* before dinner. "I'll be damned if that's going to happen. By God, we'll fight them."

"Fight who?" Andrew sat in the hotel's foyer, sipping his whisky and water and watching the world go by.

"We'll fight the French, by God," Jennings said. "And King Thibaw."

Andrew watched Mariana descend the stairs. He thought she looked immensely graceful. *Mariana has matured into an exceptionally beautiful lady. She was right to turn down my marriage proposition. She can do far better than me.*

"What are you two discussing so passionately?" Mariana asked, smiling at both as they stood for her.

"International relations," Andrew told her. "We're putting the world to rights."

Jennings was two steps ahead and pulled out a chair.

Mariana slid gracefully into the chair, politely thanked Jennings and looked around the foyer. "It's busy in here this evening."

"This French nonsense has brought people together," Jennings said. "There might be war, and that could be bad for business."

"Jennings has been telling me he's going to take the Queen's Shilling, or the

Empress's Shilling now, and chase the French out of Thibaw's kingdom." Andrew enjoyed Jennings' reaction.*

"I am not joining the army," Jennings denied immediately. "I meant Britain might fight the French, not me personally."

"Ah," Andrew said. "My apologies, Jennings. I must have misunderstood."

"I'm sure you would be a fine soldier, Mr Jennings," Mariana said. "You're tall, strong and commanding." She smiled, brushing back an imaginary loose strand of hair. "I think you'd look very dashing in a scarlet dress uniform."

Andrew looked from Mariana to Jennings and back. *What's this? Has my Mariana found another sweetheart?* Andrew lifted his glass and examined Jennings over the rim. *He is presentable, I'll grant you, if not quite to my taste. I would count my fingers after I shook his hand, but women have different ideas than men.*

Mariana caught Andrew's gaze. "Mr Jennings has been looking after me," Mariana said.

"That's good," Andrew replied with what he hoped was a smile. "Did you need looking after?"

Mariana coloured. "I was a bit lonely," she said. "You were away longer than I expected."

"I was away longer than I expected, too," Andrew replied.

"I counted the three weeks you said," Mariana said, "and then three more weeks, and another three until I quite filled my journal with little numbers and crosses."

"I am sure the good Captain was doing his duty, Miss Maxwell," Jennings said. "The *Times of India* mentioned some of your exploits, Captain Baird. You did excellent work when you rescued that little girl."

"Thank you," Andrew said. He looked up when the door banged open, and a harassed-looking lieutenant entered.

"I am looking for Captain Baird," the lieutenant announced. "Captain Andrew Baird of the Natal Dragoons."

"That's me," Andrew admitted, raising a hand.

The lieutenant approached, standing to attention a yard from the table. "The Chief Commissioner sends his compliments, sir, and would like a word with you whenever it is convenient."

Andrew glanced at the suddenly silent Mariana. "Now would be a good time," he said. "Will you be all right alone for a time, Mariana?"

"I'll be fine, Captain Baird," Mariana replied formally and forced a smile. "Mr Jennings will keep me company again. Your duty must come first."

"Sir Charles will want to tell me he's pardoned Bo Thura," Andrew said.

"Duty must always come first," Jennings echoed as Andrew followed the lieutenant out of the room.

* In 1877, the British Prime Minister, Benjamin Disraeli, proclaimed Queen Victoria as Empress of India.

Sir Charles nodded to Andrew from behind his desk. "Sit down, Captain Baird."

Andrew sat, listening to the fan creaking above his head. He glanced over the desk, hoping to see a Commissioner's Pardon.

Sir Charles looked up from an open file. "You have seen active service in Africa, I believe."

"Yes, sir, against the Galekas, Zulus and Boers."

Sir Charles nodded. "And you know something of Burma."

"Not much, sir."

"You've visited Mandalay and as far north as Bhamo, which is a damned sight more than most have done. Is that not correct?"

"Yes, sir."

Sir Charles held Andrew's gaze. "Good. We are perilously short of experienced officers here, and those blasted dacoits are causing no end of trouble."

Andrew guessed what was coming. "I only came here to rescue Mary MacConnacher, sir. As soon as you grant Bo Thura a pardon, I will let him know and get back home."

Sir Charles fixed a cold eye on Andrew. "I may grant Bo Thura a pardon, Baird. That depends on his behaviour. In the meantime, I am going to send you to the Royal Scots Fusiliers."

Andrew understood the unspoken threat. If he turned down the appointment, the Governor would not grant Bo Thura's pardon. "Yes, sir."

Sir Charles continued, "The Scots Fusiliers headquarters company is based in Rangoon Cantonments, and they have detachments all along the frontier, trying to prevent the dacoits from infiltrating from Upper Burma. They circulate their rifle companies, leaving one in Rangoon to aid the police."

"I see, sir," Andrew said.

"The colonel of the Royal Scots Fusiliers and I want you to take command of a mobile patrol of Burmese Police and Fusiliers and guard the outskirts of Rangoon from dacoits."

"Yes, sir," Andrew replied.

"Your experience fighting in South Africa will come in handy, Captain. You'll have a free hand to organise your men and a roving commission, which suits you colonial soldiers." Sir Charles smiled encouragingly.

When will I get home? I've had enough of Burma.

"You'll be keen to get started, Captain," Sir Charles said. "I hope you have success against the dacoits."

"I'll try my best, sir," Andrew promised. "And please don't forget Bo Thura's rescue of Mary MacConnacher."

"Good day to you, Captain Baird," Sir Charles replied.

"Good day, sir," Andrew left the building and saw Than Than Aye standing on the opposite side of the street.

JENNINGS SMILED AT MARIANA ACROSS THE RIM OF HIS GLASS. "CAPTAIN Andrew is no sooner back than he's away again, hobnobbing with the Chief Commissioner, no less." He sighed. "Maybe he's too good for the likes of us."

"Andrew is not that way inclined," Mariana replied.

Jennings laughed. "I didn't for a second think he was. All in jest, my dear Miss Maxwell. All in jest." He poured them both more wine. "I see your Captain Andrew brought a little friend back from Upper Burma with him."

"Yes," Mariana said. "Young Mary MacConnacher. He rescued her from the dacoits. All the papers are full of it." She sipped at her wine. "But you know that already."

"Not young Mary; I know all about her." Jennings shook his head. "The other one."

"Which other one?" Mariana asked.

"Didn't you know?" Jennings raised his eyebrows. "I thought he would have told you. When Captain Andrew returned from the Kingdom of Ava, he brought a woman with him. I happened to pass them when I was in my carriage."

"What woman?" Mariana asked with her heart thundering inside her chest.

"Surely he's introduced her to you?" Jennings shook his head. "Some oversight, then. He's probably been too busy with all his official business." He smiled. "You know how these soldiers are. Everything is duty, duty, duty, and the rest of the world gets pushed aside. He'll be with her now, like as not, or as soon as the Chief Commissioner finishes with him."

"Oh," Mariana stood up. "I must see this mysterious woman."

Jennings stood politely. "I doubt you have anything to worry about, Miss Maxwell. If you ask him, I am sure he will explain."

"Oh, it will be nothing," Mariana said, forcing a smile. "Even so, I must ask him about this lady he so conveniently forgot to mention."

"It's probably perfectly innocent," Jennings said.

"I am sure it is," Mariana replied. Lifting her skirt, she swept out of the hotel, leaving Jennings alone at the table. He smiled after her, sat down, and ordered another drink.

Mariana hurried from the hotel, ignoring the usual beggars as she paced to the Chief Commissioner's office, where Andrew had headed.

I don't believe Andrew has found another woman, but why shouldn't he? I turned him down. He has every right to find somebody else.

Mariana stopped as she saw Andrew a hundred yards ahead, talking with a woman. She was tall for a Burmese, slender and straight-backed, and her faded blue longyi fitted snugly to her body.

Oh, God, she's beautiful. Andrew!

Mariana watched as Andrew and the woman spoke together, seemingly lost in each other's company. The woman laughed and placed a proprietorial hand on Andrew's arm. Mariana could see her affection as she spoke.

She knows him well. They must have met in Mandalay. Was that why he was so long up there? Was he with that woman all this time?

Mariana slid into a doorway to watch, feeling her heart race. *Now, I am a*

Peeping Tom, spying on a man who has always done his very best for me. She again remembered rejecting Andrew's marriage proposal in Edinburgh and wondered if that had chased him away forever.

Andrew! Why didn't you understand? It's not that I don't want you, and you know I love you. I am just not ready for marriage yet. Something is missing. I don't know if you want me for myself or if you want a substitute for my sister. And there is that shadow in my mind.

I don't know, Andrew!

Andrew spoke again, and the woman replied, apparently explaining something in great detail.

What is she telling him? I wish I could hear.

Mariana tried to ease closer, but a bullock cart passed, with the two animals clopping their hooves on the ground, and the ungreased wheels squeaking so loudly they blocked out every other sound. When the cart passed, Mariana looked for Andrew and saw him walking away with the woman at his side.

Damn and blast! Mariana used one of Andrew's favourite expressions when he was frustrated. *Double damn and blast. Now, I will never know. I can't tell him I was spying on him.*

Mariana felt sick as she watched Andrew and Than Than Aye walk away.

What should I do?

CHAPTER 18

RANGOON, LOWER BURMA, JANUARY 1885

Andrew looked over his men. He had one young lieutenant, a sergeant, two corporals, and a Sikh havildar. They commanded twenty Fusiliers and twenty police, equally divided between Sikhs and local Burmese. The Fusiliers looked like typical British infantry, mostly small-made men from the industrial slums of west central Scotland with a sprinkling of beefy countrymen of Ayrshire. He had hand-picked Corporals McGhee and Rowan, remembering them from the skirmish beside the Irrawaddy. Andrew knew he would get to know the rest over the next few weeks and months.

The Sikhs were brawny, bearded, and bold, eyeing him without expression, while the Burmese were stocky, agile, and alert. Andrew recognised Sukhbir Singh, the Sikh havildar.

"We'll make these men into an efficient force," Andrew told the lieutenant.

"Yes, sir," Lieutenant Morton agreed, with the sweat beading on his sunburned face.

"We've met before, Havildar," Andrew said to Sukhbir Singh.

"Yes, Sahib," Sukhbir Singh was a tall man with a neat beard and three medal ribbons.

"I want two groups of ten police and ten soldiers. Lieutenant Morton will take one group, and I'll take the other. You know the police best, Havildar, so organise them equally."

"Yes, Sahib."

"I'll address the men first," Andrew said.

"Yes, Sahib," Sukhbir Singh replied without any facial expression.

"The dacoits have been operating at will throughout British Burma," Andrew told them. "Our intelligence people believe they intend to strike at

Rangoon soon." He waited until his words were translated. "I intend to ensure that does not happen."

After acting as a static garrison in Rangoon, the Fusiliers looked pleased at the prospect of action. The Sikhs grinned when the translator passed on the information, while the Burmese remained impassive. Andrew wondered how many understood what he said.

"We will operate at night," Andrew said. "That's when the dacoits terrorise the innocent villagers, so that is when we will hunt them down."

The men nodded again. They understood the idea, but Andrew wondered if they had the ability or training to work at night. He thought the dacoits would run rings around both British and Sikhs, while Andrew wondered if the Burmans had the motivation to be a useful force.

"We'll start training tonight," Andrew said. "The Burmese police will instruct us in the local terrain, and we'll work in the dark."

As Andrew had expected, the Burmese were better at night than the Fusiliers or the Sikhs. Most of the British stumbled, spoke loudly, and got lost; the Sikhs advanced at speed in the wrong direction, and the Burmese watched with cynical amusement.

That first night, the dacoits attacked an outlying village, killed one woman, and robbed the rest. A scared civilian told of a man with a green-tasselled yellow umbrella supervising the attack.

The following day, Andrew took his men on a route march around the area, ensuring they had a basic grasp of the local geography. He made them study maps, had the NCOs work out the fastest routes between villages, and pinpointed the most suitable places for standing patrols and pickets.

After a few hours' sleep, he trained his men again that night.

"Lift your feet high when walking; you have less chance of scuffing loose stones and breaking twigs. Watch your colleagues all the time and stop every few moments; darkness and silence are your friends."

The men listened. Andrew dismissed the least competent, drafted in others, and continued with his training.

On that second night, the dacoits penetrated the suburbs of Rangoon, robbed two shops, and set a house ablaze. Again, a witness mentioned the yellow umbrella with the green tassels.

On the third day, Andrew concentrated on his men's marksmanship and stamina. He knew he had limited time in which to work and pushed them hard. Two more men fell out, and he returned them to their regiment and brought in two keen youngsters. That night, he split his men in two. He commanded one group and Lieutenant Morton the other, and they patrolled the countryside around Rangoon.

Andrew's patrol saw the glow of another fire, arriving too late to catch the dacoits, although one of his Sikhs fired at what he claimed was a running man. The resulting venison was a welcome addition to their rations.

"What do you think, Morton?" Andrew asked.

"The men are clumsy but keen," Morton was a steady-eyed youngster. "They won't let you down."

"That's my opinion," Andrew said. "Here's what we'll do." He outlined his plans to the lieutenant, working with a large-scale plan of the area.

If only civilians understood how essential organising is for even the most minor military operation, they might have a higher opinion of the military.

"When do we start, sir?" Morton asked.

"Tonight," Andrew said. "The men will have to learn as they work. The dacoits are becoming too cocky."

Morton nodded grimly. "Yes, sir. I'll make the arrangements."

"Tell the men to watch for a dacoit with a yellow umbrella with green tassels," Andrew said. "He might be organising these attacks."

"I will, sir," Morton said.

When Andrew alerted the Rangoon police to his intentions and mentioned the umbrella, the inspector drew in his breath.

"A yellow umbrella with green tassels!" he said. "That's Buda Sein! He's probably the worst of them all and far more important than a mere dacoit. According to our sources, he's Maung Thandar's companion, maybe his relation."

Andrew grunted. "We'll see if we can curb his attacks."

The inspector looked worn and old. "I wish somebody could stop them. I am sick of ravaged villages and murdered people who depend on us for protection yet are too scared of the dacoits to help us help them."

Andrew shook his hand. "We'll do our best," he promised.

The inspector grunted. "We think the dacoits will stir up trouble inside Rangoon, Captain Baird. Could you base your men in the city, please?"

Andrew nodded, wondering if the last few nights of training were wasted. "I'll do that."

Andrew stationed his men in Rangoon's northern suburbs, the area most vulnerable to dacoit attack. He placed them in pickets of four men, with six-man mobile patrols operating between each picket.

"If the men on patrol hear or see anything suspicious, move immediately to that area," Andrew said. "If you see dacoits, attack immediately. Try to drive them to one of the static pickets so we trap them between two fires."

The men nodded. Nights with little sleep had tired them, but all were veterans of Burma and knew how difficult it was to catch the dacoits. Andrew knew they preferred actively hunting the enemy rather than waiting to react.

"We might just come across ordinary thieves, sir," Lieutenant Morton said.

"Call on them to surrender," Andrew advised. "If they don't, then assume they are dacoits."

"Yes, sir," Morton said, passing on Andrew's instructions. The men, British, Burmese, and Sikh, nodded, happy that Andrew had allowed them limited freedom.

Rangoon's streets were quiet at night, with fewer pedestrians than Andrew had expected. He placed his static pickets at strategic spots and organised patrols between them, varying their routes to ensure the dacoits did not know where the soldiers would be next.

"Don't be predictable," Andrew warned. "Keep the dacoits guessing."

On the first night of Andrew's patrolling regime, the dacoits set fire to two houses and robbed another. Andrew increased the range of his patrols to cover a larger area. The second night, the dacoits looted half a street, leaving Andrew feeling frustrated.

"Somebody will know what's happening," Morton said as they sat in their makeshift barracks in the northern suburbs. "They won't tell us anything, though, or they'll give us misinformation."

Andrew considered for a moment. "That could be useful," he said. "Let's ask around, Morton. Here's what I suggest." He unfolded new ideas.

"Do you think they will work?" Morton asked.

"I don't know," Andrew replied. "We are using their strengths against them: lies, deceit, and mistrust."

Morton shrugged. "It's worth a shot, sir."

Andrew and Morton tried bribery the following day, offering a handful of rupees to anybody who told them where the dacoits might strike next. A Burmese policeman acted as interpreter.

"This man says the dacoits will rob in the east, sahib," the interpreter said.

"He thinks the dacoits are going to attack the south," the interpreter told Andrew.

"The east of the city," the interpreter said.

When Andrew and Morton compared notes, their information was similar.

"It looks like the dacoits will target the east or the south," Morton said. "What now?"

"Now, we play them at their own game," Andrew said grimly. "Either the locals fear the dacoits, or they're in cahoots with them. I don't trust them to tell us the truth."

"Nor do I, sir," Morton agreed.

"If they have given us false information, we will use that against them."

"How?" Morton asked.

"None of our informants mentioned the west of the city," Andrew leaned back in his creaking chair. "In fact, they were careful to point us anywhere except the west."

Morton agreed.

"That suggests the dacoits are going to strike in the west," Andrew said and grinned. "We have four hours before dark. I want you to gather as much straw and old rags as possible."

Morton stared at him. "Sir?"

"Straw, old rags, and old uniforms," Andrew ordered. "Send out the men on foraging expeditions and bring everything back here."

"Yes, sir," Morton looked confused as Andrew grinned at him.

"Off you go, Morton. As quick as you can."

When the men trickled in with their bundles of rags, uniforms, and straw, Andrew had them make dummies. Muttering in discontent, the men stuffed the old uniforms with rags and straw until Andrew was satisfied the result looked vaguely like a human.

Ajit Singh, the Sikh marksman, proved himself an artist, adding watermelons for heads and drawing features on their faces.

"Well done, Ajit," Andrew said. "Well done, men." He grinned at them, with the Sikhs and Burmese responding with smiles and the Fusiliers stony-faced.

When the evening drew near, Andrew marched his men to the east side of Rangoon. He placed half his men in two large houses, making it obvious they were there.

"Make a noise, men," Andrew ordered. "Laugh, swagger and mention dacoits."

The men obeyed, watching their strange officer through suspicious eyes.

When night fell, Andrew silently withdrew the pickets, leaving dummies in their place.

"Who thought of that idea?" Morton asked.

"It is a trick we used when we fought the Boers," Andrew said. "We'll see if it's as effective against the dacoits." He marched his men quietly to the west of the city, placed them in pickets of five men and waited.

"Keep hidden," Andrew ordered his men. "Don't move unless you see the dacoits or if I give the order. Lieutenant Morton, take a section, circle to the rear of the area and wait. With luck, we'll flush out some dacoits."

If I am correct, we'll have struck the first blow at Buba Sein's dacoits. If I am wrong, the men will think I am a fool, and more civilians will suffer.

Very few people walked the night-dark streets of Rangoon as if they expected something to happen. Andrew watched a pair of police walk past, talking quietly and waited with his men behind him.

Andrew checked his watch. It was two in the morning, four hours until dawn.

"Smoke, sir!" Corporal McGhee said. "I can smell smoke!"

"Well done, McGhee!" Andrew said. "Check your rifles are loaded, boys; loosen your bayonets in their scabbards." He heard a wild scream. "Move in!" he said.

Thirty police and Fusiliers doubled towards the fire, with Andrew at their head. He felt the suppressed excitement of his men. Hunting dacoits was frustrating, with contacts few and the police and Army usually arriving too late to do more than count the cost. One successful brush would lift the military and police's spirits.

The flames glowed yellow in the night sky, a beacon directing Andrew to the dacoits.

"Morton, take your men around the rear and head off any who try to run. The rest, extended order, and watch for civilians! Corporal McGhee, take the left flank."

They hit the streets in a long line, with Sikhs and Fusiliers carrying bayoneted rifles as they ran towards the flames. The Burmese police carried carbines and moved silently. Andrew saw a group of men around a wailing woman, swore and lifted his revolver.

"Leave that woman alone!" he roared, knowing the dacoits would not understand the words.

When one of the Burmese police shouted an order, the closest two dacoits looked around, their eyes gleaming in the firelight. One lifted a *dha* as if to challenge Andrew, noticed the rapidly advancing soldiers and ran. The second was slower, and a Sikh shot him as he hesitated. The sound of the rifle alerted the others, and half a dozen men erupted from two houses, most burdened with the loot they had stolen.

One dacoit shouted something, crouched to face the soldiers, realised he was outflanked and ran.

"After them, boys!" Corporal Rowan ordered. One Fusilier dropped to his knees and fired a snapshot; the others chased the dacoits, their bayonets glittering.

More dacoits appeared; one fired at Andrew, dropped his flintlock musket and screamed as a Fusilier spitted him with his bayonet.

"Got you, you thieving bastard!"

Fleet-footed, many of the dacoits escaped, only to run against Lieutenant Morton's section. Andrew heard the scatter of shots and shouts, Morton's sharp commands and somebody laughing.

That's a Sikh laugh: Sukhbir Singh.

"Round up the prisoners," Andrew said. "We'll hand them into the nearest police station." The operation, hours in planning, was over in minutes.

He looked at the three dead dacoits on the ground. "Lieutenant Morton, look after the prisoners. The rest, try and put out the flames and look after the civilians."

Andrew felt suddenly drained. Compared to the major battles in which he had been involved, the skirmish had been simple, yet he was glad it was over.

WITH THE DACOITS DISCOURAGED FROM RAIDING RANGOON, AN INCREASED force of sixty men under his command and free rein to roam anywhere within five miles of Rangoon, Andrew felt his spirits lift. Rangoon, like every crowded city, depressed him with its narrow streets and lack of space.

The countryside was more open than Andrew expected, with fertile fields, small prosperous villages and small areas of forest. He led his men from village to village, with his Burmese police talking to the villagers and asking about possible sightings of dacoits. The replies were all the same.

"They haven't seen any dacoits, sir," the police reported.

After two days of uneventful patrolling, Andrew thought the area was safe. "It looks as if our patrols have done the work," he said.

"Maybe," Lieutenant Morton replied.

"You sound doubtful," Andrew said.

"I've been in Burma longer than you, sir," Morton reminded him. "My experience with dacoits is that they'll be wherever they are not expected."

"We'll have one more local sweep," Andrew decided, "and then we'll move to a wider circuit."

He led his men in extended order across the fertile countryside, checking each house and village for strangers.

"Sir!" Corporal Rowan shouted as they skirted a paddy field outside a village. "There's somebody on the ground here. I think she's dead."

Andrew hurried over. The woman was about forty, stark naked and fastened to a bamboo structure above the embers of a fire.

"The bastards have roasted her, sir," Rowan said, staring at the corpse.

"They have," Andrew said, calling for two Burmese police officers. "Go into the village and find out what happened," he ordered.

As the police approached, a score of men erupted from the far side and ran. One delayed for a moment to fire a single shot at the British patrol and then joined his companions.

Got you!

"Sikhs and Fusiliers! Extended order!" Andrew shouted. "Get after these men! Lieutenant Morton, secure the village!"

Andrew ran forward with the Fusiliers and Sikhs on either side. "Keep in sight of each other," Andrew ordered. "Be careful of an ambush."

The fleeing men ran into the nearest copse. A moment later, a spatter of musketry sounded.

"Fusiliers! Get in there!" Andrew roared. "Sikhs! Get around the rear of the trees and keep the dacoits inside!"

Andrew knew the dangers of moving into close country in pursuit of desperate men, but the sight of the tortured woman had angered him as much as the Fusiliers. He thrust into the trees with a Fusilier on either side.

"If you see anything moving, use your bayonet," Andrew ordered. "Don't shoot in case you hit one of the Sikhs."

They moved forward slowly, with the Fusiliers stabbing viciously at every bush or patch of undergrowth.

One man yelled and leapt backwards when he saw a snake, and then they saw movement ahead. The Fusiliers bounded forward, bayonets ready, to stop when they realised they had met the Sikhs.

"Where are the dacoits?" a Fusilier asked, raising his rifle.

"They've melted away," Sukhbir Singh replied. "They always melt away."

Andrew nodded.

If we had cavalry or even mounted infantry, we could have caught them before they entered the trees. We must adapt and improve.

CHAPTER 19

RANGOON FEBRUARY AND MARCH 1885

Finding sufficient mounts for his mounted infantry was difficult in Rangoon, but Andrew used every bit of persuasion he knew, added a few empty threats, and mustered a score of horses. True, most had seen better days, and some were more fit for putting out to pasture than chasing dacoits, but they all had four legs, a back, and a head.

They'll do, Andrew told himself. *They'll have to do.*

A check of his men found ten Sikhs who were experienced horsemen and three Fusiliers with a country background. The Burmese were experts on the river but had no knowledge of horsemanship and showed no inclination to learn.

"I need another seven mounted infantrymen," Andrew said. "If I don't find any Fusiliers, I'll recruit civilians!"

The men looked at one another, and eventually, two stepped forward. Andrew nodded to his senior NCO. "Sergeant Jardine! Find me five volunteers."

"Yes, sir!" Jardine said and rapped out five names. "You men are now mounted infantry. If you scare the horses, I'll have you. If you fall off, I expect you to land at attention. If you break your fool necks, I expect you to find a replacement to take your place."

"Thank you, Sergeant," Andrew said.

"That's all right, sir!" Jardine replied.

For the next week, Andrew split his force in two. While Morton commanded the usual patrols, he taught his mounted infantry the rudiments of drill and riding. Andrew had ridden horses since he could walk, as had some Sikhs, while most of the Fusiliers were town-bred, without equine knowledge.

"Your horse will sense your fear," Andrew told them. "Your horse will know you lack experience and confidence. Your horse will try to be your master. It is up to you to prove him wrong."

The more nervous of the mounted infantrymen eyed their mounts with trepidation. The horses returned the glances with what Andrew thought was amusement.

"Your first lesson is to take care of your horse," Andrew said. "You will feed and water him before you feed yourself. You will keep his stables clean and groom him before you have breakfast. You will treat him like your brother and get to know him as your best friend."

The men listened, some smiling nervously and others without expression.

"When we ride out, the experienced men will lead, and the others will follow," Andrew said and split his class in half. While he taught the better men the tricks he had learned fighting the Zulus and Boers, the rest struggled to remain in the saddles.

They'll improve, Andrew thought. *I hope they will improve quickly.*

"We ride to battle and dismount to fight," Andrew said. "We should have short-barrelled carbines but must make do with Sniders and Martinis."

Andrew trained them to remain in their saddles and follow simple bugle calls and hand signals. He also taught them to ride in formation and how to extend to ride line abreast to cover more ground.

"I should have months to train you," Andrew said. "I don't know how much time the dacoits will allow us, but we will train day and night until they return."

He pushed them hard, used the Sikhs as examples, praised them when needed and shouted when they hesitated. After a week, the men had lost their fear of the horses. After a month, some were becoming reasonably competent riders. Andrew forced them out when the monsoon rains lashed the ground, and they rode with heads bowed and horses splashing through the mud. He borrowed a civilian vet to inspect his horses, sent the bill to the Chief Commissioner and ignored the unpleasant reply.

The northeast monsoon season ended at the end of February, and the dry season opened with brilliant sunshine and heat that seemed to bounce off the ground. Andrew ensured the men watered their horses before they filled their water bottles and continued to drive them hard. He set section against section, Sikh against Fusilier, experimented with mixed Fusilier and Sikh sections, and returned to single units. The men sulked, grumbled, and slowly grew in confidence and ability.

As March eased away, Andrew could watch his creation ride past in columns of two and feel some justified satisfaction close to pride. He returned to their makeshift headquarters, promising to return to Wells' Britannia Hotel that evening for a rare visit to Mariana.

"Sir!" Sergeant Jardine trotted up on his Shan pony. "The dacoits are back!"

Mariana quoted Tennyson to herself as she walked to the commercial heart of Rangoon.

"Tears, idle tears, I know not what they mean,
Tears from the depths of some divine despair
Rise in the heart, and gather to the eyes,
In looking on the happy autumn fields,
And thinking of the days that are no more."

Mariana stopped at the imposing stone building that rose three storeys from the street and displayed its coat of arms of a ship in full sail above a St George's Cross. Mariana checked the firm's name, *Jennings and Stanley,* muttered to herself, stepped inside the grand front door and rang the little brass bell for service. She controlled her nerves by smiling and speaking more loudly than usual.

"I want to see Mr Jennings," Mariana said as a clerk hurried to the front desk but slowed when he saw a woman standing alone.

"Do you?" The clerk was Burmese, wearing European clothing and the smug expression of a minor official with power over all who entered his domain. He looked Mariana up and down. "What is your name, please?"

"Miss Maxwell," Mariana said coldly. "Miss Mariana Maxwell."

"Miss Mariana Maxwell," the clerk repeated the name slowly. "Wait here, please." With a last look at Mariana, he left his position and disappeared through a door at the back.

Mariana glanced around the reception area. The floor was polished teak, with panelled walls and an ornate ceiling with the expected fan. A flight of stairs curved upward, past the firm's coat of arms and pictures of ships and the Golden Pagoda.

Have I done the right thing coming here? Mariana suddenly felt like a frontier farmer's daughter, out of place in this establishment of mercantile trade and wealth.

"Miss Maxwell!" Jennings burst through the door behind the counter and strode forward, dismissed the clerk with a curt word and held out his hand. "How good to see you again. But you look troubled. Is anything the matter?"

"Indeed not, Mr Jennings," Mariana realised the clerk was listening and lowered her voice. "I wish to talk to you."

Jennings glanced at the clerk, told him sharply to be about his business and ushered Mariana to the stairs. "I have an office upstairs, Miss Maxwell. We will be more private there."

The office was teak panelled, with a carved teak desk, two deep leather armchairs and a full-length mirror. Filing cabinets and a glass-fronted, walnut drinks cabinet lined one wall, with windows overlooking the harbour on the other. A large telescope stood on a swivel beside the windows.

"I like to keep an eye on the harbour," Jennings explained. "I want to know when my merchandise is arriving and departing. Sit down, Miss Maxwell, and tell me what troubles you."

Mariana folded her skirt beneath her as she sat, with the armchair soft and yielding around her.

Jennings took his place on the second armchair, facing Mariana across two yards of polished teak floor. "I sense you want to talk, Miss Maxwell, so I won't delay matters." He raised his eyebrows, smiled, and settled back in his chair.

"Mr Jennings." Mariana hesitated for a moment. "You have twice offered to show me your house. I know this is very forward of me, but if you were to ask me a third time, I would agree."

"Then that is settled," Jennings said. He lowered his voice. "Miss Maxwell,"

"Mariana," Mariana corrected. "Please call me Mariana."

If Andrew chooses to neglect me and is probably with that Burmese woman, I am entitled to be friendly with Mr Jennings.

Jennings bowed from his chair. "That is kind of you. I am Stephen, as you know."

"Stephen," Mariana said. "I like that name."

Jennings stood, keeping his gaze on Mariana. "Miss Maxwell, Mariana, will you do me the honour of joining me for dinner in my house?"

"I would be delighted, Stephen," Mariana replied, with her heartbeat increasing. "When?"

Am I betraying Andrew? No, he has left me, and this is a simple dinner between friends, nothing else.

Stephen considered for a moment. "Shall we say tomorrow evening at six? That will give the servants time to prepare something special for you."

"I don't need anything special," Mariana said. "Please don't go to any trouble."

Jennings shook his head. "I want something special for a very special lady," he countered.

About to deny she was special, Mariana thought of Andrew with the Burmese woman. *After all the years he has known me, he finds another woman. Maybe this Burmese woman is not his first. Perhaps he knew a whole string of women in Africa and Britain.*

"Thank you, Stephen. I will come at six, prompt." Mariana lifted her head.

"I'll send a carriage for you," Jennings promised. He lowered his voice. "May I be permitted to make a confession?"

"Of course," Mariana said, prepared to forgive him anything.

"When I first saw you," Stephen spoke quietly. "I thought you were just one of the fishing fleet, but as I got to know you, I realised you were something special." He looked away, lowering his voice. "You are like no woman I have ever met before."*

Mariana bobbed in a little curtsy without leaving her seat. "Thank you, Stephen. That was lovely of you."

What would Tennyson say? He said: "Come friends, it's not too late to seek a newer

* The Fishing Fleet: single women who travelled to India to find a husband. Those who failed were known as 'returned empties.'

world." Mariana smiled despite the nervous hammer of her heart. *I am seeking a newer world with a man who has never been anything but kind to me. Stephen has paid me every attention and looked after me while Andrew was away courting that Burmese woman and pretending to be a soldier while the country is at peace.*

"Now," Jennings stepped to the drinks cabinet. "I know the sun is hardly over the yardarm, but neither of us is a sailor, so we don't have to follow that archaic custom. A brandy and water, Mariana?"

"THEY'RE BACK?" ANDREW ASKED.

"Yes, sir," Sergeant Jardine said, standing at attention at Andrew's side. "One of the standing patrols has reported that a gang of dacoits is raiding five miles north of Rangoon."

"Thank you, Sergeant," Andrew said. "Now we will see how good the mounted infantry is." *I won't be seeing Mariana tonight, then.*

"Parade dismissed! Fill up your water bottles and report back in ten minutes with fifty rounds of ammunition. We're dacoit hunting!"

Andrew had prepared for such an event. He had put Sukhbir Singh in charge of the Sikhs and Lieutenant Morton with the Fusiliers' infantry. Sergeant Jardine gave Andrew the details, and he folded a map, stuffed it in his saddlebag and grabbed more ammunition for his revolver.

"Morton, take the infantry at the double and support the horsemen."

"Yes, sir," Morton said.

"Your job is to guard the villages."

"Yes, sir," Morton ran to organise his foot soldiers.

"The rest of you, mount and ride!" Andrew addressed the assembled mounted infantry. He told them their destination and grinned. "Right, lads! It's time to put all that training to the test. Follow me!"

After months of patrolling, Andrew knew the land well and rode directly to the affected area. He saw the rising smoke a mile away and gave quick orders to his men. "Sukhbir Singh! Take your men and head them off. Your job and mine is to pursue the dacoits. Lieutenant Morton and his men will guard the villages."

"Yes, Sahib," Sukhbir grinned and saluted, with his men eager to meet the dacoits.

"The rest, follow me." Andrew glanced over his shoulder. Nobody had fallen off his horse, and the Fusiliers had kept in formation. He knew the Sikhs were better horsemen than the Fusiliers and allowed Sukhbir his head while Morton's section would guard the civilians.

Men and women working in the fields looked up as the mounted infantry passed, with a bullock cart pulling to the side to allow them passage.

"Keep the pace up!" Andrew ordered. He knew the men suffered in the heat and had prepared them by allowing looser clothing and trying to find shade whenever possible. He heard the regular crunch of hooves on the ground and felt a glow of satisfaction that he was commanding regular soldiers again in a worthwhile campaign.

We are protecting civilians against very unpleasant people. This is why I signed up, not for glory but to make a difference, to do good.

After twenty minutes, the Fusiliers heard a crackle of musketry ahead and involuntarily increased their speed.

"Push on, lads!" Andrew ordered. He could see movement ahead, the blur of galloping horsemen accompanied by hoarse shouts and sporadic firing. Andrew saw a village on the right, with smoke rising from a burning building and Sukhbir's Sikhs riding around an area of long grass.

"Fusiliers!" Andrew barked. "Move towards the grass, trot!" He had deliberately kept his instructions simple, without the complicated manoeuvres that fully trained cavalry would perform. He watched his men ride forward, keeping in approximate formation as they approached the long grass.

"Dismount!" Andrew ordered. "Form a firing line. At the double!"

The Fusiliers dismounted, with every fourth man taking control of the horses' reins while the rest ran forward to take their positions. Most of the men immediately understood what was happening, while others looked confused but obeyed orders.

"The Sikhs have flushed out the enemy," Andrew explained. "The dacoits are running for the grass to hide. Havildar Sukhbir Singh's men will drive them this way, and we will stop them."

After weeks of chasing the elusive dacoits with little result, followed by hard months of training, the Fusiliers were pleased to see them in the open.

Andrew heard the shouts of the Sikhs as they hounded the dacoits.

"Lie down!" Andrew ordered his Fusiliers. "We want to surprise the enemy."

The men obeyed, with their khaki uniforms merging with the sun-dried grass. Andrew crouched, revolver in hand, as he watched the scene unfold.

The mounted Sikhs stretched in a continuous line across the maidan. They shot at any dacoit who doubled back, herding the majority towards the supposed shelter of the grassland. Andrew heard the men plainly: the high-pitched shouts of the Burmese and the deeper voices of the Sikhs.

The first dacoit plunged into the long grass, with his companions following. With the grass obscuring his vision, Andrew could not make out details.

"Ready, lads! Make sure you're loaded," Andrew called. He felt his men's tension as they rubbed sweating palms on their legs or shook the perspiration from their eyebrows.

The dacoits were running desperately, maybe forty or fifty of them, half-naked men with firearms and *dhas*, hoping to hide in the grass as the Sikhs pursued in high excitement.

Andrew timed his orders, waiting until the dacoits were only a hundred and fifty yards away, sufficient distance for two volleys. "Ready! Aim low! Don't hit the horsemen; they're on our side!"

"I dinnae think Sergeant Jardine is on our side!" an anonymous voice called.

Andrew began the countdown. "Three, two, one. Fire!"

The Fusiliers fired with an unaimed volley that sliced into the grassland. Andrew did not know how many dacoits they hit. The shots surprised the mounted Sikhs nearly as much as the enemy, and Andrew ordered a second volley before uttering the order, "Fix bayonets! Bayonets... Fix!"

He heard the ominous snick as the Fusiliers attached the eighteen-inch-long bayonets to the barrels of their Martini-Henry's.

"Corporal McGhee, keep your section here to stop any dacoits who evade us. The rest, in open order, advance!"

With the mounted infantry behind them and the Fusiliers in front, the dacoits had nowhere to run. Some threw up their hands in surrender, others tried to fight, and a few threw themselves on the ground, hoping to look dead or invisible in the long grass. Remembering the tortured or murdered villagers and the pillaged villages, the British and Sikhs had little mercy. They shot or bayonetted until Andrew and Sergeant Jardine called for restraint. One man faced Andrew squarely, holding a long *dha* in defiance, only turning to run at the last minute.

Andrew saw the man was broad-chested, with a tattoo across his face and a gold hilt on his *dha*.

"Catch that man!" Andrew ordered, but by the time the nearest horseman could turn, the dacoit had disappeared.

Damn it! He looked like the leader of the whole bunch! He might have been Buda Sein.

The British and Sikhs rounded up five living dacoits as prisoners, and Andrew ordered a count of the dead.

"Have the prisoners dig one large grave," he said. "We'll bury them here."

The dacoits were a sorry-looking bunch. They mostly wore minimal clothing, with bare feet and rudimentary weapons. Most possessed a *dha*, and some had only short knives or heavy staves.

"Sahib!" Sukhbir Singh called out, raising a hand to Andrew. "Look at this, sahib."

Andrew marched over. "What have you found, Havildar?"

Sukhbir rolled over the nearest dead dacoit and pointed to his neck. "There, sahib."

Andrew saw the dragon tattooed on the nape. "It's a dragon, Sukhbir."

"Yes, Sahib. Only the king's soldiers have a dragon tattooed there," Sukhbir said. "This man is no ordinary loose wallah. He is one of the king's soldiers."*

Is this an isolated case of one of Thibaw's soldiers joining a dacoit raid? Or has the king sent his men to cause havoc in British Burma?

"Check the others," Andrew ordered. "See if there are any more soldiers."

Three of the dead had a dragon tattoo on their necks.

I'll have to report these tattoos to Sir Charles.

"Check the prisoners," Andrew said.

One man tried to run when the Sikhs and Fusiliers began to ask questions,

* Loosewallah – bandit, thief.

but the Sikhs were ready, and a mounted man caught him by his hair and dragged him back.

"Check them for dragon tattoos and ask who led them," Andrew said. "One of our Burmese policemen can translate."

Only the prisoner who tried to escape had a dragon tattoo.

"You'd best go for a walk, sir," Sergeant Jardine said. "I'll ask the fellow who tried to escape."

"No ugly business," Andrew said.

"No, sir," Jardine replied.

Andrew knew it was sometimes better to leave experienced men like Sergeant Jardine to perform necessary but unpleasant tasks.

After checking his men, Andrew returned to Sergeant Jardine, who saluted.

"Their leader is a fellow named Buda Sein, sir," Jardine said. "The dacoit was a stubborn fellow, but Sukhbir and I persuaded him to tell us."

Andrew saw the dacoit looking battered, bloody but alive. He remembered the woman the dacoits had roasted to death and quelled his conscience. "Thank you, Sergeant. We'll take the prisoners to the jail in Rangoon." He thought of the man with the golden-hilted *dha* and wished he had caught him.

That man, Buda Sein, is trouble. He'll return, and we'll be ready for him.

CHAPTER 20

RANGOON, APRIL TO AUGUST 1885

Mariana looked at herself in the mirror, patted her hair in place, and adjusted her earrings. She had never worn earrings before coming to Burma and would never adopt the Burmese habit of boring holes in her ears to hold cheroots. However, Mariana rather liked the idea of gold hoops that caught the light when she moved her head. She tilted her head again, watching her reflection and smiling.

What would the good people of Berwick think if they saw me like this? They'd be scandalised. Good God! Some domestic servants even hang men and women's washing on different clothes lines.

Mariana touched the gold rings, smiling.

Anyway, Stephen gave me these gold earrings so I will wear them for his sake.

Mariana sighed and looked down on herself. The dark dress contrasted nicely with her blonde hair, while the earrings connected the two. Mariana smiled at her reflection, seeing her grey eyes crinkling at the corners. She leaned closer to the mirror. *Are those lines around my eyes? Oh, Lord, I hope not; I must be getting old before my time. I am twenty-four and still unmarried. Maybe I'll end up an old maid.*

She thought again of Andrew's proposal in Edinburgh and shook her head. *If I had agreed, I'd be married to a man I rarely see. Where is he now? Is he playing at soldiers or with his Burmese woman?*

Mariana started at the tap on her door. *Andrew!* "Who is it?"

"The maid, Miss Maxwell," a light voice replied.

"Come in," Mariana called.

The maid was small in stature, efficient and friendly. "A carriage has arrived for you, Miss Maxwell."

"Thank you," Mariana replied, standing up. "How do I look?"

The maid stepped back. "Like Supayalat," she said solemnly. "Thibaw's queen. The gentleman is fortunate."

"Thank you," Mariana said, smiling. Taking a deep breath, she left her room and hurried down the stairs, passing the old Burmese woman at the foot of the pillar.

The carriage was more luxurious than anything she had ever seen, a tall wheeled blue Brougham with a matched pair of greys and a dignified coachman wearing a long blue coat and a top hat. A servant opened the door for Mariana, saw her comfortably inside and quietly closed the door. As the servant joined the coachman in front, the Brougham eased away, with the sound of hooves and whirr of well-greased wheels strangely soothing.

I am going to a gentleman's house, alone and unescorted. Mariana watched the streets pass by without interest. *I hope I am doing the right thing.*

The journey to Jennings' house on Rangoon's outskirts took a full twenty minutes, and when the Brougham came to a smooth halt, the servant dismounted to open the door for Mariana. She took a deep breath, smiled politely, and descended.

"Welcome to my humble abode, Miss Maxwell," Jennings greeted Mariana as she left the carriage. Dressed in an evening suit and tails, he bowed deeply and offered his arm.

"Thank you, Mr Jennings," Mariana replied. "I am Mariana, remember?"

"And I am Stephen. Come this way, Mariana."

The house was two-storeyed and L-shaped within immaculately groomed grounds. Stephen had arranged for the servants to stand in a double row outside the columned front door. They bowed as Stephen and Mariana passed.

"How lovely," Mariana curtseyed in return, which made Stephen smile.

The interior of the house matched the exterior with a combination of local and European furniture. Massive teak pillars held the upper floors in place, while the main reception room had a large brass Buddha on a plinth, with a six-foot-tall palm tree in an elaborate brass pot on either side.

"I've never seen anything like this before," Mariana said.

I could not imagine this in Berwick or Natal.

"Do you like it?" Stephen snapped a finger, and a graceful servant took Mariana's light coat.

"I do like it," Mariana said. "Have you converted to Buddhism, Stephen?"

"Heavens, no," Jennings smiled at the idea. "But while in Rome, you know. Anyway, it helps my Burmese visitors relax when they see I don't reject their philosophy. It is a philosophy, you know, and not a religion."

"I was not aware of that," Mariana said as Jennings paused to allow her to admire the room.

"The Buddhists don't worship the man, only the perfection he achieved," Jennings told her.

Andrew already told me that.

"I see," Mariana said, starting as somebody rang a gong, with the sound reverberating around the house.

"I am sorry," Jennings touched her arm. "I should have warned you about the gong." He smiled disarmingly. "Dinner is ready. I don't believe in waiting when one is hungry. Are you hungry, Mariana?"

"I have starved myself since breakfast," Mariana admitted. "It would be less than polite not to bring an appetite with me."

Jennings laughed. "Well said, Mariana. I do like a lady with an appetite." He stopped as a servant opened the door for them. "Do you prefer British, European or Burmese fare?" He held up a sealed envelope. "I have written your reply here."

"British," Mariana replied without hesitation.

"Open it," Jennings handed over the envelope. The slip of paper inside read "British."

"How clever you are," Mariana said, smiling. She stepped through the door into the hallway.

"I think I know you well," Jennings told her. He gave her his arm. "Shall we go into the dining room?"

Mariana smiled, with her head whirling at the attention and the novelty of the situation. "Yes, please," she said, walking at Jennings' side.

The circular table was smaller than Mariana had expected and much more intimate, with only two places set opposite each other. A single candle burned in the centre, with the light reflecting from an array of plates and glasses that Mariana found daunting. After Andrew's austere lifestyle and the reality of life on the Natal frontier, Mariana was nearly overwhelmed by such luxury.

"You look surprised, Mariana," Jennings said.

"A little," Mariana admitted. "It's lovely. It's all lovely."

Behind the table, large windows allowed a view of the garden, where coloured lanterns hung from trees to give an almost surreal and calming effect.

"I am glad you approve," Jennings said. "Are you all right with soup to begin with? Or would you prefer something else?" He smiled. "I can cater to whatever taste you prefer, Mariana."

"Soup is fine, thank you," Mariana saw that Jennings was trying his best to make her feel comfortable.

The servants moved smoothly throughout the seven-course meal, which included soup, freshly caught fish, a rather tough chicken, and some vegetables Mariana did not recognise but which Jennings explained to her with humorous asides.

They finished with fruit and laughter as Jennings entertained Mariana with a fund of humorous anecdotes about his life in Burma.

"And now wine, dear Mariana," Jennings said. He signalled to a servant. "Champagne!"

Mariana watched as the servant opened the bottle with a loud pop that made her start.

"Oh!"

"It's all right, Mariana. It's meant to do that," Jennings explained.

With the large window behind her, Mariana lifted the glass tentatively, watching the bubbles rise to the surface and explode.

"Drink," Stephen encouraged. "I bought half a dozen bottles of champagne in honour of your visit. Champagne is far too exclusive for me to drink alone."

"Thank you," Mariana said and sipped delicately. "It's very bubbly."

"Some people call champagne bubbly," Jennings said.

Mariana giggled. "It tickles my nose."

"Enjoy the sensation," Jennings watched her over the rim of his glass. "Here's a toast to us," he said. "May we have a long and happy friendship."

Mariana lifted her glass. "To us," she agreed and giggled again.

After they finished the champagne, Jennings threw the empty bottle to a servant, who caught it with practised hands.

"Where are my manners!" Jennings said. "I do apologise, Mariana. I have been so intent on introducing you to the pleasure of champagne that I neglected to show you the rest of the house."

"Oh, I don't mind," Mariana said. She smiled, seeing Jennings as a slightly blurred figure on the opposite side of the table.

"Would you like to see the rest of my house?" Jennings asked.

"I'd love to," Mariana said.

The upstairs rooms were as luxurious as those on the ground floor. Each had large windows facing the garden, while the neighbouring house was in darkness.

"How many bedrooms do you have?" Mariana asked, holding onto Jennings for support.

"One main bedroom and four guest bedrooms," Jennings replied.

"How lovely," Mariana said. She swallowed hard. "Could I go home now, please? I don't feel very well."

After their initial success against the dacoits, Baird's Mounted Infantry patrolled the ground north of Rangoon. Andrew called on every village and town to reassure the population that the British were there to protect them. The villagers greeted him politely and resumed their daily life.

When Sir Charles Crosthwaite saw Andrew's accomplishments, he increased his force to two hundred men, a mixture of mounted men and infantry.

"I only intended you to be here temporarily, Baird," Sir Charles told him. "But I want you to remain until the present crisis with King Thibaw is resolved."

"Have you thought further about Bo Thura's pardon, sir?" Andrew asked.

"I am gathering information, Baird. This Bo Thura has been a pain in our neck for some time."

"Yes, sir," Andrew said.

"Many people would not wish Bo Thura to be secure within British territory," Sir Charles said. "I have yet to make up my mind. In the meantime, keep hunting your dacoits."

"I will, sir," Andrew promised.

The mills of Sir Charles grind slowly when he wants me to clear Rangoon of dacoits. I hope Mariana is all right. I am neglecting the poor girl terribly.

❄

Mariana stood in Jennings' office with her hands folded before her, feeling like a schoolgirl standing before the headmistress.

"You look very contrite, Mariana," Jennings said. "Whatever is the matter?"

"I do apologise for my behaviour in your house," Mariana said. "I am most thoroughly ashamed of myself."

"For what?" Jennings asked, smiling. "Sit down, Mariana. For goodness' sake, sit down."

"I fear I had too much to drink," Mariana remained standing.

"That was my fault entirely," Jennings said. "I should have known you were unused to champagne. Can you forgive me?"

"Only if you forgive me," Mariana replied. The conversation had gone better than she expected.

"Then we are both forgiven," Jennings said. His smile broadened. "You were quite charming in that condition."

"Some men would have taken advantage of me," Mariana said. "You were a perfect gentleman and took me back to the hotel."

Jennings smoothed a finger over his moustache. "You must know by now that I respect you, Mariana. I would never dishonour you. Sit down, do."

Mariana sat down, smoothing her skirt beneath her. "Thank you, Stephen. I am so glad you understand."

Jennings chuckled. "You are worth understanding. Shall we try again?"

Andrew enhanced his tactics with strong pickets of police backed by infantry in the villages and mounted patrols to discourage the dacoits. His theory was simple: the infantry held the dacoits with rifle fire, and the noise would attract the nearest mounted men, who would hunt the fugitives. If the mounted men came across a party of dacoits, they drove them towards the nearest village, where the picket waited with their rifles.

Remembering the success of his deception with the dummies, Andrew had his men make another twenty, asked Ajit Singh to create their faces, clothed them in worn khaki and positioned them within the standing pickets.

"If the dacoits see these dummies," he explained. "They might think we are stronger than we are and leave us in peace."

Lieutenant Morton laughed. "Yes, sir. We've strengthened our force with men we don't have to feed or pay. Best not tell Gladstone, or he'll replace us all with dummies."

"Using dummy soldiers is not a new trick," Andrew said. "When we expected Bonaparte to invade Britain, we built the Royal Military Canal in Kent and manned it with wooden soldiers."

"Were they any good?"

"I never heard of them getting drunk," Andrew replied solemnly.

In addition to placing dummies with the standing pickets, Andrew augmented the mounted patrols with straw-filled and watermelon-headed uniforms. He did not know if his ideas fooled the dacoits, but the Sikhs found them amusing and gave names to their latest recruits.

Andrew supervised as his Sikhs and Fusiliers tied the dummies to their horses. Skilled with his hands, Fusilier Jordan carved fine wooden rifles for the latest recruits.

"There we are, sir. That should fool Johnny Dacoit." Jordan stepped back, smiling at his handiwork.

"I think so," Andrew agreed. "They'll think we have improved our armament and doubled the size of our force."

If I can clear these dacoits away, maybe Sir Charles will grant Bo Thura his pardon, and Mariana and I can get home. Why am I so concerned about a Burmese dacoit? Is it because he's family? Is blood thicker than water? I can't think of any other reason.

CHAPTER 21

RANGOON, AUGUST TO NOVEMBER 1885

Andrew watched his Mounted Infantry ride past. The Sikhs were naturals, riding like centaurs, as easy in the saddle as on foot. Despite all of Andrew's work, the Fusiliers were not as good. With a few exceptions, they looked what they were: infantrymen on horseback.

"I'll improve you," Andrew promised and continued to train them. He spent every spare moment with his men, working them until they were sick of the sight, smell, and sound of horses.

He spread his Burmese police and Sikhs around the villages and asked his Burmese to infiltrate the villages and ask questions.

"The local people will not talk to us," Andrew said, "but they might talk to you. Good intelligence is half the battle. If we know what the enemy is doing, we have a massive advantage, so ask questions. I want this Buda Sein in jail."

The Burmese police spread across the villages, some in uniform and most in plain clothes. As they asked their questions, Andrew continued to train his Mounted Infantry. In the evenings, he read over the notes the police gathered, and twice, he met Mariana for a few tense hours.

"Can't you tear yourself away from your duty for a few days, Andrew?" Mariana asked.

"I can't," Andrew told her. "People's lives are at stake."

"Well, is there a room in the barracks for me?"

Andrew thought of a lone woman sharing the barracks with his Mounted Infantry and police. "That would not be a good idea," he said.

Mariana did not hide her disappointment. "I hardly ever see you," she said.

"It won't be much longer," Andrew told her. "Then we'll be heading back home."

Andrew tried to see Mariana at least once a week but felt they were drifting apart. He wrote her letters, left them in her room and returned to duty feeling sick and depressed; the only cure was to lose himself in his duty.

Duty is what Windrushes do. We live for our duty, God help us.

After two months, Andrew thought his Fusiliers were reasonably competent Mounted Infantry. He could watch them with satisfaction and planned to spend more time with Mariana when the Burmese police handed him two reports. He read them and called for Lieutenant Morton.

"The police say the villagers in Pat Lan have stopped talking to them, Morton, and the nearby settlements are nervous."

"What does that mean, sir?" Morton asked.

"I think Buda Sein is using Pat Lan as his base," Andrew decided. "If not him, then somebody else. Either way, we'll visit Pat Lan with the mounted infantry."

"The Sikhs might feel left out," Morton said.

"The Sikhs will continue to patrol," Andrew told him. "I want to test the Fusiliers."

If they are successful, I can inform Sir Charles that his Mounted Infantrymen are fully trained, and he no longer needs me. I'll pick up Bo Thura's pardon and Mariana and we'll catch the next ship home.

WITH THE MOUNTED INFANTRY AT HIS BACK, ANDREW RODE OVER THE darkened countryside north of Rangoon. He hoped his deduction was correct, or this entire expedition was a waste of time.

Andrew stopped on a slight ridge a mile from Pat Lan, with the sun hinting at its morning appearance. He glanced behind him, counting his men. They were all present.

Good: nobody has dropped out.

Andrew gathered the Mounted Infantry around him.

"That village is Pat Lan, and I suspect that Buda Sein is in there," Andrew said. "You all know that Buda Sein is the instigator of many dacoit attacks on and around Rangoon, which means if we arrest him, we'll strike a major blow at the dacoits."

The Fusiliers nodded, grunted, or murmured assent.

Andrew continued. "We will surround the place and arrest all the men inside. If anybody resists, shoot them, and watch for a man with a yellow umbrella and green tassels." He lowered his voice. "That is Buda Sein."

The Fusiliers looked pleased, nodding, adjusting their equipment and checking their rifles.

"Corporal Rowan, take the right flank. Sergeant Jardine, go round the rear and ensure nobody escapes. Corporal McGhee, take the left flank. I'll give you ten minutes and boot in the front door with my section." He waited until the men murmured their understanding before he continued. "I expect resistance, men, so be prepared to fight."

Andrew expected the grins; after months in their company, he knew his

Royal Scots Fusiliers. He checked his watch. "Try not to be seen, men. I'll be moving in in twenty minutes; that will be ten past six. Go!"

He watched the Fusiliers disappear, noting the improvement in their riding. They were still not as good as his Sikhs but far better than they had been. After five minutes, the sections divided, vanishing in the gloom.

Andrew checked the time, watching the minute hand jerk forward. *How strange that such a small thing as a watch regulates our lives. We live by the clock as it ticks away our allotted span, three score years and ten, divided into these minuscule fragments of time.*

"Right, men!" Andrew raised a hand. "Follow me!"

Andrew's section stayed a few paces behind him as he moved forward. He wished he had Lancelot, his Kabul pony that had never let him down, but this Shan mount was an adequate replacement. Andrew had named it Shansi, a meaningless name that seemed to suit it, and he fondled the pony's ears in sudden affection.

Andrew kept his men under control, glanced at his watch, ensured his NCOs were in position and halted a hundred yards outside the village. He heard voices from the outlying houses, heard a growling man quieting a barking dog; a baby began to wail, a woman laughed, and somebody sounded a gong.

The brassy clamour wakened old memories as Andrew raised his voice.

"They've seen us!" Andrew shouted. "Forward, lads! Forward the Royal Scots Fusiliers!" He kicked in his heels. "Extended order! Round up all the men! Don't hurt any women or children."

Andrew knew he did not have to add his final order to the Fusiliers, but it was always best to remind them. In the heat of action, when men were in danger, they could fire without checking their target.

He heard his NCOs shouting, one after another, and ordered every second man to dismount to control the civilians and prisoners as he entered the village. He expected the arguments, the anger, and the frustrated disquiet from frightened wives and mothers. Andrew knew that these reactions were normal when soldiers dealt with civilians. Burma was no different from Ireland, Africa, India, or the Scottish Hebrides.

Someone fired a musket, the muzzle flare coming from the rear of the village. Andrew heard the echo of the shot and, a moment later, the reply from half a dozen Martini-Henrys.

That's my boys. Don't allow any dacoits to escape.

Andrew's section was busy, working in pairs as they kicked open doors and hauled out any men they found. Most were villagers, confused, angry, scared, but not dangerous. Women, wives, sisters, or mothers clung to their men, screaming and sobbing in fear.

Other men were truculent or looking for an escape.

"Keep the men secure," Andrew said to Corporal Rowan. "If a wife or mother claims anybody, release him. Hold the others and look for the green umbrella." He repeated the orders to Corporal McGhee.

The Fusiliers nodded, holding their rifles with grim professionalism. After months of frustrating training, hunting dacoits, and witnessing their handiwork, they had no intentions of allowing any to escape.

The firing at the rear of the village broke out again, with British volleys following scattered dacoit musketry.

"You're in charge, Corporal," Andrew said, mounting his horse. Kicking in his spurs, he rode towards the firing, pulling the rifle from its bucket holster.

Sergeant Jardine had stopped a breakout at the rear of the village, with his men in extended order and every fourth man holding the horses. The increasing light revealed a row of determined men in faded khaki with sun helmets on their heads and Martini-Henry rifles in steady hands.

A score of dacoits huddled behind the houses while two desperate men held a woman in front of them as a human shield. Andrew stretched forward, holding his rifle at arm's length. He nudged the nearest dacoit in the back of the head with the muzzle of the Martini.

"Release her!" Although Andrew doubted if the dacoit understood his words, the threat was plain. The man stepped back in fear, shouting to his companion. The second dacoit pulled his captive closer to him, snarling at Andrew. The woman screamed, struggling to free herself, with clawed hands raking the dacoit's face.

As the dacoit reared back, Andrew altered the angle of his rifle and fired. The bullet smashed into the dacoit's temple and exited at the back of his head, taking half his brain in a welter of blood and splintered bone. His hostage screamed again and ran, with the first dacoit watching his friend's death curiously, yet without visible emotion.

A young Fusilier ran up, immediately understood what had happened and jammed his Martini into the surviving dacoit's chest.

"Hands up, chum!" The Fusilier was about twenty, with an angelic face except for eyes that had already seen the worst of the world. When the dacoit hesitated, the Fusilier jerked up his rifle barrel, catching him under the chin and forcing his lower teeth into his upper lip. "Hands up, you bastard, or I'll blow your bloody head off!"

This time, the dacoit's hands shot into the air as blood dribbled from his mouth. "Now get back there!" The Fusilier glanced at Andrew. "I've got him, sir."

"So I see," Andrew reloaded his rifle. "Put him with the other prisoners, Fusilier."

"Yes, sir. Come on, you!" The Fusilier jabbed his rifle into the dacoit's bare back.

The firing at the rear of the village had ended, and Andrew pushed on, peering through drifting gunsmoke.

"Sergeant Jardine!"

"All secure, sir," Jardine replied quietly.

"Did you find Buda Sein?" Andrew dismounted to talk to Jardine.

"Not a shadow of him, sir," Jardine replied. "Unless he's pretending to be one of the ordinary dacoits."

Andrew saw a flurry of activity on his left. A Fusilier yelled, aimed, and fired as two dacoits burst from the back of a house and ran, jinking and weaving, into the surrounding fields. The first carried something in his right hand.

"That's a folded umbrella!" Sergeant Jardine shouted.

"Get these men!" Andrew jumped on his horse as the two men splashed through a paddy field, with the Fusiliers firing after them. The second man staggered as a bullet smashed into his shoulder. He turned around, his long hair loose over his shoulders as he shouted defiance. Another bullet knocked him face down into the mud, where he struggled for a minute, raised a hand, and lay still.

The first dacoit was further away, with his yellow umbrella distinct against the green forest behind. Andrew pushed Shansi beyond the village and into the paddy field until the mud became too deep, and the horse began to struggle.

"That's far enough, Shansi," Andrew murmured. "That's far enough." He heard the sergeant call "cease fire," heard a single shot, saw the umbrella twitch as a bullet hit it, and then the yellow vanished.

He's gone. Buda Sein has escaped again. Damn and blast the man!

"Gather the prisoners together, Sergeant, and we'll sort the wheat from the chaff. The good people of Burma will be pleased to hear we've removed another dangerous dacoit gang from the countryside."

"I'm sure they will, sir," Sergeant Jardine said.

Andrew stared into the forest, certain that Buda Sein was watching him from the shelter of the trees.

We'll meet again, Buda Sein!

After another month and a couple more successes that saw half a dozen dead dacoits and twelve disconsolate prisoners, the dacoits' attack on Rangoon's environs faded away.

"You did well, Baird," the Chief Commissioner said from behind his desk. "Now, I will advise the military to adopt your techniques of a combination of standing pickets and flying columns to keep the dacoit menace down all across Lower Burma."

"Thank you, sir," Andrew replied.

"Not that they will listen," Sir Charles said gloomily. "Senior military officers live in the past. If it was good enough for Wellington, they say, it's good enough for me."

"I can't imagine the Army forming a square in the middle of Burma," Andrew said.

"Don't give them ideas, Baird. Wellington cut his teeth in India, remember? He was a sepoy general before he fought in Spain." Sir Charles stood up. "I take it you have heard the news about the impending war?"

"I have been a little busy lately," Andrew said. "I know we sent an ultimatum to King Thibaw."

Sir Charles nodded. He stepped to the window and stood in silhouette with his hands behind his back. "We've had about enough of King Thibaw, his dacoits, his threats against British subjects, and his machinations with the French."

"Yes, sir," Andrew agreed. "If you'll remember, Bo Thura was first to alert you to the French negotiations in the Kingdom of Ava." *That was a hint about his long overdue pardon, sir.*

Sir Charles grunted. "Put him aside for now, Baird. We have larger issues on hand than the future of one blasted criminal."

"I see, sir," Andrew said.

"As you said, we have sent an ultimatum to the Kingdom of Ava," Sir Charles said, "and I will remind you why."

Andrew remained standing while Sir Charles stood at the window. "Recently, the French sent a new consul, Monsieur Haas, to Mandalay. He became very close to King Thibaw and negotiated the terms of the Ava-French treaty. They agreed to establish a French bank in Burma and a railway from Mandalay to the border with our territories. The French would have a major role in businesses presently controlled by the Burmese government."

"I see, sir."

Sir Charles grunted. "With French troops in Tonkin, it's only a small step for them to enter Mandalay, and with a direct railway to our border, any minor dispute could have unpleasant consequences."

"Yes, sir," Andrew agreed.

"Obviously, we don't want the French to have influence on our border, so we asked them to remove Monsieur Haas, which they did." Sir Charles nodded. "That was a satisfactory outcome, but Thibaw continues to give us trouble."

"I am aware of the dacoit incursions, sir," Andrew reminded.

"The Burmans have also imposed a fine on the Bombay Burmah Trading Corporation, as you know," Sir Charles continued. "We disputed Ava's supposed claims about under-reporting the amount of teak the company extracts and the spurious accusations of non-payment for the employees. When the Kingdom of Ava sent its officials to seize some of the company's timber, we demanded they accept an arbitrator to settle the disagreement."

"Did they agree, sir?"

Sir Charles remained in silhouette. "We told them we would appoint the arbitrator. They refused."

"Perhaps they doubted the neutrality of an arbitrator we chose, sir," Andrew narrowed his eyes against the glare from the window, trying to see the Chief Commissioner's expression.

"We're British, damn it," Sir Charles snapped. "We play by the rules. When they refused, we decided we had enough of their nonsense, and on the 22nd of October, we sent them an ultimatum."

Sir Charles stepped away from the window and paced the room before returning to his desk. "We demanded that they accept a British resident in Mandalay; that should forestall any more trouble from Monsieur Haas and his countrymen. We told them to suspend any legal action against the Bombay and Burmah Company until our resident arrives in Mandalay and that we should control the Kingdom of Ava's foreign relations. Lastly, they should grant us commercial facilities to develop trade with northern Burma and China."

Andrew considered the British demands. "I doubt any self-respecting ruler would accept these terms, sir. It removes virtually all independence from the country."

"How many villages have Thibaw's dacoits burned?" Sir Charles countered. "What will stop him from convening with the French or fining more British companies? We need a firm hand to deal with such people."

Andrew remembered the tortured women and ravaged villages. "I see, sir."

"King Thibaw's reply was not positive," Sir Charles said. "It was inadequate and said he would consult France, Germany, and Italy." The Chief Commissioner shook his head. "The cheek of the man!"

"What happens now, sir?"

"It will be war, Captain Baird, and then we'll be rid of the dacoit menace and have peace to develop trade and prosperity for the people of Burma."

"Yes, sir," Andrew said. Since his arrival in Rangoon, he had known that war with Thibaw's kingdom was possible but had hoped to return home before hostilities began.

"You'll wonder why I am telling you all this, Captain Baird," Sir Charles said. "As a keen young officer, you'll be desperate to play your part." He smiled. "I believe your nickname in the Zulu War was 'Up-and-at-'em,' and now is your chance to enhance your reputation further. When this war starts, which will be soon, I want you in the leading ship. You know the river and have proved you can master the Burmans in battle."

"I only fought dacoits, sir," Andrew reminded, but Sir Charles brushed away his objections.

"Nonsense! You soldiers! You praise yourselves too highly, or you hide beneath a modesty blanket. Now get yourself ready, Baird. Count your bullets, sharpen your sword, gird up your loins or whatever you soldiers do before battle."

"Yes, sir," Andrew was slightly dazed.

"See that girl of yours, eh? Miss Maxwell, isn't it?" Sir Charles was suddenly jovial. "Off you go, Baird. You're dismissed."

CHAPTER 22

RANGOON, NOVEMBER 1885

Andrew left the government office with his head spinning and his hopes of returning home dashed.

What will Mariana say to another indefinite period in Rangoon? Maybe I should move us out of Wells' Britannia and rent a bungalow? Hopefully, it's a short war.

When Andrew visited the British Cantonments, the talk in the Fusiliers' Officers' Mess was all about the impending war.

"I heard their Queen Mother declared the Burmans would resist to the last," a jovial major proclaimed.

"That should prolong the war, then," Major Goudie said. "Rather than two days, it will take a week." He saw Andrew and welcomed him with a handshake and a whisky and water. "You've been doing great things with the Mounted Infantry, I hear, Baird. What do you think about this war, then? Is it time to sort out old Thibaw?"

"Maybe so, sir," Andrew replied.

"There's no maybe about it, Baird. Thibaw's been sending his blasted bandits against us for months now. It's time we retaliated."

The Fusiliers' officers gave Andrew more details. "According to bazaar shaves, the Burmans are strengthening the palace fortifications and razing the houses near the ramparts to give their guns a clear field of fire."

"Thibaw's chief minister, Kinwin Mingyee or whatever he's called," a tall captain said. "He seems sensible. He told Thibaw to agree to our terms. Thibaw replied that if Mingyee was afraid of us, he should become a Buddhist monk!"

"From what little I've heard of Mingyee," Andrew said, "he's a dangerous man. I doubt he's our friend. He's more likely befriending who he thinks will be the winner."

Major Goudie gave an approving nod. "I think the same," he agreed.

"How about the civilians in Mandalay?" Andrew asked.

"We sent a steamer, *Dowoon*, upriver to evacuate them," Goudie said. "The Burmans detained it at Mandalay." He shrugged. "We don't know any more at present."

Andrew grunted. He had been so busy with the Mounted Infantry he had ignored the larger picture. He heard the officers talk about the Rangoon Port Trust lending the Army six barges to use as floating batteries, with the Royal Artillery fitting two sixty-pound howitzers to each. The Army would requisition Irrawaddy Flotilla steamers and mount twenty-five-pounder guns for a Naval Brigade to batter past the frontier forts.

"Upper Burma is a wilderness," one young lieutenant said. "We'll have to travel by river."

Andrew listened without adding many comments.

"The Burmese think Thibaw is omnipotent," the same subaltern said with the certainty of youth. "They can't conceive of disobeying him, even though they hate him." He glanced at Andrew. "What do you think, Captain Baird?"

"I think most Burmans only want to get on with their lives without being pestered by kings, dacoits or British soldiers." Andrew finished his whisky and stood up. "As do I. If you will excuse me, gentlemen, I must leave you."

How the devil can I tell Mariana that we can't leave Rangoon yet?

"NO!" MARIANA STARED AT ANDREW ACROSS THE WIDTH OF HER ROOM. "You're doing what?"

"I'm going to war," Andrew told her. "We're going to war with Thibaw, and I'm wanted."

"Why?" Mariana asked. "Don't they have enough soldiers? Why must you fight all their battles for them?"

"It's my duty," Andrew replied.

"Your duty?" Mariana tried to control her temper. She lowered her voice to a whisper. "Go and do your blessed duty, Captain Andrew Baird. Go on!" She pointed to the door. "Go!"

Andrew opened his mouth to speak, realised he had nothing to say, turned and left the room. "Damn and blast," he said when he entered his quarters and stood with his back to the door. "Damn and blast it all to hell and gone."

Andrew paced the room for a few moments, realised he needed more space and left the hotel to walk Rangoon's streets, now busy with an influx of British and Indian soldiers and officers. He strode to the docks, watching the accumulation of shipping carrying men and munitions for the forthcoming campaign.

Poor old Thibaw doesn't know what a hornet's nest he has stirred up by getting into bed with the French and fining a British company. He watched a platoon of sepoys *

* Indian soldiers.

march past, admired their bearing, and stopped when Than Than Aye stepped in front of him.

"Hello, Than Than Aye," Andrew said. "How good to see you again."

"Cousin Andrew," Than Than Aye took his arm. "Bo Thura asked me to find you. With this war coming, Maung Thandar has called up his followers to hunt my father down, and Bo Thura wants to know if Sir Charles has granted his pardon yet."

"Not yet," Andrew shook his head.

"When?" Than Than Aye asked.

"I don't know," Andrew replied.

"When it comes," Than Than Aye said, "will you bring it in person? Bo Thura doesn't trust anybody else."

"I'll try," Andrew replied.

How would Mariana react to yet another delay?

Than Than Aye read his expression, "You'll try, but Mariana would object. That's it, isn't it?"

"She's not at her best," Andrew agreed. "She's gone off me, I think."

Than Than Aye smiled, "Remember what I said, Andrew. Women need time."

"She's had years," Andrew replied.

"Wasn't she sick for most of these years?"

"Yes," Andrew admitted.

"And you said she was recovering after her illness."

"Yes," Andrew repeated.

"And she's known you as a mentor and friend," Than Than Aye said. "Now, you expect her to alter her view of you to a lover and husband." She smiled. "Give her time. She had a terrible experience a few years ago; then you took her to war. Not long after, you shifted her to a different country, in a different continent, and now to a third continent with a completely different culture. That's a lot for somebody to assimilate, let alone expecting her to marry her guardian angel."

"I'm hardly Mariana's guardian angel," Andrew said.

Than Than Aye touched his arm, "You are in her eyes, Andrew, if all you've told me is true. I know her culture and mine are very different, but women are women in any society. Give her time and learn patience."

Andrew smiled and moved away as a heavy bullock cart pulled past. "I'll take your advice, Than Than Aye."

"Next time you see the Chief Commissioner, Andrew, could you remind him about Bo Thura's pardon?"

"I always remind him," Andrew said.

Than Than Aye looked away, "Then remind him again, please. Tell him that Bo Thura will help all he can when the British invade."

"I will tell him," Andrew said. "I hope it helps."

"So do I," Than Than Aye replied. "I'll keep you in touch, Cousin. When the British invasion begins, my father will help."

"I can't guarantee Sir Charles will reciprocate," Andrew said.

Than Than Aye nodded, "If the British win, they will surely get rid of Maung Thandar and Buda Sein," she said. She smiled as she stepped back. "Don't give up on Mariana. Not yet."

Andrew nodded. "I won't. Thank you, Than Than Aye." He watched as a detachment of Madras Pioneers marched past, then turned to speak to Than Than Aye, but she was gone. He sighed and continued his walk.

❄

"MARIANA," JENNINGS SAID QUIETLY AS THEY SAT OPPOSITE EACH OTHER IN the hotel dining room. "May I ask you a personal question?"

"You may," Mariana replied and quickly added, "as long as it's not too personal."

"If you think I am being too forward," Jennings said, "tell me to keep quiet or slap my face. I will understand."

Mariana smiled, shaking her head. "I don't think I'll ever slap your face," she said. "Go on. Fire away. I'm ready." She sat erect in her chair. "I've braced myself for whatever you say."

Jennings laughed. "I know you and Captain Andrew have separate rooms in Wells' Hotel and live in the same house in Britain."

"The same house but separate rooms," Mariana forestalled Jennings' question. "We have separate rooms." She lifted her chin slightly. "And it has always been separate rooms, Stephen, and separate beds."

Jennings touched her arm. "I did not mean to imply any impropriety," he said.

Mariana relaxed. "You are an interesting man, Stephen. You are a very polite gentleman, yet you ask the most astounding questions."

"You are an example of the most amazing self-control," Jennings told her. "I know you have feelings for Captain Andrew, yet you remain, forgive me, pure."

Mariana looked away. "Captain Baird has been a good friend of mine for many years," she said. "Nothing else."

Jennings bowed from his seat. "Forgive my frankness on such a delicate subject," he said. "I had no right to ask." He lowered his voice. "With Captain Andrew's interest in his Burmese friend, I should have already known."

"I am not some delicate rose from a closeted background," Mariana kept her voice cool. "Coming from a Natal farm, I am fully aware of the facts of life. However, Stephen, I think we should discuss other matters."

HEAVILY MOUSTACHED AND STEADY-EYED, GENERAL SIR HARRY Prendergast was an Indian-born veteran of half a dozen campaigns who wore his medal ribbons with pride. Andrew saw the crimson ribbon of the Victoria Cross and knew he was facing an exceptionally brave man.

"Captain Baird," Prendergast said. "I am gathering as much information as possible about the Burmans before I lead the Queen's Army against them."

"Yes, sir." Andrew stood at attention on the opposite side of Prendergast's desk. The fan above creaked slightly as it rotated, with the draught rustling the maps on the wall.

"Thibaw and his officials have called up all their men to contest our advance," Prendergast said. "You've seen them in action, Baird. What was your impression?"

"I only saw them marching and attacking convicts and civilians," Andrew replied. "I'd say they were a tough-looking bunch but ill-armed. They carried a mixture of ancient muzzle-loading muskets and some modern rifles."

Prendergast nodded and scribbled a short note on a pad before him. He used only his right hand, with a wound during the Indian Mutiny disabling his left arm.

"Morale? Skills?"

Andrew considered for a moment, "I'd say their morale is high when they have a purpose. They carry their rations with them, so they can travel fast, without needing a commissariat, and dig trenches as protection from musketry or artillery."

"Are they all professional soldiers?"

"I don't believe so, sir. The King's Guards are full-time. One can identify them by a dragon tattoo on the nape of the neck." Andrew dredged his memory. "I don't believe Burma has a large standing army, but every man will be expected to fight during a war. Thibaw has an armoury in Mandalay, and the nation will provide food. I don't believe the king pays them."

Prendergast wrote more notes. "Artillery?"

"I didn't see any, sir, but I believe they have some," Andrew replied. "I know they have two or three Italian engineers modernising their forts, so I presume they will also have added artillery."

"That equates with my other sources," Prendergast said, spreading a map on the table. "You've sailed this route, Baird, so you can correct my mistakes."

"I'll do my best," Andrew promised, "though I am sure the captains of the Irrawaddy Flotilla steamers would be more useful."

Prendergast turned his steady eyes on Andrew. "They know the river, Baird. They can't give details of the defences like a military man can." He returned his attention to the map. "Thibaw has two groups of forts that could prove difficult for our advance up the Irrawaddy. Both lie between the frontier of British Burma and Mandalay. The first is here, about sixty miles from the border." He stabbed his finger down. "The Minhla group." He looked up at Andrew. "Would you agree, Baird?"

"I would, sir," Andrew said.

"Tell me your observations." Those steady eyes fixed on Andrew again.

"I saw two forts there, one on either bank of the river. The Minhla fort on the west side is old and looked neglected. I think recent floods have damaged it. On the eastern side is Kolegone, or Kuligon or Kuliyang; take your pick of the name. The Italian mercenaries supervised as the Burmese built it."

"Strength?"

"Kolegone is brick-built," Andrew said. "And situated on a slight eminence. I don't know how many guns it has, but a decent gunner could command the river for a couple of miles at least. The Italians are fine engineers, sir."

Prendergast grunted. "We think Kolegone has ten guns, but of small calibre. It has a large garrison of the king's troops, with Kinwin Mingyi's son-in-law in charge, which may or may not be advantageous to the Burmans. That depends on how loyal they are to Mingyi. What is your opinion, Captain Baird?"

"The position is strong, sir, but I cannot speak for the garrison. If I were to take it, I'd land a force lower down the Irrawaddy and take it from the rear, as most of the guns will face the river."

Prendergast lifted his chin. "Such a move would necessitate a long march through wooded country, Baird, which is ideal for ambushes."

"Yes, sir, but if the landing force put out flanking parties, they could cope."

Prendergast grunted again and ran his finger further up the map, following the course of the Irrawaddy. "The second group is here, the Ava or Singon group, although only God knows what the Burmese call it. These forts are only a few miles below Mandalay."

"Yes, sir," Andrew agreed.

"There are three forts, with what we call Ava or Singon fort, marginally to the west of Ava, the ancient capital on the left or west bank. On the right or eastern bank and nearly directly opposite is the Sogaing Fort, while slightly further upriver, on a small island near Ava, is Shabyadon Fort." He glanced at Andrew. "Any comments, Baird?"

"I passed them last year," Andrew said. "They are brick or masonry built, but I'd not call them strong, and I didn't notice any guns. The Burmese may have added artillery since I was there, of course. I think our men can take them without too much difficulty."

Prendergast scribbled Andrew's observations on his pad. "Thank you, Baird. That will be all for now. We are advancing up the Irrawaddy to defeat Thibaw, and when the fleet is assembled, you will be in the leading vessel."

"Yes, sir," Andrew replied.

Prendergast grinned. "Another chance to add to your laurels, eh, Captain? Your knowledge will come in useful, no doubt."

"I hope so, sir," Andrew said.

Mariana answered her door to Andrew's gentle tap. She greeted him with a smile, stepped aside and allowed him to enter.

"What did the general say?" Mariana asked.

"He said I'm returning to war," Andrew told her. He expected hot words, but instead, Mariana sighed and produced a foolscap-sized leather notebook.

"I'll keep a record of the days in here," she said.

"That's a lovely book," Andrew said. "Better than your last one."

"Yes. Stephen got me this one. Wasn't that nice of him?"

"Very nice."

Stephen. Not Mr Jennings.

"He even had it embossed with my name," Mariana said. She showed Andrew the gold lettering on the front of the book with *Mariana Maxwell* in copperplate writing.

"That was kind of him," Andrew said. "You must be very attached to Mr Jennings."

"We are good friends, Andrew," Mariana said and sighed again. "When you were out, Andrew, an army officer left a note for you." She handed it over and waited for him to open the envelope and read its contents. "What does it say?"

"It says I have to report on board the motor launch *Katherine* the day after tomorrow," Andrew said. "I am sorry, Mariana. I am leaving you alone again to go to war."

"I'll be all right," Mariana said bravely. *I won't be alone, Andrew. Stephen will look after me.*

CHAPTER 23

IRRAWADDY RIVER, NOVEMBER 1885

"You must be Captain Andrew Baird," the officer was young, freckled, and energetic. "I'm Midshipman Cosmo Birnie and the captain ordered me to look after you."

They shook hands on the quayside, where the morning sun cut through a faint mist and an array of shipping was berthed alongside or anchored in the river.

"You've to come with me to *Kathleen*," Birnie said. He looked Andrew up and down, marvelled at the campaign medals on his chest, and led the way with a rolling gait that did not disguise his long, determined stride. While Andrew wore a khaki uniform and a sun helmet, Birnie had a blue Royal Navy jacket above white trousers and a blue cap at a rakish angle on his head.

"Is that all your dunnage?" Birnie nodded at Andrew's single bag, "Or is there more to come?"

"That's it all," Andrew said.

"Good show. We don't have much space on *Kathleen*."

"Which ship is *Kathleen*?" Andrew looked at the assembled vessels, from the two-decked Irrawaddy Flotilla paddle steamers to the ocean-going steamships and three-masted clippers. He smiled when he saw Jamieson steering *Little Salamander* between two larger vessels with the cigar in his mouth, making nearly as many fumes as his vessel's smokestack.

"That's her there," Birnie pointed to a tiny steam launch with a canopy stretching her full length and a hands-breadth above the tallest crew member. "We're a gunboat with two guns, a Nordenfeldt and a shallow draught for the river. We have an eighteen-man crew and one passenger, which is you." He grinned at Andrew. "Come along, old fellow, I mean, please step this way, sir!"

He led them into a small dinghy, where two bearded seamen rowed them to the steam launch.

"Welcome aboard, Captain Baird," a long-jawed officer said, "cast off forward, cast off aft!"

Andrew had no longer stepped on board than *Kathleen* was on the move, with smoke issuing from her single funnel amidships.

"That's Lieutenant Frederick Trench in command," Birnie said in a hushed tone as he ushered Andrew to the stuffy below decks. "He's the senior lieutenant on HMS *Turquoise.* We're all from *Turquoise,* you see, and the captain—you have to call Trench captain because he's in charge—was a bit miffed having to come back to Rangoon to pick you up."

Andrew shared a cabin with Birnie, the most junior officer on board. Both had to stoop to fit in the cabin, and Andrew's bag fitted under the only bed.

"I'll sling a hammock," Birnie said cheerfully. "Do you know what's happened here?"

"No," Andrew admitted. He liked this grinning youth.

"Not many soldiers know much about the Senior Service," Birnie said. "When we heard that we might have to fight Thibaw, the Royal Navy only had a single vessel in Rangoon: HMS *Woodlark,* a gun vessel with Captain Clutterbuck in command. We in *Turquoise* were in Trincomalee, and Captain Woodward was sent to Rangoon, so we toddled over at full speed."

Andrew imagined the ship steaming across the Indian Ocean, with the crew eager to arrive in Burma before the hostilities started.

"Then Sir Charlie something-or-other got involved and ordered the Indian Marine, that's India's navy, to get the paddle steamer *Irrawaddy* and two screw steam launches ready for war. That's *Kathleen* and our sister ship *Settang,* in case you hadn't guessed. The guns and men come from HMS *Woodlark,* and Captain Clutterbuck is in overall command of the naval side of operations."

Andrew glanced out of the porthole and saw *Kathleen* was pushing hard up the river.

"*Irrawaddy* has two twenty-pounder breech-loaders and two nine-pounder muzzle-loaders. We were all sent up to Thayetmyo, on the frontier with Upper Burma, and then Cap'n Trench was ordered to come and pick you up." Birnie grinned. "That's you up to date, sir."

"Call me Baird," Andrew said, "and I'll call you Birnie."

"Baird and Birnie it is," Birnie said. "I'd better get back on deck in case the old man needs me." He scrambled up the miniature companionway to the deck above, leaving Andrew to look around the cabin.

"Is Captain Andrew away again?" Jennings asked, sitting opposite Mariana in the dining room.

"He is," Mariana replied, sipping a cup of lukewarm coffee.

Jennings shook his head. "How long for this time, Mariana?"

Mariana shrugged. "Until the war is over, I expect."

Jennings nodded. "I presume he had to do his duty, but it's hard on you, Mariana."

"I'll be all right," Mariana said.

"Remember, I am here if you want to talk to somebody," Jennings said.

Mariana looked up. "Thank you," she said. "I won't forget."

"You are always welcome in my house," Jennings told her, smiling. "We won't bother with the champagne next time."

Mariana managed to smile. "That would be best," she said.

Jennings patted her hand. "I'm sure the war will be over soon. Until then, don't hesitate to visit my office or house."

"Thank you," Mariana watched Jennings saunter from the hotel and suddenly felt very lonely.

IRRAWADDY RIVER, 12TH NOVEMBER 1885

"There's trouble ahead!" Birnie reported cheerfully.

"What's happening?" Andrew emerged from below decks to see *Kathleen* hove to in mid-channel with a vulture circling overhead.

"Your spy has informed Captain Raikes, the deputy commissioner, that Thibaw has sent a seven-gun steamer downriver from Mandalay."

"My spy?" Andrew asked.

"Yes indeed," Birnie tilted back his cap to scratch his head. "Apparently, he sent a note with your name on it."

Bo Thura has kept his word. I hope Sir Charles does likewise.

Birnie unfolded a chart of the river. "According to your friendly little spy, the Burman steamer intends to fortify Toungwia Island and land reinforcements at Singboungweh."

The names meant nothing to Andrew until Birnie pointed them out on the map. For all his excitability, Birnie's hand was steady as he traced the enemy steamer's course along the bends of the Irrawaddy.

"Thibaw's steamer will leave Mandalay on the 13th," Birnie said. "Or so your spy claims." He looked up, smiling. "Is that why you're with us, Baird? To keep communication with a Burman spy?"

"Maybe," Andrew evaded a direct reply as he studied the map. "Why choose Singboungweh?" he asked. "The river is fairly broad there. Our ships can just go to the far side."

Birnie laughed. "There speaks a land-based soldier," he said. "The river may be broad, but it's also shallow." He pointed to some figures written on the river. "These figures show the depth of water when the river was last surveyed. You'll see that they are in low single figures except for here," Birnie indicated a stretch close to Singboungweh. "This is the deep-water channel where our ships must sail, and artillery at Singboungweh will cover it."

Andrew nodded. "I understand," he said. *I had forgotten about the deep-water channel during my months fighting Buda Sein's dacoits.*

Birnie grinned. "We can't allow the enemy to reinforce his garrisons, can we? So Colonel Raikes asked Colonel Sladen for permission to steam up river and sort King Thibaw's ship out."

Andrew learned that Colonel Sladen was the field force's Chief Political Officer. Sladen spoke to General Prendergast, who granted permission for the gunboat *Irrawaddy* and *Kathleen* to steam upriver to confront Thibaw's vessel.

The much larger vessel *Irrawaddy* joined *Kathleen* when she steamed northwards out of Thayetmyo. The sun rose in glorious orange and red at their backs, and birds called from the trees. Andrew checked his watch. It was six in the morning of November 14th, 1885, and they were going to war.

They steamed gently upstream, the water chortling under their counters and the villages along the riverside already awake. Men in fishing boats eyed them curiously as women worked the paddy fields, children pointed and played, and the patient water buffalo plodded in their daily routine.

"It's all very peaceful," Andrew said.

"On the surface," Birnie replied, scanning the river with a long brass telescope. He pushed his cap further back on his head and jerked a thumb towards the riverbank. "God knows what's happening in there."

At eight that morning, the steamers crossed the frontier into Upper Burma. Andrew felt the atmosphere on *Kathleen* alter, as Lieutenant Trench ordered the men to the guns and posted a lookout aloft. Within five minutes, they passed a village, with half a dozen boats pulled up on the muddy bank but not a single villager in sight.

Kathleen edged closer to the bank, with Birnie examining the village through his telescope.

"Maybe they're scared of us, or perhaps Thibaw has ordered them to evacuate," Birnie said.

"Either way, it could be ominous," Andrew said.

Irrawaddy and *Kathleen* chugged on, with *Irrawaddy's* paddles churning the water to a cream-brown froth and the crew watching the riverbanks, alert for danger. They passed the village of Tagoumaw and trained their weapons on the Burmese soldiers who stared at them.

"Is that Thibaw's men?" Birnie asked.

"With the light jackets and the brass helmets?" Andrew said. "That's the king's soldiers."

"Remain at battle stations," Lieutenant Trench ordered, "but don't fire unless they do."

We don't want to be blamed for starting this war, and we won't be the aggressors if Thibaw's men fire the first shot.

The steamers passed Tagoumaw, with the Burmese soldiers watching without expression. *Irrawaddy's* wash caused large waves to break along the shore, sending the small fishing boats dancing as birds screeched and monkeys chattered above.

"We're deep in Thibaw's territory now," Andrew said. "Nearly two hours past the frontier."

"Steamer ahead, sir!" the lookout shouted. "I don't recognise her!"

"All hands, get ready!" Lieutenant Trench shouted, although, in such a small vessel as *Kathleen,* he could have passed the message without raising his voice. Andrew saw a stir in *Irrawaddy* as men rushed to the guns. He felt a renewed tremor of anticipation run through the launch.

"There she is!" Birnie said.

The Burmese steamer looked like an old Irrawaddy Flotilla vessel, slightly dilapidated but armed with artillery. She sailed close to the right bank, towing a flat, with both the steamer and flat dark with soldiers.

"Stand by your guns!" Lieutenant Trench ordered.

"Excuse me, Baird," Birnie said and took the three steps to the forward gun. The seamen waited, watching the Burmese steamer.

"Fire a warning shot!" Trench ordered. "Don't hit her!"

The gun crew had been waiting for the order, and the twenty-pounder banged out with a jet of smoke. *Kathleen* shuddered, and Andrew watched as the shot landed fifty yards away from the Burmese vessel, throwing a column of dirty brown water high into the air.

"They're still moving, by God!" Trench shouted. "They're getting up steam!"

Irrawaddy and *Kathleen* moved closer, with the respective commanders watching the river for shoals.

"*Irrawaddy* is sailing rather close to the right bank," Andrew said.

"She's keeping to the deep-water channel," Birnie replied. "Right at the bend of the river."

"Look ashore," Andrew said. "Burmese soldiers. And artillery inside that earthwork!"

"That's a new fortification, by George," Birnie said. "It's not marked on the chart!"

"The Burmans have been busy," Andrew agreed.

As the British vessels eased closer to the bank, the Burmese opened fire with small arms and artillery. Bullets whined around *Kathleen,* with some rebounding from the metal plates protecting the forward gun. A shell exploded nearby, sending a tall column of brown water fifteen feet into the air. When the water subsided, dead fish floated on the river's surface.

"Return fire!" Trench ordered cheerfully. "Thibaw's men have fired the first shots!"

Andrew saw the men on *Irrawaddy* also aiming and firing at the Burmese on land and afloat. With some Burmese behind the earthwork and others hidden in thick jungle, the British could hardly see their land-based attackers.

"They've got tents as well," Birnie said. "How civilised of them."

Irrawaddy was firing her Nordenfeldt multi-barrelled organ gun, with the heavy bullets ripping through the trees and raising spurts of mud and dust from the Burmese fortification. Andrew compared the weapon to the Gatling guns he had seen in Zululand, wondered at the innovations in military technology, and ducked as a bullet smashed against the rail he leaned on. He realised the Burmese were making good practice, with bullets whining and hissing around the launch and gunboat, splashing alongside the thin hulls and ricocheting from the upperworks.

"They're fighting well," Birnie said, grinning. He had pushed his cap so far back on his head that Andrew wondered why it did not fall off.

The bluejackets fired, shouting encouragement as they eased around the bend. They aimed at the Burmese camp, the king's steamer, and the crowded flat. The twenty-pounder made good practice on the camp, landing a succession of shells on the earthworks and the tents. Through his binoculars, Andrew saw the Burmese defenders firing back, with smoke billowing around the surrounding trees.

With the bend negotiated, *Irrawaddy* and *Kathleen* reached a wider stretch of deep water, with bullets hammering off the upperworks. Simultaneously, the Burmese steamer cast off the flat, with men leaping from both vessels and swimming towards the shore.

"Warm work, Lieutenant Baird!" Birnie said, grinning.

"Warm enough," Andrew replied as the bluejackets fired their Nordenfeldt. An officer had issued Martinis to the men, who used them enthusiastically and with more skill than Andrew expected.

"*Irrawaddy* is signalling, sir!" A young rating approached Lieutenant Trench. "Board the enemy steamer and carry her to Thayetmyo!"

"A prize, by God!" Trench gave a string of orders that saw *Kathleen* surge towards the Burmese steamer, and the crew responded eagerly despite the bullets that whistled overhead and splashed alongside. "Mr Birnie! Issue cutlasses to the men!"

The bluejackets buckled on the short, lethal swords that their forefathers had carried during the French wars and which their distant ancestors had used in the days of Morgan and Woodes Rogers. They cheered as *Kathleen* approached the enemy.

"That's the way, lads!" Trench encouraged. He was first to board the Burmese steamer, just as the remainder of her crew jumped overboard.

"Take over the engines!" Trench ordered. "Captain Baird, could you take a party of riflemen and make these damned Burmans keep their heads down, please?"

Andrew obeyed, and three men, all whom Trench could spare from *Kathleen*'s minuscule crew, followed him to the rail.

With *Kathleen* and the captured steamer closer to the bank than *Irrawaddy*, the Burmese concentrated on the British launch with artillery, muskets, and rifles. Andrew's few men loaded and fired, worked the Martini's underlevers to eject the spent cartridges, loaded again, and exchanged dark humour as they eased past the shore.

"There are their leaders," Birnie said, with a hand on Andrew's arm. He extended his telescope, ignoring the bullets that whistled past and knocked splinters from *Kathleen*'s woodwork. "These Burman lads had better be careful

Chips doesn't get hold of them. The carpenter won't be happy at all this work they're giving him."

"Yes, indeed," Andrew had seen the carpenter shouting at the men to take care of the deck planking. He would be incensed at the damage the Burmese bullets were doing to his woodwork. "Maybe we'd better find some cover from these marksmen."

Birnie laughed. "They're such bad shots that the safest place is directly in their line of fire. By God, Baird, I think that's Poung Woon with these lads!"

Andrew focused his binoculars, momentarily forgetting the danger. He recalled the images he had seen of the Burmese leadership. "By God, I believe you're right."

Birnie laughed. "If I remember correctly, Poung Woon promised to bring Thibaw the heads of General Prendergast and Colonel Sladen within a fortnight."

"He'll have to get a shift on, then," Andrew said. "The days are slipping away."

A burst of fire from *Irrawaddy* sent the Burmese deeper into the forest, and then *Kathleen* was past the most dangerous area. The trees screened the enemy as effectively as any camouflage.

"Did you see the fellow at Poung Woon's side?" Birnie asked as he snapped his telescope shut.

"Not properly," Andrew replied.

"Nor did I, but I thought it was Maung Thandar."

Andrew lifted his binoculars again, attempting to penetrate the dense forest. "Maung Thandar," he repeated. "He is the man who sends the dacoits into British Burma."

"Is that right?" Birnie replied. "I know he's one of Thibaw's ministers."

"He's a bad man," Andrew said.

"Back to Thayetmyo, men!" Trench shouted. "We've done our duty today."

Towing the flats and steaming with the current, *Kathleen* reached the relative sanctuary of the broader channel, but the Burmese followed, firing from the forest. Andrew occasionally glimpsed their light uniforms and yellow flashes from the muzzle flares.

"Aim at the smoke, boys!" Andrew shouted above the crackle of musketry and thumping of the engines. He saw one bullet strike the rail at his side, buckling the steel and leaving a thick blue-grey smear. The closest bluejacket laughed.

"Somebody will have to clean that up," he said, thumbed a cartridge into the breech of his rifle, aimed and fired. "That's for you, Thibaw, for damaging our new ship!"

The Burmese in the earthworks shifted their attention to *Irrawaddy*, with their artillery fire raising fountains of water that splashed her as she turned downstream. *Irrawaddy's* Nordenfeldts returned the fire, with her bullets landing more accurately than Andrew expected from a moving ship.

The Nordenfeldts don't have the power to destroy the fortification.

"*Irrawaddy*'s not damaging the earthwork!" Birnie agreed with his observation. "Captain Clutterbuck will have to land and storm the place, sir!"

Andrew shook his head as his military caution took control. "We don't have enough men," he replied. "There might be two or three hundred Burmans dug in there."

Birnie grunted and supervised as his men fired and reloaded. "If you say so, sir."

"The Burmese flat's loose," Trench said. "No, by God, two flats are loose. Let's capture them as well."

CHAPTER 24

IRRAWADDY RIVER, NOVEMBER 1885

Andrew glanced at the seamen, who all seemed pleased about returning to more dangerous waters. He knew the Royal Navy's daredevil reputation and had met the seamen of the Naval Brigades in both the Zulu and the Boer Wars, but here, on their own element of water, they seemed to welcome trouble.

"Aye, aye, sir!" the men said immediately.

"Are you coming, Captain Baird?" Midshipman Birnie asked, grinning as he buckled on a cutlass. "You were known as Up-and-at-'em in Africa, were you not?"

Andrew realised his reputation was at stake. Surrounded by eager seamen with cutlasses and Martinis-Henry, he knew he had to agree.

"I hoped you would not leave me out," he said.

A petty officer with a neat red beard clapped him on the back. "That's the spirit, sir!"

When *Kathleen* drew alongside, Birnie led half the boarding party onto a small boat.

"In you come, sir!" the petty officer said, helping Andrew into the bouncing boat. "Sixpence for a tour of the bay, threepence to capture the Burmese flats!"

Birnie sang as they headed to the flats, which floated close inshore.

"Come on, *Kathleens!*"

The Burmese greeted their arrival with a storm of musketry that splashed around the boat and knocked splinters off the gunwale.

"They don't like us very much," Birnie said, holding his cap as the passage of a bullet knocked it askew. "Come on, lads, attach a line to the flat!"

The seamen jumped onto the nearest flat, with Andrew moving to the side and firing towards the Burmese. He did not expect to hit anybody but hoped his fire might deter a little.

"That's the way, lads! Back to the boat, lively now!"

Andrew remained where he was, firing and loading as the seamen fastened a line from the flat to their boat and rowed the short distance to *Kathleen.*

"Lash her to *Kathleen*, boys!" Birnie said. "You can leave her now, Captain Baird!"

As the flats had no independent means of propulsion, the seamen fastened them to *Kathleen*, ignoring the bullets that crashed on board, splintering the wood.

"Handsomely now, lads!" Birnie ordered. "No holidays here!"

The seamen obeyed, lashing the flats to the sides of the launch with a skill that Andrew could only admire. He continued to fire at the Burmese, aware of the futility of a single rifle but determined to do something to help.

"This flat's full of gunpowder, sir," the petty officer said. "Bags and bags of it!"

Andrew looked downward. "So it is." He realised he was standing on sacks of gunpowder. *If a Burmese thought to ignite the gunpowder, they'd blow us all up.*

"Queer sort of cargo, sir," the petty officer reported. "Gunpowder, sandbags and pointed stakes. Maybe they were going to build a palisade."

"Maybe so," Andrew said. "We'll work that out when we get to Thayetmyo." Despite his experiences in previous campaigns, he did not feel comfortable standing on hundreds of pounds of highly combustible gunpowder while scores of Burmese fired rifles at him. The petty officer grinned, showing tobacco-stained teeth.

"That's something to tell your grandchildren, sir. The day you served with the Naval Brigade and sailed a cargo of gunpowder down the Irrawaddy River."

Andrew could not share the petty officer's humour. "We'd best dump the gunpowder," he said, placing his rifle at his feet.

Birnie straddled one of the sacks, ripped it open with his cutlass and lifted a handful of the contents. "Poor quality rubbish," he decided. "If it were reliable, I'd give it to the gunners, but this stuff is as likely to blow up in storage as propel a cannonball." He glanced at Andrew. "What do you suggest, Captain Baird?"

"Throw the whole damned lot overboard," Andrew said. "And as quick as possible!"

Birnie grinned. "That's the spirit, sir! Come on, lads, lighten the lighter, free the flat and dump the danger."

As *Kathleen* chugged downstream with smoke and smuts pouring from her funnel, the seamen lifted the bags and threw them into the river, delighting in the task.

"There goes another one!" a red-faced seaman roared. "Into the river with you!"

"Don't make any sparks, lads," the petty officer warned. "Or the powder will go up rather than down, and we'll all be shaking hands with Davy Jones or whoever the god of this blessed river may be."

The Burmese continued to fire on them from the riverbank, with *Kathleen* replying with rifles and her Nordenfeldt. As they moved downriver, fewer bullets hit the vessels, with only superficial damage and no casualties.

By the time they reached Thayetmyo, the flat was nearly a thousand pounds lighter, and the gunpowder bags littered the riverbed. Andrew breathed easier.

The garrison cheered as *Irrawaddy* and *Kathleen* steamed into Thayetmyo with the king's steamer and the two flats as prizes. Khaki-clad British soldiers and smiling sepoys rushed to see the Navy display their latest victory.

Officers and men joined together as somebody shouted for three cheers, and the men responded, laughing and pointing at the steamers.

"That's a jab in the eye for old Thibaw!" Birnie said. "We captured his steamer, singed his beard and returned without a single casualty."

Andrew saw *Irrawaddy's* carpenter shaking his head at the bullet holes in his ship and knew there would be hours' work ahead for the chippy and however many men he dragooned into service.

"The Navy did well," Andrew agreed. "Not bad for a campaign fought hundreds of miles away from the sea."

Birnie laughed. "The Army can't do without us now. Why, we had men fighting in Zululand, even."

"I remember," Andrew said quietly.

Captain Clutterbuck scrambled down from *Irrawaddy* and leapt onto the flats to examine the cargo.

"What have we here, gentlemen?"

"Logs and sandbags, sir," Birnie said. "We think the Burmese were going to strengthen their forts."

Clutterbuck examined the logs. "Maybe so," he mused. "And maybe not. Have you seen this, Trench?"

"No, sir," Trench joined them on the flat.

Clutterbuck descended to the shallow hold. "These logs are fastened to the bottom of the flat. Where were the explosives?"

"Dead centre, sir, and the full length of the ship."

Clutterbuck nodded, pulled himself to the deck and lit his pipe. "Do you know what I think? I think Thibaw was going to sink this vessel in the deep-water channel. The explosives were to sink the ship, and the sandbags held the logs in place. One of our vessels would come up, ram into the pointed logs and sink, effectively blocking the channel."

"Clever buggers, these Burmans," Trench said.

"They are," Clutterbuck agreed. "Unless the Italians came up with the idea." He stepped free of the flat and swung onto *Irrawaddy*. "Whoever it was, Italian or Burmese, we'll have to be aware of traps in future."

"Yes, sir," Trench replied.

Clutterbuck puffed out blue smoke. "We were fortunate that your friend warned us, Baird. I'd shake his hand if I ever met him."

"I'm sure he'd appreciate that, sir," Andrew said.

Bo Thura would much prefer the free pardon he is desperately trying to earn.

❄

ANDREW STOOD ON THE QUAY AT THAYETMYO, WATCHING AS THE FLEET formed up for the invasion of Thibaw's Kingdom of Ava. He had been on three campaigns, but this was his first when the British Army travelled mainly by water. The ships mustered in a long line, with the stately double-deckers of the Irrawaddy Flotilla Company, the clumsy-looking flats, and the Royal Navy vessels with artillery and Nordenfeldts. Between them, a host of smaller craft hurried to and fro with messages, supplies and jaunty seamen. Andrew grinned as he saw Jamieson steering *Little Salamander*, cigar in mouth and looking as disreputable and solid as ever.

"I've never seen anything like this before," he said.

Birnie pulled on his cheroot, examined the glowing tip, and threw the stub into the river. It lay on the surface for a few seconds before submerging into the dark water. "I doubt anybody has," he said. "We are witnessing history." Birnie grinned. "No, Captain Baird, we are making history. Isn't it fun?"

Andrew wondered if he had ever been as young and enthusiastic as Cosmo Birnie. "It's certainly interesting," he said.

Andrew studied the leading ship, the Indian Marine vessel *Irrawaddy*, with its twenty-five-pounder cannons and Nordenfeldts. It seemed a potent vessel to lead the British fleet upriver to Mandalay.

Immediately astern was the steam launch, *Kathleen*, with the busy bluejackets working at cables and cleaning the deck.

Trust the Navy to keep everything sparkling bright even as we go to war in a country of rivers and jungles.

Beyond *Kathleen*, the Irrawaddy Flotilla steamer *Thambyadine* carried Major General Prendergast and his HQ staff. Then came *Pulu* and *Palow*, both filled with Naval Brigade seamen. It seemed imperative that a contingent of seamen accompanied the British Army on its campaigns. Andrew remembered the seamen at Majuba, carrying cutlasses against the Boer rifles. Their uniquely nautical language coloured the air as their officers put them through cutlass drill, with their white uniforms bright in the sun.

Yunnan was next, accompanied by the barge *White Swan*, with the Cinque Ports battery of the Royal Artillery. Behind them were *Panthay* with Major Smith's mule battery and *Shwaymyo* with the Madras sappers and the Bombay Mountain Battery.

The paddle steamers look rather sad, reduced to troop carriers, with a flat barge fastened to each side of the steamer. The sepoys look efficient, though.

The steamer *Burma* carried the Hampshire Regiment and General White's HQ. Andrew wondered how the redcoats, or khaki coats now, would enjoy having a general living in luxury on the steamer while they crowded onto the flats.

Chuitsabu followed with the First Madras Pioneers and Twelfth Madras Infantry. Andrew had never served with Indian sepoys before. He watched them through a veteran's critical eyes, hoping they were up to the same standard as the men with whom he had served in Africa. *If they are half as good as the Sikh policemen, we'll be all right.*

Ashley Aden carried the Twenty-third Madras Infantry, the Hazara Mountain Battery and telegraph stores. Again, Andrew surveyed them and nodded approvingly to see *Paulang*, a hospital ship, easing nearby. Having immediate medical care available would encourage the troops. Andrew remembered watching wounded men carried down from Laing's Nek during the Boer War and loaded on an unsprung wagon. *Paulang* would save that agony.

Other Irrawaddy Flotilla ships followed. *Attran* with more artillery, *Aloungpyah* with the 23rd Royal Welsh Fusiliers, *Thuriah* with the 11th Bengal infantry and some native labourers, *Talifu* with the mounted infantry and *Rangoon* with flats, acting as a reserve hospital ship. Astern, there was *Mendoon*, a brand-new vessel acting as reserve steamer with more labourers and a supply of coal for the steamers. Finally, *Kahyn* carried the commissariat and acted as the postal steamer.

Eighteen of the twenty Irrawaddy steamers had flats lashed alongside, more than tripling their carrying capacity.

Andrew viewed the fleet, smelled the smoke that drifted from their smokestacks in the humid, oppressive air, watched the mass of men, infantry, artillery, bluejackets, labourers, and river sailors, and wondered if Thibaw realised what he had stirred up.

Let's hope for a short and decisive campaign, a British victory and a pardon for Bo Thura so I can get home with Mariana.

CHAPTER 25

IRRAWADDY RIVER, NOVEMBER 1885

Andrew stood in the bow as half the British fleet remained at Thayetmyo, and *Kathleen* scouted ahead. He listened to the rhythmic beat of the paddles as *Irrawaddy* steamed alongside, with a dozen other vessels following in a two-mile-long line. Andrew glanced astern, saw the soldiers on the flats watching the riverbanks, and wondered what they were thinking.

At that point, the east bank of the Irrawaddy River had thickly forested hills over five hundred feet high. The hills rose parallel to the river, casting a dense shadow to create a dark and forbidding atmosphere, with even the birds quiet. Monkeys watched like silent sentinels from the trees. A single fallen log projected into the Irrawaddy at the angle where it turned towards the west, with the water frothing creamy brown over the top.

The ships pushed on towards Patanayo and Maloon without the Burmese offering any resistance.

"We're easing towards Mandalay," Birnie said.

"I wonder if Thibaw will just throw in the towel," Andrew said. "If we were facing the Zulus or the Boers, we'd have to fight for every bend of the river. So far, the Burmans have not even sniped at us. We'll see what happens when we come to the first of their forts."

When the ships rounded a sharp curve, the river straightened out, with around three miles of clear water ahead. The sun reflected from the waves, causing a dappling effect near the banks.

"Over there," Birnie gestured to the north, extending his long brass telescope. He grinned at Andrew over his shoulder. "Now the fun will really begin," he said.

Andrew lifted his binoculars. The fort of Kolegone dominated the hillside to the north, with the sun glinting from its stone walls. On the opposite bank, the older Minhla looked less formidable but still defiant.

"That could be dangerous," Andrew said.

If the Burmans have armed Kolegone with long-range artillery, the guns could hit anything on the river and slow, or even stop the fleet's passage.

The ships eased to a halt, with the engines idling and smoke drifting over to both banks. General Prendergast called a conference of the officers on board *Thambyadine,* and Andrew hastened over in a small boat as the men watched, smoked, or played cards.

"We have two positions to carry, gentlemen," Prendergast said ponderously. "Minhla on one bank and Kolegone on the other. Of the two, I rate Kolegone as being the more dangerous." He looked around his officers. "We'll take Kolegone by a turning movement around the hills where it stands."

The officers nodded, with some viewing the hills through binoculars and others staring at a map of the Irrawaddy.

"That means a march through the jungle," the Liverpool Regiment's colonel said. "If King Thibaw has his army nearby, they could fall on the troops when they're among the trees."

"That's a possibility," Prendergast agreed. "I expect the Burmans to make a good defence. The position is strong, and they can do major damage to our ships from there. *Irrawaddy* will shell Kolegone to occupy the defenders as the Liverpool Regiment marches around the rear. The mule battery will accompany the infantry to give some fire from the rear of the position."

The officers nodded. The plan seemed sound.

"It's all up to the soldiers now," Birnie removed his cap to mop his steaming face. "I don't fancy marching through the forest with Thibaw's men on the prowl."

"They know what they're doing," Andrew said. He watched as the troops disembarked on the east side, looking pleased to have something to do free of the confines of the ships. Officers and NCOs barked orders as the men clattered across the gangplanks, their boots sounding hollow on the solid planking. They filed onto the riverbank, stamping their feet, talking, and exchanging jokes in the customary manner of British soldiers. Some stopped to stretch their legs; others peered into the trees while a few checked the locks of their rifles.

The officers gave brief orders. "Right, men. Column of fours, load your rifles and on we go. Lieutenant Philips, you have the skirmishers. Lieutenant Owen, you have the rearguard. At the double now!"

Andrew watched the Liverpool Regiment march away, with part of him wishing he was ashore with the infantry.

I don't feel in control of anything in a boat. The captain and seamen are in charge here, and I am merely a passenger.

"Even after we take Kolegone, there's plenty of river between here and Mandalay," Birnie sounded disappointed at the lack of Burmese resistance.

"We haven't won here yet," Andrew reminded him. He consulted his map and nodded to the opposite bank. "Don't forget Minhla village. There's another masonry redoubt there that General Prendergast will want to secure."

"There's a boat approaching!" the lookout shouted. "With a military officer on board."

The boat pulled alongside, and an officer of an Indian regiment bounded onto *Kathleen.*

"Are you Captain Andrew Baird?" the major asked.

"I am," Andrew admitted.

"Major Pollock of the Second Bengal Infantry," the major introduced himself. "Colonel Baker believes you are interested in seeing how the sepoys fought."

"Yes, sir," Andrew agreed. "I have never fought with Indian soldiers."

Major Pollock grinned. "Well, now's your opportunity, Captain. One of our lieutenants has come down with fever, so I am an officer short. Well volunteered."

"Thank you, sir," Andrew said. "I was feeling a bit of a bystander."

Andrew joined the sepoys, wondering how to give orders without understanding the soldiers' language. They returned his interest, staring at his unfamiliar uniform.

Colonel Baker was younger than Andrew expected, heavily sun-tanned and neatly bearded. He addressed his men, spoke to his officers and finally to Andrew.

"We're going to take that redoubt, Baird. It's around ninety yards long by fifty broad, and the longer side is parallel to the riverbank." Baker indicated their target. "I am the senior officer present and, therefore, in overall command of the landing party, and I expect you to lead from the front. If you lead, my Bengalis will follow. If you don't want to lead, you can remain behind." His smile faded as he glared into Andrew's eyes. "Don't let my lads down, Baird."

"I won't, sir," Andrew replied.

In addition to the Second Bengal Infantry, the Eleventh Bengal Infantry and Twelfth Madras Infantry landed on the west bank of the river. The steamers manoeuvred close to the riverbank, efficient sailors lowered the gangways, and the infantry filed ashore as orderly as if they were on a holiday excursion but with less fuss and noise. Andrew was one of the first to step onto the soft ground, expecting to hear the sharp crack of a Burmese rifle or see a screaming tattooed soldier swinging a *dha*. Only the heat and insects greeted him.

"Some place this," Petty Officer Durnford stamped his feet and touched the hilt of his cutlass. "Come on, boys, but be careful you don't drop that box!" Durnford commanded the small contingent of seamen, who carried explosives in case they had to blow open the gate of the fort.

As the sepoys filed ashore, their officers sent out pickets to watch for the enemy, and Major MacNeill of the headquarters staff spoke with Mr Phayre, a civil officer whose task was to ease relations with the Burmese.

"Head inland," Colonel Baker ordered, and the company officers gave orders that saw the sepoys moving into a thick jungle.

"Keep alert, men!" Andrew joined his regiment, with the sepoys eyeing him with as much curiosity as he had them.

They're wondering if I am good enough to be one of their officers, Andrew thought. *I can't blame them for that.*

The forest was so thick with undergrowth that the flank guards could only operate a few yards from the main body, and the advance guard was less than ten yards distant.

"We can't push through the jungle," Colonel Baker decided. "Stick to the path and watch for ambushes."

A single narrow track, overgrown in parts, penetrated the deep forest with sufficient space for men to walk two abreast at its widest. Andrew stepped ahead of his platoon of Bengalis, examining the trees on either side and expecting a volley of musketry at every step.

"Where the devil are the Burmese?" Pollock asked. "Don't they want to fight for their blessed country?"

"Maybe they don't want to fight for King Thibaw," Andrew replied.

The sepoys moved on, alert for danger, checking all around them, professional soldiers doing their job. They edged on for three nerve-wracking miles, with Andrew pushing in front to join the skirmishers of the Bengalis and the 12th Madras.

The volley came from the right as the skirmishers entered a small and welcome clearing. Andrew had time to see a village wilting under the sun when he heard the crackle of musketry and saw the smoke and muzzle flares. He felt the wind of a bullet's passage and saw a Madras sepoy gasp and crumple, holding his leg.

"Ambush! Find cover and return fire!" Andrew ordered, firing his revolver at the village, from where spurts of smoke showed the position of the attackers.

The Madras skirmishers were agile, kneeling or lying as they fired, with some moving towards the village. The Bengalis obeyed Andrew, dropping to the ground without fuss, firing, reloading, and firing again.

As his men engaged the enemy, Andrew studied the enemy's position. The king's soldiers had erected three defensive stockades within the village and placed six modern artillery pieces to fire down the only road.

Somebody knows his stuff. These stockades offer mutual protection, and the guns are well-positioned.

A large house stood within easy firing range of the village, presumably belonging to the local *woon*, the government's administrative officer.

That house would make an excellent defensive position.

A few hundred yards behind the village, three pagodas offered cover for scores of Burmese soldiers. Andrew grunted, checking his Bengalis. They were aiming and firing without any haste.

After a couple of volleys of musketry, the Burmese switched to their artillery, with solid shot bouncing down the road and crashing through the trees. One shot whistled above Andrew's head and smashed into a tree twenty yards behind him, bringing down a large bough.

"They're going to stand and fight," Colonel Baker said with satisfaction. "Keep firing, boys." He glanced around. "This damned jungle will make it hard to extend our men and keep contact." He grinned through his moustache. "Thank God we've got good quality infantry, Baird!"

The Burmese continued to fire, with a belt of smoke wreathing the village, speckled with spurts of orange and white muzzle flares.

"Dear God!" Lieutenant Sillery of the 12th Madras jerked upright and looked at the spreading stain on his tunic. He collapsed slowly, still staring at the enemy.

Baker lifted his voice. "Bring on the Second and Eleventh Bengal Infantry! I want them to support the skirmishers!"

The sepoys hurried forward, forming an extended line on the edge of the clearing.

"Fire on the village," Colonel Baker was in his element, striding from position to position without heeding the enemy's rifle bullets or artillery. "Keep their heads down," he ordered, "and move in slowly. Lieutenant Downes and Lieutenant Harris take two companies of the 11th Bengal, extend on the right, and take the village and stockades in flank. Captain Channer, take two companies of the Second Bengal and extend on the left. Let's squeeze these Burmans! Baird, you and I will push on in front."

"Yes, sir!" Andrew signalled to his men to follow. Thankfully, the havildar had a grasp of English and quickly translated Andrew's words to his men.

Major MacNeill led the 11th Bengal on the right, with Major Hill, Captain Peile and Lieutenant Drury in support. The Burmese remained under cover, firing at the advancing sepoys without giving ground. One bullet hit Lieutenant Drury, who fell, gasping and spitting out blood. Seeing their officer down, the sepoys gave a loud cry and surged forward, bayonets extended.

The Bengalis charged into the Burmese fire, desperate to drive the enemy from their defences. Major MacNeill grunted as a Burmese bullet slammed into him. He looked down at the red stain on his arm, said, "They're not stopping me," and continued to lead his men until another shot knocked him down. He rolled over, shook his head, rose and staggered on.

"Come on, men!" Andrew roared. He charged forward with Colonel Baker marginally in front and the sepoys behind him.

As the sepoys advanced, outflanking the stockades, the Burmese fire slackened, and they gradually withdrew from the village. Andrew saw a moving mass of men, some wearing the official light jackets and brass helmets but most without.

"Well done, my lads!" Baker shouted, reloading his revolver. "Come on, Baird! We'll make a sepoy officer of you yet, by God! If it was good enough for the Duke, it's good enough for anybody."

Andrew watched as the Burmese made a fighting withdrawal from the stockades to the pagodas, whose combinations of stone walls and intricate passages gave excellent cover.

"Come on, Bengalis!" Andrew shouted, running across the open ground with bullets zipping past him or burrowing into the dirt at his feet. The Burmese continued to fire, bringing down half a dozen of the advancing sepoys. Andrew was vaguely aware of Lieutenant Downes and Harris leading their men, advancing in short rushes rather than a single constant charge.

"These Burmese know how to fight," Baker said calmly. "They keep under cover and fire low."

"Unlike the Zulus," Andrew replied. "They always fired high, and so do most young British soldiers."

As the sepoys closed on the pagodas, the Burman defenders finally broke before the probing bayonets and ran towards the sanctuary of the forest.

"Shoot them!" Baker ordered. "Don't let them escape!"

The sepoys obeyed, aiming, firing, and reloading as fast as possible, hitting a score of the fleeing men before they reached the trees.

"That's cleared them out," Baker said with satisfaction. "It's a pity so many escaped, but it can't be helped. Well done, my lads. Get the *woon*'s house out of the way next, and then we'll deal with that damned redoubt."

Andrew nodded. The Bengalis were reloading, shouting abuse at the enemy, and behaving much like British infantry would in similar circumstances.

"Skirmishers!" Andrew shouted. "Advance a hundred yards on either side, and watch out for any Burmese counterattack!"

The Bengalis responded immediately, fanning out with rifles ready, finding cover and waiting for the enemy.

"Come on, boys!" Andrew led his men to their next objective.

The *woon*'s palace was impressive compared to the villagers' wooden houses, but Thibaw's soldiers did not attempt to defend it. Baker's sepoys captured the palace without opposition, moving around the sumptuous building with ease. When Baker ordered it burned, the sepoys enjoyed lighting torches and putting the palace to the flames. Andrew watched as the smoke coiled upwards, glanced at the scatter of dead and wounded Burmese soldiers, and wondered at the wasteful futility of war.

*They make a desert and call it peace, as Calgacus said. Are we any better than the Romans when they conquered much of the known world? Yes, we are: the Roman Empire was based on slavery, and we fight and abolish that horror wherever we can.**

"Right, gentlemen," Baker ordered. "Gather your sepoys together, and let's take the fort. We'll finish the day with another success."

---

* According to Tacitus, Calgacus, the leader of the Caledonians, made a rousing speech as he faced the Romans in what is now Scotland. Speaking of the Romans, he said: "These plunderers of the world, after exhausting the land by their devastations, are rifling the ocean: stimulated by avarice, if their

enemy be rich; by ambition, if poor; unsatiated by the East and by the West: the only people who behold wealth and indigence with equal avidity. To ravage, to slaughter, to usurp under false titles, they call empire; and where they make a desert, they call it peace."

Andrew checked his watch. It was one-forty in the afternoon. It had been a successful day so far, but perhaps the hardest part of the operation lay ahead.

"Wheel right," Baker ordered. "We'll march towards the river and take the redoubt from the rear." He grinned. "The defenders won't be able to retreat into the blasted jungle. It will be our bayonets or the Irrawaddy River for them."

Andrew joined his Bengalis, watching their satisfied faces. They had fought well in a difficult environment.

You'll do, lads, Andrew thought.

CHAPTER 26

IRRAWADDY RIVER, NOVEMBER 1885

The sepoys marched back into the forest, moving with a confident swing as Andrew ordered flankers on either side. His precautions proved unnecessary as they pushed through the trees without meeting any resistance. Once again, the forest closed in on Andrew, blocking out light and air, with insects buzzing around his head and the ground damp and slippery underfoot.

Moving with the skirmishers, Andrew was one of the first to see the Burmese redoubt. It stood at the edge of the clearing, rising abruptly against the hazy green backdrop of the forest with the flowing Irrawaddy in front.

"Stay under cover," Andrew whispered to his havildar, gesturing with his hand so his orders were clear. Previous campaigns had taught him only to advance when he had thoroughly reconnoitred the enemy's position to assess their strengths and weaknesses. The Boers had a nasty habit of positioning themselves where the British least expected them, and Andrew anticipated the Burmese would be experts in their environment.

Andrew took out his binoculars, lay on the ground, hoping there were no snakes, and studied the redoubt. The walls were high, but a few blocks of masonry littered the ground in front, spoiling what could have been an effective killing ground for the defenders. A small house stood to the west of the building.

"What's that house?" Andrew asked the havildar.

"That's a priest's house, sahib," the havildar seemed pleased to be asked.

Andrew nodded and continued to study the defences.

There was a gate on the ground level, heavy teak and firmly closed with an array of defenders and a gingal – a large calibre smooth-bore musket mounted on a swivel – above. The sun glinted on the defenders' brass hats and the barrels of their rifles.

The Burmese would destroy any force attacking that gate, Andrew realised. He swept his binoculars around the walls and stopped. A rough ramp sloped up the height of the wall on the western face, evidently for the defenders to drag up artillery. The road was littered with shattered stones and pitted with holes, the effects of years of neglect, but Andrew thought the ramp offered the best access for a party of determined men.

We'll need covering fire to keep the defenders occupied and a rush by a storming party of volunteers, the forlorn hope, as the military used to call such men. How does the Indian Army organise such things?

Before Andrew reported his findings to Colonel Baker, it became evident that other officers did not share Andrew's cautious technique. Major Stead led his company of the Eleventh Bengal Infantry into the clearing with the men vivid against the dull greenery of the vegetation. The Burmese must have been waiting for their first sight of the sepoys and immediately opened fire.

The mixed rifles and muskets created a chaotic cacophony of noise, with bullets and balls churning up the ground.

"Keep down!" Andrew snarled to his men, "and return fire!"

The Bengalis responded eagerly, firing and reloading, some shouting and others in grim silence.

The Burmese fired from the redoubt's northwest corner, using a nine-pounder cannon and gingals that spread balls like a giant shotgun. The cannon shot ripped into the forest, wounding two of the sepoys.

"Fire at the walls," Andrew ordered. "Aim for that nine-pounder."

He did not know if his sepoys were good marksmen but guessed that being under fire would unsettle the Burmese gunners' aim. Andrew walked behind his men, encouraging them with his presence as he tried to ignore the bullets that whined around him.

Andrew swore when he saw Lieutenant Downes suddenly dash forward with seven of his men, yelling defiance as they crossed the clearing. Caught by surprise or sheltering from the musketry of Andrew's men, the defenders did not fire until Downes reached the cover of the masonry blocks. Once they realised what was happening, the Burmese tried to shoot downwards, but the massive stone blocks shielded Downes' men.

What the devil are these men doing? Eight men cannot capture an entire fort!

As Andrew pondered, another group of men rushed across the maidan, with Lieutenant Wilkinson of the 12th Madras Infantry leading three men to join Downes' party. The Burmese fired furiously, with bullets knocking chips from the stones without hitting a single sepoy.

Twelve men now, and more needed.

"Damn and blast it to hell and gone!" Andrew said. "Cover me!" Rising from cover, he weaved and jinked to the stone blocks, seeing the small spurts of dirt as Burmese bullets kicked up the ground around him. He heard himself laugh and wondered at his stupidity.

"Welcome, Captain Baird," Downes said with a casual smile. "Where do we go from here?"

"There's a ramp on the western wall," Andrew ducked as a large calibre gingal ball smashed into the block six inches from his face. He saw the blue smear the lead left on the masonry and wondered what sort of mess a ball of that calibre would make if it hit him.

"A ramp?" Downes said. "That will do." He nodded. "Here come reinforcements!"

They watched as Colonel Simpson and Lieutenant Hill were next to cross the maidan, leading a platoon of around twenty-five men of the 12th Madras Infantry. They ran to the priest's house, threw themselves down and opened a vigorous fire on the Burmese on the redoubt's walls.

"What sort of ramp?" Wilkinson asked, as casually as if he was discussing the weather.

"A rough one, probably to haul artillery up the walls," Andrew replied. "There is broken masonry at the foot that might provide some cover."

"I say we should rush into the fort," Wilkinson suggested.

"Exactly so," Andrew agreed. "As we've come this far."

They looked up as the sepoys increased their firing, and the Burmese replied. Simpson and Hill joined them among the scattered masonry blocks, running from the priest's house without losing a man.

"Captain Baird tells me there is a ramp up the western wall, sir," Atkinson reported. "We were thinking of storming the redoubt."

"That's my plan, too," Hill said. He smoothed a finger over his whiskers. "Wait until the Burmans fire their next volley and charge before they can reload."

The officers nodded and passed on the information to their men. The sepoys seemed keen to fight, fixing bayonets without orders and tensing for the rush.

Here we go again. Thank God we are facing Burmese soldiers and not the expert Boer marksmen.

The sepoys in the forest fired, the Burmans retaliated, and Colonel Hill shouted, "Now!"

"After me, boys!" Wilkinson said, repeated his words in Urdu and ran forward, with the sepoys and other officers following in a mad jumble. Andrew was in the middle with a havildar on his right and a grinning sepoy on his left. The latter was shouting madly, the words meaningless to Andrew but seeming to inspire the sepoys' colleagues.

Wilkinson and Downes led the charge up the ramp, with men staggering on the uneven surface, recovering, and running on. Wilkinson tripped on a piece of loose rock, and one of the Burmese defenders slashed his *dha* on the officer's head. Wilkinson fell, with the defender stabbing at his prone body.

Downes was next onto the wall. He shot the *dha*-wielding Burmese with his revolver, then hit another man wearing Thibaw's Army uniform. A third defender lifted his musket to attack, so Downes shot him in the chest, knocking him off the wall into the courtyard below.

Andrew glanced upward, saw the Burmese massing on the wall, aimed his revolver and shot one man, fired again, wounded a second and pushed forward. A surge of sepoys passed the officers to swarm inside the redoubt while Simpson and Hill ran forward. Andrew shot at a stocky Burmese, saw his bullet hit the man full in the face and spray blood, bone, and brains behind him, and ran along the fort's inner rampart.

The sepoys were fanning out, slaughtering anybody who stood in their way, using bullets, rifle butts or bayonets indiscriminately.

Andrew stood on a wide terrace thirty feet above the interior courtyard. The Burmese had six nine-pounder cannon and five gingals on the terrace, covering all four sides of the redoubt. Sepoys and Burmese battled on the flights of stone stairs that led to the open interior, with Wilkinson lying badly injured amongst Burmese casualties at the head of the ramp.

Two Burmese ran at Andrew, one with an ancient musket and the other with a *dha*. The musketeer knelt, aimed, and pressed the trigger, but his weapon misfired. The gunpowder in the pan exploded without igniting the charge in the barrel.

A flash in the pan, Andrew said to himself and shot the man. The Burmese with the *dha* ran on, yelling until a Madras sepoy spitted him with his bayonet.

"Shoot them!" Hill ordered as the Burmese crammed the stairs in their frantic effort to escape the sepoys' bayonets. The sepoys obeyed, firing into the mass as the officers emptied their revolvers, hastily reloaded, and fired again. In the courtyard, a press of panicking Burmese struggled to open the great teak gates and thrust outside, some running toward the river in the east and others westward, where the sepoys waited for them with controlled volleys.

"We've taken the redoubt!" Downes shouted. "Well done, boys!"

Outside the walls, the 2nd Bengal Infantry had emerged from the forest and formed in parade ground order. They fired volleys at the fleeing Burmese, killing many. The Burmese dropped their weapons, threw off their Army uniforms and fled, with the sepoys capturing hundreds.

Andrew saw more British officers moving inside the redoubt. While he had participated in the assault up the ramp, Colonel Sladen and a handful of officers had burst open the northeast gate, and others had led the sepoys over the walls with scaling ladders.

"That was intense while it lasted," Downes said. He looked over the wall. "And here comes Colonel White's brigade."

White had landed his brigade an hour after Baker's, together with a battery of screw guns that the men had struggled to push along the narrow path.

"We captured fifteen guns," Downes said, drawing on a Burmese cheroot, "and quite a collection of prisoners." He smiled. "King Thibaw won't be very happy that we defeated his soldiers, and our gunners won't be happy because the Burmese claim our artillery didn't kill a single man." His smile expanded into a grin. "Our sepoys proved themselves a match for anybody, once again."

As the British consolidated their position, General Prendergast issued orders to the Army banning looting or abusing the villagers. "We want to keep the people of Upper Burma calm. Let them know we have no quarrel with them, and all we want is peace for the country."

"Let's hope the general's proclamation works," Downes said. "The last thing we want is a guerrilla war in this damned jungle."

Andrew thought of the dacoits he had chased around Rangoon. "Amen to that," he agreed.

The fleet sailed up from Thayetmyo and anchored off Minhla, with smoke gently easing from their smokestacks. The soldiers sat or lay on the flats, scrutinising the forest and wondering what lay ahead. Andrew watched as a procession of small craft ferried the wounded sepoys and Burmese onto the hospital ships.

Jamieson was there with *Little Salamander,* puffing on a huge cigar and steering his vessel with unconscious skill.

Birnie drew on his cheroot. "I wonder how they would deal with our wounded prisoners," he said. "Probably behead them or crucify them." He shrugged. "Please, God, they never take me alive."

Andrew looked at the forest covering, thought of the crucified dacoits, and nodded. "I'd agree to that," he said.

As the bulk of the fleet remained at anchor at Thayetmyo, with the men playing cards or lounging under the sun, *Irrawaddy* and *Kathleen* pushed ahead with most of the naval brigade. Prendergast sent strong patrols ashore to search for the enemy.

"The sojer lads are busy, sir," the bearded petty officer said, coiling a line.

"They are," Andrew agreed, staring at the riverbank.

"I heard they're finding lots of wounded Burmans from the affair at Minhla," the sailor stopped his work, pushed back his hat, and grinned at Andrew.

"I heard the same," Andrew said. "The swaddies* are taking the wounded to the hospital ships."

"That's very Christian of them," the seaman said. "They'll probably recover and try to stab the orderlies in the back."

Andrew lifted his binoculars and concentrated on one patch of jungle. "I thought I saw something move there."

"Did you?" the sailor asked. "Best tell Lieutenant Trench then, chum."

"It might only be an animal," Andrew replied. He watched as *Kathleen* churned on with smoke from her funnel drifting behind her and her wake creamy white astern. Her wash eased over the river, causing the small boats outside a fishing village to bob and nod and the fishermen to look up, no doubt cursing these intruders who disturbed the fish.

"Yes, sir," the seaman studied the forest. "It might be an animal or some of these Burmese lads. Better sure than sorry, sir. I'll pass the word on."

* Swaddies – soldiers. Today, it is more often mispronounced as "squaddies."

Lieutenant Trench listened to the report, nodded, sent a man to watch the riverbank, and pushed on. As *Kathleen* moved slowly away from Minhla, engineers and artillerymen worked at the redoubt, making the fort that the sepoys had captured with such sacrifice into a British strongpoint.

"The Burmans may double back," Prendergast explained to his officers. "They can retake this fort, add artillery and block us from either returning to British Burma or sending up reinforcements."

Andrew watched the British work to repair and strengthen the walls and create earthworks for artillery outside the redoubt. Across the river, Prendergast had placed a company of the Liverpool Regiment and two companies of the Second Bengal in the Kolegone fort, with Mr Phayre as the civil officer to ease relations with the Burmese.

"The Burmans will find the Liverpudlians and Bengalis hard to shift," Downes had said. "But I don't fancy that as a garrison duty, stuck in the middle of nowhere with a hostile forest at the rear and a river in front."

Andrew nodded. "Any border post can be frustrating," he agreed. "Months and months of boredom yet always aware the enemy could be watching, waiting for a minute when you relax your guard, then strike and run."

Now, Andrew was back on *Kathleen,* with Midshipman Birnie joining him as they pushed upstream against the current.

"The Burmans had a battery of four guns below the fort," Birnie said, looking up occasionally to watch the riverbanks. "They nearly hit us yesterday with one shot." He grinned again. "Imagine the trouble they could have caused if they had served their guns properly." He nodded backwards towards the main fleet. "If a shell exploded on one of the flats, we could wave farewell to half a battalion of swaddies, sir."

"You're right." Andrew lowered his binoculars as he saw a water buffalo emerge from a series of fields. "If they had held the forts with any determination, they could have caused carnage. I think the speed of our advance surprised them."

"The forts should have commanded the river from Minhla to Patanayo," Birnie agreed. "I heard there were Europeans helping Thibaw's men."

"Three of them, apparently, although I didn't see them," Andrew agreed. "Italians working for Thibaw. They ran before we could catch them. They jumped into a royal steamer and fled upriver."

"They ran at Kolegone, too," Birnie said. "They were waiting for a frontal assault, and General Prendergast's turning movement took them by surprise. As soon as the Liverpool regiment fired their first volley, Thibaw's men bolted."

"We seem to be winning this war," Andrew said. "Let's hope for a quick victory that brings peace to Burma."

Peace for Burma, a pardon for Bo Thura and a voyage home for Mariana and me. Andrew swatted a mosquito. Corbiestane Tower seemed even more desirable from thousands of miles away. *I wish I were at Corbiestane right now, with Mariana at my side.*

RANGOON, NOVEMBER 1885

Mariana felt her heartbeat increase as she stepped into the dark blue Brougham. She felt the slight jerk as the driver started the coach and stared out the window at the now-familiar streets of Rangoon.

Stephen won't let me down, Mariana told herself. *Stephen would never leave me alone for such a long time.*

The journey to Jennings' house seemed shorter than she remembered. Soon, she was walking to the front door, with moths fluttering around the oil lamps and her footsteps echoing in the humid air. She lifted her fist to knock, and the door opened.

"My dear Mariana!" Jennings smiled at her across the threshold. "I am so glad you came. Come in, my dear, come in!"

The warmth of Jennings' welcome dispelled Mariana's doubts, and she straightened her back, smiling as she entered the house. Everything was familiar, from the furniture to Jennings' smile, the faces of the servants, and the scents of incense. Mariana felt herself relaxing, allowed Jennings to ease off her jacket, and accepted a small glass of sherry.

"We won't try the champagne," Jennings said with a smile.

"Thank you, Stephen," Mariana replied. "That's probably for the best."

"It's simple fare today," Jennings said. "I hope that is all right with you?"

"Perfectly," Mariana said. "I am here for the company, not the food, although both were excellent on my last visit."

Jennings smiled. "And I am happy to have your company, too," he replied.

They sat in the airy front room with the fan above and the last rays of the sun easing through the tall windows to cast shadows on the floor.

"Beware of the dinner gong," Jennings said. "It gave you quite a start the first time you heard it."

Mariana smiled at the memory. "I made a bit of an idiot of myself, Stephen. I won't do that again."

Jennings leaned forward and took her hand. "Any blame was mine, Mariana. In my eyes, you could never be an idiot."

"Thank you, Stephen," Mariana said and lifted a finger as the dinner gong sounded. "There! I didn't start at all."

"Neither you did," Jennings stood and extended a hand.

Mariana accepted the hand without demur, and they walked into the candlelit dining room.

"How romantic," Mariana said, allowing Jennings to usher her into her seat.

MINHLA 19TH NOVEMBER 1885

The flotilla remained at Minhla, the ships swinging at their anchors as the Irrawaddy River surged past. The soldiers sweltered in boredom on the flats or welcomed the occasional patrol through the forest, although Thibaw's men left them severely alone. All the steamers had arrived, with the barge *White Swan*, containing the heavy battery, last to negotiate the river.

"I heard a shave that Thibaw sent three thousand men to reinforce Minhla," Birnie spoke through a cloud of cigar smoke. He smiled. "They must have turned back when we took his precious forts. We killed about sixty of the Burmans here."

Andrew nodded. "I was there," he said quietly. "They held their ground well, considering the quality of the troops they faced."

"There's somebody on the riverbank," Birnie said. "He's watching us."

Andrew turned around. *Bo Thura! What the devil are you doing here?* "I see him," he said. "Can I borrow your little dinghy? I want to talk to that man."

CHAPTER 27

IRRAWADDY RIVER, NOVEMBER 1885

"Cousin Andrew!"

Andrew smiled as Bo Thura slipped from the forest to stand at his side. "I don't have a pardon for you yet." Andrew glanced at the anchored British fleet. "Some of these lads would shoot on sight."

"They'll only see me if I let them," Bo Thura said casually.

"What the devil are you doing here?" Andrew asked.

"I've come to warn you," Bo Thura told him. "Maung Thandar is setting a trap for General Prendergast and Colonel Sladen."

"Tell me more," Andrew said. Together, Prendergast and Sladen were the directing force behind the invasion. If Maung Thandar killed or captured them, he would cause irreparable damage to the British.

"General Prendergast and Colonel Sladen are sailing in the steamer *Irrawaddy*," Bo Thura said. "They're scouting the river to see what's ahead."

"How the devil do you know that?" Andrew asked.

Bo Thura gave the wry Windrush smile. "I know what's happening before the general does; if I know, you can be sure that Maung Thandar does too."

Andrew looked up as a flock of parrots exploded from the trees. They passed overhead with a flapping of wings and a flash of bright colours to disappear upstream. "Tell me more," he said.

"I'll have to show you," Bo Thura said. "Come with me."

Andrew looked at *Kathleen*, which was moored a hundred yards out in the river with four bluejackets on guard. Birnie was watching everything he did, and there was a gentle waft of smoke from her funnel. "How long will it take?"

"A couple of hours," Bo Thura said.

Andrew checked his watch. "I'd better let the ship know where I am."

Bo Thura led at a smart trot along a path Andrew barely saw. He followed a yard behind, feeling the sweat dripping from him in the forest's humidity and ducking under the occasional low branch. The river remained a constant on their left, with the water swirling and chuckling, dappled in the sunlight, and often hung with clouds of insects.

The Irrawaddy is the lifeblood of Burma, Andrew thought. *It is the highway and the main artery.*

After thirty hard minutes, Bo Thura stopped, squatting on the path. "We'll have to skirt around a village here," he explained, "and go around a couple of paddy fields. If anybody talks to us, let me do the speaking."

Andrew nodded. "I will," he said.

Bo Thura had a British Martini-Henry in his right hand and the ubiquitous *dha* at his waist. He moved at a fast trot, with his feet making little sound. They eased around the village, keeping to a fringe of trees, while villagers continued their lives unheeding the war flickering around them. The majority of farmers were concerned with crops and their families, not politics and bloodshed.

After an hour, Bo Thura stopped at a broad field where a man guided a pair of buffalo. "Keep down," he said. "That man is spying for Maung Thandar."

Andrew watched the farmer. "How can you tell?"

"I know him. He'll relay every detail of your fleet to another of his kind, and Maung Thandar will know what's happening before the ships round the next bend. We'll have to circle this place."

Andrew followed as Bo Thura took a wide detour inland, with the farmer apparently innocently guiding his buffalo with a clear view over the river.

This detour will delay us, Andrew thought. *My two hours are ticking away.*

Once past the fields, Bo Thura moved even faster, skimming over the ground with Andrew struggling to keep up. He dashed the sweat from his forehead, took a deep breath and pushed on.

After another sweltering ten minutes, Bo Thura lifted a hand and stepped into the forest cover. Andrew did likewise, avoiding a giant tarantula spider that scuttled over his boot. He crouched, keeping his revolver handy. Bo Thura lifted a hand for silence and merged into the undergrowth.

Andrew heard the soft sound of sandals slapping on the ground and watched as a patrol of King's soldiers filed past with their curious, high-kneed step. He waited two minutes and emerged, with Bo Thura appearing simultaneously.

"Maung Thandar must be nervous to send out a patrol," Bo Thura said.

They moved again, slower now, with Bo Thura cautiously approaching each bend in the path and listening for any sound. After another ten minutes, he stopped.

"We're getting close," he said quietly. "We'll move through the forest for the last quarter mile. Keep close and don't make any noise."

Andrew had learned how to move silently in the frontier war against the Galekas, but Bo Thura walked like a ghost, making no sound as he drifted through the undergrowth. After a difficult period during which Andrew twice lost sight of him, they climbed a small, sparsely wooded rise. Bo Thura lifted his hand, and Andrew stopped.

The ridge overlooked a broad stretch of the river. Bo Thura slid to his stomach and crawled forward with Andrew at his side. They both stopped when they reached the edge of a fifty-foot-high cliff, and Bo Thura gestured downwards.

A group of Burman soldiers stood guard over a horde of near-naked Burmese labourers. The men were working on three flats, placing sandbags in the bottom and fixing pointed stakes at slight angles.

I've seen that sort of arrangement before, Andrew thought. *The Burmese will sink the flats in the deep-water channel through which the flotilla must sail and sink the leading ship, presumably the vessel with Prendergast and Sladen on board.*

Bo Thura touched Andrew's arm and raised his eyebrows in a silent question. When Andrew nodded, they crawled carefully backwards.

"You see?" Bo Thura asked when they reached the relative safety of the forest fringe.

"I see," Andrew said. "Do you know where the trap will be sprung?"

"No," Bo Thura shook his head. "I found the flats; I did not find the plans."

"I'll have to warn General Prendergast," Andrew said.

"You know the way back," Bo Thura replied.

"I do," Andrew replied.

"Don't forget to tell General Prendergast who gave you the information," Bo Thura said. "And pass that on to the Chief Commissioner. I need safety in British Burma."

"I won't forget," Andrew promised. "If I survive."

"Be careful to avoid Maung Thandar's spy," Bo Thura reminded and slid away.

PRENDERGAST LISTENED TO ANDREW'S WARNING WITH A STERN FACE. HIS fingers drummed on the desktop as his staff mustered around, wondering what right this intruder had to speak directly to the general.

"This dacoit fellow," Prendergast said. "Can he be trusted?"

"He gave you the intelligence about the king's steamer," Andrew reminded. He thought it best not to mention the documents about the secret French treaty.

"That intelligence was correct," Prendergast allowed. "Now, you know where the flats are situated, but not the site of the alleged trap. Is that correct?"

"I saw the flats, sir," Andrew said. "They could be anywhere on the river by now."

Prendergast leaned back in his chair. "Let us summarise. We know there might be an attempt to sink *Irrawaddy* while Sladen and I are on board. Any fool could work that out."

"Maybe, sir," Andrew said. "If we consult the map, we can work out the best spot for the Burmans to lay their trap. It must be somewhere the deep-water channel is narrow and maybe close to the shore."

"That could be anywhere on the blasted river," Prendergast said.

Andrew studied the map, tracing the river with his finger. "Yes, sir, but somewhere between here and Mandalay. May I borrow this map, sir? I want to consult with a pilot and see where the deep-water channel is."

Prendergast nodded. "Do that, Baird."

Jamieson looked surprised when Andrew appeared on *Little Salamander*.

"I thought the dacoits had murdered you," Jamieson said, puffing furiously at his cigar.

"Not yet," Andrew said. "I need your help again."

"Do you, now?" Jamieson's eyes narrowed. "I'm not taking you up any blasted river until we've beaten Thibaw," he said. "However much you offer me."

"I just want advice," Andrew told him.

"What sort of advice?" Jamieson asked.

"Professional advice," Andrew said and explained the situation. "Even you can't charge for that."

Jamieson grunted. "My time costs money," he said and sighed. "Unroll your chart then, Captain Baird, and let's have a look."

They squatted on the hot deck, and Jamieson pointed out the deep-water channel routes in the rainy and dry seasons.

"What's this here?" Andrew indicated an area where the river widened around half a dozen islands.

"There are channels between the islands," Jamieson said. "Surely you remember passing them on your pleasure cruise on *Little Salamander*?"

"No," Andrew shook his head.

"Typical bloody soldier," Jamieson sighed. "Some of the channels are deep and others shallow. This one," he pointed to a winding channel between two large islands, "is the most favoured, and this one," he moved his finger to the right, "is best avoided, but the channels can alter after a period of drought or heavy rain."

"Thank you," Andrew studied the chart. "If you were going to ambush a ship, Jamieson, which channel would you choose?"

Jamieson stabbed his stubby finger down. "That one, Baird, and I'll thank you for a golden boy for the information."

"A sovereign?" Andrew looked up in dismay. "You drive a hard bargain, Jamieson."

"I need to fund my luxurious lifestyle," Jamieson said. "Coal doesn't come cheap, you know, and all these blasted Army vessels are driving up prices." He held out a grubby hand in anticipation.

General Prendergast looked up when Andrew returned. "Well?"

"If I were going to attack your ship, sir," Andrew said, unrolling the map on Prendergast's desk and ignoring his staff. "I would do it there, in the channel between these islands." He indicated the spot. "The passage is very narrow so that the flats would fill the channel, and the current is fast, which would carry away any survivors."

Prendergast surveyed the chart, nodded, and looked up. "All right, Baird. You did a lot of irregular work in Africa. Let's see how good you are here. Take a platoon along the riverbank and capture or destroy these flats if they are still there."

"Yes, sir," Andrew replied. The prospect of an independent command away from the confines of superior officers was appealing. "Which regiment can I select from, sir?"

"Use the 23rd Foot, the Welsh Fusiliers," Prendergast replied.

"Thank you, sir."

"I'll contact their colonel and send *Kathleen* upriver if you need nautical support." Prendergast smiled. "The bluejackets tend to fret unless we give them something active to do."

The colonel of the Fusiliers was waiting when Andrew arrived. "I don't like my men being used on some harebrained escapade," he said. "Especially when a young officer from some obscure colonial horse regiment has a bee in his bonnet." He looked Andrew up and down, nodding at the medal ribbons on his breast. "You've been on campaign already, I see."

"Yes, sir, the Frontier War, Zululand and against the Boers."

"Well, that might count for something, I suppose. I am sending one of my officers to keep an eye on you, Baird."

"Thank you, sir," Andrew replied. He did not want a Fusilier officer watching everything he did, but one did not argue with a colonel.

"Follow me," the colonel said. He had selected forty volunteers, including a sergeant, a corporal, and a hard-faced lieutenant. They stood beside the river, dressed in faded and stained khaki, holding their Martinis at their sides and staring at this upstart young captain.

"Well, men," Andrew addressed them. "My name is Captain Andrew Baird, and we are going on an important mission."

The Fusiliers looked straight ahead without any change of expression. The sergeant looked around forty, with a breast full of medal ribbons and a face that looked like it could chop teak.

"The Burmans plan to ambush our ship *Irrawaddy* as it passes through a narrow channel, sink her, and murder the general. We are to prevent this from happening."

The lieutenant and some of the men began to look interested. The majority continued to stare directly ahead.

"Are there any questions?" Andrew knew it was highly unusual for an officer to allow his men to ask questions, but he had learned his trade with irregular horsemen, where discipline differed from regular British regiments. Some of the men looked surprised.

Lieutenant Toshack lifted his voice. "Yes, sir," he barked. "Where is this ambush?"

"We think it is about ten miles upriver," Andrew said. "Where the Irrawaddy broadens, and there are islands between the banks."

“Thank you, sir,” the lieutenant replied, glancing over his men.

“We will leave an hour before dawn tomorrow,” Andrew said. “I want everybody to carry seventy rounds of ammunition, sufficient rations to last a day and night, a full water bottle and a blanket.”

The men nodded. The first battalion, Royal Welsh Fusiliers, was a veteran regiment that knew how to fight, although they had not seen much action since the Indian Mutiny. The men had been in India for five years and were thoroughly acclimatised to the heat.

“Dismissed,” Andrew ordered and watched the men march away.

Here we go again. Tennyson’s poetry flashed into Andrew’s head.

“Half a league, half a league,
Half a league onward,
All in the valley of Death
Rode the six hundred.”

Let’s hope I’m not leading these men into the valley of Death.

CHAPTER 28

RANGOON AND THE IRRAWADDY RIVER, NOVEMBER 1885

Jennings looked at Mariana across the width of the circular table. "Did you enjoy the meal, Mariana?"

"Very much so," Mariana replied.

"More wine?" Jennings signalled to a servant, who poured red wine into their crystal glasses. "Here's a toast to us." He lifted his glass high.

"To us," Mariana echoed. The wine was sweet and cool, welcoming after the meal.

"More?" Jennings suggested. "Or shall I play for you?" He indicated the piano in the adjoining room.

"Do you play the piano?" Mariana accepted more wine. "You are a man of many talents, Stephen. I've always wanted to learn the piano."

"I can teach you," Jennings said. "Come on over."

"I'll be a hopeless duffer," Mariana told him.

"Nonsense," Jennings said. "I don't believe you'd be a duffer at anything." He extended his hand and guided Mariana to the piano. "Put your glass on top, beside mine." Sitting her on the stool, he ran a finger over the keyboard and held her hands. "Now, let's begin."

ANDREW INSPECTED THE MEN IN THE LIGHT OF A WANING MOON. THEY stood relaxed, seemingly unconcerned by the prospect of a long march and a possible skirmish at the end.

"They're a handy-looking bunch," Andrew told the lieutenant.

"They're Welsh Fusiliers," Toshack replied, as if that was answer enough.

"That explains it, then," Andrew said. He set the corporal in charge of the rearguard, with orders to ensure nobody was left behind, and led the way along the forest track Bo Thura had shown him the previous day.

Andrew moved at a steady pace, stopping every thirty minutes for a five-minute break to allow the men to drink from their water bottles as the NCOs checked nobody had dropped out. The weather was not overbearingly hot, but the patches of dense forest increased the humidity. Andrew pushed the men forward, hoping they were as fit and determined as the infantry he had worked with in Africa.

The Fusiliers responded well, ignoring the mosquitoes and watching the trees in case of ambush.

After an hour, Andrew halted them at the outskirts of a village, remembering Bo Thura's warning about Maung Thandar's spies.

Let him spy and make whatever report he chooses. I have a platoon of quality British infantry here; I'll put my money on them to defeat any number of Thibaw's soldiers.

"Lieutenant Toshack, put out two-man pickets in front, flank, and rear."

"Sir." Toshack gave crisp orders, and the men moved out. Their khaki uniforms were not as distinct as the old-fashioned scarlet but still stood out against the prevailing dull green.

Andrew allowed the men ten minutes, then moved on, pushing them hard. He skirted the village, ploughing through the shallow paddy fields without stopping. He watched the Fusiliers waving to the women working in the fields and the men lounging and smoking outside the houses.

These Fusiliers seem a decent bunch.

The sound of boots thumping on the narrow path was reassuring, with Welsh, Irish, and English accents muttering as the Fusiliers progressed. When the trees thinned and the view was open to the Irrawaddy, Andrew saw *Kathleen* steaming in the deep-water channel, seemingly serene. It was a reminder that British sea power could reach hundreds of miles inland, provided there was sufficient water to float.

"How far, sir?" Toshack asked.

"We're over halfway," Andrew said. He glanced at the Fusiliers. They were hot and sweaty but composed, moving well. Nobody had fallen out. "One more halt, and then we'll be close."

Andrew saw the movement at the edge of the next field, with Sergeant Coslett ordering two men to investigate. Andrew kept the platoon waiting until the patrol returned.

"Nothing, sir," a long-faced private reported. "If anybody was there, he bolted when he saw us coming."

"Keep an eye open," Andrew ordered. "The Burmese like to use ambushes."

"We'll watch for them, sir," Sergeant Coslett promised. "Come on, lads, back on the road."

They pushed on, tiring now as the miles slid away and the sun rose. The men were familiar with the forest sounds and sensations but wary of Burmese attack.

"Halt!" Andrew stopped them when they reached the foot of the ridge. "I'll go ahead and see what's happening."

"Best not go alone, sir," Toshack advised. "Shall I come with you?"

"No." Andrew shook his head. "Stay with the men. I'll take Sergeant Coslett. If the Burmans kill me, I'll depend on you to destroy the Burmese boats and get your men back safely."

"Yes, sir." Toshack accepted the possibility of Andrew's death as part of a soldier's duty.

"You're with me, Sergeant Coslett," Andrew said and led him up the ridge. He stopped at the cliff above the flats and crawled to the edge, relieved that the flats remained where he had seen them the previous day. "There they are, Sergeant."

"The Burmans are moving them, sir," Coslett said.

The three flats floated close inshore, with a large group of Burmese in the water working around them. The Burmese kept close inshore as they attached lines to the flats, preparatory to towing and pushing them upstream towards the islands.

"Why don't they use one of their steamers?" Coslett wondered.

"The smoke would alert *Kathleen*," Andrew replied. "She's only a couple of miles downstream. As it is, the river has cut into the bank, and the overhanging trees conceal them."

"Shall I get the men, sir?" Coslett asked.

"Yes." Andrew nodded. "Bring them up. I'll keep an eye on the flats."

He watched as Coslett hurried back along the path with his rifle at the trail. Andrew saw a group of king's soldiers surrounding a tall man and recognised Maung Thandar.

That man must be the most active opponent we have in this war.

Maung Thandar gave sharp orders that saw the labourers push and drag the flats through the water against the current. When one man stumbled, Maung Thandar snarled something, and one of the soldiers cracked the labourer over the head with the barrel of his rifle.

You're an unpleasant man, Maung Thandar.

Andrew contemplated firing at Maung Thandar until he realised the range was too long for an accurate shot and would only give away his presence without gaining any advantage. He crawled along the cliff's edge, keeping level with the Burmese and hoping nothing delayed the Fusiliers.

The islands were a mile ahead, with the Irrawaddy already beginning to widen. With Maung Thandar giving vocal encouragement and his soldiers using slaps, kicks, and jabs from their rifles, the Burman labourers were making good time pushing the flats.

If the Fusiliers don't hurry, we'll be too late. Once the Burmese sink these things in the deep-water channel, they'll be the very devil to lift. They'll delay the expedition and give Thibaw time to organise a stiffer resistance, which will cost lives.

Maung Thandar shouted again, and the labourers put even more effort into pushing the flats, easing them upstream four feet at a time.

Andrew swore. *Where is Sergeant Coslett with the Fusiliers?* He could see the islands ahead, with the deep-water channel evident and *Kathleen* nowhere in sight. A troop of monkeys chattered above, seeming to laugh at Andrew's predicament.

I'll have to slow the Burmans down, Andrew decided, drawing his revolver. *I'll get closer and shoot at Maung Thandar.*

He was aiming at Maung Thandar when he heard the hollow thump of boots behind him.

Thank God for small mercies!

"Sorry we took so long," Lieutenant Toshack said. "We found a man spying on us and had to dispose of him."

Andrew nodded. "Well done, Lieutenant."

"What's happening here, sir?"

"The Burmese are making good time with the flats," Andrew said. "Bring your men along the riverbank. Double!"

Andrew led the way, with the Fusiliers panting after him. When they came close to the Burmese, Andrew ordered them to silence, moved fifty yards away from the riverbank until they had passed the toiling Burmese, and returned to the river. The Burmese were close to the shore and a hundred yards upstream. Andrew lined his men on the riverbank, lying down and silent.

"Mark your targets, fire a volley, and then it's every man for himself," Andrew ordered. The Fusiliers looked at one another, surprised at this latitude from an officer.

"On my word!" Andrew realised the Burmese had become aware of their presence and were looking up, with Maung Thandar's guard clustering closer to him. "Fire!"

The Fusiliers fired a smart volley that felled half a dozen labourers.

Maung Thandar probably dragooned these poor devils into working.

"Aim for the soldiers as well," Andrew ordered, firing his revolver as the Fusiliers aimed and fired at the labourers.

With luck, the labourers will scatter and escape, leaving Maung Thandar without a workforce.

When the firing began, many of the Burmese immediately fled, diving into the fast-flowing river to swim away. Some splashed downstream, away from the Fusiliers' murderous fire, and a few remained, trying to shelter behind the flats or under the overhang of the banks.

Andrew aimed for Maung Thandar, fired, and saw a soldier step in front of his target. The revolver bullet hit the soldier in the face, knocking his head back. When he fell, another took his place, and then a fast Burmese boat appeared from upstream with half a dozen men paddling furiously.

"Shoot the paddlers!" Andrew shouted. "Don't let that man escape!"

The Fusiliers altered their aim as Maung Thandar scrambled into the boat. Two of the Burmese soldiers lifted rifles to return the Fusiliers' fire, with their bullets rising high above the Welshmen's heads. Splashes around the boat showed where the Fusiliers' bullets landed, while two of the paddlers crumpled, and splinters flew from the boat's bulwarks.

Maung Thandar rolled into the bottom of the boat as the crew thrust their paddles into the water and raced away. The Fusiliers hit another man, who jerked upright and slumped over the bulwark. Andrew emptied his revolver at the small boat, swore as it sped away, leaving a trail of blood, and returned to the main focus of his mission.

"Down to the river, lads. Grab those flats!"

The Fusiliers scrambled down the muddy cliff, with some men sliding and falling, to splash into the water with loud curses. Dead and wounded Burmese floated inshore, with the current carrying some away and others remaining tangled in the overhanging undergrowth.

"Get the flats!" Andrew ordered. "Sergeant Coslett! Take a section and fire at that boat!" Free of human restraint, the flats were spinning downstream, and Andrew realised the current might yet take them to the deep-water channel as a hazard to shipping.

Lieutenant Toshack led a section into the water and grabbed the most distant flat, dragging it close to the bank, where it acted as a barrier to the other two. The three clumsy craft rubbed and bumped together.

"Well done, Lieutenant!" Andrew shouted. He saw the men struggling with the weight and ordered the remainder of the platoon to help, jumping to add his strength to the Fusiliers'. Sergeant Coslett returned, shaking his head.

"Sorry, sir, the boat escaped. It crossed the river and disappeared up a tributary."

Andrew cursed silently. "It can't be helped. Give us a hand with these damned things." He saw *Kathleen* in the deep-water channel and waved to attract her attention, hoping the lookout could see him so close to the bank.

"Lieutenant Toshack! Destroy or sink these flats! Ensure Maung Thandar can't salvage them."

"Yes, sir!" Toshack answered.

Andrew watched a Burmese corpse bob past, trailing greasy blood over the water, and signalled to *Kathleen* again. "Can nobody in that damned ship see me?" Eventually, he unholstered his revolver and fired three shots in the air.

The revolver fire alerted *Kathleen,* and Lieutenant Trench launched a small boat, with two sailors pulling at the oars and Midshipman Birnie in the stern. Andrew waded waist-deep into the water to meet them and grabbed the stem. "Did you see that Burmese boat?"

"We saw a small boat," Birnie said.

"Thibaw's minister, Maung Thandar, is aboard her," Andrew said. "She escaped up a tributary. See if you can follow her and capture or kill Maung Thandar. He's the focal point for Thibaw's resistance."

"I'll pass the message on," Birnie said.

"Move!" Andrew ordered. "We'll deal with the flats." He turned away as the oarsmen pulled their boat back to *Kathleen.*

"Lieutenant Toshack," Andrew said. "If you were planning to sink a ship between two islands in a river, what else would you do?"

Toshack considered for a moment. "I'd ensure the British commanders were either dead or captured, sir."

"Exactly so," Andrew agreed. "You'd position a force of infantry and maybe a battery of artillery on the island. I'll deal with the flats; you take a section upstream and check the islands."

"Yes, sir," Toshack said. He shouted for a corporal and set off upstream at a fast march, with his men nearly jogging to keep pace with him.

"How are we doing, Sergeant?" Andrew asked.

"All right, sir," Coslett replied. "We were going to knock the bottom out of the boats and sink them, but one's half full of gunpowder." He grinned. "We're going to make a devil of a bang instead."

"That's the spirit!" Andrew approved. "Blow the things to Kingdom Come!"

Coslett laughed. "We will, sir. Best stand clear!"

"Get the men back, Coslett! And drag these wounded Burmese away. They can't hurt us now, and I'll not kill wounded men."

"Yes, sir." When Coslett barked orders, the Fusiliers hauled the Burmese casualties back from the river.

"Whenever you're ready, Sergeant," Andrew shouted.

The explosions ripped all three flats to shreds, spread splinters over a fifty-yard radius and knocked branches from the trees. The water erupted in a seventy-foot-high fountain that hovered and then collapsed, bringing mud and dead fish.

"That was some bang," Coslett looked pleased with himself as his men cheered. Andrew thought there was something very satisfying in destroying the enemy's weapons.

"You didn't leave much of the flats," Andrew approved. He saw the shattered remnants of the stakes and fragments of the flats carried away on the current.

"We didn't leave much of anything, sir," Coslett said.

As the echoes of the explosion died away, the Fusiliers heard firing from upstream. "Lieutenant Toshack's found some trouble," Andrew said. "Gather the men together, Sergeant, and we'll see what's happening up there."

"Yes, sir," Coslett said, shouting for his men.

The Fusiliers emerged from the trees, laughing at the destruction. "Form up in a column of four!" Andrew ordered. "Sergeant, take the rearguard. I'll take the advance guard, and every fourth man watch the flanks."

The shooting was louder now and more insistent, as if Toshack was involved with a large body of the enemy. Andrew led the platoon at the double with his revolver in his hand.

He rounded a bend in the path and stopped as he saw Toshack's section withdrawing towards him, firing ahead and into the forest. Andrew glanced at his men, deciding how best to form up to defend themselves on the narrow path.

"Three abreast on the path," he ordered. "Front rank kneeling, second standing and third in reserve. Open up to allow Lieutenant Toshack's section through."

Well-trained, the Fusiliers obeyed.

"When our lads have passed," Andrew continued, "the front rank will fire a volley and file back through the other two ranks. The front nine men will face along the track, and the rest will face the forest."

Toshack's section ran back, hurrying without panic.

"Get to the rear," Andrew ordered as they reached him. "Where's Lieutenant Toshack?"

"He's coming, sir," the corporal was bleeding from a wound on his shoulder.

Toshack was last to appear, firing his revolver down the path, where a host of Burmese soldiers advanced.

"Ready, lads," Andrew said. "Once the lieutenant is safe, fire three rounds rapid!"

The Fusiliers waited as Toshack strode up to them, opened ranks to let him pass, closed, and fired rolling volleys.

Andrew estimated about fifty of Thibaw's soldiers were on the path, with the sun glinting from their weapons. The Fusiliers' first bullets ripped into the leading men, knocking down two and hitting a man in the second rank. The Fusiliers reloaded and fired without orders, the heavy bullets smashing down two or more men as the Burmese closed. A spray of blood rose with pieces of a man's skull.

"Keep firing, men," Andrew ordered.

Seeing the carnage in front, the Burmese soldiers at the back hesitated. "Load!" Andrew ordered. He heard the jerking of the underlevers as the Fusiliers ejected the spent cartridges and pressed in the new.

"Come on, you bastards," a Fusilier growled, presenting his rifle to the enemy.

Andrew hoped the Martinis continued to operate, for they had an unpleasant reputation for overheating and jamming at inconvenient moments.

Another volley hammered the faltering Burmese. One man crumpled, and another fell backwards, spouting blood. The rest turned away.

"They're retiring, sir," a Fusilier reported just as firing broke out further forward in the column.

"They're in the forest!" Toshack shouted. "Volley fire, men! One rank at a time."

Andrew nodded. If all three ranks fired simultaneously, the Burmese could attack while the men reloaded. Firing one rank at a time reduced the volume of fire but retained most of the firepower if the enemy charged.

"Keep moving," Andrew ordered. "Withdraw along the path."

I've brought my men into a bad situation, with the forest on one side, the enemy behind us and no space to manoeuvre. We'll have to rely on discipline and musketry.

The Fusiliers withdrew slowly, with one section firing whenever they saw movement in the trees and the rearguard ready if the pursuing Burmese appeared on the path. Gunsmoke coiled around them, marking their progress as men fired, cursed, reloaded, and moved on, staring into the shaded trees.

"Steady, men!" Andrew shouted. "Keep together!"

The first Fusilier fell ten minutes later. A dozen Burmese fired from the forest, with one bullet striking a Fusilier high in the shoulder. The man grunted, put a hand to the wound and swore softly. "The buggers shot me," he said in disbelief.

"Help that man!" Andrew ordered and increased the speed. They had a long march ahead with an unknown number of the enemy all around. He glanced at the river, hoping for support from *Kathleen* or *Irrawaddy*, but the water remained clear of traffic. A gong sounded somewhere, encouraging Thibaw's men.

"Movement!" Coslett shouted and ordered a section to fire, with the bullets slicing leaves from the trees and chipping the wood. The platoon moved in a cloud of gunsmoke, with men watching all around.

"We could do with naval support here," Toshack echoed Andrew's thoughts. "A pity *Kathleen* is hunting Maung Thandar on the other side of the Irrawaddy."

"We must make do with what we have," Andrew replied.

A second Fusilier fell as they passed through a clearing, and the Burmese fired from behind a hastily constructed timber and earth stockade. The man grunted and crumpled to the ground with two Burmese bullets in him. He died without knowing what had killed him.

Andrew saw the enemy's brass helmets glinting behind the stockade and snarled. "Sergeant Coslett, outflank them on the left with one section, fire and get in with the bayonet. Lieutenant Toshack, get the men down and fire on the enemy; I'll take Three Section on the right flank. On my word, Coslett."

As Toshack laid down covering fire, Coslett and Andrew advanced on either flank of the earthworks. The Burmese did not wait to receive the charge but withdrew quickly, with the Fusiliers in pursuit.

"Stand and fight, you bastards!" the Fusiliers shouted. "Come back and fight!"

"Don't chase them!" Andrew ordered. He grabbed an excited Fusilier's arm. "Get back, man! They'll be waiting for you in the trees." He saw one fleet-footed Fusilier catch a Burmese soldier. The Burmese turned, drew his *dha*, and the Fusilier thrust his bayonet hilt-deep into the man's stomach.

"And that's done for you, Johnny Thibaw!"

"Reform!" Coslett bellowed. "Don't linger in the open!"

"Open order," Andrew ordered. "Don't close up until we reach the forest. Move at the double." He shuffled the ranks, moving the rearguard further up the column and men from the centre to the rear.

"Push on!"

The Fusiliers obeyed, marching and firing, with two men supporting the wounded and Andrew in the rearguard. He heard firing ahead, glanced over his shoulder and saw Coslett in the centre of the column giving brisk orders.

"Don't waste ammunition, boys! Only fire when I say!"

Andrew nodded. He had not anticipated a fighting withdrawal along the forest track, expecting *Kathleen* to provide adequate support. The appearance of Maung Thandar had altered the raid's dynamics.

"Sir!" Toshack reported. "Thibaw's soldiers hold a village ahead." The lieutenant looked calm, although rivulets of sweat had streaked lighter patches down his smoke-blackened face.

Andrew remembered the village where Thibaw's spy had lived. "Take over the rearguard, Corporal!" he shouted and hurried to the head of the column.

The Burmese had dug low earthworks around the village, and men fired muskets at the Fusiliers. The sun glinted from brass helmets, and a gong sounded ominously in the background.

"They've trapped us," Toshack said. "With a fortified village ahead, skirmishers in the forest and men behind, they've sprung a neat little ambush."

"They have," Andrew agreed. He saw a yellow umbrella in the village and knew a high-ranking officer commanded the Burmese.

I'd put good money that's Buda Sein.

CHAPTER 29

IRRAWADDY RIVER AND RANGOON, NOVEMBER 1885

"Dig in," Andrew ordered. "Form a semi-circle and hold our ground."

The Fusiliers obeyed, pulling together and finding cover wherever they could.

The longer we are here, the more reinforcements the Burmans can gather. I might have prevented Thibaw from sinking a ship and killing General Prendergast, but he'll laud the defeat of a British platoon as a significant victory. By the time the foreign propagandists have finished, it will resound like Isandhlwana or Majuba.

"Don't waste ammunition," Sergeant Coslett advised. "Only fire when I say, or you are sure of your target."

Fortunately, recent rains had softened the ground as the Fusiliers used bayonets and hands to dig out shallow shelters in the ground, all the time enduring a constant harassing fire from the Burmese.

"It's lucky they're poor shots, sir," Coslett said.

"Let's hope we are better," Andrew replied, checking his ammunition. He had twenty-four cartridges left.

With the men lying down, replying whenever a Burmese soldier showed himself, Andrew pondered his best move.

"Lieutenant Toshack," he said. "We can't stay here indefinitely. When dark falls, we'll advance against the village."

"Yes, sir," Toshack ducked as a bullet whistled overhead. "What then, sir?"

"We'll play it by ear when we capture the place," Andrew said. "There will be food in the village at least; the men must be getting hungry."

"Yes, sir. I'll pass on the word," Toshack said.

Andrew crawled around the ragged perimeter, trying to ignore the shots that buzzed overhead.

"There's one!" Coslett traversed his rifle to the right and fired. "Got him, I think."

"Good shot, Sergeant!" Andrew did not see the result of Coslett's shot, but a word of encouragement was never wasted. He admired the Fusiliers' fire discipline, for a detachment of Johnny Raws would be blasting away at every movement in the trees, while these Welshmen only fired when they had a definite target.

"How long until dark, sir?" Toshack asked.

Andrew glanced at his watch and swore when he saw it had stopped. *Is it broken? Or did I forget to wind it?* "I'd estimate an hour, Lieutenant."

Toshack glanced at the village, where yellow-white muzzle flares showed where the Burmese were firing. "It's going to be a long hour."

With the Fusiliers lying behind cover, the Burmese shots passed mainly overhead, with the occasional bullet burrowing into the damp path.

"Aim at the smoke and flashes!" Andrew advised. He saw some of the men counting their cartridges. "Don't waste ammunition."

"Sir!" Coslett spun and fired, "Behind you!"

Andrew flinched as the bullet passed so close he felt the wind and heard a yell. He turned to see a score of Burmans rising, dripping from the river.

"Two and Three Sections!" Andrew yelled. "Guard the riverbank!"

Half the Fusiliers faced around to meet this new threat, with some firing and resorting to their rifle butts and a fortunate few having their bayonets fixed. Andrew shot the nearest attacker and then joined Two and Three Sections in a furious battle with bayonet, boot and rifle butt against the Burmese dhas.

As Andrew's men struggled with the riverside attackers, the Burmese in the trees increased their fire.

Andrew pushed a man aside, pressed the muzzle of his revolver against a bare Burmese chest and squeezed the trigger. He smelled scorched flesh, saw the man's mouth and eyes open wide as he toppled backwards and saw a Fusilier thrust a bayonet into another attacker. A Burmese stabbed a Fusilier in the back, another shouted something, and then the skirmish ended.

The surviving Burmese withdrew back into the dark river, leaving a scatter of bodies on the ground and blood on the rushing water.

"Roll call!" Andrew shouted, slipping behind a tree when a bullet whined dangerously close to his head.

Sergeant Coslett called the roll.

"Ryan is dead, sir, and Collins wounded."

Andrew swore. He was losing far too many men on this expedition. The daylight was quickly fading, with long shadows across the river and insects increasing their assaults on the Fusiliers.

I didn't think the Burmese would come by river. Buda Sein is an innovative man. Unless we move soon, he'll think of another strategy to surprise us, and next time, we might not be so fortunate.

"Let's take that village," Andrew ordered. "There's more cover there than here."

Toshack lifted a hand. "Listen, sir! Can you hear that? It's an engine!"

Andrew lifted his head. "Yes, by God! You're right! Is that one of ours? Or a king's steamer?" He listened for a moment. "I can't hear any paddles thumping."

"I'll have a look, sir," Toshack slid backwards into the river, ducked under the bank and swam a few strokes. He returned within five minutes, dripping wet but smiling.

"She's ours, sir! *Kathleen*!"

"She won't see us in the dark," Andrew said as the launch's engines increased in volume. He stood up, and half a dozen Burmese fired, forcing him back down again. "That's a bit of a problem."

"She's slowing down!" Toshack reported and swore. "She's training her guns on us."

"Get down, boys!" Andrew roared. "*Kathleen* is going to fire!"

The Fusiliers tried to dig themselves deeper into the path as *Kathleen* opened up, with her shells exploding around the village and the besieged British.

"She thinks we're Burmese," a Fusilier said.

"Do I look like a bloody Burman?" another Fusilier asked.

"No, you're far too ugly to be Burmese."

Andrew heard the simple black humour of British soldiers hiding their fear as *Kathleen's* guns raked the village and forest, bringing down branches and twigs, knocking chunks from the trees and raising splashes from the river and clods of earth from the path.

"We're on your side!" a Fusilier shouted.

In the forest, the Burmese fired at *Kathleen*, bringing more shots in retaliation.

I've never been under British fire before, Andrew thought. *That's another experience I could do without.*

When the Burmese fire slackened, *Kathleen* concentrated on the village, setting two houses on fire and hammering the fortifications.

"With luck, *Kathleen* will chase the Burmese away," Toshack said.

The firing eased and started again as the Burmese fired a small-calibre artillery piece at the launch.

"Can these men not take a hint?" a Fusilier shouted. "Can't they just bugger off like sensible fellows?"

With his head close to the ground, Andrew did not see the landing party until the seamen were ashore. He heard the voices first.

"McGraw! Take five men to port. Simonds, take five to starboard, and I'll go right up the throat. Come on, *Kathleens*!"

The seamen yelled as they charged forward, with light from the burning buildings reflecting from fixed bayonets and cutlass blades. Andrew heard a scattered crackle as the defenders fired a final few shots and hurriedly withdrew, leaving the bluejackets in command of the village.

"Right, Fusiliers," Andrew stood up. "Let's make our presence known!" He strode forward. "*Kathleens*! Why the devil were you firing at us?"

Midshipman Birnie stared at Andrew. "Where did you spring from? We thought you were dead!"

"Not yet," Andrew replied, "although you did your best to kill us. Could you take us home now? We've had enough of footslogging over Burma."

❄

MARIANA LIFTED HER HAND FROM THE KEYBOARD. "THAT'S ALL YOU'RE getting from me tonight, Stephen. I'm tired."

"You will be, Mariana. Shall I sing you a song?" Jennings asked.

"Yes, please, Stephen," Mariana slid from the piano stool to allow Stephen access. She could feel the friendly warmth of his body close to hers.

"I'll start with a nonsense song," Stephen said, immediately singing in a rich baritone.

"I've seen a deal of gaiety throughout my noisy life,
With all my grand accomplishments, I ne'er could get a wife."

Stephen laughed as he sang, watching Mariana's reaction to his words. She smiled in response, drank more wine, and enjoyed his gaiety.

"For Champagne Charlie is my name,
Good for any game at night, my boys,
Champagne Charlie is my name."

Mariana shook her head. "I don't believe you are a Champagne Charlie," she said. "I think you are much more than that."

"Why, thank you, kind miss," Stephen said, bowing from the stool. "Here's an old one, and I am sure you'll know the chorus."

"I don't know many popular songs," Mariana did not object as Stephen pulled her closer.

"Mid pleasures and palaces though we may roam,
Be it ever so humble, there's no place like home!
A charm from the skies seems to hallow us there,
Which seek through the world is ne'er met elsewhere."

Stephen played the piano like a professional, with his hands dancing across the keys as he smiled at Mariana. "And now the chorus, Mariana, one, two, three..."

Mariana joined in, lifting her voice to words she recognised.

"Home! Home!
Sweet, sweet home!
There's no place like home!
There's no place like home!"

Singing together created a bond, and Mariana laughed as Jennings opened a new bottle of red wine.

"I hope you can think of this house as your home, Mariana," he said. "Rather than your stuffy little room in Wells's Britannia."

Mariana smiled as the wine and the music made her head spin. "I'd like that," she said.

"I hoped you would," Jennings said quietly. "Do you know a song called 'In the Gloaming'? It's quite melancholic."

Mariana shook her head. "I told you I don't know many popular songs."

"I'll sing you the last verse," Jennings said, topping her glass again. He lowered his voice, holding Mariana's gaze.

"In the gloaming, oh my darling,
When the lights are soft and low.
Will you think of me and love me,
As you did once long ago?"

Mariana nodded. "Yes," she whispered. "Yes, I will. I'll always remember this evening."

"Then this house and all inside it is yours, my dear," Stephen said. "Including me. Especially me."

Leaving the stool, he snaked an arm around Mariana's waist, pulled her closer, and kissed her. Mariana returned his kiss and did not object when he pulled her closer.

CHAPTER 30

IRRAWADDY RIVER, NOVEMBER 1885

Andrew put aside his official report and stared at the next sheet of blank paper on his writing pad. He always considered that writing reports was easy: all he had to do was state the facts and stick to a formula. Writing personal letters, on the other hand, entailed thought and effort.

Dear Mariana, he wrote, leaned back in the tiny cabin, and chewed the end of his pen. *What can I say to her? I doubt she'd be interested in news of the campaign.* He looked out of the porthole for inspiration, saw only the surging river, sighed, and returned to chewing the pen.

What do I want to say? I want her to reconsider her refusal. How the devil do I phrase that?

He looked out of the porthole again and saw *Thambyadine*, the vessel that held General Prendergast, steering erratically past them.

Somebody will get it in the neck for that.

He saw the boat approaching *Kathleen* and, a few moments later, heard the tap on his cabin door.

"Sorry, Baird," Birnie said cheerfully. "That's a message from General Whatshisname asking if your report is ready yet."

"I'll be a couple of minutes," Andrew replied.

"Best make them very short minutes," Birnie said. "*Thambyadine's* boat is alongside to take you to the general."

Andrew sighed, glanced at his letter to Mariana, lifted his report, and followed Birnie onto the deck. "Take me to General Prendergast," he said, stepping into the small boat.

Prendergast nodded to Andrew. "I heard you had a little skirmish with the enemy, Baird."

"Yes, sir. The Welsh Fusiliers did splendidly, and the Navy chased away the enemy." Andrew produced his written report. "It's all in there, sir."

Prendergast glanced at the document and placed it on his desk. "Thank you, Captain. I'll read it later. I believe you were once recommended for the Victoria Cross."

"Yes, sir, in Zululand," Andrew said.

"By whom?"

"Redvers Buller, sir," Andrew said.

Prendergast finger-groomed his beard. "Ah, Redvers Buller, a rising star and one of the Wolseley Ring."

"I believe so, sir," Andrew agreed.

"Why was his recommendation not approved?" Prendergast asked.

"I never heard, sir," Andrew said.

They stood in the general's study in the stern of *Thambyadine* with the great paddles thumping through the river and the troops crowding the flats. Andrew saw the hospital ship nearby, with the awnings sheltering the sick.

Why has Thambyadine chosen a different route from the rest of the fleet?

Andrew stepped to the window and stared forward.

"Which channel are we taking, sir?"

"I leave that to the captain, Baird. He follows the pilot's instructions." Prendergast sounded amused. "You've blown up the trap, Captain, so why do you ask?"

"The flotilla has been steaming line astern since we left Rangoon, sir, but now *Thambyadine* is steering a different course to the rest," Andrew said. "Could I have your permission to speak to the captain?"

"By all means," Prendergast said. "I'll come with you." They left the cabin together, with the staff officers perplexed that a general should speak to a mere captain from a colonial regiment.

Thambyadine's captain looked surprised when Prendergast and Andrew arrived at his side. "What's the trouble, General?"

Andrew did not waste time on politeness. He pointed to the smiling Burmese pilot. "That's not the usual pilot," he said. "Where's the usual pilot?"

"He's got a touch of fever," the captain explained. "This fellow took his place."

"This fellow is piloting you into the shallows," Andrew said. Reaching forward, he grabbed the pilot's shoulder and hauled him back. "What's your game, chum?"

As the man wriggled free, Andrew saw the tattoo on the nape of his neck. "That's the mark of the king's soldiers, Captain. This man is a spy!"

The pilot slid away and ran for the rail, with Andrew following. "Stop that man!" He unfastened his holster and hauled out his revolver. As the man poised on the rail and jumped into the river, Andrew fired three shots, seeing the splashes where the bullets landed. Soldiers on the flats a hundred yards away stared at them, wondering what was happening.

"I think you got him," Prendergast said. "He hasn't surfaced."

"These fellows swim like Tweed salmon," Andrew pointed out. "He's like as not doubled back and swum to the other bank."

The captain grunted. "Slow to quarter speed. Steer us behind the leading ship, helmsman; we'll follow the leader until we can find a trustworthy pilot."

Andrew nodded to *Little Salamander*. "I would recommend the master of that launch, sir. Captain Jamieson is an ex-Royal Navy man who has been plying these waters since the 1850s."

The captain stiffened his back. "I am master of *Thambyadine*, Captain Baird. I will not take orders from some ex-able seaman in a launch."

"Yes, sir," Andrew stepped back. "If you gentlemen will excuse me, I'll return to *Kathleen*."

I've done my bit here. The captain can choose his pilot.

MARIANA DRESSED SLOWLY, AWARE THAT STEPHEN WAS SITTING UP IN BED, watching her. She was not sure how she felt. Empty, perhaps; certainly not how she thought she should feel. The memories returned, hammering at her mind, tearing at her with their horror.

"I'd better get back to the hotel," she said.

Jennings slid from the bed without hiding his nakedness. Mariana looked away, not wanting to see any more.

"I'll get the coach ready," Jennings said, patting her bottom as he passed.

Mariana pulled away. "Thank you." She dressed hurriedly, averting her eyes as Stephen leisurely pulled on his clothes.

"You can stay the night if you wish," Jennings said.

Mariana shook her head. "No. No, thank you. I'd better get back." She was suddenly desperate to return to the hotel, to have familiar things around her and analyse what had happened.

"I'll see you tomorrow," Jennings said.

Mariana nodded, only wanting to be alone with her revived memories. She fought the tears that welled at the back of her eyes.

Oh, God, did that happen? I knew I could never marry Andrew.

"WHAT'S THAT?" THE LOOKOUT SHOUTED. "THERE'S SOMETHING IN THE water ahead, sir."

"Quarter speed," Lieutenant Trench ordered. "I see it."

Kathleen eased forward, barely making way against the force of the current. "What the devil is that?"

"It's a human head, Captain," Andrew focussed his field glasses on the object. "It's a human head on a stake." He swept his gaze across the river. "There are more of them, sir."

Kathleen slowed as Lieutenant Trench saw a line of human heads across the river, each thrust on the end of a pointed stake.

"Who the hell are these people?" Birnie asked.

"I don't know the answer," Andrew replied.

"Remove them," Trench ordered. "Birnie, take a boat out and lift these heads. I don't know who the poor devils were, but they deserve better than this." He glanced behind him. "Whatever you do, don't let the Press get hold of this horror. Keep it within *Kathleen*, or the journalists will have everyone howling for Burmese blood. Any Burmese blood."

"I knew some of these men, sir," Andrew said as he studied the disembodied heads. "That gentleman is named Harding, and that fellow is Marmaduke Patchley." Andrew could hear Patchley's voice proclaiming his Englishness. "The other men, I don't know." Patchley and Harding were the only Europeans on the stakes. The others were indigenous Burmese, victims of a war they had never sought nor could ever profit from, whatever the outcome.

"Bury them all," Trench said. "Whoever they were."

Andrew returned to his cabin and remembered his barely started letter for Mariana. He thought of Harding's kindness, Patchley's ignorant arrogance, and the unknown Burmese whom somebody had killed to intimidate the invaders.

War is the greatest obscenity mankind has created. It spawns every kind of evil under the excuse of defending one state or ruler against another.

Andrew sighed and returned to his letter.

When Mariana reached the landing halfway down the hotel stairs, she saw the Burmese woman standing in the foyer. She felt her heartbeat increase.

What's she doing here? Has she come to gloat that she captured my man? What should I do?

Mariana looked around for support, but the foyer was deserted except for the receptionist. Even Myat Lay Phyu was absent. Mariana steeled herself, straightened her back and approached the woman.

"Miss Maxwell," Than Than Aye said, stepping forward.

"Yes," Mariana said coldly. She held Than Than Aye's gaze, hoping to intimidate her.

Than Than Aye did not lower her eyes. "We have things to talk about."

"I can't think of anything we have to say," Mariana would have swept past if Than Than Aye had not moved into her path.

"We have to talk about Captain Andrew Baird," Than Than Aye said.

Mariana stiffened. "What about Captain Baird?"

"We have to talk about him," Than Than Aye said. "Please sit down, Miss Maxwell."

About to refuse, Mariana saw that Myat Lay Phyu had returned to her customary place at the pillar. Myat Lay Phyu nodded once and indicated a chair.

"If we must," Mariana said. She sat down, smoothing her skirt under her and keeping her back straight. "Speak."

"You are wondering who I am," Than Than Aye said. "And you think I propose stealing Captain Baird away from you."

"Is that what I am thinking?" Mariana asked coldly. "I do not believe I have made you privy to my thoughts."

"Your actions make your thoughts clear," Than Than Aye said. "Let me say you have nothing to fear from me."

Mariana was about to leave when she saw Myat Lay Phyu shake her head. "What should I have to fear from you? I do not even know who you are."

"I am Than Than Aye, Bo Thura's daughter and Andrew's cousin," Than Than Aye said.

"Oh," Mariana tried to hide her surprise.

Than Than Aye smiled, "Andrew and I are related by blood," she emphasised. "That is all."

Mariana felt the colour flood her face. "Then you are not," she searched for the word. "Intimate. You are not together."

"Not in the way you imagined," Than Than Aye said.

"Oh," Mariana said again. "I thought."

"You thought what Stephen Jennings led you to think," Than Than Aye said.

"Stephen is a good man," Mariana said, unsure of her words. "He cares for me."

"Come with me," Than Than Aye said, "and I will show you what your good friend Stephen Jennings is really like."

When Mariana looked up, Myat Lay Phyu nodded once, and Mariana wondered if there was anything that enigmatic woman did not understand.

Mariana and Than Than Aye left the hotel together, and Than Than Aye signalled for a pair of rickshaws. She gave rapid instructions to the runners, told Mariana to sit back and took her place as elegantly as any sovereign. The runners pulled their rickshaws effortlessly through the streets, avoiding the bullock carts until they pulled up close to Jennings' house.

"We'll walk the rest," Than Than Aye said. "Come along, Miss Maxwell."

Mariana followed as Than Than Aye stalked through the mansions that filled this quarter of Rangoon. They stopped opposite Jennings' house, with bright birds singing from the trees and a couple of carriages grumbling past.

"Why are we here?" Mariana asked.

"Wait, and you'll see," Than Than Aye said.

Mariana did not have long to wait. Within ten minutes, Jennings' Brougham coach rolled to his house, and the servant opened the door. Jennings stepped out with a European woman at his side. Mariana watched as Jennings offered the woman his arm.

"Oh!" Mariana said. "Perhaps that lady is Stephen's sister."

"That is a very thin straw to support her weight," Than Than Aye said. She led Mariana across the road. "He won't see you," Than Than Aye promised. "He's too engrossed in his new attraction, and she is too stupid to care. Now listen to their conversation."

Jennings was talking, holding the woman's hands. "When I first met you," he said. “I thought you were just one of the fishing fleet, but now I can tell that you are something special. You are like no woman I have ever met before.”

“Oh, the cad!” Mariana said, surprised. “He said those exact words to me.”

“And to every other girl he attempts to seduce, I expect,” Than Than Aye said. “You were not his first.”

Mariana nodded. She had too many emotions running through her to speak.

“Do you wish to see more?” Than Than Aye put a small hand on Mariana’s sleeve.

Mariana clung to her slender hope. “Yes,” she said and lifted her chin defiantly.

Than Than Aye touched her arm, “Then I’ll show you,” she said. “Come with me.”

“Where are we going?”

“You’ll see.” Than Than Aye led Mariana round the back of the neighbouring house and spoke to one of the servants. Mariana could not understand the conversation but saw Than Than Aye press something in the servant’s hand.

What’s happening? I wish I knew what was happening.

“This way, Miss Maxwell,” Than Than Aye said, beckoning her to the back door. “Inside!”

“Should we? What if the owner comes?”

“This is the servant’s area. The owner is far too important to come here,” Than Than Aye explained. “Come on, Miss Maxwell.”

The door led to a wooden staircase, which Than Than Aye rapidly mounted, with Mariana following. They stopped on the upper floor and pushed into a sparsely furnished room with a window facing Jennings’ house.

“This will do,” Than Than Aye said. “Stand at the window, Miss Maxwell, and tell me what you see.”

“Stephen’s house,” Mariana said. She looked downward, where Stephen’s large windows allowed her to see the dining room. The circular table was set as it had been for her initial visit, and Jennings sat opposite the woman who looked more composed than Mariana had felt in that situation.

“Who is she?” Mariana asked.

“His latest conquest,” Than Than Aye replied. “Her name is Ellen Ambrose, the younger daughter of Edward Ambrose of Edward Ambrose and Company.”

“How do you know that?” Mariana asked.

“I make it my business to know things,” Than Than Aye replied.

“They’re drinking my champagne!” Mariana said indignantly.

“Your champagne?” Than Than Aye asked.

Mariana nodded. “Yes. Stephen bought half a dozen bottles of champagne just for me.”

Than Than Aye shook her head. “No, Mariana. Stephen is the biggest wine and spirit importer in Rangoon. Jennings and Stanley buy champagne by the dozens of crates."

"Oh." Mariana watched Ellen Ambrose finish her glass and accept another, with Stephen drinking half as much and pouring most of the contents of his glass into one of the plant pots beside the table. "I wondered how Stephen finished his glass so quickly."

"Do you want to see any more?" Than Than Aye asked.

"Yes," Mariana replied. She knew it would hurt her, but she had to discover the truth. She felt Than Than Aye standing behind her as she waited, guessing what would happen. After half an hour, Stephen stood and extended a hand.

Ellen Ambrose took his hand and followed him upstairs. Mariana watched as they entered Stephen's bedroom.

"Oh, Lord," Mariana said as Stephen expertly undressed Ellen Ambrose. "Was he ever married?"

"Not to my knowledge," Than Than Aye said.

"No special island trips with his wife, then," Mariana turned away as Stephen shrugged off his clothes.

"No, but he does own a small house on an island. His own little love nest," Than Than Aye said. "He likes the hunt, and when he has made the kill, the bedding, he loses interest and moves to his next prey. You were a difficult target, while Ellen Ambrose was an easy conquest."

"I think I have seen sufficient," Mariana said.

Than Than Aye glanced out of the window, "I don't think I want to see any more of Stephen Jennings either. I can see more than enough from this angle."

Mariana agreed. The rear view of Jennings as he seduced Ellen Ambrose was less than appealing.

"Take me back to the hotel, please," Mariana said.

She felt Than Than Aye's unspoken sympathy as they walked silently through the streets and to her usual seat in the foyer under the friendly shade of a potted palm. Myat Lay Phyu watched from beside the pillar, somehow reassuring in her silence.

"Are you all right?" Than Than Aye asked.

Mariana shook her head. "Oh, God," she put a hand to her mouth. "I've ruined everything," she whispered. "Poor Andrew."

Than Than Aye did not talk for a few moments, "That may be so," she said eventually. "That is something you must discuss with Captain Andrew."

"Oh, God," Mariana repeated.

"Stephen Jennings led you astray," Than Than Aye said, "but it is not too late to put things right."

"It is," Mariana said. "You don't understand, Than Than Aye. In our culture, a woman must be pure, untouched before her wedding day."

Mariana saw the faces leering down at her, gloating, blood-splashed, laughing, cruelly callous. She shook away the images, unable to accept them.

Than Than Aye put a hand on Mariana's sleeve. "I doubt Captain Andrew has been a monk these past few years," she said dryly. "He knows the way of the world and will understand when you explain things to him."

"I can't tell him!" Mariana shook her head. "He will hate me forever."

Than Than Aye smiled. "He will not. You must trust him, Mariana."

"How can he trust me?" Mariana asked miserably. "After what I have done."

"Did you trust Stephen?"

"Yes," Mariana replied.

"Why?"

"I thought he loved me."

"Andrew loves you," Than Than Aye reminded. "He'll trust you."

"I don't deserve his trust," Mariana said.

"Oh, stuff and nonsense!" Than Than Aye scolded. "You are a red-blooded woman, that's all. If you want Andrew back, you must claim him and ensure you keep him. Feeling sorry for yourself doesn't help, and neither does brooding over the past."

"You sound like my sister," Mariana told her ruefully.

Than Than Aye laughed. "Good! If I were your sister, I'd give you a slap. Now straighten your back, look the world in the eye and let your man chase you until you decide to catch him."

Mariana smiled at the idea of holding a large net to ensnare Andrew.

"That's better," Than Than Aye said. "Now, let's see what's best to do."

Mariana felt fresh hope as she looked at Than Than Aye, with Myat Lay Phyu listening to every word. Myat Lay Phyu held Mariana's gaze and nodded approval.

There's more, Mariana reminded herself. *There's a lot more that I can't tell them and can never tell Andrew. He will never want me if I tell him everything.*

CHAPTER 31

IRRAWADDY RIVER, NOVEMBER 1885

Andrew stood in *Kathleen's* bows as she floated at anchor in front of the flotilla, with the Irrawaddy chuckling under her counter and birds singing above. He raised his binoculars to peer forward.

I am the foremost man in the leading vessel in the flotilla. That means that at this minute, on the 24th of November 1885, I am the most forward British soldier in Burma. How do I feel?

Empty.

I wish I had made peace with Mariana before we left Rangoon. Compared to that, Upper Burma is unimportant.

"Weigh anchors!" The call sounded from astern, bellowed by some brass-lunged naval officer.

"Weigh anchors! Quarter speed ahead!" Lieutenant Trench echoed the call, and *Kathleen's* hands rushed to obey.

Andrew constantly admired the efficiency of the flotilla and the associated Royal Navy ships as they pushed forward against the strong current. The vessels always seemed to maintain their position despite the skirmishes with the Burmese, the state of the channel or the sudden torrential rain.

Kathleen edged in front, marginally ahead of *Irrawaddy*, as Trench followed the deep-water channel, constantly consulting with the pilot.

They passed several small villages, each with a quota of fishing boats on the river. The inhabitants clustered at the water's edge to watch them pass, with one or two waving without a single hostile action.

"There's another village ahead," the lookout called. "It's larger than the last few."

"That should be Kaoung-Wah," Andrew consulted his map just as he heard the bang of artillery and saw a sudden column of water rise a hundred yards in front.

"Somebody doesn't like visitors!" a rating shouted.

Andrew raised his field glasses to trace the origin of the shot. "There's a stockade outside the village," he reported. "It looks like it's only timber and newly made."

"Hold your fire," Lieutenant Trench said as the seamen on the forward gun looked hopeful. A moment later, one of the gun barges beside *Ngawoon* opened fire, with shells exploding over and inside the stockade.

"Good shooting!" Andrew said. He saw the white smoke drift from above the now shattered timber.

"Signal from *Irrawaddy*, sir," an eager rating reported to Lieutenant Trench. "Proceed forward and see if the Burmans still occupy the stockade."

"On we go, men!" Trench shouted. "Half speed ahead and watch for any gunfire!"

Kathleen's crew were in high spirits as the launch powered forward, with the helmsman weaving slightly to disrupt any enemy gunner's aim.

"They're not firing!" the lookout shouted.

"I want a landing party to check what's happening!" In a vessel as small as *Kathleen*, there was no need even to shout, but Trench bellowed every word as if he were on the bridge of a battleship. "Six men! Captain Baird, will you lead it?"

Andrew knew Trench was master in the vessel. "Aye, aye, sir!" he replied, much to the ratings' amusement.

"We'll make a seaman out of the soldier yet," a rating observed.

"We'll have to go to sea for that," the bearded petty officer replied.

"A riverman, then."

The petty officer glanced at Andrew. "He's halfway there already."

When *Kathleen* pulled close inshore, Andrew jumped into the shallows and led his six volunteers up a steep incline to the stockade. "Extended order!" He shouted and remembered he commanded seamen and not trained soldiers. "That means spread out, lads!"

Andrew zig-zagged in front of the landing party, watching the timber stockade ahead for bobbing heads and the spurting, darting flames of musketry. Instead, he saw nothing. He reached the log wall with the landing party a few steps behind him. As Andrew looked up at the nine-foot high wall, one of the sailors threw himself up, with the others following, more dexterous than soldiers. Andrew swore and dragged himself over the pointed logs to find the interior bare and deserted, with a single dismounted gun.

The sailors drew their cutlasses and checked every corner.

"Nobody here, sir!" they reported. "The place is as empty as a public* house on a Sunday afternoon."

"Back to the ship," Andrew ordered. He reported his findings, and *Kathleen* was already heading north when a body of infantry and engineers landed to

---

* A Public – a public house, a pub.

destroy the stockade. The explosion echoed across the Irrawaddy as wood splinters rose and descended into the river.

"That's another nail in Thibaw's teak coffin," Birnie said as *Kathleen* steamed on, battling against the current as they probed deeper into the Kingdom of Ava.

At quarter past four that day, the lookout shouted another warning. "Burman soldiers ahead!"

Andrew lifted his field glasses. He saw movement on the high ground behind the village of Mingyan, with the sun reflecting from the brass helmets of royal soldiers.

"I'd say at least two hundred infantrymen," Andrew reported. "With earthworks lower down, close to the river." He scanned the area. Around and behind the earthworks, fields of grain mingled among acres of long waving grass.

Earthworks are a sure indicator that the Burmese intend to place artillery here. Once again, General Prendergast's rapid advance has caught Thibaw by surprise.

When *Kathleen* passed the information on, Prendergast sent her ahead, together with *Irrawaddy* and *White Swan*. Andrew saw the Royal Artillerymen on *White Swan* preparing for action.

"General Prendergast has ordered us to engage the enemy," Birnie said. "I hope they make a proper fight of it this time and don't cut and run."

"You bloodthirsty thing," Andrew replied.

Birnie laughed and pointed astern. "Look! Here's *Yunan* and *Ataran* coming to join us!"

Yunan was a 396-ton paddle launch, while *Ataran* was a twin-screw 140-tonner, both belonging to the Irrawaddy Flotilla Company. When a gun barge also steamed up, the British opened fire on the Burmese positions.

Andrew saw the seamen were eager to fight, loading and firing with a speed that the Royal Artillery would envy. As the gunners fired, the ships steamed forward, inching slowly against the current.

"There's another earthwork!" Andrew saw the turned-up earth and flattened grass where men had dragged a wheeled gun to its position. The Burmese waited until the British vessels were close before firing, with shells whistling overhead or falling short to churn up the Irrawaddy water.

"They're game!" Birnie shouted as if he enjoyed being under fire.

"Alter your target to that fellow, gunners," Trench ordered. He gave more precise orders, and the naval gunners returned fire.

As well as artillery, the Burmese attacked with musketry, so rifle bullets buzzed and hummed like a host of hornets, rattling against the metalwork and splintering the woodwork of the British vessels.

"This is more like it!" Birnie shouted. "Well done, Thibaw! Fight on, Burmese soldiers!"

As the ships pushed upriver, they silenced battery after battery, blowing up the earthworks and sending the Burmese riflemen running into the tall grass for the Nordenfeldts to hammer.

"We're near the village now," Birnie shouted. "It's more like a town, though."

Andrew lifted his field glasses from the latest battery to study Mingyan. "They're going to make a stand there," he said. "They have proper earthworks and larger calibre artillery."

The Burmans opened fire as the British flotilla came near, with one shell exploding in the air near *Kathleen* and spreading splinters across the launch.

"Good shot!" Birnie shouted. "Come on now, *Kathleens*! Show them what the Navy can do."

The firing was evenly matched, with the Burmese having the advantage of a stable battery while the ships had larger calibre guns. A host of riflemen supported the Burmans' battery, with bullets whistling around the ships' gun crews as smoke formed a greasy white cloud that hugged the water.

"They're making a fight of it," Birnie said as he commanded the forward gun. "Good show."

Andrew borrowed a Martini-Henry and fired whenever he had a clear target, which was not often among the gunsmoke.

The bluejackets wiped sweat off their foreheads, gulped down a mouthful of water and worked on loading and firing. Clouds of dust and dirt concealed the Burmese earthworks, split only by the flares of the Burmese artillery.

Around six in the evening, the Burmese fire eased.

"We've broken them!" Birnie said. "They put up a decent show, though."

"Somebody's still resisting," Andrew said, as a solitary Burmese rifleman fired, with the bullet zipping across the surface of the river.

Night fell swiftly, with the Burmese firing an occasional shot and the British retaliating with short bursts from the Nordenfeldts, so the flash and flare of gunshots lit up the river, the village, and the surrounding fields.

Shortly before dawn, Andrew saw a company of infantry land beneath the earthwork and march over the churned-up ground. They blew up the guns without the Burmese resisting, scouted the area, and returned to the ships at noon. A platoon remained behind to prevent the Burmese from returning.

"That was a smart little action," Birnie said with satisfaction. "By Jove, if the Burmans fight like that at Mandalay, I'll have something to tell the grandchildren, won't I just?"

"Do you have grandchildren, Birnie?" Andrew asked.

"Steady on," Birnie replied. "I haven't found a wife yet."

Andrew smiled. "Good luck. I'm sure plenty of women would love a man like you."

That evening, the flotilla anchored off Yandabo, still with *Kathleen* in the van and the rest forming a long line of ships. Andrew noticed more sick men under the awnings as the mosquitoes began their evening assaults.

"Yandabo is where we signed the treaty that ended the First Burmese War," Birnie said. "That was back in 1826, nearly sixty years ago, and we're still fighting them. Hopefully, this campaign will end any further hostilities. I don't like fighting in forests. Give me a broad horizon any time."

Andrew nodded. "I prefer the open spaces, too."

Let's end this river war so I can return to Mariana. I wonder when she'll get my letter? I hope she writes back.

CHAPTER 32

IRRAWADDY RIVER, NOVEMBER 1885

Jennings saw the letter lying on its silver tray as he stood at reception. "Is that for Miss Maxwell?" he asked.

The receptionist smiled and bowed. "Yes," she said. "That's for Miss Maxwell."

"I'll take it to her," Jennings said.

"Yes, sir," the receptionist handed it over.

Jennings slid the letter inside his jacket. *I'll burn that later,* he thought.

THE EXPEDITIONARY FORCE ANCHORED OFF PAGAN WITHOUT FURTHER opposition, despite rumours of a formidable Burmese Army gathering to defend the capital.

Elsewhere, dacoits were causing trouble around the frontier, with the British flying columns hunting them. The British plan was for the expeditionary force up the Irrawaddy to reach Mandalay simultaneously with a land-based Tounghoo brigade on the first of December.

"Catch them in a pincer movement, eh?" Birnie remarked.

"That's the plan," Andrew agreed.

Kathleen moved off again, probing cautiously northward with the river bisecting Thibaw's hostile territory.

"There's an object ahead, sir," the lookout reported. "I can't see what it is."

"Half speed ahead!" Trench ordered. "All hands stand by with grappling hooks and boathooks. Be careful of any tricks!"

Andrew moved to the starboard bow, holding an unfamiliar boathook, a long pole with a brass hook on the end, in his hands. "It's a large flat!" he shouted. "The Burmese might have filled her with explosives or some other devilment."

"Keep your gun trained on her, Birnie," Trench ordered. "There could be hundreds of Thibaw's soldiers waiting to board us!"

A lithe sailor scrambled to the highest point of the launch. "She's deserted and drifting, sir. Nobody on board that I can see."

"Grapple her!" Trench ordered, and expert hands threw grappling hooks over the surging water. The seamen fastened her to *Kathleen*'s stern and towed her away from the deep-water channel.

"Anchor her beside the bank," Trench ordered. "She's no danger to shipping there. Send a message to Captain Clutterbuck that the passage is clear."

An hour later, Andrew heard paddles thumping behind them as the British fleet moved again on their remorseless journey towards Mandalay.

"More boats, sir!" the lookout shouted as the Burmese pilot guided them along the deep-water channel.

"Birnie: take a boarding party and see what these boats are," Trench shouted.

"Aye, aye, sir!" Birnie called on six men who rowed towards the boats and inspected them individually. "Stones, sir! Each boat has a cargo of heavy stones but no crew."

"Thibaw was probably going to sink these in the channel," Trench said. "Cut them adrift, scupper them, and shove them in the shallows."

The sailors worked happily, pushing the boats clear of the fleet's passage and cheering when each one spun downstream, slowly sinking.

"That's another in the eye for Thibaw!"

"That's the way, Tom! Show the King of Ava what we think of him!"

"*Kathleen* forever!"

With the passage cleared, *Kathleen* led the flotilla upstream, with men waiting at the guns and a man in the bow, casting the lead in case the pilot proved unreliable. After Andrew's discovery of the king's soldier acting as a pilot on *Thambyadine*, the seamen were wary of the Burmese pilots.

At four in the afternoon, with the sun reflecting from the rippling water, the lookout shouted again.

"There's a rowing boat ahead, sir! A big one, flying a flag! With an armed steamer as an escort! It's not a British flag, sir."

Andrew lifted his field glasses and joined the officers with their telescopes.

"She looks like a galley," Birnie said. "A high-prowed rowing boat from the *Odyssey*."

"She's a state barge," Andrew stated. "I saw her in the moat at Mandalay."

Birnie whistled. "A state barge, is she? By Jove, that's a royal boat, I'll be bound. And she's wearing a white flag. Is it a flag of truce? Or is she surrendering?" He shifted his telescope. "It's that armed steamer that bothers me. Is she going to fight?"

"We'll see in a moment," Trench said. "Stand by the guns, men, and have a reception party ready in case it's the king himself." He closed his telescope with a snap. "Take us alongside, helmsman. Mr Birnie! Have a party ready with a line."

"Aye, aye, sir," Birnie replied.

"Which ship is General Prendergast on today?" Trench asked.

"*Thurreah*, sir," Birnie replied.

"We'll tow the state barge to *Thurreah* and let the general look after them. Baird, could you take Petty Officer McGraw and board the steamer? We'll have our guns trained on them in case anybody gives you any trouble."

"Aye, aye, sir," Andrew replied, knowing a soldier using nautical terminology always amused the sailors. McGraw was the sturdy, phlegmatic petty officer with the neat red beard.

"This way, sir," McGraw said, leading Andrew into a small boat. He tapped the cutlass at his belt and the Martini in his hand. "We might have to fight them, sir. Do you have a weapon?"

"I have a revolver," Andrew said.

It seemed foolhardy, boarding an enemy craft crowded with men with only a handful of bluejackets, but the seamen accepted the situation.

"We're British sailors," one man said with a gap-toothed grin. He pulled at his oars. "We're the Senior Service, old Britannia's first line of defence, the heirs of Nelson."

"We're the bloody Andrew," McGraw said. "Stop gabbing and get on with your duty, Brierly!"*

Andrew nodded as McGraw hooked onto the steamer and swung on board without waiting for Andrew, who followed a second later.

The Burmese crewmen stepped aside as Andrew sent McGraw to the wheelhouse to take charge of the boat. The other seamen commandeered the guns, moving the Burmese gently away without any resistance.

"It's all right, sir," McGraw said quietly. "We'll look after the ship. You look after the officers."

Andrew nodded. "That's what I'll do," he said, watching a party of bluejackets leap onto the royal barge with a line. "We're taking you in tow, lads," a grinning seaman told the confused Burmese seamen. "You're going to see our general."

The Burmese stepped back, allowing the bluejackets to tie up their craft.

"Take her easy," Trench ordered, and Kathleen eased back to the main fleet with her screw churning up the water. Andrew watched the two vessels, one an example of the most modern maritime technology and the other a boat whose design had probably not altered for a thousand years, and wondered at the juxtaposition of East and West.

Kathleen brought the barge to *Thurreah*, and a body of King Thibaw's officials boarded the British ship, looking about them as the bluejackets mounted a guard of honour with Martini-Henry rifles and shining cutlasses.

---

* The Andrew: according to folklore, in the early 19th century, an impressment officer named Andrew Miller pressed so many seamen that some seamen claimed he owned the navy. Many seamen called the Navy "The Andrew" in Miller's honour.

As the general met the officials, Captain Clutterbuck sent a detachment of sailors to the Burmese steamer.

"We'll take over now, sir," the young midshipman in charge looked only slightly surprised to see Andrew on the steamer.

"Thank you," Andrew returned to *Kathleen* with his men. McGraw chewed a wad of tobacco as though capturing an enemy ship with a handful of men was an everyday occurrence.

In the Royal Navy, Andrew thought, *it might well be an everyday occurrence.*

Kathleen waited alongside *Thurreah* as the Burmese officials handed over a letter from Kinwin Mingyi, Thibaw's chief minister, to General Prendergast.

"Either Thibaw is surrendering, or he's threatening to invade Britain and kidnap the queen," Birnie said.

"Maybe it's a proposal of marriage," Andrew suggested. "Thibaw already has a couple of wives. Perhaps he wants to add Queen Victoria to his collection."

"Good Lord! Do you think so?" Lieutenant Trench shook his head. "One wife is quite enough for anybody. Look! Thibaw's officials are returning!"

The officers on *Kathleen* waited for news while the men polished the brass-work, exercised the guns and sweltered in the heat. After an hour, Trench sent Birnie to *Thurreah* to find out what was happening.

Birnie returned in twenty minutes, grinning as he bounced back on board. "Thibaw is looking for a truce, sir," he reported, "but General Prendergast said he'd only stop fighting if Thibaw surrendered himself, his army and Mandalay."

"That's pretty unequivocal," Andrew said.

"Compared to what Thibaw did to his rivals and relatives, we are very generous," Birnie said. "The general promised to respect the lives and property of the king and his family, on one condition."

"What's the condition?" Andrew asked.

"The Europeans in Mandalay should be unharmed," Birnie replied.

"Let's hope they are," Andrew said. Like all his generation, he had heard of the massacre of British civilians in Cawnpore during the Indian Mutiny and the terrible repercussions that followed.

"Signal from Captain Clutterbuck!" Trench said. "We're moving again!"

Once again, *Kathleen* and *Irrawaddy* eased forward with the British fleet following deeper into Upper Burma. That night, as the sun sank in glorious orange-red, the flotilla cast anchor only seven miles south of Ava, the old capital of Burma.

"It's been a busy day," Andrew said. "Let's hope for success tomorrow."

Tomorrow is the crucial day. Thibaw will either decide to fight or the war will be over.

MARIANA SAT ON HER BED WITH THE FAN SLOWLY ROTATING ABOVE HER head and a bird calling outside.

What have I done? Have I awakened myself to a new life or completely ruined the old one? What would Elaine say?

Mariana lay back slowly with her hands folded behind her head.

I can't tell Andrew what happened. He'll be devastated after all he's done for me over the years. If I tell him and beg forgiveness, he'll always think he is my second choice, as I do with him and Elaine. Then there is the other thing: how can I face Andrew after that? I can't tell him. Oh, God, what a mess!

Mariana felt tears form in her eyes and thought of her past, from the happy days in Inglenook on the Natal-Zululand border to the terrible time when the renegades murdered her family and kidnapped her. Andrew had rescued her and had cared for her during the long years when she recovered from the trauma. Andrew had brought her into his life and proposed marriage when he considered her sufficiently fit.

Oh, God, what a fool I have been. Andrew!

It's too late now. I have ruined my life. Is there any point in carrying on? Should I end it now?

"I CAN SEE SOLDIERS ON AVA'S RAMPARTS," BIRNIE SAID, WITH HIS telescope pressed against his right eye.

Andrew nodded. "I see them," he said. "The sun reflects on their brass helmets."

"The Burmese have sunk a dozen boats and other assorted rubbish on the approaches to the fort," Birnie reported. "Their soldiers could make things difficult for us if they choose to oppose our landing. I would not enjoy being in a small stationary boat, under Burmese artillery and rifle fire."

Andrew nodded. "That would be unpleasant," he agreed.

Behind them, the British fleet lay at anchor in a long line of steamers and flats, with the khaki-clad troops stirring to the calls of various bugles.

"Sir!" Petty Officer McGraw approached Andrew. "You're wanted on the flagship, sir. General Prendergast has summoned all the British officers of the rank of captain and above."

"Thank you, McGraw," Andrew replied.

What's happening now?

With no room in his cabin, Prendergast addressed his officers on the deck, with the water lapping at the hull and a flight of parrots wheeling and screeching overhead.

"Mandalay is the capital and king's residence of Upper Burma," General Prendergast said, "but Ava is the heart and soul of the country. That's why Thibaw is called the King of Ava. By the look of the Burmese garrison, it looks as if we might have to storm the defences."

The officers nodded, with many glancing at the fort, assessing the difficulties and possible casualties.

"We'll start with a naval bombardment," Prendergast said. "With all the ships in the fleet present, that should be quite sufficient to soften them up.

We'll clear the obstructions when the barrage keeps them occupied, land the troops, and follow with a direct assault before the defenders recover."

"Who will make the attack, sir?"

"We'll send... what the devil?" Prendergast looked up as a naval lieutenant appeared with a slip of paper.

"Sorry to interrupt, sir," the lieutenant said with a hurried salute. "There's a Burmese vessel approaching with a flag of truce."

"Another one?" Prendergast said. "Why don't they just invite themselves in for tea."

The lieutenant smiled. "Perhaps they will, sir. There's also a message addressed to you, sir."

"I see," Prendergast took the message, tore it open and read the contents. He looked up. "Gentlemen, it appears that we won't have to take Ava by assault after all. King Thibaw has decided to surrender."

Andrew joined in the general cheer and mutual handshaking, although he felt more relief than elation.

As soon as I am free from this campaign, I'll push Sir Charles for Bo Thura's pardon, bring him to safety and return to Mariana. Maybe this time, she will accept my proposal, or perhaps she wishes to make her way in the world without me.

Prendergast boarded a small boat for the steamer *Palow*, where Captain Woodward ruled supreme, and sailed to the fort. Andrew saw the king's soldiers remaining on the battlements and hoped the Burmese had not planned any trickery.

As the general entered the fort, the fleet sailed a short distance north and anchored opposite Ava. As one of the smaller vessels, *Kathleen* probed at the sunken boats and stakes to find the best channel ashore.

"Aye, aye," Birnie jerked a thumb downstream. "Here comes the admiral. The fighting must be over right enough for the bigwigs to arrive."

Andrew saw the Irrawaddy Company paddle steamer *Palu* sail up to the fleet and cast her anchor. Rear-Admiral Sir Frederick Richards, the Naval Commander-in-Chief, boarded a small boat to *Palow*, where Prendergast had returned.

"Things are happening," Birnie said.

"It seems we're not involved," Andrew replied.

Birnie smiled. "No; we're only good for the fighting and the dirty jobs. The admirals have the champagne and the glamour."

"They're welcome to it," Andrew watched through his field glasses as regimental officers marched smartly to their troops, who filed into small boats for the bluejackets to row them ashore. When the vessels manoeuvred to the riverbank, the troops filed over the gangplanks.

Andrew watched the Indian and British troops take over the fortifications of Ava, replacing the king's troops on the battlements and at the guns.

The war is over. It was hardly a war, a procession upriver with a few skirmishes and a few dozen casualties. Once the dust has settled, I'll be free from Army regulations again.

As Andrew fretted and hoped, General Prendergast sent a brigade to garrison Sagain Fort on the right bank of the river. The sepoys moved in, the Burmese filed out peacefully, and the British relaxed a little more.

"It's all going very well," Birnie offered Andrew a cheroot, shared a match and puffed smoke contentedly around *Kathleen*. "That must be one of the easiest wars we've ever won. Not like Majuba, Old Boy, or Isandhlwana."

"No," Andrew pulled his pipe from his pocket and tamped tobacco into the bowl. "Quite the opposite. Let's hope we can defeat the dacoits as easily as we did Thibaw's army."

Birnie grunted. "That may be a false hope, Baird. We've only commandeered about two and a half thousand stand of small arms, and many of them were old Brown Bess-era muskets. I'd guess the Burmans have squirrelled the more modern weapons away."

"Time will tell," Andrew said. "What's the adage? In war, it is essential that men should know what they fight for and like what they know. Something like that. Perhaps the Burmese did not love Thibaw sufficiently to fight for him."

"Perhaps not," Birnie agreed. "My worry is they might not love us either, and we'll be stuck in a long-drawn-out, small-scale war in the forests."

"That's a chilling prospect," Andrew said. "At present, it's a bit of an anticlimax."

Please, God, let me be away before that happens. I know where Bo Thura hides; if I had that blasted pardon, I'd pick him up, make a quick dash to the Frontier, and all would be hale and hearty. That important word, if!

After a night anchored off Ava, the fleet steamed the short distance to the Mandalay landing stage. The ships anchored in the river at nine in the morning, with the officers ordering the men to look their smartest. At one that afternoon, the Naval Brigade and some of the Army disembarked and marched to Mandalay City.

"You're not required, Baird," Birnie said with false envy. "You can remain here in comfort while the rest of us don our best bibs and tuckers and swelter under the sun."

"I'll come along too," Andrew said. "I can't abide doing nothing, and anyway, I'd like to see the end of this campaign. I was in Mandalay before it began, so I'll see the climax."

Birnie laughed. "I thought you'd have seen enough of Burma."

"It gets in your blood," Andrew told him.

What did my father say about India? You hate India for a month and then love it forever. Burma has the same effect, as Jennings told us.

Andrew pulled on his uniform for the formal takeover of Thibaw's capital, marching behind the Naval Brigade as they entered the capital. While the sailors commandeered the eastern entrance of Mandalay, the soldiers filed around the walls and took over the other three gates.

Andrew remained with the Naval Brigade, observing without participating. He saw Colonel Sladen, acting in his civilian capacity, meet with Thibaw in the palace.

"It's all over," Birnie said, standing at sweating attention. "Thibaw is formally surrendering."

"With the whole flotilla and our Army here, the poor devil has no choice," Andrew said.

"Poor devil?" Birnie raised his eyebrows. "Tell that to the hundreds of people he murdered to climb to power."

Andrew was a silent witness as the Army made its triumphal entry into Mandalay. The men wore their khaki uniforms, and for a moment, Andrew sighed for the splendour of scarlet uniforms.

"War's not the same without the scarlet and pipeclay," Birnie mirrored his thoughts. "It's all professional now, ugly, sordid, and brutal. There's no glamour anymore."

"It was always ugly and sordid," Andrew said. "Colourful uniforms and flapping colours only painted over the reality."

"I know. But I do feel we are missing something. I yearn for the old days," eighteen-year-old Birnie said.

"Maybe you're right," Andrew replied.

Do we all view the past with nostalgia because we were younger and fitter there, with optimistic dreams of a future that never quite materialised? I hoped for Mariana. God, I am getting maudlin; I am only twenty-six years old. It must be the enervating climate here.

Andrew shook away his fit of depression. *I can still have Mariana if I convince her my love is genuine.*

The following day, the 30th of November 1885, Andrew saw another steamer plough up the Irrawaddy to berth alongside the fleet.

"Here comes the king's taxi," Birnie said as they stood at *Kathleen's* rail.

Commander William Morrison had brought *Tigris* to carry the king and his entourage to Indian exile.

"It's sad in a way," Andrew said. "The end of a dynasty."

"He was a murdering tyrant," Birnie gave his opinion. "Burma will be more peaceful under our rule."

Andrew remembered the tales of slaughter and the crucified men. "There is no doubt about that," he agreed. "All the same, I'll go onshore and watch the king's final departure."

"You do that, old man," Birnie said. "I'll remain onboard and have the ratings polish the gun."

Andrew stood under bright sunlight to watch Thibaw's final departure from his capital. Most of the spectators were women, looking very graceful in their colourful clothes. A few wept, either in genuine grief or with emotion at the passing of an era.

The king's two buffalo carriages rumbled over the wooden drawbridge across the moat. One carriage held Thibaw and his queens Supayalat and Supayalay, and the other carried his mother-in-law and servants, who leaned out of the coach windows, holding umbrellas. They stared at the novel sight of two long lines of khaki-clad British and Indian soldiers, one on each side of the road.

Are the soldiers intended as a guard-of-honour for the king? Or are they to stop any trouble?

The buffalos that drew the carriages were white and splendidly groomed. They marched proudly with heads held high, as if aware they were part of history, for never again would a native king grace the capital of Burma. The carriage wheels crunched on the road, the soldiers stood at attention, and only a few people in the crowd cheered.

Andrew saw a small group of lesser servants straggling in the rear of the carriages, and then they disappeared around a bend of the road. The dust settled, NCOs gave sharp orders, and the British and Indian soldiers formed up and marched away. Unsure how he felt, Andrew returned to *Kathleen.*

"And that was that," Birnie said. "We came, we saw, we conquered, and nothing was ever the same again."

"For the better, I hope," Andrew replied.

"Oh, indeed, for the better, but won't we be for the worse as well? When we've conquered all these queer, fascinating little barbaric kingdoms, won't we be the losers as well as the victors? We'll have lost what makes the world different and colourful." Birnie looked at Andrew, finished his cheroot and threw the stub into the moat, where it hissed for a second and died. "Ours not to reason why and all that."

"Ours but to bleed and die," Andrew said.

"On with life, eh? And hope the Burmans are happy with that blood-stained despot out of the way." Birnie shrugged. "They won't be, of course, and they'll blame us for everything from poor crops to the dacoits. That's the price of Empire, old boy."

Andrew thought of the dead and wounded sepoys at Minhla and the suffering sick lying under the awnings of the hospital ship. "One of the prices anyway," he agreed.

CHAPTER 33

RANGOON AND UPPER BURMA, DECEMBER 1885

Mariana entered the telegraph station in Rangoon and caught the operator's attention.

"Yes, miss?" The operator was sallow-skinned, with tired eyes and thinning hair. "What can I do for you?"

"I wish to send a telegram," Mariana said. She had never been in a telegraph office before and was unsure what to do.

"You've come to the right place, miss," the operator said, handing over a small, preprinted pad and a stubby pencil. "Just write the address and your message, and remember you have to pay for every word, so the briefer the message, the less you pay."

Mariana wrote a longer message than she expected before handing the pad back. "I don't know the address," she admitted.

"Do you know the name?" the operator asked wearily.

"General Jack Windrush," Mariana said. "He commands the troops in Southwest England."

"Fighting Jack," the operator permitted himself a slight smile. "I'll have his telegraphic address." He glanced at Mariana with renewed interest. "I served with him in Afghanistan," he said. "I won't be a jiffy, miss."

ANDREW WATCHED FROM *KATHLEEN'S* DECK AS THE ROYAL PARTY LEFT FOR the long voyage to Rangoon and eventual exile to India. Two armed vessels acted as escorts in case of any rescue attempt.

Midshipman Birnie ran to Andrew, with his cap nearly falling from his head.

"Baird, old fellow. I mean, Captain Baird, sir!"

"Yes, Cosmo?" Andrew used Birnie's Christian name to ease any formality.

"General Prendergast wants to see you, sir," Birnie said.

"Then see me he shall," Andrew replied. With the king in captivity, he imagined the war was over, he would be back in Rangoon soon, and he would patch up any difficulties with Mariana. He assumed Prendergast would be releasing him from his official duties. "Is there a boat available?"

"I'll get one, Baird," Birnie said.

"Thank you, Cosmo."

"Captain Baird," Prendergast leaned back in his chair and surveyed Andrew through musing eyes. "I believe you have some business to attend."

"Have I, sir?" Andrew asked.

"You have, sir," Prendergast replied. "Two telegrams arrived this morning, Captain. One was about you, and one was for you." He lifted two telegrams from his desk. Sir Charles Crossthwaite had sent both, one mentioning General Windrush's involvement and marked confidential. Prendergast handed the other to Andrew.

"Thank you, sir." Andrew scanned the brief message.

Full pardon and safe conduct granted for Bo Thura. Bring him into Lower Burma at your convenience. Crossthwaite.

"I take it you'll be leaving us soon," Prendergast said. He glanced at his other telegram, lying face down on the desk. "You are relieved of any duties with the expeditionary force, Captain."

"Thank you, sir. I have a man to take to Lower Burma."

"Remind me," Prendergast demanded.

"The Burmese gentleman who informed us about the French intrigues in Mandalay and helped us avoid the ambushes on the river."

"Of course," Prendergast nodded. "Loyal Burmans will always be welcome. When do you wish to depart?"

"As soon as is convenient, sir."

Prendergast smiled. "That means as soon as you can. Do you require any men? I can spare a small escort in case of dacoits."

Andrew had already considered the possibility. "No, thank you, sir. I will travel faster alone, and British troops or sepoys may complicate matters."

"As you wish, Baird. I wish you luck."

"Thank you, sir." Andrew hesitated. "May I have some food, a Martini, and a supply of cartridges?"

Prendergast nodded. "I think we can manage that, Baird. I'll also arrange a boat to take you wherever you wish to travel."

"Thank you, sir," Andrew said. "Jamieson of *Little Salamander* knows the route to Yin Pauk."

"He's your man, then," Prendergast said.

JAMIESON CLAMPED HIS CIGAR BETWEEN STRONG TEETH WHEN HE DROPPED off Andrew downstream of Yin Pauk.

"Be careful, Captain Baird," Jamieson advised as Andrew stepped onto the riverbank. He checked his kitbag and his rifle.

"I will," Andrew replied. "I'd ask you to wait for me, but I don't know how long I will be."

"It looks quiet," Jamieson said, "but looks are deceptive out here." He held out his hand. "Three sovereigns, Captain."

"Your prices are too steep," Andrew said.

"You won't need the money," Jamieson said. "A lone European out here is as good as dead."

"Thanks for the encouragement, Jamieson," Andrew said.

"Try to remain alive," Jamieson advised. "You are a good customer, and I always value your gold."

The track was familiar as Andrew pushed towards Yin Pauk. Men and women were busy in the fields as if their king had not recently fought a war with the British Empire. An elephant hauled a load of teak logs, and a group of men crouched at the entrance to a house, gambling and smoking.

Since his last visit, Andrew had learned a few Burmese phrases, sufficient to make himself understood if he spoke slowly. Stepping into the open clearing around the village to ensure he was seen, Andrew shouldered his rifle and raised his voice. "My name is Andrew Baird," he said in Burmese. "I do not intend any harm."

He heard the murmur of voices as women quickly hustled their children away and men stepped forward to face this intruder.

"I am looking for Bo Thura," Andrew said as a man emerged with a *dha* at his waist and a musket in his hand. "He might be expecting me."

The man spoke too rapidly for Andrew to understand.

"Bo Thura," Andrew repeated. "I'm looking for Bo Thura." He waited, trying to look friendly as more men appeared from doorways or the surrounding fields. One man shouted something and a familiar scar-faced figure emerged from one of the houses. Aung Thiha grinned at Andrew and indicated he should follow.

"Where are we going?" Andrew asked, without receiving a reply.

Aung Thiha led him into a small clearing two hundred yards outside the village, where birds sang from a tree, and three women chattered while preparing food. A few ramshackle huts showed where Bo Thura had set up his camp.

Aung Thiha stopped, faced Andrew, and drew his *dha*.

"What the devil?" Andrew reached for his revolver until Aung Thiha laughed, and Bo Thura stepped from behind a bush. He looked older than the last time Andrew had seen him, yet still with the same wry smile and bright eyes. "Cousin Andrew! I wondered if you would come back. Have you any news?"

"I said I would return," Andrew reminded. "I have good news. Sir Charles has issued a free pardon and agreed to let bygones be bygones." He saw the relief on Bo Thura's face and produced the telegram. "Here, read this for yourself."

Bo Thura scanned the telegram, smiling. "It could not have come at a better time," he said. "Maung Thandar and Buda Sein have been pressing us."

"Even after they lost the war?" Andrew asked. "That's surprising."

"The British have allowed Maung Thandar to retain his position," Bo Thura explained. "Until they change their mind, he will continue to encourage his dacoits and persecute those who stood against him. Thandar will attempt to twist the British around his finger as he did with Thibaw." Bo Thura glanced around. "That means he will send his warriors against me, as will Buda Sein."

Andrew nodded, accepted a cigar, and took a deep draw. "You have the Chief Commissioner's pardon and my personal guarantee that you'll be safe in Lower Burma," Andrew said. "We'll have Upper Burma pacified in a few weeks, and then you'll be safe from Bhamo to the sea." Andrew looked around at the camp, with men and women milling in happy confusion. "How about your people? How will they fare?"

"Maung Thandar and Buda Sein don't know their names," Bo Thura said. "Some will stay as dacoits; others will return to their villages or move to Mandalay." He grinned. "As soon as Sir Charles realises what sort of man Thandar is, he'll get rid of him."

Andrew nodded, accepting Bo Thura's word. "Gather your possessions and whichever followers you wish to take with you," Andrew said. "The quicker we start, the faster we'll reach British territory." He looked around, "I know we've deposed Thibaw, but Upper Burma will remain dangerous until we have properly pacified it."

"I'll tell my people what is happening," Bo Thura said.

Andrew waited as Bo Thura gathered his followers into the centre of the camp and addressed them in a loud voice. Andrew listened, understanding the gist as Bo Thura told them he was heading south into British-controlled Burma and that they would be safer without him. Andrew could see the disappointment on many faces.

When Bo Thura finished, the crowd slowly dissipated. A few waited to speak privately to him and then drifted away.

"You'll miss them," Andrew said.

"They'll be alive," Bo Thura said. "If they stay with me, they may not survive."

"Let's move then," Andrew replied. "We'll find a boat and once we reach the Irrawaddy, we can catch one of the Flotilla steamers."

Bo Thura smiled. "I have a much smaller vessel than my old war boat, now."

"As long as it floats," Andrew said.

Bo Thura had hidden his boat in the undergrowth. High prowed and brightly-painted, it was only sufficiently large to hold four people. Aung Thiha and San Kyi eased it free and shoved it onto the river, where it floated as a symbol of hope for the future.

"We'll head for Kandaw," Bo Thura said. "It's a small village about twenty miles away. They know me in Kandaw, and we can plan what to do next."

"We head for British territory," Andrew told him, "and report to the first official we see."

Bo Thura shook his head. "They might not know Sir Charles has granted me a pardon. And how about my people?"

"I'll speak up for them," Andrew promised. "And I have Sir Charles's telegram in my pocket."

Bo Thura gave that wry smile that was so like Andrew's father. "Will a colonel or a general, or even worse, a civic official, listen to the words of a mere captain?"

"They'd better, by God," Andrew said, "or I'll have my father on them." He stopped, realising he was contemplating something he had vowed never to do, using his father's influence.

Burma is altering me.

"Don't waste time," Andrew said.

They paddled with the current, keeping to the centre of the river in case of ambush and watching every bend. Andrew sat in the bows with his Martini in his lap while Aung Thiha, San Kyi and Bo Thura paddled. Insects clouded from the undergrowth, and birds and monkeys chattered overhead.

It was evening when they arrived at Kandaw, with the light fading and the smell of cooking fires aromatic in the air. Bo Thura guided the boat to the riverbank, and they disembarked, with Aung Thiha and San Kyi smiling at the throng which gathered to greet them.

The headman welcomed Bo Thura and looked enquiringly at Andrew.

"He's a friend," Bo Thura said.

The headman faced Andrew, smiled, and ushered them all into his village. They ate a simple meal of rice with vegetables and stewed melon sauce, and the headman showed them to an empty house.

"We'll sleep here tonight," Andrew took control. "Leave before dawn and try to reach the Irrawaddy in a couple of days. There are plenty of British boats on the river, and we'll be safe."

He slept with an easy mind, knowing he was among friends and his path home was clear.

I'll see you soon, Mariana, and we'll sort things out between us.

"Andrew!" Bo Thura shook Andrew awake. "Get up!"

"What's happening?" Andrew rolled from his bed, grabbed his revolver, and stood, dazed with sleep. He heard the brassy clamour of a gong, men shouting and a long, drawn-out scream.

"We are betrayed," Bo Thura said. "The headman has betrayed us to Buda Sein!"

Glad he had not undressed, Andrew followed Bo Thura out the door. He saw Aung Thiha slicing at a man with his *dha* and San Kyi running away, having given the warning with his gong.

A horde of men ran at Bo Thura, some with the jackets of the king's soldiers, others bare-chested, and all armed. Andrew fired his revolver, wounding the nearest man. The others hesitated, and Aung Thiha hacked a soldier down.

"*Pyay! Suuthoetko pyan htein htarrmaal!*" Aung Thiha shouted. "Run! I'll hold them back!"

"Andrew!" Bo Thura pushed Andrew to the village boundary. "Get out!"

"We can't leave Aung Thiha behind!"

"*Pyay!*" Aung Thiha shouted. "Run!" He jumped into the middle of the advancing men, slashing right and left, laughing as he fought.

"Run!" Bo Thura said.

Andrew hesitated, firing his revolver into the mass. He saw one man fall and another stagger, holding his leg. He saw Aung Thiha slice a man's arm clean off and then parry a knife thrust at his throat. Aung Thiha turned, killed the knifeman, and shouted something Andrew could not catch.

He saw the headman at the back of the mob. Lifting his revolver, Andrew aimed quickly and fired.

"We haven't time!" Bo Thura shouted. "Run, Andrew!"

Andrew saw the headman spin around, holding his arm, and then Bo Thura shoved him ahead and into the forest.

The noise behind them rose and ended in a nearly painful silence.

"That's Aung Thiha gone," Bo Thura said. "He was a good man."

"He would have fitted in any British infantry regiment," Andrew agreed. "Where's San Kyi?"

"He'll catch up," Bo Thura said, pushing Andrew ahead. "He's the most agile man I have ever known."

They hurried on, with Bo Thura setting the pace and Andrew struggling to keep up. After half an hour, they left the path, and Bo Thura led Andrew into the forest, ducking under low branches and plunging through tangled undergrowth.

"How about snakes?" Andrew gasped.

"They'll run when they hear us coming," Bo Thura said. He paused when they reached a small clearing. "Wait."

Knowing that Bo Thura was his master in the forest, Andrew stopped.

"Listen," Bo Thura ordered.

They crouched beside a thick-trunked teak tree, with insects clouding around their heads and the bird calls harsh in the air.

Andrew heard the muted murmur of voices in the distance. He put his hand flat on the ground, then lay down to listen. "About a dozen men," he said. "It's in the vibrations."

Bo Thura frowned. "Who taught you that trick?"

"A frontiersman in the Natal Dragoons," Andrew said. "It might not be as accurate in the forest as in the African bush."

"It may come in useful," Bo Thura said thoughtfully. "San Kyi hasn't found us yet. I thought he'd be here by now."

They crouched as a group of hunters approached and walked silently past, looking to the right and left. Andrew began to stand until Bo Thura placed a hand on his shoulder and shook his head.

Andrew remained still as two more men padded past. Bo Thura lifted a finger. "Wait," he mouthed.

A few moments later, another two men passed, both carrying rifles.

Bo Thura waited another few minutes.

"This way," he said, heading at an angle away from the path. Andrew followed, admiring the way Bo Thura could move without making a sound.

They travelled for two hours, with Bo Thura following half-hidden animal paths in the undergrowth. He stopped at a small clearing, where trees overhung a small temple, and monkeys chattered all around.

"We can stop here for the night," Bo Thura said. "Nobody comes here."

"Will we shelter inside the temple?" Andrew asked, checking his rifle.

"No. The monkeys have made it their own," Bo Thura said. "They would tear us to pieces. We are safe if we remain outside." He glanced around. "I hoped that San Kyi would be here. We often use this clearing as a rendezvous."

They slept in a hollow in the ground a hundred yards from the temple, and apart from the ubiquitous insects and the chattering of the monkeys, nothing bothered them. Andrew woke at dawn to find Bo Thura scavenging for fruit.

"We're lucky the monkeys left us something," Bo Thura said. When he smiled, the tattoos on his face merged, yet his eyes wore Andrew's father's expression.

"How far are we from the old border with Lower Burma?" Andrew asked.

Bo Thura screwed up his face. "Seven or eight days if we are lucky."

"That's where we're headed," Andrew said. "There are police posts there and regular Army patrols."

"Maung Thandar and Buda Sein will undoubtedly have his men watching the river ports for me," Bo Thura considered for a moment. "I can't think of a better plan than yours, except the police posts only have a small garrison."

"It's a sanctuary," Andrew said. "The alternative is a much longer journey to Thayetmyo, which Buda Sein will be watching, or wait for a steamer on the river."

"The river which Buda Sein will have well-guarded," Bo Thura said. "He'll have every villager along the bank looking for us."

"Can you get us to the old border?" Andrew asked. "Without Buda Sein's men seeing us?"

"Can you keep pace with me?" Bo Thura responded.

They grinned at each other. "Lead on, cousin," Andrew said.

CHAPTER 34

UPPER BURMA, DECEMBER 1885 AND JANUARY 1886

Bo Thura stopped without warning, holding up his hand. "Can you smell it?"

"Petroleum," Andrew said after a second. "Earth-oil."

"That's right," Bo Thura agreed. "Over this way." Moving quietly, he led Andrew to a small clearing with a crucified man in the centre.

"A message for us," Bo Thura said. "That's San Kyi."

Buda Sein's men had stripped San Kyi, coated him in petroleum, crucified him and left him to die slowly.

"He was a good man," Bo Thura said. "One of the most loyal."

Andrew remembered San Kyi keeping pace with *Little Salamander* from Thayetmyo to Mandalay. Now, he was tortured, roasted, and murdered.

"Do you want to bury him?" Andrew asked.

"We'll leave him," Bo Thura decided. "Buddhists don't believe in burial, and a cremation fire would alert Buda Sein."

"Another good man gone," Andrew said. "Buda Sein has a lot to answer for."

"Buda Sein or Maung Thandar," Bo Thura added. He glanced at San Kyi. "Goodbye, my friend. Come on, Cousin Andrew."

Bo Thura moved faster now, threading through the forest without any sign of fatigue. Andrew lost count of the days as Bo Thura took charge, travelling by night and resting through the day. They bypassed villages or raided store-houses for food under cover of darkness, eased through tangled undergrowth on paths Andrew could not see, and listened to the sounds of jungle animals and birds.

Andrew learned to relish lizards and red ants as a nutritious meal, drank unfiltered water from muddy streams and watched as parties of dacoits questioned villagers with threats and violence.

"Can't we help?" Andrew asked.

"If we do, Buda Sein will return, destroy the village and massacre the people," Bo Thura told him.

They moved on, lean and ragged, spotted with jungle sores and insect bites, until Bo Thura stopped at the edge of a man-made clearing.

"There," Bo Thura said. "There's the police post of Ban Hteik Chaung." He grinned at Andrew. "We made it!"

Andrew stared ahead, hardly daring to believe that they had reached sanctuary.

A Union flag drooped from a white-painted pole, with a small, walled encampment beneath. Andrew saw the colourful turbans of Sikh policemen and a smartly uniformed British officer.

Oh, thank God.

"Are you alright, Cousin?" Bo Thura asked curiously.

"Yes," Andrew replied. "Come on, Bo Thura, let's make ourselves known."

The Sikh sentry lifted his rifle when Andrew and Bo Thura emerged from the forest's edge. He shouted something, and a Burmese policeman ran to his side and called out a challenge.

"They want to know who we are," Bo Thura said.

Andrew nodded. "I bet they do. We're like two walking scarecrows." He raised his voice. "I am Captain Andrew Baird of the Natal Dragoons, and my companion is Bo Thura, a friend and ally of the British."

At the sound of a British voice, the officer stepped beside the Sikh. "Who did you say you were?"

"Captain Andrew Baird of the Natal Dragoons," Andrew repeated.

"Good Lord," the officer said. "Are you not the fellow who brought back young Mary MacConnacher from the dacoits?"

"That's right," Andrew said. "And this gentleman," he indicated Bo Thura, "rescued her."

"Good Lord," the officer repeated. "Come in. I am Lieutenant Hanley," the officer held out his hand. "Martin Hanley. What the devil have you been up to?"

"Buda Sein's men have chased Bo Thura and me from Kandaw to here," Andrew entered the police post with Bo Thura at his side.

"Good Lord," Hanley said for the third time.

Four buildings were within the compound, with the largest forming half the boundary wall and providing accommodation for the twenty Sikh and ten Burmese policemen. The smallest building acted as Lieutenant Hanley's office and living quarters; the others were a lock-up for prisoners and an armoury and storehouse.

"You'll need to wash, and you must be hungry," Hanley ushered them into his office-cum-living-accommodation. "I can't offer anything luxurious, I am afraid; we're a bit spartan here, but what I have is yours."

"Thank you," Andrew said. He sat down and closed his eyes, breathing in the smell of fresh coffee. Bo Thura looked nervous inside the police post until Andrew reassured him he was safe.

"Why is Buda Sein chasing you?" Hanley asked, looking from Andrew to Bo Thura and back.

"Buda Sein was one of Maung Thandar's accomplices," Andrew explained. "When Bo Thura refused to pay him tribute, he got annoyed."

Hanley frowned. "Bo Thura! I know that name! He's a notorious dacoit! A wanted man!"

"Not anymore," Andrew said calmly. "The Chief Commissioner has granted him a full pardon for helping rescue Mary MacConnacher, alerting us to the French interference in Mandalay and aiding us during the late war."

"Good Lord," Hanley eyed Bo Thura, immediately calmed. "You helped rescue little Mary MacConnacher, did you? Well done, Bo Thura."

They all looked up when one of the Sikhs shouted something.

"Don't be alarmed," Hanley said. "That's only my havildar returning with the regular patrol. Sukhbir Singh is a good man."

Andrew smiled. "I know him well," he replied. "We worked together before the war started. Sukhbir Singh is one of the best."

Holding his coffee mug in his right hand, Andrew strolled to the door to greet the havildar.

Sukhbir Singh arrived at the run. "Close the gate, Sahib!" he shouted. "The dacoits are all around us!"

As Sukhbir Singh spoke, a fusillade sounded from the forest.

"Good Lord," Hanley said and raised his voice, immediately dropping the façade as his professionalism took over. "Everyone to their positions! Rifles and forty rounds of ammunition! Sukhbir Singh! Take the east and south walls!"

"Here they come!" Andrew said as a horde of dacoits burst onto the maidan around the police post.

"Aim low, men," Hanley ordered. "Drive them back."

The Sikhs needed no encouragement as they ran to the outside wall with the Burmese police only a few seconds behind them.

There are too few men to defend this perimeter, Andrew thought. He joined them, with Bo Thura at his side.

"On my word!" Hanley said, watching the dacoits advance across the maidan. "By Jove, there are a lot of them. Wait for it! Wait! Fire!"

The police volley was as controlled as that of any British infantry regiment. Half a dozen dacoits fell, two to lie prone and the others to struggle and kick. The dacoits charged on, yelling.

Andrew aimed, fired, and saw his man fly backwards as the Martini bullet caught him high in the chest. He worked the rifle's underlever, pushed in a cartridge, and aimed again.

"Reload!" Hanley shouted. "Aim! Fire!"

The police fired, with Andrew and Bo Thura's rifles joining the general melee. The dacoits fired from the forest, with most of their bullets high.

We have time for one more volley, and then it will be hand-to-hand, Andrew thought.

"Reload!" Hanley shouted again. "Aim! Fire! Fix bayonets!"

As the police clicked on the formidable eighteen-inch bayonets, the dacoits turned and fled.

"Reload!" Hanley shouted. "Stand firm, Sukhbir Singh!"

Andrew saw the havildar halfway over the wall, preparing to follow the retreating dacoits.

"They'll be waiting in the trees, Havildar," Andrew said. "Ten or twenty of them for every one of us."

The police settled down as the dacoits occupied the forest, with both sides sniping whenever they saw an opportunity.

"What is your normal procedure when the dacoits attack?" Andrew asked.

Hanley reloaded his rifle. "They rarely attack police posts," he said. "When they do, it's in smaller numbers, more like a nuisance raid than a full-scale assault. This situation is highly unusual." He glanced at the sky. "It will be night soon, which might give them an advantage."

"Do the Royal Scots Fusiliers still patrol this area?" Andrew asked.

"They do," Hanley said. "One of their flying patrols is due here late tomorrow, and as soon as the Army appears, the dacoits will flee like snow off a dyke. We only have to hold out until then."

"It's me they want," Bo Thura said, stepping towards Hanley. "If I leave, they'll likely go away."

"You'll stay!" Andrew snapped. "We'll have to face the dacoits sometime. Buda Sein has been a thorn in our side for months."

The gongs began half an hour later, just as the sun faded.

"Scare tactics," Hanley said. "They hope to play on our nerves. Light the lanterns, Havildar."

"Yes, Sahib," Sukhbir Singh replied.

Hanley had placed twenty oil lanterns around the perimeter, each illuminating a five-yard radius. The lanterns also attracted moths and other flying insects that fluttered and burned their wings on the hot glass bowls.

"If you see anything moving beyond the lamplight," Hanley ordered. "Shoot." He translated his words into Sikh and Burmese.

Andrew nodded. He knew it was going to be a long night. He listened to the gongs, wondering if they were summoning more men or were only intended to intimidate.

Sukhbir Singh grinned at him. "They're trying to frighten us," he said and laughed. "Do I look afraid?"

"It would take more than gongs to frighten a Sikh," Andrew replied.

"I want three-man patrols to check the perimeter," Hanley said, "vary the routes and times, and don't leave anybody behind."

"I'll take a patrol," Andrew volunteered.

"Are you sufficiently fit?" Hanley asked. "You look like death's young brother!"

"I'm fit," Andrew replied.

The gongs continued, surrounding the police post with noise, disturbing sleep, and stretching nerves.

When Andrew returned from an uneventful circuit of the perimeter, Hanley asked, "Do you think they will attack?"

"I don't know how these dacoits fight," Andrew replied. He ducked as a rifle cracked and a bullet whined overhead. "It could be a long night."

"I could lead a sortie," Hanley suggested, "attack them rather than sit waiting."

"You'll be taking your men into their territory," Andrew replied. "The dacoits would cut them to pieces."

Both looked around as a dozen rifles fired together, smashing one of the guard lanterns. The police replied, aiming at the muzzle flares deep in the forest. A moment later, another volley smashed a second lamp.

"They're putting out the lights," Hanley said.

"Prepare a fire," Andrew said. "Darkness will give them an advantage."

Hanley looked at him for a moment, then raised his voice. "Gather anything that will burn!" he ordered. "We need light!"

As the Burmese fired at the lamps, smashing them one by one, half the police replied to the musketry, and the rest gathered tables, chairs, and spare furniture.

"Keep these patrols out!" Andrew shouted. "Watch for any incursions."

"Do you think they'll try to infiltrate?" Hanley asked.

"I would," Andrew replied, "and these lads are no slouches when it comes to raiding and small-scale warfare."

When the final two lanterns exploded in a welter of splinters and spluttering oil, the flames rose briefly and died. The darkness seemed total, enhanced by sudden silence as the gongs ceased.

"What now?" Hanley asked.

"Now we light the fire," Andrew replied.

He heard the warning shout from Sukhbir Singh, and then a volley of shots came from the forest, with bullets ripping overhead and crashing into the buildings.

"Return fire!" Hanley ordered, hurrying to the wall.

The Sikhs responded eagerly, with some standing to get a better shot and others hurrying from quieter posts to reinforce the front. The Burmese police joined them, muttering to each other as they took their positions.

"Keep under cover," Andrew roared. He lifted his head, with his instincts, or perhaps his experience, warning him that something was wrong.

"Watch the rear," Andrew warned. "We've got too many men in one place."

Before Andrew finished talking, one of the Sikhs gave a long moan and collapsed, with a dacoit withdrawing a bloody *dha* from his back.

"Every second man! Watch your rear!" Hanley shouted. "The dacoits are inside the compound!"

The dacoits came with a rush, attacking the police from the rear. They killed the first man, a lithe Burmese policeman who tried to stop them, and thrust a *dha* into the back of a second Sikh.

Hanley lifted his revolver and shot one man in the chest, fired at a second, and gasped as a dacoit slid low across the floor and slashed at his thigh.

"You dirty hound!" Andrew shot the dacoit, saw Ajit Singh thrust his bayonet through another, and then more police joined in, shooting and stabbing with controlled ferocity. The dacoits within the post melted away while the firing outside intensified.

"Get them out!" Hanley ordered. He staggered as a bullet slammed into his chest, fired at the retreating dacoits, and swore as another bullet knocked him off his feet.

"Hanley!" Andrew leapt to his side. He saw Sukhbir Singh organise his men to eradicate the last of the invaders, and then the firing outside ended.

"I'm all right," Hanley said, smiling. "Let me rest for a moment to get my breath back. They've winded me."

Andrew saw the blood bubble from Hanley's mouth as he spoke and knew he was hard hit. "That must be it," he said. "Get back to your positions, men, and make sure all these dacoits are dead or in a cell. We don't want them coming back to life and stabbing us in the back."

"Light the fire!" Andrew ordered. "Keep it fed!"

The fire gave flickering light to the post, illuminating the men, from the bearded Sikhs to the smaller, stocky Burmese.

The gongs continued all night as the Burmese sniped without attacking. At dawn, they began to muster in the fringes, shouting insults at the police.

"They are gathering their courage for a final assault," Sukhbir Singh said. "Now we will see who the real warriors are!"

When one of the dacoits shouted something, the Burmese police fled, leaving the police even more short-handed.

"We're better off without them," Bo Thura said. "We don't know when they will join the enemy. Look!" He pointed with the muzzle of his rifle.

Andrew swore when he saw the rising sun catch the yellow umbrella. "That's Buda Sein," he said. "He's come in person for the final assault."

"Here they come," Bo Thura said as Andrew lifted his rifle. "And there are more." He pointed to the right, where another force of dacoits filtered through the trees.

CHAPTER 35

UPPER BURMA AND RANGOON, JANUARY 1885

"Who the devil are these lads?" Andrew asked as the new force of dacoits arrived on the flank of Buda Sein's men.

"Trouble," Hanley said, struggling to his feet. Using a Martini-Henry as a crutch, he hobbled to the wall, dribbling blood from his mouth.

As dacoits began to fire from the trees, the two groups moved slowly towards the police post, with the gongs clamouring in the background and Buda Sein in the centre under his yellow umbrella.

"Ready!" Hanley shouted and coughed, spitting blood.

Andrew put a hand on Hanley's shoulder. "Permit me, Lieutenant," he said. "Present!"

The Sikhs aimed their rifles, facing their enemy without a trace of fear.

"Don't fire!" Bo Thura shouted. "Not yet!"

"What the devil?" Andrew asked. "What's wrong, Bo Thura?"

"Look!" Bo Thura pointed. "Look what's happening!"

The second group of dacoits had altered direction. Rather than advancing on the police post, they charged towards Buda Sein's men, fired their rifles and drew their dhas.

"What the devil?" Andrew asked again.

"That's Aung Thiha!" Bo Thura said, pointing. "Look!"

"Dear God! I thought Buda Sein's men had killed him!"

Aung Thiha led his force against Buda Sein's dacoits, slashing with their *dhas*. Taken by surprise, Buda Sein's men faltered. The advance stopped as they faced this unexpected attack.

"Sukhbir Singh ran to Hanley. "Permission to charge them, sir?"

"No," Hanley shook his head. "We don't know who is friendly and who is not. Stay put, Havildar!"

"Yes, Sahib!" Sukhbir Singh did not hide his disappointment.

"Stay here, Cousin Andrew," Bo Thura grinned as he slipped over the wall. Andrew watched him march unhesitatingly towards Buda Sein's men. The fighting was intense as Aung Thiha pushed forward, with men falling on both sides. Bo Thura had nearly reached Buda Sein when Andrew saw the yellow umbrella begin to withdraw.

Aung Thiha reached Buda Sein first. Andrew saw the flash of steel as he lifted his *dha*. Buda Sein crumpled to the ground; Aung Thiha stooped, sawed at his neck, and lifted Buda Sein's disembodied head.

With the death of their leader, Buda Sein's dacoits fled, leaving their dead and wounded on the ground. Bo Thura embraced Aung Thiha, spoke briefly, and returned to the police post.

"Well, Cousin Andrew," he said. "Take me to Rangoon."

Hanley lifted a hand. "Hark!" he said as a half-company of the Royal Scots Fusiliers marched towards the post. "The flying column has arrived."

Andrew nodded and looked forward, where dead and dying men carpeted the open ground. "Thank God for Aung Thiha. Thank God for the *kyawal.*"

"ANDREW," MARIANA TOUCHED ANDREW'S ARM AND STEPPED BACK. "I HAVE to talk to you."

They stood outside the Golden Pagoda, with the rising sun reflecting from the roofs and the tinkle of temple bells in the breeze.

"This is a good place to talk," Andrew replied.

They were silent for a moment, both gathering their courage.

"When we were in Edinburgh," Mariana said quietly. "You asked me to marry you."

"I did," Andrew agreed.

"I turned you down," Mariana said, facing the temple. "I wasn't sure why I turned you down. I thought it was because of Elaine."

Andrew listened, allowing her to take her time. He did not interrupt.

"I was worried in case you only wanted to marry me for Elaine's sake," Mariana said.

Andrew slid his hand into hers, feeling her tremble. She was quiet for two minutes, ordering her thoughts.

"Yet, I knew there was more," Mariana said. "There was a shadow I could not fathom." She squeezed his hand, wriggled it free, and stepped away. "Andrew, if I had agreed to marry you on our wedding night, you would not be my first man."

Andrew took a deep breath. He did not interrupt.

Mariana continued. "When the renegades murdered everybody and kidnapped me, they did more." She remembered the horror, the laughing, mocking faces, the knowing, bloodstained hands tearing at her clothes, the leering, gasping men with urgent, demanding bodies violating her.

Andrew listened as Mariana told everything in an outpouring of horror that he knew she needed to cleanse her memory. He allowed her space to talk as the sun rose higher and yellow-robed monks began their day of prayer and meditation. The temple bells tinkled, somehow peaceful.

When Mariana stopped, she was no longer shaking. Her voice was unemotional as if talking had drained her of the past.

Andrew took her hand again. "You've been through hell," he said. "Could you not tell me this earlier?"

"No," Mariana said. "I had forgotten. Or rather, I pushed the memories away, stored them in some dark part of my mind and locked them in." She turned slightly, facing him with her eyes narrow. "Until something turned a key in the lock and released them all."

Andrew had to ask. "What was the key?"

"Stephen Jennings," Mariana replied.

Myat Lay Phyu stood on the pagoda steps, watching them without speaking. Her eyes were deep with knowledge.

"How did he do that?" Andrew guessed the answer.

"I shared his bed," Mariana told him.

"Did he rape you?" Andrew used the brutal term as his anger rose. He could picture himself killing Jennings with his bare hands, tearing him to bloody shreds.

"No. He did not," Mariana replied. She lifted her chin. "I was compliant."

"Do you love him?" Andrew asked.

"No." Mariana shook her head.

Myat Lay Phyu had not moved. She held Mariana's gaze, unsmiling yet encouraging.

"Do you want to see him again?" Andrew asked.

"No," Mariana shook her head.

"I could kill him," Andrew said, meaning every word.

"Please don't," Mariana said.

"Will you marry me?"

"If you still want me," Mariana replied.

"If you want me," Andrew replied, "after I neglected you, leaving you alone with a predator like Stephen Jennings."

Mariana sought his hand. "I want to marry you."

"That is settled then," Andrew told her.

Myat Lay Phyu smiled and walked away, her feet making no sound on the stone steps.

"Andrew, stand here and watch," Mariana said as Than Than Aye approached Jennings outside Jennings and Stanley's office building. When Than Than Aye slipped on the uneven ground, he instinctively caught him.

"Thank you, sir," Than Than Aye said, momentarily pressing against him.

"My pleasure, my dear," Jennings said. "You speak English very well."

"Thank you," Than Than Aye said, lowering her eyes demurely. "A kind missionary taught me." She remained at Jennings' side.

"He taught you well, I must say," Jennings said, eyeing her up and down.

"He taught me many things about your culture," Than Than Aye said. "Many things, sir."

"I can only imagine," Jennings replied.

"Do you know who that woman is?" Andrew asked.

"That woman is called Than Than Aye," Mariana said. "We're old friends."

"Are you indeed?" Andrew asked. "You'll have to tell me more."

"Maybe later," Mariana said. "A girl needs some secrets."

They watched as Than Than Aye slid closer to Jennings so her hip touched his. "I have heard that you are a kind man," she said.

"Where did you hear that?" Jennings asked.

"I heard you were good to girls," Than Than Aye said. She moved away again, pouting.

"Now, wait a minute," Jennings followed, putting a hand on her shoulder. "Where are you going?"

"Wherever you want to go," Than Than Aye replied.

"Would you like to see my house?" Jennings asked.

Than Than Aye widened her eyes. "That would be a pleasure, sir," she said. "I've never been with a European before."

Jennings smiled. "When I first saw you," he said. "I thought you were just another beautiful Burmese woman, but now I can tell that you are something special. You are like no woman I have ever met before."

Than Than Aye snuggled closer. "Thank you, sir. I am sure I can surprise you."

"Why are we watching this?" Andrew asked as Jennings ushered Than Than Aye into his Brougham.

"You'll see tomorrow," Mariana said.

"Tell me now," Andrew said.

When Mariana smiled, shaking her head, Andrew realised he was witnessing a new, mischievous side of her character.

No, he told himself. *It's not a new side. This is the old Mariana I saw before her abduction. Mariana is back to normal at last.* "I can wait," he said.

WELLS PLACED A FOLDED NEWSPAPER ON THEIR TABLE AT BREAKFAST THE following morning. He nodded to Andrew and walked on to another customer.

Mariana watched as Andrew glanced at the newspaper, lifted it, and read one of the articles. He looked across the table at Mariana.

"Did you know about this?"

"Did I know about what?" Mariana asked innocently.

"This!" Andrew prodded his finger at an article as he passed the newspaper to her. "Somebody broke into Jennings' stables and stole his horses while he was otherwise engaged." Andrew leaned back in his chair. "You and I know what he was doing. Our mutual friend Than Than Aye had him fully occupied. We also both know that Bo Thura is the best horse thief this side of India."

Mariana smiled slowly. "I said you'd see tomorrow," she said. "Stephen Jennings was proud of his horses."

"Bo Thura!" Andrew exclaimed. "Damn and blast the man! I went to a lot of trouble to rescue that fellow, and his first action is to steal the finest horses in Rangoon."

Mariana laughed. "I wonder if that was his plan all along," she said. "Was he playing a game with us?"

Maybe he was. Maybe my beloved cousin was pulling my strings like a puppet-master, working me to his advantage as he planned to steal the finest bloodstock horses in Burma.

Andrew put the newspaper back on the table. "I doubt we'll ever know," he said. "Come on, Mariana. We must buy our shipping tickets."

As they left the British India offices beside the harbour, Mariana watched the launch steam slowly upriver, with the grey-bearded man in the wheelhouse calmly smoking a cheroot. The flat attached to the launch floated light on the water as though it carried little weight, so they made good time against the current. She idly noted the name on the launch's stern, *Little Salamander,* and smiled when she saw a horse poke its head over the side.

"A bribe for Kiugkwek-li," Andrew had also seen the horse. "Now that Sir Charles has removed Maung Thandar from power, Kiugkwek-li is suitably bribed, and Buda Sein suitably dead, Bo Thura can resume the only life he knows." He placed the steamship tickets in his inside pocket and took Mariana's hand. "Come on, Mariana, we have packing to complete." He watched *Little Salamander* steam slowly upstream. "I wonder what Jamieson charged Bo Thura for that cargo. These two rogues are well suited."

YORLING CHAPTER 36

EDINBURGH, SCOTLAND, JUNE 1886

The sun eased through low clouds as Andrew walked under the portcullis and into Edinburgh Castle. The Governor had formed up the garrison as a guard of honour, with the men immaculate in their brilliant scarlet tunics and blue trousers. They presented arms as Andrew marched past on his way to St Margaret's Chapel.

Friends that Andrew had known since childhood packed the chapel. The garrison chaplain waited at the altar, Bible in hand and a benevolent smile on his face. Andrew's mother sat at the front, greeting him with a silent smile and a nod of encouragement. Andrew heard the echo of his boots as he marched the few paces to face the chaplain and slammed to attention as if he were before the regimental colonel rather than the Lord God Almighty.

"Relax, Captain Baird," the chaplain said quietly. "She'll be here."

"Yes, sir," Andrew realised how tense he was and stood at ease, feeling his heart thumping. He heard the murmur of the small congregation and wondered what they were discussing and how long he would have to wait before Mariana appeared.

What if she has changed her mind? She already embarrassed me in this castle. Is she going to do that again, jilting me at the altar?

As the thought crossed his mind, Andrew heard footsteps behind him, the heavy tread of a man with a slight limp from a wound in the Second Burmese War and the lighter patter of a woman. He glanced behind him and saw his father, General Jack Windrush, with Mariana holding on to the crook of his elbow. As Mariana had no surviving relatives, Jack Windrush acted as her father to give away the bride.

Andrew thought that Mariana had never looked more elegant in her flowing white wedding dress with the veil obscuring her face and two bridesmaids, chosen from the garrison children, holding her train.

"Face your front, Captain," the chaplain advised. "She'll be with you shortly."

Andrew obeyed, trying to control the surge of relief and the grin that threatened to split his face. He heard the heavy footsteps halt behind him. The lighter patter continued for two more steps, and then Mariana was at his side, where she belonged. Andrew looked sideways as Mariana swept back her veil.

"Are you both ready?" the chaplain asked softly.

"Yes," Andrew replied as Mariana nodded.

Andrew felt as if he were somebody else, looking down as the chaplain intoned the words of the wedding ceremony. His father stood behind him, and Mariana was at his side. He could feel his mother's eyes fixed on his back and knew she was encouraging him, as always.

Memories of Zululand, the Transvaal, and Burma returned to him in an array of faces and incidents. He allowed his mind to wander and only returned when he sensed the chaplain's eyes fixed on him.

"I now pronounce you man and wife," the chaplain announced. "You may kiss the bride."

Andrew could not contain his smile as he turned towards his wife. He heard somebody cheer as he touched her lightly on the lips.

"Now we're married," Mrs Mariana Baird said.

"So we are," Andrew agreed.

He heard somebody call for three cheers, but the rest of that day was only a happy blur.

ANDREW'S HOUSE ON BERWICK'S WALLS WAS WARM AND WELCOMING AS HE carried his new wife over the threshold.

"I have something for you," he said, placing her gently on the ground. "Wait here." He ran upstairs to his study, fumbled for the desk key, and withdrew the brown-paper-wrapped parcel he had placed there when Mariana refused his offer at Edinburgh Castle.

"What is it?" Mariana asked as Andrew returned with the parcel.

"Why not open it and see?" Andrew suggested. He watched with an indulgent smile as Mariana ripped off the paper.

"Books," Mariana said. "Leather bound with gold embossed titles." She held up the first. "Tennyson's poems, including the Morte d'Arthur and the Lady of Shalott."

Andrew nodded. It had cost him a small fortune to buy the books and have a bookbinder add a leather cover with gold lettering.

"What's this? Another *Morte d'Arthur*? By Sir Thomas Malory?" Mariana looked up quizzically.

"It's a copy of the Fifteenth Century original," Andrew explained. "You can compare the two versions. Malory's is much longer."

Mariana lifted the third and by far the slimmest book. She read the title. "*The Gododdin* by Aneirin," she said. "That's the poem you mentioned that day in Edinburgh."

"Yes," Andrew said. He had the heroic poem specially printed and bound for Mariana, with her name written inside, as she saw when she opened it up.

"Oh," Mariana said. "What a lovely wedding present."

Andrew nodded. He did not tell her the books had been intended as an engagement present. Some things were better left unsaid.

Mariana lifted the books, smelled the leather, and smiled. "Thank you, Andrew," she said and extended her hand. "Come with me." She smiled. "We've waited a long time for this, husband," she said, leading him upstairs.

HISTORICAL NOTE

THE KIDNAPPING OF MARY WINCHESTER

I based the kidnapping of Mary MacConnacher on actual events. The Lushais were a tribe that lived on the Northeast frontier of India, in the hill country between Bengal and Burma. They occasionally raided the British-run tea plantations to plunder and kidnap, continuing their depredations despite the British sending men on punitive expeditions.

In 1871, the Lushais grabbed a young British girl, Mary Winchester, who was reportedly golden-haired. The British sent an expedition to recover Mary, with men dying from diseases and accidents, as well as from brushes with the tribal warriors. When a relief column found young Mary, she was in perfect health, spoke Lushai better than English, and smoked cheroots. The Lushais were upset about losing her and asked for a lock of her golden hair as a keepsake.

As both Mary's parents were dead, she was sent to Britain to live with relatives. Sometimes, one wonders if she would not have been happier with the Lushais.

THE THIRD BURMESE WAR

The Third Burmese War was a short affair that the British won after a couple of skirmishes. However, the British found that occupying the country was one thing and pacifying or conquering it was something else. Dacoity continued well into the 1890s, with the British blaming any act of resistance on dacoits or bandits. It is possible that many of the perpetrators may have intended to remove British rule rather than simple robbery and mayhem.

THE IRRAWADDY FLOTILLA COMPANY

Rudyard Kipling immortalised the Irrawaddy Flotilla Company in his poem *Mandalay* when he wrote:

"Come you back to Mandalay,
Where the old Flotilla lay:
Can't you 'ear their paddles chunkin' from Rangoon to Mandalay?"

The Irrawaddy Flotilla Company was owned and managed in Glasgow, Scotland with its headquarters in Rangoon. It operated from 1865 until the 1940s and, at one time, boasted the largest river boat fleet in the world. The ships were built in sections in Glasgow, sent to Rangoon and reassembled in the Flotilla Company's shipyard.

ABOUT THE AUTHOR

Born in Edinburgh, Scotland and educated at the University of Dundee, Malcolm Archibald has written in a variety of genres, from academic history to folklore, historical novels to fantasy. He won the Dundee International Book Prize with *Whales for the Wizard* in 2005 and the Society of Army Historical Research prize for Historical Military Fiction with *Blood Oath* in 2021.

Happily married for over 42 years, Malcolm has three grown children and lives outside Dundee in Scotland.

To learn more about Malcolm Archibald and discover more Next Chapter authors, visit our website at www.nextchapter.pub.

NOTES

CHAPTER 1

1. Amabutho - Zulu regiments were known as amabutho and formed of men of the same age. After months of training, they were allowed home and usually reformed only to guard their local area in times of war or for national festivals.

CHAPTER 2

1. *The Charge of the Light Brigade,* by Alfred, Lord Tennyson

CHAPTER 4

1. Quote from *The Charge of the Light Brigade,* by Alfred, Lord Tennyson.
2. *Ode on the Duke of Wellington*, by Alfred, Lord Tennyson.
3. Quote from *The Lady of Shalott,* by Alfred, Lord Tennyson.
4. Quote from *The Holy Grail,* by Alfred, Lord Tennyson.

CHAPTER 5

1. Quote from *Ulysses,* Alfred, Lord Tennyson.

CHAPTER 6

1. Isicoco- a band of fibre sewn into the hair, coated with gum, polished, and worn with pride.

CHAPTER 7

1. Quote from *The Lady of Shalott,* by Alfred, Lord Tennyson

CHAPTER 8

1. *Idylls of the King,* by Alfred, Lord Tennyson
2. *The Lady of Shalott,* by Alfred, Lord Tennyson

CHAPTER 9

1. The Byrne Settlers were immigrants to Natal brought out by the company J. C. Byrne between 1849 and 1851.

CHAPTER 10

1. *The Lay of the Last Minstrel,* by Sir Walter Scott.
2. The transformation occurred in 1879, but I pushed it forward a year for the purposes of the story.

CHAPTER 11

1. *Morte d'Arthur,* by Alfred, Lord Tennyson

CHAPTER 12

1. Cameronians- a Scottish Lowland infantry regiment.

CHAPTER 15

1. From *Idylls of the King,* by Alfred, Lord Tennyson.

CHAPTER 16

1. Rorke's Drift

CHAPTER 24

1. Bundook - Rifle

CHAPTER 27

1. Beresford and O'Toole got the Victoria Cross for the rescue. Originally the award was granted only to Beresford, but he refused the honour unless O'Toole was also granted the medal.

CHAPTER 33

1. *Ulysses,* by Alfred, Lord Tennyson

CHAPTER 1

1. See 'The Noise of Zulu Battle' by Malcolm Archibald, published by Next Chapter in May 2023.

CHAPTER 2

1. Redvers Buller was one of the foremost British soldiers in the closing decades of the Nineteenth century. Andrew fought beside him during the Zulu War.

CHAPTER 5

1. Sandwala: a slang term for Isandhlwana, where the Zulus defeated a British army in January 1879.
2. A Commandant Robertse, of the besieging Boers, was wounded in this opening skirmish of the war.

CHAPTER 6

1. The Siege of Lucknow during the Indian Mutiny (1857).

CHAPTER 7

1. The ambush at Bronkhorst Spruit lasted fifteen minutes and cost the British 56 men killed and 92 wounded. Colonel Anstruther later died of his wounds. The Boers lost two dead and five wounded, with most of the British fire going above the Boers' heads. Conductor Egerton of the Commissariat and Transport Department and Sergeant Bradley smuggled the Colours to safety. Three soldiers' wives were awarded the Royal Red Cross for their courage and for attending to the wounded.

CHAPTER 8

1. The Battle of Boomplats was fought on 29th August 1848 between a British force led by Sir Harry Smith and Commandant General Andreas Pretorius. The British won the skirmish and later annexed territory to the British Empire.
2. Kriegsraad – a pre-battle meeting to discuss tactics.
3. The flag above the fort was homemade. Lieutenant Rundle of the Royal Artillery provided a cloak, with Lieutenant Lindsell a coat and an unnamed sergeant his scarlet tunic. The flag remained in place for the duration of the siege. In 1912, Rundle, then General Sir Leslie Rundle, presented the flag to the 2nd Battalion Royal Scots Fusiliers.
4. Nine of Ou Griet's balls either hit the walls of the fort or landed inside in the attack on the First of January 1881. They did some minor damage without killing or injuring a single soldier. During the entire siege, Ou Griet was accredited with killing one man and wounding five others. The other cannonballs passed over the fort. Private Dobbs of the 21st Foot was killed during this attack.

CHAPTER 9

1. Scoff or skoff became accepted as a slang word for food after the Second Boer War of 1899-1902, but British soldiers based in South Africa would have added it to their vocabulary in the late 1870s or early 1880s.

CHAPTER 10

1. The Battle of Maiwand, fought on the 27th of July 1880, was an Afghan victory over a British army.
2. The Battle of Laing's Nek was the last occasion British redcoats marched to battle with the colours displayed.
3. Lieutenant Hill gained the Victoria Cross for rescuing wounded men under fire during the action at Laing's Nek.

CHAPTER 11

1. Wolseley Ring: General Sir Garnet Wolseley formed a group of the brightest and best officers known as the Wolseley Ring. They included Colley, Redvers Buller and other prominent late Nineteenth century officers.
2. Lieutenant Lindsell led this all-volunteer party on the 7th of January 1881.

CHAPTER 12

1. Out of a total strength of twenty-seven officers and men, the Royal Artillery lost thirteen killed and wounded in the battle of Schuinschoogte. Lieutenant Parsons was one of the wounded.
2. The Ingogo claimed three men that night, and one more next day when Captain Wilkinson of the Rifles drowned trying to bring medical help to the wounded.

CHAPTER 13

1. On the 22nd of January, 1881, Lieutenant Dalrymple-Hay of the 21st Foot, the Royal Scots Fusiliers, won the DCM for leading twelve men to clear a Boer trench. He rose to become a major, and his son, John Dalrymple-Hay of the Gordon Highlanders, died of enteric fever in the Second Boer War.
2. The wound to Private Colvin created an exchange of letters between Colonel Winsloe and General Cronje. The missile may have been a bullet fired by an 8-bore elephant gun.
3. Sir Garnet Wolseley was one of Britain's foremost soldiers of the period. Sir Evelyn Wood was another distinguished officer and a favourite of Queen Victoria.

CHAPTER 15

1. The Gordons recruited Ghazi, an Afghan hound in Afghanistan. The dog was wounded at Majuba but made it home. He kept regular watch with the men, drew his rations and guarded the other regimental pets.
2. The Battle of Blood River was fought on the 16th of December 1838, when a few hundred Boer Voortrekkers defeated a Zulu impi at least fifteen thousand strong.

CHAPTER 17

1. Alfred, Lord Tennyson: *The Princess*.
2. Forlorn Hope: a near suicide mission.

CHAPTER 18

1. This incident occurred at the Battle of Warburg, 31st of July 1760.
2. "Remember Majuba" became a common war cry during the Second Boer War of 1899 to 1902.

CHAPTER 19

1. When the Zulus killed Louis Napoleon, Prince Imperial of France, during the Zulu War, the Bonaparte dynasty ended. Some people in France thought the British had allowed the Zulus to kill him, or French Republicans or even Queen Victoria.
2. This incident was based on a similar event during the Second Boer War, 1899-1902, when a Boer marksman fired at them from a range Captain Doyle of Doyle's Australian Scouts calculated at 2300 yards. The rifle was an 1877 Steyr with a drop-block breech and a .303 bore. The marksman was an old man with a long beard. Captain Doyle's son, the late Douglas Doyle, informed me of the encounter.

CHAPTER 21

1. Weenen: The Place of Weeping, where the Zulus massacred many Boer settlers.

The Soldier's Son - Books 1-3
ISBN: 978-4-82419-612-5
Hardcover Edition

Published by
Next Chapter
2-5-6 SANNO
SANNO BRIDGE
143-0023 Ota-Ku, Tokyo
+818035793528

25th July 2024

Milton Keynes UK
Ingram Content Group UK Ltd.
UKHW041834121124
451129UK00006B/91